DINNER AT THE HOMESICK RESTAURANT,

THE ACCIDENTAL TOURIST

and

BREATHING LESSONS

DINNER AT THE HOMESICK RESTAURANT,

THE ACCIDENTAL TOURIST

and

BREATHING LESSONS

Three Novels by

ANNE TYLER

Chatto & Windus
LONDON

Published in 1992 by
Chatto & Windus Ltd
20 Vauxhall Bridge Road
London SW1V 2SA

Dinner at the Homesick Restaurant
first published by Chatto & Windus in 1982
This edition reset from the second impression
of the above edition of 1983
The Accidental Tourist first published by
Chatto & Windus in 1985
Breathing Lessons first published by
Chatto & Windus in 1989

A CIP catalogue record for this book is
available from the British Library.

ISBN 0 7011 3958 7

Typeset by SX Composing Limited, Rayleigh, Essex
Printed and bound in Great Britain by
Mackays of Chatham PLC, Chatham, Kent

CONTENTS

DINNER AT THE HOMESICK RESTAURANT

1

Something You
Should Know

While Pearl Tull was dying, a funny thought occurred to her. It twitched her lips and rustled her breath, and she felt her son lean forward from where he kept watch by her bed. "Get . . ." she told him. "You should have got . . ."

You should have got an extra mother, was what she meant to say, the way we started extra children after the first child fell so ill. Cody, that was; the older boy. Not Ezra here beside her bed but Cody the troublemaker—a difficult baby, born late in her life. They had decided on no more. Then he developed croup. This was in 1931, when croup was something serious. She'd been frantic. Over his crib she had draped a flannel sheet, and she set out skillets, saucepans, buckets full of water that she'd heated on the stove. She lifted the flannel sheet to catch the steam. The baby's breathing was choked and rough, like something pulled through tightly packed gravel. His skin was blazing and his hair was plastered stiffly to his temples. Toward morning, he slept. Pearl's head sagged in the rocking chair and she slept too, fingers still gripping the ivory metal crib rail. Beck was away on business—came home when the worst was over, Cody toddling around again with nothing more than a runny nose and a loose, unalarming cough that Beck didn't even notice. "I want more children," Pearl told him. He acted surprised, though pleased. He reminded her that she hadn't felt she could face another delivery. But "I want some extra," she said, for it had struck her during the croup: if Cody died, what would she have left? This little rented house, fixed up so carefully and pathetically; the nursery with its Mother Goose theme; and Beck, of course, but he was so busy with the Tanner Corporation, away from home more often than not, and even when home always fuming over business: who was on the rise and who was on the skids, who had spread damaging rumors behind his back, what chance he had of being let go now that times were so hard.

"I don't know why I thought just one little boy would suffice," said Pearl.

But it wasn't as simple as she had supposed. The second child was Ezra, so sweet and clumsy it could break your heart. She was more endangered than ever. It would have been best to stop at Cody. She still hadn't learned, though. After Ezra came Jenny, the girl—such fun to dress, to fix her hair in different styles. Girls were a kind of luxury, Pearl felt. But she couldn't give Jenny up, either. What she had now was not one loss to fear but three. Still, she thought, it had seemed a good idea once upon a time: spare children, like spare tires, or those extra lisle stockings they used to package free with each pair.

"You should have arranged for a second-string mother, Ezra," she said. Or she meant to say. "How shortsighted of you." But evidently she failed to form the words, for she heard him sit back again without comment and turn a page of his magazine.

She had not seen Ezra clearly since the spring of '75, four and a half years ago, when she first started losing her vision. She'd had a little trouble with blurring. She went to the doctor for glasses. It was arteries, he told her; something to do with her arteries. She was eighty-one years old, after all. But he was certain it could be treated. He sent her to a specialist, who sent

2

her to someone else . . . well, to make a long story short, they found they couldn't help her. Something had shriveled away behind her eyes. "I'm falling into disrepair," she told the children. "I've outlived myself." She gave a little laugh. To tell the truth, she hadn't believed it. She had made the appropriate sounds of dismay, then acceptance, then plucky cheer; but inwardly, she'd determined not to allow it. She just wouldn't hear of it, that was all. She had always been a strong-willed woman. Once, when Beck was away on business, she'd walked around with a broken arm for a day and a half till he could come stay with the babies. (It was just after one of his transfers. She was a stranger in town and had no one to turn to.) She didn't even hold with aspirin; didn't hold with depending, requesting. "The doctor says I'm going blind," she told the children, but privately, she'd intended to do no such thing.

Yet every day, her sight had faded. The light, she felt, was somehow thinning and retreating. Her son Ezra, his calm face that she loved to linger on—he grew dim. Even in bright sunshine, now, she had difficulty making out his shape. She could barely discern his silhouette as he came near her—that large, sloping body settling into softness a bit in his middle age. She felt his flannel warmth when he sat next to her on the couch, describing what was on her TV or going through her drawer of snapshots the way she liked to have him do. "What's that you've got, Ezra?" she would ask.

"It seems to be some people on a picnic," he would say.

"Picnic? What kind of picnic?"

"White tablecloth in the grass. Wicker basket. Lady wearing a middy blouse."

"Maybe that's Aunt Bessie."

"I'd recognize your Aunt Bessie, by now."

"Or Cousin Elsa. *She* favored middy blouses, I recall."

Ezra said, "I never knew you had a cousin."

"Oh, I had cousins," she said.

She tipped her head back and recollected cousins, aunts,

uncles, a grandpa whose breath had smelled of mothballs. It was peculiar how her memory seemed to be going blind with the rest of her. She didn't so much see their faces as hear their fluid voices, feel the crisp ruching of the ladies' shirtwaists, smell their pomades and lavender water and the sharp-scented bottle of crystals that sickly Cousin Bertha had carried to ward off fainting spells.

"I had cousins aplenty," she told Ezra.

They had thought she would be an old maid. They'd grown tactful—insultingly tactful. Talk of others' weddings and confinements halted when Pearl stepped out on the porch. A college education was offered by Uncle Seward—at Meredith College, right there in Raleigh, so she wouldn't have to leave home. No doubt he feared having to support her forever: a millstone, an orphaned spinster niece tying up his spare bedroom. But she told him she had no use for college. She felt that going to college would be an admission of defeat.

Oh, what was the trouble, exactly? She was not bad-looking. She was small and slender with fair skin and fair, piled hair, but the hair was growing dry as dust and the strain was beginning to show around the curled and mobile corners of her mouth. She'd had suitors in abundance, more than she could name; yet they never lasted, somehow. It seemed there was some magical word that everyone knew but Pearl—those streams of girls, years younger than she, effortlessly tumbling into marriage. Whas she too serious? Should she unbend more? Lower herself to giggle like those mindless, silly Winston twins? Uncle Seward, *you* can tell me. But Uncle Seward just puffed on his pipe and suggested a secretarial course.

Then she met Beck Tull. She was thirty years old. He was twenty-four—a salesman with the Tanner Corporation, which sold its farm and garden equipment all over the eastern seaboard and where he would surely, surely rise, a smart young fellow like him. In those days, he was lean and rangy. His black hair waved extravagantly, and his eyes were a brilliant shade of blue

4

that seemed not quite real. Some might say he was . . . well, a little extreme. Flamboyant. Not quite of Pearl's class. And certainly too young for her. She knew there were some thoughts to that effect. But what did she care? She felt reckless and dashing, bursting with possibilities.

She met him at a church—at the Charity Baptist Church, which Pearl was only visiting because her girlfriend Emmaline was a member. Pearl was not a Baptist herself. She was Episcopalian, but truthfully not even that; she thought of herself as a nonbeliever. Still, when she went to the Baptist church and saw Beck Tull standing there, a stranger, glossily shaved and wearing a shiny blue suit, and he asked within two minutes if he might be allowed to call, she related it in some superstitious way to the church itself—as if Beck were her reward for attending with the Baptists. She did not dare *stop* attending. She became a member, to her family's horror, and was married at Charity Baptist and went to one Baptist church or another, in one town or another, her entire married life, just so her reward would not be snatched away. (Didn't that maybe, it occurred to her, imply some kind of faith after all?)

Courting her, he brought chocolates and flowers and then—more serious—pamphlets describing the products of the Tanner Corporation. He started telling her in detail about his work and his plans for advancement. He paid her compliments that made her uncomfortable till she could get off alone in her room and savor them. She was the most cultured and refined little lady that he had ever known, he said, and the best mannered, and the daintiest. He liked to place her hand to his, palm to palm, and marvel at its tiny size. Despite the reputation of salesmen, he was respectful to a fault and never grabbed at her the way some other men might.

Then he received his transfer, and after that things sped up so; for he wouldn't hear of leaving her behind but must marry her immediately and take her with him. So they had their Baptist wedding—both of them out of breath, Pearl always pictured later—and spent their honeymoon moving to Newport News. She never even got to enjoy her new status among her girlfriends. She didn't have time to show off a single one of her trousseau dresses, or to flash her two gold rings—the narrow wedding band and the engagement ring, set with a pearl, inscribed *To a Pearl among Women*. Everything seemed so unsatisfying.

They moved, and they moved again. For the first six years they had no children and the moves were fairly easy. She'd gaze at each new town with hopeful eyes and think: This may be where I'll have my son. (For pregnancy, now, took on the luster that marriage had once had—it was the treasure that came so easily to everyone but her.) Then Cody was born, and moving seemed much harder. Children had a way of complicating things, she noticed. There were the doctors and the school transcripts and this, that, and the other. Meanwhile she looked around and saw that somehow, without her noticing, she'd been cut off from most of her relatives. Aunts and uncles had died while she'd been too far away to do more than send a sympathy note. The house where she was born was sold to a man from Michigan; cousins married strangers with last names she'd never heard of; even the street names were changed so she'd be lost if she ever went back. And it struck her once, in her forties, that she really had no notion what had become of that grandpa with the mothball breath. He couldn't still be living, could he? Had he died and no one thought to inform her? Or maybe they'd sent the news to an out-of-date address, three or four years behind times. Or she might have heard but simply forgotten, in the rush of some transfer or other. Anything was possible.

Oh, those transfers. Always there was some incentive—a chance of promotion, or richer territory. But it seldom amounted to much. Was it Beck's fault? He claimed it wasn't, but she didn't know; she really didn't know. He claimed that he was haunted by ill-wishers. There were so many petty people in

6

this world, he said. She pursed her lips and studied him. "Why do you look at me that way?" he asked. "What are you thinking? At least," he said, "I provide for you. I've never let my family go hungry." She admitted that, but still she felt a constant itch of anxiety. It seemed her forehead was always tight and puckered. This was not a person she could lean on, she felt—this slangy, loud-voiced salesman peering at his reflection with too much interest when he tied his tie in the mornings, combing his pompadour tall and damp and frilly and then replacing the comb in a shirt pocket full of pencils, pens, ruler, appointment book, and tire gauge, all bearing catchy printed slogans for various firms.

Over his beer in the evening (but he was not a drinking man; don't get her wrong), Beck liked to sing and pull at his face. She didn't know why beer made him tug his skin that way—work it around like a rubber mask, so by bedtime his cheeks had a stretched-out, slackened look. He sang "Nobody Knows the Trouble I've Seen"—his favorite song. Nobody knows but Jesus. She supposed it must be true. What were his private thoughts, inside his spreading face, under the crest of black hair? She didn't have the faintest idea.

One Sunday night in 1944, he said he didn't want to stay married. They were sending him to Norfolk, he said; but he thought it best if he went alone. Pearl felt she was sinking in at the center, like someone given a stomach punch. Yet part of her experienced an alert form of interest, as if this were happening in a story. "Why?" she asked him, calmly enough. He didn't answer. "Beck? Why?" All he did was study his fists. He looked like a young and belligerent schoolboy waiting out a scolding. She made her voice even quieter. It was important to learn the reason. Wouldn't he just tell her what it was? He'd told her, he said. She lowered herself, shaking, in to the chair across from him. She looked at his left temple, in which a pulse ticked. He was just passing through some mood, was all. He would change his mind in the morning. "We'll sleep on it," she told him.

But he said, "It's tonight I'm going."

He went to the bedroom for his suitcase, and he took his other suit from the wardrobe. Meanwhile Pearl, desperate for time, asked couldn't they talk this over? Think it through? No need to be hasty, was there? He crossed from bureau to bed, from wardrobe to bed, packing his belongings. There weren't that many. He was done in twenty minutes. He drew in his breath and she thought, Now he'll tell me. But all he said was, "I'm not an irresponsible person. I do plan to send you money."

"And the children," she said, clutching new hope. "You'll want to visit the children."

(He would come with presents for them and she'd be the one to open the door—perfumed, in her Sunday dress, maybe wearing a bit of rouge. She'd always thought false color looked cheap, but she could have been wrong.)

Beck said, "No."

"What?"

"I won't be visiting the children."

She sat down on the bed.

"I don't understand you," she said.

There ought to be a whole separate language, she thought, for words that are truer than other words—for perfect, absolute truth. It was the purest fact of her life: she did not understand him, and she never would.

At the time, they were living in Baltimore, in a row house on Calvert Street. The children were fourteen, eleven, and nine. They were old enough to suspect something wrong, if she didn't take care. She took infinite care. The morning after Beck left she rose and dressed, piled her hair on her head the same as always, and cooked oatmeal for the children's breakfast. Cody and Jenny ate without speaking; Ezra told a long, rambling dream. (He was the only one cheerful in the mornings.) There was some disappointment that the oatmeal lacked raisins. Nobody asked where Beck was. After all, he often left before

8

they woke on a Monday. And there'd been times—many times—when he'd stayed away the whole week. It wasn't so unusual.

When Friday night rolled around, she said he'd been delayed. He'd promised to take them to the Midget Circus, and she told them she would do it instead. Another week passed. She had no close friends, but if she met a chance acquaintance in the grocery store, she remarked that luckily, she wouldn't have to use any meat points today. Her husband was away on business, she said. People nodded, showing no interest. He was almost always away on business. Few had ever met him.

Nights, especially Friday nights, she lay in bed in the dark and listened to the gritty click of heels on the sidewalk. Footsteps would come close and then pass. She would let out her breath. A new set of footsteps approached. Surely *this* was Beck. She knew how hesitantly he would let himself in, expecting the worst—his children's tears, his wife's reproaches. But instead, he'd find everything unchanged. The children would greet him offhandedly. Pearl would peck his cheek and ask if he'd had a good trip. Later, he would thank her for keeping his secret. He would be so easily readmitted, since only the two of them knew he'd left; outsiders would go on believing the Tulls were a happy family. Which they were, in fact. Oh, they'd always been so happy! They'd depended only on each other, because of moving around so much. It had made them very close. He'd be back.

Her Uncle Seward's widow wrote to wish her a happy birthday. (Pearl had forgotten all about it.) Pearl responded immediately, thanking her. *We celebrated at home,* she wrote. *Beck surprised me with the prettiest necklace . . . Say hello to the others,* she added, and she pictured them all in her uncle's parlor; she ached for them, but drew herself up and recalled how they had been so sure no man would marry her. She could never tell them what had happened.

Her old friend Emmaline stopped by, on her way to visit a

9

sister in Philadelphia. Pearl said Beck was out of town; the two of them were in luck; they could talk girl-talk to their hearts' content. She put Emmaline in the double bed with her, instead of in the guest room. They stayed awake half the night gossiping and giggling. Once Pearl almost set a hand on Emmaline's arm and said, "Emmaline. Listen. I feel so horrible, Emmaline." But fortunately, she caught herself. The moment passed. In the morning they overslept, and Pearl had to rush to get the children off to school; so there wasn't much said. "We should do this more often," Emmaline told her as she left, and Pearl said Beck would be sorry he had missed her. "You know he's always liked you," she said. Although actually, Beck used to claim that Emmaline reminded him of a woodchuck.

Easter came, and Jenny had a part in her school's Easter pageant. When the day arrived and Beck was still not home, Jenny cried. Couldn't he *ever* be home? It wasn't his fault, Pearl told her. There was a war on, production speeded up; he couldn't help it if his company needed him more now. They ought to be proud, she said. Jenny dried her tears and told everyone that her daddy had to help with the war effort. The war was so old by now, grinding on; no one was impressed. Still, it made Jenny feel better. Pearl went to the Easter pageant alone, wearing a rakish, visored hat that was patterned after the hats the WACs wore.

When Beck had been gone a month, he sent a note from Norfolk saying he was fine and hoped that she and the kids did not lack for anything. He enclosed a check for fifty dollars. It wasn't nearly enough. Pearl spent a morning pacing the house. First she went over his note in her mind, picking apart his words for underlying meanings. But not much could underlie *right good apartment with hotplate* and *sales manager seems to think well of me.* Then she considered the money. Around lunchtime, she put on her coat and her WACs hat and walked around the corner to Sweeney Bros. Grocery and Fine Produce, where a CASHIER WANTED sign had been yellowing in the window for weeks. They were tickled to death to hire her. The younger Sweeney brother showed her how to work the cash register and said she could start the next morning. When her children came home from school that day, she told them she was taking a job to fill in time. She needed something to keep her busy, she said, now that they were growing up and going off on their own more.

Two months passed. Three months. Fifty dollars a month from Beck. When the second check arrived, no letter came with it. She tore the envelope apart, thinking it must have got stuck inside, but there wasn't a word. With the third check, though, he wrote that he was moving to Cleveland, where the company planned to open a new branch. He said it was a good sign they'd decided on this transfer—or "invite," he called it. He never called it a transfer; he called it an invite. An invite to this important expansion westward. He began the letter, *Dear Pearl & kids*, but Pearl didn't show it to the children. She folded it neatly and put it with the first letter, in a hosiery box in her bureau, where even that meddlesome Cody wouldn't think to look. In the fourth envelope, again, there was only a check. She saw that he was not in *communication* with her (was how she phrased it), but was merely touching base from time to time. Really, all he was doing was saying, *Please find enclosed*. It didn't occur to her to answer him. Yet she went on saving his letters.

Sometimes she had strange thoughts that surprised her. For instance: At least I have more closet space now. And more drawer space.

At night she dreamed that Beck was new and wonderful again, someone she'd just become acquainted with. He gazed at her adoringly, overturning some unfamiliar center deep inside her. He helped her cross streets, climb steps. His hand cupped her elbow warmly or circled her waist or steadied the small of her back. She felt cherished. When she woke, her only thought was to sink back into her dream. She would keep her

11

eyes shut. Superstitiously, she would play possum, not stirring, trying to persuade the dream that she was still asleep. But it never worked. Finally she would rise, whatever the hour, and go downstairs to make a pot of coffee. Standing at the kitchen window with her cup, watching the sky whiten over the rooftops, she would catch sight of her dark, transparent reflection—her small face and round chin that was taking on a dented look, these past few years; the worried tent of her colorless eyebrows; the pale frazzle of hair that failed to hide the crease across her forehead. That crease was not a wrinkle but a scar, the mark of a childhood accident. Oh, she was not so old! She was not so very old! But then she remembered the accident: she'd been trying to ride a cousin's bicycle, the very first in the family. A "wheel" was what they called it. Trying to ride a wheel. And here it was 1944 and bicycles were everywhere, but so modernized they were hardly the same breed of beast. All three of her children knew how to ride and would, in fact, have had bikes of their own if not for the war. How had she come so far? She had just passed her fiftieth birthday. There was not a hope of Beck's return. He'd found someone younger, someone glamorous and merry, still capable of bearing children. They were laughing at her—at how she'd always been an old maid, really, always an old maid at heart. How she flinched when he turned to her in the dark, still startled, after all these years, by the concreteness of him—by his scratchy whiskers, salty-smelling skin, weighty body. How she had to have things just perfect, the linens on labeled shelves in the cupboard and the shades pulled evenly in the windows. How she'd never learned to let go, to give in, to float on the current of a day, but must always fuss and pull at stray threads and straighten the corners of things; and worst of all, how she *knew* she did that, knew while she was doing it, but still could not stop herself.

He was never coming back.

It was time to tell the children. She was amazed, in fact, that she'd managed to keep it from them for so long. Had they always been this easy to fool? One good thing about telling them: they would rally around her better. She didn't like to admit it but she was losing control of the boys. Instead of supporting her—taking out the garbage, helping her in various manly and protective ways—they seemed to be running wild; yes, even Ezra. They didn't even do the chores they used to do, let alone take on new ones. Cody in fact was hardly ever home. Ezra was dreamy and forgetful and would like as not walk off in the middle of a task. When she told them what was what, she thought, they'd be horrified at how they'd let her down. They'd ask why she'd hidden it all this time, what she could have been thinking of.

Only she couldn't tell them.

She planned how she would do it: she would gather them around her on the sofa, in the lamplight, some evening after supper. "Children. Dear ones," she would say. "There's something you should know." But she wouldn't be able to continue; she might cry. It was unthinkable to cry in front of the children. Or in front of anyone. Oh, she had her pride! She was not a tranquil woman; she often lost her temper, snapped, slapped the nearest cheek, said things she later regretted—but thank the Lord, she didn't expose her tears. She didn't *allow* any tears. She was Pearl Cody Tull, who'd ridden out of Raleigh triumphant with her new husband and never looked back. Even now, even standing at the kitchen window, all alone, watching her tense and aging face, she didn't cry.

Every morning, then, she went off to Sweeney Bros. She continued to wear her hat, giving the impression that she had merely dropped in and was helping out as a favor, in a pinch. As each customer approached (generally someone she knew, at least by sight), she would give a firm nod and then squint, implying a smile. She rang up the purchases efficiently while a boy named Alexander bagged them. "Thank you, and good day," she said at the end, with another shorthand smile. She liked to seem crisp and professional. When neighbors showed up,

13

people she knew more closely, she felt she was dying inside but she didn't lose her composure. With them she was even crisper. She had a little rhythm between the key stabbing and the sliding of groceries along the wooden counter; it kept her mind off things. If she allowed herself to think, she started worrying. Summer had arrived and her children were out of school all day. No telling what they might be up to.

At five-thirty she walked home, past crowds of youngsters playing hopscotch or huddled over marble games, past babies set to air in their carriages, women perched on their stoops fanning themselves in the heat. She'd climb her steps and be met at the door with bad news: "Jenny fell down the stairs today and bit her lower lip clean through and had to go to Mrs. Simmons's house for ice and gauze."

"Oh, Jenny, honey!"

It seemed they greeted her with disaster, saved up all their accidents especially for her. She'd want to take off her hat and shoes and fall back on to the sofa; but no, it was "The toilet's stopped up," and "I tore my pants," and "Cody hit Ezra with the orange juice pitcher."

"Can't you just let me be?" she would ask. "Can't you just give me a minute to myself?"

She'd make supper from tins she'd brought home, nothing fancy. She would listen to the radio while she washed dishes. Jenny was supposed to dry but was off playing tag with the boys. Stepping out the back door to heave her dishpan of water into the yard, Pearl paused to watch them—Cody and Jenny dark and quick, high-pitched, overcome with laughter; Ezra pale, a glimmer in the twilight, slower and more wandery in his movements. Sometimes there'd be neighbor children, too, but more often just the three of them. They stuck together, mostly.

She shampooed her hair and rinsed out a slip. Called to Cody to fetch the other two and come inside now.

Nights, she worked on the house. To look at her—an out-of-date kind of woman, frail boned, deep bosomed, as if those pout-fronted gowns of her girlhood had somehow formed her figure—you would never guess it, but Pearl was clever with tools. She patched a crack, glazed a window, replaced two basement stair treads. She mended a lamp switch and painted the kitchen cupboards. Even in the old days, she had done such things; Beck was not very handy. "This whole, entire house is resting on my shoulders," she would tell him, and she meant it as an accusation; but the thought was also reassuring, in a way. She knew that she was competent. From early in their marriage, from the moment she had realized how often they would be moving, she had concentrated on making each house perfect—airtight and rustproof and waterproof. She dropped the effort of continually meeting new neighbors, and she stopped returning (freshly filled) the cake tins they brought over when she arrived. All she cared about was sealing up the house, as if for a hurricane. She woke nights wondering if the basement were dry, and went down barefoot to make sure. She couldn't enjoy their Sunday outings because the house might have burned to the ground in her absence. (How vividly she could picture their return! There'd be an open space where the house used to stand, and a tattered hole for the basement.) Here in Baltimore, she gathered, she was thought to be unfriendly, even spooky—the witch of Calvert Street. What a notion! She'd known such witches in her childhood; she was nothing like them. All she wanted was to be allowed to get on with what mattered: calk the windows; weatherstrip the door. With tools she was her true self, capable and strong. She felt an indulgent kind of scorn for her children, who had not inherited her skill. Cody lacked the patience, Ezra was inept, Jenny too flighty. It was remarkable, Pearl thought, how people displayed their characters in every little thing they undertook.

Hammering down a loose floorboard, with a bristle of nails in her mouth, she would let time slip away from her. It would get to be ten-thirty or eleven. Her children would be standing in the doorway all sweaty and grass stained, blinking in the sudden brightness. "Heavens! Get to bed," she told them. "I thought I called you in hours ago." But a while after they left she'd start to feel deserted, even though they hadn't been much company. She would lay aside her hammer and rise and walk the house, smoothing her skirt, absently touching her hair where it was falling out of its bun. Up the stairs to the hall, past the little room where Jenny slept, and into her own room, with its buckling cardboard wardrobe streaked to look like wood grain, the bare-topped bureau, the cavernous bed. Then out again and up more stairs to the boys' room, a third-floor dormitory that smelled of heat. The trustful sound of her sons' breathing made her envious. She turned and descended the stairs, all the way down to the kitchen. The back door stood open and the screen door fluttered with moths. Neighboring houses rang with someone's laughter, a few cracked notes from a trumpet, an out-of-tune piano playing "Chattanooga Choo-Choo." She closed the door and locked it and pulled down the paper shade. She climbed the stairs once more and took off her clothing, piece by piece, and put on her nightgown and went to bed.

She dreamed he wore that aftershave that he'd used when they were courting. She hadn't smelled it in years, hadn't given it a thought, but now it came back to her distinctly—something pungent, prickled with spice. A swaggery and self-vaunting scent, she had known even then; but catching wind of it, when he arrived on Uncle Seward's front porch to pick her up, she had felt adventurous. She had flung the door open so widely that it banged against the wall, and he had laughed and said, "Well, now. Hey, now," as she stood there, smiling out at him.

She had heard you could not dream a smell, or recall a smell in its absence; so when she woke she was convinced, for a moment, that Beck had let himself into the house and was seated on the edge of the bed, watching while she slept. But there was no one there.

*

16

Dance? Oh, I don't think so, she said inside her head. I'm in charge of this whole affair, you see, and all I'd have to do is turn my back one instant for the party to go to pieces, just fall into little pieces. Whoever it was drew away. Ezra turned a page of his magazine. "Ezra," she said. She felt him grow still. He had this habit—he had always had it—of becoming totally motionless when people spoke to him. It was endearing, but also in some ways a strain, for then whatever she said to him ("I feel a draft," or "The paper boy is late again") was bound to disappoint him, wasn't it? How could she live up to Ezra's expectations? She plucked her her quilt. "If I could just have some water," she told him.

He poured it from the pitcher on the bureau. She heard no ice cubes clinking; they must have melted. Yet it seemed just minutes ago that he'd brought in a whole new supply. He raised her head, rested it on his shoulder, and tipped the glass to her lips. Yes, lukewarm—not that she minded. She drank gratefully, keeping her eyes closed. His shoulder felt steady and comforting. He laid her back down on the pillow.

"Dr. Vincent's coming at ten," he told her.

"What time is it now?"

"Eight-thirty."

"Eight-thirty in the morning?"

"Yes."

"Have you been here all night?" she asked.

"I slept a little."

"Sleep now. I won't be needing you."

"Well, maybe after the doctor comes."

It was important to Pearl that she deceive the doctor. She didn't want to go to the hospital. Her illness was pneumonia, she was almost certain; she guessed it from a past experience. She recognized the way it settled into her back. If Dr. Vincent found out he would sent her off to Union Memorial, tent her over with plastic. "Maybe you should cancel the doctor altogether," she told Ezra. "I'm very much improved, I believe."

17

"Let him decide that."

"Well, I know how my own self feels, Ezra."

"We won't argue about it just now," he said.

He could surprise you, Ezra could. He'd let a person walk all over him but then display, at odd moments, a deep and rock-hard stubbornness. She sighed and smoothed her quilt. It seemed he'd spilled some water on it.

She remembered when Ezra was a child, still in elementary school. "Mother," he had said, "if it turned out that money grew on trees, just for one day and never again, would you let me stay home from school and pick it?"

"No," she told him.

"Why not?"

"Your education is more important."

"Other kids' mothers would let them, I bet."

"Other mothers don't have plans for their children to amount to something."

"But just for one day?"

"Pick it *after* school. Or before. Wake up extra early; set your alarm clock ahead an hour."

"An hour!" he said. "One little hour, for something that happens only once in all the world."

"Ezra, will you let it be? Must you keep at me this way? Why are you so obstinate?" Pearl had asked him.

It only now occurred to her, under her damp quilt, to wonder why she hadn't said yes, he could stay home. If money decided to grow on trees one day, let him pick all he liked! she should have said. What difference would it have made?

Oh, she'd been an angry sort of mother. She'd been continually on edge; she'd felt too burdened, too much alone. And after Beck left, she'd been so preoccupied with paying the rent and juggling the budget and keeping those great, clod-footed children in new shoes. It was she who called the doctor at two a.m. when Jenny got appendicitis; it was she who marched downstairs with a baseball bat the night they heard that scary

18

noise. She'd kept the furnace stoked with coal, confronted the neighborhood bully when Ezra got beaten up, hosed the roof during Mrs. Simmons's chimney fire. And when Cody came home drunk from some girl's birthday party, who had to deal with that? Pearl Tull, who'd never taken anything stronger than a glass of wine at Christmas. She sat him smartly in a kitchen chair, ignored his groans, leaned across the table to him—and couldn't think of a thing to say.

Then Cody graduated from high school, and Ezra was a sophomore, and Jenny was a tall young lady in eighth grade. Beck would not have known them. And they, perhaps, would not have known Beck. They never asked about him. Didn't that show how little importance a father has? The invisible man. The absent presence. Pearl felt a twinge of angry joy. Apparently she had carried this off—made the transition so smoothly that not a single person guessed. It was the greatest triumph of her life. My one true accomplishment, she thought. (What a pity there was no one to whom she could boast of it.) Without noticing, even, she had gradually stopped attending the Baptist church. She stopped referring to Beck in conversation—although still, writing her Christmas cards to relatives in Raleigh, she remarked that Beck was doing well and sent them his regards.

One night, she threw away his letters. It wasn't a planned decision. She was just cleaning her bureau, was all, and couldn't think of any good reason to save them. She sat by her bedroom wastebasket and dropped in *looks like I will be moving up the ladder* and *litle place convenient to the railway station* and *told me I was doing mighty well*. There weren't very many—three or so in the past year. When had she quit ripping open the envelopes with shaking hands and rapidly, greedily scanning the lines? It occurred to her that the man she still mourned, late on sleepless nights, bore no relation whatsoever to the man who sent these tiresome messages. *Ed Ball is retiring in June,* she read with infinite boredom, *and I step into his terri-*

tory which has the highest per capitta income in Delaware. It was a great satisfaction to her that he had misspelled *capita.*

Her children grew up and embarked on lives of their own. Her sons started helping out financially, and Pearl was glad to accept. (She had never been ashamed about taking money — from Uncle Seward in the olden days, or from Beck, or now from the boys. Where she came from, a woman *expected* the men to provide.) And when Cody became so successful, he bought the row house she'd been renting all these years and presented her with the deed one Christmas morning. She could have retired from the grocery store right then, but she put it off till her sight began failing. What else would she do with her time? "Empty nest," they called it. Nowadays, that was the term they used. It was funny, in her old age, to look back and see for how short a period her nest had *not* been empty. Relatively speaking, it was nothing — empty far longer than full. So much of herself had been invested in those children; who could believe how briefly they'd been with her?

When she thought of them in their various stages — first clinging to her, then separating and drifting off — she thought of the hall lamp she used to leave on so they wouldn't be scared in the dark. Then later she'd left just the bathroom light on, further down the hall of whatever house they'd been living in; and later still just the downstairs light if one of them was out for the evening. Their growing up amounted, therefore, to a gradual dimming of the light at her bedroom door, as if they took some radiance with them as they moved away from her. She should have planned for it better, she sometimes thought. She should have made a few friends or joined a club. But she wasn't the type. It wouldn't have consoled her.

Last summer, she'd been half-awakened by a hymn on her clock radio — "In the Sweet Bye and Bye," mournfully sung by some popular singer just before Norman Vincent Peale's sermonette. *We shall meet on that beautiful shore* . . . She'd slipped into a dream in which a stranger told her that the beautiful shore was Wrightsville Beach, North Carolina, where she and Beck and the children had once spent a summer vacation. They were meeting on the shore after changing into swimsuits, for the very first swim of their very first day. Beck was handsome and Pearl felt graceful and the children were still very small; they had round, excited, joyous faces and chubby little bodies. She was astounded by their innocence—by her own and Beck's as well. She stretched her arms toward the children, but woke. Later, speaking to Cody on the phone, she happened to mention the dream. Wouldn't it be nice, she said, if heaven were Wrightsville Beach? If, after dying, they'd open their eyes and find themselves back on that warm, sunny sand, everyone young and happy again, those long-ago waves rolling in to shore? But Cody hadn't entered into the spirit of the thing. *Nice?* he had asked. He asked, was that all she thought of heaven? Wrightsville Beach, where as he recalled she had fretted for two solid weeks that she might have left the oven on at home? And had she taken into account, he asked, his own wishes in the matter? Did she suppose that he wanted to spend eternity as a child? "Why, Cody, all I meant was—" she said.

Something was very wrong with him. Something was wrong with all of her children. They were so frustrating—attractive, likable people, the three of them, but closed off from her in some perverse way that she couldn't quite put her finger on. And she sensed a kind of trademark flaw in each of their lives. Cody was prone to unreasonable rages; Jenny was so flippant; Ezra hadn't really lived up to his potential. (He ran a restaurant on St. Paul Street—not at all what she had planned for him.) She wondered if her children blamed her for something. Sitting close at family gatherings (with the spouses and offspring slightly apart, nonmembers forever), they tended to recall only poverty and loneliness—toys she couldn't afford for them, parties where they weren't invited. Cody, in particular, referred continually to Pearl's short temper, displaying it against a background of stunned, childish faces so sad and bewildered that Pearl herself hardly recognized them. Honestly, she thought, wasn't there some statute of limitations here? When was he going to absolve her? He was middle-aged. He had no business holding her responsible any more.

And Beck: well, he was still alive, if it mattered. By now he'd be old. She would bet he'd aged poorly. She would bet he wore a toupee, or false teeth too white and regular, or some flowing, youthful hairdo that made him look ridiculous. His ties would be too colorful and his suits too bold a plaid. What had she ever seen in him? She chewed the insides of her lips. Her one mistake: a simple error in judgment. It should not have had such far-reaching effects. You would think that life could be a little more forgiving.

One or twice a year, even now, his letters arrived. (Though the money had stopped when Jenny turned eighteen—or two months *after* she turned eighteen, which meant he'd lost track of her birthday, Pearl supposed.) It was typical of him that he lacked the taste to make a final exit. He spent too long at his farewells, chatting on the doorway, letting in the cold. He had retired from the Tanner Corporation, he wrote. He remained at his last place of transfer, Richmond, like something washed up from a flood; but evidently he still traveled some. In 1967 he sent her a postcard from the World's Fair in Montreal, and another in '72 from Atlantic City, New Jersey. He seemed spurred into action by various overblown occasions—when man first walked on the moon, for instance (an event of no concern to Pearl, or to any other serious person). *Well!* he wrote, *Looks like we made it*. His enthusiasm seemed flushed, perhaps alcohol induced. She winced and tore the letter into squares.

Later, when her eyes went, she saved her mail for Ezra. She'd hold up an envelope. "Where's this from? I can't quite make it out."

"National Rifle Association."

"Throw it away. What's this?"

"Republican Party."

"Throw it away. And this?"

"Something in longhand, from Richmond."

"Throw it away."

He didn't ask why. None of her children possessed a shred of curiosity.

She dreamed her uncle hitched up Prince and took her to a medal contest, but she had failed to memorize a piece and stood onstage like a dumb thing with everybody whispering. When she woke, she was cross with herself. She should have done "Dat Boy Fritz"; she'd always been good at dialect. And she knew it off by heart still, too. Her memory had not faded in the slightest. She rearranged her pillow, irritably. Her edges felt uneven, was how she put it to herself. She slept again and dreamed the house was on fire. Her skin dried out from the heat and her hair seemed to sizzle in her ears. Jenny rushed upstairs to save her costume jewelry and her footsteps died away all at once, as if she'd fallen into space. "Stop!" Pearl shouted. She opened her eyes. Someone was sitting next to her, in that leather armchair that creaked. "Jenny?" she said.

"It's Ezra, Mother."

Poor Ezra, he must be exhausted. Wasn't it supposed to be the daughter who came and nursed you? She knew she should send him away but she couldn't make herself do it. "I guess you want to get back to that restaurant," she told him.

"No, no."

"You're like a mother hen about that place," she said. She sniffed. Then she said, "Ezra, do you smell smoke?"

"Why do you ask?" he said (cautious as ever).

"I dreamed the house burned down."

"It didn't really."

"Ah."

She waited, holding herself in. Her muscles were so tense, she ached all over. Finally she said, "Ezra?"

23

"Yes, Mother?"

"Maybe you could just check."

"Check what?"

"The house, of course. Check if it's on fire."

She could tell he didn't want to.

"For my sake," she told him.

"Well, all right."

She heard him rise and shamble out. He must be in his stocking feet; she recognized that shushing sound. He was gone so long that she began to fear the worst. She strained for the roar of the flames but heard only the horns of passing cars, the clock radio's electric murmur, a bicycle bell tinkling beneath the window. Then here he came, heavy and slow on the stairs. Evidently there was no emergency. He settled into his chair again. "Everything's fine," he told her.

"Thank you, Ezra," she said humbly.

"You're welcome."

She heard him pick up his magazine.

"Ezra," she said, "I've had a thought. Did you happen to check the basement?"

"Yes."

"You went clear to the bottom of the steps."

"Yes, Mother."

"I don't much care for how that furnace sounds."

"It's fine," he told her.

It was fine. She resolved to believe him. She soothed herself by wandering, mentally, from one end of the house to the other, cataloguing how well she'd managed. The fireplace flue was shut against the cold. The drains were clear and the faucets were tight and she'd bled the radiators herself—sightless, turning her key back sharply the instant she heard the hiss of water. The gutters were swept and the roof did not leak and the refrigerator hummed in the kitchen. Everything was proceeding according to instructions.

"Ezra," she said.

"Yes, Mother."

"You know that address book in my desk."

"What address book?"

"Pay attention, Ezra. I only have the one. Not the little red book for telephone numbers but the black one, in my stationery drawer."

"Oh, yes."

"I want everybody in it invited to my funeral."

There was a thrumming silence, as if she had said a bad word. Then Ezra said, "*Funeral*, Mother? You're not dying?"

"No, of course not," she assured him. "But someday," she said craftily. "Just in the eventuality, you see . . ."

"Let's not talk about it," he said.

She paused, assembling patience. What did he expect—that she'd go on forever? It was so tiring. But that was Ezra for you. "All I'm saying," she said, "is I'd like those people invited. Are you listening? The people in my address book."

Ezra didn't answer.

"The address book in my stationery drawer."

"Stationery drawer," Ezra echoed.

Good; he'd got it. He flicked a magazine page, said nothing further, but she knew he'd got it.

She thought of how that address book must have aged by now—smelling mousy, turning brittle. It dated back to long before her sight had started dimming. Emmaline was in it, and Emmaline had been dead for twenty years or more. So was Mrs. Simmons dead, down in St. Petersburg, Florida, and Uncle Seward's widow and perhaps his daughter too. Why, everybody in that book was six feet under, she supposed, except for Beck.

She remembered that he took a whole page—one town after another crossed out. She'd kept it up to date because she'd imagined needing to call him in an emergency. What emergency had she had in mind? She couldn't think of any that would be eased in the slightest by his presence. She'd like to see his face when he received an invitation to her funeral. An "invite," he would call it. "Imagine that!" he would say, shocked. "She left me first, after all. Here's the invite to her funeral." She could hear him now.

She laughed.

The doctor came, stamping his feet. "Is it snowing out?" she asked him.

"Snowing? No."

"You were stamping your feet."

"No," he said, "it's just cold." He settled on the edge of her bed. "Feels like my toes are falling off," he told her. "My knee bones say we're going to have a frost tonight."

She waved away the small talk. "Listen here," she said. "Ezra called you over by mistake."

"Is that so."

"I'm really feeling fine. Maybe earlier I was under the weather, but now I'm much improved."

"I see," he said. He took her wrist in his icy, wrinkled fingers. (He was nearly as old as she was, and had all but given up his practice.) He held it for what seemed to be several minutes. Then he said, "How long has *this* been going on?"

"I don't know what you're talking about."

"Where's the phone?" he asked Ezra.

"Wait! Dr. Vincent! Wait!" Pearl cried.

He had laid down her wrist, but now he set his hand on hers and she felt him leaning over her, breathing pipe tobacco. "Yes?" he said.

"I'm not going to any hospital."

"Of course you're going."

She spoke clearly, maybe a little too loudly, directing her voice toward the ceiling. "Now, I've thought this through," she told him. "I don't want those crank-up beds and professional smells. It would kill me."

"Dear lady—"

"And you know they wouldn't be able to give me

26

penicillin."

"Penicillin, no . . ."

"That's what I took in forty-three."

"Don't tire yourself," the doctor said. "I remember all about it."

Or maybe it was '44. But Beck had not yet left. He'd been away on a business trip, anad brought back an archery set for the children. The things he spent his money on! When they were never well off, in the best of times. He took the set on their Sunday drive to a field outside the city — nailed the canvas target to a tree trunk. Oh, he never gave a thought to danger. He was not the type to lie awake nights listing all that could go wrong. Well, anyway. She couldn't say just how it had happened (she was arranging a bouquet of winter grasses at the time, as she no longer partook in sports), but somehow, she got hit. It was Cody who drew the bowstring, but that was incidental; Cody was not the one she had blamed, after the first little flurry. She blamed Beck, who through sheer thoughtlessness if not inention had shot her through the heart; or not the heart exactly but the fleshy part above it, between breast and shoulder. It was the queerest sensation, like being slapped — no sting whatsoever, but a jarring and then a disk of bright blood on her favorite blouse. "Oh!" she said, and she looked down, and went on holding her weeds. Then the pain began. Beck, white faced, pulled the arrow out. Jenny started crying. They drove straight home, forgetting to untack the target from the tree, but by the time they arrived the bleeding had stopped and it appeared there was no real danger. Pearl dressed the wound herself — iodine and gauze. Two days later, she noticed something amiss. The wound was not better but worse, inflamed, and she had a fever. Beck was on another trip, and she had to go to the doctor alone, rushing off breathless and hastily hatted because she wanted to get home again before the children returned from school. In those days, Dr. Vincent was just building up his practice after a tour of duty in the army. She remembered he still had a full

head of hair, and he wasn't yet wearing glasses. He gave her a
shot of penicillin—a miracle drug he'd first used overseas, he
said. Walking home, she felt a tremendous sense of well-being,
the way you always do when a doctor has taken upon himself
the burden of your illness; but that night, she collapsed. First
there was a rash, then chills, then a hazy and swarming landscape. It was Cody who called the ambulance. In the hospital,
once the crisis was past, everyone acted stern and reproachful,
as if it had been her fault. "You almost died," a nurse told her.
But that was nonsense. Of course she wouldn't have died; she
had children. When you have children, you're obligated to
live. She closed her eyes against the nurse's words. Then two
doctors came in and pulled up chairs beside her bed and
solemnly, portentously explained about penicillin. She must
never, never take it again, and must keep instructions to that
effect in her pocketbook at all times. Pearl wasn't paying much
heed (she was framing a request to be released, so she could get
on home to her children), but she did remember they said,
"Once is your limit. Twice will kill you." That impressed her. It
was like something in a fairy tale—like a magic potion you
could use only once and never again. And here she'd wasted it
on such a paltry occurrence: a bow-and-arrow wound. No more
miracles! In later years, when penicillin was a household word
and her grandchildren took it for every little thing, she would go
on and on about it. "Lucky you. Poor me. I'd just better not get
an infection, is all I can say, or come down with strep throat or
pneumonia."

Pneumonia.

There was a watery, roaring sound in her ears that made it
hard to hear her own voice. She had to wait for it to subside
before she spoke. "Dr. Vincent," she said.

"I'm here."

His hand was still on hers. It was no longer icy. He had
warmed himself on her skin as if she were a stove. She gathered
her voice and said, "Tell Ezra I'm staying."

"But—" he said.

"I know what I'm doing."

He was silent.

"Tell him," she said forcefully, "that this is nothing. You understand? I don't want any hospitals. It would kill me, just kill me to hear those loudspeakers paging doctors I have never heard of. This is just a cold. Tell him."

"Well," said Dr. Vincent. He cleared his throat. He removed his hand from hers. "Are you sure?" he asked.

"I'm sure."

He seemed to be thinking. He turned away and said to Ezra, "You hear what she says?"

"Yes," said Ezra, closer than Pearl had expected.

"I suggest we call your brother and sister, though."

Pearl felt a stirring of interest.

"But if it's that serious . . ." Ezra said.

"Let's just see what happens," the doctor told him. He laid a palm on Pearl's forehead.

After that, he must have left. The roar came back to her ears and she didn't quite hear him go. She was dwelling on thoughts of Cody and Jenny; it would be lovely to have all her children together. Then suddenly a heavy chill spread across her chest. Why, she thought. Dr. Vincent is going to allow this! Yes, he's really going to allow it. This is it, then!

Surely not.

She'd been preoccupied with death for several years now; but one aspect had never before crossed her mind: dying, you don't get to see how it all turns out. Questions you have asked will go unanswered forever. Will this one of my children settle down? Will that one be happier? Will I ever discover what was meant by such-and-such? All these years, it emerged, she'd been expecting to run into Beck again. How odd; she hadn't realized. She had also supposed that there would be some turning point, a flash of light in which she'd suddenly find out the secret; one day she'd wake up wiser and more contented and accepting. But it hadn't happened. Now it never would. She'd supposed that on her deathbed . . . deathbed! Why, that was this everyday, ordinary Posturepedic, not the ornate brass affair that she had always envisioned. She had supposed that on her deathbed, she would have something final to tell her children when they gathered round. But nothing was final. She didn't have anything to tell them. She felt a kind of shyness; she felt inadequate. She stirred her feet fretfully and searched for a cooler place on the pillow.

"Children," she had said. This was just before Cody left for college, the day she'd burned Beck's letters. She said, "Children, there's something I want to discuss with you."

Cody was talking about a job. He had to find one in order to help with the tuition fees. "I could work in the cafeteria," he was saying, "or maybe off-campus. I don't know which." Then he heard his mother and looked over at her.

"It's about your father," Pearl said.

Jenny said, "I'd choose the cafeteria."

"You know, my darlings," Pearl told them, "how I always say your father's away on business."

"But off-campus they might pay more," said Cody, "and every penny counts."

"At the cafeteria you'd be with your classmates, though," Ezra said.

"Yes, I thought of that."

"All those coeds," Jenny said. "Cheerleaders. Girls in their little white bobby sox."

"Sweater girls," Cody said.

"There's something I want to explain about your father," Pearl told them.

"Choose the cafeteria," Ezra said.

"Children?"

"The cafeteria," they said.

And all three gazed at her coolly, out of gray, unblinking, level eyes exactly like her own.

*

30

She dreamed it was her nineteenth birthday and that devilish John Dupree had brought her a tin of chocolates and a burnt-leather ornament for her hair. "Why, John, how cunning! Have a sweet," she told him. In the dream, it puzzled her to know that John Dupree had been dead for sixty-one years. He was killed in the Argonne Forest by the Huns. She remembered paying a visit of condolence to his mother, who, however, was not receiving guests. "It's all been a mistake, apparently," Pearl told John Dupree. And she fastened up her hair with the burnt-leather ornament.

"There's no question," Jenny said. "We have to call an ambulance. What's got into Dr. Vincent? Is he senile?"

"He does all right, for his age," Ezra said. As usual, he seemed to have missed some central point; even Pearl could see that. Jenny sighed, or perhaps just made some impatient rustling sound with her clothes.

"It's lucky you called me," she said. "I come and find everything falling apart."

"Nothing's falling apart."

"And why is she lying flat? She's obviously having trouble breathing. Where's that big green cushion Becky made her?"

Pearl had been skidding through time, for a moment— preparing to go by ambulance to have her arrow wound treated. She was braced for the precarious, tilting trip down the stairs on a stretcher. It was mention of Becky that set her straight. Becky was her grandchild, Jenny's oldest daughter. "Jenny?" she said.

"How are you feeling?" Jenny asked.

"Is Cody here too?"

Apparently not. Jenny leaned over the bed to give her a kiss. Pearl patted Jenny's hair and found it badly cut, choppy to the touch, but for once she didn't scold. (Jenny had lovely thick hair that she tended to ignore, to mistreat, as if looks didn't really matter.) "It was nice of you to come," Pearl told her.

"Well, goodness, I was worried," said Jenny. "You're the

only mother we have."

Pearl felt she had come full circle. "You should have got an extra," she said.

"Excuse me?"

She didn't repeat it. She turned her face on the pillow and was overtaken by a sudden jolt of anger. Why hadn't they arranged for an extra? All those years when she was the only one, the sole support, the lone tall tree in the pasture just waiting for the lightning to strike . . . well. She seemed to be losing track of her thoughts. "Did you bring the children?" she said.

"Not this time. I left them with Joe."

Joe? Oh, yes, her husband. "Why isn't Cody here?" Pearl asked.

"Well, you know," said Ezra, "it's always so hard to locate him . . ."

"We think you should go to the hospital," Jenny told Pearl.

"Oh, thank you, dear, but I don't believe I care to."

"You're not breathing right. Where's that cushion Becky made when she was little? The one with the uplifting motto," Jenny said. "*Sleep, o faithful warrior, upon thy carven pillow.*" She gave a little snort of laughter, and Pearl smiled, picturing Jenny's habit of covering her mouth with her hand as if overcome, as if struck absolutely helpless by life's silliness. "Anyhow," Jenny said, pulling herself together. "Ezra, *you* agree with me, don't you?"

"Agree?"

"About the hospital."

"Ah . . ." said Ezra.

There was a pause. You could pluck this single moment out of all time, Pearl thought, and still discover so much about her children—even about Cody, for his very absence was a characteristic, perhaps his main one. And Jenny was so brisk and breezy but . . . oh, you might say somewhat opaque, a reflecting surface flashing your own self back at you, giving no hint of *her* self. And Ezra, mild Ezra: no doubt confusedly

32

tugging at the shock of fair hair that hung over his forehead, considering and reconsidering . . . "Well," he said, "I don't know . . . I mean, maybe if we waited a while . . ."

"But how long? How long can we afford to wait?"

"Oh, maybe just till tonight, or tomorrow . . ."

"Tomorrow! What if it's, say, pneumonia?"

"Or it could be only a cold, you see."

"Yes, but—"

"And we wouldn't want her to go if it makes her unhappy."

"No, but—"

Pearl listened, smiling. She knew the outcome now. They would deliberate for hours, echoing each other's answers, repeating and rephrasing questions, evading, retreating, arguing for argument's sake, ultimately going nowhere. "You never did face up to things," she said kindly.

"Mother?"

"You always were duckers and dodgers."

"Dodgers?"

She smiled again, and closed her eyes.

It was such a relief to drift, finally. Why had she spent so long learning how? The traffic sounds—horns and bells and rags of music—flowed around the voices in her room. She kept mislaying her place in time, but it made no difference; all she remembered was equally pleasant. She remembered the feel of wind on summer nights—how it billows through the house and wafts the curtains and smells of tar and roses. How a sleeping baby weighs so heavily on your shoulder, like ripe fruit. What privacy it is to walk in the rain beneath the drip and crackle of your own umbrella. She remembered a country auction she'd attended forty years ago, where they'd offered up an antique brass bed complete with all its bedclothes—sheets and blankets, pillow in a linen case embroidered with forget-me-nots. Two men wheeled it on to the platform, and its ruffled coverlet stirred like a young girl's petticoats. Behind her eyelids, Pearl

Tull climbed in and laid her head on the pillow and was borne away to the beach, where three small children ran toward her, laughing, across the sunlit sand.

2

Teaching the Cat to Yawn

While Cody's father nailed the target to the tree trunk, Cody tested the bow. He drew the string back, laid his cheek against it, and narrowed his eyes at the target. His father was pounding in tacks with his shoe; he hadn't thought of bringing a hammer. He looked like a fool, Cody thought. He owned no weekend clothes, as other fathers did, but had driven to this field in the strained-looking brown striped salesman suit, white starched shirt, and navy tie with multicolored squares and circles scattered randomly across it. The only way you could tell this was a Sunday was when he turned, having pounded in the final tack; he didn't have his tie pulled up close to his collar. It hung loose and slightly crooked, like a drunkard's tie. A cockscomb of hair, as black as Cody's but wavy, stood up on his forehead.

"There!" he said, plodding back. He still carried the shoe. He walked lopsided, either smiling at Cody or squinting in the sunlight. It was nowhere near spring yet, but the air felt unseasonably warm and a pale sun poured heat like a liquid over Cody's shoulders. Cody bent and pulled an arrow from a cardboard tube. He laid it against the string. "Wait, now, son," his father said. "You want to do things right, now."

Naturally, this would have to be an educational experience.

There were bound to be lectures and criticisms attached. Cody sighed and lowered the bow. His father stooped to put his shoe on, squirming his foot in without undoing the laces, the way Cody's mother hated. The heel of his black rayon sock was worn so thin it was translucent. Cody looked off in another direction. He was fourteen years old—too big to be dragged on family outings any more and definitely too big for bows and arrows, unless of course you'd just leave the equipment to him and his friends, alone, and let them horse around or have themselves a contest or shatter windowpanes and streetlights for the hell of it. How did his father come up with these ideas? This was turning out to be even less successful than most. Cody's mother, who was not the slightest bit athletic, picked dried flowers beside a fence. His sister buttoned her sweater with chapped and bluish hands. His brother, Ezra, eleven years old, chewed a straw and hummed. He was missing his whistle, no doubt—a bamboo pipe, with six finger holes, on which he played tunes endlessly. He'd smuggled it along but their father had made him leave it in the car.

At that moment, Cody's two best friends were attending a movie: *Air Force*, with John Garfield and Faye Emerson. Cody would have given anything to be with them.

"Now, your left arm goes like this," his father said, positioning him. "You want to keep your wrist from getting stung, you see. And stand up straight. It was archery gave us our notions of proper posture; says so in the instruction book. Used to be that people slouched around any old how, all except the archers. I bet you didn't know that, did you?"

No, he didn't know that. He stood like something made of clay while his father poked him here and prodded him there, molding him into shape. "In the olden days . . ." his father said.

Cody let go of the bowstring. *Thwack.* The arrow hit the edge of the target, more sidewise than endwise, bounced off harmlessly and fell among the tree roots. "Now! What'd you go and do that for?" his father asked him. "Did I tell you to shoot yet? Did I?"

"It slipped," said Cody.

"Slipped!"

"And anyhow, it couldn't have stuck in the target. Not with that hard fat tree trunk behind it."

"It most certainly could have," his father said. "Like always, you just had to jump on in. Impulsive. Had to have it your way. When are you going to start keeping a better rein on yourself?"

Cody's father (who never kept any sort of rein on himself whatsoever, as Cody's mother constantly reminded him) lunged off toward the target, muttering and grabbing fistfuls of weed heads which he then threw away. Seeds and dry hulls spangled the air around him. "Willful boy; never listens. Don't know why I bother."

Cody's mother shaded her eyes and called, "Did he hit it?"

"No, he didn't hit it. How could he; I wasn't even through explaining."

"People have been known to hit a target without a person explaining it beforehand," Cody muttered.

"What say?"

"Let Ezra try," Cody's mother suggested.

His father picked up the arrow and jammed it into the bull's eye, dead center. "Want to tell me it can't stick?" he asked Cody. He pointed to the arrow, which stayed firm. "Look at that: steel-tipped. Of course it sticks. And spongy bark on the tree. I chose that tree. Of course it sticks. You could have lodged it in easy."

"Ha," said Cody, kicking a clod of earth.

"What say, son?"

"Let Ezra try," Pearl called again. "Beck? Let Ezra try."

Ezra was her favorite, her pet. The entire family knew it. Ezra looked embarrassed and switched the straw to the other side of his mouth. Beck waded back to them. "Oh, I don't know, I don't know. I wonder sometimes," he said.

"Ezra? See if you can hit it, honey," Pearl called.

Beck's glance at Cody might have been sympathy, or else disgust. He pulled another arrow from the cardboard tube. "All right, Ezra, come on and try," he said. "Just don't get carried away like Cody here did."

Ezra came over, still nibbling his straw, and accepted the bow from Cody. Well, this would be a laugh. There was no one as clumsy as Ezra. When he took his stance he did it all wrong, he just *looked* all wrong, in some way you couldn't put your finger on. His elbows jutted out, winglike; his floppy yellow hair feathered in his eyes. "Now, wait, now," Beck kept saying. "What's the trouble here?" He moved around realigning Ezra's shoulders, adjusting his grip on the bow. Ezra stayed patient. In fact, he might have had his mind on something else altogether; it seemed his attention had been caught by a cloud formation over to the south. "Oh, well," Beck said finally, giving up. "Let her fly, I guess, Ezra. Ezra?"

Ezra's fingers loosened on the string. The arrow sped in a straight, swift path, no arc to it at all. As if guided by an invisible thread—or worse, by the purest and most natural luck—it split the length of the arrow that Beck had already jammed in and it landed at the center of the bull's-eye, quivering. There was a sharp, caught silence. Then Beck said, "Will you look at that."

"Why, Ezra," Pearl said.

"Ezra," their sister Jenny cried. "Ezra, look what you did! What you went and did to that arrow!"

Ezra took the straw from his mouth. "I'm sorry," he told Beck. (He was so used to breaking things.)

"Sorry?" said Beck.

He seemed to be hunting the proper tone of voice. Then he found it. "Well, son," he said, "this just goes to show that it pays to follow instructions. See there, Cody? See what happens? A bull's-eye. I'll be damned. If you'd listened close like Ezra did, and not gone off half-cocked . . ."

He was moving toward the target as he spoke, oaring

through the weeds, and Jenny was running to get there first. Cody couldn't take his turn at shooting, therefore, although he was itching to. He was absolutely obligated to split that second arrow as Ezra had split the first. It was unthinkable not to. What were the odds against it? He felt a springy twanging inside, as if he himself were the bowstring. He bent down and pulled a new arrow from the tube and fitted it to the bow. He drew and aimed at a clump of shrubbery, then at his father's dusty blue Nash, and then at Ezra, who was already wandering off again dreamy as ever. Longingly, Cody focused on Ezra's fair, ruffled head. "Zing. *Wham.* Aagh, you got me!" he said. Imagine the satisfaction. Ezra turned slowly and caught sight of him. "No!" he cried.

"Huh?"

Ezra ran toward him, flapping his arms like an idiot and stammering, "Stop, stop, stop! No! Stop!" Did he really think Cody would shoot him? Cody stared, keeping the bow drawn. Ezra took a flying leap with his arms outstretched like a lover. He caught Cody in a kind of bear hug and slammed him flat on his back. It knocked the wind out of Cody; all he could do was gasp beneath Ezra's warm, bony weight. And meanwhile, what had happened to the arrow? It was minutes before he could struggle to a sitting position, elbowing Ezra off of him. He looked across the field and found his mother leaning on his father's arm, hobbling in his direction with a perfect circle of blood gleaming on the shoulder of her blouse. "Pearl, my God. Oh, Pearl," his father was saying. Cody turned and looked at Ezra, whose face was pale and shocked. "See there?" Cody asked him. "See what you've gone and done?"

"Did *I* do that?"

"Gone and done it to me again," Cody said, and he staggered to his feet and walked away.

On a weekday when his father was out of town, his mother shopping for supper, his brother and sister doing homework in their rooms, Cody took his BB gun and shot a hole in the kitchen window. Then he slipped outdoors and poked a length of fishing line through the hole. From the kitchen, he pulled the line until the rusty wrench that he'd tied to the other end was flush against the outside of the glass. He held it there by anchoring the line beneath a begonia pot. When his mother returned from shopping, Cody was seated at the kitchen table coloring a map of Asia.

After their homework was finished, Jenny and Ezra went out back. Ezra had been showing Jenny, all week, how to hit a softball. (It seemed her classmates chose her last whenever they had a game.) As soon as they had walked through, Cody rose and went to the window. He saw them take their places in the darkening yard, bounded on either side by the neighbors' hedges. They were a comically short distance apart. Jenny stood closest to the house and held her bat straight up, gingerly, as if preparing to club to death some small animal. Ezra tossed her a gentle pitch. (He was no great player himself.) Jenny took a whizzing swing, missed, and retrieved the ball from among the trash cans beside the back door. She threw it in an overhand so stiff and deformed that Cody wondered why Ezra bothered. Ezra caught it and pitched again. As the ball arched toward the bat, Cody felt for the fishing line beneath the begonia pot. He gave a quick tug. The windowpane clattered inward, breaking in several pieces. Jenny spun around and stared. Ezra's mouth dropped open. "What was that?" Pearl called from the dining room.

"Just Ezra breaking another window," Cody told her.

One weekend their father didn't come home, and he didn't come the next weekend either, or the next. Or rather, one morning Cody woke up and saw that it had been a while since their father was around. He couldn't say that he had noticed from the start. His mother offered no excuses. Cody, watchful as a spy, studied her furrowed, distracted expression and the way that her hands plucked at each other. It troubled him to realize that he couldn't picture his father's most recent time with them. Trying to find some scene that would explain Beck's leaving, he could only come up with *general* scenes, blended from a dozen repetitions: meals shattered by quarrels, other meals disrupted when Ezra spilled his milk, drives in the country where his father lost the way and his mother snapped out pained and exasperated directions. He thought of once when the Nash's radiator had erupted in steam and his father, looking helpless, had flung his suit coat over it. "Oh, honestly," his mother had said. But that was way back; it was years ago, wasn't it? Cody journeyed through the various cubbies and crannies of the house, hunting up the trappings of his father's "phases" (as his mother called them). There were the badminton racquets, the butterfly net, the archery set, the camera with its unwieldy flashgun, and the shoe box full of foreign stamps still in their glassine envelopes. But it meant nothing that these objects remained behind. What was alarming was his father's half of the bureau: an empty sock drawer, an empty underwear drawer. In the shirt drawer, one unused sports shirt, purchased by the three children for Beck's last birthday, his forty-fourth. And a full assortment of pajamas; but then, he always slept in his underwear. In the wardrobe, just a hanger strung with ties—his oldest, dullest, most frayed and spotted ties—and a pair of shoes so ancient that the toes curled up.

Cody's brother and sister were staggeringly unobservant. They flitted in and out of the house like birds—Ezra playing his whistle, Jenny singing parts of jump-rope songs. Cody had the impression that musical notes filled their heads to over-flowing; they left no room for anything serious. *Auntie Sue got dressed in blue*, Jenny sang, *put on shoes and rubbers too* . . . Her plain, flat voice and heedlessly swinging braids somehow reassured him. After all, what could go so wrong, when she skipped past with her ragged rope? What could go so very wrong?

Then one Saturday she said, "I'm worried about Daddy."

41

"Why?" Cody asked.

"Cody," she said, in her elderly way, "you can see that he doesn't come home any more. I think he's left us."

"Don't be silly," Cody told her.

She surveyed him for a moment, with a composure that made him uneasy, and when he didn't say any more she turned and went out on the porch. He heard the glider creak as she settled into it. But she didn't start singing. In fact, the house was unusually quiet. The only sound was his mother's heels, clicking back and forth overhead as she put away the laundry. And Ezra wasn't playing his whistle. Cody had no idea where Ezra was.

He went upstairs to his mother's bedroom. She was folding a sheet. "What're you doing?" he asked. She gave him a look. He settled in a ladder-backed chair to watch her work. She was wearing a housedress that he very much disliked, cream colored with deep red streaks across it like paintbrush strokes. The shoulders were shaped by triangular pads that unbuttoned and removed when it was time to wash the dress. Cody had often thought of stealing those pads. With her shoulders broadened, his mother looked powerful and sharp and scary. On her feet were open-toed shoes and short white socks. She traveled rapidly between the laundry basket and the bed, laying out stacks of clothing. There was no stack for his father.

"When is Dad coming home?" he asked.

"Oh," she said, "pretty soon."

She didn't meet his eyes.

Cody looked around him and noticed, for the first time, that there was something pinched and starved about the way this house was decorated. Not a single perfume bottle or china figurine sat upon his mother's bureau. No pictures hung on the walls. Even the bedside tables were completely bare; and in all the drawers in this room, he knew, every object would be aligned and squared precisely—the clothing organized by type and color, whites grading into pastels and then to darks; comb and brush parallel; gloves paired and folded like a row of clenched fists. Who *wouldn't* leave such a place? He straightened, feeling panicky. His mother chose that moment to come over and smooth his hair down. "My," she told him, smiling, "you're getting so big! I can't believe it."

He shrank back in his seat.

"You're getting big enough for me to start relying on," she said.

"I'm only fourteen," Cody told her.

He slipped off the chair and left the room. The bathroom door was closed; he heard the shower running and Ezra singing "Greensleeves." He opened the door just a crack, snaked one arm in, and turned on the hot water in the sink. Then he traveled through the rest of the house, from kitchen to downstairs bathroom to basement, methodically opening every hot water faucet to its fullest. But you couldn't really say his heart was in it.

"Tull?" the man asked.

"Yes."

"Is this the Tull residence?"

"Yes, it is."

"Darryl Peters," the man said, showing a business card.

Cody took a swig of beer and accepted the card. While he was reading it, he sloshed the beer bottle absently to get a good head of suds. He was wearing dungarees and nothing else; it was a blistering day in August. The house, however, was fairly cool—the living room dim, the paper shades pulled all the way down and glowing yellow with the afternoon sun. Mr. Peters looked in wistfully, but remained on the porch with his hat in his hand. He was way overdressed, for August.

"So," said Cody. He nudged the screen door open with his bare foot. Mr. Peters caught hold of it and stepped inside.

"Would your mother be in?" he asked.

"She's taken a job."

"Well, then, your . . . is Ezra Tull your father?"

"He's my brother."

"Brother. Ah."

"*He's* in."

"Well, then," Mr. Peters said.

"I'll go get him."

Cody went upstairs and into Jenny's room. Jenny and Ezra were playing checkers on the floor. Ezra, wearing shorts and a sleeveless undershirt full of holes, stroked his cat, Alicia, and frowned at the board. "Someone to see you," Cody told him.

Ezra looked up. "Who is it?" he asked.

Cody shrugged.

Ezra rose, still hugging the cat. Cody went with him as far as the stairs. He stopped there and leaned over the banister to eavesdrop, grinning. Ezra arrived in the living room. "You want *me?*" Cody heard him ask.

"Ezra Tull?" said Mr. Peters.

"Yes."

"Well, ah . . . maybe there's been a mistake."

"What kind of mistake?"

"I'm from Peaceful Hills Memorial Gardens," Mr. Peters said. "I thought you wished to purchase a resting place."

"Resting place?"

"I thought you filled out this mail-in coupon: Ezra Tull, your signature. *Yes, I would like an eternal home for myself and/or my loved ones. I understand that a sales representative will call.*"

"It wasn't me," said Ezra.

"You didn't fill this out. You're not interested in a plot."

"No, thank you."

"I should have known," said Mr. Peters.

"I'm sorry," Ezra told him.

"Never mind, I can see it's not your doing."

"Maybe when I'm older, or something . . ."

"That's all right, son. Never mind."

44

Cody climbed to the stuffy, hot third floor, where Lorena Schmidt sat on his bed with her back against the wall. She was new to the neighborhood—a tawny girl with long black hair, one lock of which she was twining around a finger. "Who was that?" she asked Cody.

"A cemetery salesman."

"Ugh."

"He came to see Ezra."

"Who's Ezra?"

"My *brother* Ezra, dummy."

"Well? How should I know?" Lorena said. "You mean that brother downstairs? Blondish kid, good-looking?"

"Good-looking! Ezra?"

"I liked his kind of serious face," Lorena said. "And those pale gray eyes."

"*My* eyes are gray."

"Well. Anyhow," Lorena said.

"Besides," said Cody, "he gets fits."

"He does?"

"He'll fool you. He'll look as normal as anyone else and then all of a sudden, splat! He's flat on the floor, foaming at the mouth."

"I don't believe you," Lorena said.

"Some people think he's dangerous. I'm the only one brave enough to go near him, when he gets that way."

"I don't believe a word of it," Lorena said.

She twisted around to the head of Cody's bed and lifted a corner of the window shade. "I see your mother coming," she said.

"What? Where?"

She turned and flashed him a grin. One of her front teeth was chipped, which made her look unstable, lacking in self-control. "I was teasing," she said.

"Oh."

"You ought to've seen your face. Ha! I haven't even met

your mother. How would I know if she was coming?"

"You must have met her," Cody said. "She's a cashier now at Sweeney Brothers Grocery. Folks around this neighborhood call her the Sweeney Meanie."

"Well, we do our shopping at Esmond's."

"So would I," said Cody.

"How come she works? Where's your father?"

"Missing in action," he told her.

"Oops, sorry."

He gave her a casual wave of his hand and took a swallow of beer. "She runs the cash register," he said. "Look in Sweeney's window, next time you go past. You'll know her right off. Walk in and say, 'Ma'am, this soup can's dented. Can I have a reduction?' 'Soup's soup,' she'll say. 'Full price, please.'"

"Oh, one of those," Lorena said.

"Tight little bun on the back of her head. Mouth like it's holding straight pins. Anybody dawdles, tries to pass the time of day, she'll say, 'Move along, please. Please move along.'"

He was smiling at Lorena as he spoke, but inside he felt a sudden pang. He pictured his mother at the register, with that anxious line like a strand of hair or a faint, fragile dressmaker's seam running across her forehead.

Cody took every blanket and sheet from Ezra's bed and removed the pillow and the mattress. Underneath were four wooden slats, laid across the frame. He lifted them out and stored them in the wardrobe. With great care, he set the mattress back on the frame. He drew a breath and waited. The mattress held. He replaced the bedclothes and he puffed the pillow and laid it delicately at the head. He lugged a pile of magazines from their hiding place in his bureau, opened them, and scattered them on the floor. Then he turned off the light and went to his own bed, across the room.

Ezra padded in barefoot, eating a sandwich. He wore pajama bottoms with a trailing drawstring. "Oh, me," he said, and he sank into bed. There was a crash. The floor shook, and their mother shrieked and came pounding up the stairs. When she turned on the light, Cody raised his head and stared at her with a sleepy, befuddled expression. She had a hand pressed to her heart. She was taking in gulps of air. Jenny shivered behind her, hugging a worn stuffed rabbit. "Good Lord preserve us," their mother said.

Ezra looked like someone in a bathtub full of cloth. He was having trouble disentangling himself from the sheets. One hand, upraised, still clutched the half-eaten sandwich. "Ezra, honey," Pearl said, but then she said, "Why, Ezra." She was looking at the magazines. They were opened to pictures of women in nightgowns, in bathing suits, in garter belts and black lace brassieres, in bath towels, in useless wisps of transparent drapery, or in nothing whatsoever. "Ezra Tull!" she said.

Ezra worked his way up to peer over the edge of his bed frame.

"Truly, Ezra, I never suspected that you would be such a person," she told him. Then she turned and left the room, taking Jenny with her.

Ezra emerged from his bed, flew through the air, and landed on Cody. He grabbed a handful of hair and started shaking Cody's head. All Cody could say was, "Mmf! Mmf!" because he didn't want their mother to hear. Finally he managed to bite Ezra's knee and Ezra rolled off, panting and sobbing. He must have knocked into something at some earlier point, because his left eye was swelling. It made him look sad. Cody got up and showed him where he'd stashed the slats. They fitted them into place, heaved the mattress back on the frame, and attempted to smooth the blankets. Then Cody turned out the light, and they climbed into their beds and went to sleep.

Sometimes Cody dreamed about his father. He would be stepping through the doorway, wearing one of his salesman suits, bringing the afternoon paper as he always did on Friday. His ordinariness was astounding—his thick strings of hair and the tired, yellowish puffs beneath his eyes. (In waking memories, lately, he was not so real, but had blurred and leveled and lost his details.) "How was your week?" he asked, tediously. Cody's mother answered, "Oh, all right."

In these dreams, Cody was not his present self. He had somehow slid backward and become a toddler again, rushing around on tiny, fat legs, feverishly showing off. "See this? And this? See me somersault? See me pull my wagon?" His smallness colored every act; he was conscious of a desperate need to learn to *manage*, to take charge of his surroundings. Waking in the dark, the first thing he did was stretch his long legs and lift his arms, which were becoming veiny and roped with muscle. He thought of how it would be if his father returned some time in the future, when Cody was a man. "Look at what I've accomplished," Cody would tell him. "Notice where I've got to, how far I've come without you."

Was it something I said? Was it something I did? Was it something I didn't do, that made you go away?

School started, and Cody entered ninth grade. He and his two best friends landed in the same homeroom. Sometimes Pete and Boyd came home with him; they all walked the long way, avoiding the grocery store where Cody's mother worked. Cody had to keep things separate—his friends in one half of his life and his family in the other half. His mother hated for Cody to mix with outsiders. "Why don't you ever have someone over?" she would ask, but she didn't deceive him for a moment. He'd say, "Nah, I don't need anybody," and she would look pleased. "I guess your family's enough for you, isn't it?" she would ask. "Aren't we lucky to have each other?"

He only allowed his friends in the house when his mother was at work, and sometimes for no reason he could name he would lead them through her belongings. He would open her smallest top drawer and show them the real gold brooch that his

48

father had given her when they were courting. "He thinks a lot of her," he would say. "He's given her heaps of stuff. Heaps. There's heaps of other stuff that I just don't happen to have on hand." His friends looked bored. Switching tactics, Cody would show them her ironed handkerchiefs stacked so exactly that they seemed encased by an invisible square box. "I mean," he said, "*your* mothers don't do that, do they? Do they? Women!" he said, and then, musing over some mysterious metal clasp or something that was evidently used to hold up stockings, "Who can understand them? Really: can you figure them out? She likes Ezra best, my dumb brother Ezra. Sissy old Ezra. I mean, if it were Jenny, I could see it—Jenny being a girl and all. But Ezra! Who could like Ezra? Can you give me a single reason why?"

His friends shrugged, idly gazing around the room and jingling the loose change in their pockets.

He hid Ezra's left sneaker, his arithmetic homework, his baseball mitt, his fountain pen, and his favorite sweater. He shut Ezra's cat in the linen cupboard. He took Ezra's bamboo whistle to school and put it in the jacket of Josiah Payson, Ezra's best friend—a wild-eyed boy, the size of a full-grown man, who was thought by some to be feebleminded. It was typical of Ezra that he loved Josiah with all his heart, and would even have had him to the house if their mother weren't scared of him. Cody stopped by when Ezra's class was at lunch, and he slipped behind the cloakroom partition and stuck the whistle in the pocket of Josiah's enormous black peacoat. After that there was a stretch of Indian summer and Josiah evidently left his jacket where it hung, so the whistle stayed lost for days. Ezra was very upset about it. "Have you seen my whistle?" he asked everybody. For once, Cody didn't have to listen to "Greensleeves" and "The Ash Grove," played on that breathy little pipe, whose range was so limited that for high notes, Ezra had to blow extra hard and split people's eardrums. "You took it," Ezra told

Cody. "Didn't you? I know you did."

"What would I want with a stupid toy whistle?" Cody asked.

He was hoping that when it turned up in Josiah Payson's pocket, Ezra would blame Josiah. But it didn't happen that way. Whatever passed between them was settled without any fuss, and the two of them continued to be friends. Once again, a cracked, foggy "Ash Grove" burbled in every corner of the house.

Their mother went on one of her rampages. "Pearl has hit the warpath," Cody told his brother and sister. He always called her Pearl at such times. "Better look out," he said. "She's dumped all Jenny's bureau drawers."

"Oh-oh," Ezra said.

"She's slamming things around and talking to herself."

"*Oh*, boy," Jenny said.

Cody had met the other two on the porch; they'd stayed late at school. He silently opened the door for them, and they crept up the stairs. Each took a great, lunging stride over the step that creaked—although surely their mother would not have heard them. She was making too much noise in the kitchen. Throwing pots through windowpanes, was what it sounded like.

They tiptoed across the hall to Jenny's room. "What a mess!" Ezra breathed. Heaps of clothing covered the floor. Empty drawers had been hurled everywhere. The wardrobe stood open, its hangers stripped, and Jenny's puff-sleeved dresses lay in a heap. Jenny stared from the doorway. "Jen?" Cody asked her. "What did you do?"

"Nothing," Jenny said in a quavery voice.

"Think! Some little thing, something you've forgotten about . . ."

"Nothing. I promise."

"Well, help me get these drawers back in," he said to Ezra.

It was a two-man job. The drawers were oak, cumbersome and inclined to stick. Cody and Ezra grunted as they fitted them into the bureau. Jenny traveled around the room collecting her clothes. Tears had filled her eyes, and she kept dapping at her nose with one or another rolled pair of socks. "Stop that," Cody told her. "She'll do it all again, if she finds snot on your socks."

He and Ezra gathered slips and hair ribbons, shook out blouses, tried to get the dresses back on their hangers the way they'd been before. Some were hopelessly wrinkled, and those they smoothed as best they could and hid at the rear of the wardrobe. Meanwhile Jenny knelt on the floor, sniffling and folding undershirts.

"I wish we could just go off," Ezra said, "and not come back till it's over."

"It won't be over till she's had her scene," Cody told him. "You know that. There's no way we can get around it."

"I wish Daddy were here."

"Well, he's not, so shut up."

Ezra straightened a sash.

After they'd put everything in order, the three of them sat in a row on Jenny's bed. The sounds from the kitchen were different now—cutlery rattling, glassware clinking. Their mother must be setting the table. Pretty soon she'd serve supper. Cody had such a loaded feeling in his throat, he never wanted to eat again. No doubt the others felt the same; Ezra kept swallowing. Jenny said, "Let's run away from home."

"We don't have anyplace to run to," Cody said.

Their mother came to the foot of the stairs and called them. Her voice was thin, like the sound of a gnat. "Children."

They filed down, dragging their feet. They stopped at the first-floor bathroom and meticulously scrubbed their hands, taking extra pains with the backs. Each one waited for the others. Then they went into the kitchen. their mother was slicing a brick of Spam. She didn't look at them, but she started speaking the instant they were seated. "It's not enough that I should have to work till five p.m., no; then I come home and find nothing seen to, no chores done, you children off till all hours with disreputable characters in the alleys or wasting your time with school chorus, club meetings; table not set, breakfast dishes not washed, supper not cooked, floors not swept, mail in a heap on the mat . . . and not a sign of any of you. Oh, I know what's going on! I know what you three are up to! Neighborhood savages, that's what you are, mingling with each and all. How am I supposed to deal with this? How am I expected to cope? Useless daughter, great unruly bruising boys . . . *I* know what people are saying. You think my customers aren't glad to tell me? Coming in simpering, 'Well, Mrs. Tull, that oldest boy of yours is certainly growing up. I saw him with a pack of Camels in the street in front of the Barlow girl's house.' And I have to smile and take it. Have to stand there on exhibit while they're all thinking, 'Poor Mrs. Tull, I don't know how she can hold her head up. It's clear she doesn't have the least ability to handle those children; look at how they're disgracing her.' Sticking potatoes on people's exhaust pipes and letting the air out of tires and shooting at streetlights with BB guns and stealing hubcaps and making off with traffic signs and moving Mrs. Correlli's madonna to Sonny Boy Brown's kitchen stoop and hanging around the hydrants with girls no better than tramps, girls in tight sweaters and ankle chains, oh, I hear about it everywhere . . ."

"But not me, Mama," Jenny said.

"I beg your pardon?"

"I don't do those things."

Well, of course she didn't (only Cody did), but she shouldn't have pointed that out. Now she'd drawn attention to herself. Pearl turned, gathered force, and plunged. "You! I know about you. I couldn't believe my ears. What should I be doing but coming down the church steps Sunday when I see you with that Melanie Miller from your Bible class. 'Oh, Melanie . . .'" She made her voice shrill and prissy, nothing like Jenny's, really. "'Melanie, I just love your dress. I wish *I* had a dress like that.' Understand," she said, turning to the boys, "this was a cheap little number from Sears. The plaid wasn't matched; there was a ruffle at the hem like a . . . square dance outfit and a bunch of artificial flowers pinned to the waist. A totally inappropriate dress for a nine-year-old, or for anyone. But 'Oh, I wish I had that,' your sister says, so everyone thinks, 'Poor Mrs. Tull, she can't even afford a Sears and Roebuck dress with artificial flowers; I don't know how she manages, slaving away at that grocery all day and struggling over her budget at night, cutting here and cutting there, wondering will she scrape by, hoping nobody runs up a doctor bill, praying her children's feet will stop growing . . .'

"And Melanie's mother, well it's just like opening the door to such a person. First thing you know she'll be walking in here big as life: 'Mrs. Tull, I happen to have the catalogue we ordered Melanie's dress from, if you would care for one for Jenny.' As if I'd want to dress my daughter like an orphan! As if I'd like for her to duplicate some other child! 'No, thank you, Mrs. Miller,' I'll say. 'I may not be able to afford so very much but at least when I do buy, I buy with finished seams. No, Mrs. Miller, you keep your so-called wish book, your quarter-inch hem allowances, smashed felt flowers . . .' What's wrong with us, I'd like to know? Aren't we good enough for my own blood daughter? Doesn't she feel I'm doing my best, my level best, to provide? Does she have to pick up riffraff? Does she have to bring home scum? We're a family! We used to be so close! What happened to us? Why would she act so disloyal?"

She sat down serenely, as if finished with the subject forever, and reached for a bowl of peas. Jenny's face was streaming with tears, but she wasn't making a sound and Pearl seemed unaware of her. Cody cleared his throat.

"But that was Sunday," he said.

Pearl's serving spoon paused, midway between the bowl and her plate. She looked politely interested. "Yes?" she said.

"This is Wednesday."

"Yes."

"It's Wednesday, dammit; it's three days later. So why bring up something from Sunday?"

Pearl threw the spoon in his face. "You upstart," she said. She rose and slapped him across the cheek. "You wretch, you ugly horror." She grabbed one of Jenny's braids and yanked it so Jenny was pulled off her chair. "Stupid clod," she said to Ezra, and she took the bowl of peas and brought it down on his head. It didn't break, but peas flew everywhere. Ezra cowered, shielding his head with his arms. "Parasites," she told them. "I wish you'd all die, and let me go free. I wish I'd find you dead in your beds."

After that, she went upstairs. The three of them washed the dishes, dried them, and put them away in the cupboards. They wiped the table and countertops and swept the kitchen floor. The sight of any crumb or stain was a relief, a pleasure; they attacked it with Bon Ami. They pulled the shades in the windows and locked the back door. Outside, the neighborhood children were organizing a game of hide-and-seek, but their voices were so faint that they seemed removed in time as well as in space. They were like people from long ago, laughing and calling only in memory, or in one of those eerily lifelike dreams that begin on the edge of sleep.

Shortly before Thanksgiving, a girl named Edith Taber transferred to their school. Cody had been new to so many schools himself, he recognized that defiant tilt of the head when she stepped into his homeroom. She carried a zippered notebook that wasn't the right kind at all, and over her skirt she wore what appeared to be a grown man's shirt, which no one had ever heard of doing. But she had thick black hair and the kind of gypsy look that Cody liked; and he was also drawn by the proud and scornful way she walked alone to her classes—as friendless as Cody was, he thought, or at least, as friendless as he felt inside. So that afternoon he walked a short distance behind her (it turned out she lived just one block north of him), and the next

54

afternoon he caught up and walked beside her. She seemed to welcome his company and talked to him nearly nonstop, every now and then clutching her coat collar tight against her throat in a gesture that struck him as sophisticated. Her brother was in the navy, she said, and had promised to bring her a silk kimono if he made it through the war. And she didn't find that Baltimore was very cosmopolitan, and she thought Miss Saunders, the English teacher, resembled Lana Turner. She said she felt it was really attractive when boys didn't slick their hair back but let it fall over their foreheads, straight, the way Cody did. Cody raked his fingers through his hair and said, well, he didn't know about that; he'd always sort of supposed that girls preferred a little wave or curl or something. She said she just despised for a boy to have curls. They walked the rest of the way without speaking, although from time to time Cody whistled parts of the only tune that came to his mind, which happened to be "The Ash Grove."

He couldn't walk her home on Wednesday because he had to stay late for detention, and the following day was Thanksgiving. There wouldn't be any more school till Monday. All Thursday morning, he hung around the front porch in the damp November chill, gazing northward to Edith's street and then wheeling away and taking midair punches at a cushion from the glider. Finally his mother emerged, rosy from the kitchen, and coaxed him inside. "Cody, honey, you'll freeze to death. Come and shell me some pecans." They were having a meager meal — no turkey — but she'd promised to make a pie for dessert. Already the house smelled different: spicier, more festive. Cody would have stayed on the porch forever, though, if he'd thought there was a chance of seeing Edith.

After dinner they all played Monopoly. Generally, Cody's family didn't allow him in their games; he had this problem with winning. He absolutely insisted on winning any game he played. And he did win too — by sheer fierceness, by caring the most. (Also, he'd been known to cheat.) Sometimes, he would even win when no one else suspected it was a contest. He would eat more peanuts, get his corn shucked the fastest, or finish his page of the comics first. "Go away," his family would say when he approached (nonchalantly shuffling cards or tossing a pair of dice). "You know what we said. Never again!" But this afternoon, they let him play. He tried to hold back, but once he'd bought a hotel on the Boardwalk, things got out of hand. "Oh, my, I should have remembered," his mother said. "What's he doing in this game?" But she was smiling. She wore her blue wool dress and her hair was coming out of its bun, which made her look relaxed. Her token was the flatiron. She skipped right over the Boardwalk, but Ezra was next and he hit it. He didn't have anywhere near enough money. Cody tried to lend him some; he hated it when people just gave up. He liked to get everybody thousands of dollars in debt, struggling to the bitter end. But Ezra said, "No, no, I quit," and backed off, holding up one palm in that old-mannish way he had. So Cody had to go on with just Jenny and his mother, and eventually with just his mother. They played right down to the line, when she landed on the Boardwalk with three dollar bills to her name. As a matter of fact, Cody had a pretty good time.

Then the younger two talked Cody and Pearl into putting on their old skit: "The Mortgage Overdue." "Oh, come on! Please! It wouldn't feel like a holiday without it." Cody and Pearl ended up agreeing to it, even though they were rusty and Cody couldn't remember the dance step that came at the finish. This was something salvaged from his mother's girlhood, the kind of piece performed at amateur recital contests or campfire circles. Pearl played Ivy, the maiden in distress, and Cody was the villain twirling his waxed mustache. *Ivy, sweet sweet Ivy, lean upon my arm,* he cajoled her with an evil leer, while Pearl rolled her eyes and shrank into a corner. She could have been an actress, her children thought; she had it letter-perfect, the blushing gaze and the old-fashioned singsong of her responses. At the end the hero came and rescued her. Ezra and Jenny always claimed to be too shy, so Cody had to take the hero's part as well. "*I will pay the money for the mortgage on the farm,*" he told the maiden, and he danced her into the dining room. The dance step came back to him after all, but his mother's tongue got twisted and instead of *wedded life* she said *leaded wife* and collapsed in a heap of giggles. Jenny and Ezra gave them three curtain calls.

That evening, Cody went out to the porch and looked northward some more in the twilight. Ezra came too and sat in the glider, pushing back and forth with the heel of one sneaker. "Want to walk toward Sloop Street?" Cody asked him.

"What's on Sloop Street?"

"Nothing much. This girl I know, Edith Taber."

"Oh, yes. Edith," Ezra said.

"You know who she is?"

"She's got this whistle," Ezra said, "that plays sharps and flats with hardly any extra trouble."

"Edith *Taber?*"

"A recorder."

"You're thinking of someone else," Cody told him.

"Well, maybe so."

Cody was silent a moment, leaning on the porch railing. Ezra creaked companionably in the glider. Then Cody said, "A black-haired girl. Ninth-grader."

"New in town," Ezra agreed.

"When'd you see her?"

"Just yesterday," Ezra said. "I was walking home from school, playing my whistle, and she caught up with me and said she liked it and asked if I wanted to see her recorder. So I went to her house and I saw it."

"To her *house?* Did she know you were my brother?"

"Well, no, I don't think so," Ezra said. "She has a parakeet that burps and says, 'Forgive me.' Her mother served us cookies."

57

"You met her mother?"

"It would be nice to have a recorder, someday."

"She's too old for you," Cody said.

Ezra looked surprised. "Well, of course," he said. "She's fourteen and a half."

"What would she want with a little sixth-grader?"

"She wanted to show me her whistle," Ezra said.

"Shoot," said Cody.

"Cody? Are we going to walk toward Sloop Street?"

"Nah," said Cody. He kicked a pillar.

"If I asked Mother," Ezra said, "do you think she would get me one of those recorders for Christmas?"

"You dunce," said Cody. "You raving idiot. Do you think she's got money to spare for goddamn *whistles?*"

"Well, no, I guess not," Ezra said.

Then Cody went into the house and locked the door, and when Ezra started pounding on it Cody told their mother it was only Mr. Milledge, having one of his crazy spells.

Monday morning, he looked for Edith on the way to school but he didn't see her. As it turned out, she was tardy. She arrived in homeroom just after the bell. He tried to catch her eye but she didn't glance his way; only gazed fixedly at the teacher all during announcements. And when the first bell rang she walked to class with Sue Meeks and Harriet Smith. Evidently, she was no longer friendless.

By third period, it was clear she was avoiding him. He couldn't even get near her; she had a constant bodyguard. But what had he done wrong? He cornered Barbara Pace—a plump, cheerful redhead who served as a kind of central switchboard for ninth-grade couples. "What's the matter with Edith?" he asked.

"Who?"

"Edith Taber. We were getting along just fine and now she won't speak."

"Oh," she said. She shifted her books. She was wearing a man-sized shirt with the tails out. Come to think of it, so were half the other girls. "Well," she said, "I guess she likes somebody else now."

"Is it my brother?" Cody asked.

"Who's your brother?"

"Ezra. My brother, Ezra."

"I didn't know you had a brother," she said, peering at him.

"Well, she liked me well enough last week. What happened?"

"See," she told him patiently, "now she's been to a couple of parties and naturally she's developed new interests. She's got a sort of . . . broader view, and also she didn't realize about your reputation."

"What reputation?"

"Well, you do drink, Cody. And you hung around with that cheap Lorena Schmidt all summer; you smell like a walking cigarette; and you almost got arrested over Halloween."

"Did my brother tell her that?"

"What's this about your brother? Everybody told her. It's not exactly a secret."

"Well, I never claimed to be a saint," Cody said.

"She says you're real good-looking and all but she wants a boy she can respect," said Barbara. "She thinks she might like Francis Elburn now."

"Francis Elburn! That fairy."

"He's really more her type," said Barbara.

"His hair is curly."

"So?"

"Francis Elburn; Jesus Christ."

"There's no need to use profanity," Barbara told him.

Cody walked home alone, long after the others had left, choosing streets where he'd be certain not to run into Edith or her friends. Once he turned down the wrong alley and it struck him that he was still an outsider, unfamiliar with the neighborhood. His classmates had been born and raised here, most of them, and were more comfortable with each other than he could ever hope to be. Look at his two best friends: their parents went to the movies together; their mothers talked on the telephone. *His* mother . . . He kicked a signpost. What he wouldn't give to have a mother who acted like other mothers! He longed to see her gossiping with a little gang of women in the kitchen, letting them roll her hair up in pincurls, trading beauty secrets, playing cards, losing track of time—"Oh, goodness, look at the clock! And supper not even started; my husband will kill me. Run along, girls." He wished she had some outside connection, something beyond that suffocating house.

And his father: he had uprooted the family continually, tearing them away as soon as they were settled and plunking them someplace new. But where was he now that Cody *wanted* to be uprooted, now that he was saddled with a reputation and desperate to leave and start over? His father had ruined their lives, Cody thought—first in one way and then in another. He thought of tracking him down and arriving on his doorstep: "I'm in trouble; it's all your fault. I've got a bad name, I need to leave town, you'll have to take me in." But that would only be another unknown city, another new school to walk into alone. And there too, probably, his grades would begin to slip and the neighbors would complain and the teachers would start to suspect him first when any little thing went wrong; and then Ezra would follow shortly in his dogged, earnest, devoted way and everybody would say to Cody, "Why can't you be more like your brother?"

He let himself into the house, which smelled of last night's cabbage. It was almost dark and the air seemed thick; he felt he had to labor to move through it. He climbed the stairs wearily. He passed Jenny's room, where she sat doing her homework in a tiny dull circle of yellow from the lamp. Her face was thin and shadowed and she didn't bother greeting him. He climbed on up to his own room and flicked on the light switch. He had set his books on the bureau before he realized Ezra was there. Asleep, as usual — curled on his bed with a sheaf of homework papers. Oh, Ezra was so slow and dazed; he could sleep anytime. His lips were parted. His cat, Alicia, lay in the crook of his arm, purring and looking self-satisfied.

Cody knelt beside his bed and pulled from beneath it a half-filled bottle of bourbon, an empty gin bottle, five empty beer bottles, a crumpled pack of Camels, and a box of pretzels. He strewed them around Ezra, arranging them just right. He went to the hall storage closet and took out his father's Six-20 Brownie camera. In the doorway of his room, he aimed and paused and clicked the shutter. Ezra didn't wake, amazingly enough. (The light from the flashgun was so powerful, you'd see swimming blue globes for minutes after being photographed.) But the cat seemed mildly disturbed. She got to her feet and yawned. What a yawn! — huge and disdainful. It would have made a wonderful picture: deadbeat Ezra and his no-account cat, both with gaping mouths. Cody wondered if she'd do it again. "Yawn," he told her, and he advanced the film for another photo. "Alicia? Yawn." She only smirked and settled down again. He yawned himself, demonstrating, but apparently cats didn't find such things contagious. He lowered the camera and came closer to pat her head, scratch beneath her chin, stroke her throat. Nothing worked. "Yawn, dammit," he said, and he tried to pry her teeth apart by force. She drew up sharply, eyes wide and glaring. Ezra woke.

"Your cat is *retarded*," Cody told him.

"Huh?"

"I can't get her to yawn."

Ezra reached over, matter-of-factly, and circled the cat with his arm. She gave a luxurious yawn and nestled down against him, and Ezra went back to sleep. Cody didn't try for another picture, though. He'd never seen anyone take the fun out of things the way Ezra did.

*

61

Cody and Ezra and Jenny went shopping for a Christmas present for their mother. Each of them had saved four weeks' allowance, which meant forty cents apiece, and Cody had a dollar extra that he'd taken from Miss Saunders's center desk drawer. That made two dollars and twenty cents—enough for some winter gloves, Cody suggested. Jenny said gloves were boring and she wanted to buy a diamond ring. "That's really stupid," Cody told her. "Even you ought to know you can't buy a diamond ring for two-twenty."

"I don't mean a real one, I mean glass. Or anything, just so it's pretty and not useful."

They were forced to shop in the stores near home, since they didn't want to spend money on carfare. It was mid-December and crowds of other people were shopping too—plowing past with their arms full of packages, breathing white clouds in the frosty air. Further downtown the department store windows would be as rich and bright as the insides of jewel boxes, and there'd be carols and clanging brass bells and festoons of tinsel on the traffic lights, but in this neighborhood the shops were smaller, darker, decorated with a single wreath on the door or a cardboard Santa Claus carrying a carton of Chesterfield cigarettes. Soldiers on leave straggled by in clumps, looking lost. The shoppers had something grim and determined about them—even those with the gaudiest packages. They seemed likely to mow down anyone in their path. Cody took a pinch of Jenny's coat sleeve so as not to lose her.

"I'm serious," she was saying. "I don't want to get her anything warm. Anything necessary. Anything—"

"Serviceable," Ezra said.

They all grimaced.

"If we bought her a ring, though," Ezra said, "she might feel bad about the wastefulness. She might not really enjoy it."

Cody hated the radiant, grave expression that Ezra wore sometimes; it showed that he realized full well how considerate he was being. "What do *you* want for Christmas?" Cody asked him roughly. "World peace?"

"World what? I'd like a recorder," Ezra said.

They crossed an intersection with a swarm of sailors. "Well," said Cody, "you're not getting one."

"I know that."

"You're getting a cap with turn-down earflaps and a pair of corduroy pants."

"Cody!" said Jenny. "You weren't supposed to tell."

"It doesn't matter," Ezra said.

They separated for a woman who had stopped to fit her child's mittens on. "It used to be," Jenny said, "that we got toys for Christmas, and candy. Remember how nice last Christmas was?"

"This one's going to be nice too," Ezra told her.

"Remember down in Virginia, when Daddy bought us a sled, and Mother said it was silly because it hardly ever snowed but December twenty-sixth we woke up and there was snow all over everything?"

"That was fun," Ezra said.

"We had the only sled in town," Jenny said. "Cody started charging for rides. Daddy showed us how to wax the runners and we pulled it to the top of that hill . . . What was the name of that hill? It had such a funny—"

Then she stopped short on the sidewalk. Pedestrians jostled all around her. "Why," she said.

Cody and Ezra looked at her.

"He's really not ever coming home again. Is he," she said.

No one answered. After a minute they resumed walking, three abreast, and Cody took a pinch of Ezra's sleeve, too, so they wouldn't drift apart in the crowd.

Cody sorted the mail, setting aside for his mother a couple of envelopes that looked like Christmas cards. He threw away a department store flyer and a letter from his school. He pocketed an envelope with a Cleveland postmark.

He went upstairs to his room and switched on the goose-necked lamp beside his bed. While the lightbulb warmed, he whistled and stared out the window. Then he tested the bulb with his fingers and, finding it hot enough, wrapped the envelope around it and counted slowly to thirty. After that he pried open the flap with ease and pulled out a single sheet of paper and a check.

. . . says they should be producing to capacity by June of '45 . . . his father wrote. *Sorry the enclosed is a little smaller than expected as I have incurred some . . .* It was his usual letter, nothing different. Cody folded it again and slid it back in the envelope, though it hardly seemed worth the effort. Then he heard the front door slam. "Ezra Tull?" Pearl called. Her cloppy high heels started rapidly up the stairs. Cody tucked the envelope into his bureau and shut the drawer. "Ezra!"

"He's not here," Cody said.

She came to stand in the doorway. "Where is he?" she asked. She was out of breath, untidy-looking. Her hat was on crooked and she still wore her coat.

"He went to get the laundry, like you told him to."

"What do you know about this?"

She bore down on him, holding out a stack of snapshots. The one on top was so blurred and gray that Cody had trouble deciphering it. He took the whole collection from her hand. Ah, yes: Ezra lay in a stupor, surrounded by liquor bottles. Cody grinned. He'd forgotten that picture completely.

"What could it mean?" his mother asked. "I take a roll of film to the drugstore and I come back with the shock of my life. I just wanted to get the camera ready for Christmas. I was expecting maybe some scenes from last summer, or Jenny's birthday cake . . . and here I find Ezra like a derelict! A common drunk! Could this be what it looks like? Answer me!"

"He's not as perfect as you think he is," Cody told her.

"But he's never given me a moment's worry."

"He's done a lot that might surprise you."

Pearl sat down on his bed. She was shaking her head, looking stunned. "Oh, Cody, it's such a battle, raising children," she said. "I know you must think I'm difficult. I lose my temper, I carry on like a shrew sometimes, but if you could just realize how . . . helpless I feel! How scary it is to know that everyone I love depends on me! I'm afraid I'll do something wrong."

She reached up—for the photos, he thought, and he held them out to her; but no, what she wanted was his hand. She took it and pulled him down beside her. Her skin felt hot and dry. "I've probably been too hard on you," she said. "But I look to you for support now, Cody. You're the only person I can turn to; it may be you and I are more alike than you think. Cody, what am I going to do?"

She leaned closer, and Cody drew back. Even her eyes seemed to give off heat. "Uh, well . . ." he said.

"Who took that picture, anyhow? Was it you?"

"Look," he said. "It was a joke."

"Joke?"

"Ezra didn't drink that stuff. I just set some bottles around him."

Her gaze flicked back and forth across his face.

"He's never touched a drop," Cody told her.

"I see," she said. She freed his hand. She said, "Well, all I can say is, that's some joke, young man." Then she stood up and took several steps away from him. "That's some sense of humor you've got," she said.

Cody shrugged.

"Oh, I suppose it must seem very funny, scaring your mother half out of her wits. Letting her babble on like a fool. Slandering your little brother. It must seem hilarious, to someone like you."

"I'm just naturally mean, I guess," Cody said.

"You've been mean since the day you were born," she told him.

After she had walked out, he went to work resealing his father's letter.

Ezra landed on Park Place and Cody said, "Aha! Park Place with one hotel. Fifteen hundred dollars."

"Poor, poor Ezra," Jenny said.

"How'd you do that?" Ezra asked Cody.

"How'd I do what?"

"How'd you get a hotel on Park Place? A minute ago it was mortgaged."

"Oh, I scrimped and saved," Cody said.

"There's something peculiar going on here."

"Mother!" Jenny called. "Cody's cheating again!"

Their mother was stringing the Christmas tree lights. She looked over and said, "Cody."

"What did I do?" Cody asked.

"What did he do, children?"

"He's the banker," Jenny said. "He made us let him keep the bank and the deeds and the houses. Now he's got a hotel on Park Place and all this extra money. It's not fair!"

Pearl set down the box of lights and came over to where they were sitting. She said, "All right, Cody, put it back. Jenny keeps the deeds from now on; Ezra keeps the bank. Is that clear?"

Jenny reached for the deeds. Ezra began collecting the money.

"And I tell you this," Pearl said. "If I hear one more word, Cody Tull, you're out of the game. Forever! Understood?" She bent to help Ezra. "Always cheating, tormenting, causing trouble . . ." She laid the fives beside the ones, the tens beside the fives. "Cody? You hear what I say?"

He heard, but he didn't bother answering. He sat back and smiled, safe and removed, watching her stack the money.

3

Destroyed by Love

Supposedly, Jenny Tull was going to be a beauty someday, but the people who told her that were so old they might easily be dead by the time that day arrived, and no one her own age saw much promise in her. At seventeen, she was skinny and severe and studious-looking. Her bones were so sharp, they seemed likely to puncture her skin. She had coarse dark hair that she was always hacking at, much to her mother's disapproval—one week chopping it to a blunt, square shape; the next week cutting bangs that accidentally slanted toward the left; and then, to correct her error, shortening the bangs so drastically that they appeared damaged and painful. While her classmates were wearing (in 1952) bouffant skirts and perky blouses with the collars turned up in back, Jenny's clothes were hand-me-downs from her mother: limp, skimpy dresses fashionable in the forties, with too much shoulder and not enough skirt. And since her mother despised the sloppiness of loafers, Jenny's shoes were the same kind of sturdy brown oxfords that her brothers wore. Every morning she clomped off to school looking uncomfortable and cross. No wonder hardly anyone bothered to speak to her.

She was about to be, for the very first time, the only child at home. Her brother Cody was away at college. Her brother Ezra had refused to go to college and started instead what his mother openly hoped was a temporary job in Scarlatti's Restaurant, chopping vegetables for salads; but just as he was advancing to sauces, notice came that he'd been drafted. None of his family could envision it: placid Ezra slogging through Korea, tripping over his bayonet at every opportunity. Surely something would be wrong with him, some weakness of spine or eyesight that would save him. But no, he was found to be in perfect health, and in February was ordered off to a training camp down south. Jenny sat on his bed while he packed. She was touched by the fact that he was taking along his little pearwood recorder, the one he'd bought with his first week's wages. It didn't seem to her that he had a very clear idea of what he was getting into. He moved in his cautious, deliberate way, sorting out what he would send to the basement for storage. Since their mother had plans for renting his room, he couldn't just leave things as they were. Already his brother Cody's bed was freshly made up for a boarder, the blankets tight as drumskins on the narrow mattress, and Cody's sports equipment was packed away in cartons.

She watched Ezra empty a drawer of undershirts, most of them full of holes. (Somehow, he always managed to look like an orphan.) He had grown to be a large-boned man, but his face was still childishly rounded, with the wide eyes, the downy cheeks, the delicate lips of a schoolboy. His hair seemed formed of layers of silk in various shades of yellow and beige. Girls were always after him, Jenny knew, but he was too shy to take advantage of it—or maybe even to be aware of it. He proceeded through life absentmindedly, meditatively, as if considering some complex mathematical puzzle from which he was bound to look up, you would think, as soon as he found the solution. But he never did.

"After I leave," he told Jenny, "will you stop in at Scarlatti's

68

Restaurant from time to time?"

"Stop in and do what?"

"Well, talk with Mrs. Scarlatti, I mean. Just make sure she's all right."

Mrs. Scarlatti had been without a husband for years, if she'd ever had one, and her only son had recently been killed in action. Jenny knew she must be lonely. But she was a bleak and striking woman, so fashionably dressed that it seemed an insult to her particular section of Baltimore. Jenny couldn't imagine holding a conversation with her. Still, anything for Ezra. She nodded.

"And Josiah too," Ezra said.

Josiah was even more difficult—downright terrifying, in fact: Ezra's friend Josiah Payson, close to seven feet tall, excitable, and incoherent. It was generally understood that he wasn't quite right in the head. Back in grade school, the other children had teased him, and they had teased Ezra too and asked Jenny why her brother hung out with dummies. "Everybody knows Josiah should be sent away," they told her. "He ought to go to the crazy house; everybody says so."

She said, "Ezra, I can't talk to Josiah. I wouldn't understand him."

"Of course you'd understand," said Ezra. "He speaks English, doesn't he?"

"He jibbers, he jabbers, he stutters!"

"You must have only seen him when they're picking on him. The rest of the time he's fine. Oh, if Mother'd let me have him to the house once, you would know. He's fine! He's as bright as you or me, and maybe brighter."

"Well, if you say so," Jenny told him.

But she wasn't convinced.

After Ezra was gone, it occurred to her that he'd only mentioned outsiders. He hadn't said anything about taking care of their mother. Maybe he assumed that Pearl could manage on her own. She could manage very well, it was true, but Ezra's leaving seemed to take something out of her. She delayed the renting of his room. "I know we need the money," she told Jenny, "but I really can't face it right now. It still has his smell. Maybe if I aired it a while . . . It still has his shape in it, know what I mean? I look in and the air feels full of something warm. I think we ought to wait a bit."

So they lived in the house alone. Jenny felt even slighter than usual, overwhelmed by so much empty space. In the afternoons when she came home from school, her mother would still be at work, and Jenny would open the door and hesitantly step inside. Sometimes it seemed there was a startled motion, or a stopping of motion, somewhere deep in the house just as she crossed the threshold. She'd pause then, heart thumping, alert as a deer, but it never turned out to be anything real. She'd close the door behind her and go upstairs to her room, turn on her study lamp, change out of her school clothes. She was an orderly, conscientious girl who always hung things up and took good care of her belongings. She would set her books out neatly on her desk, align her pencils, and adjust the lamp so it shone at the proper angle. Then she'd work her way systematically through her assignments. Her greatest dream was to be a doctor, which meant she'd have to win a scholarship. In three years of high school, she had never received a grade below an A.

At five o'clock she would go downstairs to scrub the potatoes or start the chicken frying—whatever was instructed in her mother's note on the kitchen table. Soon afterward her mother would arrive. "Well! I tell you that old Pendle woman is a trial and a nuisance, just a nuisance, lets me ring up all her groceries and then says, 'Wait now, let me see, why, I don't have near enough money for such a bill as this.' Goes fumbling through her ratty cloth change purse while everyone behind her shifts from foot to foot . . ." She would tie an apron over her dress and take Jenny's place at the stove. "Honey, hand me the salt, will you? I see there's no mail from the boys. They've forgotten all about us, it seems. It's only you and me now."

It was only the two of them, yes, but there were echoes of the others all around—wicked, funny Cody, peaceful Ezra, setting up a loaded silence as Jenny and her mother seated themselves at the table. "Pour the milk, will you, dear? Help yourself to some beans." Sometimes Jenny imagined that even her father made his absence felt, though she couldn't picture his face and had little recollection of the time before he'd left them. Of course she never mentioned this to her mother. Their talk was small talk, little dibs and dabs of things, safely skating over whatever might lie beneath. "How is that poor Carroll girl, Jenny? Has she lost any weight that you've noticed?"

Jenny knew that, in reality, her mother was a dangerous person—hot breathed and full of rage and unpredictable. The dry, straw texture of her lashes could seem the result of some conflagration, and her pale hair could crackle electrically from its bun and her eyes could get small as hatpins. Which of her children had not felt her stinging slap, with the claw-encased pearl in her engagement ring that could bloody a lip at one flick? Jenny had seen her hurl Cody down a flight of stairs. She'd seen Ezra ducking, elbows raised, warding off an attack. She herself, more than once, had been slammed against a wall, been called "serpent," "cockroach," "hideous little sniveling guttersnipe." But here Pearl sat, decorously inquiring about Julia Carroll's weight problem. Jenny had a faint, tremulous hope that times had changed. Perhaps it was the boys' fault. Maybe she and her mother—intelligent women, after all—could live without such scenes forever. But she never felt entirely secure, and at night, when Pearl had placed a kiss on the center of Jenny's forehead, Jenny went off to bed and dreamed what she had always dreamed: her mother laughed a witch's shrieking laugh; dragged Jenny out of hiding as the Nazis tramped up the stairs; accused her of sins and crimes that had never crossed Jenny's mind. Her mother told her, in an informative and considerate tone of voice, that she was raising Jenny to eat her.

*

71

Cody wrote almost never, and what letters he did write were curt and factual. *I won't be coming home for spring vacation. All my grades are fine except French. This new job pays better than the old one did.* Ezra sent a postcard the moment he arrived in camp, and followed that three days later with a letter describing his surroundings. It was longer than several of Cody's put together, but still it didn't tell Jenny what she wanted to know. *There's somebody two blocks down who's from Maryland too I hear but I haven't had a chance to talk to him and I don't think he's from Baltimore anyway but some other place I wouldn't know about so I doubt we'd have much to . . .* What was he saying, exactly? Had he, or had he not, made any friends? If people lived so close together, you'd think they would have talked. Jenny pictured the others ignoring him and making fun of his incompetence. He simply was not a soldier. But *I have learned right much about my rifle,* he wrote. *Cody would be surprised* She tried to imagine his long, sensitive fingers cleaning and oiling a gun. She understood that he must be surviving, more or less, but she couldn't figure out how. She thought of him on his belly, in the dust of the rifle range, squeezing a trigger. His gaze was so reflective, how would he hit a target? *They say the whole bunch of us will be joining the Korean Conflict as soon as we are . . .* Why, they'd pick him off like a fly! He'd never do more to defend himself than dodge and shield his head.

I think a lot about Scarlatti's Restaurant and how nice the lettuce smelled when I tore it into the bowl, he wrote—his only mention of homesickness, if that was what it was. Pearl gave a jealous sniff. "As if lettuce had a smell!" Jenny was jealous too; he could have remembered, instead, how he and she used to lie on the floor in front of the Philco on Monday nights, listening to the Cities Service Band of America. What did he see in that restaurant, anyhow? Then a little knob of discomfort started nudging inside her chest. There was something she hadn't done, something unpleasant that she didn't want to do . . . Check on Mrs. Scarlatti. She wondered if Ezra had really meant for her to keep her promise. He couldn't actually expect that of her, could he? But she supposed he could. He was a literal-minded kind of person.

So she folded Ezra's letter and put it in her pocket. Then she slipped her coat on and walked to St. Paul Street, to a narrow brick building set in a strip of shops and businesses.

Scarlatti's was the neighborhood's one formal elegant eating place. It served only supper, mostly to people from better parts of the city. At this hour—five-thirty or so—it wouldn't even be open. She went to the rear, where she'd been a couple of times with Ezra. She circled two garbage cans overflowing with wilted greens, and she climbed the steps and knocked on the door. Then she cupped a hand to the windowpane and peered in.

Men in dirty aprons were rushing around the kitchen, which was a mass of steam and stainless steel, pot lids clattering, bowls as big as birdbaths heaped with sliced vegetables. No wonder they hadn't heard her. She turned the knob, but the door was locked. And before she could knock any harder, she caught sight of Mrs. Scarlatti. She was slouched in the dining room entranceway, holding a lit cigarette—a white-faced woman in a stark black knife of a dress. Whatever she was saying, Jenny couldn't catch it, but she heard the gravelly, careless sound of her voice. And she saw how Mrs. Scarlatti's black hair was swept completely to the right, like one of those extreme Vogue magazine model's, and how she leaned her head to the right as well so that she seemed to be burdened, cruelly misused, bearing up under an exhausting weight that had something to do with men and experience. Imagine Ezra knowing such a person! Imagine him at ease with her, close enough to worry about her. Jenny backed away. She understood, all at once, that her brothers had grown up and gone. Her mental pictures of them were outdated—Ezra playing the bamboo whistle he used to have in grade school, Cody triumphantly rattling his dice over their old Monopoly board. She thought of a faded flannel shirt that Ezra had worn so often, it was like a second skin. She thought of how he would rock back and forth with his hands in his rear pockets when he was lost for something to say, or dig a hole in the ground with his sneaker. And how when Jenny was shattered by one of her mother's rages, he would slip downstairs to the kitchen and fix her a mug of hot milk laced with honey, sprinkled over with cinnamon. He was always so quick to catch his family's moods, and to offer food and drink and unspoken support.

She traveled down the alley and, instead of heading home, took Bushnell Street and then Putnam. It was getting colder; she had to button her coat. Three blocks down Putnam stood a building so weathered and dismal, you'd think it was an abandoned warehouse till you saw the sign: TOM 'N' EDDIE'S BODY SHOP. She had often come here to fetch Ezra home, but she'd only called his name at the drive-in doorway; she had never been inside. Now she stepped into the gloom and looked around her. Tom and Eddie (she assumed) were talking to a man in a business suit; one of them held a clipboard. In the background, Josiah Payson swung a gigantic rubber mallet against the fender of a pickup. Jenny was hit by a piece of memory, a mystifying fragment: Josiah in the school yard, long ago, violently flailing a pipe or a metal bar of some sort, cutting a desperate, whizzing circle in the air and shouting something unintelligible while Ezra stood guard between him and a mob of children. "Everything will be fine; just go away," Ezra was telling the others. But what had happened next? How had it ended? How had it started? She felt confused. Meanwhile Josiah swung his mallet. He was grotesquely tall, as gaunt as the armature for some statue never completed. His cropped black hair bristled all over his head, his skull of a face glistened, and he clenched a set of teeth so ragged and white and crowded, so jumbled together and overlapping, that it seemed he had chewed them up and was preparing to spit them out.

"Josiah," she called timidly.

He stopped to look at her. Or was he looking someplace

74

else? His eyes were dead black—lidless and almost Oriental. It was impossible to tell where they were directed. He heaved the hammer onto a stack of burlap bags and lunged toward her, his face alight with happiness. "Ezra's sister!" he said. "Ezra!"

She smiled and hugged her elbows.

Directly in front of her, he came to a halt and smoothed his stubble of hair. His arms seemed longer than they should have been. "Is Ezra okay?" he asked her.

"He's fine."

"Not wounded or—"

"No."

Ezra was right: Josiah spoke as distinctly as anyone, in a grown man's rumbling voice. But he had trouble finding something to do with his hands, and ended up scraping them together as if trying to rid his palms of dirt or grease, or even of a layer of skin. She was aware of Tom and Eddie glancing over at her curiously, losing track of their conversation. "Come outside," she told Josiah. "I'll let you see his letter."

Outside it was twilight, almost too dark to read, but Josiah took the letter anyway and scanned the lines. There was a crease between his eyebrows as deep as if someone had pressed an ax blade there. She noticed that his coveralls, pathetically well washed, were so short for him that his fallen white socks and hairy shinbones showed. His lips could barely close over that chaos of teeth; his mouth had a bunchy look and his chin was elongated from the effort.

He handed the letter back to her. She had no way of knowing what he had got out of it. "If they'd let me," he said, "I'd have gone with him. Oh, I wouldn't mind going. But they claimed I was too tall."

"Too tall?"

She'd never heard of such a thing.

"So I had to stay behind," he said, "but I didn't want to. I don't want to work in a body shop all my life; I plan to do something different."

"Like what?"

"Oh, I don't know. Find something with Ezra, I guess, once he gets out of the army. Ezra, he would always come to visit me here and look around and say, 'How can you stand it? All the noise,' he'd say. 'We got to find you something different.' But I didn't know where to start hunting, and now Ezra's gone away. It's not the noise that's so bad, but it's hot in summer and cold in winter. My feet get bothered by the cold, get these itchy things all over the toes."

"Chilblains, maybe," Jenny suggested. She felt pleasantly bored; it seemed she had known Josiah forever. She ran a thumbnail down the crease of Ezra's letter. Josiah gazed either at her or straight through her (it was hard to tell which) and cracked his knuckles.

"Probably what I'll do is work for Ezra," he said, "once Ezra opens his restaurant."

"What are you talking about? Ezra's not opening a restaurant."

"Sure he is."

"Why would he want to do that? As soon as he pulls himself together he's going off to college, studying to be a teacher."

"Who says so?" Josiah asked.

"Well, my mother does. He's got the patience for it, she says. Maybe he'll be a professor, even," Jenny told him. But she wasn't so certain now. "I mean, it's not a lifework, restaurants."

"Why isn't it?"

She couldn't answer.

"Ezra's going to have him a place where people come just like to a family dinner," Josiah said. "He'll cook them one thing special each day and dish it out on their plates and everything will be solid and wholesome, really homelike."

"Ezra told you that?"

"Really just like home."

"Well, I don't know, maybe people go to restaurants to get *away* from home."

"It's going to be famous," Josiah said.

"You have the wrong idea entirely," Jenny told him. "How did you come up with such a crazy notion?"

Then without warning, Josiah went back to being his old self—or her old picture of him. He dropped his head, like a marionette whose strings had snapped. "I got to go," he told her.

"Josiah?"

"Don't want those people yelling at me."

He loped away without saying goodbye. Jenny watched after him as regretfully as if he were Ezra himself. He didn't look back.

Cody wrote that he was being interviewed by several corporations. He wanted a job in business after he finished school. Ezra wrote that he could march twenty miles at a go now without much tiring. It began to seem less incongruous, even perfectly natural, that Ezra should be a soldier. After all, wasn't he an enduring sort, uncomplaining, cheerful in performing his duties? Jenny had worried needlessly. Her mother too seemed to relax somewhat. "Really it's for the best, when you think about it," she said. "A stint in the service is often just the ticket; gives a boy time to get hold of himself. I bet when he comes back, he'll want to go to college. I bet he'll want to teach someplace."

Jenny didn't tell her about his restaurant.

Twice, after her first visit to Josiah, she looked in on him again. She would stop by the body shop after school, and Josiah would come outside a moment to swing his arms and gaze beyond her and speak of Ezra. "Got a letter from him myself, over at the house. Claimed he was marching a lot."

"Twenty miles," Jenny said.

"Some of it uphill."

"He must be in pretty good shape by now."

"He always did like to walk."

The third time she came, it was almost dark. She'd stayed

late for chorus. Josiah was just leaving work. He was getting into his jacket, which was made of a large, shaggy plaid in muted shades of navy and maroon. She thought of the jackets that little boys wore in the lower grades of school. "That Tom," Josiah said, jabbing his fists in his pockets. "That Eddie." He strode rapidly down the sidewalk. Jenny had trouble keeping up. "They don't care how they talk to a fellow," he said. "Don't give a thought to what he might feel; feelings just like anyone else . . ."

She dropped back, deciding that he'd rather be alone, but partway down the block he stopped and turned and waited. "Aren't I a human being?" he asked when she arrived at his side. "Don't I feel bad if someone shouts at me? I wish I were out in the woods someplace, none of these people to bother me. Camping out in a dead, dead quiet with a little private tent from L. L. Bean and a L. L. Bean sleeping bag." He turned and rushed on; Jenny had to run. "I've half a mind to give notice," he said.

"Why don't you, then?"

"My mama needs the money."

"You could find something else."

"Oh, no, it isn't easy."

"Why not?"

He didn't answer. They raced past a discount jewelry store, a bakery, a bank of private apartments with inviting yellow windows. Then he said, "Come and have supper at our house."

"What? Oh, I can't."

"Ezra used to come," he said, "back before he worked in the restaurant and couldn't get away. My mama was always glad to set an extra plate out, always, anytime. But *your* mother didn't often let him; your mother doesn't like me."

"Oh, well . . ."

"I wish you'd just have supper with us."

She paused. Then she said, "I'd be happy to."

He didn't seem surprised. (Jenny was astonished, herself.)

He grunted and continued to tear along. His whisks of black hair stood out around his head. He led her down a side street, then through an alley that Jenny wasn't familiar with.

From the front, his house must have been very much like hers—a brick row house set in a tiny yard. But they approached it from the rear, where a tacked-on, gray frame addition gave it a ramshackle look. The addition turned out to be an unheated pantry with a cracked linoleum floor. Josiah stopped there to work himself free of his jacket, and then he reached for Jenny's coat and hung them both on hooks beside the door. "Mama?" he called. He showed Jenny into the kitchen. "Got company for supper, Mama."

Mrs. Payson stood at the stove—a small, chubby woman dressed in earth tones. She reminded Jenny of some modest brown bird. Her face was round and smooth and shining. She looked up and smiled, and since Josiah failed to make the introduction Jenny said, "I'm Jenny Tull."

"Oh, any kin to Ezra?"

"I'm his sister."

"My, I'm just so fond of that boy," Mrs. Payson said. She lifted the pot from the stove and set it on the table. "When he was called up I cried, did Josiah tell you? I sat right down and cried. Why, he has been like a son to me, always in and out of the house . . ." She laid three place settings while Josiah poured the milk. "I'll never forget," she said, "back when Josiah's daddy died, Ezra came and sat with us, and fixed us meals, and made us cocoa. I said, 'Ezra, I feel selfish, taking you from your family,' but he said, 'Don't you worry about it, Mrs. Payson.'"

Jenny wondered when that could have been. Ezra had never mentioned Mr. Payson's dying.

Supper was spaghetti and a salad, with chocolate cake for dessert. Jenny ate sparingly, planning to eat again when she got home so her mother wouldn't guess; but Josiah had several helpings of everything. Mrs. Payson kept refilling his plate. "To look at him," she said, "you'd never know he eats so much, would you? Skinny as a fence post. I reckon he's still a growing boy." She laughed, and Josiah grinned bashfully with his eyes cast down—a skeletal, stooped, hunkering man. Jenny had never thought about the fact that Josiah was somebody's son, some woman's greatest treasure. His stubby black lashes were lowered; his prickly head was bent over his plate. He was so certain of being loved, here if no place else. She looked away.

After supper she helped with the dishes, placing each clean plate and glass on open wooden shelves whose edges had grown soft from too many coats of paint. Her mother would be frantic by now, but Jenny lingered over the wiping of each fork. Then Josiah walked her home. "Come back and see us!" Mrs. Payson called from the doorway. "Make sure you're buttoned up!" Jenny thought of . . . . was it "Jack and the Beanstalk"? . . . or perhaps some other fairy tale, where the humble widow, honest and warmhearted, lives in a cottage with her son. Everything else—the cold dark of the streets, the picture of her own bustling mother—seemed brittle by comparison, lacking the smoothly rounded completeness of Josiah's life.

They walked up Calvert Street without talking, puffing clouds of steam. They crossed to Jenny's house and climbed the porch steps. "Well," said Jenny, "thank you for inviting me, Josiah."

Josiah made some awkward, jerky motion that she assumed was an effort toward speech. He stumbled closer, enveloped her in a circle of rough plaid, and kissed her on the lips. She had trouble, at first, understanding what was happening. Then she felt a terrible dismay, not so much for herself as for Josiah. Oh, it was sad, he had misread everything; he would be so embarrassed! But how could he have made such an error? Thinking it over (pressed willy-nilly against his whiskery chin, against the knobbiness of his mouth), she saw things suddenly from his viewpoint: their gentle little "romance" (was what he must call it), as seamless as the Widow Payson's fairy tale existence. She longed for it; she wished it were true. She ached, with something like nostalgia, for a contented life with his mother in her snug house, for an innocent, protective marriage. She kissed him back, feeling even through all those layers of wool how he tensed and trembled.

Then light burst out, the front door slammed open, and her mother's voice broke over them. "What? What! What is the meaning of this?"

They leapt apart.

"You piece of trash," Pearl said to Jenny. "You tramp. You trashy thing. So this is what you've been up to! Not so much as notifying me where you are, supper not started, I'm losing my mind with worry—then here I find you! Necking! Necking with a, with a—"

For lack of a word, it seemed, she struck out. She slapped Jenny hard across the cheek. Jenny's eyes filled with tears. Josiah, as if it were he who'd been struck, averted his face sharply and stared away at some distant point. His mouth was working but no sound came forth.

"With a crazy! A dummy! A retarded person. You did it to spite me, didn't you," Pearl told Jenny. "It's your way of making mock of me. All these afternoons that I've been slaving in the grocery store, you were off in some alleyway, weren't you, off with this animal, this gorilla, letting him take his pleasure, just to shame me."

Josiah said, "But-but-but—"

"Just to show me up when I had such great plans for you. Cutting school, no doubt, lying with him in bushes and back seats of cars and maybe this very house, for all I know, while I'm off slaving at Sweeney Brothers—"

"But! But! Aagh!" Josiah shouted, and he sputtered so that Jenny saw white flecks flying in the lamplight. Then he flung out his scarecrow arms and plunged down the steps and disappeared.

She didn't see him again, of course. She chose her routes carefully and never again came near him, never approached any place that he was likely to be found; and she assumed he did the same. It was as if, by mutual agreement, they had split the city between them.

And besides, she had no reason to see him: Ezra's letters stopped. Ezra appeared in person. One Sunday morning, there he was, sitting in the kitchen when Jenny came down to breakfast. He wore his old civilian clothes that had been packed away in mothballs—jeans and a scruffy blue sweater. They hung on him like something borrowed. It was alarming how much weight he had lost. His hair was unbecomingly short and his face was paler, older, shadowed beneath the eyes. He sat slumped, clamping his hands between his knees, while Pearl scraped a piece of scorched toast into the sink. "Jam or honey, which?" she was asking. "Jenny, look who's here! It's Ezra, safe and sound! Let me pour you more coffee, Ezra." Ezra didn't speak, but he gave Jenny a tired smile.

He'd been discharged, as it turned out. For sleepwalking. He had no memory of sleepwalking, but every night he dreamed the same dream: he was marching through an unchanging terrain of cracked mud flats without a tree or a sprig of grass, with a blank blue bowl of sky overhead. He would set one foot in front of the other and march and march and march. In the morning, his muscles would ache. He'd thought it was from his *waking* marches, till they told him differently. All night, they told him, he roamed the camp, plodding between the rows of cots. Soldiers would stir and sit up and say, "Tull? That you?" and he would leave. He wouldn't answer, wouldn't wake, but simply went someplace else. To some of the soldiers, the youngest ones, his silence was frightening. There were complaints. He was sent to a doctor, who gave him a box of yellow pills. With the pills he still walked, but he would fall down from time to time and just lie where he fell until morning. Once he must have landed on his face; when they roused him, his nose was bloody and they thought it might be broken. It wasn't, but

82

for several days he had purple circles under his eyes. Then they sent him to a chaplain, who asked if Ezra had anything particular on his mind. Was there some trouble back home, perhaps? Woman trouble? Illness in his family? Ezra said no. He told the chaplain things were fine; he couldn't for the life of him think what this was all about. The chaplain asked if he liked the army and Ezra said, well, it wasn't something you would like or dislike; it was something you had to get through, was more to the point. He said the army wasn't his style, exactly—what with the shouting, the noise—but still, he was coming along. He guessed he was doing all right. The chaplain said just to try not to sleepwalk again, in that case; but the very next night Ezra walked directly into town, four and a half miles in his olive-drab underwear with his eyes wide open but flat as windows, and a waitress in a diner had to wake him up and get her brother-in-law to drive him back to camp. The next day they called another doctor in, and the doctor asked him a series of questions and signed some papers and sent him home. "So here I am," Ezra said in a toneless voice. "Discharged."

"But honorably," said his mother.

"Oh, yes."

"The thought! All the while this was going on, you never said a word."

"Well, how could you have helped?" he asked.

The question seemed to age her. She sagged.

After breakfast he went upstairs and fell on his bed and slept through the day, and Jenny had to wake him for supper. Even then he could barely keep his eyes open. He sat groggily swaying, eating almost nothing, nodding off in the middle of a mouthful. Then he went back to bed. Jenny wandered through the house and fidgeted with the cords of window shades. Was this how he was going to be, now? Had he changed forever?

But Monday morning, he was Ezra again. She heard his little pearwood recorder playing "Greensleeves" before she was even dressed. When she came downstairs he was scrambling eggs the way she liked, with cheese and bits of green pepper, while Pearl read the paper. And at breakfast he said, "I guess I'll go get my old job back." Pearl glanced over at him but said nothing. "How come you didn't call on Mrs. Scarlatti?" Ezra asked Jenny. "She wrote and said you never came."

Jenny said, "Oh, well, I meant to . . ."

She lowered her eyes and held her breath, waiting. Now was when he would mention Josiah. But he didn't. She looked up and found him buttering a piece of toast, and she let out her breath. She was never going to be certain of what Ezra knew, or didn't know.

II

By the time Jenny reached college, she'd grown to be the beauty that everyone predicted. Or was it only that she'd come into fashion? Her mirror showed the same face, so far as she could tell, but most of her dormitory's phone calls seemed to be for her, and if she hadn't been working her way through school (waiting tables, folding laundry, shelving books in the library stacks), she could have gone out every night. Away from Baltimore, her looks lost a little of their primness. She let her hair grow and she developed a breathless, flyaway air. But she never forgot about medical school. Her future was always clear to her: a straightforward path to a pediatric practice in a medium-sized city, preferably not too far from a coast. (She liked knowing she could get out anytime. Wouldn't mid-westerners feel claustrophobic?) Friends teased her about her single-mindedness. Her roommate objected to Jenny's study light, was exasperated by the finicky way she aligned her materials on her desk. In this respect, at least, Jenny hadn't changed.

Meanwhile, her brother Cody had become a success—shot ahead through several firms, mainly because of his ideas for using the workers' time better; and then branched out on his own to become an efficiency expert. And Ezra still worked for Mrs. Scarlatti, but he had advanced as well. He really ran the kitchen now, while Mrs. Scarlatti played hostess out in front. Jenny's mother wrote to say it was a shame, a crime and a shame. *I tell him the longer he piddles about in that woman's restaurant the harder he'll find it to get back on track, you know he always intended to go to college . . .*

Pearl still clerked at the grocery store but was better dressed, looking less careworn, since Jenny's scholarship and part-time jobs had relieved the financial strain. Jenny saw her twice a year—at Christmas and just before the start of school each September. She made excuses for the other holidays, and during the summers she worked at a clothing shop in a small town near her college. It wasn't that she didn't want to see her mother. She often thought of her wiry energy, the strength she had shown in raising her children single-handed, and her unfailing interest in their progress. But whenever Jenny returned, she was dampened almost instantly by the atmosphere of the house—by its lack of light, the cramped feeling of its papered rooms, a certain grim spareness. She almost wondered if she had some kind of allergy. It was like a respiratory ailment; on occasion, she believed she might be smothering. Her head grew stuffy, as it did when she had studied too long without a break. She snapped at people. Even Ezra irritated her, with his calm and his docility.

So she kept her distance, and after missing her family a while began to discard the very thought of them. She grew brisker, busier, more hurried. Ezra's letters—as ponderous as his conversation, just this side of dull—would turn up on the edge of the bathroom sink or crumpled among the bedclothes, where Jenny had laid them aside in midsentence. Her mind just drifted, that was all. And twice, during her first two years in college, Cody stopped to see her while traveling through Pennsylvania on business, and both times she was happy at the prospect (he was so dashing and good-looking, she was proud to show him off), but she felt muffled, gradually, once he'd arrived. It wasn't her fault; it was his. It seemed that everything she said carried, for him, the echo of their mother. She saw him stiffen. She knew exactly what he was thinking. "How are you fixed for money?" he would ask her. "You need a few new dresses?" She would say, "No, thanks, Cody, I'm fine"—really meaning it, needing nothing; but she saw, from his expression, what he had understood her to say: "No, no," in Pearl's thin voice, "never mind me . . ." She could not straighten his tie, or compliment his suit, or inquire about his present life without setting up that guarded look in his face. It made her feel unjustly accused. Did he really imagine she would be so domineering, or reproachful, or meddlesome? "Look," she tried once. "Let's start over. I didn't intend what you think I intended." But his wary, sidelong glance told her that he suspected even this. There was no way to cut themselves out of the tangle. She let him leave. Back in her dorm room she studied her reflection, her swing of dark hair and her narrow-waisted figure. Then she acted gayer than usual, for a while, and had a sense of having clapped her hands to free them of some thick and clinging dust.

Late in her senior year, she fell in love. She had been in love before, of course—once with an English major who'd grown too possessive, bit by bit; and once with a barrel-necked football star who seemed now, when she looked back, to be a symptom of some temporary insanity. But this was different. This was Harley Baines, a genius, a boy of such intelligence that even his smudged tortoiseshell glasses, pure white skin, and adenoidal voice struck awe in his classmates. He was not outside Jenny's group so much as above it, beyond it—a group in himself. It was rumored that he could have had a Ph.D. at twelve but was kept from it by his parents, who wanted him to enjoy a normal childhood. Next year he'd be at Paulham University, outside Philadelphia, doing advanced research in the field of genetics. Jenny was going to Paulham too; she had just been accepted by its medical school. That was what made her notice Harley

Baines. Secure in the center of her own noisy group (which would not be hers much longer, which would soon be scattered by graduation, leaving her defenseless), she looked across the campus and saw Harley Baines passing with his stork-like gait, wearing unstylish, pleated flannel trousers and bulky pullover obviously knitted by his mother. His hair, which could have used a shampoo, was a particularly dense shade of black. She wondered if he knew she was entering Paulham. She wondered if he would care, if he found girls beneath his notice. Was he impervious? Unobtainable? Her friends had to call her name several times, laughing at her bemused expression.

It was the spring of 1957—an unusually late and gradual spring. Professors opened the classroom windows with long, hooked poles, and the smell of lilacs floated in. Jenny wore sleeveless blouses and full skirts and ballerina flats. Harley Baines laid aside his home-knit sweater. Bared, his arms were muscular, thick with black hair. Around his neck he wore a gold or brass disk of some kind. She was dying to know what it was. One day in German class, she asked. He said it was a medal he'd won in a high school science fair, for setting up an experiment on the metabolic rate of white rats. She thought it was a funny thing to go on wearing all this time, but she didn't say so. Instead, she touched the medal lightly with her fingertips. It hung just inside his shirt, and it was almost hot.

She asked him at other times (catching up with him in a corridor, arranging to stand behind him in the cafeteria line) whether he was looking forward to Paulham University, and what sort of housing he would have there, and what he'd heard about Paulham's public transportation system. Offering these questions in an even, noncommittal voice, she felt like one of those circus trainers who take care to present to an animal only the curled-in backs of their hands, showing they pose no threat. She didn't want to alarm him. But Harley didn't act alarmed at all, and answered her courteously, matter-of-factly. (Was that good or bad?) When exams began, she came to him with her genetics notes and asked if he could help her study. They sat outdoors in the grass, in front of the Student Union, on a blue chenille bedspread she'd brought from her room. Their class-mates lounged on other bedspreads all around them—including some of Jenny's friends, who cast her startled, doubtful looks and then glanced quickly past her. She'd been hoping they would stroll over, make Harley a part of the group. But on second thought, she could see that would never happen.

While she framed her queries (acting not so slow-witted as to put him off, but still in need of his assistance), Harley listened and stripped a grass blade. He wore heavy, dressy shoes that seemed out of place on the bedspread. In his probing hands, the grass blade took on the look of a scientific experiment. He answered her levelly, with no question marks after his sen-tences; he took it for granted that she would understand him. Which she did, in fact, and would have even if she hadn't known her subject ahead of time. His logic proceeded steadily from A to B to C. In his slowness and his thoroughness, he re-minded her of Ezra—though otherwise, how different they were! When he finished, he asked if everything was clear now. "Yes, thank you," she said, and he nodded and rose to go. Was that *it?* She rose too, and felt suddenly dizzy—not from stand-ing, she believed, but from love. He had actually managed to bowl her over. She wondered what he would do if she threw her arms around him and collapsed against him, laid her face on his white, white chest, burned her cheek on his scientific medal. Instead she asked, "Will you help me fold the bedspread, please?" He bent to lift one end, and she lifted the other. They advanced. He gave his end to her and then soberly brushed off every wisp of grass, every flower petal and grain of pollen, from his side of the spread. After that he took the spread back again, evidently assuming that she would brush off her side. She looked up into his face. He stepped forward, flipped the spread around him like a hooded cloak, and wrapped her inside its darkness and kissed her. His glasses knocked against her nose. It was an unskillful kiss anyhow, too abrupt, and she couldn't help imagining the picture they made—a blue chenille pillar in the middle of the campus, a twin-sized mummy. She laughed. He dropped the spread and turned on his heel and walked off very fast. A plume of hair bobbed on the back of his head like a rooster's tail.

Jenny returned to her room and took a bath and changed to a ruffled dress. She leaned out her open window, humming. Harley didn't come. Eventually she went to supper, but he wasn't in the cafeteria, either. The next day, after her last exam, she phoned his dormitory. Some sleepy-sounding, gruff boy answered. "Baines has left for home," he said.

"Home? But we haven't had graduation yet."

"He's not planning to go through with that."

"Oh," said Jenny. She hadn't thought of graduation as "going through" with anything, although it was true you could simply have your diploma mailed out. To people like Harley Baines, she supposed, a degree was unimportant. (While Jenny's family was coming all the way to Summerfield for this event.) She said, "Well, thank you anyhow," and hung up, hoping her voice didn't sound as forlorn to Harley's roommate as it did to her.

That summer, after graduation, she worked again at Molly's Togs in the little town near the college. It had always seemed a pleasant job, but this year she was depressed by the studied casualness of married women's clothes—their Bermuda shorts for golfing and their wide-hipped khaki skirts. She gazed away unhelpfully when her customers asked, "Does it suit me? Do you think it's too youthful?" Next year at this time, she would be at Paulham. She wondered how soon she could start wearing a starched white coat.

In July, a letter arrived from Harley Baines, forwarded from home by her mother. When Jenny returned to her boarding-house after work, she found it on the hall table. She stood looking at it a moment. Then she slipped it into her straw purse and climbed the stairs. She let herself into her room, threw her purse on the bed, and opened the window. She took a square tin from a drawer and fed the two goldfish in the bowl on the bureau. All before opening Harley's letter.

Did she guess, ahead of time, what it would say?

Later, she imagined that she must have.

His handwriting was as small and separate as typing. She would have imagined something more headlong from a genius. He used a colon after the greeting, as if it were a business letter.

18 July, 1958
Dear Jenny:

I unreasonably took offense at what was, in fact, a natural reaction on your part. I must have seemed ridiculous.

What I had intended, before our misunderstanding, was that we might become better acquainted over the summer and then marry in the fall. I still find marriage a viable option. I know this must seem sudden—we haven't exactly had a normal American courtship—but after all, we are neither of us frivolous people.

Bear in mind that we will both be at Paulham next year and could share a single apartment, buy groceries in economy lots, etc. Also, I sense that your finances have been something of a problem, and I would be glad to assume that responsibility.

The above sounds more pragmatic than I'd intended. Actually, I find I love you, and am awaiting your earliest reply. Sincerely, Harley Baines

P.S. I know that you're intelligent. You didn't have to make up all those questions about genetics.

The postscript, she thought, was the most affecting part of the letter. It was written in a looser hand, as if impulsively, while the rest seemed copied and perhaps recopied from a rough draft.

She read the letter again, and then folded it and set it on her bed. She went over to study her goldfish, who had left too much food floating on the surface of the water. She would have to cut down on their rations. *Dear Harley*, she practiced. *It was such a surprise to . . .* No. He wouldn't care for gushiness. *Dear Harley: I have considered your terms and . . .* What she was trying to say was "Yes." She was pulled only very slightly by the feelings she'd had for him earlier (which now seemed faded and shallow, a schoolgirl crush brought on by senior panic). What appealed to her more was the *angularity* of the situation—the mighty leap into space with someone she hardly knew. Wasn't that what a marriage ought to be? Like one of those movie-style disasters—shipwrecks or earthquakes or enemy prisons—where strangers, trapped in close quarters by circumstances, show their real strengths and weaknesses.

Lately, her life had seemed to be narrowing. She could predict so easily the successive stages of medical school, internship, and residency. She had looked in a mirror, not so long ago, and realized all at once that the clear, fragile skin around her eyes would someday develop lines. She was going to grow old like anyone else.

She took paper from a bureau drawer, sat down on her bed, and uncapped her fountain pen. *Dear Harley:* she wrote. She plucked a microscopic hair from the pen point. She thought a while. Then she wrote, *All right*, and signed her name—the ultimate in no-nonsense communication. Even Harley couldn't find it excessive.

The following evening, just before supper, Jenny arrived in Baltimore. She had burned all her bridges: quit her job, given away her goldfish, and packed everything in her room. It was the most reckless behavior she had ever shown. On the Greyhound bus she sat grandly upright, periodically shrugging off the snoring soldier who drooped against her. When she reached the terminal she hailed a cab, instead of waiting for a city bus, and rode home in style.

No one had been told she was coming, so she was puzzled by the fact that while she was paying off the driver, the front door of her house opened wide and her mother proceeded across the porch and down the steps in a flowing, flowered dress, high-heeled pumps, and a hat whose black net veil was dotted with what looked like beauty spots. Behind her came Ezra in unpressed clothes that were a little too full cut, and last was Cody, dark and handsome and New Yorkish in a fine-textured, fitted gray suit and striped silk tie. For a second, Jenny fancied they were headed for her funeral. This was how they would look—formally dressed and refraining from battle—if Jenny were no longer among them. Then she shook the thought away, and smiled and climbed out of the taxi.

Her mother halted on the sidewalk. "My stars!" she said. "Ezra, when you say family dinner, you *mean* family dinner!" She raised her veil to kiss Jenny's cheek. "Why didn't you tell us you were coming? Ezra, did you plan it this way?"

"I didn't know a thing about it," Ezra said. "I thought of writing you, Jenny, but I didn't think you'd come all this distance just for supper."

"Supper?" Jenny asked.

"It's some idea of Ezra's," Pearl told her. "He found out Cody was passing through, maybe spending the night, and he said, 'I want both of you to get all dressed up—'"

"I am *not* spending the *night*," Cody said. "I'm running on a schedule here, when will you see that? I shouldn't even be staying for supper. I ought to be in Delaware."

"Ezra's got something he wants to say," Pearl said, picking a thread off Jenny's sundress, "some announcement he wants to make, and is taking us to Scarlatti's Restaurant. Though hot as it is, I believe a leaf of lettuce is just about all I could manage. Jenny, honey, you're thin as a stick! And what's in this big suitcase? How long are you planning to stay?"

"Oh, well . . . not long," Jenny said. She felt shy about

telling her news. "Maybe I ought to change clothes. I'm not as dressed up as the rest of you."

"No, no, you're fine," Ezra told her. He was rubbing his hands together, the way he always did when he was pleased. "Oh, it's working out so well!" he said. "A real family dinner! It's just like fate."

Cody took Jenny's suitcase inside the house. Meanwhile, her mother fussed: smoothing Jenny's hair, clucking at her bare legs. "No stockings! On a public conveyance." Cody came back and opened the door of a shiny blue car at the curb. He helped Pearl in, cupping her elbow. "What do you think of my car?" he said to Jenny.

"It's very nice. Did you buy it new?"

"How else? A Pontiac. Smell that new-car smell," he said. He walked around to the driver's seat. Jenny and Ezra settled in the rear; Ezra's knobbly wrists dangled between his knees.

"Of course, it's not yet paid for," Cody said, pulling into traffic, "but it will be very soon."

"Cody Tull!" his mother said. "You didn't go in debt for this."

"Why not? I'm getting rich, I tell you. Five years from now I can walk into an auto dealer, any dealer—Cadillac—and slap cold cash on the counter and say, 'I'll take three. Or on second thought, make that four.'"

"But not now," said Pearl. "Not yet. You know how I feel about buying on time."

"Time is what I deal with," Cody said. He laughed, and shot through an amber light. "What could be more fitting? Ten years more, you'll be riding in a limousine."

"Why would I want to do that?"

"And Ezra can go to Princeton, if he likes. And I can buy Jenny a clinic all of her own. I can pay for her to specialize in every field, one by one."

Now was the moment for Jenny to mention Harley, but she watched the scenery and said nothing.

At Scarlatti's, they were shown to a table in the corner, at the end of the long, brocade-draped dining room. It was early evening, not yet dark. The restaurant was almost empty. Jenny wondered where Mrs Scarlatti was. She started to ask about her, but Ezra was too busy overseeing their meal. He had ordered ahead, evidently, and now wanted it known that four would be eating instead of three. "We have my sister with us too. It's going to be a real family dinner." The waiter, who seemed fond of Ezra, nodded and went to the kitchen.

Ezra sat back and smiled at the others. Pearl was polishing a fork with her napkin. Cody was still talking about money. "I plan to buy a place in Baltimore County," he said, "in the not-too-distant future. There's no particular reason that I should be based in New York. I always did want land, that rolling Maryland farmland. I might raise horses."

"Horses! Oh, Cody, really, that's just not our style," Pearl said. "What would you want with horses?"

"Mother," Cody said, "anything's our style. Don't you see? There's no limit. Mother, do you know who called for my services last week? The Tanner Corporation."

Pearl set her fork down. Jenny tried to remember where she had heard that name before. It rang just the dimmest bell; it was like some lowly household object that you never look at, and only notice when you return after years of absence. "Tanner?" she asked Cody. "What's that?"

"It's where our father worked."

"Oh, yes."

"Where he still may, for all I know. But, Jenny, you should have seen it. Such a nickel-and-dime operation . . . I mean, not small, good Lord, with that mess of branch offices over-lapping and conflicting, but so . . . . tacky. Really so easily en-compassed. And I was thinking: imagine, just like that, I have them in my power. The Tanner Corporation! The great, almighty Tanner Corporation. That afternoon, I went out and ordered my Pontiac."

94

"There was never," Pearl said, "the slightest thing tacky about the Tanner Corporation."

Their appetizers arrived on chilled plates, along with a slender, pale green bottle of wine. The waiter poured a sip for Ezra, who tasted it as if it were important. "Good," he said. (It was strange to see him in a position of command.) "Cody? Try this wine."

"Never," said Pearl, "was there anything nickel-and-dime, in the smallest, tiniest way, ever in this world, about the Tanner Corporation."

"Oh, Mother, face it," Cody told her. "It's a trash heap. I'm going to strip it to the bones."

You would think he was speaking of something alive—an animal, some creature that would suffer. Pearl must have thought so, too. She said, "Cody, why must you act toward me in this manner?"

"I'm not acting in any manner."

"Have I ever wronged you, knowingly? Ever done you harm?"

"Please," Ezra said. "Mother? Cody? It's a family dinner! Jenny? Let's have a toast."

Jenny hastily raised her glass. "A toast," she said. "Mother? A toast."

Pearl's eyes went reluctantly to Ezra's face. "Oh," she said, after a pause. "Thank you, dear, but wine in all this heat would settle on my stomach like a rock."

"It's a toast to *me*, Mother. To my future. A toast," said Ezra, "to the new full partner of Scarlatti's Restaurant."

"Partner? Who would that be?"

"Me, Mother."

Then the double doors to the kitchen opened and in came Mrs. Scarlatti, glamorous as ever, striding on rangy, loose-strung legs and tossing back her asymmetrical hairdo. She must have been waiting for her cue—eavesdropping, in fact. "So!" she said, setting a hand on Ezra's shoulder. "What do you think of my boy here?"

"I don't understand," said Pearl.

"Well, you know he's been my right hand for so long, ever since my son died, really *better* than my son, if the truth be told; poor Billy never cared all that much for the restaurant business . . ."

Ezra was rising, as if something momentous were about to happen. While Mrs. Scarlatti went on speaking in her rasping, used-up voice—telling his own mother what an angel Ezra was, a sweetie, so gifted, such a respect for food, for decent food served decently, such a "divine" (she said) instinct for seasonings—he pulled his leather billfold from his pocket. He peered into it, looked anxious for a moment, and then said, "Ah!" and held up a ragged dollar bill. "Mrs. Scarlatti," he said, "with this dollar I hereby purchase a partnership in Scarlatti's Restaurant."

"It's yours, dear heart," said Mrs. Scarlatti, taking the money.

"What's going on here?" Pearl asked.

"We signed the papers in my lawyer's office yesterday afternoon," Mrs. Scarlatti said. "Well, it makes good sense, doesn't it? Who would I leave this damn place to when I kick off—my chihuahua? Ezra knows it inside out by now. Ezra, pour me a glass of wine."

"But I thought you were going to college," Pearl told Ezra.

"I was?"

"I thought you were planning to be a teacher! Maybe a professor. I don't understand what's happened. Oh, I know it's none of my affair. I've never been the type to meddle. Only let me tell you this: it's going to look very, very peculiar to people who don't have all the facts. Accepting such a gift! And from a woman, to boot! It's a favor; partnerships don't cost a dollar; you'll be beholden all your life. Ezra, we Tulls depend on ourselves, only on each other. We don't look to the rest of the world for any help whatsoever. How could you lend yourself to this?"

"Mother, I like making meals for people," Ezra said.

"He's a marvel," said Mrs. Scarlatti.

"But the obligation!"

Cody said, "Let him be, Mother."

She swung on him so quickly, it was more like pouncing. "I know you're enjoying this," she said.

"It's his life."

"What do you care about his life? You only want to see us break up, dissolve in the outside world."

"Please," said Ezra.

But Pearl rose and marched toward the door. "You haven't eaten!" Ezra cried. She didn't stop. In her straight-backed posture, Jenny saw the first signs of her mother's old age—her stringy tendons and breakable bones. "Oh, dear," Ezra said, "I wanted this to be such a good meal." He tore off after Pearl. Scattered diners raised their heads, thought a moment, and went back to eating.

That left Cody, Jenny, and Mrs. Scarlatti. Mrs. Scarlatti didn't seem particularly distressed. "Mothers," she said mildly. She tucked the dollar bill inside her black linen bosom.

Cody said, "Well? Does that wrap it up? Because I should have been in Delaware an hour ago. Can I give you a lift, Jenny?"

"I guess I'll walk," Jenny said.

The last she saw of Mrs. Scarlatti, she was standing there all alone, surveying the untouched appetizers with an amused expression on her face.

After Cody had driven off, Jenny walked slowly toward home. She didn't see Pearl or Ezra anywhere ahead of her. It was twilight—a sticky evening, smelling of hot tires. As she floated past shops in her sundress, she began to feel like someone's romantic vision of a young girl. She tried out a daydream of Harley Baines, but it didn't work. What did Jenny know about marriage? Why would she even want to get married? She was only a child; she would always be a child. Her wedding plans seemed makeshift and contrived—a charade. She felt foolish. She tried to remember Harley's kiss but it had vanished altogether, and Harley himself was no more real to her than a little paper man in a mail-order catalogue.

In the candy store, two children argued while their mother pressed a hand to her forehead. Next came the pharmacy and then the fortune-teller's—a smudged plate glass window with MRS. EMMA PARKINS—READINGS AND ADVICE arched in curly gold letters that were flaking around the edges. Handmade signs sat propped on the sill like afterthoughts: STRICTEST CONFI-DENCE and NO PAYMENT IF NOT FULLY SATISFIED. In the light from a dusty globe lamp, Mrs. Parkins herself paced the room—a fat, drab old woman with a cardboard fan on a Popsi-cle stick.

Jenny reached the corner, paused, and then turned. She went back to the fortune-teller's door. Should she knock, or just walk on in? She tried the handle. The door swung open and a little bell above it tinkled. Mrs. Parkins lowered her fan and said, "Do tell! A customer."

Jenny hugged her purse to her chest.

"Keeping warm?" Mrs. Parkins asked her.

"Yes," said Jenny. She thought she smelled cough syrup, the bitter, dark, cherry-flavored kind.

"Why don't you have a seat," Mrs. Parkins said.

There were two armchairs, puffy, facing each other across the little round table that held the lamp. Jenny sat in the chair nearest the door. Mrs. Parkins plucked her dress from the backs of her thighs and settled down with a groan, still gripping her fan. "Radio says the weather ought to break tomorrow," she said, "but I don't know if I can last that long. Seems like every year, the heat just hits me harder."

Yet her hand, when she reached for Jenny's, was cool and dry, with tough little pads at the fingertips. She fanned herself while she studied Jenny's palm. It made her work look com-monplace. "Long life, good career line . . ." she murmured, as if riffling through a file. Jenny relaxed.

"I suppose there's something special you want to know about," Mrs. Parkins said.

"Oh, well . . ."

"No sense beating around the bush."

Jenny said, "Should I get . . . well . . . married?"

"Married," said Mrs. Parkins.

"I mean, I could. I have this chance. I've been asked."

Mrs. Parkins went on scrutinizing Jenny's hand. Then she beckoned for the other one, which she barely glanced at. Then she sat back and fanned herself some more, gazing at the ceiling.

"Married," she said finally. "Well, I tell you. You could, or you could not. If you don't, you *will* get other offers. Surely. But here is my advice: you go ahead and do it."

"What, get married?"

"If you don't, see," Mrs. Parkins said, "you'll run into a lot of heartbreak. Lot of trouble in your romantic life. From various different people. What I mean to say," she said, "if you don't go on and get married, you'll be destroyed by love."

"Oh," Jenny said.

"That'll be two dollars, please."

Searching through her purse, Jenny had an interesting thought. By Ezra's rate of exchange, she could have bought a couple of restaurants for the same amount of money.

She married Harley late in August, in the little Baptist church that the Tulls had attended off and on. Cody gave Jenny away and Ezra was the usher. The guests he ushered in were: Pearl, Mr. and Mrs. Baines, and an aunt on Harley's mother's side. Jenny wore a white eyelet dress and sandals. Harley wore a black suit, white button-down shirt, and snub-nosed, dull black shoes. Jenny looked down at those shoes all during the ceremony. They reminded her of licorice jellybeans.

Pearl did not shed a tear, because, she said, she was so glad things had worked out this way, even though certain people might have informed her sooner. It was a relief to see your daughter handed over safely, she said—a burden off. Mrs. Baines cried steadily, but that was the kind of woman she was. She told Jenny after the wedding that it certainly didn't mean she had anything against the marriage.

Then Harley and Jenny took a train to Paulham University, where they'd rented a small apartment. They had no furniture yet and spent their wedding night on the floor. Jenny was worried about Harley's inexperience. She was certain he'd always been above such things as sex; he wouldn't know what to do, and neither would she, and they would end up failing at something the rest of the world managed without a thought. But actually, Harley knew very well what to do. She suspected he'd researched it. She had an image of Harley at a library desk, comparing the theories of experts, industriously making notes in the proper outline form.

III

"On old Olympus's torrid top," Jenny told the scenery rushing past her window, "a Finn and German picked some hops."

This was supposed to remind her of the cranial nerves: olfactory, optic, oculomotor . . . She frowned and checked in her textbook. It was 1958—the start of the first weekend in May, but not a weekend she could spare. She was paying a visit to Baltimore when she should have been holed up in Paulham, studying. She had telephoned her mother long-distance. "Could you ask Ezra to meet my train?"

"I thought you had so much work to do."

"I can work down there just as well."

"Are you bringing Harley?"

"No."

"Is anything wrong?"

100

"Of course not."

"I don't like the sound of this, young lady."

On the telephone, Pearl's voice was dim and staticky, easily dealt with. Jenny had said, "Oh, Mother, really." But now the train was drawing into Baltimore, and the sight of factory smokestacks, soot-blackened bricks, and billboards peeling in the rain—a landscape she associated with home—made her feel less sure of herself. She hoped that Ezra would meet her alone. She rubbed a clean spot on the window and stared out at acres of railroad track, then at the first metal posts flying by, then at slower posts, better defined, and a dark flight of stairs. The train shrieked and jerked to a stop. Jenny closed her book. She stood up, edged past a sleeping woman, and took a small suitcase from the rack overhead.

This station always seemed to be under some kind of construction, she thought. When she arrived at the top of the stairs, she heard the whine of a power tool—an electric drill or saw. The sound was almost lost beneath the high ceiling. Ezra stood waiting, smiling at her, with his hands in his windbreaker pockets. "How was your trip?" he asked.

"Fine."

He took her suitcase. "Harley all right?"

"Oh, yes."

They threaded through a sparse crowd of people in raincoats. "Mother's still at work," Ezra said, "but she ought to be home by the time we get there. And I've put in a call to Cody. I thought we might all have dinner at the restaurant tomorrow night; he's supposed to be passing through."

"How *is* the restaurant?"

Ezra looked unhappy. He guided Jenny through the door, into a dripping mist that felt cool on her skin. "She's not at all well," he said.

Jenny wondered why he called the restaurant "she," as if it were a ship. But then he said, "The treatments are making her worse. She can't keep anything down," and she understood that he must mean Mrs. Scarlatti. Last fall, Mrs. Scarlatti had been hospitalized for a cancer operation—her second, though up until then no one had known of the first. Ezra had taken it very hard. Mournfully trudging down a row of taxis, he said, "She hardly ever complains, but I know she's suffering."

"Are you running the restaurant alone, then?"

"Oh, yes, I've been doing that since November. Everything: the hiring and the firing, bringing in new help as people quit. A restaurant is not all food, you know. Sometimes it seems that food is the least of it. I feel the place is falling apart on me, but Mrs. Scarlatti says not to worry. It always looks like that, she says. Life is a continual shoring up, she says, against one thing and another just eroding and crumbling away. I'm beginning to think she's right."

They had reached his car, a dented gray Chevy. He opened the door for her and heaved her suitcase into the rear, which was already a chaos of *Restaurateur's Weeklys*, soiled clothing, and some kind of tongs or skewers in a Kitchen Korner shopping bag. "Sorry about the mess," he said when he'd slid behind the wheel. He started the engine and backed out of his parking slot. "Have you learned to drive yet?"

"Yes, Harley taught me. Now I drive him everywhere; he likes to be free to think."

They were on Charles Street. The rain was so fine that Ezra hadn't bothered to turn on his windshield wipers, and the glass began to film over. Jenny peered ahead. "Can you see?" she asked Ezra.

He nodded.

"First he wants me to drive," she said, "and then he criticizes every last little thing about how I do it. He's so clever; you don't know how far his cleverness can extend. I mean, it's not just math or genetics he knows all about but the most efficient temperature for cooking pot roast, the best way to organize my kitchen—everything, all charted out in his mind. When I'm driving he says, 'Now, Jennifer, you know full well that three

102

blocks from here is that transit stop where you have to veer left, so what are you doing in the right-hand lane? You ought to plan ahead more,' he says. 'Three blocks!' I say. 'Good grief! I'll get to it when I get to it,' and he says, 'That's exactly what your trouble is, Jenny.' 'Between here and that transit stop,' I tell him, 'anything might happen,' and he says, 'Not really. No, not really. In all three intersections there's a left-turn lane, as you'll recall, so you wouldn't have to wait for . . .' Nothing is unplanned, for Harley. You can see the numbered pages leafing over inside his head. There's never a single mistake."

"Well," Ezra said, "I guess it's like a whole different outlook, being a genius."

"It's not as if I hadn't been warned," said Jenny, "but I didn't realize it was a warning. I was too young to read the signals. I thought he was only like me, you know—a *careful* person; I always was careful, but now compared to Harley I don't seem careful at all. I should have guessed when I went to meet his parents before the wedding, and all the books in his room were arranged by height and blocks of color. Alphabetized I could have understood; or separated by subject matter. But this arbitrary, fixed pattern of things, a foot of red, a foot of black, no hardbacks mingling with the paperbacks . . . it's worse than Mother's bureau drawers. It's out of the frying pan, into the fire! The first time Harley kissed me, he had to brush off this bedspread beforehand that we'd been sitting on. Wouldn't you think that might have told me something? Every night now before he goes to sleep he perches on the edge of the bed and brushes off the soles of his feet. These bare white feet, untouched . . . what could have dirtied them? He wears shoes every waking moment and slippers if he takes one step in the night. But no, there he sits, so methodical, so exact, everything in its proper sequence, brush-brush . . . sometimes I think I'll hit him. I'm fascinated, I stand there watching him brush his left foot first, his right foot second, not letting either touch the floor once he's finished with it, and I think, 'I'm going to bash your head in for you, Harley.'"

Ezra cleared his throat. "It's the adjustment," he said. "Yes, that's it: adjustment. The first year of marriage. I'm sure that's all it is."

"Well, maybe so," Jenny said.

She wished she hadn't talked so much.

When they reached home, therefore—where their mother had just arrived herself—Jenny said nothing at all about Harley. (Pearl thought Harley was wonderful, admirable—maybe not so easy to hold a conversation with but the perfect person to marry her daughter.) "Now tell me," Pearl said when she'd kissed her. "How come you didn't bring that husband of yours? You haven't had some silly kind of quarrel."

"No, no. It's only my work. The strain of work," Jenny said. "I wanted to come and rest, and Harley couldn't leave his lab."

It was true that the house seemed restful, suddenly. After Ezra left for Scarlatti's, her mother led Jenny to the kitchen and brewed her a cup of tea. One thing Pearl never skimped on was tea. She moved around the room, heating the speckled brown teapot, humming some old, wavery hymn. The damp weather had frizzed her hair into little corkscrews and the steam had turned her cheeks pink; she looked almost pretty. (What kind of marriage had she had? Something must have gone terribly wrong with it, but Jenny couldn't help imagining it as perfect, all of a piece, her parents permanently joined. That her father had left was only a fluke—some misunderstanding still not cleared up.)

"I thought we'd have a very light supper," said her mother. "Maybe a salad or something."

"That would be fine," Jenny said.

"Something plain and simple."

Plain and simple was just what Jenny needed. She loosened; she was safe at last, in the only place where people knew exactly who she was and loved her anyhow.

So it was all the odder that after supper, touring the house, she felt a flash of pity for Ezra when she looked in upon his room. Still here! she thought, seeing his boyish tartan blanket on the bed, his worn recorder on the windowsill, the stamped metal tray on his bureau heaped with ancient, green-tinged pennies. How can he bear it? she wondered, and she went back down the stairs, shaking her head and marveling.

This was what Jenny had brought with her: a change of clothes, her anatomy textbook, Harley's letter proposing marriage, and his photo in a sterling silver frame. Unpacking, she set the photo firmly on her desk and examined it. She had brought it not for sentimental reasons but because she planned to think Harley over, to sum him up, and she didn't want distance to alter her judgment. She foresaw that she might be so misguided as to miss him. This picture would remind her not to. He was a stiff and stodgy man; you could see it in the thickened line of his jaw and in the opaque, bespectacled gaze he directed at the camera. He disapproved of her reasoning methods—too rushed and haphazard, he said. He didn't like her chattery friends. He thought her clothes lacked style. He criticized her table manners. "Twenty-five chews per bite," he would tell her. "That's my advice. Not only is it more healthful, but you'll find yourself not eating so much." He was obsessed by the fear that she might grow fat. Since Jenny could count every one of her ribs, she wondered if he had a kind of mad spot—if he were insane not through and through, but in one isolated area. It was the un-controllability he feared, perhaps: he would not like to see Jenny ballooning, the pounds collecting unrestrained; he wouldn't like to see her getting out of hand. That must be it. But she did begin to wonder if she might be gaining weight. She started stepping on the scales every morning. She stood in front of the full-length mirror, sucking in her stomach. Was it possible her hips were widening? Out in public, though, she noticed that the fleshy women were the ones who caught Harley's eye—the burgeoning and dimpled ones, blondes, a little blowzy. It was a mystery, really.

Jenny's grades were not very good. She wasn't failing, or anything like that; but neither was she making A's, and her lab work was often slipshod. Sometimes it seemed to her that she'd been hollow, all these years, and was finally caving in on herself. They'd found her out: at heart, there was nothing to her.

Packing for this trip (which Harley saw as a waste of time and money), she had strode across the bedroom to where his photo sat on the bureau. Harley was standing in front of it. "Move, please," she told him. He looked offended and stepped aside. Then, when he saw what she wanted, his face had . . . well, flown open, you might say. His glare had softened, his lips had parted to speak. He was touched. And *she* was touched that *he* was touched. Nothing was ever simple; there were always these complications. But what he said was, "I don't understand you. Your mother has frightened and mistreated you all your life, and now you want to visit her for no apparent reason."

Probably what he was saying was "Please don't go."

You had to be a trained decoder to read the man.

She shook open his letter of proposal. See how he had dated it: *18 July, 1957*—a form that struck her as pretentious, unless of course he happened to be English. She wondered how she could have overlooked the pompous language, the *American courtship* (as if his superior intelligence placed him on a whole separate continent), and most of all, the letter itself, the very fact that it was written, advancing the project of marriage like a corporation merger.

Well, she *had* overlooked it. She'd chosen not to see. She knew she had acted deviously in this whole business—making up her mind to win him, marrying him for practical reasons. She had calculated, was what it was. But she felt the punishment was greater than the crime. It wasn't such a terrible crime. She'd had no idea (would any unmarried person?) what a serious business she was playing with, how long it lasts, how deep it goes. And now look: the joke was on her. Having got what she was after, she found it was she who'd been got. Talk about calculating! He was going to run her life, arrange it perfectly by height and color. He was going to sit in the passenger seat with that censorious expression on his face and dictate every turn she took and every shift of gears.

Because she knew it would make Ezra happy, she went to visit the restaurant late in the evening. The rain had stopped, but there was still a mist. She felt she was walking underwater, in one of those dreams where a person can breathe as easily as on land. There were only a few other people out—all of them hurrying, locked in themselves, shrouded by raincoats and plastic scarves. Traffic swished by; reflections of the headlights wavered on the streets.

The restaurant's kitchen seemed overcrowded; it was a miracle that an acceptable plate of food could emerge from it. Ezra stood at the stove, supervising the skimming of some broth or soup. A young girl lifted ladles full of steaming liquid and emptied them into a bowl. "When you're done—" Ezra was saying, and then he said, "Why, hello, Jenny," and came to the door where she waited. Over his jeans he wore a long white apron; he looked like one of the cooks. He took her around to meet the others; sweaty men chopping or straining or stirring. "This is my sister, Jenny," he would say, but then he'd get sidetracked by some detail and stand there discussing food. "Can I offer you something to eat?" he asked finally.

"No, I had supper at home."

"Or maybe a drink from the bar?"

"No, thanks."

"This is our headwaiter, Oakes. And this is Josiah Payson; you remember him."

She looked up and up, into Josiah's face. He was all in white, spotless (how had they found a uniform to fit him?), but his hair still bristled wildly. And it was no easier than ever to see where he was directing his gaze. Not at her; that was certain. He was avoiding her. He seemed completely blind to the sight of her.

"When the Boyces come," Ezra was saying to Oakes, "tell them we have the cream of mussel soup. There's only enough for the two of them; it's waiting on the back burner."

"How are you, Josiah?" Jenny asked.

"Oh, not bad."

"So you work here now."

"I'm the salad chef. Mostly, I cut things up."

His spidery hands twisted in front of him. The crease in his forehead seemed deeper than ever.

"I've thought of you often," Jenny said.

She didn't mean it, at first. But then she understood, with a rush to her head that was something like illness, that she spoke the truth: she had been thinking of him all these years without knowing it. It seemed he had never once left her mind. Even Harley, she saw, was just a reverse kind of Josiah, a Josiah turned inside out: equally alien, black-and-white, incomprehensible to anyone but Jenny.

"Is your mother well?" she asked him.

"She died."

"Died!"

"A long time ago. She went out shopping and she died. I live in my house all alone now."

"I'm sorry," Jenny said.

But still he wouldn't meet her eyes.

Ezra turned from Oakes and asked, "Are you sure I can't get you a snack, Jenny?"

"I have to leave," she told him.

Going home, she wondered why the walk seemed so long. Her feet felt unusually heavy, and there was some old, rusty pain deep inside her chest.

The ash grove, how graceful, Ezra's recorder piped out, *how sweetly 'tis singing* . . . Waking slowly, still webbed in bits of dreams, Jenny found it strange that a pearwood recorder should put forth plums—perfectly round, pure, plummy notes arriving in a spill on her bed. She sat up and thought for a moment. Then she pushed her blankets back and reached for her clothes.

Ezra was playing "Le Godiveau de Poisson" when she left for the house.

Down this street, and then that one, and then another that turned out to be a mistake. She had to retrace her path. It was going to be a beautiful day. The sidewalks were still wet, but the sun was rising in a pearly pink sky above the chimneys. She dug her hands in her coat pockets. She met an old man walking a poodle, but no one else, and even he passed soundlessly and vanished.

When she reached the street she wanted, nothing looked familiar and she had to take the alley. She could only find the house from the rear. She recognized that makeshift gray addition behind the kitchen, and the buckling steps that gave beneath her feet, and the wooden door with most of its paint worn off. She looked for a bell to ring but there wasn't one; she had to knock. There was the scraping of furniture somewhere inside the house—chair legs pushing back. Josiah, when he came, was so tall that he darkened the window she peered through.

He opened the door. "Jenny?" he said.

"Hello, Josiah."

He looked around him, as if supposing she had come to see someone else. She noticed his breakfast on the kitchen table: a slice of white bread spread with peanut butter. In the scuffed linoleum and the sink full of dirty dishes, in his tattered jeans and raveling brown sweater, she read neglect and hopelessness. She pulled her coat tighter around her.

"What are you, what are you here for?" he asked.

"I did everything wrong," she told him.

"What are you talking about?"

"You must feel I'm just like the others! Just like the ones you want to escape from, off in the woods with your sleeping bag."

"Oh, no, Jenny," he said. "I would never believe you're like that."

"You wouldn't?"

"Nobody would; you're too pretty."

"But I mean—" she said.

She set a hand on his sleeve. He didn't pull away. Then she stepped closer and slipped her arms around him. She could feel, even through her coat, how thin and bony his rib cage was, and how he warmed his skimpy sweater. She laid her ear against his chest, and he slowly, hesitantly raised his hands to her shoulders. "I should have gone on kissing you," she said. "I should have told my mother, 'Go away. Leave us alone.' I should have stood up for you and not been such a coward."

"No, no," she heard him say. "I don't think about it. I don't think about it."

She drew back and looked up at him.

"I don't talk about it," he said.

"Josiah," she said, "won't you at least tell me it's all right now?"

"Sure," he said. "It's all right, Jenny."

After that, there was really nothing else to discuss. She stood on tiptoe to kiss him goodbye, and she thought he looked directly at her when he smiled and let her go.

"To everybody's good health," Cody said, raising his glass. "To Ezra's food. To Scarlatti's Restaurant."

"To a happy family dinner," Ezra said.

"Oh, well, that too, if you like."

They all drank, even Pearl—or maybe the little sip she took was only make-believe. She was wearing her netted hat and a beige tailored suit so new that it failed to sit back when she did. Jenny was in an ordinary skirt and blouse, but still she felt dressed up. She felt wonderful, in fact—perfectly untroubled.

She kept beaming at the others, pleased to have them around her.

But really, were they all here? In Jenny's new mood, her family seemed too small. These three young people and this shrunken mother, she thought, were not enough to sustain the occasion. They could have used several more members—a family clown, for instance; and a genuine black sheep, blacker than Cody; and maybe one of those managerial older sisters who holds a group together by force. As things were, it was Ezra who had to hold them together. He wasn't doing a very good job. He was too absorbed in the food. Right now he was conferring with the waiter, gesturing toward the soup, which had arrived a touch too cool, he said—though to Jenny it seemed fine. And now Pearl was collecting her purse and sliding back her chair. "Powder room," she mouthed to Jenny. Ezra would be all the more upset, once he noticed she'd gone. He liked the family in a group, a cluster, and he hated Pearl's habit of constantly "freshening up" in a restaurant, just as he hated for Cody to smoke his slim cigars between courses. "I wish just once," he was always saying, "we could get through a meal from start to finish," and he would say it again as soon as he discovered Pearl was missing. But now he was telling the waiter, "If Andrew would keep the china hot—"

"He mostly does, I swear it, but the warming oven's broke."

"What's your opinion?" Cody whispered, setting his face close to Jenny's. "Has Ezra ever slept with Mrs. Scarlatti? Or has he not."

Jenny's mouth dropped open.

"Well?" he asked.

"Cody Tull!"

"Don't tell me it hasn't occurred to you. A lonely rich widow, or whatever she is; nice-looking boy with no prospects . . ."

"That's disgusting," Jenny told him.

"Not at all," Cody said blandly, sitting back. He had a way

of surveying people from under half-lowered lids which made him look tolerant and worldly. "There's nothing wrong," he said, "with taking advantage of your luck. And you have to admit Ezra's lucky; *born* lucky. Have you ever noticed what happens when I bring around my girlfriends? They fall all over him. They have ever since we were kids. What do they see in him, anyway? How does he do it? *Is* it luck? You're a woman; what's his secret?"

"Honestly, Cody," Jenny said, "I wish you'd grow out of this."

Ezra finished his conversation with the waiter. "Where's Mother?" he asked. "I turn my back one second and she disappears."

"Powder room," said Cody, lighting a cigar.

"Oh, why does she always do that? More soup is coming, fresh off the stove, piping hot this time."

"Are you having it brought in by barefoot runners?" Cody asked.

Jenny said, "Don't worry, Ezra. I'll go call her."

She made her way between the tables, toward a corridor with an EXIT sign over the archway. But just before the ladies' room, in front of a swinging, leather-covered door, she caught sight of Josiah. He had his white uniform on and was carrying an aqua plastic dishpan full of chicory leaves. "Josiah," she said.

He stopped short and his face lit up. "Hi, Jenny," he said.

They stood smiling at each other, not speaking. She reached out to touch his wrist.

"Oh, no!" her mother cried.

Jenny snatched her hand back and spun around.

"Oh, Jenny. Oh, my God," Pearl said. Her eyes were no longer gray; they were black, and she gripped her shiny black purse. "Well, I understand it all now," she said.

"No, wait," Jenny said. Her heart was beating so fast, it seemed she was vibrating where she stood.

"Visiting for no apparent reason," said Pearl, "and slipping away this morning to meet him like a tramp, some cheap little tramp—"

"Mother, you've got it wrong!" Jenny told her. "It's nothing, don't you see?" She felt she had run out of breath. Gasping for air, she gestured toward Josiah, who merely stood there with his mouth agape. "He just . . . we just met in the hall and . . . it's not that way at all, he's *nothing* to me, don't you see?"

But she had to say this to Pearl's back, hurrying after her through the dining room. Pearl reached their table and said, "Ezra, I cannot stay here."

Ezra stood up. "Mother?"

"I simply cannot," she said. She gathered up her coat and walked away.

"But what happened?" Ezra asked, turning to Jenny. "What's bothering her?"

Cody said, "That lukewarm soup, no doubt," and he rocked back comfortably in his chair with a cigar between his teeth.

"I wish just once," Ezra said, "we could eat a meal from start to finish."

"I don't feel well," Jenny told him.

In fact, her lips were numb. It was a symptom she seemed to remember from before, from some long-forgotten moment, or maybe from a nightmare.

She left her coat behind, and she rushed thorough the dining room and out to the street. At first, she thought her mother had disappeared. Then she found her, half a block ahead—a militant figure walking briskly. Oh, what if she wouldn't even turn around? Or worse, would turn and lash out, slap, snap, her clawed pearl ring, her knowing face . . . But Jenny ran to catch up with her, anyway. "Mother," she said.

In the light from the liquor store window, she saw her mother reassemble her expression—take a cool, unperturbed look.

"You've got it all wrong," Jenny told her. "I'm not a tramp! I'm not cheap! Mother, listen to me."

"It doesn't matter," Pearl said politely.

"Of course it matters!"

"You're over twenty-one. If you don't know good from bad by now, there's nothing more I can do about it."

"I felt sorry for him," Jenny said.

They crossed a street and started up the next block.

"He told me his mother had died," Jenny said.

They veered around a gang of teen-aged boys.

"She was all he had—his father's dead too. She was the center of his life."

"Well," said Pearl, "I suppose it can't have been easy for her."

"I don't know how he's going to manage now she's gone."

"I believe I saw her in the grocery once," said Pearl. "A brown-haired woman?"

"Plumpish, sort of."

"Full in the face?"

"Like a wood thrush," Jenny said.

"Oh, Jenny," said her mother, and she gave a little laugh. "The things you come up with, sometimes!"

They passed the candy store, and then the pharmacy. Jenny and her mother fell in to step. They passed the fortune-teller's window. The same dusty lamp glowed on the table. Jenny, looking in, thought that Mrs. Parkins had not been much of a prophet. Why, she had even had to listen to the radio for tomorrow's weather! And she should have guessed from the very first instant, from the briefest, most cursory glance, that Jenny was not capable of being destroyed by love.

4

Heart Rumors

The first few times that Mrs. Scarlatti stayed in the hospital, Ezra had no trouble getting in to visit her. But the last time was harder. "Relative?" the nurse would ask.

"No, ah, I'm her business partner."

"Sorry, relatives only."

"But she doesn't have any relatives. I'm all she's got. See, she and I own this restaurant together."

"And what's in that jar?"

"Her soup."

"Soup," said the nurse.

"I make the soup she likes."

"Mrs. Scarlatti isn't keeping things down."

"I know that, but I wanted to give her something."

This would earn him a slantwise glance, before he was led brusquely into Mrs. Scarlatti's room.

In the past, she had chosen to stay in a ward. (She was an extremely social woman.) She'd sit up straight in her dramatic black robe, a batik scarf hiding her hair, and "Sweetie!" she'd say as he entered. For a moment the other women would grow all sly and alert, till they realized how young he was—way too young for Mrs. Scarlatti. But now she had a private room, and the most she could do when he arrived was open her eyes and then wearily close them. He wasn't even sure that he was welcome any more.

He knew that after he left, someone would discard his soup. But this was his special gizzard soup that she had always loved. There were twenty cloves of garlic in it. Mrs. Scarlatti used to claim it settled her stomach, soothed her nerves—changed her whole perception of the day, she said. (However, it wasn't on the restaurant's menu because it was a bit "hearty"—her word—and Scarlatti's Restaurant was very fine and formal. This hurt Ezra's feelings, a little.) When she was well enough to be home, he had often brewed single portions in the restaurant kitchen and carried them upstairs to her apartment. Even in the hospital, those first few times, she could manage a small-sized bowl of it. But now she was beyond that. He only brought the soup out of helplessness, he would have preferred to kneel by her bed and rest his head on her sheets, to take her hands in his and tell her, "Mrs. Scarlatti, come back." But she was such a no-nonsense woman; she would have looked shocked. All he could do was offer this soup.

He sat in a corner of the room in a green vinyl chair with steel arms. It was October and the steam heat had come on; the air felt sharp and dry. Mrs. Scarlatti's bed was cranked upward slightly to help her breathe. From time to time, without opening her eyes, she said, "Oh, God." Then Ezra would ask, "What? What is it?" and she would sigh. (Or maybe that was the radiator.) Ezra never brought anything to read, and he never made conversation with the nurses who squeaked in and out on their rubber soles. He only sat, looking down at his pale, oversized hands, which lay loosely on his knees.

Previously, he had put on weight. He'd been nowhere near fat, but he'd softened and spread in that mild way that fair-haired men often do. Now the weight fell off. Like Mrs. Scarlatti, he was having trouble keeping things down. His large, floppy clothes covered a large, floppy frame that seemed oddly two-dimensional. Wide in front and wide behind, he was flat as paper when viewed from the side. His hair fell forward in a sheaf, like wheat. He didn't bother pushing it back.

He and Mrs. Scarlatti had been through a lot together, he would have said, if asked—but what, exactly? She had had a bad husband (a matter of luck, she made it seem, like a bad bottle of wine) and ditched him; she had lost her only son, Ezra's age, during the Korean War. But both these events she had suffered alone, before her partnership with Ezra began. And Ezra himself: well, he had not actually been through anything yet. He was twenty-five years old and still without wife or children, still living at home with his mother. What he and Mrs. Scarlatti had survived, it appeared, was year after year of standing still. Her life that had slid off somewhere in the past, his that kept delaying its arrival—they'd combined, they held each other up in empty space. Ezra was grateful to Mrs. Scarlatti for rescuing him from an aimless, careerless existence and teaching him all she knew; but more than that, for the fact that she depended on him. If not for her, whom would he have? His brother and sister were out in the world; he loved his mother dearly but there was something overemotional about her that kept him eternally wary. By other people's standards, even he and Mrs. Scarlatti would not have seemed particularly close. He always called her "Mrs. Scarlatti." She called Ezra her boy, her angel, but was otherwise remarkably distant, and asked no questions at all about his life outside the restaurant.

He knew the restaurant would be fully his when she died. She had told him so, just before this last hospital stay. "I don't want it," he had said. She was silent. She must have understood that it was only his manner of speaking. Of course he didn't *want* it, in the sense of coveting it (he never thought much about money), but what would he do otherwise? Anyway, she had no one else to leave it to. She lifted a hand and let it drop. They didn't mention the subject again.

*

Once, Ezra persuaded his mother to come and visit too. He liked for the various people in his life to get along, although he knew that would be difficult in his mother's case. She spoke of Mrs. Scarlatti distrustfully, even jealously. "What you see in such a person I can't imagine. She's downright . . . tough, is what she is, in spite of her high-fashion clothes. It looks like her face is not trying. Know what I mean? Like she can't be bothered putting out the effort. Not a bit of lipstick, and those crayony black lines around her eyes . . . and she hardly ever smiles at people."

But now that Mrs. Scarlatti was so sick, his mother kept her thoughts to herself. She dressed carefully for her visit and wore her netted hat, which made Ezra happy. He associated that hat with important family occasions. He was pleased that she'd chosen her Sunday black coat, even though it wasn't as warm as her everyday maroon.

In the hospital, she told Mrs. Scarlatti, "Why, you look the picture of health! No one would ever guess."

This was not true. But it was nice of her to say it.

"After I die," Mrs. Scarlatti said in her grainy voice, "Ezra must move to my apartment."

His mother said, "Now, let's have none of that silly talk."

"Which is silly?" Mrs. Scarlatti asked, but then she was over-taken by exhaustion, and she closed her eyes. Ezra's mother misunderstood. She must have thought she'd asked *what* was silly, a rhetorical question, and she blithely smoothed her skirt around her and said, "Total foolishness, I never heard such rot." Only Ezra grasped Mrs. Scarlatti's meaning. Which was silly, she was asking—her dying, or Ezra's moving? But he didn't bother explaining that to his mother.

Another time, he got special permission from the nurses' office to bring a few men from the restaurant—Todd Duckett, Josiah Payson, and Raymond the sauce maker. He could tell that Mrs. Scarlatti was glad to see them, although it was an awkward visit. The men stood around the outer edges of the room and cleared their throats repeatedly and would not take seats. "Well?" said Mrs. Scarlatti. "Are you still buying everything fresh?" From the inappropriateness of the question (none of them was remotely involved with the purchasing), Ezra realized how out of touch she had grown. But these people, too, were tactful. Todd Duckett gave a mumbled cough and then said, "Yes, ma'am, just how you would've liked it."

"I'm tired now," Mrs. Scarlatti said.

Down the hall lay an emaciated woman in a coma, and an old, old man with a tiny wife who was allowed to sleep on a cot in his room, and a dark-skinned foreigner whose masses of visiting relatives gave the place the look of a gypsy circus. Ezra knew that the comatose woman had cancer, the old man a rare type of blood disease, and the foreigner some cardiac problem—it wasn't clear what. "Heart rumor," he was told by a dusky, exotic child who was surely too young to be visiting hospitals. She was standing outside the foreigner's door, delicately reeling in a yo-yo.

"Heart *murmur*, maybe?"

"No, rumor."

Ezra was starting to feel lonely here and would have liked to make a friend. The nurses were always sending him away while they did something mysterious to Mrs. Scarlatti, and much of any visit he spent leaning dejectedly against the wall outside her room or gazing from the windows of the conservatory at the end of the corridor. But no one seemed approachable. This wing was different from the others—more hushed—and all the people he encountered wore a withdrawn, forbidding look. Only the foreign child spoke to him. "I think he's going to die," she said. But then she went back to her yo-yo. Ezra hung around a while longer, but it was obvious she didn't find him very interesting.

Bibb lettuce, Boston lettuce, chicory, escarole, dripping on the counter in the center of the kitchen. While other restaurants' vegetables were delivered by anonymous, dank, garbage-smelling trucks, Scarlatti's had a man named Mr. Purdy, who shopped personally for them each morning before the sun came up. He brought everything to the kitchen in splintery bushel baskets, along about eight a.m., and Ezra made a point of being there so that he would know what foods he had to deal with that day. Sometimes there were no eggplants, sometimes twice as many as planned. In periods like this—dead November, now—nothing grew locally, and Mr. Purdy had to resort to vegetables raised elsewhere, limp carrots and waxy cucumbers shipped in from out of state. And the tomatoes! They were a crime. "Just look," said Mr. Purdy, picking one up. "Vine-grown, the fellow tells me. Vine-*grown*, yes. I'd like to see them grown on anything else. 'But ripened?' I say. 'However was they ripened?' 'Vine-ripened, too,' fellow assures me. Well, maybe so. But nowadays, I don't know, all them taste anyhow like they spent six weeks on a windowsill. Like they was *made* of windowsill, of celluloid, or pencil erasers. Well, I tell you, Ezra: I apologize. It breaks my heart to bring you such rubbage as this here; I'd sooner not show up at all."

Mr. Purdy was a pinched and prunish man in overalls, a white shirt, and a shiny black suit coat. He had a narrow face that seemed eternally disapproving, even during the growing season. Only Ezra knew that inwardly, there was something nourishing and generous about him. Mr. Purdy rejoiced in food as much as Ezra did, and for the same reasons—less for eating himself than for serving to others. He had once invited Ezra to his home, a silver-colored trailer out on Ritchie Highway, and given him a meal consisting solely of new asparagus, which both he and Ezra agreed had the haunting taste of oysters. Mrs. Purdy, a smiling, round-faced woman in a wheelchair, had claimed they talked like lunatics, but she finished two large helpings while both men tenderly watched. It was a satisfaction to see how she polished her buttery plate.

"If this restaurant was just mine," Ezra said now, "I wouldn't serve tomatoes in the winter. People would ask for tomatoes and I'd say, 'What can you be thinking of, this is not the season.' I'd give them something better."

"They'd stomp out directly," Mr. Purdy said.

"No, they might surprise you. And I'd put up a blackboard, write on it every day just two or three good dishes. Of course! In France, they do that all the time. Or I'd offer no choice at all; examine people and say, 'You look a little tired. I'll bring you an oxtail stew.'"

"Mrs. Scarlatti would just die," said Mr. Purdy.

There was a silence. He rubbed his bristly chin, and then corrected himself: "She'd rotate in her grave."

They stood around a while.

"I don't really want a restaurant anyhow," Ezra said.

"Sure," Mr. Purdy said. "I know that."

Then he put his black felt hat on, and thought a moment, and left.

The foreign child slept in the conservatory, her head resting on the stainless steel arm of a chair like the one in Mrs. Scarlatti's room. It made Ezra wince. He wanted to fold his coat and slide it beneath her cheek, but he worried that would wake her. He kept his distance, therefore, and stood at one of the windows gazing down on pedestrians far below. How small and determined their feet looked, emerging from their foreshortened figures! The perseverance of human beings suddenly amazed him.

A woman entered the room—one of the foreigners. She was lighter skinned than the others, but he knew she was foreign because of her slippers, which contrasted with her expensive wool dress. The whole family, he had noticed, changed into slippers as soon as they arrived each morning. They made themselves at home in every possible way—setting out bags of seeds and nuts and spicy-smelling foods, once even brewing a quart of yogurt on the conservatory radiator. The men smoked cigarettes in the hall, and the women murmured together while knitting brightly colored sweaters.

Now the woman approached the child, bent over her, and tucked her hair back. Then she lifted her in her arms and settled in the chair. The child didn't wake. She only nestled closer and sighed. So after all, Ezra could have put his coat beneath her head. He had missed an opportunity. It was like missing a train—or something more important, something that would never come again. There was no explanation for the grief that suddenly filled him.

He decided to start serving his gizzard soup in the restaurant. He had the waiters announce it to patrons when they handed over the menu. "In addition to the soups you see here, we are pleased to offer tonight . . ." One of the waiters had failed to show up and Ezra hired a woman to replace him—strictly against Mrs. Scarlatti's policy. (Waitresses, she said, belonged in truck stops.) The woman did much better than the men with Ezra's soup. "Try our gizzard soup," she would say. "It's really hot and garlicky and it's made with love." Outside it was bitter cold, and the woman was so warm and helpful, more and more people followed her suggestion. Ezra thought that the next time a waiter left, he would hire a second woman, and maybe another after that, and so on.

He experimented the following week with a spiced crab casserole of his own invention, and then with a spinach bisque, and when the waiters complained about all they had to memorize he finally went ahead and bought a blackboard. SPECIALS, he wrote at the top. But in the hospital, when Mrs. Scarlatti asked how things were going, he didn't mention any of this. Instead, he sat forward and clasped his hands tight and said, "Fine. Um . . . fine." If she noticed anything strange in his voice, she didn't comment on it.

*

Mrs. Scarlatti had always been a lean, dark, slouching woman, with a faintly scornful manner. It was true, as Ezra's mother said, that she gave the impression of not caring what people thought of her. But that had been part of her charm—her sleepy eyes, hardly troubling to stay open, and her indifferent tone of voice. Now, she went too far. Her skin took on the pallid look of stone, and her face began to seem sphinxlike, all flat planes and straight lines. Even her hair was sphinxlike—a short, black wedge, a *clump* of hair, dulled and rough. Sometimes Ezra believed that she was not dying but petrifying. He had trouble remembering her low laugh, her casual arrogance. ("Sweetie," she used to say, ordering him off to some task, trilling languid fingers. "Angel boy . . .") He had never felt more than twelve years old around her, but now he was ancient, her parent or grandparent. He soothed and humored her. Not all she said was quite clear these days. "At least," she whispered once, "I never made myself ridiculous, Ezra, did I?"

"Ridiculous?" he asked.

"With you."

"With me? Of course not."

He was puzzled, and must have shown it; she smiled and rocked her head on the pillow. "Oh, you always were a much-loved child," she told him. It must have been a momentary wandering of the brain. (She hadn't known him as a child.) "You take it all for granted," she said. Maybe she was confusing him with Billy, her son. She turned her face away from him and closed her eyes. He felt suddenly anxious. He was reminded of that time his mother had nearly died, wounded by a misfired arrow—entirely Ezra's fault; Ezra, the family stumbler. "I'm so sorry, I'm sorry, I'm sorry," he had cried, but the apology had never been accepted because his brother had been blamed instead, and his father, who had purchased the archery set. Ezra, his mother's favorite, had got off scot-free. He'd been left unforgiven—not relieved, as you might expect, but forever burdened. "You're mistaken," he said now, and Mrs. Scarlatti's eyelids fluttered into crepe but failed to open. "I wish you'd get me straight. See who I *am*, I'm Ezra," he said, and then (for no logical reason) he bent close and said, "Mrs. Scarlatti. Remember when I left the army? Discharged for sleepwalking? Sent home? Mrs. Scarlatti, I wasn't really all the way asleep. I mean, I knew what I was doing. I didn't *plan* to sleepwalk, but part of me was conscious, and observed what was going on, and could have wakened the rest of me if I'd tried. I had this feeling like watching a dream, where you know you can break it off at any moment. But I didn't; I wanted to go home. I just wanted to leave that army, Mrs. Scarlatti. So I didn't stop myself."

If she had heard (with her only son, Billy, blown to bits in Korea), she would have risen up, sick as she was, and shouted, "Out! Out of my life!" So she must have missed it, for she only rocked her head again and smiled and went on sleeping.

Just after Thanksgiving the woman who'd been in a coma died, and the tiny old man either died or went home, but the foreigner stayed on and his relatives continued to visit. Now that they knew Ezra by sight, they hailed him as he passed. "Come!" they would call, and he would step in, shy and pleased, and stand around for several minutes with his fists locked in his armpits. The sick man was yellow and sunken, hooked to a number of tubes, but he always tried to smile at Ezra's entrance. Ezra had the impression that he knew no English. The others spoke English according to their ages—the child perfectly, the young adults with a strong, attractive accent, the old ones in ragged segments. Eventually, though, even the most fluent forgot themselves and drifted into their native language—a musical one, with rounded vowels that gave their lips a muscled, pouched, commiserative shape, as if they were perpetually tut-tutting. Ezra loved to listen. When you couldn't understand what people said, he thought, how clearly the links and joints in their relationships stood out! A woman's face lit and bloomed as she turned to a certain man; a barbed

124

sound of pain leapt from the patient and his wife doubled over. The child, when upset, stroked her mother's gold wristwatch band for solace.

Once a young girl in braids sang a song with almost no tune. It wandered from note to note as if by accident. Then a man with a heavy black mustache recited what must have been a poem. He spoke so grandly and unselfconsciously that passersby glanced in, and when he had finished he translated it for Ezra. *"O dead one, why did you die in the springtime? You haven't yet tasted the squash, or the cucumber salad."*

Why, even their poetry touched matters close to Ezra's heart.

By December he had replaced three of the somber-suited waiters with cheery, motherly waitresses, and he'd scrapped the thick beige menus and started listing each day's dishes on the blackboard. This meant, of course, that the cooks all left (none of the dishes were theirs, or even their type), so he did most of the cooking himself, with the help of a woman from New Orleans and a Mexican. These two had recipes of their own as well, some of which Ezra had never tasted before; he was entranced. It was true that the customers seemed surprised, but they adjusted, Ezra thought. Or most of them did.

Now he grew feverish with new ideas, and woke in the night longing to share them with someone. Why not a restaurant full of refrigerators, where people came and chose the food they wanted? They could fix it themselves on a long, long stove lining one wall of the dining room. Or maybe he could install a giant fireplace, with a whole steer turning slowly on a spit. You'd slice what you liked on to your plate and sit around in armchairs eating and talking with the guests at large. Then again, maybe he would start serving only street food. Of course! He'd cook what people felt homesick for—tacos like those from vendors' carts in California, which the Mexican was always pining after; and that wonderful vinegary North Carolina barbecue that Todd Duckett had to have brought by his mother several times a year in cardboard cups. He would call it the Homesick Restaurant. He'd take down the old black and gilt sign . . .

But then he saw the sign, SCARLATTI'S, and he groaned and pressed his fingers to his eyes and turned over in his bed.

"You have a beautiful country," the light-skinned woman said.

"Thank you," said Ezra.

"All that green! And so many birds. Last summer, before my father-in-law fell ill, we were renting a house in New Jersey. The Garden State, they call it. There were roses everywhere. We could sit on the lawn after supper and listen to the nightingales."

"The what?" said Ezra.

"The nightingales."

"Nightingales? In New Jersey?"

"Of course," she said. "Also we liked shopping. In particular, Korvette's. My husband likes the . . . how do you say? Drip and dry suits."

The sick man moaned and tossed, nearly dislodging a tube that entered the back of his wrist. His wife, an ancient, papery lady, leaned toward him and stroked his hand. She murmured something, and then she turned to the younger woman. Ezra saw that she was crying. She didn't attempt to hide it but wept openly, tears streaming down her cheeks. "Ah," the younger woman said, and she left Ezra's side and bent over the wife. She gathered her up in arms as she'd gathered the child earlier. Ezra knew he should leave, but he didn't. Instead he turned and gazed out the window, slightly tilting his head and looking nonchalant, as some men do when they have rung a doorbell and are standing on the porch, waiting to be noticed and invited in.

Ezra's sister, Jenny, sat at the desk in her old bedroom, reading a battered textbook. She was strikingly pretty, even in reading glasses and the no-color quilted bathrobe she always left on a closet hook for her visits home. Ezra stopped at her doorway and peered in. "Jenny?" he asked. "What are you doing here?"

"I thought I'd take a breather," she said. She removed her glasses and gave him a blurry, unfocused look.

"It isn't semester break yet, is it?"

"Semester break! Do you think medical students have time for such things?"

"No, well," he said.

But lately she'd been home more often than not, it appeared to him. And she never mentioned Harley, her husband. She hadn't referred to him once all fall, and maybe even all summer. "It's my opinion she's left him," Ezra's mother had said recently. "Oh, don't act so surprised! It must have crossed your mind. Here she suddenly moves to a new address—closer to the school, she claims—and then can't have us to visit, anytime I offer; always too busy or preparing for some quiz, and when I call, you notice, it's never Harley who answers, never once Harley who picks up the phone. Doesn't that strike you as odd? But I'm unable to broach the subject. I mean, she deflects me, if you know what I mean. Somehow I just never . . . *you* could, though. She always did feel closer to you than to me or Cody. Won't you just ask her what's what?"

But now when he lounged in the doorway, trying to find some way to sidle into a conversation, Jenny put her glasses back on and returned to her book. He felt dismissed. "Um," he said. "How are things in Paulham?"

"Fine," she said, eyes scanning the print.

"Harley all right?"

There was a deep, studious silence.

"It doesn't seem we ever get to see him any more," Ezra said.

"He's okay," Jenny said.

She turned a page.

Ezra waited a while longer, and then he straightened up from the doorway and went downstairs. He found his mother in the kitchen, unpacking groceries. "Well?" she asked him.

"Well, what?"

"Did you talk to Jenny?"

"Ah . . ."

She still had her coat on; she thrust her hands in her pockets and faced him squarely, with her bun slipping down the back of her head. "You promised me," she told him. "You swore you'd talk to her."

"I didn't swear to, Mother."

"You took a solemn oath," she told him.

"I notice she still wears a ring," he said hopefully.

"So what," said his mother. She went back to her groceries.

"She wouldn't wear a ring if she and Harley were separated, would she?"

"She would if she wanted to fool us."

"Well, I don't know, if she wants to fool us maybe we ought to *act* fooled. I don't know."

"All my life," his mother said, "people have been trying to shut me out. Even my children. Especially my children. If I so much as ask that girl how she's been, she shies away like I'd inquired into the deepest, darkest part of her. Now, why should she be so standoffish?"

Ezra said, "Maybe she cares more about what *you* think than what outsiders think."

"Ha," said his mother. She lifted a carton of eggs from the grocery bag.

"I'm worried I don't know how to get in touch with people," Ezra said.

"Hmm?"

"I'm worried if I come too close, they'll say I'm overstepping. They'll say I'm pushy, or . . . emotional, you know. But if I back off, they might think I don't care. I really, honestly believe I missed some rule that everyone else takes for granted; I must have been absent from school that day. There's this narrow little dividing line I somehow never located."

"Nonsense; I don't know what you're talking about," said his mother, and then she held up an egg. "Will you look at this? Out of one dozen eggs, four are cracked. Two are *smushed*. I can't imagine what Sweeney Brothers is coming to, these days."

Ezra waited a while, but she didn't say any more. Finally, he left.

He tore down the wall between the restaurant kitchen and the dining room, doing most of the work in a single night. He slung a sledgehammer in a steady rhythm, then ripped away at hunks of plaster till a thick white dust had settled over everything. then he came upon a mass of pipes and electrical wires and he had to call in professionals to finish off the job. The damage was so extensive that he was forced to stay closed for four straight weekdays, losing a good deal of money.

He figured that while he was at it, he might as well redecorate the dining room. He raced around the windows and dragged down the stiff brocade draperies; he peeled up the carpeting and persuaded a brigade of workmen to sand and polish the floorboards.

By the evening of the fourth day, he was so tired that he could feel the hinging of every muscle. Even so, he washed the white from his hair and changed out of his speckled jeans and went to pay a visit to Mrs. Scarlatti. She lay in her usual position, slightly propped, but her expression was alert and she even managed a smile when he entered. "Guess what, angel," she whispered. "Tomorrow they're letting me leave."

"Leave?"

"I asked the doctor, and he's letting me go home."

"Home?"

"As long as I hire a nurse, he says . . . Well, don't just stand there, Ezra. I need for you to see about a nurse. If you'll look in that nightstand . . ."

It was more talking than she'd done in weeks. Ezra felt

almost buoyant with new hope; underneath, it seemed, it must have given up on her. But of course, he was also worried about the restaurant. What would she think when she saw it? What would she say to him? "Everything must go back again, just the way it was," he could imagine. "Really, Ezra. Put up that wall this instant, and fetch my carpets and my curtains." He suspected that he had very poor taste, much inferior to Mrs. Scarlatti's. She would say, "Dear heart, how could you be so *chintzy?*"—a favorite word of hers. He wondered if he could keep her from finding out, if he could convince her to stay in her apartment till he had returned things to normal.

He thanked his stars that he hadn't changed the sign that hung outside.

It was Ezra who settled the bill at the business office, the following morning. Then he spoke briefly with her doctor, whom he chanced to meet in the corridor. "This is wonderful about Mrs. Scarlatti," Ezra said. "I really didn't expect it."

"Oh," said the doctor. "Well."

"I was getting sort of discouraged, if you want to know the truth."

"Well," the doctor said again, and he held out his hand so suddenly that it took Ezra a second to respond. After that, the doctor walked off. Ezra felt there was a lot more the man could have said, as a matter of fact.

Mrs. Scarlatti went home by ambulance. Ezra drove behind, catching glimpses of her through the tinted window. She lay on a stretcher, and next to her was another stretcher holding a man in two full leg casts. His wife perched beside him, evidently talking nonstop. Ezra could see the feathers on her hat bob up and down with her words.

Mrs. Scarlatti was let off first. The ambulance men unloaded her while Ezra stood around feeling useless. "Oh, smell that air," said Mrs. Scarlatti. "Isn't it fresh and beautiful." Actually, it was terrible air—wintry and rainy and harsh with soot. "I never told you this, Ezra," she said, as they wheeled her through the building's front entrance, "but I really didn't believe I would see this place again. My little apartment, my restaurant . . ." Then she raised a palm—her old, peremptory gesture, directed toward the ambulance men. They were preparing to guide her stetcher through the right-hand door and up the stairs. "Dear fellow," she said to the nearest one, "could you just open that door on the left and let me take a peek?"

It happened so fast, Ezra didn't have time to protest. The man reached back in a preoccupied way and opened the door to the restaurant. Then he resumed his study of the stairs; there was an angle at the top that was going to pose a problem. Mrs. Scarlatti, meanwhile, turned her face with some effort and gazed through the door.

There was a moment, just a flicker of a second, when Ezra dared to hope that she might approve after all. But looking past her, he realized that was impossible. The restaurant was a warehouse, a barn, a gymnasium—a total catastrophe. Tables and upended chairs huddled in one corner, underneath bald, barren windows. Buckling plank footbridges led across the varnished floor, which had somehow picked up a film of white dust, and the missing kitchen wall was as horrifying as a toothless smile. Only two broad, plaster pillars separated the kitchen from the dining room. Everything was exposed—sinks and garbage cans, the blackened stove, the hanging pots with their tarnished bottoms, a calendar showing a girl in a sheer black nightgown, and a windowsill bearing two dead plants and a Brillo pad and Todd Duckett's asthma inhalant.

"Oh, my God," said Mrs. Scarlatti.

She looked up into his eyes. Her face seemed stripped. "You might at least have waited till I died," she said.

"Oh!" said Ezra. "No, you don't understand; you don't know. It wasn't what you think. It was just . . . I can't explain, I went wild somehow!"

But she raised that palm of hers and sailed up the stairs to

131

her apartment. Even lying flat, she had an air of speed and power.

She didn't refuse to see him again—nothing like that. Every morning he paid her a visit, and was admitted by her day nurse. He sat on the edge of the ladylike chair in the bedroom and reported on bills and health inspections and linen deliveries. Mrs. Scarlatti was unfailingly polite, nodding in all the right places, but she never said much in return. Eventually, she would close her eyes as a sign that the visit was finished. Then Ezra would leave, often jostling her bed by accident or overturning his chair. He had always been a clumsy man, but now was more so than usual. It seemed to him his hands were too big, forever getting in the way. If only he could have done something with them! He would have liked to fix her a meal—a sustaining meal, with a depth of flavors, a complicated meal that would require a whole day of chopping things small, and grinding, and blending. In the kitchen, as nowhere else, Ezra came into his own, like someone crippled on dry land but effortlessly graceful once he takes to water. However, Mrs. Scarlatti still wasn't eating. There was nothing he could offer her.

Or he would have liked to seize her by the shoulders and shout, "Listen! Listen!" But something closed-off about her face kept stopping him. Almost in plain words, she was telling him that she preferred he not do such a thing. So he didn't.

After a visit, he would go downstairs and look in on the restaurant, which at this hour was vacant and echoing. He might check the freezer, or erase the blackboard, and then perhaps just wander a while, touching this and that. The wallpaper in the back hall was too cluttered and he ripped it off the wall. He tore away the ornate gilt sconces beside the telephone. He yanked the old-fashioned silhouettes from the restroom doors. Sometimes he did so much damage that there was barely time to cover it up before opening, but everybody pitched in and it always got done somehow or other. By six o'clock, when the

132

first customers arrived, the food was cooked and the tables were laid and the waitresses were calm and smiling. Everything was smoothed over.

Mrs. Scarlatti died in March, on a bitter, icy afternoon. When the nurse phoned Ezra, he felt a crushing sense of shock. You would think this death was unexpected. He said, "Oh, no," and hung up, and had to call back to ask the proper questions. Had the end been peaceful? Had Mrs. Scarlatti been awake? Had she said any words in particular? Nothing, said the nurse. Really, nothing at all; just slipped away, like. "But she mentioned you this morning," she added. "I almost wondered, you know? It was almost like she sensed it. She said, 'Tell Ezra to change the sign.'"

"Sign?"

" 'It's not Scarlatti's Restaurant any more,' she said. Or something like that. 'It isn't Scarlatti's.' I think that's what she said."

From the pain he felt, Mrs. Scarlatti might as well have reached out from death and slapped him across the face. It made things easier, in a way. He was almost angry; he was almost relieved that she was gone. He noticed how the trees outside sparkled like something newly minted.

He was the one who made the arrangements, working from a list that Mrs. Scarlatti had given him months before. He knew which funeral home to call and which pastor, and which acquaintances she had wanted at the service. A peculiar thing: he thought of phoning the hospital and inviting that foreign family. Of course he didn't, but it was true they would have made wonderful mourners. Certainly they'd have done better than those who did come, and who later stood stiffly around her frozen grave. Ezra, too, was stiff—a sad, tired man in a flapping coat, holding his mother's arm. Something ached behind his eyes. If he had cried, Mrs. Scarlatti would have said, "Jesus, Ezra. For God's sake, sweetie."

Afterward, he was glad to go to the restaurant. It helped to keep busy—stirring and seasoning and tasting, stumbling over the patch in the floor where the center counter had once stood. Later, he circulated among the diners as Mrs. Scarlatti herself used to do. He urged upon them his oyster stew, his artichoke salad, his spinach bisque and his chili-bean soup and his gizzard soup that was made with love.

5

The Country Cook

Cody Tull always had a girlfriend, one girl after another, and all the girls were wild about him till they met his brother, Ezra. Something about Ezra just hooked their attention, it seemed. In his presence they took on a bright, sharp, arrested look, as if listening to a sound that others hadn't caught yet. Ezra didn't even notice this. Cody did, of course. He would give an exaggerated sigh, pretending to be amused. Then the girl would collect herself. It was already too late, though; Cody never allowed second chances. He had a talent for mentally withdrawing. An Indian-faced man with smooth black hair, with level, balanced features, he could manage, when he tried, to seem perfectly blank, like a plaster clothing model. Meanwhile, his ragged, dirty, unloved younger self, with failing grades, with a U in deportment, clenched his fists and howled, "Why? Why always Ezra? Why that sissy pale goody-goody Ezra?"

But Ezra just gazed into space from behind his clear gray eyes, from under his shock of soft, fair hair, and went on thinking his private thoughts. You could say this for Ezra: he seemed honestly unaware of the effect he had on women. No one could accuse him of stealing them deliberately. But that made it all the worse, in a way.

Cody half believed that Ezra had some lack—a lack that worked in his favor, that made him immune, that set him apart from ordinary men. There was something almost monkish about him. Women never really managed to penetrate his meditations, although he was unfailingly courteous to them, and considerate. He was likely to contemplate them in silence for an inappropriate length of time, and then ask something completely out of the blue. For instance: "How did you get those little gold circles through your ears?" It was ridiculous—a man reaches the age of twenty-seven without having heard of pierced earrings. However, it must not have seemed ridiculous to the woman he was addressing. She raised a finger to an earlobe in a startled, mesmerized way. She was spellbound. Was it Ezra's unexpectedness? The narrowness of his focus? (He'd passed up her low-cut dress, powdered cleavage, long silky legs.) Or his innocence, perhaps. He was a tourist on a female planet, was what he was saying. But he didn't realize he was saying it, and failed to understand the look she gave him. Or didn't care, if he did understand.

Only one of Cody's girlfriends had not been attracted to his brother. This was a social worker named Carol, or maybe Karen. Upon meeting Ezra, she had fixed him with a cool stare. Later, she had remarked to Cody that she disliked motherly men. "Always feeding, hovering," she said (for she'd met him at his restaurant), "but acting so clumsy and shy, in the end it's *you* that takes care of *them*. Ever notice that?" However, she hardly counted; Cody had so soon afterward lost interest in her.

You might wonder why he went on making these introductions, considering his unfortunate experiences—the earliest dating from the year he turned fourteen, the latest as recent as a month ago. After all, he lived in New York City and his family lived in Baltimore; he didn't really have to bring these women home on weekends. In fact, he often swore that he would stop it. He would meet somebody, marry her, and not mention her even to his mother. But that would mean a life-time of suspense. He'd keep watching his wife uncomfortably, suspiciously. He'd keep waiting for the inevitable—like Sleeping Beauty's parents, waiting for the needle that was bound to prick her finger in spite of their precautions.

He was thirty years old by now, successful in his business, certainly ready to marry. He considered his New York apartment temporary, a matter of minor convenience; he had recently purchased a farmhouse in Baltimore County with forty acres of land. Weekends, he traded his slim gray suit for corduroys and he roamed his property, making plans. There was a sunny backyard where his wife could have her kitchen garden. There were bedrooms waiting to be stocked with children. He imagined them tumbling out to meet him every Friday afternoon when he came home. He felt rich and lordly. Poor Ezra: all he had was that disorganized restaurant, in the cramped, stunted center of the city.

Once, Cody invited Ezra to hunt rabbits with him in the woods behind the farm. It wasn't a success. First Ezra fell into a yellowjackets' nest. Then he got his rifle wet in the stream. And when they paused on a hilltop for lunch, he whipped out his battered recorder and commenced to tootling "Greensleeves," scaring off all living creatures within a five-mile radius—which might have been his intention. Cody wasn't even talking to him, at the end; Ezra had to chatter on by himself. Cody stalked well ahead of him in total silence, trying to remember why this outing had seemed such a good idea. Ezra sang "Mister Rabbit." "*Every little soul,*" he sang, blissfully off-key, "*must shine, shine . . .*"

No wonder Cody was a cuticle chewer, a floor pacer, a hair rummager. No wonder, when he slept at night, he ground his teeth so hard that his jaws ached every morning.

Early in the spring of 1960, his sister, Jenny, wrote him a letter. Her divorce was coming through in June, she said—two more months, and then she'd be free to marry Sam Wiley. Cody didn't think much of Wiley, and he flicked this news aside like a gnat and read on. *Though it looks,* she said, *as if Ezra might beat me down the aisle. Her name is Ruth but I don't know any more than that.* Then she said she was seriously considering dropping out of medical school. The complications of her personal life, she said, were using up so much energy that she had none left over for anything else. Also, she had gained three pounds in the last six weeks and was perfectly obese, a whale, living now on lettuce leaves and lemon water. Cody was accustomed to Jenny's crazy diets (she was painfully thin), so he skimmed that part. He finished the letter and folded it.

Ruth?

He opened it again.

. . . *as if Ezra might beat me down the aisle,* he read. He tried to think of some other kind of aisle—airplane, supermarket, movie house—but in the end, he had to believe it: Ezra was getting married. Well, at least now Cody could keep his own girls. (This gave him, for some reason, a little twinge of uneasiness.) But Ezra! Married? That walking accident? Imagine him in a formal wedding—forgetting license, ring, and responses, losing track of the service while smiling out the window at a hummingbird. Imagine him in bed with a woman. (Cody snorted.) He pictured the woman as dark and Biblical, because of her name: Ruth. Shadowed eyes and creamy skin. Torrents of loose black hair. Cody had a weakness for black-haired women; he didn't like blondes at all. He pictured her bare shouldered, in a red satin nightgown, and he crumpled Jenny's letter roughly and dropped it in the wastebasket.

The next day at work, Ruth's image hung over him. He was doing a time-and-motion study of a power-drill factory in New Jersey, a dinosaur of a place. It would take him weeks to sort it out. *Joining object K to object L: right-hand transport unloaded, search, grasp, transport loaded . . .* He passed down the assembly line with his clipboard, attracting hostile glances.

Ruth's black hair billowed in the rafters. *Unavoidable delays: 3.* Avoidable delays: 9. No doubt her eyes were plum shaped, slightly tilted. No doubt her hands were heavily ringed, with long, oval fingernails painted scarlet.

When he returned to his apartment that evening, there was a letter from Ezra. It was an invitation to his restaurant this coming Saturday night. *You are cordially invited* was centered on the page like something engraved—Ezra's idea of a joke. (Or maybe not; maybe he meant it in earnest.) Oh, Lord, not another one of Ezra's dinners. There would be toasts and a fumbling, sentimental speech leading up to some weighty announcement—in this case, his engagement. Cody thought of declining, but what good would that do? Ezra would be desolate if a single person was missing. He'd cancel the whole affair and keep on rescheduling till Cody accepted. Cody might as well go and be done with it.

Besides, he wouldn't at all mind meeting this Ruth.

Ezra was listening to a customer—or a one-time customer, from the sound of it. "Used to be," the man was saying, "this place had class. You follow me?"

Ezra nodded, watching him with such a sympathetic, kindly expression that Cody wondered if his mind weren't somewhere else altogether. "Used to be there was fine French cuisine, flamed at the tables and all," said the man. "And chandeliers. And a hat-check girl. And waiters in black tie. What happened to your waiters?"

"They put people off," Ezra said. "They seemed to think the customers were taking an exam of some kind, not just ordering a meal. They were uppish."

"I liked your waiters."

"Nowadays our staff is homier," Ezra said, and he gestured toward a passing waitress—a tall, stooped, colorless girl, open mouthed with concentration, fiercely intent upon the coffee mug that she carried in both hands. She inched across the floor, breathing adenoidally. She proceeded directly between Ezra and the customer. Ezra stepped back to give her room.

The customer said, " 'Nettie,' I said, 'you've just got to see Scarlatti's. Don't knock Baltimore,' I tell her, 'till you see Scarlatti's.' Then we come upon it and even the sign's gone. Home-sick Restaurant, you call it now. What kind of a name is that? And the decor! Why, it looks like . . . why, a gigantic roadside diner!"

He was right. Cody agreed with him. Dining room walls lined with home preserves, kitchen laid open to the public, un-kempt cooks milling around compiling their favorite dishes (health food, street food, foreign food, whatever popped into their heads) . . . Ever since Ezra had inherited this place—from a woman, wouldn't you know—he'd been systematically wrecking it. He was fully capable of serving a single entrée all one evening, bringing it to your table himself as soon as you were seated. Other nights he'd offer more choice, four or five selections chalked up on the blackboard. But still you might not get what you asked for. "The Smithfield ham," you'd say, and up would come the okra stew. "With that cough of yours, I know this will suit you better," Ezra would explain. But even if he'd judged correctly, was that any way to run a restaurant? You order ham, ham is what you get. Otherwise, you might as well eat at home. "You'll go bankrupt in a year," Cody had promised, and Ezra almost did go bankrupt; most of the regular patrons disappeared. Some hung on, though; and others dis-covered it. There were several older people who ate here every night, sitting alone at their regular tables in the barnlike, plank-floored dining room. They could afford it because the prices weren't written but recited instead by the staff, evidently accord-ing to whim, altering with the customer. (Wasn't that illegal?) Ezra worried about what these older people did on Sundays, when he closed. Cody, on the other hand, worried about Ezra's account books, but didn't offer to go over them. He would find a disaster, he was sure—errors and bad debts, if not outright, naive crookery. Better not to know; better not to get involved.

"It's true there've been some changes," Ezra was telling his ex-customer, "but if you'll just try our food, you'll see that we're still a fine restaurant. Tonight it's all one dish—pot roast."

"Pot roast!"

"A really special kind—consoling."

"Pot roast I can get at home," said the man. He clamped a felt hat on his head and walked out.

"Oh, well," Ezra told Cody. "You can't please everybody, I guess."

They made their way to the far corner, where a RESERVED sign sat upon the table that Ezra always chose for family dinners. Jenny and their mother weren't there yet. Jenny, who'd arrived on the afternoon train, had asked her mother's help in shopping for a dress to be married in. Now Ezra worried they'd be late. "Everything's planned for six-thirty," he said. "What's keeping them?"

"Well, no problem if it's only pot roast."

"It's not *only* pot roast," Ezra said. He sat in a chair. His suit had a way of waffling around him, as if purchased for a much larger man. "This is something more. I mean, pot roast is really not the right name; it's more like . . . what you long for when you're sad and everyone's been wearing you down. See, there's the cook, this real country cook, and pot roast is the least of what she does. There's also pan-fried potatoes, black-eyed peas, beaten biscuits genuinely beat on a stump with the back of an ax—"

"Here they come," Cody said.

Jenny and her mother were just walking across the dining room. They carried no parcels, but something made it clear they'd been shopping—perhaps the frazzled, cross look they shared. Jenny's lipstick was chewed off. Pearl's hat was knocked crooked and her hair was frizzier than ever. "What took you so long?" Ezra asked, jumping up. "We were starting to worry."

"Oh, this Jenny and her notions," said Pearl. "Her size

141

eight figure and no bright colors, no pastels, no gathers or puckers or trim, nothing to make her look fat, so-called . . . Why are there five places set?"

The question took them all off guard. It was true, Cody saw. There were five plates and five crystal wineglasses. "How come?" Pearl asked Ezra.

"Oh . . . I'll get to that in a minute. Have a seat, Mother, over there."

But she kept standing. "Then at last we find just the right thing," she said. "A nice soft gray with a crocheted collar, Jenny all the way. 'It's you,' I tell her. And guess what she does. She has a tantrum in the middle of Hutzler's department store."

"Not a *tantrum*, Mother," Jenny told her. "I merely said—"

"Said, 'It isn't a funeral, Mother; I'm not going into mourning.' You'd think I'd chosen widow's weeds. This was a nice pale gray, very ladylike, very suitable for a second marriage."

"Anthracite," Jenny told Cody.

"Pardon?"

"Anthracite was what the saleslady called it. In other words: coal. Our mother thinks it suitable to marry me off in a coal-black wedding dress."

"Uh," said Ezra, looking around at the other diners, "maybe we should be seated now."

But Pearl just stood straighter. "And *then*," she told her sons, "then, without the slightest bit of thought, doing it only to spite me, she goes rushing over to the nearest rack and pulls out something white as snow."

"It was cream colored," Jenny said.

"Cream, white—what's the difference? Both are inappropriate, if you're marrying for the second time and the divorce hasn't yet been granted and the man has no steady employment. 'I'll take this one,' she says, and it's not even the proper size, miles too big, had to be left at the store for alterations."

"I happened to like it," Jenny said.

142

"You were lost in it."

"It made me look thin."

"Maybe you could wear a shawl or something, brown," said her mother. "That might tone it down some."

"I can't wear a shawl in a wedding."

"Why not? Or a little jacket, say a brown linen jacket."

"I look fat in jackets."

"Not in a short one, Chanel-type."

"I hate Chanel."

"Well," said Pearl, "I can see that nothing will satisfy you."

"Mother," Jenny said, "I'm already satisfied. I'm satisfied with my cream-colored dress, just the way it is. I love it. Will you please just get off my back?"

"Did you hear that?" Pearl asked her sons. "Well, I don't have to stand here and take it." And she turned and marched back across the dining room, erect as a little wind-up doll.

Ezra said, "Huh?"

Jenny opened a plastic compact, looked into it, and then snapped it shut, as if merely making certain that she was still there.

"Please, Jenny, won't you go after her?" Ezra asked.

"Not on your life."

"*You're* the one she fought with. *I* can't persuade her."

"Oh, Ezra, let's for once just drop it," Cody said. "I don't think I'm up to all this."

"What are you saying? Not have dinner at all?"

"I could only eat lettuce leaves anyhow," Jenny told him.

"But this is important! It was going to be an occasion. Oh, just . . . wait. Wait here a minute, will you?"

Ezra turned and rushed off to the kitchen. From the swarm of assorted cooks at the counter, he plucked a small person in overalls. It was a girl, Cody guessed—a weasel-faced little redhead. She followed Ezra jauntily, almost stiff-legged, wiping her palms on her backside. "I'd like you to meet Ruth," Ezra said.

Cody said, "Ruth?"

"We're getting married in September."

"Oh," said Cody.

Then Jenny said, "Well, congratulations," and kissed Ruth's bony, freckled cheek, and Cody said, "Uh, yes," and shook her hand. There were calluses like pebbles on her palm. "How do," she told him. He thought of the phrase *banty hen*, although he had never seen a banty hen. Or maybe she was more of a rooster. Her brisk, carroty hair was cut so short that it seemed too scant for her skull. Her blue eyes were round as marbles, and her skin was so thin and tight (as if, like her hair, it had been skimped on) that he could see the white cartilage across the bridge of her nose. "So," he said. "Ruth."

"Are you surprised?" Ezra asked him.

"Yes, very surprised."

"I wanted to do it right; I was going to announce it over drinks and then call her in to join the family dinner. But, honey," Ezra said, turning to Ruth, "I guess Mother was over-tired. It didn't work out the way I'd planned."

"Shit, that's okay," Ruth told him.

Cody said, "Surely. Certainly. We can always do it later."

Then Jenny started asking about the wedding, and Cody excused himself and said he thought he'd go see how their mother was. Outside in the dark, walking up the street toward home, he had the strangest feeling of loss. It was as if someone had died, or had left him forever—the beautiful, black-haired Ruth of his dreams.

"I knew what that dinner was going to be, tonight," Pearl told Cody. "I'm not so dumb. I knew. He's got himself engaged; he's going to marry the country cook. I knew that anyway but it all came home to me when I walked in the restaurant and saw those five plates and glasses. Well, I acted badly. Very badly. You don't have to tell me, Cody. It was just that I saw those plates and something broke inside of me. I thought, 'Well, all

144

right, if that's how it's got to be, but not tonight, just not tonight, Lord, right on top of buying wedding dress number two for my only daughter.' So then, why, I went and made a scene that caused the dinner to be canceled, exactly as if I'd planned it all ahead of time, which of course I hadn't. You believe me, don't you? I'm not blind. I know when I'm being unreasonable. Sometimes I stand outside my body and just watch it all, totally separate. 'Now, stop,' I say to myself, but it's like I'm . . . elated; I've got to rush on, got to keep going. 'Yes, yes, I'll stop,' I think, 'only let me say this one more thing, just this one more thing . . .'

"Cody, don't you believe I want you three to be happy? Of course I do. Naturally. Why, I wouldn't hold Ezra back for the world, if he's so set on marrying that girl—though I don't know what he sees in her, she's so scrappy and hoydenish; I think she's from Garrett County or some such place and hardly wears shoes—you ought to see the soles of her feet sometime—but what I want to say is, I've never been one of those mothers who try to keep their sons for themselves. I honestly hope Ezra marries. I truly mean that. I want somebody taking care of him, *especially* him. You can manage on your own but Ezra is so, I don't know, defenseless . . . Of course I love you all the same amount, every bit the same, but . . . well, Ezra is so *good*. You know? Anyway, now he has this Ruth person and it's changed his whole outlook; watch him sometime when she walks into a room, or swaggers, or whatever you want to call it. He adores her. They get all playful together, like two puppies. Yes, often they remind me of puppies, snuggling down and giggling, or bounding about the kitchen or listening to that hill-billy music that Ruth seems to be so crazy about. But, Cody. Promise not to tell this to anyone. Promise? Cody, sometimes I stand there watching them and I see they believe they're completely special, the first, the only people ever to feel the way they're feeling. They believe they'll live happily ever after, that all the other marriages going on around them—those ordinary, worn-

145

down, flattened-in arrangements—why, those are nothing like what *they'll* have. They'll never settle for so little. And it makes me mad. I can't help it, Cody. I know it's selfish, but I can't help it. I want to ask them, 'Who do you think you are, anyhow? Do you imagine you're unique? Do you really suppose I was always this difficult old woman?'

"Cody, listen. I was special too, once, to someone. I could just reach out and lay a fingertip on his arm while he was talking and he would instantly fall silent and get all confused. I had hopes; I was courted; I had the most beautiful wedding. I had three lovely pregnancies, where every morning I woke up knowing something perfect would happen in nine months, eight months, seven . . . so it seemed I was full of light; it was light and plans that filled me. And then while you children were little, why, I was the center of your worlds! I was everything to you! It was Mother this and Mother that, and 'Where's Mother? Where's she gone to?' and the moment you came in from school, 'Mother? Are you home?' It's not fair, Cody. It's really not fair; now I'm old and I walk along unnoticed, just like anyone else. It strikes me as unjust, Cody. But don't tell the others I said so."

At work that next week, charting the steps by which power drills were fitted into their housings, Cody watched the old, dark Ruth fade from the rafters and hallways, until at last she was completely gone and he forgot why she had moved him so. Now a new Ruth appeared. Skinny and boyish, overalls flapping around her shinbones, she raced giggling down the assembly line with Ezra hot on her heels. Ezra's hair was tousled. (He was not immune at all, it appeared, but had only been waiting in his stubbornly trustful way for the proper person to arrive.) He caught her in the supervisor's office and they scuffled like . . . yes, like two puppies. A cowlick bounced on the crown of Ruth's head. Her lips were chapped and cracked. Her nails were bitten into tiny pink cushions and there were scrapes and burns across her knuckles, scars from her country cooking.

Cody called his mother and said he'd be down for the week-end, and would Ruth be around, did she think? After all, he said, it was time he got to know his future sister-in-law.

He arrived on Saturday morning bringing flowers, copper-colored roses. He found Ruth and Ezra playing gin on the living room floor. Ruth's reality, after his week of dreaming, struck him like a blow. She seemed clearer, plainer, harder edged than anybody he'd known. She wore jeans and a shirt of some ugly brown plaid. She was so absorbed in her game that she hardly glanced up when Cody walked in. "Ruth," he said, and he held out the flowers. "These are for you."

She looked at them, and then drew a card. "What are they?" she asked.

"Well, roses."

"Roses? This early in the year?"

"Greenhouse roses. I especially ordered copper, to go with your hair."

"You leave my hair out of this," she said.

"Honey, he meant it as a compliment," Ezra told her.

"Oh."

"Certainly," said Cody. "See, it's my way of saying wel-come. Welcome to our family, Ruth."

"Oh. Well, thanks."

"Cody, that was awfully nice of you," Ezra said.

"Gin," said Ruth.

Late that afternoon, when it was time to go to the restaurant, Cody walked over with Ruth and Ezra. He'd had a long, im-mobile day—standing outside other people's lives, mostly—and he needed the exercise.

It had been raining, off and on, and there were puddles on the sidewalk. Ruth strode straight through every one of them, which was fine since her shoes were brown leather combat boots. Cody wondered if her style were deliberate. What would she do, for instance, if he gave her a pair of high-heeled evening sandals? The question began to fascinate him. He became obsessed; he developed an almost physical thirst for the sight of her blunt little feet in silver straps.

There was no explaining his craving for the gigantic watch—black faced and intricately calibrated, capable of withstanding a deep-sea dive—whose stainless steel expansion band hung loose on her wiry wrist.

Ezra had his pearwood recorder. He played it as he walked, serious and absorbed, with his lashes lowered on his cheeks. "Le Godiveau de Poisson," he played. Passersby looked at him and smiled. Ruth hummed along with some notes, fell into her own thoughts at others. Then Ezra put his recorder in the pocket of his shabby lumber jacket, and he and Ruth began discussing the menu. It was good they were serving the rice dish, Ruth said; that always made the Arab family happy. She ran her fingers through her sprouty red hair. Cody, walking on the other side of her, felt her shift of weight when Ezra circled her with one arm and pulled her close.

In the restaurant, she was a whirlwind. Ezra cooked in a dream, tasting and reflecting; the others (losers, all of them, in Cody's opinion) floated around the kitchen vaguely, but Ruth spun and pounced and jabbed at food as if doing battle. She was in charge of a chicken casserole and something that looked like potato cakes. Cody watched her from a corner well out of the way, but still people seemed to keep tripping over him.

"Where did you learn to cook?" he asked Ruth.

"No place," she said.

"Is this chicken some regional thing?"

"Taste," she snapped, and she speared a piece and held it out to him.

"I can't," he said.

"Why not?"

"I feel too full."

148

In fact, he felt full of *her*. He'd taken her in all day, consumed her. Every spiky movement—slamming of pot lids, toss of head—nourished him. It came to him like a gift, while he was studying her narrow back, that she actually wore an undershirt, one of those knitted singlets he remembered from his childhood. He could make out the seams of it beneath the brown plaid. He filed the information with care, to be treasured once he was alone.

The restaurant opened and customers began to trickle in. The large, beaming hostess seated them all in one area, as if tucking them under her wing.

"Find a table," Ezra told Cody. "I'll bring you some of Ruth's cooking."

"I'm honestly not hungry," Cody said.

"He's *full*," said Ruth, spitting it out.

"Well, what'll you do, then? Isn't this boring for you?"

"No, no, I'm interested," Cody said.

He could look across the counter and into the dining room, where people sat chewing and swallowing and drinking, patting their mouths with napkins, breaking off chunks of bread. He wondered how Ezra could stand to spend his life at this.

When the first real flurry was over, Ruth and Ezra settled at the scrubbed wooden table in the center of the kitchen, and Cody joined them. Ezra ate some of Ruth's chicken casserole. Ruth lit a small brown cigarette and tipped back in her chair to watch him. The cigarette smelled as if it were burning only by accident—like something spilled on the floor of an oven, or stuck to the underside of a saucepan. Cody, seated across from her, drank it in. "Eat, Cody, eat," Ezra urged him. Cody just shook his head, not wanting to lose his chestful of Ruth's smoke.

Meanwhile, the other cooks came and went, some of them sitting also to wolf various odd assortments of food while their kettles simmered untended. Ezra's boyhood friend Josiah appeared, metamorphosed into an efficient grown man in starchy white, and he and Ruth had a talk about peeling the apples for the pie. Cody could not have cared less about her pie, but he was riveted by her offhand, slangy style of speech. She held her cigarette between thumb and index finger, with her elbow propped against her rib cage. She hunkered forward to consider some decision, and beneath her knotted brows her eyes were so pale a blue that he was startled.

They left the restaurant before it closed. Josiah would lock up, Ezra said. They took a roundabout route home, down a quiet, one-way street, to drop Ruth off at the house where she rented a room. When Ezra accompanied her up the front steps, Cody waited on the curb. He watched Ezra kiss her good night—a bumbling, inadequate kiss, Cody judged it; and he felt some satisfaction. Then Ezra rejoined him and galumphed along beside him, big footed and blithe. "Isn't she something?" he asked Cody. "Don't you just love her?"

"Mm."

"But there's so much I need to find out from you! I want to take good care of her, but I don't know how. What about life insurance? Things like that! So much is expected of husbands, Cody. Will you help me figure it out?"

"I'll be glad to," Cody said. He meant it, too. Anything: any little crack that would provide him with an entrance.

Eventually, Ezra subsided, although he continued to give the impression of inwardly bubbling and chortling. From time to time, he hummed a few bars of something underneath his breath. And then when they were almost home—passing houses totally dark, where everyone had long since gone to sleep—what should he do but pull out that damned recorder of his and start piping away. It was embarrassing. It was infuriating: "Le Godiveau de Poisson," once again. Depend on Ezra, Cody thought, to have as his theme song a recipe for a seafood dish. He walked along in silence, hoping someone would call the police. Or at least, that they'd open a window.

"You there! Quiet!" But no one did. It was so typical: Ezra the golden boy, everybody's favorite, tootling down the streets scot-free.

On Sunday morning, Cody presented himself at Ruth's door—or rather, at the door of the faded, doughy lady who owned the house Ruth stayed in. This lady toyed so fearfully with the locket at her throat that Cody felt compelled to take a step backward, proving he was not a knock-and-rob man. He gave her his most gentlemanly smile. "Good morning," he said. "Is Ruth home?"

"Ruth?"

He realized he didn't know Ruth's last name. "I'm Ezra Tull's brother," he said.

"Oh, *Ezra*," she said, and she stood back to let him enter.

He followed her deep into the interior, past a tumult of over-stuffed furniture and dusty wax fruit and heaps of magazines. In the kitchen, Ruth slouched at the table spooning up cornflakes and reading a newspaper propped against a cereal box. A pale, pudgy man stood gazing into an open refrigerator. Cody had an impression of inertia and frittered lives. He felt charged with energy. It ought to be so easy to win her away from all this!

"Good morning," he said. Ruth looked up. The pudgy man retreated behind the refrigerator door.

"I hope you're not too far into that cereal," Cody said. "I came to invite you to breakfast."

"What for?" Ruth asked, frowning.

"Well . . . not for any *purpose*. I'm just out walking and I thought you might want to walk with me, stop off for doughnuts and coffee someplace."

"Now?"

"Of course."

"Isn't it raining?"

"Only a little bit."

"No, thanks," she said.

Her eyes dropped back to her newspaper. The landlady slid her locket along its chain with a miniature zipping sound.

"What's going on in the world?" Cody asked.

"What world?" said Ruth.

"The news. What does the newspaper say?"

Ruth raised her eyes, and Cody saw the page she had turned to. "Oh," he said. "The comics."

"No, my horoscope."

"Your horoscope." He looked to the landlady for help. The landlady gazed off toward a cabinet full of jelly glasses. "Well, what . . . um, symbol are you?" Cody asked Ruth.

"Hmm?"

"What astrological symbol?"

"Sign," she corrected him. She sighed and stood up, finally forced to recognize his presence. Snatching her paper from the table, she stalked off toward the parlor. Cody made way for her and then trailed after. Her jeans, he guessed, had been bought at a little boys' clothing store. She had no hips whatsoever. Her sweater was transparent at the elbows.

"I'm Taurus," she said over her shoulder, "but all that's rubbish, anyhow. Total garbage."

"Oh, I agree," Cody said, relieved.

She stopped in the center of the parlor and turned to him. "Look at here," she said, and she jabbed her finger at a line of newsprint. *"Powerful ally will come to your rescue. Accent today on high finance."* She lowered the paper. "I mean, who do they reckon they're dealing with? What kind of business am I supposed to be involved in?"

"Ridiculous," said Cody. He was hypnotized by her eyebrows. They were the color of orange sherbet, and whenever she spoke with any heat the skin around them grew pink, darker than the eyebrows themselves.

"Ignore innuendos from long-time foe," she read, running a finger down the column. "Or listen to this other one: *Clandes-*

tine meeting could solve mystery. Almighty God!" she said, and she tossed the paper into an armchair. "You got to lead quite a life, to get anything out of your horoscope."

"Well, I don't know," Cody said. "Maybe it's truer than you realize."

"Come again?"

"Maybe it's saying you *ought* to lead such a life. Ought to be more adventurous, not just slave away in some restaurant, mope around a gloomy old boardinghouse . . ."

"It's not so gloomy," Ruth said, lifting her chin.

"Well, but—"

"And anyhow, I won't always be here. Me and Ezra, after we marry, we're moving in above the Homesick. Then once we get us some money we plan on a house."

"But still," said Cody, "you won't have anywhere near what those horoscopes are calling for. Why, there's all the outside world! New York, for instance. Ever been to New York?"

She shook her head, watching him narrowly.

"You ought to come; it's springtime there."

"It's springtime here," she said.

"But a different kind."

"I don't see what you're getting at," she told him.

"Well, all I want to say is, Ruth: why settle down so soon, when there's so much you haven't seen yet?"

"Soon?" she said. "I'm pretty near twenty years old. Been rattling around on my own since my sixteenth birthday. Only thing I *want* is to settle down, sooner the better."

"Oh," said Cody.

"Well, have a good walk."

"Oh, yes, walk . . ."

"Don't drown," she told him, callously.

At the door, he turned. He said, "Ruth?"

"What."

"I don't know your last name."

"Spivey," she said.

153

He thought it was the loveliest sound he had ever heard in his life.

The following weekend, he drove her out to see his farm. "I have seen all the farms I care to," she said, but Ezra said, "Oh, you ought to go, Ruth. It's pretty this time of year." Ezra himself had to stay behind; he was supervising the installation of a new meat locker for the restaurant. Cody had known that before he invited her.

This time he brought her jonquils. She said, "I don't know what I want with *these*; there's a whole mess in back by the walkway."

Cody smiled at her.

He settled her in his Cadillac, which smelled of new leather. She looked unimpressed. Perversely, she was wearing a skirt, on the one occasion when jeans would have been more suitable. Her legs were very white, almost chalky. He had not seen short socks like hers since his schooldays, and her tattered sneakers were as small and stubby as a child's.

On the drive out, he talked about his plans for the farm. "It's where I'd like to live," he said. "Where I want to raise my family. It's a perfect place for children."

"What makes you think so?" she asked. "When I was a kid, all I cared about was getting to the city."

"Yes, but fresh air and home-grown vegetables, and the animals . . . Right now, the man down the road is tending my livestock, but once I move in full-time I'm going to do it all myself."

"*That* I'd like to see," said Ruth. "You ever slopped a hog? Shoveled out a stable?"

"I can learn," he told her.

She shrugged and said no more.

When they reached the farm he showed her around the grounds, where she stared a cow down and gave a clump of hens the evil eye. Then he led her into the house. He'd bought it

154

lock, stock, and barrel—complete with plush sofa and kerosene stove in the parlor, rickety kitchen table with its drawerful of rusted flatware, 1958 calendar on the wall advertising Mallardy's oystershell mixture for layers, extra rich in calcium. The man who'd lived here—a widower—had died upstairs in the four-poster bed. Cody had replaced the bedclothes with new ones, sheets and a quilt and down pillows, but that was his only change. "I do plan to fix things up," he told Ruth, "but I'm waiting till I marry. I know my wife might like to have a say in it."

Ruth removed a window lock easily from its crumbling wooden sash. She turned it over and peered at the underside.

"I want a wife very much," said Cody.

She put back the lock. "I hate to be the one to tell you," she said, "but smell that smell? Kind of sweetish smell? You got dry rot here."

"Ruth," he said, "do you dislike me for any reason?"

"Huh?"

"Your attitude. The way you put me off. You don't think much of me, do you?" he said.

She gave him an edgy, skewed look, evasive, and moved over to the stairway. "Oh," she said, "I like you a fair amount."

"You do?"

"But I know your type," she said.

"What type?"

"There were plenty like you in my school," she said. "Oh, sure! Some in every class, on every team—tall and real good-looking, stylish, athletic, witty. *Smooth*-mannered boys that everything always came easy to, that always knew the proper way of doing things, and never dated any but the cheerleader girls, or the homecoming queen, or her maids of honor at the lowest. Passing me in the halls not even knowing who I was, nor guessing I existed. Or making fun of me sometimes, I'm almost certain—laughing at how poor I dressed and mocking my freckly face and my old red hair—"

155

"Laughing! When have I ever done such a thing?"

"I'm not naming you in particular," she said, "but you sure do put me in mind of a type."

"Ruth. I wouldn't mock you. I think you're perfect," he said. "You're the most beautiful woman I've ever laid eyes on."

"See there?" she asked, and she raised her chin, spun about, and marched down the stairs. She wouldn't answer anything else he said to her, all during the long drive home.

It was a campaign, was what it was—a long and arduous battle campaign, extending through April and all of May. There were moments when he despaired. He'd had too late a start, was out of the running; he'd wasted his time with those unoriginal, obvious brunettes whom he'd thought he was so clever to snare while Ezra, not even trying, had somehow divined the jewel. Lucky Ezra! His whole life rested on luck, and Cody would probably never manage to figure out how he did it.

Often, after leaving Ruth, Cody would be muttering to himself as he strode away. He would slam a fist in his palm or kick his own car. But at the same time, he had an underlying sense of exhilaration. Yes, he would have to say that he'd never felt more alive, never more eager for each new day. Now he understood why he'd lost interest in Carol or Karen, what's-her-name, the social worker who hadn't found Ezra appealing. She'd made it too easy. What he liked was the competition, the hope of emerging triumphant from a neck-and-neck struggle with Ezra, his oldest enemy. He even liked biding his time, holding himself in check, hiding his feelings from Ruth till the most advantageous moment. (Was *patience* Ezra's secret?) For, of course, this wasn't an open competition. One of the contestants didn't even know he *was* a contestant. "Gosh, Cody," Ezra said, "it's been nice to have you around so much lately." And to Ruth, "Go, go; you'll enjoy it," when Cody invited her anywhere.

Once, baiting Ezra, Cody stole one of Ruth's brown cigarettes and smoked it in the farmhouse. (The scent of burning tar filled his bedroom. If he'd had a telephone, he would have forgotten all his strategies and called her that instant to confess he loved her.) He stubbed out the butt in a plastic ashtray beside his bed. Then later he invited Ezra to look at his new calves, took him upstairs to discuss a leak in the roof, and led him to the nightstand where the ashtray sat. But Ezra just said, "Oh, was Ruth here?" and launched into praise for an herb garden she was planting on top of the restaurant. Cody couldn't believe that anyone would be so blind, so credulous. Also, he would have died for the privilege of having Ruth plant herbs for him. He thought of the yard out back, where he'd always envisioned his wife's kitchen garden. Rosemary! Basil! Lemon balm!

"Why didn't she come to me?" he asked Ezra. "She could always grow her herbs on my farm."

"Oh, well, the closer to home the fresher," said Ezra. "But you're kind to offer, Cody."

Oiling his rifles that night, Cody seriously considered shooting Ezra thorugh the heart.

When he complimented Ruth, she bristled. When he brought her the gifts he'd so craftily chosen (gold chains and crystal flasks of perfume, music boxes, silk flowers, all intended to contrast with the ugly, mottled marble rolling pin that Ezra presented, clumsily wrapped, on her twentieth birthday), she generally lost them right away or left them wherever she happened to be. And when he invited her places, she only came along for the outing. He would take her arm and she'd say, "Jeepers, I'm not some old lady." She would scramble over rocks and through forests in her combat boots, and Cody would follow, bemused and dazzled, literally sick with love. He had lost eight pounds, could not eat—a myth, he'd always thought that was—and hardly slept at night. When he did sleep, he willed himself to dream of Ruth but never did; she was impishly, defiantly absent, and daytimes when they next met he thought he saw something taunting in the look she gave him.

He often found it difficult to keep their conversations going. It struck him sometimes—in the middle of the week, when he was far from Baltimore—that this whole idea was deranged. They would never be anything but strangers. What single interest, even, did they have in common? But every weekend he was staggered, all over again, by her strutting walk, her belligerent chin and endearing scowl. He was moved by her musty, little-boyish smell; he imagined how her small body could nestle into his. Oh, it was Ruth herself they had in common. He would reach out to touch the spurs of her knuckles. She would ruffle and draw back. "What are you doing?" she would ask. He didn't answer.

"I know what you're up to," his mother told him.

"I beg your pardon?"

"I see through you like a sheet of glass."

"Well? What am I up to, then?" he asked. He really did hope to hear; he had reached the stage where he'd angle and connive just to get someone to utter Ruth's name.

"You don't fool me for an instant," said his mother. "Why are you so contrary? You've got no earthly use for that girl. She's not your type in the slightest; she belongs to your brother, Ezra, and she's the only thing in this world he's ever wanted. If you were to win her away, tell me what you'd do with her! You'd drop her flat. You'd say, 'Oh, my goodness, what am I doing with *this* little person?'"

"You don't understand," said Cody.

"This may come as a shock," his mother told him, "but I understand you perfectly. With the rest of the world I might not be so smart, but with my three children, why, not the least little thing escapes me. I know everything you're after. I see everything in your heart, Cody Tull."

"Just like God," Cody said.

"Just like God," she agreed.

Ezra arranged a celebration dinner for the evening before

Jenny's wedding—a Friday. But Thursday night, Jenny phoned Cody at his apartment. It was a local call; she said she wasn't ten blocks away, staying at a hotel with Sam Wiley. "We got married yesterday morning," she said, "and now we're on our honeymoon. So there won't be any dinner after all."

"Well, how did all *this* come about?" Cody asked.

"Mother and Sam had a little disagreement."

"I see."

"Mother said . . . and Sam told her . . . and I said, 'Oh, Sam, why not let's just . . .' Only I do feel bad about Ezra. I know how much trouble he's gone to."

"By now, he ought to be used to this," Cody said.

"He was going to serve a suckling pig."

Hadn't Ezra noticed (Cody wondered) that the family as a whole had never yet finished one of his dinners? That they'd fight and stamp off halfway through, or sometimes not even manage to get seated in the first place? Well, of course he must have *noticed*, but was it clear to him as a pattern, a theme? No, perhaps he viewed each dinner as a unit in itself, unconnected to the others. Maybe he never linked them in his mind.

Assuming he was a total idiot.

It was true that once—to celebrate Cody's new business— they had made it all the way to dessert; so if they hadn't ordered dessert you could say they'd completed the meal. But the fact was, they did order dessert, which was left to sag on the plates when their mother accused Cody of deliberately setting up shop as far from home as possible. There was a stiff-backed little quarrel. Conversation fell apart. Cody walked out. So technically, even that meal could not be considered finished. Why did Ezra go on trying?

Why did the rest of them go on showing up, was more to the point.

In fact, they probably saw more of each other than happy families did. It was almost as if what they couldn't get right, they had to keep returning to. (So if they ever did finish a dinner, would they rise and say goodbye forever after?)

Once Jenny had hung up, Cody sat on the couch and leafed through the morning's mail. Something made him feel unsettled. He wondered how Jenny could have married Sam Wiley—a scrawny little artist type, shifty eyed and cocky. He wondered if Ezra would cancel his dinner altogether or merely postpone it till after the honeymoon. He pictured Ruth in the restaurant kitchen, her wrinkled little fingers patting flour on drumsticks. He scanned an ad for life insurance and wondered why no one depended on him—not even enough to require his insurance money if he should happen to die.

He ripped open an envelope marked AMAZING OFFER! and found three stationery samples and a glossy order blank. One sample was blue, with *LMR* embossed at the top. Another had a lacy *PAULA*, the *P* entwined with a morning-glory vine, and the third was one of those letters that form their own envelopes when folded. The flap was printed with butterflies and *Mrs. Harold Alexander III*, 219 Saint Beulah Boulevard, Dallas, Texas. He studied that for a moment. Then he took a pen from his shirt pocket, and started writing in an unaccustomed, backhand slant:

Dear Ruth,

Just a line to say hey from all of us. How's the job going? What do you think of Baltimore? Harold says ask if you met a young man yet. He had the funniest dream last night, dreamed he saw you with someone tall, black hair and gray eyes and gray suit. I said well, I certainly hope it's a dream that comes true!

We have all been fine tho Linda was out of school one day last week. A case of "math test-itis" it looked like to me, ha ha! She says to send you lots of hugs and kisses. Drop us a line real soon, hear?

Cody felt he had just found the proper tone toward the end; he was sorry to run out of space. He signed the letter *Luv, Sue*

(*Mrs. Harold Alexander III*), and sealed, stamped, and addressed it. Then he placed it in a business envelope, and wrote a note to his old college roommate in Dallas, asking if he would please drop the enclosed in the nearest mailbox.

That weekend he didn't go home, and his reward was to dream about Ruth. She was waiting for a train that he was traveling on. He saw her on the platform, peering into the windows of each passenger car as it slid by. He was so eager to reach her, to watch her expression ease when she caught sight of him, that he called her name aloud and woke himself up. He heard it echoing in the dark—not her name, after all, but some meaningless sleep sound. For hours after that he tried to burrow back inside the dream, but he had lost it.

The next morning he began another letter, on the sheet headed *PAULA*. In a curlicued script, he wrote:

Dear Ruthie,

You old thing, don't you keep in touch with your friends any more? I told Mama the other day, Mama that Ruth Spivey has forgotten all about us I believe.

Things here are not going too good. I guess you might have heard that me and Norman are separated. I know you liked him, but you had no idea how tiresome he could be, always so slow and quiet, he got on my nerves. Ruthie stay clear of those pale blond thoughtful kind of men, they're a real disappointment. Go for someone dark and interesting who will take you lots of places you've never been. I'm serious, I know what I'm talking about.

Mama sends you greetings and asks do you want her to sew you anything. She's real crippled now with the arthritis in her knees and can only sit in her chair, has plenty of time for sewing.

See ya, Paula

That letter he mailed from Pennsylvania, when he visited a packing-crate plant the following Tuesday. And on Wednesday, from New York, he sent the blue sheet with *LMR* at the top.

Dear Ruth,

    Had lunch with Donna the other day and she told me you were going with a real nice fellow. Was kind of hazy on the particulars but when she said his name was Tull and he came from Baltimore I knew it must be Cody. Everybody here knows Cody, we all just love him, he really is a good man at heart and has been misjudged for years by people who don't understand him. Well, Ruthie, I guess you're smarter than I gave you credit for, I always thought you'd settle for one of those dime-a-dozen blond types but now I see I was wrong.

    I'll be waiting for the details.

Love, Laurie May

"You went too far with that last letter," Ruth told him.

"I don't know what you're talking about."

He was sitting on a kitchen stool, watching her cube meat. He'd come directly to the restaurant this Saturday—bypassing home, bypassing the farm—hoping to find her altered somehow, mystified, perhaps tossing him a speculative glance from time to time. Instead, she seemed cross. She slammed her cleaver on the chopping board. "Do you realize," she asked, "that I went ahead and answered that first note? Not wanting someone to worry, I sent it back and said it wasn't mine, there must be some mistake; went out specially and bought a stamp to mail it with. And would've sent the second back, too, only it didn't have a return address. Then the third comes; well, you went too far."

"I tend to do that," Cody said regretfully.

Ruth slung the cleaver with a thunking sound. Cody was afraid the others—only Todd Duckett and Josiah, this early—would wonder what was wrong, but they didn't even look around. Ezra was out front, chalking up tonight's menu.

"Just what is your *problem?*" Ruth asked him. "Do you have something against me? You think I'm some Garrett County hick that you don't want marrying your brother?"

"Of course I don't want you marrying him," Cody said. "I love you."

"Huh?"

This wasn't the moment he had planned, but he rushed on anyway, as if drunk. "I mean it," he said, "I feel driven. I feel pulled. I have to have you. You're all I ever think about."

She was staring at him, astonished, with one hand cupped to scoop the meat cubes into a skillet.

"I guess I'm not saying it right," he told her.

"Saying what? What are you talking about?"

"Ruth. I really, truly love you," he said. "I'm sick over you. I can't even eat. Look at me! I've lost eleven pounds."

He held out his arms, demonstrating. His jacket hung loose at the sides. Lately he'd moved his belt in a notch; his suits no longer fit so smoothly but seemed rumpled, gathered, bunchy.

"It's true you're kind of skinny," Ruth said slowly.

"Even my shoes feel too big."

"What's the matter with you?" she asked.

"You haven't heard a word I said!"

"Over *me*, you said. You must be making fun."

"Ruth, I swear—" he said.

"You're used to New York City girls, models, actresses; you could have anyone."

"It's you I'll have."

She studied him a moment. It began to seem he'd finally broken through; they were having a conversation. Then she said, "We got to get that weight back on you."

He groaned.

"See there?" she asked. "You never eat a thing I offer you."

"I can't," he told her.

"I don't believe you ever once tasted my cooking."

She set the skillet aside and went over to the tall black kettle that was simmering on the stove. "Country vegetable," she said, lifting the lid.

"Really, Ruth . . ."

163

She filled a small crockery bowl and set it on the table. "Sit down," she said. "Eat. When you've tried it, I'll tell you the secret ingredient."

Steam rose from the bowl, with a smell so deep and spicy that already he felt overfed. He accepted the spoon that she held out. He dipped it in the soup reluctantly and took a sip.

"Well?" she asked.

"It's very good," he said.

In fact, it was delicious, if you cared about such things. He'd never tasted soup so good. There were chunks of fresh vegetables, and the broth was rich and heavy. He took another mouthful. Ruth stood over him, her thumbs hooked into her blue jeans pockets. "Chicken feet," she said.

"Pardon?"

"Chicken feet is the secret ingredient."

He lowered the spoon and looked down into the bowl.

"Eat up," she told him. "Put some meat on your bones."

He dipped the spoon in again.

After that, she brought him a salad made with the herbs she'd grown on the roof and a basketful of rolls she'd baked that afternoon—a recipe from home, she said. Cody ate everything. As long as he ate, she watched him. When she brought him more butter for his rolls, she leaned close over him and he felt the warmth she gave off.

Now two more cooks had arrived and a Chinese boy was sautéing black mushrooms, and Ezra was running a mixer near the sink. Ruth sat down next to Cody, hooking her combat boots on the rung of his chair and hugging her ribs. Cody cut into a huge edge of pie and gave some thought to food—to its inexplicable, loaded meaning in other people's lives. Couldn't you classify a person, he wondered, purely by examining his attitude toward food? Look at Cody's mother—a nonfeeder, if ever there was one. Even back in his childhood, when they'd depended on her for nourishment . . . why, mention you were hungry and she'd suddenly act rushed and harassed, fretful, out of breath, distracted. He remembered her coming home from work in the evening and tearing irritably around the kitchen. Tins toppled out of the cupboards and fell all over her—pork 'n' beans, Spam, oily tuna fish, peas canned olive-drab. She cooked in her hat, most of the time. She whimpered when she burned things. She burned things you would not imagine it possible to burn and served others half-raw, adding jarring extras of her own design such as crushed pineapple in the mashed potatoes. (Anything, as long as it was a leftover, might as well be dumped in the pan with anything else.) Her only seasonings were salt and pepper. Her only gravy was Campbell's cream of mushroom soup, undiluted. And till Cody was grown, he had assumed that roast beef had to be stringy—not something you sliced, but a leathery dry object which you separated with a fork, one strand from the other, and dropped with a clunk upon your plate.

Though during illness, he remembered, you could count on her to bring liquids. Hot tea: she was good at that. And canned consommé. Thin things, watery things. Then she'd stand in the door with her arms folded while you drank it. He remembered that her expression, when others ate or drank, conveyed a mild distaste. She ate little herself, often toyed with her food; and she implied some criticism of those who acted hungry or over-interested in what they were served. Neediness: she disapproved of neediness in people. Whenever there was a family argument, she most often chose to start it over dinner.

Biting into Ruth's flaky, shattering crust, Cody considered his mother's three children—Jenny, for instance, with her lemon-water and lettuce-leaf diets, never allowing herself a sweet, skipping meals altogether, as if continually bearing in mind that disapproving expression of her mother's. And Cody himself was not much different, when you came right down to it. It seemed that food didn't count, with him; food was something required by others, so that for their sakes—on dates, at business luncheons—he would obligingly order a meal for himself just to keep them company. But all you'd find in his refrigerator was cream for his coffee and limes for his gin and tonics. He never ate breakfast; he often forgot lunch. Sometimes a gnawing feeling hit his stomach in the afternoon and he sent his secretary out for food. "What kind of food?" she would ask. He would say, "Anything, I don't care." She'd bring a Danish or an eggroll or a liverwurst on rye; it was all the same to him. Half the time, he wouldn't even notice what it was—would take a bite, go on dictating, leave the rest to be disposed of by the cleaning lady. A woman he'd once had dinner with had claimed that this was a sign of some flaw. Watching him dissect his fish but then fail to eat it, noticing how he refused dessert and then benignly, tolerantly waited for her to finish a giant chocolate mousse, she had accused him of . . . what had she called it? Lack of enjoyment. Lack of ability to enjoy himself. He hadn't understood, back then, how she could draw so many implications from a single meal. And still he didn't agree with her.

Yes, only Ezra, he would say, had managed to escape all this. Ezra was so impervious—so thickheaded, really; nothing ever touched him. He ate heartily, whether it was his mother's cooking or his own. He liked anything that was offered him, especially bread—would have to watch his weight as he got older. But above all else, he was a feeder. He would set a dish before you and then stand there with his face expectant, his hands clasped tightly under his chin, his eyes following your fork. There was something tender, almost loving, about his attitude toward people who were eating what he'd cooked them.

Like Ruth, Cody thought.

He asked her for another slice of pie.

Mornings, now, he called her from New York, often getting her landlady out of bed; and Ruth when she answered was still creaky voiced from sleep—or was it from bewilderment, even now? Reluctantly, each time, she warmed to his questions, speaking shortly at first. Yes, she was fine. The restaurant was fine. Dinner last night had gone well. And then (letting her sentences stretch gradually longer, as if giving in to him all over again) she told him that this house was starting to wear her down—creepy boarders padding around in their slippers at all hours, no one ever *going* anywhere, landlady planted eternally in front of her TV. This landlady, a widow, believed that Perry Como's eyebrows quirked upward as they did because he was by nature a bass, and singing such high notes gave him constant pain; she had heard that Arthur Godfrey, too, had been enduring constant pain for years, smiling a courageous smile and wheeling about on his stool because the slightest step would stab him like a knife. Yes, everything, to Mrs. Pauling, was a constant pain; *life* was a constant pain, and Ruth had started looking around her and wondering how she stood this place.

Weekends—Friday and Saturday nights—Ruth tore through the restaurant kitchen slapping haunches of beef and whipping egg whites. Ezra worked more quietly. Cody sat at the wooden table. Now and then, Ruth would place some new dish in front of him and Cody would eat it dutifully. Every mouthful was a declaration of love. Ruth knew that. She was tense and watchful. She gave him sideways, piercing glances when he forked up one of her dumplings, and he was careful to leave nothing on his plate.

Then on Sunday mornings, yellow summer mornings at her boardinghouse, he rang her doorbell and pulled her close to him when she answered. Anytime he kissed her, he was visited by the curious impression that some other self of hers was still moving through the house behind her, spunky and lighthearted and uncatchable even yet, checking under pot lids, slamming cupboard doors, humming and tossing her head and wiping her hands on her blue jeans.

"I don't understand," Ezra told them.

"Let me start over," said Cody.

Ezra said, "Is this some kind of a joke? Is that what it is?

What is it?"

"Ruth and I—" Cody began.

But Ruth said, "Ezra, honey. Listen." She stepped forward. She was wearing the navy suit that Cody had bought her to go away in, and high-heeled shoes with slender straps. Although it was a glaring day in August, her skin had a chilled, dry, powdery look, and her freckles stood out sharply. She said, "Ezra, we surely never planned on this. We never had the least intention, not me or Cody neither one."

Ezra waited, evidently still not comprehending. He was backed against the huge old restaurant stove, as if retreating from their news.

"It just happened, like," said Ruth.

"You don't know what you're saying," said Ezra.

"Ezra, honey—"

"You would never do this. It's not true."

"See, I don't know how it came about but me and Cody . . . and I should've told you sooner but I kept thinking, oh, this is just some . . . I mean, this is silly; he's so sophisticated, he isn't someone for *me*; this is just some . . . daydream, see . . ."

"There's bound to be an explanation," Ezra said.

"I feel real bad about it, Ezra."

"I'm sure I'll understand in a minute," he said. "Just give me time. Just wait a minute. Let me think it through."

They waited, but he didn't say anything more. He pressed two fingers against his forehead, as if working out some complicated puzzle. After a while, Cody touched Ruth's arm. She said, "Well, Ezra, goodbye, I guess." Then she and Cody left.

In the car, she cried a little—not making any fuss but sniffling quietly and keeping her face turned toward the side window. "Are you all right?" Cody asked.

She nodded.

"You're sure you still want to go on with this."

She nodded again.

They were planning to travel by train—Ruth's idea; she had

168

never set foot on a train—to New York City, where they would be married in a civil ceremony. Ruth's people, she said, were mostly dead or wouldn't much care; so there wasn't any point having the wedding in her hometown. And it went without saying that *Cody's* people . . . well. For the next little bit, they might as well stay in New York. By and by, things would simmer down.

Ruth took off one of her gloves, already gray at the seams, and crumpled it into a ball and blotted both her eyes.

Near Penn Station, Cody found a parking lot that offered weekly rates. It was a good deal of trouble, traveling by train, but worth it for Ruth's sake. She was already perking up. She asked him if he thought there'd be a dining car—an "eating car," she called it. Cody said he imagined so. He accepted the ticket the parking attendant gave him and slid out from behind the steering wheel, grunting a little; lately he'd put on a few pounds around the waist. He took Ruth's suitcase from the trunk. Ruth wasn't used to high heels and she hobbled along unsteadily, every now and then making a loud, scraping sound on the sidewalk. "I hope to get the knack of these things before long," she told Cody.

"You don't have to wear them, you know."

"Oh, I surely *do*," she said.

Cody guided her into the station. The sudden, echoing coolness seemed to stun her into silence. She stood looking around her while Cody went to the ticket window. A lady at the head of the line was arguing about the cost of her fare. A man in a crisp white suit rolled his eyes at Cody, implying exasperation at the wait. Cody pretended not to notice. He turned away as if checking the length of the line behind him, and a plump young woman with a child smiled instantly, fully prepared, and said, "Cody Tull!"

"Um—"

"I'm Jane Lowry. Remember me?"

"Oh, Jane! Jane Lowry! Well, good to see you, how nice to

". . . and is this your little girl?"

"Yes; say hello to Mr. Tull, Betsy. Mr. Tull and Mommy used to go to school together."

"So you're married," Cody said, moving forward in line. "Well, what a—"

"Remember the day I came to visit you, uninvited?" she asked. She laughed, and he saw, in the tilt of her head, a flash of the young girl he had known. She had lived on Bushnell Street, he remembered now; she had had the most beautiful hair, which still showed its chips of gold light, although she wore it short now. "I had such a crush on you," she said. "Lord, I made a total fool of myself."

"You played a game of checkers with Ezra," he reminded her.

"Ezra?"

"My brother."

"You had a brother?"

"I certainly did; do. You played checkers with him all afternoon."

"How funny; I thought you only had a sister. What was her name? Jenny. She was so skinny, I envied her for years. Anything she wanted, she could eat and not have it show. What's Jenny doing now?"

"Oh, she's in medical school. And Ezra: he runs a restaurant."

"In those days," said Jane, "my fondest wish was to wake up one morning and find I'd turned into Jenny Tull. But I'd forgotten you had a brother."

Cody opened his mouth to speak, but the man in white had moved away and it was Cody's turn at the window. And by the time he'd bought his tickets, Jane had switched to the other line and was busy buying hers.

He didn't see her again—though he looked for her on the train—but it was odd how she'd plunged him into the past. Swaying on the seat next to Ruth, holding her small, rough

170

hand but finding very little to say to her, he was startled by fragments of buried memories. The scent of chalk in geometry
class; the balmy, laden feeling of the last day of school every
spring; the crack of a baseball bat on the playground. He found
himself in a summer evening at a drive-in hamburger stand,
with its blinding lights surrounded by darkness, its hot, salty,
greasy smell of French fries, and all his friends horsing around
at the curb. He could hear an old girlfriend from years ago, her
droning, dissatisfied voice: "You ask me to the movies and I say
yes and then you change your mind and ask me bowling instead
and I say yes to that but you say wait, let's make it another night,
as if anything you can have is something it turns out you don't
want . . . " He heard his mother telling Jenny not to slouch,
telling Cody not to swear, asking Ezra why he wouldn't stand up
to the neighborhood bully. "I'm trying to get through life as a
liquid," Ezra had said, and Cody (trying to get through life as a
rock) had laughed; he could hear himself still. "Why aren't
cucumbers prickly any more?" he heard Ezra ask. And "Cody?
Don't you want to walk to school with me?" He saw Ezra aiming a red-feathered dart, his chapped, childish wrist awkwardly
angled; he saw him running for the telephone—"I'll get it! I'll
get it!"—hopeful and joyous, years and years younger. He remembered Carol, or was it Karen, reciting Ezra's faults—a
motherly man, she'd said; what had she said?—and it occurred
to him that the reason he had dropped her was, she really hadn't
understood Ezra; she hadn't appreciated what he was all about.
Then Ruth squeezed his hand and said, "I intend to ride trains
forever; it's so much better than the bus. Isn't it, Cody? Cody?
Isn't it?" The train rounded a curve with a high, thin, whistling
sound that took him by surprise. He honestly believed, for an
instant, that what he'd heard was music—a tune piped, a burble
of notes, a little scrap of melody floating by on the wind and
breaking his heart.

6

Beaches on the Moon

Twice or maybe three times a year, she goes out to the farm to make sure things are in order. She has her son Ezra drive her there, and she takes along a broom, a dustpan, rags, a grocery bag for trash and a bucket and a box of cleanser. Ezra asks why she can't just keep these supplies in the farmhouse, but she knows they wouldn't be safe. The trespassers would get them. Oh, the trespassers—the small boys and courting couples and the teen-aged gangs. It makes her mad to think of them. As the car turns off the main road, rattling up the rutted driveway, she already sees their litter—the beer cans tossed among the scrubby weeds, the scraps of toilet paper dangling from the bushes. This land has been let go and the vegetation is matted and wild, bristly, scratchy, no shade at all from the blazing sun. There are little spangles of bottle tops embedded in the dirt of the road. And the yard (which is not truly mown but sickled by Jared Peers, once or twice a summer) is flocked with white paper plates and Dixie cups, napkins, sandwich bags, red-striped straws, and those peculiarly long-lived, accordioned worms of paper that the straws were wrapped in.

Ezra parks the car beneath an oak tree. "It's a shame. A disgrace and a shame," Pearl says, stepping out. She wears a seersucker dress that will wash, and her oldest shoes. On her head is a broad-brimmed straw hat. It will keep the dust from her hair—from all but one faded, blondish frizz bordering each temple. "It's a national crime," she says, and she stands looking around her while Ezra unloads her cleaning supplies. The house has two stories. It is a ghostly, rubbed-out gray. The ridgepole sags and the front porch has buckled and many of the window-panes are broken—more every time she comes.

She remembers when Cody first showed her this place. "Imagine what can be done with it, Mother. Picture the possibilities," he said. He was planning to marry and raise a family here—provide her with lots of grandchildren. He even kept the livestock on, paying Jared Peers to tend it till Cody moved in.

That was years ago, though, and all that remains of those animals now is a couple of ragged hens gone wild, clucking in the mulberry tree out behind the barn.

She has a key to the warped rear door but it isn't needed. The padlock's missing and the rusted hasp hangs open. "Not again," she says. She turns the knob and enters, warily. (One of these days, she'll surprise someone and get her head blown off for her trouble.) The kitchen smells stale and cold, even in the heat of the day. There's a fly buzzing over the table, a rust spot smearing the back of the sink, a single tatter of cloudy plastic curtain trailing next to the window. The linoleum's worn patternless near the counters.

Ezra follows, burdened with household supplies. He sets them down and stands wiping his face on the sleeve of his work shirt. More than once he's told her he fails to see the use of this: cleaning up only to clean again, the next time they come out. What's the purpose, he wants to know. Why go to all this trouble, what does she have in mind? But he's an obliging man, and when she insists, he says no more. He runs his fingers through his hair, which the sweat has turned a dark, streaked yellow. He tests the kitchen faucet. First it explodes and then it yields a coppery trickle of water.

There are half a dozen empty bottles lying on the floor—Wild Turkey, Old Crow, Southern Comfort. "Look! And look," says Pearl. She nudges a Marlboro pack with her toe. She scrapes at a scorch on the table. She discreetly looks away while Ezra hooks an unmentionable rubber something with the broom handle and drops it into the trash bag.

"Cody," she used to say, "you could hire a man to come and haul this furniture off to the dump. Surely you don't want it for yourself. Cody, there's a Sunday suit in the bedroom closet. There are shoes at the top of the cellar stairs—chunky, muddy old garden shoes. You ought to hire a man to come haul them for you." But Cody paid no attention—he was hardly ever there. He was mostly in New York; and privately, Pearl had expected that that was where he would stay. Which of those girl-friends of his would agree to a life in the country? "You'd just better watch out who you marry," she had told him. "None of your dates that *I've* met would do—those black-haired, flashy, beauty-queen types."

But if only he'd married one of them! If only he'd been satis-fied with that! Instead, one afternoon Ezra had come into the kitchen, had stood there looking sick. "What's wrong?" she'd asked. She knew it was something. "Ezra? Why aren't you at work?"

"It's Cody," he said.

"Cody?"

She clutched at her chest, picturing him dead—her most difficult, most distant child, and now she would never have the answer to him.

But Ezra said, "He's gone off to get married."

"Oh, married," she said, and she dropped her hand. "Well? Who to?"

"To Ruth," he said.

"*Your* Ruth?"

"My Ruth."

"Oh, sweetheart," she said.

Not that she hadn't had some inkling. She had seen it coming for weeks, she believed, though she hadn't exactly seen marriage—more likely a fling, a flirtation, another of Cody's teases. Should she have hinted to Ezra? He wouldn't have listened. He was so gullible, and so much in love. Ruth was the center of his world, for some reason. And anyway, who would have thought that Cody would let it get so serious? "He's just doing it to be mean, sweetheart," she told Ezra. She was right, too, as she'd been right the other times she'd said it—oh, those other times! Those inconsequential spats, those childhood quarrels, arguments, practical jokes! "Cody, stop it this instant," she used to tell him. "You think I don't see what you're up to? Let your poor brother alone. Ezra, pay no mind. He's only being mean." Back then, Ezra had listened and nodded, hoping to believe her; he had doted on his older brother. But now he said, "What does it matter why he did it? He did it, that's all. He stole her away."

"If she could be stolen, honey, why, you don't want her anyhow."

Ezra just looked at her—bleak faced, grim, a walking ache of a man. She knew how he felt. Hadn't she been through it? She remembered from when her husband left—a wound, she'd been, a deep, hollow hole, surrounded by shreds of her former self.

She sweeps all the trash to the center of the floor, collects the bottles and the cigarette packs. Meanwhile, Ezra tapes squares of cardboard to the broken windowpanes. He works steadily, doggedly. She looks up once and sees how the sweat has made an eagle-shaped stain across his back. There are other cardboard squares on other panes, broken earlier. In a few more seasons, it occurs to her, they'll be working in the dark. It's as if they're sealing themselves in, windowpane by windowpane.

When Cody came back with Ruth, after the honeymoon, he was better-looking than ever, sleek and dark and well dressed, but Ruth was her same homely self: a little muskrat of a girl with wickety red hair and freckles, her skin that tissue-thin kind subject to lip sores and pink splotches, her twiggish body awkward in a matronly brown suit that must have been bought especially for this occasion. (Though Pearl was to find, in later years, that all Ruth's clothes struck her that way; nothing seemed as natural as those little-boy dungarees she used to wear with Ezra.) Pearl watched the two of them sharply, closely, anxious to come to some conclusion about their marriage, but they gave away no secrets. Ruth sat pressing her palms together; Cody kept his arm across the back of the couch, not touching her but claiming her, at least. He talked at length about the farm. They were heading out there directly, settling in that night. It was too late for sowing a garden but at least they could clean the place up, begin to make plans for next spring. Ruth was going to get started on that while Cody went back to New York. Ruth nodded at this, and cleared her throat and fumbled with the pocket of her suit jacket. Pearl thought she was reaching for one of her little cigars, but after a moment she stopped fumbling and placed her palms together again. And in fact, Pearl never saw her smoke another one of those cigars.

Then Ezra arrived—not whistling, oddly quiet, as he'd been since Ruth had left. He stopped inside the door and looked at them. "Ezra," Cody said easily, and Ruth stood up and held out her hand. She seemed frightened. This made Pearl like her, a little. (Ruth, at least, recognized the magnitude of what they'd done.) "How you doing, Ezra," Ruth said, quavering. And Ezra had said . . . oh, something or other, he'd managed something; and stood around a while shifting from foot to foot and answering their small talk. So it looked, on the surface, as if they might eventually smooth things over. Yes, after all, this choosing of mates was such a small, brief stage in a family's history.

But Ezra no longer played tunes on his recorder, and he continued to look limp and beaten, and he went to bed every night with no more than a "Good night, Mother." She grieved for him. She longed to say, "Ezra, believe me, she's nothing! You're worth a dozen Ruth Spiveys! A dozen of both of them, to be frank, even if Cody *is* my son . . . " Though of course she loved Cody dearly. But from infancy, he had batted her away; and his sister had been so evasive, somehow; so whom did that leave but Ezra? Ezra was all she had. He was the only one who would let her in. Sometimes, in his childhood, she had worried that he would die young—one of life's ironic twists, to take what you valued most. She had watched him trudging down the street to school, his duck-yellow head bowed in thought, and she would have a sudden presentiment that this was the last she would see of him. Then when he returned, full of news about friends and ball games, how solid, how commonplace—even how irritating—he seemed! And sometimes, long ago when he was small, he might climb up into her lap and place his thin little arms around her neck, and she would drink in his smell of warm biscuits and think, "Really, this is what it's all about. This is what I'm alive for." Then, reluctantly, she allowed him to slip away again. (They claimed she was possessive, pushy. Little did they know.) As a child, he'd had a chirpy style of talking that was so cheerful, ringing through the house like a trill of water . . . when had that begun to change? As an older boy he grew shy and withdrawn, gazing out of shining gray eyes and saying next to nothing. She'd worried when he didn't date. "Wouldn't you like to bring someone home? Ask someone to Sunday dinner?" He shook his head, tongue-tied. He blushed and lowered his long lashes. Pearl wondered, seeing the blush, whether he thought much about girls and such as that. His father had left by then and Cody was no help, three years older, off tomcatting someplace or other. Then as a man, Ezra was . . . well, to be honest, he was not much different from when he was a boy. In a way, he was an *eternal* boy, never got boastful and brash like most men but stayed gentle, somber, contentedly running that restaurant of his and coming home peaceful and tired.

It was a shock when he introduced her to Ruth. What an urchin she was! But plainly, Ezra adored her. "Mother, I'd like you to meet my—meet Ruth." Pearl had stalled a little, at first. Maybe she had failed to act properly welcoming. Well, who could blame her? And now, seeing how things had turned out, who could say she'd been wrong? But she can't help wondering, anyhow . . . If she'd been a little more encouraging, they might have married sooner. They might have married before Cody could work his mischief. Or if she had let herself *realize* . . . Yes, she wonders over and over again: if she'd mentioned Cody's plot to Ezra, stopped that situation that was not so much a courtship as a landslide, a kind of gathering and falling of events . . .

Ridiculous, of course, to imagine that anything she did could have mattered. What happens, happens. It's no one's fault. (Or it's only Cody's fault, for he has always been striving and competitive, a natural-born player of games, has had to win absolutely everything, even something he doesn't want like a runty little redhead far below his usual standards.)

She opens the farmhouse parlor to air it. It smells like skunk. She leaves the front door ajar, taking care not to step onto the porch, which could very well give way beneath her. She remembers how, toward the end of that first week after the honeymoon, she asked Ezra to bring out to Ruth a few odds and ends for the farm—some extra pans, some linens, a carpet sweeper she had no use for. Was there an ulterior motive in her suggestion? If not, why didn't she accompany him, visit the bride like any good mother-in-law? "Please, I don't want to," Ezra said, but she said, "Honey. Go." She hadn't had any conscious design—truly, none at all—but it was a fact that later that morning, dawdling over the dishes, she'd allowed herself a little daydream: Ezra coming up behind Ruth, setting his arms around her, Ruth protesting only briefly before collapsing against him . . . Oh, shouldn't it be possible to undo what was done? What all of them had done?

But Ezra when he returned was as subdued as ever, and only said that Ruth thanked Pearl for the pans and linens but was sending back the carpet sweeper as the farmhouse had no carpets.

Then Saturday, Cody came storming in with everything Ezra had taken to Ruth. "What's all this?" he asked Pearl.

"Why, Cody, pots and sheets, as you can surely see."

"How come Ezra brought them out?"

"I asked him to," she said.

"I won't have it! Won't have him hanging around the farm."

"Cody. It was at my request. Believe me," she told him.

"I do," he said.

She tried to get Ezra to go again the following week—taking the rug from the dining room and the carpet sweeper, once more—but he wouldn't. "I'm not comfortable there," he said. "There's no point. What's the point?" She supposed he was right. Yes, she thought, let Ruth wonder where he'd got to! People who leave us will be sorry in the end. She imagined Ruth alone in the farmhouse, roaming from room to room and peering sadly through the bare windows.

The next weekend, Pearl asked Ezra to drive her out. He couldn't very well refuse; he was her only means of transportation. They both, without discussing it, wore Sunday clothing—formal, guestlike clothing. They found the house looking sealed and abandoned. A lone hound nudged at a bone in the yard, but he surely didn't belong there.

Back home, Pearl placed a call to Cody in New York. "Aren't you coming to the farm any more?"

"Things are kind of busy."

"Won't Ruth be there during the week?"

"I want her here with me," he said. "After all, we just did get married."

"Well, when will we see you?"

"Pretty soon, not too long, I'm sure we'll be down in a while . . ."

But they weren't; or if they were, they didn't tell Pearl, and she was too proud to ask again. The summer ended and leaves turned all colors, but Ezra dragged himself along with no change. "Sweetheart," Pearl told him, as in his boyhood, "isn't there someone you'd like to have home? Some friend to dinner? Anyone," she said. Ezra said no.

From time to time, Pearl called Cody in New York again. He was courteous and noncommittal. Ruth, if she spoke, gave flustered replies and didn't seem to have her wits about her. Then in October, two full weeks went by when no one answered the phone at all. Pearl wondered if they'd gone to the farm, and she begged Ezra to investigate. But when he finally agreed to, he found nobody there. "Someone's shattered four window-panes," he reported. "Threw rocks at them, or shot them out." This made Pearl feel frightened. The world was closing in on them; even here on her own familiar streets, she no longer felt safe. And who knew what might have become of Ruth and Cody? They could be lying dead in their apartment, victims of a burglary or some bizarre, New York-type accident, their bodies undiscovered for weeks. Oh, this was what happened when you broke off all ties with your family! It wasn't right; with your family, if with no one else, you have to keep on trying.

She called frantically, day after day, often letting the phone ring thirty or forty times. There was something calming about that faraway purling sound. She was, at least, connected—though only to an object in Cody's apartment.

Then he answered. It was late in October. She was so taken aback that she didn't know what to say. It seemed the monotonous ring of the phone had grown to be enough for her. "Um, Cody . . ." she said.

"Oh. Mother."

"Cody, where have you *been?*"

"I had a job to see to in Ohio. I took Ruth along."

"You didn't answer the phone for weeks, and we looked for

you out at the farm and some of the windows were broken."

"Damn! I thought I was paying Jared to keep that kind of thing from happening."

"You can't imagine how I felt, Cody. When I heard about the windows I felt . . . You're letting that place go to rack and ruin and we never get to see you any more."

"I do have a job to do, Mother."

"I thought that once you married, you were moving down to Baltimore. You were doing over the farmhouse and planting a garden and all."

"Yes, definitely. That's a definite possibility," said Cody. "Get Ezra to tape those windows, will you? And tell him to speak to Jared. I can't have the place depreciating."

"All right, Cody," she said.

Then she asked about Thanksgiving. "Will you be coming down? You know how Ezra likes to have us at the restaurant."

"Oh, Ezra and his restaurant . . ."

"Please. We've hardly seen you," she said.

"Well, maybe."

So in November they returned—Cody looking elegant and casual, Ruth incongruous in a large, ornate blue dress. Her hair was so stubby, her head so small, that the dress appeared to be drowning her. She staggered in her high-heeled shoes. She still would not meet Ezra's gaze.

"What have you two been up to?" Pearl asked Ruth, as they rode in Cody's Cadillac to the restaurant.

"Oh, nothing so much."

"Are you decorating Cody's apartment?"

"Decorating? No."

"We've hardly seen it," Cody said. "I'm taking on longer-term jobs. In December I start reorganizing a textile plant in Georgia, a *big* thing, five or six months. I thought maybe Ruth could come with me; we could rent us a little house of some kind. There's not much point in commuting."

"December? But then you'd miss Christmas," said Pearl.

Cody looked surprised. He said, "Why would we miss it?"

"I mean, would you still make the trip to Baltimore?"

"Oh. Well, no, I guess not," he said. "But we're here for Thanksgiving, aren't we?"

She resolved to say no more. She had her dignity.

They sat at their regular family table, surrounded by a fair-sized crowd. (In those days—the start of the sixties—shaggy young people had just discovered Ezra's restaurant, with its stripped wood and pure, fresh food, and they thronged there every evening.) It was sad that Jenny couldn't come; she was spending the holiday with her in-laws. But Ruth, at least, rounded out their number. Pearl smiled across the table at her. Ruth said, "It feels right funny to be eating where I used to be cooking."

"Would you like to visit the kitchen?" Ezra asked. "The staff would enjoy seeing you."

"I don't mind if I do," she said. It was the first time since her marriage that she'd looked at him directly—or the first that Pearl knew about.

So Ezra scraped back his chair and rose, and guided Ruth into the kitchen. Pearl could tell that Cody wasn't pleased. He stopped in the act of unfolding his napkin and gazed after them, even taking a breath as if preparing to object. Then he must have thought better of it. He shook out the napkin angrily, saying nothing.

"So," said Pearl. "When do you move to the farm?"

"Farm? Oh, I don't know," he said. "Everything's so changed; the whole character of my work has changed." He looked again toward the kitchen.

"But you'd planned on raising a family there. It was all you ever talked about."

"Yes, well, and these long-term contracts," he said, as if he hadn't heard her.

Pearl said, "You had your heart just set on it."

But he continued watching the other two. He was not the

least bit interested in what she might be saying. The kitchen was fully exposed, and could not have concealed the smallest secret. So why was Cody nervous? Ezra and Ruth stood talking with one of the cooks, their backs to the dining room. Ezra gestured as he spoke. He lifted both arms wide, one arm behind Ruth but not touching her, not brushing her shoulder, surely not encircling her or anything like that. Even so, Cody rose abruptly from his chair. "Cody!" Pearl said. He strode toward the kitchen, with his napkin crumpled in one fist. Pearl stood up and hurried after him, and arrived in time to hear him say, "Let's go, Ruth."

"Go?"

"I didn't come here to watch you and Ezra chumming it up in the kitchen."

Ruth looked scared. Her face seemed to grow more pointed.

"Come on," said Cody, and he took her elbow. "Goodbye," he told Pearl and Ezra.

"Oh!" said Pearl, running after them. "Oh, Cody, what can you be thinking of? How can you act so foolish?"

Cody yanked Ruth's coat from a brass hook in passing. He opened the front door and pulled Ruth into the street and shut the door behind them.

Ezra said, "I don't understand."

Pearl said, "Why does it always turn out this way? How come we end up quarreling? Don't we all love each other? Everything else aside," she said, "don't we all want the best for one another?"

"Certainly we do," Ezra said.

His answer was so level and firm that she felt comforted. She knew things were bound to work out someday. She let him lead her back to the table, and the two of them had a forlorn turkey dinner on the wide expanse of white linen.

Upstairs there are four bedrooms, sparsely furnished, musty. The beds are so sunken-looking, evidently even the courting couples have not been tempted by them. They're untouched, the drab, dirty quilts still smooth. But a dead bird lies beneath one window. Pearl calls down the stairwell. "Ezra? Ezra, come here this instant. Bring the broom and trash bag."

He mounts the stairs obediently. She looks down and sees, with a pang, that his lovely fair hair is thinning on the back of his head. He is thirty-seven years old, will be thirty-eight in December. He will probably never marry. He will never do anything but run that peculiar restaurant of his, with its hodge-podge of food, its unskilled waitresses, its foreign cooks with questionable papers. You could say, in a way, that Ezra has suffered a tragedy, although it's a very small tragedy in the eyes of the world. You could say that he and Ruth, together, have suffered a tragedy. Something has been done to them; something has been taken away from them. They have lost it. They *are* lost. It doesn't help at all that Cody in fact is a very nice man—that he's bright and funny and genuinely kind, to everyone but Ezra.

You could almost say that Cody, too, has suffered a tragedy. In 1964, when she went out to Illinois to visit them, she felt in their house the thin, tight atmosphere of an unhappy marriage. Not a really terrible marriage—no sign of hatred, spitefulness, violence. Just a sense of something missing. A certain failure to connect, between the two of them. Everything seemed so tenuous. Or was it her imagination? Maybe she was wrong. Maybe it was the house itself—a ranch house in a development, rented for the four months or so that Cody would need to reorganize a plastics plant in Chicago. Plainly the place was expensive, with wall-to-wall carpeting and long, low, modern furniture; but there were no trees anywhere nearby, not even a bush or a shrub—just that raw brick cube rising starkly from the flatness. And outside it was so white-hot, so insufferably hot, that they were confined to the house with its artificial, refrigerated air. They were *imprisoned* by the house, dependent upon it like spacemen in a spaceship, and when they went out it was only to dash through a crushing weight of heat to Cody's air-conditioned Mercedes. Ruth, going about her chores every day, had the clenched expression of someone determined to survive no matter what. Cody came home in the evening gasping for oxygen—barely crawling over the doorsill, Pearl fantasized—but did not seem all that relieved to have arrived. When he greeted Ruth, they touched cheeks and moved apart again.

It was the first time Pearl had ever visited them, the first and only time, and this was after years of very little contact at all. They seldom came to Baltimore. They never returned to the farm. And Cody wrote almost no letters, though he would telephone on birthdays and holidays. He was more like an acquaintance, Pearl thought. A not very cordial acquaintance.

Once she and Ezra were driving down a road in West Virginia, on an outing to Harper's Ferry, when they chanced to come up behind a man in jogging shorts. He was running along the edge of the highway, a tall man, dark, with a certain confident, easy swing to his shoulders . . . Cody! Out here in the middle of nowhere, by sheer coincidence, Cody Tull! Ezra slammed on his brakes, and Pearl said, "Well, did you ever." But then the jogger, hearing their car, had turned his face and he wasn't Cody after all. He was someone entirely different, beefy jawed, nowhere near as handsome. Ezra sped up again. Pearl said, "How silly of me, I know full well that Cody's in, ah . . ."

"Indiana," said Ezra.

"Indiana; I don't know why I thought . . ."

They were both quiet for several minutes after that, and in those minutes Pearl imagined the scene if it really had been Cody—if he had turned, astonished, as they sailed past. Oddly enough, she didn't envision stopping. She thought of how his mouth would fall open as he recognized their faces behind the glass; and how they would gaze out at him, and smile and wave, and skim on by.

Whenever he phoned he was cheerful and hearty. "How've you been, Mother?"

"Why, Cody!"

"Everything all right? How's Ezra?"

Oh, on the phone he was so nice about Ezra, interested and affectionate like any other brother. And on the rare occasions when he and Ruth came through Baltimore—heading somewhere else, just briefly dropping in—he seemed so pleased to shake hands with Ezra and clap him on the back and ask what he'd been up to. At first.

Only at first.

Then: "Ruth! What are you and Ezra talking about, over there?" Or: "Ezra? Do you mind not standing so close to my wife?" When Ezra and Ruth were hardly speaking, really. They were so cautious with each other, it hurt to watch.

"Cody. Please. What are you imagining?" Pearl would ask him, and then he would turn on her: "Naturally, *you* wouldn't see it. Naturally, he can do no wrong, can he, Mother. Your precious boy. Can he."

She had given up, finally, on ever being asked to visit. When Cody called and told her Ruth was pregnant, some two or three years into the marriage, Pearl said, "Oh, Cody, if she'd like it at all, I mean when the baby arrives . . . if she'd like me to come take care of things . . ." But evidently, she wasn't needed. And when he called to say that Luke was born—nine pounds, three ounces; everything was fine—she said, "I can't wait to see him. I honestly can't wait." But Cody let that pass.

They sent her photos: Luke in an infant seat, blond and stern. Luke creeping bear-style across the carpet, on hands and feet instead of knees. (Cody had crept that way too.) Luke uncertainly walking, with a clothespin in each fat fist. He had to have the clothespins, Ruth wrote, because then he thought he was holding on to something. Otherwise, he fell. Now that photos were arriving, letters came too, generally written by Ruth. Her grammar was shocking and she couldn't spell. She said, *Me and Cody wrecken Luke's eyes are going to stay blue,* but what did Pearl care about grammar? She saved every letter and put Luke's pictures on her desk in little gilt frames she bought as Kresge's.

I think I ought to come see Luke before he's grown, she wrote. No one answered. She wrote again. *Would June be all right?* Then Cody wrote that they were moving to Illinois in June, but if she really wanted then maybe she could come in July.

So she went to Illinois in July, traveling with a trainload of fresh-faced boy soldiers on their way to Vietnam, and she spent a week in that treeless house barricaded against the elements. It was a shock, even to her, how instantly and how deeply she loved her grandson. He was not quite two years old by then, a beautiful baby with a head that seemed adult in its shape — sharply defined, the golden hair trimmed close and neat. His firm, straight lips seemed adult as well, and he had an un-childlike way of walking. There was a bit of slump in his posture, a little droop to his shoulders, nothing physically wrong but an air of resignation that was almost comical in someone so small. Pearl sat on the floor with him for hours, playing with his trucks and cars. "Vroom. Vroom. Roll it back to Granny, now." She was touched by his stillness. He had a sizable vocabulary but he used it only when necessary; he was not a spend-thrift. He was careful. He lacked gaiety. Was he happy? Was this a fit life for a child?

She saw Cody had a sprinkling of gray in his sideburns, a more leathery look to his cheeks; but that Ruth was still a scrappy little thing in too-short hair and unbecoming dresses. She had not grown fuller or softer with age. She was like certain supermarket vegetables that turn from green to withered without ever ripening. In the evenings, when Cody came home from work, Ruth clattered around the kitchen cooking great quantities of country food that Cody would hardly touch; and Cody had a gin and tonic and watched the news. The two of them asked each other, "How was your day?" and "Everything fine?" but they didn't seem to listen to the answers. Pearl could believe that in the morning, waking in their king-sized bed, they asked politely, "Did you sleep all right?" She felt oppressed and uncomfortable, but instead of averting her gaze she was for some reason compelled to delve deeper into their lives; she sent them out one night to a movie, promising to watch Luke, and then ransacked all the desk drawers but found only tax receipts, and bank statements, and a photo album belonging to the people who really lived here. Anyway, she couldn't have said what it was she was looking for.

Coming home, jouncing on the train amid another group of soldiers, she felt weary and hopeless. She arrived in Baltimore seven hours late, with a racking headache. Then as she entered the station, she saw Ezra walking toward her in his plodding way and she felt such a stab of . . . well, recognition. It was Luke's walk, solemn little Luke. Life was so sad, she thought, that she almost couldn't bear it. But kissing Ezra, she felt her sorrow overtaken by something very like annoyance. She wondered why he put up with this, why he let things go on this way. Could it be that he took some *satisfaction* in his grief? (As if he were paying for something, she thought. But what would he be paying for?) In the car, he asked, "How'd you like Luke?" and she said, "Don't you ever think of just going there and trying to get her back?"

"I couldn't," he said, unsurprised, and he maneuvered the car laboriously from its parking slot.

"Well, I don't see why not," she told him.

"It's not right. It's wrong."

She wasn't given to philosophy, but during the drive home she stared at the grimy Baltimore scenery and considered the question of right and wrong: of theoretical virtue, existing in a vacuum; of whether there was any point to it all. When they reached home, she got out of the car and entered the house without a word, and climbed the stairs to her room.

*

Ezra scoops the dead bird into a piece of cardboard and slides it into the trash bag. Then he tapes the cardboard to the broken windowpane where the bird must have entered. Pearl, meanwhile, sweeps up the shards of glass. She leaves them in a pyramid and goes downstairs for the dustpan. Already, she sees, the house has a bit more life to it—the sunny pattern of leaves shimmering on the parlor floor in front of the open door, the smell of hot grass wafting through the rooms. "It was never all that practical," Cody said on the phone just recently, referring to the farm. "It was only a half-baked idea that I had when I was young." But if he really meant that, why doesn't he go on and sell? No, he couldn't possibly; she has spent so much time sweeping this place, preparing it for him, opening and shutting bureau drawers as if she'd find his secrets there. She can imagine Ruth in this kitchen, Cody out surveying the lines or whatever it is men do on farms. She can picture Luke running through the yard in denim overalls. He is old enough to go fishing now, to swim in the creek beyond the pasture, maybe even to tend the animals. In August, he'll be eight. Is it eight? Or nine. She's lost track. She hardly ever sees him, and must conquer his shyness all over again whenever he and his parents pass through Baltimore. Each visit, his interests have changed: from popguns to marbles to stamp collecting. Last time he was here, some two or three years back, she got out her husband's stamp album—its maroon, fake-leather cover gone gray with mildew—only to find that Luke had switched to model airplanes. He was assembling a balsa wood jet, he told her, that would actually fly. And he was planning to be an astronaut. "By the time I'm grown," he said, "astronauts will be ordinary. People will be taking rockets like you would take a bus. They'll spend their summers on Venus. They won't go to Ocean City; they'll go to beaches on the moon." "Ah," she said, "isn't that wonderful!" But she was too old for such things. She couldn't keep up, and the very thought of traveling to the moon made her feel desolate.

And nowadays—well, who can guess? Luke must be involved in something entirely different. It's so long since he was here, and she's not sure he'll ever be back. During that last visit, Ezra got his old pearwood recorder from the closet and showed Luke how to play a tune. Pearl knows very little about recorders, but evidently something happens—the wood dries up, or warps, or something—when they're not played enough; and this one hadn't been played in a decade, at least. Its voice had gone splintery and cracked. How startled she'd been, hearing three ancient notes tumble forth after such a silence! Ezra and Luke walked south on Calvert Street to buy some linseed oil. Not two minutes after they left, Cody asked where they'd got to. "Why, off to buy oil for Ezra's recorder," Pearl told him. "Didn't you see them go?" Cody excused himself and went outside to pace in front of the house. Ruth stayed in the living room, discussing schools. Pearl hardly listened. She could look through the window and see Cody pacing, turning, pacing, his suit coat whipping out behind him. She could tell when Ezra and Luke returned, even before she saw them, by the way that Cody stiffened. "Where have you been?" she heard him ask. "What have you two been doing?"

Luke never did learn how to play the recorder. Cody said they had to go. "Oh, but Cody!" Pearl said. "I thought you were spending the night!"

"Wrong," he told her. "Wrong again. I can't stay here; this place is not safe. Don't you see what Ezra's up to?"

"What, Cody? What is he up to?"

"Don't you see he's out to steal my son?" he asked. "The same way he always stole everybody? Don't you *see*?"

In the end, they left. Ezra wanted to give Luke the recorder for keeps, but Cody told Luke to leave it; he'd get him a newer one, fancier, finer. One that wasn't all dried up, he said.

Pearl believes now that her family has failed. Neither of her sons is happy, and her daughter can't seem to stay married. There is no one to accept the blame for this but Pearl herself, who raised these children single-handed and did make mistakes, oh, a bushel of mistakes. Still, she sometimes has the feeling that it's simply fate, and not a matter for blame at all. She feels that everything has been assigned, has been preordained; everyone must play his role. Certainly she never intended to foster one of those good son/bad son arrangements, but what can you do when one son is consistently good and the other consistently bad? What can the sons do, even? "Don't you *see?*" Cody had cried, and she had imagined, for an instant, that he was inviting her to look at his whole existence—his years of hurt and bafflement.

Often, like a child peering over the fence at somebody else's party, she gazes wistfully at other families and wonders what their secret is. They seem so close. Is it that they're more religious? Or stricter, or more lenient? Could it be the fact that they participate in sports? Read books together? Have some common hobby? Recently, she overheard a neighbor woman discussing her plans for Independence Day: her family was having a picnic. Every member—child or grownup— was cooking his or her specialty. Those who were too little to cook were in charge of the paper plates.

Pearl felt such a wave of longing that her knees went weak.

Ezra has finished taping the glass. Pearl drifts through the other bedrooms, checking the other windows. In the smallest bedroom, a nursery, a little old lady in a hat approaches. It's Pearl, in the speckled mirror above a bureau. She leans closer and traces the lines around her eyes. Her age does not surprise her. She's grown used to it by now. You're old for so much longer than you're young, she thinks. Really it hardly seems fair. And then she thinks, for no earthly reason, of a girl she went to school with, Linda Lou something-or-other—such a pretty, flighty girl, someone she'd always envied. In the middle of their senior year, Linda Lou disappeared. There were rumors, later confirmed —an affair with the school's only male teacher, a married man; and a baby on the way. How horrified her class-mates had been! It had thrilled them: that they actually knew such a person, had borrowed her history notes, helped her retie a loose sash, perhaps even brushed her hand accidentally—that hand that may have touched . . . well, who knew what. It occurs to Pearl, peering into the glass, that the baby born of that scandal must be sixty years old by now. He would have gray hair and liver spots, perhaps false teeth, bifocals, a tedious burden of a life. Yet Linda Lou, wearing white, still dances in Pearl's mind, the prettiest girl at the senior social.

"Don't you *see?*" Cody has asked, and Pearl has said, "Honey, I just can't understand you."

Then he shrugged, and his normal, amused expression returned to his face. "Ah, well," he said, "I can't either, I guess. After all, what do I care, now I'm grown? Why should it matter any more?"

She doesn't recall if she managed any reply to that.

She steps away from the mirror. Ezra comes in, bearing the trash bag. "All finished, Mother," he says.

"It looks a lot better, doesn't it?"

"It looks just fine," he tells her.

They descend the stairs, and close the door, and carry their supplies to the car. As they drive away Pearl glances back, like any good housewife checking what she's cleaned, and it seems to her that even that buckling front porch is straighter and more solid. She has a feeling of accomplishment. Others might have given up and let the trespassers take the place over, but never Pearl. Next season she will come again, and the season after, and the season after that, and Ezra will go on bringing her—the two of them bumping down the driveway, loyal and responsible, together forever.

7

Dr. Tull Is Not a Toy

"Whoever's the first to mention divorce has to take the children," Jenny said. "This has kept us together more times than I can count."

She was joking, but the priest didn't laugh. He may have been too young to catch it. All he did was shift uncomfortably in his chair. Meanwhile the children milled around him like something bubbling, like something churning, and the baby dribbled on his shoes. He withdrew his feet imperceptibly, as if trying not to hurt the baby's feelings.

"Yet I believe," he said, appearing to choose his words, "that you yourself have been divorced, have you not?"

"Twice," said Jenny. She giggled, but he only looked worried. "And once for Joe here," she added.

Her husband smiled at her from the sofa.

"If I hadn't had the foresight to keep my maiden name," Jenny said, "my medical diploma would read like one of those address books where people have moved a lot. Names crossed out and added, crossed out and added—a mess! Dr. Jenny Marie Tull Baines Wiley St. Ambrose."

The priest was one of those very blond men with glasslike hair, and his color was so high that Jenny wondered about his blood pressure. Or maybe he was just embarrassed. "Well," he said. "Mrs., um—or Dr. —"

"Tull."

"Dr. Tull, I only thought that the . . . instability, the lack of stability, might be causing Slevin's problems. The turnover in fathers, you might say."

"In fathers? What are you talking about?" Jenny asked. "Slevin's not *my* son. He's Joe's."

"Ah?"

"*Joe* is his father and always has been."

"Oh, excuse me," said the priest.

He grew even pinker—as well he ought, Jenny felt; for slow, plump Slevin with his ashy hair was obviously Joe's. Jenny was small and dark; Joe a massive, blond, bearded bear of a man with Slevin's slanted blue eyes. (She had often felt drawn to overweight men. They made her feel tidy.) "Slevin," she told the priest, "is Joe's by Greta, his previous wife, and so are most of the others you see here. All except for Becky; Becky's mine. The other six are his." She bent to take the dog's bone from the baby. "Anyway . . . but Joe's wife, Greta: she left."

"Left," said the priest.

"Left me flat," Joe said cheerfully. "Cleared clean out of Baltimore. Parked the kids with a neighbor one day, while I was off at work. Hired an Allied van and departed with all we owned, everything but the children's clothes in neat little piles on the floor."

"Oh, my stars," said the priest.

"Even took their beds. Can you explain that? Took the crib and the changing table. Only thing I can figure, she was so used to life with children that she really couldn't imagine; really assumed she would need a crib no matter where she went. First thing I had to do when I got home that night was go out and buy a fleet of beds from Sears. They must've thought I was opening a motel."

"Picture it," Jenny said. "Joe in an apron. Joe mixing

Similac. Well, he was lost, of course. Utterly lost. The way we met: he called me at home in the dead of night when his baby got roseola. That's how out of touch he was; it's been twenty years at least since pediatricians made house calls. But I came, I don't know why. Well, he lived only two blocks away. And he was so desperate—answered the door in striped pajamas, jiggling the baby—"

"I fell in love with her the moment she walked in," said Joe. He stroked his beard; golden frizz flew up around his stubby fingers.

"He thought I was Lady Bountiful," Jenny said, "bearing a medical bag instead of a basket of food. It's hard to resist a man who needs you."

"Need had nothing to do with it," Joe told her.

"Well, who admires you, then. He asked if I had children of my own, and how I managed while I worked. And when I said I mostly played it by ear, with teen-aged sitters one minute and old ladies the next, my mother filling in when she could or my brother or a neighbor, or Becky sometimes just camping in my waiting room with her math assignment—"

"I could see she wasn't a skimpy woman," Joe told the priest. "Not rigid. Not constricted. Not that super-serious kind."

"No," said the priest, glancing around him. (It hadn't been a day when Jenny could get to the housework.)

Jenny said, "He said he liked the way I let his children crawl all over me. He said his wife had found them irritating, the last few years. Well, you see how it began. I had promised myself I'd never remarry, Becky and I would rather manage on our own, that's what I was best at; but I don't know, there Joe *was*, and his children. And his baby was so little and so recently abandoned that she turned her head and opened her mouth when I held her horizontal; you could tell she still remembered. Anyway," she said, and she smiled at the priest, who really was shockingly young—a wide-eyed boy, was all.

195

"How did we get on this subject?"

"Uh, Slevin," said the priest. "We were discussing Slevin."

"Oh, yes, Slevin."

It was a rainy, blowy April afternoon, with the trees turning inside out and beating against the windowpanes, and the living room had reached just that shade of dusk where no one had realized, quite yet, that it was time to switch on the lights. The air seemed thick and grainy. The children were winding down like little clocks and fussing for their suppers; but the priest, lacking children of his own, failed to notice this. He leaned forward, setting his fingertips together. "I've been concerned," he said, "by Slevin's behavior at C.Y.O. meetings. He's not sociable at all, has no friends, seems moody, withdrawn. Of course it could be his age, but . . . he's fourteen, is he?"

"Thirteen," said Joe, after thinking it over.

"Thirteen years old, naturally a difficult . . . I wouldn't even mention it, except that when I suggested we have a talk he just wrenched away and ran out, and never returned. Now we notice that you, Mr. St. Ambrose, that you drop him off for mass every Sunday, but in fact he's stopped coming inside and simply sits out front on the steps and watches the traffic. He's, you might say, playing hooky, but—"

"Shoot," said Joe. "I get up specially on a Sunday morning to drive him there and he plays *hooky*?"

"But my point is—"

"I don't know why he wants to go anyhow. He's the only one of them that does."

"But it's his withdrawn behavior that worries me," the priest said, "more than his church attendance. Though it might not be a bad idea if, perhaps, you accompanied him to mass sometime."

"Me? Hell, I'm not even Catholic."

"Or I don't suppose *you*, Dr. Tull . . ."

Both men seemed to be waiting for her. Jenny was wondering about the baby's diaper, which bulged suspiciously, but she

196

gathered her thoughts and said, "Oh, no, goodness, I really wouldn't have the faintest—" She laughed, covering her mouth—a gesture she had. "Besides," she said, "it was Greta who was the Catholic. Slevin's mother."

"I see. Well, the important thing—"

"I don't know why Slevin goes to church. And to Greta's church, her old one, clear across town."

"Does he communicate with his mother now?"

"Oh, no, she's never been back. Got a quickie divorce in Idaho and that's the last we heard."

"Are there any, ah, step-family problems?"

"Step-family?" Jenny said. "Well, no. Or yes. I don't know. There *would* be, probably; of course these things are never easy . . . only life is so rushed around here, there really isn't time."

"Slevin is very fond of Jenny," Joe told the priest.

"Why, thank you, honey," Jenny said.

"She won him right over; she's got him trailing after her anyplace she goes. She's so cool and jokey with kids, you know."

"Well, I try," Jenny said. "I do make an effort. But you never can be sure. That age is very secretive."

"Perhaps I'll suggest that he stop by and visit me," the priest said.

"If you like."

"Just to gab, I'll say, chew the fat . . ."

Jenny could see that it would never work out.

She walked with him to the door, strolling with her hands deep in her skirt pockets. "I hope," she said, "you haven't got the wrong idea about us. I mean, Joe's an excellent father, honestly he is; he's always been good with Slevin."

"Yes, of course."

"Oh, when I compare him with some others I could name!" Jenny said. She had a habit, with disapproving people, of talking a little too much, and she knew it. As they crossed the hall, she said, "Sam Wiley, for instance—my second husband.

197

Becky's father. You'd die if you ever saw Sam. He was a painter, one of those graceful compact *small* types I've never trusted since. Totally shiftless. Totally unreliable. He left me before Becky was born, moved in with a model named Adar Bagned."

She opened the front door. A fine, fresh mist blew in and she took a deep breath. "Oh, lovely," she said. "But isn't that a hilarious name? For the longest time I kept trying to turn it around, thinking it must make more sense if I read it off backward. Goodbye, then, Father. Thanks for dropping in."

She closed the door on him and went off to fix the children's supper.

This would be a very nice house, Jenny was fond of saying, if only the third-floor bathtub didn't drain through the dining room ceiling. It was a tall, trim Bolton Hill row house; she'd bought it back in '64, when prices weren't yet sky-high. In those days, it had seemed enormous; but seven years later, with six extra children, it didn't feel so big any more. It was inconvenient, warrenlike, poorly arranged. There were so many doors and radiators, it was hard to find space for the furniture.

She cooked at a sticky, stilt-legged stove, rinsed greens at a yellowed sink skirted with chintz, set plates on a table that was carved with another family's initials. "Here, children, everyone get his own silver, now—"

"You gave Jacob more peas than me."

"She did not."

"Did too."

"Did not."

"Did too."

"Take them! I don't even like them."

"Where's Slevin?" Jenny asked.

"Who needs Slevin anyhow, the old grouch."

The telephone rang and Joe came in with the baby. "That's your answering service, they want to know—"

"I'm not on; it's Dan's night on. What are they calling *me* for?"

"That's what I thought, but they said—"

He wandered off again, and returned a minute later to settle at the table with the baby in his lap. "Here's her meat," Jenny said, flying past. "Her spoon is on the . . ."

She left the kitchen, climbed the stairs to the second floor and called up to the third. "Slevin?" No answer. She climbed the rest of the way, quickly growing breathless. How out of shape she was! It was true, as her mother was forever telling her, that she had let herself go—a crime, her mother said, for anyone with Jenny's good looks. It was true that she'd become a bit haggard, slackened somewhat, her skin turning sallow and her eyebrows shaggy and her wide, amused mouth a dry brownish color now that she wore no lipstick. "Your hair!" her mother mourned. "Your lovely hair!"—which wasn't lovely at all: a thick, blunt, gray-threaded clump with boxy bangs. "You used to be such a beauty," Pearl would say, and Jenny would laugh. A fat lot of good it had done her! She liked to think that she was wearing her beauty out—using it up, she liked to think. She took some satisfaction in it, like a housewife industriously making her way through a jar of something she did not enjoy, would not buy again, but couldn't just discard, of course.

Panting, clutching a handful of denim skirt, she arrived on the third floor. It was the older children's floor, not her territory, and it had a musty, atticky smell. "Slevin?" she called. She knocked at his door. "Supper, Slevin!"

She opened the door a crack and peered in. Slevin lay on his unmade bed with his forearm over his eyes. A wide strip of blubbery belly showed, as it nearly always did, between jeans and T-shirt. He had his earphones on; that was why he hadn't heard. She crossed the room and lifted the earphones from his head. A miniature Janis Joplin song rang out tinnily: "Me and Bobby McGee." He blinked and gave her a puzzled look, like someone just waking. "Suppertime," she told him.

"I'm not hungry."

"Not hungry! What kind of talk is that?"

"Jenny, honest, I just don't want to get up."

But she was already pulling him to his feet—a burly boy nearly Jenny's height and considerably heavier but still babyish, creamy skinned. She propelled him to the door, pushing from behind with both palms flat on the small of his back. "You're the only one of them that I have to carry bodily to meals," she said. She sang him down the stairs:

"Oh, they had to carry Harry to the ferry,
And they had to carry Harry to the shore . . ."

"Seriously, Jenny," Slevin said.

They entered the kitchen. Joe made a trumpet of his hands above the baby's head and said, "Ta-ra! Ta-ra! He approaches!" Slevin groaned. The others didn't look up from their meal.

Sitting in her place next to Joe, gazing around at the tableful of children, Jenny felt pleased. They were doing well, she decided—even the older ones, who'd acted so wary and hostile when she had first met them.

Then she had an unsettling thought: it occurred to her that this would have to be her permanent situation. Having taken on these children, straightened their upturned lives and slowly, steadily won their trust, she could not in good conscience let them down. Here she was, forever. "It's lucky we get along," she said to Joe.

"It's extremely lucky," he said, and patted her hand and asked for the mustard.

"Isn't it amazing how school always smells like school," Jenny told Slevin's teacher. "You can add all the modern conveniences you like—audiovisual things and computers—it still smells like book glue and that cheap gray paper they used to have for arithmetic and also . . . what's that other smell?

There's another smell besides. I know it but I can't quite name it."

"Have a seat, Dr. Tull," the teacher said.

"Radiator dust," said Jenny.

"Pardon?"

"*That's* the other smell."

"I called you in for a purpose," said the teacher, opening the file that lay before her. She was a tiny thing, surely not out of her twenties, perky and freckled with horn-rimmed glasses dwarfing her pointed nose. Jenny wondered how she'd learned to be so intimidating so quickly. "I know you're a busy woman, Dr. Tull, but I'm genuinely anxious about Slevin's school performance and I thought you ought to be informed."

"Oh, really?" Jenny said. She decided she would feel better if she too wore glasses, though hers were only needed for reading. She dug through her purse and a pink plastic pacifier fell out. She pretended it hadn't happened.

"Slevin is very, very intelligent," the teacher said. She glared at Jenny accusingly. "He goes straight off the top of the charts."

"Yes, I figured that."

"But his English average . . ." the teacher said, flipping through papers. "It's F. Well, maybe D minus."

Jenny clicked her tongue.

"Math: C. History: D. And science . . . and gym . . . He's had so many absences, I finally asked if he'd been cutting school. 'Yes, ma'am,' he said—came right out with it. 'What did you cut?' I asked him. 'February,' he said."

Jenny laughed. The teacher looked at her.

Jenny straightened her glasses and said, "Do you think it might be puberty?"

"*All* these children are going through puberty," the teacher told her.

"Or . . . I don't know; boredom. You said yourself he's intelligent. Why, you ought to see him at home! Monkeying around with machinery, wiring stereos . . . He's got a tape recorder of his own, he worked for it and bought it himself, some superduper model, offhand I can't think of the name. I'm such a dunce about these things, when he talked about head cleaners I thought he meant shampoo; but Slevin knows all about it and—"

"Mr. Davies suggests," said the teacher, "—that's our assistant principal—he suggests that Slevin may be experiencing emotional problems due to the adjustments at home."

"What adjustments?"

"He says Slevin's mother abandoned him and Slevin was moved to your household almost immediately thereafter and had to get used to a brand-new mother and sister."

"Oh, that," said Jenny, waving her hand.

"Mr. Davies suggests that Slevin might need professional counseling."

"Nonsense," Jenny said. "What's a little adjustment? And anyhow, that happened a good six months ago. It's not as if . . . why, look at my daughter! She's had to get used to *seven* new people and she's never said a word of complaint. Oh, we're all coping! In fact my husband was saying, just the other day, we should think about having more children now. We ought to have at least one *joint* child, he says, but I'm not so sure myself. After all, I'm thirty-six years old. It probably wouldn't be wise."

"Mr. Davies suggests—"

"Though I suppose if it means so much to him, it's all the same to me."

"The same!" said the teacher. "What about the population explosion?"

"The what? You're getting me off the subject, here . . . My point is," Jenny said, "I don't see the need to blame adjustment, broken homes, bad parents, that sort of thing. We make our own luck, right? You have to overcome your setbacks. You can't take them too much to heart. I'll explain all that to Slevin. I'll tell him this evening. I'm certain his grades will improve."

Then she bent to pick up the pacifier, and shook hands with the teacher and left.

On the wall in Jenny's office was a varnished wooden plaque: DR. TULL IS NOT A TOY. Joe had made it for her in his workshop. He was incensed by the scrapes and bruises that Jenny gathered daily in her raucous games with her patients. "Make them show some respect," he told her. "Maintain a little dignity." But the sign was all but lost among her patients' snapshots (on beaches, on seesaws, on photographers' blanketed tables, or behind lit birthday cakes) and the crayoned self-portraits they'd brought her. Anyhow, most of them were too young to read. She scooped up Billy Burnham and carried him, squawking and giggling, to the nurse for his tetanus shot. "Now, it's possible," she called back to Mrs. Burnham, "that tonight he'll experience a little soreness in his left—" Billy squirmed, and a button popped off Jenny's white coat.

The Albright baby was due for a DPT shot. The Carroll baby had to have her formula switched. Lucy Brandon's constant sniffle looked like an allergy; Jenny told Mrs. Brandon where she could take her for testing. Both the Morris twins' tonsils were swollen.

She asked the receptionist to order her a sandwich, but the receptionist said, "Aren't you eating out? Your brother's here; he's been waiting half an hour, at least."

"Oh, my Lord, I forgot all about him," Jenny said. She went into the waiting room. Ezra was seated on the vinyl couch, surrounded by pull toys and building blocks and oilcloth picture books. A family of Spanish-speaking children, probably patients of Dr. Ramirez, played at his feet, but you'd never mistake Ezra for a parent. His shaggy yellow hair was soft as a child's; he wore faded work clothes, and his face was wide and expectant.

"Ezra, honey," Jenny told him, "I clean forgot. My next appointment's in twenty minutes; do you suppose we could just grab a hamburger?"

"Oh, surely," Ezra said.

He waited while she took off her white coat and put on a raincoat. Then they rode the elevator down to the marble-paved lobby, and pushed through the revolving door on to a spattery, overcast street. There was a smell like wet coal. Huddled people hurried by and buses wheezed and cathedral bells rang far away.

"I feel dumb," Jenny said, "taking you of all people to a hamburger joint."

She was thinking of his restaurant, which always intimidated her a little. Recently, Ezra had remodeled the living quarters above it into a series of tiny, elegant private dining rooms like those in old movies—the velvet-hung compartments where the villain attempts to seduce the heroine. They'd be perfect for anniversary couples, Ezra said. (Like most unmarried men, he was comically, annoyingly sentimental about marriage.) But so far, only business groups and heavily jeweled Baltimore politicians had asked to use the rooms.

Now he said, "A hamburger's fine; I'm crazy about hamburgers." And when they walked through the plate glass doorway, into a slick, tiled area lined with glaring photos of onion rings and milkshakes, he looked around him happily. Secretaries clustered at some tables, construction workers at others. "It's getting like a collective farm," Ezra said. "All these chain places that everyone comes to for breakfast, lunch, sometimes supper . . . like a commune or a kibbutz or something. Pretty soon we won't have private kitchens at all; you just drop by your local Gino's or McDonald's. I kind of like it."

Jenny wondered if there were any eating place he wouldn't like. At a soup kitchen, no doubt, he'd be pleased by the obvious hunger of the customers. At a urine-smelling tavern he'd discover some wonderful pickled eggs that he'd never seen anywhere else. Oh, if it had to do with food, he was endlessly appreciative.

While he ordered for them, she settled herself at a table. She took off her raincoat, smoothed her hair, and scraped at a Pablum spot on her blouse. It felt strange to be sitting alone. Always there was someone—children, patients, colleagues. The empty space on either side of her gave her an echoing, weightless feeling, as if she lacked ballast and might at any moment float upward.

Ezra returned with their hamburgers. "How's Joe?" he asked, sitting down.

"Oh, fine. How's Mother?"

"Doing well, sends her love . . . I brought you something," he said. He set aside his burger to rummage through his windbreaker pockets. Eventually, he came up with a worn white envelope. "Pictures," he said.

"Pictures?"

"Photos. Mother's got all these photos; I just discovered them. I thought maybe you'd be interested in having a few."

Jenny sighed. Poor Ezra: he was turning into the family custodian, tending their mother and guarding their past and faithfully phoning his sister for lunch. "Why don't you keep them," she said. "You know I'd just lose them."

"But a lot of these are of you," he said. He spilled the envelope on to the table. "I figured the children might like them. For instance, somewhere here . . ." He shuffled various versions of a younger, sterner Jenny. "Here," he said. "Don't you see Becky in this?"

It was Jenny in a plaid tam-o'-shanter, unsmiling. "Ugh," she said, stirring her coffee.

"You were a really nice little girl," said Ezra. He returned to his burger but kept the photo before him. On the back of it, Jenny saw, something had been written in pencil. She tried to make it out. Ezra noticed and said, "Fall, 1947. I got Mother to write the dates down. And I'm going to send Cody some, too."

Jenny could just imagine Cody's face when he got them. "Ezra," she said, "to tell the truth, I wouldn't waste the postage."

"Don't you think he'd like to compare these with how Luke looks, growing up?"

"Believe me," she said, "he'd burn them. You know Cody."

"Maybe he's changed," Ezra said.

"He hasn't," said Jenny, "and I doubt he ever will. Just mention something—one little harmless memory from our childhood—and his mouth turns down. *You* know how his mouth does. I said to him once, I said, 'Cody, you're no better than the Lawsons.' Remember the Lawsons? They moved into our neighborhood from Nashville, Tennessee, and the very first week all four children got mumps. Mrs. Lawson said, 'This city is unlucky, I believe.' The next week a pipe in their basement burst and she said, 'Well, that's Baltimore.' Then their daughter broke her wrist . . . When they moved back to Tennessee, I went over to say goodbye. They were loading up their car trunk and they happened to slam the lid down smack on the fingers of their youngest boy. When they drove off he was screaming, and Mrs. Lawson called out, 'Isn't this a fitting way to leave? I always did say Baltimore was unlucky.'"

"Well, now, I'm trying to follow you, here," Ezra said.

"It's whether you add up the list or not," Jenny said. "I mean, if you catalogue grudges, anything looks bad. And Cody certainly catalogues; he's ruining his life with his catalogues. But after all, I told him, we made it, didn't we? We did grow up. Why, the three of us turned out fine, just fine!"

"It's true," said Ezra, his forehead smoothing. "You especially, Jenny. Look at you: a doctor."

"Oh, shoo, I'm nothing but a baby weigher," Jenny said. But she was pleased, and when they rose to go she took along the photographs to make him happy.

Joe said if they did have a baby, he'd like it to be a girl. He'd looked around and noticed they were a little short on girls.

"How can you say that?" Jenny asked. She ticked the girls off on her fingers: "Phoebe, Becky, Jane . . ."

When her voice trailed away, he stood watching her. She was expecting him to speak, but he didn't. "Well?" she asked.

"That's only three."

She felt a little rush of confusion. "Have I left one out?"

"No, you haven't left one out. Has she left one out," he told the wall. He snorted. "Has she left one out, she asks. What a question! No, you haven't left one out. Three is all we have. Three girls."

"Well, there's no need to act so cross about it."

"I'm not cross, I'm frustrated," he said. "I'm trying to have a conversation here."

"Isn't that what we're doing?"

"Yes, yes . . ."

"Then where's the problem?"

He wouldn't say. He stood in the kitchen doorway with his arms folded tight across his chest. He gazed off to one side, scowling. Jenny was puzzled. Where they quarreling, or what? When the silence stretched on, she gradually, imperceptibly, returned to slicing the cucumbers for supper. She brought the knife down as quietly as possible, and without a sound scooped the disks of cucumber into a bowl. (When she and Joe had first met, he'd said, "Do you put cucumber on your skin?" "*Cucumbers?*" she'd asked, astonished. "You look so cool," he told her, "I thought of this bottle of cucumber milk my aunt used to keep on her vanity table.")

Two of the children, Jacob and Peter, were playing with the Ouija board in front of the refrigerator. Jenny had to step over them when she went to get the tomatoes. "Excuse me," she told them. "You're in my way." But they ignored her; they were intent on the board. "What will I be when I grow up?" Jacob asked, and he set his fingertips delicately upon the pointer. "Upper middle class, middle middle class, or lower middle class: which?"

Jenny laughed, and Joe glared at her and wheeled and stamped out of the kitchen.

On the evening news, a helicopter crewman who'd been killed in Laos was buried with full military honors. An American flag, folded into a cushiony triangle, was handed to the parents—a gray-haired, square-chinned gentleman and his fragile wife. The wife wore a trim beige raincoat and little white gloves. It was she who accepted the flag. The husband had turned away and was weeping, would not even say a few words to the microphone somebody offered him. "Sir? Sir?" a reporter asked.

One white glove reached out and took the microphone. "What my husband means to say, I believe," the wife declared in a feathery, Southern voice, "is we thank all those who've gathered here, and we know we're just going to be fine. We're strong, and we're going to be fine."

"Hogwash," Slevin said.

"Why, Slevin," said Jenny. "*I* didn't know you were political."

"I'm not; it's just a bunch of hogwash," he told her. "She ought to say, 'Take your old flag! I object! I give up!'"

"My goodness," Jenny said mildly. She was sorting Ezra's photos; she held one out to distract him. "Look," she said. 'Your Uncle Cody, at age fifteen."

"He's not my uncle."

"Of course he is."

"He's not my real uncle."

"You wouldn't say that if you knew him. You'd like him," Jenny said. "I wish he'd come for a visit. He's so . . . unbrotherly or something; I don't know. And look!" she said, alighting on another photo. "Isn't my mother pretty?"

"*I* think she looks like a lizard," Slevin said.

"Oh, but when she was a girl, I mean . . . isn't it sad how carefree she was."

"Half the time, she forgets my name," Slevin said.

"Well, she's old," Jenny told him.

"Not that old. What she's saying is, I'm not worth her bother. Old biddy. Sits at the head of the table with a piece of bread on her plate and sets both hands down flat and just stares around at us, stares around, face like one of those rotating fans, waiting for the butter but never asking, never saying a word. Till finally you or Dad says, 'Mother? Could we pass you the butter?' and she says, 'Why, *thank* you,' like she was wondering when you'd realize."

"She hasn't had an easy life," Jenny said.

"I wish just once we'd get all through the meal and nobody offer her the butter."

"She raised us on her own, you know," Jenny told him. "Don't you think it must have been hard? My father walked out and left her when I was nine years old."

"He did?" Slevin asked. He stared at her.

"He left her, absolutely. We never set eyes on him again."

"Bastard," Slevin said.

"Oh, well," said Jenny. She leafed through some more photos.

"Jesus! These people! They try to do you in."

"You're overreacting," Jenny told him. "I can't even remember the man, if you want to know the truth. Wouldn't know him if I saw him. And my mother managed fine. It all worked out. Look at this, Slevin: see Ezra's old-fashioned haircut?"

Slevin shrugged and switched the TV channel.

"And see what I was like at your age?" She handed him the picture with the tam-o'-shanter.

He glanced over. He frowned. He said, "Who did you say that was?"

"Me."

"No, it's not."

"Yes, it is. Me at thirteen. Mother wrote the date on the back."

"It's not!" he said. His voice was unusually high; he sounded like a much younger child. "It isn't! Look at it! Why, it's like a . . . concentration camp person, a victim, Anne Frank! It's terrible! It's so sad!"

Surprised, she turned the photo around and looked again. True, the picture wasn't particularly happy—it showed a dark little girl with a thin, watchful face—but it wasn't as bad as all that. "So what?" she asked, and she held it out to him once more. He drew back sharply.

"It's somebody else," he told her. "Not you; you're always laughing and having fun. It's not you."

"Oh, fine, it's not me, then," she said, and she returned to the rest of the photos.

"I want to talk to you about that oldest boy," her mother said on the phone. "What's his name? Kevin?"

"Slevin, Mother. Honestly."

"Well, he stole my vacuum cleaner."

"He did what?"

"Sunday afternoon, when you all came to visit, he slipped into my pantry and made off with my Hoover upright."

Jenny sat down on her bed. She said, "Let me get this straight."

"It's been missing all week," her mother said, "and I couldn't understand it. I knew we hadn't been burglarized, and even if we had, what would anyone want with my old Hoover?"

"But why accuse Slevin?"

"My neighbor told me, just this afternoon. Mrs. Arthur. Said, 'Was that your grandson I saw Sunday? Kind of hefty boy? Loading your Hoover upright into your daughter's car trunk?'"

"That's impossible," Jenny said.

"Now, how do you know that? How do you know what is or is not possible? He's hardly more than a stranger, Jenny. I mean, you got those children the way other people get weekend guests."

"You're exaggerating," Jenny told her.

"Well, all I ask is for you to go check Slevin's bedroom. Just check."

"What, this minute?"

"There's lint specks all over my carpet."

"Oh, all right," Jenny said.

She laid the receiver on her pillow and climbed from the second floor to the third. Slevin's door was open and he wasn't in his room, although his radio rocked with the Jefferson Airplane. She stepped stealthily over Slevin's knapsack, avoided a teetering pile of *Popular Science* magazines, opened his closet door, and found herself staring at her mother's vacuum cleaner. She would know it anywhere: an elderly machine with a gray cloth dust bag. Its cord was coiled neatly and it seemed unharmed. If he'd taken it apart to learn how it worked, she might have understood. Or if he'd smashed it, out of some rage toward her mother. But there it sat, entire. She stood puzzling over it for several seconds. Then she wheeled it out of the closet and lugged it down the stairs, to where her mother's voice was twanging impatiently from the receiver. "Jenny? Jenny?"

"Well, you're right," Jenny said. "I found it in his room."

There was a pause in which Pearl could have said, "I told you so," but kindly did not. Then she said, "I wonder if he might be calling for help in some way."

"By stealing a *vacuum* cleaner?"

"He's really a very sweet boy," Pearl said. "I can see that. Maybe he's asking for a psychologist or some such."

"More likely he's asking for a neater house," Jenny said. "The dust balls on his closet floor have started raising a family."

She pictured Slevin, in desperation, stealing an arsenal of cleaning supplies—this neighbor's broom, that neighbor's Ajax, gathered with the same feverish zeal he showed in collecting Indian head pennies. She was attacked by a sudden spurt of laughter.

"Oh, Jenny," her mother said sadly. "Do you have to see

everything as a joke?"

"It's not *my* fault if funny things happen," Jenny said.

"It most certainly is," said her mother, but instead of explaining herself, she all at once grew brisk and requested the return of her vacuum cleaner by tomorrow morning.

Jenny and Joe and every child except the baby were watching television. It was long past bedtime for most of them, but this was a special occasion: the Late, Late Show was *A Taste of Honey*. Everyone in the house had heard of *A Taste of Honey*. It was Jenny's all-time favorite movie. She had seen it once, back in 1963, and never forgotten it. Nothing else had ever measured up to it, she was fond of saying, and after returning from some other movie she was sure to announce, "Well, it was all right, I guess, but it wasn't *A Taste of Honey*." By now, any one of the children could finish that sentence before she got it halfway out. They'd ask as soon as she walked in the door, "Was it *A Taste of Honey*, Jenny? Was it?" and Phoebe was once heard telling Peter, "I like the new teacher okay, I guess, but she isn't *A Taste of Honey*."

When they learned it was coming to television, they had all begged to stay up and watch. The older ones made cocoa and the younger ones set out potato chips. Becky and Slevin arranged a ring of chairs around the TV set in the living room.

"You know what's going to happen," Joe told Jenny. "After all this time, even *A Taste of Honey* won't be *A Taste of Honey*."

In a way, he was right. Not that she didn't still love it—yes, yes, she assured the children, it was just as she'd remembered—but after all, she was a different person watching it. The movie wrenched her with pity, now, when before it had made her feel hopeful. And wasn't it odd, wasn't it downright queer, that she'd never identified the story with her own? In 1963, she was a resident in pediatrics, struggling to care for a two-year-old born six weeks after her marriage dissolved. Yet she'd watched a movie about an unwed, unsupported pregnant girl with the most detached enjoyment, dreamily making her way through a box of pretzels. (And what had she been doing in a movie theater, anyway? How had she found the time, during such a frantic schedule?)

When it was over, she switched off the TV and shooed the children up the stairs. Quinn, the youngest, who had not been all that impressed with A Taste of Honey, was sound asleep and had to be carried by Joe. Even the older ones were groggy and blinking. "Wake up," she told them. "Come on, now," and she tugged at Jacob, who had dropped in a bundle on the topmost step. One by one she guided them to their beds and kissed them good night. How noisy their rooms seemed, even in silence! — that riotous clamor of toys and flung-off clothes, their vibrant, clashing rock star posters and anti-war bumper stickers and Orioles banners. Three of the children wouldn't use sheets but slept in sleeping bags instead—garishly patterned, zippered cocoons sprawled on top of the blankets; and Phoebe didn't like beds at all but curled in a quilt on the floor, most often out in the hall in front of her parents' room. She lay across the doorway like a bodyguard, and you had to watch your step in the dark so as not to trip on her.

"I want that radio *down*," Jenny said, and she kissed the top of Becky's head. Then she peeked into Slevin's room, knocked on the frame of his open door, and entered. He wore his daytime clothes to bed, as always—even his wide tooled belt with the trucker's buckle—and he lay on top of the covers. She had been kissing him good night ever since she'd married Joe, but still he acted bashful. All she really did was brush her cheek against his, allowing him his dignity. "Sleep well," she told him.

He said, "I see you found the vacuum cleaner."

"Vacuum cleaner," she said, stalling for time.

"I'm sorry I took it," he said. "I guess your mom is pretty mad, huh? But it wasn't stealing; honest. I just needed to borrow it for a spell."

She sat on the edge of the bed. "Needed to borrow it for what?" she said.

He said, "Well, for . . . I don't know. Just for . . . See, there it was in the pantry. It was exactly like my mother's. Just exactly. You know how you never think about a thing, or realize you remember it, and then all at once something will bring it all back? I forgot how it had that rubber strip around the edge so it wouldn't scuff the furniture, and that tall, puffy bag I used to be scared of when I was a kid. It even smelled the same. It had that same clothy smell, just like my mother's. You know? So I wanted to take it home. But once I got it here, well, it didn't work out. It's like I had lost the connection. It wasn't the same after all."

"That's all right, Slevin," she said. "Heavens, honey, that's all right." Then she worried her voice had shown too much, would make him bashful again, so she laughed a little and said, "Shall we get you a Hoover of your own for your birthday?"

He turned over on his side.

"Or we could have it made up in calico," she told him, giggling. "A tiny stuffed calico vacuum cleaner to take to bed with you."

But Slevin just closed his eyes, so after a while she wished him good night and left.

She dreamed she was back with Sam Wiley, her second husband and the one she'd loved the best. She'd made a fool of herself over Sam. She dreamed he was twirling on that high wooden stool they used to have in their kitchen in Paulham. He was preening the scrolls of his handlebar mustache and singing "Let It Be." Which hadn't even existed, at the time.

She opened her eyes and heard "Let It Be" on one of the children's radios, sailing out across the dark hall. How often had she told them? She got up and made her way to Peter's room—stepping over Phoebe. Radios late at night sounded so different, she thought—so far away and crackling with static, almost gritty, as if the music had had to travel above miles of railroad tracks and deserted superhighways, past coal yards and auto dumps, oil derricks and factory smokestacks and electrical transformers. She switched off the radio and pulled Peter's sleeping bag up around his shoulders. She checked on the baby in her crib. Then she returned to bed, shivering slightly, and huddled against Joe's hulking back for warmth.

"Mack the Knife," Sam used to sing, and "Greenfields"— yes, that had been around. She remembered how operatic he'd get, rolling his eyes, pounding his chest, trying to make her laugh. (She'd been an earnest young medical student, in those days.) Then she remembered the tender, aching line that the examining table had pressed across the mound of the baby, when Jenny was an intern bending over a patient. Six months pregnant, seven months . . . By her eighth month the marriage was finished, and Jenny was walking around in a daze. She saw that she had always been doomed to fail, had been unlovable, had lacked some singular quality that would keep a husband. She had never known this consciously, before, but the pain she felt was eerily familiar—like a suspicion, long held, at last confirmed.

She wore uniforms designed for male physicians with forty-inch waists; there were no maternity lab coats. On rounds, professors would give her doubtful glances and ask if she were sure she was up to this. Sympathetic nurses brought her so many cups of coffee that she thought she would float away. One of those nurses stayed with her through most of her labor. Other women had their husbands, but Jenny had Rosa Perez, who let her squeeze her fingers as hard as needed and never said a word of complaint.

And what was the name of that neighbor who used to watch the baby? Mary something—Mary Lee, Mary Lou—some fellow intern's wife, as poor as Jenny and the mother of two children under two. She baby-sat for a pittance, but even that was more than Jenny could afford. And the schedule! Months of nights on duty, thirty-six hours on call and twelve off, emergency room, obstetrics, trauma surgery . . . and her residency was not much better. Meanwhile, Becky changed from an infant to a little girl, an outsider really, a lively child with Sam Wiley's snapping black eyes, unrelated to Jenny. Though it was a shock, sometimes, to see her give that level, considering stare so typical of the Tulls. Was it possible, after all, that this small stranger might constitute a family? She learned to walk; she learned to talk. "No!" she would say, in her firm, spunky voice; and Jenny, trying to stay awake at three in the morning or three in the afternoon, whatever bit of time they had together, dropped her head in her hands. "No!" said Becky, and Jenny hauled off and slapped her hard across the mouth, then shook her till her head lolled, then flung her aside and ran out of the apartment to . . . where? (A movie, perhaps?) In those days, objects wobbled and grew extra edges. She was so exhausted that the sight of her patients' white pillows could mesmerize her. Sounds were thick, as if underwater. Words on a chart were meaningless—so many K's and G's, such a choppy language English was, short syllables, clumps of consonants, she'd never noticed; like Icelandic, maybe, or Eskimo. She slammed Becky's face into her Peter Rabbit dinner plate and gave her a bloody nose. She yanked a handful of her hair. All of her childhood returned to her: her mother's blows and slaps and curses, her mother's pointed fingernails digging into Jenny's arm, her mother shrieking, "Guttersnipe! Ugly little rodent!" and some scrap of memory—she couldn't quite place it—Cody catching hold of Pearl's wrist and fending her off while Jenny shrank against the wall.

Was this what it came to—that you never could escape? That certain things were doomed to continue, generation after generation? She failed to see a curb and sprained her ankle, hobbled to work in agony. She misdiagnosed a case of viral pneumonia. She let a greenstick fracture slip right past her. She brought Becky a drink of water in the middle of the night and then suddenly, without the slightest intention, screamed, "Take it! Take it!" and threw the cup into Becky's face. Becky shivered and caught her breath for hours afterward, even in her sleep, though Jenny held her tightly on her lap.

Then her mother called from Baltimore and said, "Jenny? Don't you write your family any more?"

"Well, I've been so busy," Jenny meant to say. Or: "Leave me alone, I remember all about you. It's all come back. Write? Why should I write? You've damaged me; you've injured me. Why would I want to write?"

Instead, she started . . . not crying, exactly, but something worse. She was torn by dry, ragged sobs; she ran out of air; there was a grating sound in her chest. Her mother said, calmly, "Jenny, hang up. You know that couch in your living room? Go lie down on it. I'll be there just as soon as Ezra can drive me."

Pearl stayed two weeks, using all of her vacation time. The first thing she did was call Jenny's hospital and arrange for sick leave. Then she set about putting the world in order again. She smoothed clean sheets on Jenny's bed, brought her tea and bracing broths, shampooed her hair, placed flowers on her bureau. Becky, who had hardly seen her grandmother till now, fell in love with her. Pearl called Becky "Rebecca" and treated her formally, respectfully, as if she were not quite sure how much she was allowed. Every morning she walked Becky to the playground and swung her on the swings. In the afternoon they went shopping together. She bought Becky an old-fashioned dress that made her look solemn and reasonable. She bought picture books—nursery rhymes and fairy tales and *The Little House*. Jenny had forgotten about *The Little House*. Why, she had loved that book! She'd requested it every evening, she remembered now. She'd sat on that homely old sofa and listened while her mother, with endless patience, read it three times, four times, five . . . Now Becky said, "Read it again," and Pearl returned to page one, and Jenny listened just as closely as Becky did.

Sundays, when his restaurant closed, Ezra drove up from Baltimore. He was not, in spite of his innocent face, an open sort of person, and rather than speak outright of Jenny's new breakability he kept smiling serenely at some point just beyond her. She took comfort in this. There was already too much openness in the world, she felt—everyone raging and weeping and rejoicing. She imagined that Ezra was not subject to the ups and downs that jolted other people. She liked to have him read the papers to her (trouble in Honduras, trouble in Saigon, natural disasters in Haiti and Cuba and Italy) while she listened from a nest of deep blue blankets and a nightgown still warm from her mother's iron.

On the second weekend, Cody blew in from wherever he'd vanished to most recently. He traveled on a breeze of energy and money; Jenny was impressed. He used her telephone for two hours like the wheeler-dealer he always was and arranged to pay for a full-time sitter, a slim young woman named Delilah Greening who turned out to be better help than Jenny would ever have again. Then he slung his suit coat over one shoulder, gave her a little salute, and was gone.

She slept, sometimes, for twelve and fourteen hours straight. She woke dislocated, frightened by the sunlit, tickling silence of the apartment. She mixed up dreams and real life. "How did it happen—?" she might ask her mother, before she remembered that it hadn't happened (the Shriners' parade through her bedroom, the elderly gentleman hanging by his heels from her curtain rod like a piece of fruit). Sometimes at night, voices came vividly out of the dark. "Dr. Tull. Dr. Tull," they'd say, urgently, officially. Or, "Six hundred fifty milligrams of quinine sulfate . . ." Her own pulse thudded in her eardrums. She held her hand toward the light from the streetlamp and marveled at how white and bloodless she had become.

When her mother left and Delilah arrived, Jenny got up

and returned to work. For a while, she carried herself as gently as a cup of liquid. She kept level and steady, careful not to spill over. But she was fine, she saw; she really was fine. Weekends, her mother and Ezra paid brief visits, or Jenny took Becky down to Baltimore on the train. They both dressed up for these trips and sat very still so as not to muss their clothes. Jenny felt purified, like someone who had been drained by a dangerous fever.

And the following summer, when she could have accepted more lucrative offers in Philadelphia or Newark, she chose Baltimore instead. She joined two older pediatricians, entered Becky in nursery school, and shortly thereafter purchased her Bolton Hill row house. She continued to feel fragile, though. She went on guarding a trembly, fluid center. Sometimes, loud noises made her heart race—her mother speaking her name without warning, or the telephone jangling late at night. Then she would take herself in hand. She would remind herself to draw back, to loosen hold. It seemed to her that the people she admired (one of her partners, who was a wry, funny man named Dan Charles; and her brother Ezra; and her neighbor Leah Hume) had this in common: they gazed at the world from a distance. There was something sheeted about them—some obliqueness that made them difficult to grasp. Dan, for instance, kept up such a steady, easy banter that you never could ask him about his wife, who was forever in and out of mental institutions. And Leah: she could laugh off the repeated failures of her crazy business ventures like so many pratfalls. How untouched she looked, and how untouchable, chuckling to herself and covering her mouth with a shapely, badly kept hand! Jenny studied her; you could almost say she took notes. She was learning how to make it through life on a slant. She was trying to lose her intensity.

"You've changed," her mother said ((all intensity herself). "You've grown so different, Jenny. I can't quite put my finger on what's wrong, but *something* is." She wanted Jenny to remarry; she hoped for a dozen grandchildren, at least; she was always after Jenny to get out and mingle, socialize, make herself more attractive, meet some nice young man. What Jenny didn't tell her was, she simply couldn't be bothered with all that. She felt textureless, so that events just slid right off her with no friction whatsoever; and the thought of the heartfelt conversations required by a courtship filled her with impatience.

Then she met Joe with his flanks of children—his padding, his moat, his barricade of children, all in urgent need of her brisk and competent attention. No conversation *there*—she and Joe had hardly found a moment to speak to each other seriously. They were always trying to be heard above the sound of toy trucks and xylophones. She didn't even have time for thinking any more.

"Of course, the material object is nothing," said the priest. He winced at a squeal from the waiting room. "That's unimportant, the least of my concerns. Though it did have some historical value. It was donated, I believe, by the missionary brother of one of our parishioners."

Jenny leaned back against the receptionist's window and touched a hand to her forehead. "Well, I don't . . ." she said. "*What* did you say this was?"

"A rhinoceros foot," said the priest, "in the shape of an umbrella stand. Or an umbrella stand in the shape of a rhinoceros foot. It was an actual rhinoceros foot from . . . wherever rhinoceri come from."

A naked toddler shot out a door like a stray piece of popcorn, pursued by a nurse with a hypodermic needle. The priest stood back to give them room. "We know it was there in the morning," he said. "But at four o'clock, it was gone. And Slevin was in just previously; I'd asked him to come for a chat. Only I was on the phone when he arrived. By the time I'd hung up he was gone, and so was the rhinoceros foot."

Jenny said, "I wonder if his mother had a rhinoceros foot."

"Pardon?" said the priest.

She realized how this must have sounded, and she laughed. "No," she said, "I don't mean *she* had rhinoceros feet . . . oh, Lord . . ."

The priest said, "Dr. Tull, don't you see this is serious? We have a child in trouble here, don't you see that? Don't you think that something ought to be done? Where do you *stand*, Dr. Tull?"

Jenny's smile faded and she looked into his face. "I don't know," she said, after a pause. She felt suddenly bereft, as if something were missing, as if she'd giving something up. She hadn't *always* been like this! she wanted to tell him. But aloud she said, "I only meant, you see . . . I believe he steals what reminds him of his mother. Hoovers and umbrella stands. Doesn't that make sense?"

"Ah," said the priest.

"What's next, I wonder," Jenny said. She mused for a moment. "Picture it! Grand pianos. Kitchen sinks. Why, we'll have his mother's whole household," she said, "her photo albums and her grade-school yearbooks, her college roommate asleep on our bed and her high school boyfriends in our living room." She pictured a row of dressed-up boys from the fifties, their hair slicked down wetly, their shirts ironed crisply, perched on her couch like mannequins with heart-shaped boxes of chocolates on their knees. She laughed. The priest groaned. A little blue plastic helicopter buzzed across the waiting room and landed in Jenny's hair.

8

This Really Happened

The summer before Luke Tull turned fourteen, his father had a serious accident at the factory he was inspecting. A girder swung around on its cable, hit Luke's father and the foreman standing next to him, and swept them both off the walkway and down to the lower level of the factory. The foreman was killed. Cody lived, by some miracle, but he was badly hurt. For two days he lay in a coma. There was a question of brain damage, till he woke and, in his normal, crusty way, asked who the hell was in charge around here.

Three weeks later, he came home by ambulance. His thick black hair had been shaved off one side of his head, where a gauze patch covered the worst of his wounds. His face—ordinarily lean and tanned—was swollen across one cheekbone and turning different shades of yellow from slowly fading bruises. His ribs were taped and an arm and a leg were in casts—the right arm and the left leg, so he couldn't use crutches. He was forced to lie in bed, cursing the game shows on TV. "Fools. Jackasses. Who do they think would be watching this crap?"

Luke's mother, who had always been so spirited, lost something important to the accident. First, in the terrible coma days, she drifted around in a wash of tears—a small, wan, pink-eyed woman. Her red hair seemed drained of color. Luke would say, "Mom?" and she wouldn't hear, would sometimes snatch up her car keys as if mistaking who had called and go tearing off to the hospital again, leaving Luke alone. Even after the coma ended, it didn't seem she came back completely. When Cody was brought home, she sat by his bed for hours saying nothing, lightly stroking one thick vein that ran down the inside of his wrist. She watched the game shows with a tremulous smile. "Jesus, look at them squawk," Cody said disgustedly, and Ruth bent down and laid her cheek against his hand as if he'd uttered something wonderful.

Luke, who had once been the center of her world, now hung around the fringes. It was July and he had nothing to do. They'd only been living here—in a suburb of Petersburg, Virginia—since the end of the school year, and he didn't know any boys his own age. The children on his block were all younger, thin voiced and excitable. It annoyed him to hear their shrieking games of roll-a-bat and the sputtery *ksh! kshew!* of their imaginary rifles. Toddlers were packed into flowered vinyl wading pools which they spent their mornings emptying, measuring cup by measuring cup, till every yard was a sea of mud. Luke could not remember ever being that young. Floating through the icy, white and gold elegance of the rented colonial-style house, he surfaced in various gilt-framed mirrors: someone awkward and unwanted, lurching on legs grown too long to manage, his face past cuteness but not yet solidified into anything better—an oval, fragile face, a sweep of streaky blond hair, a mouthful of braces that made his lips appear irregular and vulnerable. His jeans were getting too short but he had no idea how to go about buying new ones. He was accustomed to relying on his mother for such things. In the old days, his mother had done everything for him. She had got on his nerves, as a matter of fact.

Now he made his own breakfast—Cheerios or shredded wheat—and a sandwich for lunch. His mother cooked supper, but it was something slapped together, not her usual style at all; and mostly she would let Luke eat alone in the kitchen while she and Cody shared a tray in the bedroom. Or if she stayed with Luke, her *talk* was still of Cody. She never asked Luke about himself, no; it was "your daddy" this and "your daddy" that, never a thing but "your daddy." How well he was bearing up, how he'd always borne up, always been so dependable from the earliest time she had known him. "I was not but nineteen when I met him," she said, "and he was thirty years old. I was a homely chit of a girl and he was the handsomest thing you ever saw, so fine mannered and wearing this perfect gray suit. At the time, I was all set to marry Ezra, your daddy's brother. I bet you didn't know that, did you? Oh, I got around, in those days! Then your daddy stepped in. He was brazen as you please. Didn't care how it looked, didn't have an ounce of shame, just moved right in and claimed me for his own. Well, first I thought he was teasing. He could have had anyone, any girl he liked, somebody beautiful even. Then I saw he meant it. I didn't know which way to turn, for I did love your Uncle Ezra, though he was not so . . . I mean, Ezra was a much plainer person, more like me, you would say. But your daddy'd walk into the room and it seemed like, I don't know, the air just came alive, somehow. He put his hands on my shoulders one day and I told him please, I was engaged to marry Ezra, and he said that he knew that. He stepped up close and I said really, Ezra was a good, good man, and he said yes, he was; and we hugged each other like two people sharing some bereavement and I said, 'Why, you're near about my brother-in-law!' and he said, 'Very nearly, yes,' and he kissed me on the lips."

Luke lowered his lashes. He wished she wouldn't talk about such things.

"And if we've had our ups and downs," she said, "well, I just want you to know that it wasn't *his* fault, Luke. Look at me! I'm nothing but a little backwoods Garrett County farm girl, hardly educated. And I'm not so easy to get along with, either. I'm not so easygoing. You mustn't blame him. Why, once—oh, you were in nursery school, I bet you don't remember this—I packed you up and left him. I told him he didn't love me and never had, only married me to spite his brother, Ezra, that he'd always been so jealous of. I accused him of terrible things, just terrible, and then while he was at work I carried you off to the railroad station and . . . this is funny now when I tell it, but it wasn't then: while we were waiting on the bench a Marine threw up in my pocketbook. Came time to board the train and I just couldn't make myself put my fingers in and get out the tickets, assuming they were still usable; and couldn't bear to reach in for the money to buy more tickets, either. So I called your daddy on the telephone, begged a dime from a nun and said, 'Cody, come and get me; this isn't really what I want to be doing. Oh, Cody,' I said, 'we've got so interwoven; even if you didn't love me at all, now we're so entwined. It's you I have to stay with.' And he left off work and drove down to collect me, all steady and sure in his fine gray suit, nothing like the rest of the world. Don't you remember that? You've forgotten all about it," she said. "It's just as well, I reckon. Luke, when you almost lose a person, everything comes so clear! You see how much he matters, how there's no one the least bit like him; he's irreplaceable. How he always puts us first; I mean, has never, in all his days, left you and me behind when he's off on business, but carts us to every new town he's called to because he won't do like his father, he says: travel about forgetting his own relations. It's not true that he brings us along because he doesn't trust me. He really cares for our welfare. When I think now," she said, "about your daddy kissing me that first time—'Very nearly, yes,' he said. 'Yes, very nearly your brother-in-law,' and kissed me so quiet but definite, insisting, like he wouldn't take no for an answer—why, I see now that's when my *life* began! But at the time I had no notion, didn't grasp the importance. I didn't know back then that one person can have such effect on another."

But even if she was changed (if even Luke was changed—

fading into someone transparent, he imagined), Cody was absolutely the same. After all, Cody hadn't suffered the strain of that coma; he'd been absent from it. He hadn't worried he would die, once he came to, because it wouldn't occur to him that he was the *type* to die. He'd sailed through the whole experience with his usual combination of nonchalance and belligerence, and now he lay thrashing on his bed wondering when he could get up again. "What I mainly am is mad," he told Luke. "This whole damn business has left me mad as hell. I felt that girder hit, you know that? I really felt it hit, and it hurt, and all the time I was flying through the air I wanted to hit it back, punch somebody; and now it seems I'm still waiting for the chance. When do I get to get even? And don't talk to me about lawsuits, compensation. The only thing I want to do is hit that girder back."

"Mom says would you like some soup," said Luke, wiping his palms nervously down his thighs.

"No, I wouldn't like soup. What's she always trying to feed me for? Listen, Luke. If your grandma calls again today, I want you to tell her I've gone back to work."

"To work?"

"I can't stand to hear her fret on the phone any more."

"But all along," Luke said, "you've been telling her you were too sick for company. Yesterday you were too sick and today you've gone back to *work?* What'll she think?"

"It's nothing to me what she thinks," said Cody. He never sounded very fond of Grandma Tull, who had called from Baltimore every day since the accident. Luke enjoyed her, the little he knew of her, but Cody said looks were deceiving. "She puts on a good front," he told Luke. "You don't know what she's like. You don't know what it was like growing up with her."

Luke felt he did know (hadn't he heard it all a million times?) but his father had got started now and wouldn't be stopped. "Let me give you an example," he said. "Listen, now. This really happened." That was the way he always introduced

226

his childhood. "This really happened," he would say, as if it were unthinkable, beyond belief, but then what followed never seemed so terrible to Luke. "I swear it: your grandma had this friend named Emmaline that she hadn't seen in years. Only friend she ever mentioned. And Emmaline lived in . . . I forget. Anyhow, someplace far away. So one Christmas I saved up the money to buy a Greyhound bus ticket to wherever this Emmaline lived. I slaved and borrowed and *stole* the money, and presented my mother with the ticket on Christmas morning. I was seventeen at the time, old enough to take care of the others, and I said, 'You leave tomorrow, stay a week, and I'll watch over things till you get back.' And you know what she said? Listen; you won't believe this. 'But Cody, honey,' she said. 'Day after tomorrow is your brother's birthday.'"

He looked over at Luke. Luke waited for him to go on.

"See,' Cody said, "December twenty-seventh was Ezra's birthday."

"So?" Luke asked.

"So she wouldn't leave her precious boy on his birthday! Not even to visit her oldest, dearest, only friend, that her other boy had given her a ticket for."

"I wouldn't like for Mom to leave me on my birthday, either," Luke said.

"No, no, you're missing the point. She wouldn't leave Ezra, her favorite. Me or my sister, she would surely leave."

"How do you know that?" Luke asked him. "Did you ever try giving her a ticket on *your* birthday? I bet she'd have said the same thing."

"My birthday is in February," Cody said. "Nowhere near any occasion for gift giving. Oh, I don't know why I bother talking to you. You're an only child, that's your trouble. You haven't the faintest idea what I'm trying to get across." And he turned his pillow over and settled back with a sigh.

Luke went out in the yard and threw his baseball against the garage. It thudded and bounced back, shimmering in the sunlight. In the old days, his mother had practiced throwing with him. She had taught him to bat and pitch overhand, too. She was good at sports. He saw glimpses in her, sometimes, of the scatty little tomboy she must once have been. But it had always seemed, when they played ball together, this this was only a preparation for the *real* game, with his father. It was like cramming for an exam. Then on weekends Cody came home and pitched the ball to him and said, "Not bad. Not bad at all," when Luke hit it out of the yard. At these moments Luke was conscious of adding a certain swagger to his walk, a certain swing to his shoulders. He imagined he was growing to be more like his father. Sauntering into the house after practice, he'd pass Cody's parked car and ask, "She still getting pretty good mileage?" He would stand in front of the open refrigerator and swig iced tea directly from the pitcher—something his mother detested. Oh, it was time to put his mother behind him now— all those years of following her through the house, enmeshed in her routine, dragging his toy broom after her big one or leaning both elbows on her dressing table to watch, entranced, as she dusted powder on her freckled nose. The dailiness of women's lives! He knew all he cared to know about it. He was exhausted by the trivia of measuring out the soap flakes, waiting for the plumber. High time to move to his father's side. But his father lay on his back in the bedroom, cursing steadily. "What the hell is the matter with this TV? Why bother buying a Sony if there's no one who will fix it?"

"I'll find us a repairman today," Ruth's new, soft voice floated out.

Ruth wore dresses all the time now because Cody said he was tired of her pantsuits. "Everlasting polyester pantsuits," he said, and it was true she didn't look as stylish as most other women, though Luke wasn't so sure that the pantsuits were to blame. Even after she changed to dresses, something seemed to be wrong. They were too big, or too hard-surfaced, or too shiny; they looked less like clothes than . . . housing, Luke thought.

"Is this better?" she asked his father, and she stood hopefully in the doorway, flat on her penny loafers because in Garrett County, she said, they had never learned her to walk in high heels. By then, Cody had recovered from his mood. He said, "Sure, honey. Sure. It's fine." He wasn't *always* evil tempered. It was the strain of lying immobile. It was the constant discomfort. He did make an effort. But then, not two hours later: "Ruth, will you explain why I have to live in a place that looks like a candy dish? Is it necessary to rent a house where everything is white and gold and curlicued? You think of that as class?"

It was the nature of Cody's job that he worked alone. As soon as he finished streamlining whatever factory had called him in, he moved on. His partner, a man named Sloan, lived in New York City and invented the devices that Cody determined a need for—sorting racks, folding aids, single hand tools combining the tasks of several. Consequently, there were no fellow workers to pay Cody visits, unless you counted that one edgy call by the owner of the factory where he'd had his accident. And they didn't know any of the neighbors. They were on their own, just the three of them. They might have been castaways. No wonder Cody acted so irritable. The only time Luke and his mother got out was once a week, when they went for groceries. Backing her white Mercedes from the garage, Ruth sat erect and alert, not looking behind her, already anxious about Cody. "Maybe I should've made you stay. If he needs to go to the bathroom—"

"He can good and *wait*," Luke said through his teeth.

"Why, Luke!"

"Let him pee in the bed."

"Luke Tull!"

Luke stared out the window.

"It's been hard on you," his mother said. "We've got to find you some friends."

"I don't need friends."

"Everybody needs friends. We don't have a one, in this town. I feel like I'm drying up. Sometimes I wonder," she said, "if this life is really . . ." But she didn't say any more.

When they returned, Cody was pleasant and cheerful, as if he'd made some resolutions in their absence. Or maybe he'd been refreshed by the solitude. "Talked to Sloan," he told Ruth. "He called from New York. I said to him, soon as I get this cast off I'm going to finish up at the factory and clear on out. I can't take much more of this place."

"Oh, good, Cody, honey."

"Bring me my briefcase, will you? I want to jot down some ideas. There's lots I could be doing in bed."

"I picked out some of those pears you like."

"No, no, just my briefcase, and that pen on the desk in my study. I'm going to see if my fingers are up to writing yet."

He told Luke, "Work is what I need. I've been *starved* for work. It's made me a little snappish."

Luke scratched his rib cage. He said, "That's all right."

"You make sure you get a job you enjoy, once you're grown. You've got to enjoy what you're doing. That's important."

"I know."

"Me, I deal with time," said Cody. He accepted a ball-point pen from Ruth. "Time is my favorite thing of all."

Luke loved it when his father talked about time.

"Time is my obsession: not to waste it, not to lose it. It's like . . . I don't know, an object, to me; something you can almost take hold of. If I could just collect enough of it in one clump, I always think. If I could pass it back and forth and sideways, you know? If only Einstein were right and time were a kind of river you could choose to step into at any place along the shore."

He clicked his pen point in and out, frowning into space. "If they had a time machine, I'd go on it," he said. "It wouldn't much matter to me where. Past or future: just out of my time. Just someplace else."

Luke felt a pang. "But then you wouldn't know *me*," he said.

"Hmm?"

"Sure he would," Ruth said briskly. She was opening the latches of Cody's briefcase. "He'd take you with him. Only mind," she told Cody, "if Luke goes too you've got to bring penicillin, and his hay fever pills, and his fluoride toothpaste, you hear?"

Cody laughed, but he didn't say one way or another about taking Luke along.

That was the evening that Cody first got his strange notion. It came about so suddenly: they were playing Monopoly on Cody's bed, the three of them, and Cody was winning as usual and offering Luke a loan to keep going. "Oh, well, no, I guess I've lost," said Luke.

There was the briefest pause—a skipped beat. Cody looked over at Ruth, who was counting her deed cards. "He sounds just like Ezra," he told her.

She frowned at Baltic Avenue.

"Didn't you hear what he said? He said it just like Ezra."

"Really?"

"*Ezra* would do that," Cody told Luke. "Your Uncle Ezra. It was no fun beating him at all. He'd never take a loan and he wouldn't mortgage the least little thing, not even a railroad or the waterworks. He'd just cave right in and give up."

"Well, it's only that . . . you can see that I've lost," Luke said. "It's only a matter of time."

"Sometimes it's more like you're Ezra's child, not mine."

"Cody Tull! What a thought," said Ruth.

But it was too late. The words hung in the air. Luke felt miserable; he had all he could do to finish the game. (He knew his father had never thought much of Ezra.) And Cody, though he dropped the subject, remained dissatisfied in some way. "Sit up straighter," he kept telling Luke. "Don't *hunch*. Sit straight.

God. You look like a rabbit."

As soon as he could, Luke said good night and went off to bed.

The following morning, everything was fine again. Cody did some work on his papers and had another talk with Sloan. Ruth cooked a chicken for a nice cold summer supper. Anytime Luke wandered by, Cody said something cheerful to him. "Why so long in the face?" he'd ask, or, "Feeling bored, son?" It sounded funny, calling Luke "son." Cody didn't usually do that.

They all had lunch in the bedroom—sandwiches and potato salad, like a picnic. The telephone, buried among the sheets, started ringing halfway through the meal, and Cody said not to answer it. It was bound to be his mother, he said. They kept perfectly silent, as if the caller could somehow hear them. After the ringing stopped, though, Ruth said, "That poor, poor woman."

"Poor!" Cody snorted.

"Aren't we awful?"

"You wouldn't call her poor if you knew her better."

Luke went back to his room and sorted through his old model airplanes. His parents' voices drifted after him. "Listen," Cody was telling Ruth. "This really happened. For my mother's birthday I saved up all my money, fourteen dollars. And Ezra didn't have a penny, see . . ."

Luke scrabbled through his wooden footlocker, the one piece of furniture that really belonged to him. It had accompanied all their moves since before he could remember. He was hunting the missing wing of a jet. He didn't find the wing but he did find a leather bag of marbles—the kind he used to like, with spritzy bubbles like ginger ale inside them. And a slingshot made from a strip of inner tube. And a tonette—a dusty black plastic whistle on which, for Mother's Day back in first grade, he'd played "White Coral Bells" along with his classmates. He tried it now: *White coral bells, upon a slender stalk . . .* It returned to him, note by note. He rose and went to his parents' room to play it through to the end. *Lilies of the valley deck my—*

His father said, "I can't stand it."

Luke lowered the tonette.

"Are you doing this on purpose?" Cody asked. "Are you determined to torment me?"

"Huh?"

"Cody, honey . . ." Ruth said.

"You're haunting me, isn't that it? I can't get away from him! I spend half my life with meek-and-mild Ezra and his blasted wooden whistle; I make my escape at last, and now look: here we go again. It's like a conspiracy! Like some kind of plot where someone decided, long before I was born, I would live out my days surrounded by people who were . . . nicer than I am, just naturally nicer without even having to try, people that other people preferred; and everywhere I go there's something, just that goddamn forgiving smile or some demented folk song floating out a window—"

"Cody, Luke will be thinking you have lost your senses," Ruth said.

"And you!" Cody told her. "Look at you! Ah, Lord," he said. "Some people fit together forever, don't they? And you haven't a hope in heaven of prying them apart. Married or not, you've always loved Ezra better than me."

"Cody, what are you *talking* about?"

"Admit it," Cody said. "Isn't Ezra the real, true father of Luke?"

There was a silence.

"You didn't say that. You couldn't have," Ruth told him.

"Admit it!"

"You know you don't seriously believe such a thing."

"Isn't it the truth? Tell me! I won't get angry, I promise."

Luke went back to his room and closed the door.

All that afternoon he lay on his bed, rereading an old horse book from his childhood because he didn't have anything else to do. The story struck him as foolish now, although once he'd loved it. When his mother called him for supper, he walked very firmly into the kitchen. He was going to refuse, absolutely, to eat in the bedroom with Cody any more. But his mother had already set two places at the kitchen table. She sat across from him while they ate, not eating much herself. Luke shoveled in various cold foods and refused to meet her eyes. The fact was that she was stupid. He didn't know when he'd seen such a weak and stupid woman.

After supper he went back to his room and listened to a radio show where people called up a tired-sounding host and offered their opinions. They discussed drunken drivers and battered wives. It grew dark, but Luke didn't turn on the light. His mother tapped hesitantly on his door, paused, and left.

Then he must have fallen asleep. When he woke it was darker than ever, and his neck was stiff, and a woman on the radio was saying, "Now, I'm not denying I signed the papers but that was only his fast talk, only him talking me into it. 'Just put your John Doe right here,' he tells me . . ."

"I assume you mean John Hancock," the host said wearily.

"Whatever," said the woman.

Then beneath these voices, murmuring through the wall, came Cody's grumble and Ruth's pale answers. Luke covered his head with his pillow.

He tried to recall his Uncle Ezra. It was several years since they'd met. And even that was such a brief visit, his father taking them away in a huff before they'd got well settled. Finding Ezra was something like hunting through that footlocker; he had to burrow past a dozen other memories, and more came trailing up along with what he was after. He smelled the burned toast in his grandma's kitchen and remembered Ezra's bedroom, which had once been Ezra's and Cody's together, where boyhood treasures (a football-shaped bookend, a peeling hockey stick) had sat in their places so long that to Ezra, they were invisible. Anything that caught Luke's attention, Ezra had seemed surprised to see. "Oh! Would you like to have that?" he would ask, and when Luke politely declined, not wanting to seem greedy, Ezra said, "Please. I can't think what it's still doing here." His room had been large—a sort of dormitory arrangement, occupying the whole third floor—but its stuffy smell of used sheets and twice-worn clothes had made it seem smaller. There was a lock inside the bathroom door downstairs, Luke recalled, that looked exactly like a little silver cashew; and the bathroom itself was tall and echoing, ancient, cold floored, with a porcelain knob in the tub reading WASTE.

He tried to picture his cousins—Aunt Jenny's children—but only came up with another room: his cousin Becky's ruffled bedroom, with its throng of shabby stuffed animals densely encircling her bed. How could she sleep? he had wondered. But she told him she had no trouble sleeping at all; and whenever she went away to spend the night, she said, she took the whole menagerie in a giant canvas suitcase and set it out first thing around the new bed, even before unpacking her pajamas; and most of her friends did the same. It was Luke's first inkling that girls were different. He was mystified and charmed, and he treated her protectively for the rest of that short visit—though she was a year older than he and half a head taller.

If Ezra were really his father, Luke thought, then Luke could live in Baltimore where houses were dark and deep and secretive. Relatives would surround him—a loving grandma, funny Aunt Jenny, those rafts of cousins. Ezra would let him help out in his restaurant. He would talk about food and how people need to be fed with care; Luke could hear his ambling way of speaking. Yes, now he had it: the memory homed in. Ezra wore a flannel shirt of soft blue plaid, washed into oblivion. His hair was yellow . . . why! It was Luke's kind of yellow, all streaky and layered. And his eyes were Luke's kind of gray, a full shade lighter than Cody's, and his skin had that same golden cast that caused it to blend into his hair almost without demarcation.

Luke let himself believe in some unimaginable moment between Ruth and Ezra, fourteen years ago. He skipped across it quickly to the time when Ezra would arrive to claim him. "You're old enough to be told now, son . . ."

Knitting this scene in the dark, doubling back to correct a false note or racing forward to a good part, Luke forgot himself and took the pillow off his head. Instantly, he heard Cody's voice behind the wall. "Everything I've ever wanted, Ezra got it. Anything in life I wanted. Even things I thought I had won, Ezra won in the end. And he didn't even seem to be trying; that's the hell of it."

"You won the damn *Monopoly* games, didn't you?" Luke shouted.

Cody said nothing.

The next morning, Cody seemed unusually quiet. Ruth took him into the doctor's to get his walking cast—a moment they'd been waiting for, but Cody didn't act interested now. Luke had to go along to serve as a crutch. He flinched when Cody first laid his heavy arm cast across his shoulders; he felt there was some danger hovering. But Cody was a dead weight, grunting as he walked, evidently thinking about other matters. He heaved himself into the car and stared bleakly ahead of him. In the doctor's waiting room, while Luke and his mother read magazines, Cody just sat empty faced. And after he got his walking cast, he hobbled back to the car unassisted, ignoring Luke's offer of help. He fell into bed as soon as they reached home and lay gazing at the ceiling. "Cody, honey? Remember the doctor said to give that leg some exercise," Ruth told him.

He didn't answer.

Luke went out to the yard and kicked at the grass a while as if he were hunting for something. Next door, a cluster of toddlers in their wading pool stared at him. He wanted to shout, "Turn away! Stop looking at me; you have no business." But instead it was he who turned, wandering out of the yard and down the street. More wading pools; more round-eyed, judging stares. A Welsh corgi, squat and dignified, bustled down the sidewalk, followed by a lady in a flowing caftan. "Toulouse! Toulouse!" she called. The heat was throbbing; it almost breathed. Luke's face became filmed with sweat and his T-shirt stuck to his back. He kept wiping his upper lip. He passed rows of colonial houses similar to his, each with some object featured like a museum piece in the living-room window: a bulbous lamp, a china horse, a vase of stiff-necked marigolds. (And what did his own window have? He couldn't recall. He'd wanted to say a weeping fig tree, but that was from an apartment they'd rented, three or four towns back.) Sprinklers spun lazily. It was a satisfaction to stop, from time to time, and watch a lawn soak up the spangled water drops.

Now here came some busy lady with her baby in a stroller, small children all around her. He crossed the street to avoid them, took a right turn, and arrived on Willow Bough Avenue with its whizzing traffic, discount drugstores, real estate offices and billboards and service stations. He waited at an inter-section, pondering where to go next. One of the things about moving so often was, he never really knew where he was. He believed his sense of direction had been blunted. He couldn't understand how some people seemed to carry a kind of detailed, internal map of the town they lived in.

A Trailways bus zipped past him reading BALTIMORE. Imagine hailing it. (Could you hail a Trailways bus?) Imagine boarding it—assuming he had the money, which he didn't—and riding off to Baltimore, arriving at Ezra's restaurant and strolling in. "Here I am." "*There* you are," Ezra would say. Oh, if only he'd brought his money! Another bus passed, but that was a local. Then a gigantic truck drew up, braking for an amber light. Luke, as if obeying orders, stuck out a thumb. The driver leaned across the seat and opened the door on the passenger side. "Hop on in," he told Luke.

No RIDERS, a label on the window read. None of this was

happening. Slowly, like someone being pushed from behind, Luke climbed into the cab. It was filled with loud music and a leathery, sweaty, masculine smell that made him feel instantly comfortable. He slammed the door and settled back. The driver—a knife-faced man, unshaven—squinted up at the traffic light and asked, "Whereabouts you headed, son?"

Luke said, "Baltimore, Maryland."

"Folks know you're going?"

"Sure," said Luke.

The driver shot him a glance.

"Why, my folks . . . *live* in Baltimore," Luke told him.

"Oh, then."

The truck started up again. They rumbled past the shopping mall where Luke's mother went for groceries. A green sign swung overhead, listing points north. "Well," said the driver, adjusting his mirror, "I tell you: I can carry you as far as Richmond. That's where I have to veer west."

"Okay," said Luke.

Even Richmond, after all, was farther than he'd ever meant to go.

On the radio, Billy Swan was singing "I Can Help." The driver hummed along in a creaky voice that never quite hit the right note. His thin gray hair, Luke saw, had recently been combed; it lay close to his skull in damp parallel lines. He held a cigarette between his fingers but he didn't light it. His fingernails were so thick and ridged, they might have been cut from yellow corduroy.

"In the summer of fifty-six," he said, "I was passing along this very road with my wife in a Safeway grocery truck when she commences to go into labor. Not but eight months gone and she proceeds directly into labor. Lord God! I recall to this day. She says, 'Clement, I think it's my time.' Well, I was young then. Inexperienced. I thought a baby came one-two-three. I thought we didn't have a moment to spare. And also, you know what they say: a seven-month baby will turn out good but an eight-month baby won't make it. I can't figure why *that* should be. So anyhow, I put on the brakes, I'm shaking all over. My brake foot is so shaky we're just wobbling down the highway. You see that sign over there? Leading off to the right? See that hospital sign? Well, that is where I take her. Straight up that there road. I never come by here but what I recall it."

Luke looked politely at the hospital sign, and then swiveled his neck to go on looking after they had passed. It was the only response he could think of.

"Labor lasted thirty-two hours," the driver said. "Safeway thought I'd hijacked their rig."

"Well," said Luke, "but the baby got born okay."

"Sure," the driver told him. "Five-pound girl. Lisa Michelle." He thought a moment. Then he said, "She died later on, though."

Luke cleared his throat.

"Crib death is what they call it nowadays," said the driver. He swerved around a trailer. "Ever hear of it?"

"No, sir, I haven't."

"Sudden crib death. Six months old. Light of my life. Bright as a button, too—loved me to bits. I'd come home and she would just rev right up—wheel her arms and legs like a windmill soon as she set eyes on me. Then she went and died."

"Well, gosh," said Luke.

"Now I got others," the driver said. "Want to see them? Turn down that sun visor over your head."

Luke turned down the visor. A color photo, held in place by a pink plastic clothespin, showed three plain girls in dresses so new and starchy that it must have been Easter Sunday.

"The youngest is near about your age," the driver said. "What are you: thirteen, fourteen?" He honked at a station wagon that had cut too close in front. "They're nice girls," he said, "but I don't know. It's not the same, somehow. Seems like I lost the . . . attachment. Lost the knack of getting attached. I mean, I like them; shoot, I love them, but I just don't have the

. . . seems to me I can't get up the energy no more."

A lady on the radio was advertising Chevrolets. The driver switched stations and Barbra Streisand came on, showing off as usual. "But you ought to see my wife!" the driver said. "Isn't it amazing? She loves those kids like the very first one. She just started in all over. I don't know what to make of her. I look at her and I can't believe it. 'Dotty,' I say, 'really it all comes down to nothing. It's not for anything,' I say. 'Dotty, how come you can go *on* like this?' See, me, I never bounced back so good. I pass that hospital road and you know? I halfway believe if I made the turnoff, things would be just like before. Dotty'd be holding my hand, and Lisa Michelle would be waiting to be born."

Luke rubbed his palms on his jeans. The driver said, "Well, now. Listen to me! Just gabbing along; I guess you think I talk too much." And for the rest of the trip he was quiet, only whistling through his teeth when the radio played a familiar song.

He said goodbye near Richmond, going out of his way to leave Luke at a ramp just past a rest center. "You wait right here and you'll get a ride in no time," he said. "Here they're traveling slow anyhow, and won't mind stopping." Then he raised his hand stiffly and drove off. From a distance, his truck looked as bright and chunky as a toy.

But it seemed he took some purpose with him, some atmosphere of speed and assurance. All at once . . . what was Luke *doing* here? What could he be thinking of? He saw himself, alone in the fierce white glare of the sun, cocking his thumb at an amateurish angle on a road in the middle of nowhere. He couldn't even visualize how far he had to go. (He'd never done well in geography.) Although it was hot—the peak of the afternoon, by now—he wished for a windbreaker: protection. He wished for his billfold, not so much for the small amount of money it held as for the i.d. card that had come with it when he bought it. If he were killed on this road, how would they know whom to notify? He wondered if—homeless, parentless—he would have to wear these braces on his teeth for the rest of his

240

life. He pictured himself as an old man, still hiding a mouthful of metal whenever he smiled.

Then an out-of-date, fin-tailed car stopped next to him and the door swung open. "Need a lift?" the driver asked. In the back, a little tow-headed boy bounced up and down, calling "Come on! Come on! Get in and have a ride. Come on in and ride with us!"

Luke got in. He found the driver smiling at him—a sun-tanned man in blue jeans, with deep lines around his eyes. "My name's Dan Smollett," he said. "That's Sammy in the back seat."

"I'm Luke."

"We're heading toward D.C. That do you any good?"

"It's fine," said Luke. "I guess," he added, still unsure of his geography. "I'm on my way to Baltimore."

"Baltimore!" said Sammy, still bouncing. "Daddy, can we go to Baltimore?"

"We have to go to Washington, Sammy."

"Don't we know someone in Baltimore too? Kitty? Susie? Betsy?"

"Now, Sammy, settle down, please."

"We're looking up Daddy's old girlfriends," Sammy told Luke.

"Oh," said Luke.

"We just came from Raleigh and saw Carla."

"No, no, Carla was in Durham," his father told him. "It was DeeDee you saw in Raleigh."

"Carla was nice," said Sammy. "She was the best of the bunch. You would've liked her, Luke."

"I would?"

"It's too bad she was married."

"Sammy, Luke doesn't want to hear about our private lives."

"Oh, that's all right," said Luke. He wasn't sure what he was hearing, anyhow.

241

They were back on the freeway by now, staying in the slow lane—perhaps because of the grinding noise that came whenever Dan accelerated. Luke had never been in a car as old as this one. Its interior was a dusty gray felt, the floors awash in paper cups and Frito bags. The glove compartment—doorless—spilled out maps that were splitting at the seams, along with loose change, Lifesavers, and miniature tractors and dump trucks. In the rear, Sammy bounced among blankets and grayish pillows. "Settle down," his father kept saying, but it didn't do any good. "He gets a little restless, along about afternoon," Dan told Luke.

"How long have you been traveling?" Luke asked.

"Oh, three weeks or so."

"Three weeks!"

"We left just after summer school. I'm a high school English teacher; I had to teach this grammar course first."

"Lookit here," Sammy said, and on his next bounce upward he thrust a wad of paper into Luke's face. Evidently, someone had been chewing on it. It was four sheets, mangled together, bearing typed columns of names and addresses. "Daddy's old girlfriends," Sammy said.

Luke stared.

"They are not," said his father. "Really, Sammy." He told Luke, "That's my graduating class in high school. Boys *and* girls. Last year they had a reunion; I didn't go but they sent us this address list."

"Now we're looking up the girls," Sammy said.

"Not all the girls, Sammy."

"The girls that you went out with."

"My wife is divorcing me," Dan told Luke. He seemed to think this explained everything. He faced forward again, and Luke said, "Oh." Another rest center floated by, a distant forest of Texaco and Amoco signs. A moving van honked obligingly when Sammy gave the signal out the window. Sammy squealed and bounced all the harder—a spiky mass of bones and striped

T-shirt, flapping shorts, torn sneakers.

"What year are you in school?" Dan asked Luke.

"I'm going into ninth grade."

"Read any Hemingway? *Catcher in the Rye?* What are they giving you to read?"

"I don't know yet. I'm new," said Luke.

He could easily picture Dan as a teacher. He would wear his jeans in the classroom. He'd be one of those casual, comradely types that Luke had never quite trusted. Better to have him in suit and tie; at least then you knew where you stood.

"In Washington," Sammy said, "there's *two* girls, Patty and Lena."

"Don't say girls, say women," Dan told him.

"Patty Sears and Lena Sparrow."

"I'm better on the S's," Dan said to Luke. "They were in the homeroom."

"Lena we hear is separated," Sammy said.

Luke said, "But what do you do when you visit? What is there to do?"

"Oh, sit around," Sammy said. "Stay a few days if they ask us. Play with their dogs and their cats and their kids. Most of them do have kids. And husbands."

"Well, then," said Luke. "If they've got husbands . . . "

"But we don't know that till we get there. Do we," Sammy said.

"Sammy's a little mixed up," Dan said. "It's not as though we're hunting replacements. We're just traveling. This divorce has come as a shock and I'm just, oh, traveling back. I'm visiting old friends."

"But only *girl*friends," Sammy pointed out.

"They're girls I used to get along fine with. Not sweethearts, necessarily. But they liked me; they thought I was fine. Or at least, they seemed to. I assumed they did. *I* don't know. Maybe they were just acting polite. Maybe I was a mess all along."

Luke couldn't think what to say.

"So listen!" Dan told him. "You read *The Great Gatsby* yet?"

"I don't think so."

"How about *Lord of the Flies*? You get to *Lord of the Flies*?"

"I haven't read anything," said Luke. "I've been moved around a lot; anyplace I go they're doing *Silas Marner*."

This seemed to throw Dan into some kind of depression. His shoulders sagged and he said no more.

Sammy finally stopped bouncing and sat back with a *Jack and Jill*. Pages turned, rattling in the hot wind that blew through the car. On the seat between Dan and Luke, Dan's address list fluttered. It didn't seem very long. Four or five sheets of paper, two columns to a sheet; it would be used up in no time. Luke said, "Um . . ."

Dan looked over at him.

"You must have gone to college," Luke said.

"Yes."

"Or even graduate school."

"Just college."

"Don't you have some addresses from there?"

"College isn't the same," said Dan. "I wouldn't be going far enough back. Why," he said, struck by a thought, "college is where I met my wife!"

"Oh, I see," Luke said.

Outside Washington, Dan stopped the car to let him off. On the horizon was a haze of buildings that Dan said was Alexandria. "Alexandria, Virginia?" Luke asked. He didn't understand what that had to do with Washington. But Dan, who seemed in a hurry, was already glancing in his side-view mirror. Sammy hung out the window calling, "Bye, Luke! When will I see you again? Will you come and visit when we find a place? Write me a letter, Luke!"

"Sure," said Luke, waving. The car rolled off.

By now it must be four o'clock, at least, but it didn't seem to

Luke that he felt any cooler. His eyes ached from squinting in the sunlight. His hair had grown stringy and stiff. Something about this road, though—the foreign smells of tar and diesel fuel, or the roar of traffic—made him believe for the first time that he really was getting somewhere. He was confident he'd be picked up sooner or later. He thumbed a while, walked a few yards, stopped to thumb again. He had turned to begin another walk when a car slammed on its brakes, veering to the shoulder in front of him. "For God's sake," a woman called. "Get in this instant, you hear?"

He opened the door and got in. It was a Dodge, not nearly as old as Dan's car but almost as worn-looking, as if it had been used a great deal. The woman inside was plump and fortyish. Her eyes were swollen and tears had streaked her cheeks, but he trusted her anyhow; you'd think she was his mother, the way she scolded him. "Are you out of your mind? Do you want to get killed? Do you know the kind of perverts in this world? Make sure your door's shut. *Lock* it, dammit; we're not in downtown Sleepy Hollow. Fasten your seat belt. Hook up your shoulder harness."

He was happy to obey. He adjusted some complicated kind of buckle while the woman, sniffling, ground the gears and shot back into traffic. "What's your name?" she asked him.

"Luke."

"Well, Luke, are you a total idiot? Does your mother know you're hitching rides? Where are your parents in all of this?"

"Oh, ah, Baltimore," he said. "I don't guess you would be going there."

"God, no, what would I want with Baltimore?"

"Well, where *are* you going?"

"I don't know," she told him.

"You don't know?"

He looked at her. The tears were streaming down her cheeks again. "Um, maybe—" he said.

"Oh, relax. Never mind, I'll take you on to Baltimore."

"You will?"

"It's better than circling the Beltway forever."

"Golly, thanks," he said.

"They're letting infants out on their own these days."

"I'm not an infant."

"Don't you read the papers? Sex crimes! Muggings! Murders! Things that make no sense."

"So what? I've been traveling on my own a *long* time. Years," he said. "Ever since I was born, almost."

"For all you know," she told him, "I could be holding you for ransom."

This startled a laugh out of him. She glanced over and gave a sad smile. There was something reassuring about the comfortable mound of her stomach, the denim skirt riding up her stocky legs, the grayish-white tennis shoes. Periodically, she swabbed at the tip of her nose with her knuckles. He noticed that she wore a wedding ring, and had worn it for so long it looked embedded in her finger.

"Just two or three miles ahead, not a month ago," she said, "a boy in a sports car stopped to pick up a girl and she smashed in his skull with a flashlight, rolled him down an embankment and drove away in his sports car."

"That proves it's you doing something dangerous, not me," he pointed out. (How easy it was to fall into the bantering, argumentative tone reserved for mothers!) "What did you pick me up for? I could be planning to kill you."

"Oh, indeed," she said, sniffling again. "You wouldn't happen to have a Kleenex on you, by any chance?"

"No, sorry."

"I'd never stop for just anyone," she told him. "Only if they're in danger—I mean young girls alone, or infants like you."

"I am not an—"

"Yesterday it was a girl in short shorts, can you believe it? I told her; I said, 'Honey, you're inviting trouble, dressed like that.' Day before, it was a twelve-year-old boy. He said he'd been robbed of his bus fare and had to get home as best he could. Day before that—"

"What, you drive here every day?"

"Most days."

He looked out the window at the vans and oil tankers, interstate buses, cars with their overloaded luggage racks. "I had sort of thought this was a long-*range* highway," he said.

"Oh, no. Heavens, no. No, I live right nearby," she told him.

"Then what are you driving around for?"

Her chin crumpled in. "None of your business," she said.

"Oh."

"What it is, you see, I generally do this from two or three in the afternoon till suppertime. Sometimes I go to Annapolis, sometimes off in Virginia someplace. Sometimes just round and round the Beltway. It all depends," she said. She tossed him a look, as if expecting him to ask what it all depended on, but he had been insulted and said nothing. She sighed. "Two or three o'clock is when my daughter wakes up. My daughter is fourteen years old. Just about your age, right? How old are you?"

He drummed his fingers and looked out the window.

"In the summer, she sleeps forever. My husband says, 'Jeepers, Mag.' He says, 'Why do you let her sleep so late?' Well, I'll tell you why. It's because she's impossible. Truly impossible I mean, it isn't believable that she could be so awful. She comes downstairs in her bathrobe, yawning. Finds me in the kitchen. Says, 'Well, Ma, I see you're wearing your insecticide perfume again. DDT Number Five.' Then she floats away. Leaving me sniffing my wrists and wondering. I say, 'Liddie, are you going to clean your room today?' and she says, 'Listen to you, sniping and griping; you sound exactly like your mother.' I make a little joke; she says, 'Very funny, Ma. Ha ha. The big comedian.' I find she's stolen my best lace bra that I only wear on my anniversary and she flings it back all grimy at the seams: 'Take it, who wants it, it's too flat-chested anyhow.' To my face, she calls me a bitch, says I'm fat and homely, says she hates me, and I say, 'Listen here, young lady, it's time we got a few things straight,' but all she does is yawn and start chewing one of those plastic price-tag strings off the sleeve of her blouse. I tell my husband, 'Speak to her,' so he says, 'Liddie, *you* know how your mother gets. Why do you upset her?' I say, 'How I get? What do you mean, how I get?' and before you know, it's him and me fighting, which may have been her plan all along. Division. Disruption. Chaos. That's what she enjoys. She's got this boyfriend, treats him terribly. Finally he broke up with her, and she cried all night and asked a hundred times, 'Why did I act like I did? What can I do to change his mind?' I told her to be honest, just phone him and say she didn't know what had got into her; so next morning she phoned, and they made up, and everything was wonderful and she came and thanked me for my good advice. Her life was back in order, it looked like. So she sat at the table a while, calm as I've seen her. Then she started swinging her foot. Then she started picking her fingernails. Then she went and phoned her boyfriend again. Said, 'Roger, I didn't want to tell you this but I thought it's time you knew. The doctor says I'm dying of leukemia.'"

Luke laughed. She looked over at him innocently, but he noticed a wry, proud twist at the corners of her mouth. "Around two or three o'clock," she said, "I get in my car and start driving. At first, I'm talking out loud. You ought to see me. 'I'm never coming back,' I say. I'm cursing through my teeth; I'm honking at crippled old ladies. 'That little wretch, that pest, that spoiled brat,' I say. 'She'll be sorry!' I speed along—oh, you ought to see my traffic record! One more point on my license and I'll have to take that Saturday course on the evils of reckless driving; have to watch that movie where the lady ends up decapitated. Well, at least it'll get me out of the house. I sling the car around and don't let other cars ahead of me and I picture how my husband will come home and say, 'Liddie? Where is your mother? What did you *do* to her, Liddie?' and Liddie will feel just awful . . . but then I think of my husband. I have a really nice husband. It's not him I want to leave. And I wonder if I could sneak back home at night and tell him, 'Psst! Let's *both* leave. Let's elope,' I'll say. But I know he wouldn't do it. He's not as much involved. She annoys him but he's not around enough to make any serious mistakes with her. That's what kills me: making mistakes. Overreacting, letting her get to me . . . oh, I can think of so many! You could say that what I'm leaving behind is my own poor view of me, right? So then I start driving slower. I start remembering things. I think of Liddie when she was small: she always stood so straight. You could pick her out of a crowd by her straight little back. And for one whole year she would only eat with chopsticks. Click-click against her plate . . . you ought to have seen the mess! But I didn't mind. In those days, she liked me a lot. I was a really good mother, and she liked me."

"Maybe she *still* likes you," Luke said doubtfully.

"No," said the woman. "She doesn't."

They passed a sign for Baltimore. The countryside seemed endlessly the same—fields of high grass, then the backsides of housing developments with clotheslines and motorcycles and aboveground, circular swimming pools, then fields of high grass again, as if the scenery came around regularly on a giant conveyor belt.

"What it is," said the woman, "it's like I'm driving till I find her past self. You know? And *my* past self. Then mile by mile, I simmer down. I let up on the gas a bit more. So by suppertime, I'm ready to come home again."

Luke checked the clock on her dashboard. It was four thirty-five.

"Tonight I'll just fix a tuna salad," she said.

"Well, I appreciate your doing this."

"It's nothing," she said, and she gave a final swipe to her nose.

By five o'clock, they had reached the outskirts of Baltimore. It was something like entering a piece of machinery, Luke thought—all sooty and cluttered and churning. The woman seemed used to it; she drove without comment. "Now, tell me what to do after Russell Street," she said.

"Ma'am?"

"How do I find your house?"

"Oh," he said, "why don't you just drop me off downtown."

"Where downtown?"

"Anyplace will do."

She looked over at him.

He said, "I live so near, I mean . . ."

"Near to where?"

"Why, to anywhere."

"Now, listen, Luke," she said. "I'm getting a very odd feeling here. I want to know exactly where your parents are."

He wondered what she would do if he told her he had to look them up in the telephone book. He'd been away so long, he would say, at summer camp or someplace, the address had just slipped his . . . no. But the fact was, he had never known Ezra's street address. It was just a house they arrived at, Cody driving, Luke sitting in back.

"The thing of it is," he said, "they're both at work. They own this restaurant, the Homesick Restaurant. Maybe you could drop me off at the restaurant."

"Where is that?"

"Ah . . ."

"There is no such place, is there," she said. "I knew it! Homesick Restaurant, indeed."

"There is! Believe me," he said. "But it's new. They just did buy it, and I haven't been there yet."

"Look it up," she told him.

She stopped so suddenly, he was glad he'd fastened his seat belt. A telephone booth stood beside them. "Go on! Look it

250

up," she told him. She must have thought she was calling his bluff.

Luke said, "All right, I will."

Then in the phone booth—the old, fully enclosed kind, a glass and aluminum boxful of heat—he ran a finger past *Homeland Racquet Club, Homeseekers Realty,* and found himself so surprised by *Homesick Restaurant* that it might have been a bluff after all. "It's on St. Paul Street," he said when he came back to the car. "You can drop me off anywhere; I'll find the number."

But no, she had to take him to the doorstep, though it meant a good deal of doubling back because St. Paul, it turned out, was one-way and she kept miscalculating the cross streets. When she parked in front of the restaurant, she said, "Well, I'll be! It exists."

"Thank you for the ride," Luke said.

She peered at him. "Are you going to be all right, Luke?" she asked.

"Of course I am."

"And you're certain your parents are here."

"Of course they are."

But she waited, anyhow. (It reminded him of the grade-school parties given by his classmates—his mother making sure he got in before she drove away.) He tried the restaurant's door and found it locked. He would have to go around to the rear. The woman leaned out her window and called, "What's the trouble, Luke?"

"I forgot, I have to use the kitchen entrance."

"What if that's locked, too?"

"It isn't."

"You listen, Luke," she called to him. "Everything is changing; things aren't safe like in the old days. Every alley in this city is full of muggers, are you hearing what I say? Every doorway and vacant buidling. Luke, every street in Baltimore."

He waved and disappeared. A moment later he heard the

car take off again—but reluctantly, without its usual verve, as if she were still absorbed in her catalogue of dangers.

He knew the restaurant so well, he must have carried its image constantly within him: its clatter of pans and crash of china, smell of cut celery simmering in butter, broom-shaped bundles of herbs dangling from the rafters, gallon jars of wrinkly Greek olives, bushel baskets of parsley, steaming black kettles watched devotedly by a boy no older than Luke. Beyond the kitchen, hardly separate from it, stretched the dining room with its white-draped tables and dusty sunbeams. There were so many decorations in the dining room—gifts and mementos, accumulated over the years—that Luke was always reminded of someone's home, one of those teeming family houses where kindgarten drawings are taped above the mantel and then forgotten. He recognized the six-foot collage of Ezra's hearts-of-palm salad, presented by an artist who often ate here, and he saw the colored paper chain that he and his cousins had festooned around a light fixture for some long-ago Christmas dinner. (Ezra had never taken it down, though the dinner had broken off in a quarrel and the chain was now brittle and faded.) Luke knew that in one corner, out of his line of vision, sat a heavy antique bicycle that Ezra had bought in a Timonium flea market. MERCURIO'S CULINARY DELICACIES was lettered importantly across its wooden basket, which was filled with frosty glass pears and bananas contributed by a customer. Astride the bicycle stood a cardboard Marilyn Monroe with her dress blowing up—the prank of unknown persons, but no one had ever removed her and Marilyn rode on, her neck creased nearly to the breaking point, her smile growing paler season by season and her accordion-pleated skirt curling at the edges.

Hot, flushed workers darted around the kitchen, intent on their private tasks, weaving between the others like those Model T's in silent comedies—*zip!*, just missing, never once colliding, their paths crisscrossing but miraculously slipping past disaster. Luke stood in the doorway unnoticed. His trip had been such a process in itself; he had almost lost sight of his purpose. What was he doing here, anyhow? But then he saw Ezra. Ezra was piling biscuits in a crude rush basket. He wore not the blue plaid shirt that Luke remembered—which was flannel, after all, unsuitable for summer—but a chambray shirt with the sleeves rolled up. He thoughtfully set each biscuit in its place, his large, blunt hands deliberate. Luke made his way across the kitchen. He was surprised by a flash of shyness. His heart was beating too fast. He arrived in front of Ezra and said, "Hi."

Ezra looked up, still thoughtful. "Hi," he said.

He didn't know who this was.

Luke was stricken, at first. Then he began to feel pleased. Why, he must have changed immeasurably! He'd shot up a foot; his voice was getting croaky; he was practically a man. And there was some safety, a kind of shield, in Ezra's flat gaze. Luke rearranged his plans. He squared his shoulders. "I'd like a job," he said firmly.

Ezra grew still. "Luke?" he said.

"If that boy over there can tend the kettles—" Luke was saying. He stopped. "Pardon?"

"It's Cody's Luke. Isn't it."

"How'd you guess?"

"I could tell when you did your shoulders that way, just like your dad, just exactly like your dad. How funny! And something about the tone of your voice, all set to do battle . . . well, Luke!" He shook Luke's hand very hard. His fingers had a sandy feel from the biscuits. "Where are your parents? Back at the house?"

"I'm here on my own."

"On your own?" Ezra said. He was smiling genially, uncertainly, like someone hoping to understand a joke. "You mean, with nobody else?"

"I wanted to ask if I could stay with you."

Ezra stopped smiling. "It's Cody," he said.

"Excuse me?"

"Something's happened to him."

"Nothing's happened."

"I should have gone down; I knew I should. I shouldn't have let him stop me. The accident was worse than they let on."

"No! He's fine."

Ezra surveyed him for a long, silent moment.

"He's already got his walking cast," Luke told him.

"Yes, but his other wounds, his head?"

"Everything's okay."

"You swear it?"

"Yes! Gosh."

"See, I don't have any other brothers," Ezra said.

"I swear. I cross my heart," said Luke.

"Then where is he?"

"He's in Virginia," said Luke. "I left him there. I ran away."

Ezra thought this over. A waitress sidled past him with a tray of delicately clinking, trembling glasses.

"I didn't plan to," Luke told him. "But he said to me . . . see, he said . . ."

Oh, there was no point in telling Ezra what Cody had said. It was nonsense, one of those remarks that pop up out of nowhere. And here was Luke, much too far from home, faltering under his uncle's kindly gaze. "I can't explain," he said.

But just as if he *had* explained, Ezra said gently, "You mustn't take it to heart. He didn't mean it. He wouldn't hurt you for anything in the world."

"I know that," Luke said.

On the telephone with Ruth, Ezra was jocular and brotherly, elaborately casual, playing down what had happened. "Now, Ruth, I'm sitting here looking straight at him and he's perfectly all right . . . police? What for? Well, call them back, tell them he's safe and sound. A lot of fuss over nothing, tell them."

Luke listened, smiling anxiously as if his mother could see

254

him. He laced the spirals of the telephone between his fingers. They were in Ezra's little office behind the kitchen. Ezra sat at a desk piled with cookbooks, bills, magazines, a pot of chives, a copper pan with a cracked enamel lining, and a framed news photo of two men in aprons holding an entire long fish on a platter.

Then evidently, Cody took over the phone. Ezra sounded more serious now. "We could maybe keep him a while," he said. "We'd like to have him visit. I hope you'll let him." In the directness and soberness of his tone, even in his short sentences, Luke read a kind of caution. He worried that Cody was shouting on the other end of the line; he dropped the cord and wandered away, pretending to be interested in the books in Ezra's bookcase. He felt embarrassed for his father. But there must not have been any shouting after all; for Ezra said serenely, "All right, Cody. Yes, I can understand that."

When he'd hung up, he told Luke, "They'll be here as soon as possible. He'd rather come get you now, he said."

Luke felt a little notch of dread beginning in his stomach. He wondered how angry his father was. He wondered how he could have thought of doing this—coming all this distance! So alone! It seemed like something he had floated through in a dream.

His grandmother's house still had its burned-toast smell, its dusky corners, its atmosphere of secrecy. If you moved in here, Luke thought, wouldn't you go on finding unexpected cubbyholes and closets for weeks or even months afterward? (Yes, imagine moving in. Imagine sharing the cozy living room, Grandma's peaceful kitchen). His grandmother skittered around him, adding tiny dishes of food to what was already on the table. Ezra kept telling her, "Mother, take it easy. Don't fuss so." But Luke enjoyed the fuss. He liked the way she would stop in the midst of preparing something to come running over and cup his face. "Look at you! Just look!" She was shorter than he was, now. And she had aged a great deal, or else he'd been too young before to notice. There was something scratchy and fly-away about her little screwed-tight topknot, once blond but now colorless, and her face sectioned deeply by pockets of lines and her wrinkled, spotted hands. He saw how much she loved him, purely from her hungry touch on his cheeks, and he wondered how his father could have misjudged her so.

"It's not right that your parents just come and take you back," she told him. "We'll make them stay. We'll just make them. I'll change the sheets in Jenny's old room. You can have the guest room. Oh, Luke! I wouldn't have known you. I wouldn't have dreamed it was you if I'd seen you on the street; it's been that long. Though I would have said . . . yes, I would have thought to myself as I passed, 'My, that child reminds me of my Cody years ago; doesn't he? Just fairer haired, is all.' I would have had this little pang and then forgotten, and then later, maybe, making tea at home, I'd think, 'Wait now, some-thing was disturbing me back there . . .'"

She tried to pour a bowl of leftover green beans into a sauce-pan but missed, and slopped most of the liquid on to the counter, and swabbed it with wads of paper towels while laugh-ing at herself. "What an old lady! What a silly old lady, you're thinking. My eyesight isn't what it used to be. No, no, Ezra, I can manage, dear."

"Mother, why don't you let me take over?"

"I can certainly manage in my own kitchen, Ezra," she said. "Wouldn't you like to go back to the restaurant? No telling what those people of yours are up to."

"You just want to have Luke to yourself," Ezra teased her.

"Oh, I admit it! I admit it!"

She turned on the flame beneath the saucepan. "Every-thing is coming together," she told Luke. "I've been so worried, just sick with worry, picturing Cody in pain and longing to go to him, and of course he wouldn't let me; he's been like that ever since he was a baby, so . . . thorny, so bristly, just always has his back up. And now a little trouble or something—no, don't look so uneasy! I won't ask any questions, I promise; Ezra told me; it's none of our business, but . . . a little trouble of some kind brings you here to us, I don't know, maybe an argument? One of Cody's tempers?"

"*Mother*," said Ezra.

"And so," she went on hastily, "we get to see him after all. He's really going to show himself. But, Luke. Be truthful. He isn't, he's not . . . scarred or anything, is he? His face, I mean. He hasn't got any disfiguring scars."

"Just bruises," said Luke. "Nothing that'll last. In fact," he added, "they're mostly gone by now."

It surprised him to find that he had held on to the picture of a broken Cody all this time, when really the bruises had faded, come to think of it, and the swellings had disappeared and the hair had almost completely grown over his head wound.

"He always was so handsome," Pearl said. "It was part of his identity."

Ezra moved around the table, setting out plates and silver-ware. The saucepan hissed on the stove. Luke sat down on a kitchen chair and tipped back against a radiator. Its sharply sculptured ribs and tall pipes made him think of old-fashioned, comforting places—a church he'd visited with a kindergarten friend, for instance, or his second-grade classroom, where once, when a snowstorm started during lunch hour, he had imagined a blizzard developing and keeping all the children snugly marooned for days, drinking cups of soup sent up from the cafeteria.

After supper, he and Pearl watched TV while Ezra went back to check the restaurant. Pearl kept the living room completely dark, lit only by the flickering blue TV screen. Both the front windows were open and they could hear the noises from the street—a game of prisoner's base, a Good Humor bell, a woman calling her children. Around nine o'clock, when the twilight had finally given way to night and the stuffy air had cooled some, Luke caught the distinctive, tightly woven hum of a Mercedes drawing up to the curb. He tensed. Pearl, who wouldn't have recognized the sound, went on placidly watching TV. "Who's that, dear?" she asked him, but it was some actor she referred to; she was peering at the television set. There were footsteps across the porch. "Eh?" she said. "Already?" She rose, fumbling first for the arms of her chair in two or three blind passes. She opened the front door and said, "Cody?"

Cody stood looming, larger than Luke had expected, his arm and leg casts glowing whitely in the dark. "Hello, Mother," he said.

"Why, Cody, let me look at you! And Ruth: hello, dear. Cody, are you all right? I can't make out your face. Are you really feeling better?"

"I'm fine," Cody told her. He kissed her cheek and then limped in.

"Hey, Dad," Luke said, rising awkwardly.

Cody said, "May I ask what you thought you were up to?"

"Well, I don't know . . ."

"Don't know! Is that all you have to say? You scared the hell out of us! Your mother's been beside herself."

"Oh, honey, we were so worried!" Ruth cried. She pulled him close and kissed him. Her dress—a magenta polyester that she wore on special occasions—crumpled its sharp ruffles against his chest. He smelled her familiar, grassy smell that he'd never really noticed before.

"We near about lost our minds," Ruth told Pearl. "I believe I must've aged a quarter-century. I felt if I looked out that same front window one more time I'd go mad, go stark, raving mad—same old curve in the road, same old sidewalk, empty. You just don't know."

"I do know. I do know," said Pearl.

She was feeling for the switch to a lamp that sat on a table. The silk shade rustled and tilted. Then Ezra arrived in the door.

258

"Cody?" he said. "Is that you?" He strode in fast and first encountered Ruth—almost ran her down—and seized her hand and pumped it. "Good to see you, Ruth," he said. Meanwhile, Cody found the switch for his mother and turned the lamp on. It was coincidental; he was only being helpful, but Luke felt he'd turned on the lamp to *examine* them. Ruth and Ezra, face to face. Ezra blinked in the sudden light and then gave Cody a bear hug. Cody stood unresisting. "How's your arm? How's your leg?" Ezra asked. "What, no crutches?"

Cody went on studying Ruth and Ezra. "He says he can't use them," said Ruth. "He says with his opposite arm in a cast . . . " She reached out and smoothed Luke's T-shirt, which didn't need smoothing. She pushed his hair off his forehead. "And now that he's got this walking cast . . ." she said absently. "Oh, Luke, sweetheart, didn't you think you'd be missed?"

Cody turned away and sank into an armchair. "Would you two like some iced tea?" Pearl asked.

"No, thanks," said Cody.

"Or coffee? A nice cup of coffee?"

"No! God. Nothing," said Cody.

Luke expected Pearl to look hurt, but she only gave Cody a curiously satisfied smile. "You always were a grump when you weren't feeling well," she told him.

In fact, how surprising this whole visit was!—low-keyed and uneventful, even boring. Luke started out sitting rigidly erect, but gradually he relaxed and let his attention drift to a variety show on TV. The grown-ups murmured around him without any emphasis, discussing money. Cody wanted Pearl to get a new furnace; he would pay for it, he said. Pearl said she had a little savings, but Cody kept insisting, as if there were something gratifying, something triumphant in buying a person a furnace. Oh, money, money, money. You'd think they could come up with some more interesting subject.

Luke pressed a lever in his armchair and found himself

flung back, his feet raised suddenly on some sort of footrest. Now Pearl was asking where they would go after Petersburg, and Cody was saying he didn't know; Sloan and he were hoping to take on this cosmetics firm down in . . . His reasonable tone of voice made Luke feel hoodwinked, betrayed. Why, all this time he'd been hearing such terrible tales! He'd been told of such ill will and bitterness! But Cody and Pearl conversed pleasantly, like any civilized adults. They discussed whether the North or the South was a better place to live. They had a mild, dull, uninvested sort of argument about it, till it emerged that Pearl was assuming Baltimore was North and Cody was assuming it was South. She asked if this new factory might be as dangerous as the last one. "Any place is dangerous," said Cody, "if idiots are running it."

"Cody, I worry so," she told him. "If you knew how frantic I've been! Hearing my oldest, my firstborn son is in critical condition and I'm not allowed to come see him."

"Critical condition! I'm walking around, aren't I?"

"The walking *wounded*," she said, and she threw her hands up. "Isn't it ironic? I'd always thought disasters were . . . lower class. I would read these hard-luck stories in the paper: lady evicted when she's trying to raise the seven children of her daughter who was shot to death in a bar, and one of the children's retarded and another has to be taken for dialysis so many times per week by city bus, transferring twice . . . well, of course I feel sorry for such people but also, I don't know, impatient, as if they'd brought it on themselves some way. There's a limit, I want to tell them; only so much of life is luck. But now look: my eyesight's poorly and my oldest son's had a serious accident and *his* son's run away from home for reasons we're not told, and I haven't seen my daughter in weeks because she's all tied up with her little girl who's got that disease, what's it called, Anor Exia—"

"How's Becky doing, anyhow?" Cody asked, and Luke had an image of Cody's reaching into a wild snarl of strings and tugging on the one short piece that wasn't all tangled with the others.

"No one knows," Pearl said, rocking.

Ruth massaged her forehead, which had the strained, roughened look it always got after a difficult day. Ezra laughed at something on TV. Cody, who was watching the two of them, sighed sharply and turned back to his mother.

"We'd better be going," he told her.

She straightened. "What?" she said. "You're leaving?"

"We've got a long drive."

"But that's exactly why you're staying!" she told him. "Rest tonight. Start fresh in the morning."

"We can't," said Cody.

"Why can't you?"

"We have to . . . ah, feed the dog."

"I didn't know you had a dog."

"A Doberman."

"But Dobermans are vicious!"

"That's why we better hurry back and feed him," Cody said. "Don't want him eating up the neighbors."

He reached out a hand toward Luke, and Luke clambered off the reclining chair to help him to his feet. When Cody's fingers closed on his, Luke imagined some extra tightness—a secret handshake, a nudge at the joke they'd put over on Pearl. He kept his face deliberately expressionless.

"Listen, all," Ezra said. "It isn't long till Thanksgiving, you know."

Everybody stared at him.

"Will you come back here for Thanksgiving? We could have a family dinner at the restaurant."

"Oh, Ezra, no telling where we'll be by then," said Cody.

"What," said Pearl. "You never heard of airplanes? Amtrak? Modern transportation?"

"We'll talk about it when the time gets closer," Cody said, patting her shoulder. "Ruth, you got everything? So long, Ezra, let me know how it's going."

There was a flurry of hugs and handshakes. Later, Luke wasn't sure he'd said thank you to Ezra—though what did he want to thank him for, exactly? Something or other . . . They made their way down the sidewalk and into Cody's car, which still had the stale, blank smell of air-conditioned air. Everyone called out parts of sentences, as if trying to give the impression that they had so much left to say to each other, there wasn't room to fit it all in. "Now, you be sure to—" "It sure was good to—" "Tell Jenny we wish—" "And drive defensively, hear?"

They pulled away from the curb, waving through the window. Pearl and Ezra fell behind. Luke, sitting in back, faced forward and found his father at the wheel. Ruth was in the passenger seat. "Mom?" Luke said. "Don't you think you ought to drive?"

"He insisted," Ruth said. "He drove all the way here, too." She turned and looked at Luke meaningfully, over the back of the seat. "He said he wanted it to be him that drove to get you."

"Oh," said Luke.

What was she waiting for? She went on looking at him for some time, but then gave up and turned away again. Trying his best, Luke sat forward to observe how Cody managed.

"Well, I guess it wouldn't be all that hard," he said, "except for shifting the gears."

"Shifting's easy," Cody told him.

"Oh."

"And luckily there's no clutch."

"No."

They passed rows and rows of houses, many with their porches full of people rocking in the dark. They turned down a block where there were stoops instead of porches, white stoops set close to the street. On one of these a whole family perched, with a beer cooler and an oscillating fan and a baby in a mesh crib on the sidewalk. A TV sat on a car hood at the curb so if you happened by on foot, you'd have to cross between TV and

262

audience, muttering, "Excuse me, please," just as if you'd walked through someone's living room. Luke gazed back at that family as long as they were in sight. They were replaced by a strip of bars and cafés, and then by an unlit alley.

"Isn't it funny," Luke told his father, "no one's ever asked you to reorganize anything in Baltimore."

"Very funny," Cody said.

"We could live with Grandma then, couldn't we?"

Cody said nothing.

They left the city for the expressway, entering a world of high, cold lights and a blue-black sky. Ruth slid slowly against the window. Her small head bobbed with every dip in the road.

"Mom's asleep," Luke said.

"She's tired," said Cody.

Perhaps he meant it as a reproach. Was this where the scolding started? Luke kept very quiet for a while. But what Cody said next was, "It wears her out, that house. Your grandma's so difficult to deal with."

"Grandma's not difficult."

"Not for you, maybe. For other people she is. For your mother. Grandma believes your mother is 'scrappy.' She told me that, once. Called her 'scrappy and hoydenish.'" He laughed, recalling something, so that Luke started smiling expectantly. "One time," Cody said, "—I bet you don't remember this—your mother and I had this silly little spat and she packed you up and ran off to Ezra. Then as soon as she got to the station, she started thinking what life would be like with your grandma and she called and asked me to come drive her home."

Luke's smile faded. "Ran off to *where?*" he asked.

"To Ezra. But never mind, it was only one of those—"

"She didn't run to Ezra. She was planning to go to her folks," Luke said.

"What folks?" Cody asked him.

Luke didn't know.

"She's an orphan," Cody said. "What folks?"

263

"Well, maybe—"

"She was planning to go to Ezra," Cody said. "I can see it now! I can picture how they'd take up their marriage, right where ours left off. Oh, I believe I've always had the feeling it wasn't my marriage, anyhow. It was someone else's. It was theirs. Sometimes I seemed to enjoy it better when I imagined I was seeing it through someone else's eyes."

"Why are you *telling* me this?" Luke asked him.

"All I meant was—"

"What are you, crazy? How come you go on hanging *on* to these things, year after year after year?"

"Now, wait a minute, now . . ."

"Mom?" Luke shook her shoulder. "Mom! Wake up!"

Ruth's head sagged over to the other side.

"Let her rest," Cody said. "Goddammit, Luke—"

"Wake up, Mom!"

"Hmm," said Ruth, not waking.

"Mom? I want to ask you. Mom? Remember when you packed me up and left Dad?"

"Mm."

"Remember?"

"Yes," she murmured, curling tighter.

"Where were we going to go, Mom?"

She raised her head, with her hair all frowsy, and gave him a blurry, dazed stare. "What?" she said. "Garrett County, where my uncle lives. Who wants to know?"

"Nobody. Go back to sleep," Cody told her.

She went back to sleep. Cody rubbed his chin thoughtfully.

They sped through a corridor of light that was bounded on both sides by the deepest darkness. They met and passed solitary cars that disappeared in an instant. Luke's eyelids drooped.

"What I mean to say," Cody said. "What I drove all this way to say . . ."

But then he trailed off. And when he started speaking again, it was on a whole different subject: time. How time was under-

264

estimated. How time was so important and all. Luke felt re-lieved. He listened comfortably, lulled by his father's words. "Everything," his father said, "comes down to time in the end—to the passing of time, to changing. Ever thought of that? Anything that makes you happy or sad, isn't it all based on minutes going by? Isn't happiness expecting something time is going to bring you? Isn't sadness wishing time back again? Even *big* things—even mourning a death: aren't you really just wish-ing to have the time back when that person was alive? Or photos—ever notice old photographs? How wistful they make you feel? Long-ago people smiling, a child who would be an old lady now, a cat that died, a flowering plant that's long since withered away and the pot itself broken or misplaced . . . Isn't it just that time for once is stopped that makes you wistful? If only you could turn it back again, you think. If only you could change this or that, undo what you have done, if only you could roll the minutes the other way, for once."

He didn't seem to expect an answer, which was lucky. Luke was too sleepy to manage one. He felt heavy, weighted with other people's stories. He imagined he was slipping or falling. He believed he was gliding away, streaming down a great, wide, light-filled river of time along with all the people he had met today. He let his head nod over, and he closed his eyes and slept.

9

Apple Apple

One morning Ezra Tull got up and shaved, brushed his teeth, stepped into his trousers, and encountered a lump in the bend of his right thigh. His fingers glanced over it accidentally and faltered and returned. In the bedroom mirror, his broad, fair face had a frozen look. The word cancer came on its own, as if someone had whispered it into his ear, but what caused his shocked expression was the thought that flew in after it: All right. Let it happen. I'll go ahead and die.

He shook that away, of course. He was forty-six years old, a calm and sensible man, and later he would make an appointment with Dr. Vincent. Meanwhile he put on a shirt, and buttoned it, and unrolled a pair of socks. Twice, without planning to, he tested the lump again with his fingertips. It was nearly the size of an acorn, sensitive but not painful. It rolled beneath his skin as smoothly as an eyeball.

It wasn't that he really wanted to die. Naturally not. He was only giving in to a passing mood, he decided as he went downstairs; this summer hadn't been going well. His mother, whose vision had been failing since 1975, was now (in 1979) almost totally blind, but still did not fully admit it, which made it all the harder to care for her; and his brother was too far away and

266

his sister too busy to offer him much help. His restaurant was floundering even more than usual; his finest cook had quit because her horoscope advised it; and a heat wave seemed to be stupefying the entire city of Baltimore. Things were so bad that the most inconsequential sights served to confirm his despair— the neighbor's dog panting on the sidewalk, or his mother's one puny hydrangea bush wilting and sagging by two o'clock every afternoon. Even the postman signified catastrophe; his wife had been murdered in a burglary last spring, and now he lugged his leather pouch through the neighborhood as if it were heavy beyond endurance, as if it would eventually drag him to a halt. His feet went slower and slower; his shoulders bent closer to the ground. Every day the mail arrived later.

Ezra stood with his coffee at the window and watched the postman moping past and wondered if there were any point to life.

Then his mother came downstairs, planting her feet just so. "Oh, look," she said, "what a sunny morning!" She could feel it, he supposed—warming her skin in squares when she stood next to him at the window. Or perhaps she could even see it, since evidently she still distinguished light from dark. But her dress was done up wrong. She had drawn her wispy gray-blond hair into its customary bun, and deftly applied a single spark of pink to the center of her dry, pursed lips, but one side of her collar stuck up at an angle and the flowered material pouched outward, showing her slip in the gap between two buttons.

"It's going to be another scorcher," Ezra told her.

"Oh, poor Ezra, I hate to see you go to work in this."

All she said carried references to sight. He couldn't tell if she planned it that way.

She let him bring her a cup of coffee but she turned down breakfast, and instead sat beside him in the living room while he read the paper. This was their only time together—morning and noon, after which he left for the restaurant and did not return till very late at night, long past her bedtime. He had trouble imagining what she did in his absence. Sometimes he telephoned from work and she always sounded so brisk—"Just fixing myself some iced tea," she would say, or "Sorting through my stockings." But in the background he would hear the ominous, syrupy strains of organ music from some television soap opera, and he suspected that she simply sat before the TV much of the day, with a cardigan draped graciously over her shoulders even in this heat and her chilled hands folded in her lap. Certainly she saw no friends; she had none. As near as he could recall, she had never had friends. She had lived through her children; the gossip they brought was all she knew of the outside world, and their activities provided her only sense of motion. Even back when she worked at the grocery store, she had not consorted with the customers or the other cashiers. And now that she had retired, none of her fellow workers came to visit her.

No, this was the high point of her day, no doubt: these slow midmorning hours, the rustling of Ezra's paper, his spotty news reports. "Another taxi driver mugged, it says here."

"Oh, my goodness."

"Another shoot-out down on the Block."

"Where will it all end?" his mother wondered.

"Terrorist bomb in Madrid."

Newspapers, letters, photos, magazines—those he could help her with. With those she let herself gaze straight ahead, blank eyed, while he acted as interpreter. But in all other situations, she was fiercely independent. What, exactly, was the nature of their understanding? She admitted only that her sight was not what it had once been—that it was impaired enough to make reading a nuisance. "She's blind," her doctor said, and she reported, "He thinks I'm blind," not arguing but managing to imply, somehow, that this was a matter of opinion—or of will, of what you're willing to allow and what you're not. Ezra had learned to offer clues in the casual, slantwise style that she would accept. If he were to say, for instance, "It's raining,

Mother," when they were setting out for somewhere, she would bridle and tell him, "Well, *I* know that." He learned to say, "Weatherman claims this will keep up. Better bring your umbrella." Then her face would alter and smooth, adjusting to the information. "Frankly, I don't believe him," she would say, although it was one of those misty rains that falls without a sound, and he knew she hadn't detected it. She concealed her surprise so well that only her children, accustomed to her stubborn denial of anything that might weaken her, could have seen what lay behind that challenging gray stare.

Last month, Ezra's sister had reported that their mother had called to ask a strange question. "She wanted to know if it were true," she said, "that lying on her back a long time would give her pneumonia. 'What for?' I asked her. 'Why do you care?' 'I was only curious,' she said."

Ezra lowered his paper, and he cautiously placed two fingertips at the bend of his thigh.

After they'd finished their coffee, he washed out the cups and straightened the kitchen, which nowadays had an unclean look no matter what he did to it. There were problems he didn't know how to handle—the curtains graying beside the stove, and the lace doily growing stiff with dust beneath the condiment set on the table. Did you actually launder such things? Just throw them in the machine? He could have asked his mother, but didn't. It would only upset her. She would wonder, then, what else she'd missed.

She came out to him, testing her way so carefully that her small black pumps seemed like quivering, delicate, ultrasensitive organs. "Ezra," she said, "what are your plans for this morning?"

"No plans, Mother."

"You're certain, now."

"What is it you want to do?"

"I was thinking we could sort through my desk drawers, but

if you're busy—"

"I'm not busy."

"You just say so if you are."

"I'll be glad to help."

"When you were little," she said, "it made you angry to see me sick or in need of aid."

"Well, that was when I was little."

"Isn't it funny? It was you that was the kindest, the closest, the sweetest child; the others were always up to something, off with their own affairs. But when I felt sick, you would turn so coldhearted! 'Does this mean we don't get to go to the movies?' you'd ask. It was your brother who'd take over then—the one I'd least expect it of. I would say, 'Ezra, could you just fetch me an afghan, please?' and you would turn stony and pretend not to hear. You seemed to think I'd done something *to* you—got a headache out of malice."

"I was very young then," Ezra said.

Although it was odd how clenched he felt, even now—not so much angry as defenseless; and he'd felt defenseless as a child, too, he believed. He had trusted his mother to be everything for him. When she cut a finger with a paring knife, he had felt defeated by her incompetence. How could he depend on such a person? Why had she let him down so?

He took her by the upper arm and led her back to the living room. (He was conscious, suddenly, of his height and his solid, comfortable weight.) He seated her on the couch and went over to the desk to remove the bottom drawer.

This was something he had done many times before. It wasn't, certainly, that the drawer needed cleaning, although to an outsider it might appear disorganized. Cascades of unmounted photos slid about as he worked; others poked from the moldy, crumbling albums stacked to one side. There was a shoe box full of his mother's girlhood diaries; an incomplete baby book for Cody; and a Schrafft's candy box containing old letters, all with the stamps snipped off the envelopes. There was a dim, lavender-colored corsage squashed as stiff and hard as a dried-up mouse carcass; a single kid glove hardened with age; and a musty-smelling report card for Pearl E. Cody, fourth year, 1903, with the grades entered in a script so elegant that someone might have laid A-shaped tendrils of fine brown hair next to every subject. Ezra was fond of these belongings. He willingly went over them again and again, describing them for his mother. "There's that picture of your Aunt Melinda on her wedding day."

"Ah?"

"You are standing next to her with a fan made out of feathers."

"We'll save it," said his mother. She was still pretending they were merely sorting.

But soon enough, she forgot about that and settled back, musing, while he recited what he'd found. "Here is a picture of someone's porch."

"Porch? Whose porch?"

"I can't tell."

"What does it look like?"

"Two pillars and a dark floor, clay pot full of geraniums . . ."

"Am I in it?"

"No."

"Oh, well," she said, waving a hand, "maybe that was Luna's porch."

He had never heard of Luna.

To tell the truth, he didn't believe that relatives were what his mother was after. Ladies and gentlemen drifted by in a blur; he did his best to learn their names, but his mother dismissed them airily. It was herself she was hunting, he sensed. "Do you see me, at all? Is that the dinner where I wore the pale blue?" Her single-mindedness sometimes amused him, sometimes annoyed him. There was greed in the forward jutting of her chin as she waited to hear of her whereabouts. "Am *I* in that group? Was *I* on that picnic?"

He opened a maroon velvet album, each of its pulpy gray pages grown bright yellow as urine around the edges. None of the photos here was properly glued down. A sepia portrait of a bearded man was jammed into the binding alongside a Kodachrome of a pink baby in a flashy vinyl wading pool, with SEPT '63 stamped on the border. His mother poked her face out, expectant. He said, "Here's a man with a beard. I think it's your father."

"Possibly," she said, without interest.

He turned the page. "Here's a group of ladies underneath a tree."

"Ladies?"

"None of them look familiar."

"What are they wearing?"

"Long, baggy dresses," he told her. "Everything seems to be sagging at the waist."

"That would be nineteen-ten or so. Maybe Iola's engagement party."

"Who was Iola?"

"Look for me in a navy stripe," she told him.

"There's no stripes here."

"Pass on."

She had never been the type to gaze backward, had not filled his childhood with "When I was your age," as so many mothers did. And even now, she didn't use these photos as an excuse for reminiscing. She hardly discussed them at all, in fact—even those in which she appeared. Instead, she listened, alert, to any details he could give her about her past self. Was it that she wanted an outsider's view of her? Or did she hope to solve some mystery? "Am I smiling, or am I frowning? Would you say that I seemed happy?"

When Ezra tried to ask *her* any questions, she grew bored. "What was your mother like?" he would ask.

"Oh, that was a long time ago," she told him.

She hadn't had much of a life, it seemed to him. He wondered what, in all her history, she would enjoy returning to. Her courtship, even knowing how it would end? Childbirth? Young motherhood? She did speak often and wistfully of the years when her children were little. But most of the photos in this drawer dated from long before then, from back in the early part of the century, and it was those she searched most diligently. "The Baker family reunion, that would be. Nineteen-o-eight. Beulah's sweet sixteen party. Lucy and Harold's silver anniversary." The events she catalogued were other people's; she just hung around the fringes, watching. "Katherine Rose, the summer she looked so beautiful and met her future husband."

He peered at Katherine Rose. "She doesn't look so beautiful to *me*," he said.

"It faded soon enough."

Katherine Rose, whoever she was, wore a severe and complicated dress of a type not seen in sixty years or more. He was judging her rabbity face as if she were a contemporary, some girl he'd glimpsed in a bar, but she had probably been dead for decades. He felt he was being tugged back through layers of generations.

He flipped open tiny diaries, several no bigger than a lady's compact, and read his mother's cramped entries aloud. "*December eighth, nineteen-twelve. Paid call on Edwina Barrett. Spilled half-pint of top cream in the buggy coming home and had a nice job cleaning it off the cushions I can assure you . . .*" "*April fourth, nineteen-o-eight. Went into town with Alice and weighed on the new weighing machine in Mr. Salter's store. Alice is one hundred thirteen pounds, I am one hundred ten and a half.*" His mother listened, tensed and still, as if expecting something momentous, but all he found was *purchased ten yards heliotrope brilliantine*, and *made chocolate blanc-mange for the Girls' Culture Circle*, and *weighed again at Mr. Salter's store*. During the summer of 1908—her fourteenth summer, as near as he could figure—she had weighed herself about every

273

two days, hitching up her pony Prince and riding clear down-town to do so. "*August seventh,*" he read. "*Had my measure-ments taken at the dressmaker's and she gave me a copy to keep. I have developed in every possible sense.*" He laughed, but his mother made an impatient little movement with one hand. "*September ninth,*" he read, and then all at once had the feeling that the ground had rushed away beneath his feet. Why, that perky young girl was this old woman! This blind old woman sit-ting next to him! She had once been a whole different person, had a whole different life separate from his, had spent her time *swinging clubs with the Junior Amazons* and *cutting up with the Neal boys something dreadful* and *taking first prize at the Autumn Recital Contest.* (*I hoped that poor Nadine would win,* she wrote in a chubby, innocent script, *but of course it was nice to get it myself.*) His mother sat silent, absently stroking the dead corsage. "Never mind," she told him.

"Shall I stop?"

"It wasn't what I wanted after all."

On his way to the restaurant, Ezra ducked into a bookstore and located a Merck Manual in the Family Health section. He checked the index for *lump,* but all he found was *lumpy jaw (actinomycosis).* Evidently you had to know the name of your disease first—in which case, why bother looking it up? He thought through what he remembered of his high school biology course, and decided to check under *lymph gland.* The very phrase was reassuring; lymph glands swelled all the time. He had a couple in his neck that grew pecan sized anytime he developed a sniffle. But there were no lymph glands listed in the index, and it stopped him cold to see *lymphatic leukemia* and *lymphohematogenous tuberculosis.* He shut the book quickly and replaced it on the shelf.

Josiah had already opened the restaurant, and two helpers were busy chopping vegetables in the kitchen. A salesman in a plaid suit was trying to interest Josiah in some new product.

"But," Josiah kept saying. "But I don't think—" Josiah was so gawky and confused-looking—an emaciated giant in white, with his black and gray hair sticking out in frenzied tufts as if he'd grabbed handfuls in desperation—that Ezra felt a rush of love for him. He said, "Josiah, what's the problem?" and Josiah turned to him gratefully. "Uh, see, this gentleman here—"

"Murphy's the name. J. R. Murphy," said the salesman. "I sell soy sauce, private brand. I sell it by the case."

"We could never manage a case," said Ezra. "We hardly ever use it."

"You will, though," the salesman told him. "Soy sauce is the coming thing; better get it while you can. This here is the antidote for radiation."

"For what?"

"Nucular accidents! Atom bums! Just take a look at the facts: those folks in Hiroshima didn't get near as many side effects as expected. Want to know why? It was all that Japanese food with soy sauce. Plain old soy sauce. Keep a case of this around and you'll have no more worries over Three Mile Island."

"But I don't even like soy sauce."

"Who says you've got to like it?"

"Well, maybe just a few bottles . . ." Ezra said.

He wondered if there were some cryptic, cultish mark on his door that told all the crazy people he'd have trouble saying no.

He went to check on the dining room. Two waitresses were shaking out tablecloths and spreading them with a crisp, ripping sound. Josiah was lugging in bales of laundered napkins. There was always a moment, this early in the day, when Ezra found his restaurant disheartening. He was chilled by the empty tables, the looming, uncurtained windows, the bitter smell of last night's cigarettes. What kind of occupation was this? People gulped down his food without a thought, too busy courting or arguing or negotiating to notice what they ate; then they went home and forgot it. Nothing amounted to anything. And Ezra was a middle-aged man with his hair growing transparent at the back of his head; but here he was, where he'd been at twenty, living with his mother in a Calvert Street row house and reading himself to sleep with cookbooks. He had never married, never fathered children, and lost the one girl he had loved out of sheer fatalism, lack of force, a willing assumption of defeat. (*Let it be* was the theme that ran through his life. He was ruled by a dreamy mood of acceptance that was partly the source of all his happiness and partly his undoing.)

Josiah came to stand before him. "See my boots?" he asked.

Ezra surfaced and looked down at Josiah's boots. They poked from beneath the white uniform—gigantic, rubber-coated canvas boots that could weather a flood, a snowstorm, an avalanche.

"L. L. Bean," Josiah said.

"Ah."

L. L. Bean was where Josiah got his mystery gifts. Once or twice a year they arrived: a one-man tent; a goose-down sleeping bag; hunting shoes in his unwieldy, hard-to-find size; an olive-drab poncho that could see him through a monsoon; a pocket survival kit containing compass, flint, signal mirror, and metallic blanket. All this for a man who'd been born and reared in the city and seemed inclined to stay there. There was never any card or note of explanation. Josiah had written the company, but L. L. Bean replied that the donor preferred to stay anonymous. Ezra had spent hours helping Josiah think of possibilities. "Remember that old lady whose walk you used to shovel? Maybe it's her."

"She'd be dead by now, Ezra."

"Remember Molly Kane, with her wheelchair? You used to wheel her to Algebra One."

"But she said, 'Let go my chair, you big ree-tard!'"

"Maybe now she regrets it."

"Oh, no. Not her. Not Molly Kane."

"Maybe just someone you changed a tire for and never gave

276

it another thought. Someone you opened a door for. Maybe
. . . I don't know."

Ordinarily he enjoyed these speculations, but now,
looking down at Josiah's mammoth boots, he was struck by the
fact that even Josiah—lanky, buck-toothed, stammering
Josiah—had a human being all his own that he was linked to,
whether or not he knew that person's name, and lived in a
nest of gifts and secrets and special care that Ezra was excluded
from.

"*New Year's Day, nineteen-fourteen,*" Ezra read aloud. "*I hope
this little diary will not get lost as last year's did. I hope I will not
put anything foolish in it as I have been known to do before.*"

His mother hid a smile, unsuccessfully. What foolishness
could she have been up to so long ago? Ezra's eyes slipped down
the page to a line that had been crossed out. "There's something
here I can't read," he said.

"I never was known for my penmanship."

"No, I mean you scribbled over it with so many loops and
things—"

"Apple apple," his mother said.

"Excuse me?"

"That's what we wrote over words that we wanted kept
secret. *Appleappleapple* all joined together, so no one could
guess what was written underneath."

"Well, it certainly worked," Ezra said.

"Move on," his mother told him.

"Oh. Um . . . *put a flaxseed poultice on my finger . . .
started some gartlets of pale pink ribbon . . . popped some popcorn and buttered half, made cracker-jack of the rest . . .*"

His mother sighed. Ezra skimmed several pages in silence.

How plotless real life was! In novels, events led up to something. In his mother's diaries, they flitted past with no apparent
direction. Frank brought her perfumed blotters and a box of
"cocoa-nut" candy; Roy paid quite a call and couldn't seem to

tear himself away; Burt Tansy took her to the comic opera and afterward presented her with a folio of the songs; but none of these people was ever mentioned again. Someone named Arthur wrote her a letter that was *the softest thing*, she said. *I didn't know he could be so silly. It was all in form though and I am not very mad.* A certain Clark Allensby promised to visit and did not; *I suppose it is all for the best*, she said, *but I can't understand his actions as to-morrow he is leaving.* And while she was stretching the curtains, she said, *the darkie announced a young man come to visit. I looked like a freak but went in anyhow and there sat Hugh McKinley. He was heading for the seed store so just HAPPENED to stop by, and staid some while* . . .

Ezra began to see that for his mother (or for the young girl she had been), there was a plot, after all. She had imagined a perfectly wonderful plot—a significance to every chance meeting, the possibility of whirlwind courtships, grand white weddings, flawless bliss forever after. *James Wrayson came to call most shockingly late,* she wrote. *Stole my picture off the piano and put it in his pocket. Acted too comical for words. I'm sure I don't know what will come of this.*

Well, nothing had come of it. Nothing came of anything. She married a salesman for the Tanner Corporation and he left her and never came back. "Ezra? Why aren't you reading to me?" his mother asked.

"I'm tired," he said.

He took her to an afternoon ball game. In her old age, she had become a great Orioles fan. She would listen on the radio if she couldn't attend in person, even staying up past her bedtime if the game went into extra innings. Baseball was the only sport that made sense, she said: clear as Parcheesi, clever as chess. She looked pleased with herself for thinking of this, but Ezra suspected that it had something in common too with those soap operas she enjoyed. Certainly she viewed each game as a drama, and fretted over the gossip that Ezra culled for her from the sports pages—players' injuries, rivalries, slumps, mournful tales of young rookies so nervous they flubbed their only chances. She liked to think of the Orioles as poverty-stricken and virtuous, unable to simply *buy* their talent as richer teams did. Players' looks mattered to her as deeply as if they were movie stars: Ken Singleton's high, shining cheekbones, as described by one of her granddaughters, sent her into a little trance of admiration. She liked to hear how Al Bumbry wiggled his bat so jauntily before a hit; how Stanhouse drove people crazy delaying on the mound. She wished Doug De Cinces would shave off his mustache and Kiko Garcia would get himself a haircut. She thought Earl Weaver was not fatherly enough to be a proper manager and often, when he replaced some poor sad pitcher who'd barely had a chance, she would speak severely into the radio, calling him "Merle Beaver" for spite and spitting out her words. "Just because he grows his own tomatoes," she said, "doesn't necessarily mean a person has a heart."

Sometimes Ezra would quote her to his friends at the restaurant, and halfway through a sentence he would think, Why, I'm making her out to be a . . . character; and all he'd said would feel like a lie, although of course it had happened. The fact was that she was a very strong woman (even a frightening one, in his childhood), and she might have shrunk and aged but her true, interior self was still enormous, larger than life, powerful. Overwhelming.

They got to the stadium early so his mother could walk at her own pace, which was so slow and halting that by the time they were settled, the lineup was already being announced. Their seats were good ones, close to home plate. His mother sank down gratefully but then had to stand, almost at once, for the national anthem. For *two* national anthems; the other team was Toronto. Halfway through the second song, Ezra noticed that his mother's knees were trembling. "Do you want to sit down?" he asked her. She shook her head. It was a very hot day but her arm, when he took hold of it, was cool and almost unnaturally dry, as if filmed with powder.

How clear a green the grass was! He could see his mother's point: precise and level and brightly colored, the playing field did have the look of a board game. Players stood about idly swinging their arms. Toronto's batter hit a high fly ball and the center fielder plucked it from the sky with ease, almost absentmindedly. "Well!" said Ezra. "That was quick. First out in no time."

There was a knack to his commentary. He informed her without appearing to, as if he were making small talk. "Gosh. Look at that change-up." And "Call that a ball? Skimmed right past his knees. Call that a ball?" His mother listened, face uplifted and receptive, like someone at a concert.

What did she get out of this? She'd have followed more closely, he thought, if she had stayed at home beside her radio. (And she'd never *bring* a radio; she worried people might think it was a hearing aid.) He supposed she liked the atmosphere, the cheering and excitement and the smell of popcorn. She even let him buy her a Styrofoam cup of beer, which was allowed to grow warm after one sip; and when the bugle sounded she called, "Charge," very softly, with an embarrassed little half-smile curling her lips. Three men were getting drunk behind her—booing and whistling and shouting insults to passing girls—but Ezra's mother stayed untroubled, facing forward. "When you come in person," she told Ezra, "you direct your own focus, you know? The TV or the radio men, they might focus on the pitcher when you want to see what first base is doing; and you don't have any choice but to accept it."

A batter swung a a low ball and connected, and Ezra (eyes in every direction) saw how the field came instantaneously alive, with each man following his appointed course. The short-stop, as if strung on rubber bands, sprang upward without a second's preparation and caught the ball; the outfield closed in like a kaleidoscope; the second-base runner pivoted and the shortstop tagged him out. "Yo, Garcia!" a drunk yelled behind them, in that gravelly, raucous voice that some men adopt in ball parks; and he sloshed cold beer down the back of Ezra's neck. "Well . . ." Ezra said to his mother. But he couldn't think how to encompass all that had happened, so finally he said, "We're up, it looks like."

She didn't answer. He turned to her and found her caving in on herself, her head falling forward, the Styrofoam cup slipping from her fingers. "Mother? Mother!" Everyone around him rose and milled and fussed. "Give her air," they told him, and then somehow they had her stretched out on her back, lying where their feet had been. Her face was paper white, immobile, like a crumpled rock. One of the drunks stepped forward to smooth her skirt decorously over her knees, and another stroked her hair off her forehead. "She'll be all right," he told Ezra. "Don't worry. It's only the heat. Folks, make room! Let her breathe!"

Ezra's mother opened her eyes. The air was bright as knife blades, shimmering with a brassy, hard light, but she didn't even squint; and for the first time Ezra fully understood that she was blind. It seemed that before, he hadn't taken it in. He reeled back, squatting at the feet of strangers, and imagined having to stay here forever: the two of them, helpless, flattened beneath the glaring summer sky.

That night he dreamed he was walking among the tables in his restaurant. A long-time customer, Mr. Rosen, was dithering over the menu. "What do you recommend?" he asked Ezra. "I see you've got your stroganoff, but I don't know, that's a little heavy. I mean I'm not so very hungry, just peckish, got a little weight on my stomach right here beneath my rib cage, know what I mean? What do you think might be good for that? What had I ought to eat?"

This was how Mr. Rosen behaved in real life, as well, and Ezra expected it and always responded kindly and solicitously.

But in the dream, he was overtaken by a most untypical panic. "I have nothing! Nothing!" he cried. "I don't know what you want! I don't have anything! Stop asking!" And he wrung his hands at the thought of his empty, gleaming refrigerator and idle stove.

He woke sweating, tangled in damp sheets. There was a certain white quality to the darkness that made him believe it was close to dawn. He climbed out of bed, hitching up his pajama bottoms, and went downstairs and poured a glass of milk. Then he wandered into the living room for a magazine, but the only ones he found were months old. Finally he settled on the rug beside his mother's desk and opened the bottom drawer.

A recipe for marmalade cake: *From the kitchen of* . . . with no name filled in. Someone's diploma, rolled and secured with a draggled blue ribbon. A clipping from a newspaper: *Bristlecone pines, in times of stress, hoard all their life in a single streak and allow the rest to die*. A photo of his sister in an evening dress with gardenias looped around her wrist. A diary for 1909, with a violet pressed between its pages. *Washed my yellow gown, made salt-rising bread, played Basket Ball*, he read. *Bought a hat shape at Warner's and trimmed it with green grosgrain. Preserved tomatoes. Went to Marching Drill. Learned progressive jackstraws*.

Her vitality hummed in the room around him. She was forever doing something to her "waists," which Ezra assumed to be blouses. Embroidering waists or mending waists or buying goods for a waist or sewing fresh braid on a waist, putting insertion on a waist, ripping insertion *off* a waist, tucking her red plaid waist until the tucker got out of fix, attaching new sleeves to a waist—even, for one entire week, attending a course called "Fashioning the Shirtwaist." She pressed a bodice, sewed a corset cover, darned her stockings, altered a girdle, stitched a comforter, monogrammed a handkerchief, cut outing flannel for skirts. (Yet in all the time he'd known her, Ezra had never seen her so much as hem a dish towel.) She went to hear a lecture entitled "Thunder Tones from the Guillotine." She pestered the vet about Prince's ailment—an injured stifle, whatever that was. She sold tickets to socials, amateur theatricals, and Mission Society picnics. She paid a call on her uncle but found his door double-locked and only a parlor window open.

In Ezra's slumbering, motionless household, the loudest sound came from fifteen-year-old Pearl, hitching up her underskirts to clamber through that long-ago window.

Daily, in various bookstores, he proceeded from the Merck Manual to other books, simpler to use, intended for laymen. Several were indexed by symptoms, including *lump*. He found that his lump could indeed be a lymph node—a temporary swelling in reaction to some minor infection. Or it could also be a hernia. Or it could be something worse. *Consult your doctor,* he read. But he didn't. Every morning, still in his pajamas, he tested the lump with his fingers and resolved to call Dr. Vincent, but later he would change his mind. Suppose it did turn out to be cancer: why would he want to endure those treatments—the radiation and the toxic drugs? Better just to die.

He noticed that he thought of dying as a kind of adventure, something new that he hadn't yet experienced. Like an unusual vacation trip.

His sister, Jenny, stopped by with her children. It was a Wednesday, her morning off. She took over the house with no trouble at all. "Where's your ironing? Give me your ironing," she said, and "What do you need in the way of shopping?" and "Quinn, get down from there." She had so much energy; she spent herself with such recklessness. In her worn-looking clothes, run-down shoes, with her dark hair lifting behind her, she flew around the living room. "I think you should buy an air-conditioner, Mother. Have you heard the latest pollution count? For someone in your state of health . . ."

Her mother, bleakly speechless, withstood this storm of

words and then lifted one white hand. "Come closer so I can see your hair," she said.

Jenny came closer and submitted to her touch. Her mother stroked her hair with a dissatisfied expression on her face. "I don't know why you can't take better care of your looks," she said. "How long since you've been to a beauty parlor?"

"I'm a busy woman, Mother."

"How much time would you need for a haircut? And you're not wearing makeup, are you. Are you? In this light, it's hard to tell. Oh, Jenny. What must your husband think? He'll think you're not trying. You've let yourself go. I expect I could pass you on the street and not know you."

Her favorite expression, it seemed to Ezra: I wouldn't know you if I saw you on the street. She used it when referring to Jenny's poor grooming, to Cody's sparse visits, to Ezra's tendency to put on weight. Ezra caught a sudden glimpse of a wide, vacant sidewalk and his various family members strolling down it, their faces averted from one another.

Jenny's children ambled through the house, looking bored and disgusted. The baby chewed on a curtain pull. Jane, the nine-year-old, perched on Ezra's knee as casually as if he were a piece of furniture. She smelled of crayons and peanut butter— homely smells that warmed his heart. "What are you fixing in your restaurant tonight?" she asked.

"Cold things. Salads. Soups."

"Soups are hot," she said.

"Not necessarily."

"Oh."

She paused, perhaps to store this information in some tidy filing cabinet inside her head. Ezra was touched by her willingness to adjust—by her amiable adaptability. Was it possible, he sometimes wondered, that children *humored* grown-ups? If grown-ups insisted on toilet training, on *please* and *thank you*—well, all right, since it seemed to mean so much to them. It wasn't important enough to argue about. This is a transitive

284

verb, some grown-up would say, and the children would go along with it; though to them it was immaterial, frankly. Transitive, intransitive, who cared? What difference did it make? It was all a foreign language anyhow.

"Maybe you could invite me to your restaurant for supper," Jane told Ezra.

"I'd be delighted to invite you for supper."

"Maybe I could bring a friend."

"Certainly."

"I'll bring Barbie."

"That would be wonderful," Ezra said.

"You bring a friend, too."

"All my friends work in the restaurant."

"Don't you ever date?"

"Of course I date."

"I don't mean just some of those lady cooks you pal around with."

"Oh, I've dated in my time."

She filed that away also.

Jenny was criticizing their mother's doctor. She said he was too old, too old-fashioned—too general, she said. "You need a good internist. I happen to know a man on—"

"I've been going to Dr. Vincent as long as I've lived in Baltimore," her mother said.

"What's that got to do with it?"

"We don't all just change for change's sake."

Jenny rolled her eyes at Ezra.

Ezra said, "Maybe *you* could be her doctor."

"I'm her relative, Ezra."

"So much the better," Ezra said.

"Besides, my field is pediatrics."

"Jenny," said Ezra. "What would you say—"

He stopped. Jenny raised her eyebrows.

"What would you say is your patients' most common disease?"

"Mother-itis," she told him.

"Oh."

"Why do you ask?"

"It's not, um, cancer or anything."

"Why do you ask?" she said again.

He only shrugged.

After she'd collected the ironing, and made a shopping list, and rounded up the children, she said that she had to be off. She brushed her cheek against her mother's and patted Ezra's arm. "I'll walk you to the car," he said.

"Never mind."

He walked her anyway, relieving her of the laundry bag while she carried the baby astride her hip. They passed the mailman. He was bent so low to the ground that he didn't even notice them.

Out by the car, Ezra said, "I've got this lump."

"Oh?" said Jenny. "Where?"

He touched his groin. "In the morning it starts out small," he said, "but by evening it's so big, it's like a rock of something in my trouser pocket. I'm wondering if it's, you know. Cancer."

"It's not cancer. More likely a hernia, from the sound of it," she said. "Go see a doctor." She got in the car and buckled the baby into her carrier. Then she leaned out the open window. "Do I have all the children?" she asked.

"Yes."

She waved and drove off.

Back in the house, his mother was hovering at the window exactly as if she could see. "That girl has too big a family," she said. "I suppose her looks must be ruined by now."

"No, I haven't noticed it."

"And her hair. Honestly. Ezra, tell me the truth," she said. "How does Jenny seem to you?"

"Oh, the same as always."

"I mean, don't you think she's let herself go? What about what she was wearing, for instance?"

He tried to remember. It was something faded, but perfectly acceptable, he guessed. Was it blue? Gray? He tried to picture her hairdo, the style of her shoes, but only came up with the chiseled lines that had always, even in her girlhood, encircled her neck—rings of lines that gave her a lush look. For some reason, those lines made him sad now, and so did Jenny's olive hands with the ragged, oval fingernails, and the crinkles at the corners of her eyes, and the news that his life would, after all, go on and on and on.

"*February sixth, nineteen-ten,*" Ezra read aloud. "*I baked a few Scottish Fancies but they wouldn't do to take to a tea.*"

His mother, listening intently, thought that over a while. Then she made her gesture of dismissal and started rocking again in her rocker.

"*I hitched up Prince and rode downtown for brown silk gloves and an ice bag. Then got out my hat frames and washed my straw hat. For supper fixed a batch of—*"

"Move on," his mother said.

He riffled through the pages, glimpsing *buttonhole stitch* and *watermelon social* and *set of fine furs for* $22.50. "Early this morning," he read to his mother, "*I went out behind the house to weed. Was kneeling in the dirt by the stable with my pinafore a mess and the perspiration rolling down my back, wiped my face on my sleeve, reached for the trowel, and all at once thought, Why I believe that at just this moment I am absolutely happy.*"

His mother stopped rocking and grew very still.

"*The Bedloe girl's piano scales were floating out her window,*" he read, "*and a bottle fly was buzzing in the grass, and I saw that I was kneeling on such a beautiful green little planet. I don't care what else might come about, I have had this moment. It belongs to me.*"

That was the end of the entry. He fell silent.

"Thank you, Ezra," his mother said. "There's no need to read any more."

Then she fumbled up from her chair, and let him lead her to the kitchen for lunch. He guided her gently, inch by inch. It seemed to him that he had to be very careful with her. They were traversing the curve of the earth, small and steadfast, surrounded by companions: Jenny flying past with her children, the drunks at the stadium sobering the instant their help was needed, the baseball players obediently springing upward in the sunlight, and Josiah connected to his unknown gift giver as deeply, and as mysteriously, as Ezra himself was connected to this woman beside him.

10

Dinner at the Homesick Restaurant

When Pearl Tull died, Cody was off on a goose hunt and couldn't be reached for two days. He and Luke were staying in a cabin owned by his business partner. It didn't have a telephone, and the roads were little more than logging trails.

Late Sunday, when they returned, Ruth came out to the driveway. The night was chilly, and she wore no sweater but hugged herself as she walked toward the car, her white, freckled face oddly set and her faded red hair standing up in the wind. That was how Cody guessed something was wrong. Ruth hated cold weather, and ordinarily would have waited inside the house.

"It's bad news," she said. "I'm sorry."

"What happened?"

"Your mother's passed away."

"Grandma *died?*" asked Luke, as if correcting her.

Ruth kissed Luke's cheek but kept her eyes on Cody, maybe trying to gauge the damage. Cody himself, wearily closing the car door behind him, was uncertain of the damage. His mother had been a difficult woman, of course. But even so . . .

"She died in her sleep, early yesterday," Ruth said. She took Cody's hand in both of hers and gripped it, tightly, so that the pain he felt right then was purely physical. He stood for a while, allowing her; then he gently pulled away and went to open the car trunk.

They had not bagged any geese—the hunt had been a lame excuse, really, to spend some time with Luke, who was now a senior in high school and would not be around for much longer. All Cody had to unload was the rifles in their canvas cases and a duffel bag. Luke brought the ice chest. They walked toward the house in silence. Cody had still not responded.

"The funeral's tomorrow at eleven," said Ruth. "I told Ezra we'd be there in the morning."

"How is he taking it?" Cody asked.

"He sounded all right."

Inside the front door, Cody set down the duffel bag and propped the rifles against the wall. He decided that he felt not so much sad as heavy. Although he was lean bodied, still in good shape, he imagined that he had suddenly sunk in on himself and grown denser. His eyes were weighty and dry, and his step seemed too solid for the narrow, polished floorboards in the hall.

"Well, Luke," he said.

Luke seemed dazed, or perhaps just sleepy. He squinted palely under the bright light.

"Do you want to go to the funeral?" Cody asked him.

"Sure, I guess," said Luke.

"You wouldn't have to."

"I don't mind."

"Of course he's going," said Ruth. "He's her grandson."

"That doesn't obligate him," Cody told her.

"Of course it obligates him."

This was where they differed. They could have argued about it all night, except that Cody was so tired.

For their journey south, Cody drove Ruth's car because his own was still splattered with mud from the goose hunt. He supposed

290

they would have to ride in some shiny, formal funeral procession. But when he happened to mention this to Ruth, halfway down the turnpike, she told him that Ezra had said their mother had requested cremation. ("Golly," Luke breathed.) There would only be the service, therefore—no cemetery trip and no burial. "Very sensible," Cody said. He thought of the tidy framework of his mother's bones, the crinkly bun on the back of her head. Did that fierce little figure exist any more? Was it already ashes? "Ah, God, it's barbaric, however you look at it," he told Ruth.

"What, cremation?" she asked.

"Death."

They sped along—Cody in his finest gray suit, Ruth in stiff black beside him. Luke sat in the rear, gazing out the side window. They were traveling the Beltway now, approaching Baltimore. They passed trees ablaze with red and yellow leaves and shopping malls full of ordinary, Monday morning traffic. "When I was a boy, this was country," Cody said to Luke.

"You told me."

"Baltimore was nothing but a little harbor town."

There was no answer. Cody searched for Luke in the rearview mirror. "Hey," he said. "You want to drive the rest of the way?"

"No, that's all right."

"Really. You want to?"

"Let him be," Ruth whispered.

"What?"

"He's upset."

"What about?"

"Your mother, Cody. You know he always felt close to her."

Cody couldn't figure how anyone could feel close to his mother—not counting Ezra, who was thought by some to be a saint. He checked Luke's face in the mirror again, but what could you tell from that impassive stare? "Hell," he said to

Ruth, "all I asked was did he want to drive."

The city seemed even more ruined than usual, tumbling under a wan, blue sky. "Look at there," Cody said. "Linsey's Candy and Tobacco. They sold cigarettes to minors. Bobbie Jo's Barbecue. And there's my old school."

On Calvert Street, the row houses stood in two endless lines. "I don't see how you knew which one was home," Luke had told him once, and Cody had been amazed. Oh, if you lived here you knew. They weren't alike at all, not really. One had dozens of roses struggling in its tiny front yard, another an illuminated madonna glowing night and day in the parlor window. Some had their trim painted in astonishing colors, assertively, like people with their chins thrust out. The fact that they were *attached* didn't mean a thing.

He parked in front of his mother's house. He slid from the car and stretched, waiting for Ruth and Luke.

By now, Pearl would have been out the door and halfway down the steps, reaching for the three of them with those eager, itchy fingers of hers.

"Is that your sister's car?" Ruth asked him.

"I don't know what kind of car she drives."

They climbed the steps. Ruth had her hand hooked in the back of Luke's belt. He was too tall for her to cup the nape of his neck, as she used to do.

When Cody first left home, he would knock when he returned for a visit. It was a deliberate, planned act; it was an insult to his mother. She had known that and objected. "Can't you walk straight in? Do you have to act like company?" "But company is what I am," he'd said. She had started outwitting him; she had lain in wait, rushing to meet him at the very first sound of his shoes on the sidewalk. (So it was, perhaps, not solely love that had sent her plunging down the steps.) Now, crossing the porch, Cody didn't know whether to knock or just open the door. Well, he supposed this house belonged to Ezra now. He knocked.

Ezra looked sad and exhausted, loosely filling a lightweight khaki suit that only he would have thought appropriate. As always, he seemed whiskerless, boy faced. There was a space between his collar and the knot of his tie. A handkerchief bunched messily out of his jacket pocket. "Cody. Come in," he said. He touched Cody's arm in that tentative way he had—something more than a handshake, less than a hug. "Ruth? Luke? We were starting to worry about you."

From the gloomy depths of the house, Jenny stepped forward to kiss everyone. She smelled of some complicated perfume but had her usual hastily assembled look—her tailored coat unbuttoned, her dark hair rough and tossed. Her husband ambled behind her, fat and bearded, good-natured. He clapped Cody on the shoulder. "Nice to see you. Too bad about your mother."

"Thank you, Joe."

"We're supposed to be starting for the church this very minute," Jenny said. "We have to leave early because we're picking up some of the children on the way."

"*I'm* all set," Cody said.

Ezra asked, "But don't you want coffee first?"

"No, no, let's get going."

"See," Ezra said, "I had planned on coffee and pastries before we started out. I'd assumed you'd be coming earlier."

"We've already had breakfast," Cody told him.

"But everything's on the table."

Cody felt his old, familiar irritation beginning. "Ezra—" he said.

"That was thoughtful of you," Ruth told Ezra, "but really, we're fine, and we wouldn't want to hold people up."

Ezra checked his watch. He glanced behind him, toward the dining room. "It's only ten-fifteen," he said. He walked over to a front window and lifted the curtain.

Now that it was apparent he had something on his mind, the others stood waiting. (He could be maddeningly slow, and all the slower if pushed.)

"It's like this," he said finally.

He coughed.

"I was kind of expecting Dad," he said.

There was a blank, flat pause.

"Who?" Cody asked.

"Our father."

"But how would he know?"

"Well, ah, I invited him."

"Ezra, for God's sake," Cody said.

"It wasn't *my* idea," Ezra said. "It was Mother's. She talked about it when she got so sick. She said, 'Look in my address book. Ask everybody in it to my funeral.' I wondered who she meant, at first. You know she never wrote anyone, and most of her relatives are dead. But as soon as I opened the address book I saw it: Beck Tull. I didn't even realize she knew where he had run off to."

"He wrote her; that's how she knew," Cody said.

"He did?"

"From time to time he sent these letters, boasting, bragging. *Doing fine . . . expecting a raise . . .* I peeked inside when Mother wasn't looking."

"I never even guessed," said Ezra.

"What difference would it have made?"

"Oh, I don't know . . ."

"He ditched us," Cody said, "when we were kids. What do you care about him now?"

"Well, I don't," said Ezra. And Cody, who had so often been exasperated by Ezra's soft heart, saw that in this case, it was true: he really didn't care. He looked directly at Cody with his peculiarly clear, light-filled eyes, and he said, "It was Mother who asked; not me. All I did was call him up and say, 'This is Ezra. Mother has died and we're holding her funeral Monday at eleven.'"

"That was *all*?" Cody said.

"Well, and then I told him he could stop by the house first, if he got here early."

"But you didn't ask, 'How are you?' or 'Where've you been?' or 'Why'd you go?' "

"I just said, 'This is Ezra. Mother has died and—'"

Cody laughed.

"At any rate," Jenny said, "it doesn't seem he's coming."

"No," said Cody, "but think about it. I mean, don't you get it? First he leaves and Mother pretends he hasn't. Out of pride, or spite, or *some*thing, she never says a word about it, makes believe to all of us that he's only on a business trip. A thirty-five-year business trip. Then Ezra calls him on the phone and does the very same thing. 'This is Ezra,' he says, as if he'd seen Dad just yesterday—"

Jenny said, "Can we get started now? My children will be freezing to death."

"Oh, surely," Ruth told her. "Cody, honey, her children are waiting on us."

"Mother would have done that, just exactly," Cody said. "If Dad had walked in she would have said, 'Ah, yes, there you are. Can you tell me if my slip is showing?'"

Joe gave a little bark of laughter. Ezra smiled, but his eyes filmed over with tears. "That's true," he said. "She would have. You know? She really would have."

"Fine, then, she would have," Jenny said. "Shall we go?"

She had been so young when their father left, anyhow. She claimed to have forgotten all about him.

At the funeral, the minister, who had never met their mother, delivered a eulogy so vague, so general, so universally applicable that Cody thought of that parlor game where people fill in words at random and then giggle hysterically at the story that results. Pearl Tull, the minister said, was a devoted wife and loving mother and a pillar of the community. She had lived a long, full life and died in the bosom of her family, who grieved for her but took comfort in knowing that she'd gone to a far finer place.

It slipped the minister's mind, or perhaps he hadn't heard, that she hadn't been anyone's wife for over a third of a century; that she'd been a frantic, angry, sometimes terrifying mother; and that she'd never shown the faintest interest in her community but dwelt in it like a visitor from a superior neighborhood, always wearing her hat when out walking, keeping her doors tightly shut when at home. That her life had been very long indeed but never full; *stunted* was more like it. Or crabbed. Or . . . what was the word Cody wanted? Espaliered. Twisted and flattened to the wall—all the more so as she'd aged and wizened, lost her sight, and grown to lean too heavily on Ezra. That she was not at all religious, hadn't set foot in this church for decades; and though in certain wistful moods she might have mentioned the possibility of paradise, Cody didn't take much comfort in the notion of her residing there, fidgeting and finding fault and stirring up dissatisfactions.

Cody sat in the right front pew, the picture of a bereaved and dutiful son. But skeptical thoughts flowed through his head so loudly that he almost believed they might be heard by the congregation. He was back to his boyhood, it seemed, fearing that his mother could read his mind as unhesitatingly as she read the inner temperature of a roasting hen by giving its thigh a single, contemptuous pinch. He glanced sideways at Ruth, but she was listening to the minister.

The minister anounced the closing hymn, which Pearl had requested in her funeral instructions: "We'll Understand It All By and By." Raising his long, boneless face to lead the singing, Reverend Thurman did appear bewildered—perhaps less by the Lord's mysterious ways than by the unresponsive nature of this group of mourners. Most were just staring into open hymnbooks, following each stanza silently. And there were so few of them: a couple of Ezra's co-workers, some surly teen-aged grandchildren sulking in scattered pews, and five or six anonymous old people, who were probably there as church members but gave the impression of having wandered in off the streets for shelter, dragging their string-handled shopping bags.

When the service was finished, the minister descended from the pulpit and stopped to offer Cody, as firstborn, a handshake and condolences. "All my sympathy . . . know what a loss . . ."

"Thank you," said Cody, and he and Ruth and the minister proceeded down the aisle. Jenny and Joe followed, and last came Ezra, blowing his nose. By rights the grandchildren should have risen too, but if they had there would have been hardly any guests remaining.

Outside, the cold was a relief, and Cody was grateful for the lumbering noise of the traffic in the street. He stood between Jenny and Ruth and accepted the murmurs of strangers. "Beautiful service," they told him.

"Thank you," he said.

He heard a woman say to Ezra, over by the church doorway, "I'm so sorry for your trouble," and Ezra said, kindly, "Oh, that's all right"—although for Ezra alone, of the three of them, this death was clearly *not* all right. What would he fill his life with now? He had been his mother's eyes. Lately, he had been her hands and feet as well. Now that she was gone he would come home every night and . . . do what? What would he do? Just sit on the couch by himself, Cody pictured; or lie on his bed, fully dressed, staring into the swarming, brownish air above his bed.

Jenny said, "Did Ezra tell you we're meeting at his restaurant afterward?"

Cody groaned. He shook an old man's hand and said to Jenny, "I knew it. I just knew it." Hadn't he told Ruth, in fact? In the car coming down, he'd said, "Oh, God, I suppose there'll be one of those dinners. We'll have to have one of those eternal family dinners at Ezra's restaurant."

"He's probably too upset," Ruth said. "I doubt he'd give a dinner now."

297

This showed she didn't know Ezra as well as she'd always imagined. Certainly he would give a dinner. Any excuse would do—wedding or engagement or nephew's name on the honor roll. "Dinner at the Homesick Restaurant! Everyone in the family! Just a cozy family gathering"—and he'd rub his hands together in that annoying way he had. He no doubt had his staff at work even this moment, preparing the . . . what were they called? The funeral baked meats. Cody sighed. But he suspected they would have to attend.

The old man must have spoken; he was waiting for Cody to answer. He tilted his flushed, tight-skinned face beneath an elaborate plume of silver hair that let the light shine through. "Thank you," Cody said. Evidently, this was the wrong response. The old man made some disappointed adjustment to his mouth. "Um . . . " said Cody.

"I said," the old man told him, "I said, 'Cody? Do you know me?'"

Cody knew him.

It shouldn't have taken him so long. There were clues he should have picked up at once: that fan-shaped pompadour, still thick and sharply crimped; the brilliant blue of his eyes; the gangsterish air of his pinstriped, ill-fitting navy blue suit.

"Yes," the old man said, with a triumphant nod. "It's your father speaking, Cody."

Cody said to Jenny, "I'm not sure if Ezra remembered to set a place for Dad."

"What?" Jenny said. She looked at Beck Tull. "Oh," she said.

"At the restaurant. Did he remember?"

"Oh, well, probably," she said.

"Nothing fancy," Cody told Beck.

Beck gaped at him.

"Just a light repast at the Homesick."

"What are you talking about?" Beck asked.

"Dinner afterward, of course, at the Homesick Restaurant."

Beck passed a hand across his forehead. He said, "Is this here Jenny?"

"Yes," Jenny told him.

"Jenny, last time I set eyes on you you were just about eight years old," said Beck. "Was it eight? Or nine. Your favorite song was 'Mairzy Doats.' You babbled that thing night and day."

"Oh, yes," Jenny said distantly. "And little lambs eat ivy."

Beck, who had drawn a breath to go on speaking, paused and shut his mouth.

"*You* remember Ruth," said Cody.

"Ruth?"

"My wife."

"Why should I remember her? I've been away! I haven't been here!"

Ruth stepped forward to offer her hand. "So Cody's married," said Beck. "Fancy that. Any children?"

"Well, Luke, of course," Cody said.

"I'm a grandfather!" He turned to Jenny. "How about you? Are you married?"

"Yes, but he's left to pick up the little ones," Jenny said. She waved goodbye to somebody.

"And Ezra?" Beck asked. "Where's Ezra?"

"Over there by the steps," Cody said.

"Ah."

Beck set off jauntily, running a hand through his crest of hair. Jenny and Cody gazed after him.

"If I just saw him on the street," Jenny said, "I would have passed him by."

"We *are* just seeing him on the street," Cody told her.

"Well. Yes."

They watched Beck arrive before Ezra with a bounce, like a child presenting some accomplishment. Ezra bent his head courteously to hear Beck's words, then gave him a mild smile and shook his hand.

"Imagine!" they heard Beck say. "Look at you! Both my sons are bigger than I am."

"Dinner is at my restaurant," Ezra told him calmly.

Beck's expression faltered once again, but recovered itself. "Wonderful!" he said. He moved toward the teen-agers, who had got wind of what was going on and stood in a clump nearby—silent, staring, hostile as usual. Beck seemed not to notice. "I'm your grandpa," he told them. "Your Grandpa Tull. Ever heard of me?" Probably they hadn't, unless they'd thought to inquire. He moved down the line, beaming. "I'm your long-lost grandpa. And you are—? What a handsome young fellow!"

He pumped the hand of the tallest teen-ager, who unfortunately was not a grandson at all but one of Ezra's salad boys.

Cody and Ruth and Jenny led the way to the restaurant on foot. The others lagged behind untidily. The first group turned on to St. Paul Street and passed various bustling little buildings—a dry cleaner's and a drugstore and a florist. All the other pedestrians were black; most held jangling radios to their ears, so that scraps of songs about love and jealousy and hardhearted women kept approaching and fading away. Then Ezra's wooden sign swung overhead, and the three of them climbed the steps and walked in.

In the chilly light from the windows, the restaurant seemed glaringly empty. One long table was covered with white linen, set with crystal and china. Thirteen places, Cody counted; for Jenny's Joe would be bringing more children, those too small to have sat through the service. A sweet-faced, plump waitress in a calico smock was drawing up a high chair for the baby. When she saw them come in, she stopped to give Jenny a hug. "I'm so sorry for your trouble," she said. "You and all your family, hear?"

"Thank you, Mrs. Potter," Jenny said. "Do you know my

brother Cody? And this is Ruth, his wife."

Mrs. Potter clicked her tongue. "It's a terrible day for you," she said.

Cody turned toward the door in time to see Beck and Ezra enter, trailed by teen-agers. Ezra had obviously relaxed and grown talkative; he never could be cool to anyone for long. "So I tore out that wall there . . ." he was saying.

"Very nice. Very classy," said Beck.

"Stripped down these floors . . ."

"I hope you don't serve that kind of food a fellow can't identify."

"Oh, no."

"A *mish*mash of food, one thing not separate from another."

"No, never," Ezra said.

Cody watched with interest. (Ezra very often served such food.) Ezra led Beck through the room, waving an arm here and there. "See, these tables can be moved together if anyone should . . . and this is the kitchen . . . and these are two of my cooks, Sam and Myron. They've come in especially for our dinner. At night I have three more: Josiah, Chenille, and Mohammad."

"Quite an operation," said Beck.

The others, meanwhile, hung around their table. No one took a seat. Cody's son, Luke, and Jenny's son Peter—both unnaturally formal in white shirts and ties—wrestled together in an aimless, self-conscious way, tossing hidden glances at Beck. Probably these children saw him as a brand-new chance—a fresh start, someone to appreciate them at last. Yet when they finally sat down, no one chose a place near Beck. It was shyness, maybe. Even Ezra settled some distance away. Since Joe and the younger ones had still not arrived, this meant that Beck found himself flanked by several empty chairs. He didn't seem to notice. Kinglike, he sat alone, folding his hands before his plate and beaming around at the others. A tracery of red veins, distinct as mapped rivers and tributaries, showed in his cheeks. "So," he said. "My son owns a fancy restaurant."

Ezra looked pleased and embarrassed.

"And my daughter's a doctor," said Beck. "But Cody? What about you?"

Cody said, "Why, *you* know: I'm an efficiency consultant."

"A, how's that?"

Cody didn't answer. Ezra said. "He checks out factories. He tells them how to do things more efficiently."

"Ah! A time-study man."

"He's one of the very best," said Ezra. "He's always getting written up in articles."

"Is that so. Well, I sure am proud of you, son."

Cody had a sudden intimation that tomorrow, it would be more than he could manage to drag himself off to work. His success had finally filled its purpose. Was this all he had been striving for—this one brief moment of respect flitting across his father's face?

"I often wondered about you, Cody," Beck said, leaning toward him. "I often thought about you after I went away."

"Oh?" said Cody, politely. "Have you been away?"

His father sat back.

"Anyhow," Ezra said. He cleared his throat. "Well. Dad. Are you still working for the Tanner Corporation?"

"No, no, I'm retired. Retired in sixty-five. They gave me a wonderful banquet and a sterling silver pen-and-pencil set. Forty-two years of service I put in."

Ruth murmured—an admiring, womanly sound. He turned to her and said, "To tell you the truth, I kind of miss it. Miss the contacts, miss the life . . . A salesman's life has a lot of action, know what I mean? Lot of activity. Oftentimes now it doesn't seem there's quite enough to keep me busy. But I do a bit of socializing, cardplaying. Got a few buddies at my hotel. Got a lady friend I see." He peeked around at the others from under his tufted eyebrows. "I bet you think I'm too old for such things," he said. "I know what you're thinking! But this is a really fine lady; she puts a lot of stock in me. And you understand I mean no disrespect to your mother, but now that she's gone and I'm free to remarry . . ."

Somehow, it had never occurred to Cody that his parents were still married. Jenny and Ezra, too, blinked and drew back slightly.

"Only trouble is this lady's daughter," Beck told them. "She's got this daughter, no-good daughter, thirty-five years old if she's a day but still residing at home. Eustacia Lee. No good whatsoever. Lost two fingers in a drill press years ago and never worked since, spent her compensation money on a snowmobile. I'm not too sure I want to live with her."

No one seemed able to think of any comment.

Then Joe arrived. He burst through the door, traveling in an envelope of fresh-smelling air, carrying the baby and towing a whole raft of children. Really there were only three, but it seemed like more; they were so chattery and jumbled. "Mrs. Nesbitt almost didn't let me out of school," and "You'll never guess what the baby ate," and "Phoebe had to stay in for being prejudiced in math." "Who's this?" a child asked, facing Beck.

"Your Grandpa Tull."

"Oh," she said, taking a seat. "Do us kids get wine?"

"Joe, I'd like you to meet my father," Jenny said.

"Really?" said Joe. "Gosh." But then he had to figure out the high-chair strap.

The last two children slipped into the empty chairs on either side of Beck. They twined their feet through the rungs, set pointy elbows on the table. Surrounded, Beck gazed first to his left and then to his right. "Will you look at this!" he said.

"Pardon?" Jenny asked.

"This group. This gathering. This . . . assemblage!"

"Oh," said Jenny, taking a bib from her purse. "Yes, it's quite a crowd."

"Eleven, twelve . . . thirteen . . . counting the baby, it's fourteen people!"

"There would have been fifteen, but Slevin's off at college," Jenny said.

Beck shook his head. Jenny tied the bib around the baby's neck.

"What we've got," said Beck, "is a . . . well, a crew. A whole crew."

Phoebe, who was religious, started loudly reciting a blessing. Mrs. Potter set a steaming bowl of soup before Beck. He sniffed it, looking doubtful.

"It's eggplant soup," Ezra told him.

"Ah, well, I don't believe . . ."

"Eggplant Soup Ursula. A recipe left behind by one of my very best cooks."

"On this day of death," Phoebe said, "the least some people could do is let a person pray in silence."

"She cooked by astrology," Ezra said. "I'd tell her, 'Let's have the endive salad tonight,' and she'd say, 'Nothing vinegary, the stars are wrong,' and up would come some dish I'd never thought of, something I would assume was a clear mistake, but it worked; it always worked. There might be something *to* this horoscope business, you know? But last summer the stars advised her to leave, and she left, and this place has never been the same."

"Tell us the secret ingredient," Jenny teased him.

"Who says there's a secret ingredient?"

"Isn't there always a secret ingredient? Some special, surprising trick that you'd only share with blood kin?"

"Well," said Ezra. "It's bananas."

"Aha."

"Without bananas, this soup is nothing."

"On this day of death," Phoebe said, "do we have to talk about food?"

"It is not a day of death," Jenny told her. "Use your napkin."

"The thing is," Beck said. He stopped. "What I mean to say," he said, "it looks like this is one of those great big, jolly, noisy, rambling . . . why, *families!*"

The grown-ups looked around the table. The children went on slurping soup. Beck, who so far hadn't even dipped his spoon in, sat forward earnestly. "A clan, I'm talking about," he said. "Like something on TV. Lots of cousins and uncles, jokes, reunions—"

"It's not really that way at all," Cody told him.

"How's that?"

"Don't let them mislead you. It's not the way it appears. Why, not more than two or three of these kids are even related to you. The rest are Joe's, by a previous wife. As for me, well, I haven't been with these people in years—couldn't tell you what that baby's name is. Is it a boy or a girl, by the way? Was I even informed of its birth? So don't count *me* in your clan. And Becky down there, at the end of the table—"

"Becky?" said Beck. "Does she happen to be named for me, by any chance?"

Cody stopped, with his mouth open. He turned to Jenny.

"No," said Jenny, wiping the baby's chin. "Her name's Rebecca."

"You think we're a family," Cody said, turning back. "You think we're some jolly, situation-comedy family when we're in particles, torn apart, torn all over the place, and our mother was a witch."

"Oh, Cody," Ezra said.

"A raving, shrieking, unpredictable witch," Cody told Beck. "She slammed us against the wall and called us scum and vipers, said she wished us dead, shook us till our teeth rattled, screamed in our faces. We never knew from one day to the next, was she all right? Was she not? The tiniest thing could set her off. 'I'm going to throw you through that window,' she used to tell me. 'I'll look out that window and laugh at your brains splashed all over the pavement.'"

The main course was set before them, on tiptoe, by Mrs. Potter and another woman who smiled steadily, as if determined not to hear. But nobody picked up his fork. The baby crooned softly to a mushroom button. The other children watched Cody with horrified, bleached faces, while the grown-ups seemed to be thinking of something else. They kept their eyes lowered. Even Beck did.

"It wasn't like that," Ezra said finally.

"You're going to deny it?" Cody asked him.

"No, but she wasn't *always* angry. Really she was angry very seldom, only a few times, widely spaced, that happened to stick in your mind."

Cody felt drained. He looked at his dinner and found pink-centered lamb and bright vegetables—a perfect arrangement of colors and textures, one of Ezra's masterpieces, but he couldn't take a bite.

"Think of the other side," Ezra told him. "Think of how she used to play Monopoly with us. Listened to Fred Allen with us. Sang that little song with you—what was the name of that song you two sang? *Ivy, sweet sweet Ivy* . . . and you'd do a little soft-shoe. The two of you would link arms and soft-shoe into the kitchen."

"Is that right!" said Beck. "*I* didn't remember Pearl could soft-shoe."

Mrs. Potter poured wine into Cody's glass. He set his fingers around the stem but then couldn't lift it. He was conscious of Ruth, to his right, watching him with concern.

Then Ezra said, "So! What do you think of this wine, Dad?"

"Oh, afraid I'm not much for wine, son," said Beck.

"This is a really good one."

"Little shot of bourbon is more my style," said Beck.

"And best of all's the dessert wine. They make it with these grapes that have suffered from a special kind of mold, you see—"

306

"Well, wait now," Beck said. "Mold?"

"You're going to love it."

"And what is this here whitish stuff?"

"It's kasha."

"I don't believe I've heard of that."

"You'll love it," Ezra said.

Beck shook his head, but he looked gratified, as if he liked to think that Ezra had traveled so far beyond him.

Then Cody pushed his plate away. "I've got this partner, Sloan," he said. "A bachelor all his life. He never married."

Everyone took on an exaggerated attentiveness—even the children.

"Last year," Cody said, "Sloan ran into some old girlfriend, a woman he'd known years ago, and she had her little daughter with her. They were celebrating the daughter's birthday. Sloan asked which birthday it was, just making conversation, and when the woman told him, something rang a bell. He calculated the dates, and he said, 'Why! My God! She must be mine!' The woman looked over at him, sort of vaguely, and then she collected her thoughts and said, 'Oh. Yes, she is, as a matter of fact.'"

They waited. Cody smiled and gave them a little salute, implying that they could go back to their food.

"Well. What a strange lady," Beck said finally.

"Not at all," Cody told him.

"You'd think she'd at least have—"

"What she was saying was, the man had nothing to do with them. He wasn't ever there, you see, so he didn't count. He wasn't part of the family."

Beck drew back sharply. His eyes no longer seemed so blue; they had darkened to a color nearer navy.

Then Joe said, "The baby!"

The baby was struggling soundlessly, convulsively, mouth open and face going purple. "She's strangling," Jenny said. Several people leapt up and a wineglass overturned. Joe was trying to pull the baby from the high chair, but Jenny stopped him. "Never mind that! Let me at her!" It seemed the tray was strapped in place and they couldn't get the baby out from under it. An older child started crying. Something crashed to the floor. Jenny punched the baby in the midriff and a mushroom button shot on to the table. The baby wailed and turned pink. Hiccuping, she was dragged from the high chair and placed on her mother's lap, where she settled down cheerfully and started pursuing a pea around the rim of Jenny's plate.

"Will I live to see them grown?" Jenny asked the others.

"He's gone," said Ezra.

They knew instantly whom he meant. Everyone looked toward Beck's chair. It was empty. His napkin was tossed aside, one corner dipping into his plate and soaking up gravy.

"Wait here," Ezra said.

They not only waited; they suspended talk, suspended movement, while Ezra rushed across the dining room and out the front door. There was a pause, during which even the baby said nothing. Then Ezra came back, running his fingers distractedly through his hair. "He's nowhere in sight," he said. "But it's only been a minute. We can catch him! Come on, all of you."

Still, no one moved.

"Please!" said Ezra. "Please. For once, I want this family to finish a meal together. Why, every dinner we've ever had, something has gone wrong. Someone has left in a huff, or in tears, everything's fallen apart . . . Come on! Everybody out, cover the area, track him down! We could gather back here when we find him and take up where we left off."

"Or," Cody pointed out, "we could finish the meal *without* him. That's always a possibility."

But it wasn't; even he could see that. One empty place at the table ruined everything. The chair itself, with its harp-shaped wooden back, had a desolate, reproachful look. Slowly, people rose. The children grouped around Ezra, who was issuing directives like a military strategist. "You and the little ones try Bushnell Street . . . rendezvous with Joe on Prima . . ." Then Ruth stood up too, to take the baby while Jenny put her coat on. They headed for the door. "Good hunting!" Cody called, and he tipped his chair back expansively and asked Mrs. Potter for another glass of wine.

Inwardly, though, he felt chastened. He thought of times in grade school when he'd teased some classmate to tears, taken things a little too far, and then looked around to find that all of his friends had stopped laughing. Wasn't there the same hollow silence in this dining room, among these sheeted tables? Mrs. Potter replaced the wine bottle upon a silver-rimmed coaster. She stepped back and folded her hands across her stomach.

"I believe I'll just go check on how they're doing," Cody told her.

Outside, the sky had deepened to a blue that was almost gaudy. A weak sun lit the tops of the buildings, and it didn't seem so cold. Cody stood with his hands at his hips, his feet spread wide—unperturbed, to all appearances—and looked up and down the street. One section of the search party was just disappearing around a corner: Joe and the teen-agers. A stately black woman with her head wrapped in bandannas had stopped to redistribute the contents of two grocery bags.

Cody took the alley to the right of the doorway, a narrow strip of concrete lined with old packing crates and garbage cans battered shapeless. He passed the restaurant's kitchen window, where an exhaust fan blew him with a memory of Ezra's lamb. He skirted a spindly, starved cat with a tail as matted as a worn-out bottle brush. The back of his neck took on that special alertness required on Baltimore streets, but he walked at an easy, sauntering pace with his hands in his trouser pockets.

"Always have a purpose," his father used to tell him. "Act like you're heading someplace purposeful, and none of the low-life will mess with you." He had also said, "Never trust a man who starts his sentences with 'Frankly,'" and "Nine tenths of a good sidearm pitch is in the flick of the wrist," and, "If you want to sell a person something, look off elsewhere as you're speaking, not straight into his eyes."

"All we have is each other," Ezra would say, justifying one of his everlasting dinners. "We've got to stick together; nobody else has the same past that we have." But in that meager handful of advice offered by Beck Tull—truly the sole advice Cody could remember from him—there didn't seem much of a past to build on. From the sound of it, you would imagine that the three of them shared only a purposeful appearance, a mistrust of frankness, a deft wrist, and an evasive gaze.

Cody suddenly longed for his son—for Luke's fair head and hunched shoulders. (He would rather die than desert a child of his. He had promised himself when he was a boy: anything but that.) He thought back to their goose hunt, where they hadn't had much to say to each other; they had been shy and stand-offish together. He wondered whether Sloan would lend him the cabin again next weekend, so they could give it another try.

He came out on Bushnell—sunnier than the alley and almost empty. He shaded his eyes with his hand and looked around him and—why! There was Luke, as if conjured up, sitting for some reason on the stoop of a boarded-over building. Cody started toward him, walking fast. Luke heard his footsteps and raised his head as Cody arrived. But it wasn't Luke. It was Beck. His silver hair appeared yellow in the sunlight, and he had taken off his suit coat to expose his white shirt and his sharp, cocked shoulders so oddly like Luke's. Cody came to a halt.

"I was just looking for the Trailways station," Beck told him. "I thought I could make it walking, but now I'm not so sure."

Cody took out his handkerchief to wipe his forehead.

"See, Claudette will be expecting me," said Beck. "That's the lady friend I mentioned. I figured I better go on and find a bus. Sorry to eat and run, but you know how it is with women. I told her I'd be home before supper. She's depending on me."

Cody replaced the handkerchief.

"I guess she'll want to get married, after this," said Beck. "She knows about Pearl's passing. She's sure to be making plans."

He held up his jacket, as if inspecting it for flaws. He folded it carefully, inside out, and laid it over his arm. The lining was something silky, faintly rainbow hued, like the sheen on aging meat.

"To tell the truth," Beck said, "I don't much want to marry her. It's not only that daughter; it's me. It's really me. You think I haven't had girlfriends before? Oh, sure, and could have married almost any one of them. Lots have begged me, 'Write your wife. Get a divorce. Let's tie the knot.' 'Well, maybe in a while,' I'd tell them, but I never did. I don't know, I just never did."

"You left us in her clutches," Cody said.

Beck looked up. He said, "Huh?"

"How could you do that?" Cody asked him. "How could you just dump us on our mother's mercy?" He bent closer, close enough to smell the camphorish scent of Beck's suit. "We were kids, we were only kids, we had no way of protecting ourselves. We looked to you for help. We listened for your step at the door so we'd be safe, but you just turned your back on us. You didn't lift a finger to defend us."

Beck stared past Cody at the traffic.

"She wore me out," he told Cody finally.

"Wore you out?"

"Used up my good points. Used up all my good points."

Cody straightened.

"Oh, at the start," Beck said, "she thought I was wonderful. You ought to have seen her face when I walked into a room. When I met her, she was an old maid already. She'd given up. No one had courted her for years; her girlfriends were asking her to baby-sit; their children called her Aunt Pearl. Then I came along. I made her so happy! There's my downfall, son. I mean with anyone, any one of these lady friends, I just can't resist a person I make happy. Why, she might be gap-toothed, or homely, or heavyset—all the better! I expect that if I'd got that divorce from your mother I'd have married six times over, just moving on to each new woman that cheered up some when she saw me, moving on again when she got close to me and didn't act so pleased any more. Oh, it's closeness that does you in. Never get too close to people, son—did I tell you that when you were young? When your mother and I were first married, everything was perfect. It seemed I could do no wrong. Then bit by bit I guess she saw my faults. I'd never hid them, but now it seemed they mattered after all. I made mistakes and she saw them. She saw that I was away from home too much and not enough support to her, didn't get ahead in my work, put on weight, drank too much, talked wrong, ate wrong, dressed wrong, drove a car wrong. No matter how hard I tried, seemed like everything I did got muddled. Spoiled. Turned into an accident. I'd bring home a simple toy, say, to cheer you all up when I came, and it would somehow start a fight—your mother saying it was too expensive or too dangerous or too difficult, and the three of you kids bickering over who got to play with it first. Do you recall the archery set? I thought it would be such fun, bring us all together—a family drive to the country, where we'd set up a target on a tree trunk and shoot our bows and arrows. But it didn't work out like I'd planned. First Pearl claims she's not athletic, then Jenny says it's too cold, then you and Ezra get in some kind of, I don't know, argument or quarrel, end up scuffling, shoot off an arrow, and wing your mother."

"I remember that," said Cody.

"Shot her through the shoulder. A disaster, a typical disaster. Then next week, while I'm away, something goes wrong with the wound. I come home from a sales trip and she tells me she nearly died. Something, I don't know, some infection or other. For me, it was the very last straw. I was sitting over a beer in the kitchen that Sunday evening and all at once, not even knowing I'd do it, I said, 'Pearl, I'm leaving.'"

312

Cody said, "You mean *that* was when you left?"

"I packed a bag and walked out," said Beck.

Cody sat down on the stoop.

"See," said Beck, "what it was, I guess: it was the grayness; grayness of things; a half-right-and-half-wrongness of things. Everything tangled, mingled, not perfect any more. I couldn't take that. Your mother could, but not me. Yes sir, I have to hand it to your mother."

He sighed and stroked the lining of his jacket.

"I'll be honest," he said, "when I left I didn't think I'd ever care to see you folks again. But later, I started having these thoughts. 'What do you suppose Cody's doing now? What's Ezra up to, and Jenny?' 'My family wasn't so much,' I thought, 'but it's all there really is, in the end.' By then, it was maybe two, three years since I'd left. One night I was passing through Baltimore and I parked a block away, got out and walked to the house. Pretty near froze to death, standing across the street and waiting. I guess I was going to introduce myself or something, if anybody came out. It was you that came. First I didn't even know you, wondered if someone else had moved in. Then I realized it was just that you had grown so. You were almost a man. You came down the walk and you bent for the evening paper and as you straightened, you kind of flipped it in the air and caught it again, and I saw that you could live without me. You could do that carefree a thing, you see—flip a paper and catch it. You were going to turn out fine. And I was right, wasn't I? Look! Haven't you all turned out fine—leading good lives, the three of you? She did it; Pearl did it. I knew she would manage. I turned and walked back to my car.

"After that, I just stuck to my own routine. Had a few pals, a lady friend from time to time. Somebody'd start to think the world of me and I would tell myself, 'I wish Pearl could see this.' I'd even write her a note, now and then. I'd write and give her my latest address, anyplace I moved to, but what I was really writing to say was, 'There's this new important boss we've got who regards me very highly.' Or, 'There's a lady here who acts extremely thrilled when I drop by.' Crazy, isn't it? I do believe that all these years, anytime I had any success, I've kind of, like, held it up in my imagination for your mother to admire. Just take a look at *this*, Pearl, I'd be thinking. Oh, what will I do now she's gone?"

He shook his head.

Cody, searching for something to say, happened to look toward Prima Street and see his family rounding the corner, opening like a fan. The children came first, running, and the teen-agers loped behind, and the grown-ups—trying to keep pace—were very nearly running themselves, so that they all looked unexpectedly joyful. The drab colors of their funeral clothes turned their faces bright. The children's arms and legs flew out and the baby bounced on Joe's shoulders. Cody felt surprised and touched. He felt that they were pulling him toward them—that it wasn't they who were traveling, but Cody himself.

"They've found us," he told Beck. "Let's go finish our dinner."

"Oh, well, I'm not so sure," Beck said. But he allowed himself to be helped to his feet. "Oh, well, maybe this one last course," he said, "but I warn you, I plan to leave before that dessert wine's poured."

Cody held on to his elbow and led him toward the others. Overhead, seagulls drifted through a sky so clear and blue that it brought back all the outings of his boyhood—the drives, the picnics, the autumn hikes, the wildflower walks in the spring. He remembered the archery trip, and it seemed to him now that he even remembered that arrow sailing in its graceful, fluttering path. He remembered his mother's upright form along the grasses, her hair lit gold, her small hands smoothing her bouquet while the arrow journeyed on. And high above, he seemed to recall, there had been a little brown airplane, almost motionless, droning through the sunshine like a bumblebee.

THE ACCIDENTAL
TOURIST

1

They were supposed to stay at the beach a week, but neither of them had the heart for it and they decided to come back early. Macon drove. Sarah sat next to him, leaning her head against the side window. Chips of cloudy sky showed through her tangled brown curls.

Macon wore a formal summer suit, his traveling suit—much more logical for traveling than jeans, he always said. Jeans had those stiff, hard seams and those rivets. Sarah wore a strapless terry beach dress. They might have been returning from two entirely different trips. Sarah had a tan but Macon didn't. He was a tall, pale, gray-eyed man, with straight fair hair cut close to his head, and his skin was that thin kind that easily burns. He'd kept away from the sun during the middle part of every day.

Just past the start of the divided highway, the sky grew almost black and several enormous drops spattered the windshield. Sarah sat up straight. "Let's hope it doesn't rain," she said.

"I don't mind a little rain," Macon said.

Sarah sat back again, but she kept her eyes on the road.

It was a Thursday morning. There wasn't much traffic. They passed a pickup truck, then a van all covered with stickers from a hundred scenic attractions. The drops on the windshield grew closer together. Macon switched his wipers on. Tick-*swoosh*, they went—a lulling sound; and there was a gentle patter on the roof. Every now and then a gust of wind blew up. Rain flattened the long, pale grass at the sides of the road. It slanted across the boat lots, lumberyards, and discount furniture outlets, which already had a darkened look as if here it might have been raining for some time.

"Can you see all right?" Sarah asked.

"Of course," Macon said. "This is nothing."

They arrived behind a trailer truck whose rear wheels sent out arcs of spray. Macon swung to the left and passed. There was a moment of watery blindness till the truck had dropped behind. Sarah gripped the dashboard with one hand.

"I don't know how you can see to drive," she said.

"Maybe you should put on your glasses."

"Putting on my glasses would help you to see?"

"Not me; you," Macon said. "You're focused on the windshield instead of the road."

Sarah continued to grip the dashboard. She had a broad, smooth face that gave an impression of calm, but if you looked closely you'd notice the tension at the corners of her eyes.

The car drew in around them like a room. Their breaths fogged the windows. Earlier the air conditioner had been running and now some artificial chill remained, quickly turning dank, carrying with it the smell of mildew. They shot through an underpass. The rain stopped completely for one blank, startling second. Sarah gave a little gasp of relief, but even before it was uttered, the hammering on the roof resumed. She turned and gazed back longingly at the underpass. Macon sped ahead, with his hands relaxed on the wheel.

"Did you notice that boy with the motorcycle?" Sarah

318

asked. She had to raise her voice; a steady, insistent roaring sound engulfed them.

"What boy?"

"He was parked beneath the underpass."

"It's crazy to ride a motorcycle on a day like today," Macon said. "Crazy to ride one any day. You're so exposed to the elements."

"We could do that," Sarah said. "Stop and wait it out."

"Sarah, if I felt we were in the slightest danger I'd have pulled over long ago."

"Well, I don't know that you would have," Sarah said.

They passed a field where the rain seemed to fall in sheets, layers and layers of rain beating down the cornstalks, flooding the rutted soil. Great lashings of water flung themselves at the windshield. Macon switched his wiper blades to high.

"I don't know that you really care that much," Sarah said. "Do you."

Macon said, "Care?"

"I said to you the other day, I said, 'Macon, now that Ethan's dead I sometimes wonder if there's any point to life.' Do you remember what you answered?"

"Well, not offhand," Macon said.

"You said, 'Honey, to tell the truth, it never seemed to me there was all that much point to begin with.' Those were your exact words."

"Um . . ."

"And you don't even know what was wrong with that."

"No, I guess I don't," Macon said.

He passed a line of cars that had parked at the side of the road, their windows opaque, their gleaming surfaces bouncing back the rain in shallow explosions. One car was slightly tipped, as if about to fall into the muddy torrent that churned and raced in the gully. Macon kept a steady speed.

"You're not a comfort, Macon," Sarah said.

319

"Honey, I'm trying to be."

"You just go on your same old way like before. Your little routines and rituals, depressing habits, day after day. No comfort at all."

"Shouldn't I need comfort too?" Macon asked. "You're not the only one, Sarah. I don't know why you feel it's your loss alone."

"Well, I just do, sometimes," Sarah said.

They were quiet a moment. A wide lake, it seemed, in the center of the highway crashed against the underside of the car and slammed it to the right. Macon pumped his brakes and drove on.

"This rain, for instance," Sarah said. "You know it makes me nervous. What harm would it do to wait it out? You'd be showing some concern. You'd be telling me we're in this together."

Macon peered through the windshield, which was streaming so that it seemed marbled. He said, "I've got a system, Sarah. You know I drive according to a system."

"You and your systems!"

"Also," he said, "if you don't see any point to life, I can't figure why a rainstorm would make you nervous."

Sarah slumped in her seat.

"Will you look at that!" he said. "A mobile home's washed clear across that trailer park."

"Macon, I want a divorce," Sarah told him.

Macon braked and glanced over at her. "What?" he said. The car swerved. He had to face forward again. "What did I say?" he asked. "What did it mean?"

"I just can't live with you anymore," Sarah said.

Macon went on watching the road, but his nose seemed sharper and whiter, as if the skin of his face had been pulled tight. He cleared his throat. He said, "Honey. Listen. It's been a hard year. We've had a hard time. People who lose a

320

child often feel this way; everybody says so; everybody says it's a terrible strain on a marriage—"

"I'd like to find a place of my own as soon as we get back," Sarah told him.

"Place of your own," Macon echoed, but he spoke so softly, and the rain beat so loudly on the roof, it looked as if he were only moving his lips. "Well," he said. "All right. If that's what you really want."

"You can keep the house," Sarah said. "You never did like moving."

For some reason, it was this that made her finally break down. She turned away sharply. Macon switched his right blinker on. He pulled into a Texaco station, parked beneath the overhang, and cut off the engine. Then he started rubbing his knees with his palms. Sarah huddled in her corner. The only sound was the drumming of rain on the overhang far above them.

2

After his wife left him, Macon had thought the house would seem larger. Instead, he felt more crowded. The windows shrank. The ceilings lowered. There was something insistent about the furniture, as if it were pressing in on him.

Of course Sarah's personal belongings were gone, the little things like clothes and jewelry. But it emerged that some of the big things were more personal than he'd imagined. There was the drop-leaf desk in the living room, its pigeonholes stuffed with her clutter of torn envelopes and unanswered letters. There was the radio in the kitchen, set to play 98 Rock. (She liked to keep in touch with her students, she used to say in the old days, as she hummed and jittered her way around the breakfast table.) There was the chaise out back where she had sunbathed, planted in the only spot that got any sun at all. He looked at the flowered cushions and marveled at how an empty space could be so full of a person—her faint scent of coconut oil that always made him wish for a piña colada; her wide, gleaming face inscrutable behind dark glasses; her compact body in the skirted swimsuit she had tearfully insisted on buying after her fortieth birthday. Threads of her exuberant hair showed up at the bottom of the sink. Her shelf in the medicine cabinet, stripped, was splashed with drops of liquid rouge in a particular plummy shade that brought her instantly to Macon's mind. He had always disapproved of her messiness but now those spills seemed touching, like colorful toys left on the floor after a child has gone to bed.

The house itself was medium-sized, unexceptional to look at, standing on a street of such houses in an older part of Baltimore. Heavy oak trees hung over it, shading it from the hot summer sun but also blocking breezes. The rooms inside were square and dim. All that remained in Sarah's closet was a brown silk sash hanging on a hook; in her bureau drawers, lint balls and empty perfume bottles. Their son's old room was neatly made up, as sleek as a room in a Holiday Inn. Some places, the walls gave off a kind of echo. Still, Macon noticed he had a tendency to hold his arms close to his body, to walk past furniture sideways, as if he imagined the house could barely accommodate him. He felt too tall. His long, clumsy feet seemed unusually distant. He ducked his head in doorways.

Now was his chance to reorganize, he told himself. He was struck by an incongruous little jolt of interest. The fact was that running a house required some sort of system, and Sarah had never understood that. She was the sort of woman who stored her flatware intermingled. She thought nothing of running a dishwasher with only a handful of forks stacked inside. Macon found that distressing. He was opposed to dishwashers in general; he believed they wasted energy. Energy saving was a hobby of his, you might say.

He started keeping the kitchen sink filled at all times, adding some chlorine bleach for disinfectant. As he finished using each dish, he dropped it in. On alternate days he pulled the plug and sprayed everything with very hot water. Then he stacked the rinsed dishes in the empty dishwasher—which had become, under his new system, a gigantic storage area.

When he hunkered over the sink to let the spray attachment run, he often had the feeling that Sarah was watching. He sensed that if he slid his eyes just slightly to the left, he would find her with her arms folded across her chest, her head tipped and her full, curved lips meditatively pursed. At first glance she was simply studying his procedure; at second glance (he knew) she was laughing at him. There was a secret little gleam in her eyes that he was all too familiar with. "I see," she would say, nodding at some lengthy explanation of his; then he'd look up and catch the gleam and the telltale tuck at one corner of her mouth.

In this vision of her—if you could call it a vision, considering that he never did glance over at her—she was wearing a bright blue dress from the early days of their marriage. He had no idea when she had given that dress up, but certainly it was years and years ago. He almost felt that Sarah was a ghost— that she was dead. In a way (he thought, turning off the faucet), she *was* dead, that young, vivid Sarah from their first enthusiastic apartment on Cold Spring Lane. When he tried to recall those days, any image of Sarah was altered by the fact that she had left him. When he pictured their introduction—back when they were barely out of childhood—it seemed nothing more than the beginning of their parting. When she had looked up at him that first night and rattled the ice cubes in her paper cup, they were already moving toward their last edgy, miserable year together, toward those months when anything either of them said was wrong, toward that sense of narrowly missed connections. They were like people who run to meet, holding out their arms, but their aim is wrong; they pass each other and keep running. It had all amounted to nothing, in the end. He gazed down at the sink, and the warmth from the dishes drifted gently up into his face.

Well, you have to carry on. You have to carry on. He decided to switch his shower from morning to night. This showed adaptability, he felt—some freshness of spirit. While he showered he let the water collect in the tub, and he stalked around in noisy circles, sloshing the day's dirty clothes underfoot. Later he wrung out the clothes and hung them on hangers to dry. Then he dressed in tomorrow's underwear so he wouldn't have to launder any pajamas. In fact, his only real laundry was a load of towels and sheets once a week—just two towels, but quite a lot of sheets. This was because he had developed a system that enabled him to sleep in clean sheets every night without the trouble of bed changing. He'd been proposing the system to Sarah for years, but she was so set in her ways. What he did was strip the mattress of all linens, replacing them with a giant sort of envelope made from one of the seven sheets he had folded and stitched together on the sewing machine. He thought of this invention as a Macon Leary Body Bag. A body bag required no tucking in, was unmussable, easily changeable, and the perfect weight for summer nights. In winter he would have to devise something warmer, but he couldn't think of winter yet. He was barely making it from one day to the next as it was.

At moments—while he was skidding on the mangled clothes in the bathtub or struggling into his body bag on the naked, rust-stained mattress—he realized that he might be carrying things too far. He couldn't explain why, either. He'd always had a fondness for method, but not what you would call a mania. Thinking then of Sarah's lack of method, he wondered if that had got out of hand now too. Maybe all these years, they'd been keeping each other on a reasonable track. Separated, demagnetized somehow, they wandered wildly off course. He pictured Sarah's new apartment, which he had never seen, as chaotic to the point of madness, with sneakers in the oven and the sofa heaped with china. The mere thought of it upset him. He looked gratefully at his own surroundings.

Most of his work was done at home; otherwise he might not have cared so about the mechanics of the household. He had a little study in the spare room off the kitchen. Seated in a stenographer's chair, tapping away at a typewriter that had served him through four years of college, he wrote a series of guidebooks for people forced to travel on business. Ridiculous, when you thought about it: Macon hated travel. He careened through foreign territories on a desperate kind of blitz—squinching his eyes shut and holding his breath and hanging on for dear life, he sometimes imagined—and then settled back home with a sigh of relief to produce his chunky, passport-sized paperbacks. *Accidental Tourist in France. Accidental Tourist in Germany. In Belgium.* No author's name, just a logo: a winged armchair on the cover.

He covered only the cities in these guides, for people taking business trips flew into cities and out again and didn't see the countryside at all. They didn't see the cities, for that matter. Their concern was how to pretend they had never left home. What hotels in Madrid boasted king-sized Beautyrest mattresses? What restaurants in Tokyo offered Sweet'n'-Low? Did Amsterdam have a McDonald's? Did Mexico City have a Taco Bell? Did any place in Rome serve Chef Boyardee ravioli? Other travelers hoped to discover distinctive local wines; Macon's readers searched for pasteurized and homogenized milk.

As much as he hated the travel, he loved the writing—the virtuous delights of organizing a disorganized country, stripping away the inessential and the second-rate, classifying all that remained in neat, terse paragraphs. He cribbed from other guidebooks, seizing small kernels of value and discarding the rest. He spent pleasurable hours dithering over questions of punctuation. Righteously, mercilessly, he weeded out the passive voice. The effort of typing made the corners of his mouth turn down, so that no one could have guessed how much he was enjoying himself. *I am happy to say,* he pecked out, but his face remained glum and intense. *I am happy to say that it's possible now to buy Kentucky Fried Chicken in Stockholm. Pita bread, too,* he added as an afterthought. He wasn't sure how it had happened, but lately pita had grown to seem as American as hot dogs.

"Of course you're managing," his sister told him over the phone. "Did I say you weren't? But at least you could have let us know. Three weeks, it's been! Sarah's been gone three weeks and I only hear about it today. And by chance, at that. If I hadn't asked to speak to her, would you ever have told us she'd left you?"

"She didn't *leave* me," Macon said. "I mean it's not the way you make it sound. We discussed it like adults and decided to separate, that's all. The last thing I need is my family gathered around me saying, 'Oh, poor Macon, how could Sarah do this to you—' "

"Why would I say that?" Rose asked. "Everybody knows the Leary men are difficult to live with."

"Oh," Macon said.

"Where is she?"

"She's got a place downtown," he said. "And look," he added, "you don't have to bend over backwards, either, and go asking her to dinner or something. She does have a family of her own. You're supposed to take my side in this."

"I thought you didn't want us to take sides."

"No, no, I don't. I mean you shouldn't take *her* side, is what I'm trying to say."

"When Charles's wife got her divorce," Rose said, "we went on having her to dinner every Christmas, just like always. Remember?"

"I remember," Macon said wearily. Charles was their oldest brother.

"I suppose she'd still be coming, if she hadn't got remarried to someone so far away."

"What? If her husband had been a Baltimore man you'd have gone on inviting them both?"

"She and Porter's wife and Sarah used to sit around the kitchen—this was before Porter's wife got *her* divorce—and they'd go on and on about the Leary men. Oh, it was the Leary men this, the Leary men that: how they always had to have everything just so, always so well thought out before-hand, always clamping down on the world as if they really thought they could keep it in line. The Leary men! I can hear them still. I had to laugh: One Thanksgiving Porter and June were getting ready to leave, back when their children were small, and June was heading toward the door with the baby in her arms and Danny hanging onto her coat and this load of toys and supplies when Porter called out, 'Halt!' and started reading from one of those cash-register tapes that he always writes his lists on: *blanket, bottles, diaper bag, formula out of the fridge* . . . June just looked over at the other two and rolled her eyes."

"Well, it wasn't such a bad idea," Macon said, "when you consider June."

"No, and you notice it was alphabetical, too," Rose said. "I do think alphabetizing helps to sort things out a little."

Rose had a kitchen that was so completely alphabetized, you'd find the allspice next to the ant poison. She was a fine one to talk about the Leary men.

"At any rate," she said. "Has Sarah been in touch since she left?"

"She's come by once or twice. Once, actually," Macon said. "For things she needed."

"What kind of things?"

"Well, a double boiler. Things like that."

"It's an excuse, then," Rose said promptly. "She could get a double boiler at any dimestore."

"She said she liked ours."

328

"She was checking to see how you're doing. She still cares. Did you talk at all?"

"No," Macon said, "I just handed her the double boiler. Also that gadget that unscrews bottle tops."

"Oh, Macon. You might have asked her in."

"I was scared she'd say no," he said.

There was a silence. "Well. Anyhow," Rose said finally.

"But I'm getting along!"

"Yes, of course you are," she told him.

Then she said she had something in the oven and hung up.

Macon went over to his study window. It was a hot day in early July, the sky so blue it made his eyes ache. He rested his forehead against the glass and stared out at the yard, keeping his hands stuffed deep in the rear pockets of his khakis. Up in one of the oak trees, a bird sang what sounded like the first three notes of "My Little Gypsy Sweetheart." "Slum . . . ber . . . on . . ." it sang. Macon wondered if even this moment would become, one day, something he looked back upon wistfully. He couldn't imagine it; he couldn't think of any period bleaker than this in all his life, but he'd noticed how time had a way of coloring things. That bird, for instance, had such a pure, sweet, piercing voice.

He turned away from the window, covered his typewriter, and left the room.

He didn't eat real meals anymore. When he was hungry he drank a glass of milk, or he spooned a bit of ice cream directly from the carton. After the smallest snack he felt overfed and heavy, but he noticed when he dressed in the mornings that he seemed to be losing weight. His shirt collar stood out around his neck. The vertical groove between his nose and mouth had deepened so that he had trouble shaving it. His hair, which Sarah used to cut for him, jutted over his forehead like a shelf. And something had caused his lower lids to droop. He used to have narrow gray slits of eyes; now they were wide and startled. Could this be a sign of malnutrition?

Breakfast: Breakfast was your most important meal. He hooked up the percolator and the electric skillet to the clock radio on his bedroom windowsill. Of course he was asking for food poisoning, letting two raw eggs wait all night at room temperature, but once he'd changed menus there was no problem. You had to be flexible about these matters. He was awakened now by the smell of fresh coffee and hot buttered popcorn, and he could partake of both without getting out of bed. Oh, he was managing fine, just fine. All things considered.

But his nights were terrible.

It wasn't that he had trouble getting to sleep in the first place. That was easy. He'd watch TV till his eyes burned; then he'd climb the stairs. He would start the shower running and spread his clothes in the tub. At times he thought of skipping this part, except there was such a danger in falling behind with your system. So he carried out each step: hanging the laundry, setting up the breakfast things, flossing his teeth. He couldn't go to bed without flossing his teeth. For some reason, Sarah had found this irritating. If Macon were condemned to death, she'd said once, and they told him he'd be executed by firing squad at dawn, he would no doubt still insist on flossing the night before. Macon, after thinking it over, had agreed. Yes, of course he would. Hadn't he flossed while in the depths of pneumonia? In the hospital with gallstones? In a motel the night his son was killed? He checked his teeth in the mirror. They were never entirely white, in spite of all his care. And now it seemed his skin was taking on a yellowish cast as well.

He turned off the lights, moved the cat over, helped the dog up onto the bed. The dog was a Welsh corgi, very short-legged, but he did love to sleep in a bed, and so every night he stood erect and propped his elbows on the mattress and gazed at Macon expectantly till Macon gave him a boost.

Then they'd all three settle themselves. Macon slipped into his envelope, the cat fitted her shape to the warm spot under his arm, and the dog plopped down near his feet. Then Macon closed his eyes and drifted off.

But eventually he found himself conscious of his dreams—not borne along by them but tediously constructing them, quibbling over details. When it dawned on him that he was awake, he would open his eyes and squint at the clock radio. But it was only one a.m. At the latest, two. There were all those hours still to be survived.

His brain buzzed with little worries. Had he left the back door unlocked? Forgotten to put the milk away? Made out a check for his bank balance instead of his gas bill? He remembered all in a rush that he'd opened a can of V-8 juice and then put the can in the icebox. Oxidation of the metal seams! Resulting in lead poisoning!

The worries changed, grew deeper. He wondered what had gone wrong with his marriage. Sarah had been his first and only girlfriend; now he thought he should have practiced on someone else beforehand. During the twenty years of their marriage there'd been moments—there'd been months—when he didn't feel they had really formed a unit the way couples were supposed to. No, they'd stayed two distinct people, and not always even friends. Sometimes they'd seemed more like rivals, elbowing each other, competing over who was the better style of person. Was it Sarah, haphazard, mercurial? Was it Macon, methodical and steady?

When Ethan was born, he only brought out more of their differences. Things they had learned to ignore in each other resurfaced. Sarah never got their son on any kind of schedule at all, was lax and unconcerned. And Macon (oh, he knew it, he admitted it) had been so intent on preparing him for every eventuality that he hadn't had time to enjoy him. Ethan at two, at four floated up into his vision as clearly as a color film projected upon the bedroom ceiling. A chortling, sunny

331

little boy, he'd been, with Macon a stooped shape above him wringing his hands. Macon had been fierce in teaching him, at age six, how to swing a bat; it would have wrenched his soul to have Ethan chosen last for any team. "Why?" Sarah had asked. "If he's chosen last, he's chosen last. Let it be, why don't you." Let it be! Life was so full of things you couldn't do anything about; you had to avert what you could. She laughed when Macon spent one fall collecting Wacky Packs, which had these jokey stickers inside that Ethan liked to plaster his bedroom door with. He'd have more than anyone in the whole third grade, Macon vowed. Long after Ethan had lost interest, Macon was still doggedly bringing them home. He knew it was absurd, but still, there was this one last sticker they had not yet managed to get hold of . . .

Ethan went away to camp when he was twelve—a year ago, almost exactly. Most boys started earlier, but Macon had kept delaying it. Why have a child at all, he asked Sarah, if you were only going to ship him off to some godforsaken spot in Virginia? By the time he finally gave in, Ethan was in the top age group—a tall blond sprout of a boy with an open, friendly face and an endearing habit of bouncing on the balls of his feet when he was nervous.

Don't think about it.

He was murdered in a Burger Bonanza his second night at camp. It was one of those deaths that make no sense—the kind where the holdup man has collected his money and is free to go but decides, instead, first to shoot each and every person through the back of the skull.

Ethan wasn't even supposed to be there. He had snuck away from camp with a cabinmate, who waited outside as a lookout.

Blame the camp for not supervising. Blame Burger Bonanza for poor security. Blame the cabinmate for not going in too and altering, perhaps, what took place. (Lookout for what, for God's sake?) Blame Sarah for allowing Ethan to leave home; blame Macon for agreeing; blame even (hell, yes) Ethan. Blame Ethan for wanting to attend that camp and for sneaking off from it, and for entering Burger Bonanza like some headstrong fool while a holdup was in progress. Blame him for so meekly moving to the kitchen with the others, for placing his hands flat against the wall as he was ordered and no doubt bouncing slightly on the balls of his feet . . .

Don't think about it.

The director of the camp, not wanting to break the news on the phone, had driven to Baltimore to tell them in person. Then he'd driven them back to Virginia. Macon often recalled that director. Jim, his name was, Jim Robinson or maybe Robertson—a burly, white-whiskered man with a crew cut, wearing a suit coat, as if in respect, over a Redskins T-shirt. He'd seemed uncomfortable with silence and did his best to fill it with abrupt little fragments of chitchat. Macon hadn't listened, or he'd thought he hadn't; but now all the fragments came back to him. How Jim's mother had been a Baltimorean herself, born the year Babe Ruth was playing for the Orioles. How Jim's tomato plants had been acting queerly, producing only tiny green marbles that fell off the vines before they ripened. How Jim's wife was terrified of driving in reverse and avoided any situation that required it. Macon gave a lot of thought to that now, lying in his bed at night. Could you really drive a car without reversing? What about at intersections, where a bus driver pokes his head out his window and asks you to roll on back a few yards so he can turn? Would she refuse? Macon imagined her, staunch and defiant, glaring straight in front of her and pretending not to notice. The driver escalating into curses, horns blowing, other drivers shouting, "Aw, lady!" It made a nice picture. He kept it firmly in mind.

Finally he would sit up and wriggle out of his sheet. The dog, sighing, roused himself and dropped off the bed to pad downstairs behind him. The floorboards were cool underfoot, the kitchen linoleum cooler still; there was a glow from the refrigerator as Macon poured himself a glass of milk. He went to the living room and turned on the TV. Generally some black-and-white movie was running—men in suits and felt hats, women with padded shoulders. He didn't try to follow the plot. He took small, steady sips of milk, feeling the calcium traveling to his bones. Hadn't he read that calcium cures insomnia? He absently stroked the cat, who had somehow crept into his lap. It was much too hot to have a cat in his lap, especially this one—a loose-strung, gray tweed female who seemed made of some unusually dense substance. And the dog, most often, would be lying on top of his feet. "It's just you and me, old buddies," Macon would tell them. The cat made a comma of sweat across his bare thighs.

At last he would slip out from under the animals and turn off the TV. He would put his glass in the chlorine solution in the kitchen sink. He would climb the stairs. He'd stand at the bedroom window looking over the neighborhood—black branches scrawled on a purple night sky, a glimmer of white clapboard here and there, occasionally a light. Macon always took comfort if he found a light. Someone else had trouble sleeping too, he assumed. He didn't like to consider any other possibility—a party, for instance, or a heart-to-heart talk with old friends. He preferred to believe that someone else was on his own, sitting up wide awake fending off his thoughts. That made him feel much better. He returned to his bed. He lay down. He closed his eyes and without even trying, he dropped off the edge into sleep.

3

Sarah telephoned Macon and asked if she could come get the navy blue rug from the dining room.

"Navy blue rug," Macon repeated. (He was stalling for time.)

"I wouldn't mention it except you never liked it," Sarah told him. "You said it was a mistake to have a rug where people were eating."

Yes, he had said that. A crumb catcher, he'd said. Unsanitary. Then why did he feel this sudden, wrenching need to keep the rug for himself?

"Macon, are you there?"

"Yes, I'm here."

"So would you mind if I came and got it?"

"No, I guess not."

"Oh, good. My apartment has these bare floors and you've no idea how—"

She would stop by for the rug and he'd invite her in. He'd offer her a glass of sherry. They would sit on the couch with their sherry and he would say, "Sarah, have you missed me?" Or no, he'd say, "I've missed you, Sarah."

She would say . . .

335

She said, "I thought I'd drop over Saturday morning, if that's convenient."

But people don't drink sherry in the morning.

And besides: He wouldn't even be here then. "I leave for England tomorrow afternoon," he said.

"Oh, is it time for England again?"

"Maybe you could come this evening."

"No, my car's in the shop."

"Your car? What's wrong with it?"

"Well, I was driving along and . . . you know that little red light on the lefthand side of the dash?"

"What, the oil pressure light?"

"Yes, and so I thought, 'Well, I'll be late for the dentist if I stop and see to it now and anyway, the car does seem to be running all right, so—' "

"Wait. Are you saying the light lit up? And then you went on driving?"

"Well, nothing sounded any different and nothing *acted* any different, so I figured—"

"Jesus, Sarah."

"What's so terrible about that?"

"You've probably ruined the engine."

"No, I did not ruin the engine, for your information. I just need this single, simple repair job but unfortunately it's going to take a few days to do it. Well, never mind. I've got a house key; I'll just let myself in on Saturday."

"Maybe I could bring the rug over."

"I'll wait till Saturday."

"That way I could see your apartment," Macon said. "I've never been inside, you know."

"No, it's not fixed up yet."

"I don't care if it's fixed up."

"It's a disaster. Nothing's been done."

"How could nothing be done? You've been living there over a month."

336

"Well, I'm not so wonderfully perfectly efficient as you are, Macon."

"You wouldn't have to be efficient to—"

"Some days," Sarah said, "I can't even make it out of my bathrobe."

Macon was silent.

"I should have agreed to teach summer school," Sarah said. "Something to give some shape to things. I open my eyes in the morning and think, 'Why bother getting up?' "

"Me too," Macon said.

"Why bother eating? Why bother breathing?"

"Me too, sweetheart."

"Macon, do you suppose that person has any idea? I want to go see him in prison, Macon. I want to sit on the other side of the grid or the screen or whatever they have and I'll say, 'Look at me. Look. Look at what you did. You didn't just kill the people you shot; you killed other people besides. What you did goes on and on forever. You didn't just kill my son; you killed me; you killed my husband. I mean I can't even manage to put up my curtains; do you understand what you did?' Then when I'm sure that he does understand, that he really does realize, that he feels just terrible, I'm going to open my purse and pull out a gun and shoot him between the eyes."

"Oh, well, sweetheart—"

"You think I'm just raving, don't you. But Macon, I swear, I can feel that little kick against my palm when I fire the gun. I've never fired a gun in my life—Lord, I don't think I've ever *seen* a gun. Isn't it odd? Ethan's seen one; Ethan's had an experience you and I have no notion of. But sometimes I hold my hand out with the thumb cocked like when kids play cowboy, and I fold my trigger finger and feel what a satisfaction it would be."

"Sarah, it's bad for you to talk like this."

"Oh? How am I supposed to talk?"

"I mean if you let yourself get angry you'll be . . . consumed. You'll burn up. It's not productive."

"Oh, productive! Well, goodness, no, let's not waste our time on anything unproductive."

Macon massaged his forehead. He said, "Sarah, I just feel we can't afford to have these thoughts."

"Easy for you to say."

"No, it is not easy for me to say, dammit—"

"Just shut the door, Macon. Just walk away. Just pretend it never happened. Go rearrange your tools, why don't you; line up your wrenches from biggest to smallest instead of from smallest to biggest; that's always fun."

"Goddammit, Sarah—"

"Don't you curse at me, Macon Leary!"

They paused.

Macon said, "Well."

Sarah said, "Well, anyhow."

"So I guess you'll come by while I'm gone," he said.

"If that's all right."

"Yes, certainly," he said.

Although he felt a curious uneasiness when he hung up, as if he were letting a stranger come. As if she might walk off with more than just the dining room rug.

For his trip to England, he dressed in his most comfortable suit. *One suit is plenty,* he counseled in his guidebooks, *if you take along some travel-size packets of spot remover.* (Macon knew every item that came in travel-size packets, from deodorant to shoe polish.) *The suit should be a medium gray. Gray not only hides the dirt; it's handy for sudden funerals and other formal events. At the same time, it isn't too somber for everyday.*

He packed a minimum of clothes and a shaving kit. A copy of his most recent guide to England. A novel to read on the plane.

Bring only what fits in a carry-on bag. Checking your luggage is asking for trouble. Add several travel-size packets of detergent so you won't fall into the hands of foreign laundries.

When he'd finished packing, he sat on the couch to rest. Or not to rest, exactly, but to collect himself—like a man taking several deep breaths before diving into a river.

The furniture was all straight lines and soothing curves. Dust motes hung in a slant of sunlight. What a peaceful life he led here! If this were any other day he'd be making some instant coffee. He would drop the spoon in the sink and stand sipping from his mug while the cat wove between his feet. Then maybe he'd open the mail. Those acts seemed dear and gentle now. How could he have complained of boredom? At home he had everything set up around him so he hardly needed to think. On trips, even the smallest task required effort and decisions.

When it was two hours till takeoff, he stood up. The airport was a thirty-minute drive at the most, but he hated feeling rushed. He made a final tour of the house, stopping off at the downstairs bathroom—the last *real* bathroom (was how he thought of it) that he'd see for the next week. He whistled for the dog. He picked up his bag and stepped out the front door. The heat slammed into him like something solid.

The dog was going with him only as far as the vet's. If he'd known that, he never would have jumped into the car. He sat next to Macon, panting enthusiastically, his keg-shaped body alert with expectation. Macon talked to him in what he hoped was an unalarming tone. "Hot, isn't it, Edward. You want the air conditioner on?" He adjusted the controls. "There now. Feeling better?" He heard something unctuous in his voice. Maybe Edward did, too, for he stopped panting and gave Macon a sudden suspicious look. Macon decided to say no more.

They rolled through the neighborhood, down streets roofed over with trees. They turned into a sunnier section full of stores and service stations. As they neared Murray Avenue, Edward started whimpering. In the parking lot of the Murray Avenue Veterinary Hospital, he somehow became a much smaller animal.

Macon got out of the car and walked around to open the door. When he took hold of Edward's collar, Edward dug his toenails into the upholstery. He had to be dragged all the way to the building, scritching across the hot concrete.

The waiting room was empty. A goldfish tank bubbled in one corner, with a full-color poster above it illustrating the life cycle of the heartworm. There was a girl on a stool behind the counter, a waifish little person in a halter top.

"I've brought my dog for boarding," Macon said. He had to raise his voice to be heard above Edward's moans.

Chewing her gum steadily, the girl handed him a printed form and a pencil. "Ever been here before?" she asked.

"Yes, often."

"What's the last name?"

"Leary."

"Leary. Leary," she said, riffling through a box of index cards. Macon started filling out the form. Edward was standing upright now and clinging to Macon's knees, like a toddler scared of nursery school.

"Whoa," the girl said.

She frowned at the card she'd pulled.

"Edward?" she said. "On Rayford Road?"

"That's right."

"We can't accept him."

"What?"

"Says here he bit an attendant. Says, 'Bit Barry in the ankle, do not readmit.' "

"Nobody told me that."

"Well, they should have."

"Nobody said a word! I left him in June when we went to the beach; I came back and they handed him over."

340

The girl blinked at him, expressionless.

"Look," Macon said. "I'm on my way to the airport, right this minute. I've got a plane to catch."

"I'm only following orders," the girl said.

"And what set him off, anyhow?" Macon asked. "Did anyone think to wonder? Maybe Edward had good reason!"

The girl blinked again. Edward had dropped to all fours by now and was gazing upward with interest, as if following the conversation.

"Ah, the hell with it," Macon said. "Come on, Edward."

He didn't have to take hold of Edward's collar when they left. Edward galloped ahead of him all the way across the parking lot.

In that short time, the car had turned into an oven. Macon opened his window and sat there with the motor idling. What now? He considered going to his sister's, but she probably wouldn't want Edward either. To tell the truth, this wasn't the first time there had been complaints. Last week, for instance, Macon's brother Charles had stopped by to borrow a router, and Edward had darted in a complete circle around his feet, taking furious little nibbles of his trouser cuffs. Charles was so astonished that he just turned his head slowly, gaping down. "What's got into him?" he asked. "He never *used* to do this." Then when Macon grabbed his collar, Edward had snarled. He'd curled his upper lip and snarled. Could a dog have a nervous breakdown?

Macon wasn't very familiar with dogs. He preferred cats. He liked the way cats kept their own counsel. It was only lately that he'd given Edward any thought at all. Now that he was alone so much he had taken to talking out loud to him, or sometimes he just sat studying him. He admired Edward's intelligent brown eyes and his foxy little face. He appreciated the honey-colored whorls that radiated so symmetrically from the bridge of his nose. And his walk! Ethan used to say that Edward walked as if he had sand in his bathing suit. His rear end waddled busily; his stubby legs seemed hinged by some more primitive mechanism than the legs of taller dogs.

Macon was driving toward home now, for lack of any better idea. He wondered what would happen if he left Edward in the house the way he left the cat, with plenty of food and water. No. Or could Sarah come see to him, two or three times a day? He recoiled from that; it meant asking her. It meant dialing that number he'd never used and asking her for a favor.

MEOW-BOW ANIMAL HOSPITAL, a sign across the street read. Macon braked and Edward lurched forward. "Sorry," Macon told him. He made a left turn into the parking lot.

The waiting room at the Meow-Bow smelled strongly of disinfectant. Behind the counter stood a thin young woman in a ruffled peasant blouse. She had aggressively frizzy black hair that burgeoned to her shoulders like an Arab headdress. "Hi, there," she said to Macon.

Macon said, "Do you board dogs?"

"Sure."

"I'd like to board Edward, here."

She leaned over the counter to look at Edward. Edward panted up at her cheerfully. It was clear he hadn't yet realized what kind of place this was.

"You have a reservation?" the woman asked Macon.

"Reservation! No."

"Most people reserve."

"Well, I didn't know that."

"Especially in the summer."

"Couldn't you make an exception?"

She thought it over, frowning down at Edward. Her eyes were very small, like caraway seeds, and her face was sharp and colorless.

342

"Please," Macon said. "I'm about to catch a plane. I'm leaving for a week, and I don't have a soul to look after him. I'm desperate, I tell you."

From the glance she shot at him, he sensed he had surprised her in some way. "Can't you leave him home with your wife?" she asked.

He wondered how on earth her mind worked.

"If I could do that," he said, "why would I be standing here?"

"Oh," she said. "You're not married?"

"Well, I am, but she's . . . living elsewhere. They don't allow pets."

"Oh."

She came out from behind the counter. She was wearing very short red shorts; her legs were like sticks. "I'm a divorsy myself," she said. "I know what you're going through."

"And see," Macon said, "there's this place I usually board him but they suddenly claim he bites. Claim he bit an attendant and they can't admit him anymore."

"Edward? Do you bite?" the woman said.

Macon realized he should not have mentioned that, but she seemed to take it in stride. "How could you do such a thing?" she asked Edward. Edward grinned up at her and folded his ears back, inviting a pat. She bent and stroked his head.

"So will you keep him?" Macon said.

"Oh, I guess," she said, straightening. "If you're desperate." She stressed the word—fixing Macon with those small brown eyes—as if giving it more weight than he had intended. "Fill this out," she told him, and she handed him a form from a stack on the counter. "Your name and address and when you'll be back. Don't forget to put when you'll be back."

Macon nodded, uncapping his fountain pen.

"I'll most likely see you again when you come to pick him up," she said. "I mean if you put the time of day to expect you. My name's Muriel."

"Is this place open evenings?" Macon asked.

"Every evening but Sundays. Till eight."

"Oh, good."

"Muriel Pritchett," she said.

Macon filled out the form while the woman knelt to unbuckle Edward's collar. Edward licked her cheekbone; he must have thought she was just being friendly. So when Macon had finished, he didn't say good-bye. He left the form on the counter and walked out very quickly, keeping a hand in his pocket to silence his keys.

On the flight to New York, he sat next to a foreign-looking man with a mustache. Clamped to the man's ears was a headset for one of those miniature tape recorders. Perfect: no danger of conversation. Macon leaned back in his seat contentedly.

He approved of planes. When the weather was calm, you couldn't even tell you were moving. You could pretend you were sitting safe at home. The view from the window was always the same—air and more air—and the interior of one plane was practically interchangeable with the interior of any other.

He accepted nothing from the beverage cart, but the man beside him took off his headset to order a Bloody Mary. A tinny, intricate, Middle Eastern melody came whispering out of the pink sponge earplugs. Macon stared down at the little machine and wondered if he should buy one. Not for the music, heaven knows—there was far too much noise in the world already—but for insulation. He could plug himself into it and no one would disturb him. He could play a blank tape: thirty full minutes of silence. Turn the tape over and play thirty minutes more.

344

They landed at Kennedy and he took a shuttle bus to his connecting flight, which wasn't due to leave till evening. Once settled in the terminal, he began filling out a crossword puzzle that he'd saved for this occasion from last Sunday's *New York Times*. He sat inside a kind of barricade—his bag on one chair, his suit coat on another. People milled around him but he kept his eyes on the page, progressing smoothly to the acrostic as soon as he'd finished the crossword. By the time he'd solved both puzzles, they were beginning to board the plane.

His seatmate was a gray-haired woman with glasses. She had brought her own knitted afghan. This was not a good sign, Macon felt, but he could handle it. First he bustled about, loosening his tie and taking off his shoes and removing a book from his bag. Then he opened the book and ostentatiously started reading.

The name of his book was *Miss MacIntosh, My Darling*, and it was 1,198 pages long. (*Always bring a book, as protection against strangers. Magazines don't last. Newspapers from home will make you homesick, and newspapers from elsewhere will remind you you don't belong. You know how alien another paper's typeface seems.*) He'd been lugging around *Miss MacIntosh* for years. It had the advantage of being plotless, as far as he could tell, but invariably interesting, so he could dip into it at random. Any time he raised his eyes, he was careful to mark a paragraph with his finger and to keep a bemused expression on his face.

There was the usual mellifluous murmur from the loudspeaker about seatbelts, emergency exits, oxygen masks. He wondered why stewardesses accented such unlikely words. "*On* our flight this evening we *will* be offering . . ." The woman next to him asked if he wanted a Lifesaver. "No, thank you," Macon said, and he went on with his book. She rustled some little bit of paper, and shortly afterward the smell of spearmint drifted over to him.

He refused a cocktail and he refused a supper tray, although he did accept the milk that was offered with it. He ate an apple and a little box of raisins from his bag, drank the milk, and went off to the lavatory to floss and brush his teeth. When he returned the plane was darker, dotted here and there with reading lamps. Some of the passengers were already asleep. His seatmate had rolled her hair into little O's and X-ed them over with bobby pins. Macon found it amazing that people could be so unself-conscious on airplanes. He'd seen men in whole suits of pajamas; he'd seen women slathered in face cream. You would think they felt no need to be on guard.

He angled his book beneath a slender shaft of light and turned a page. The engines had a weary, dogged sound. It was the period he thought of as the long haul—the gulf between supper and breakfast when they were suspended over the ocean, waiting for that lightening of the sky that was supposed to be morning although, of course, it was nowhere near morning back home. In Macon's opinion, morning in other time zones was like something staged—a curtain painted with a rising sun, superimposed upon the real dark.

He let his head tip back against the seat and closed his eyes. A stewardess's voice, somewhere near the front of the plane, threaded in and out of the droning of the engines. "We just sat and sat and there wasn't a thing to do and all we had was the Wednesday paper and you know how news just never seems to happen on a Wednesday . . ."

Macon heard a man speaking levelly in his ear. "Macon." But he didn't even turn his head. By now he knew these tricks of sound on planes at night. He saw behind his eyelids the soap dish on the kitchen sink at home—another trick, this concreteness of vision. It was an oval china soap dish painted with yellow roses, containing a worn-down sliver of soap and Sarah's rings, her engagement ring and her wedding band, just as she had left them when she walked out.

"I got the tickets," he heard Ethan say. "And they're opening the doors in five minutes."

"All right," Macon told him, "let's plan our strategy."

"Strategy?"

"Where we're going to sit."

"Why would we need strategy for that?"

"It's you who asked to see this movie, Ethan. I would think you'd take an interest in where you're sitting. Now, here's my plan. You go around to that line on the left. Count the little kids. I'll count the line on the right."

"Aw, Dad—"

"Do you want to sit next to some noisy little kid?"

"Well, no."

"And which do you prefer: an aisle seat?"

"I don't care."

"Aisle, Ethan? Or middle of the row? You must have some opinion."

"Not really."

"Middle of the row?"

"It doesn't make any difference."

"Ethan. It makes a great deal of difference. Aisle, you can get out quicker. So if you plan to buy a snack or go to the restroom, you'll want to sit on the aisle. On the other hand, everyone'll be squeezing past you there. So if you don't think you'll be leaving your seat, then I suggest—"

"Aw, Dad, for Christ's sake!" Ethan said.

"Well," Macon said. "If that's the tone you're going to take, we'll just sit any damn place we happen to end up."

"Fine," Ethan said.

"Fine," Macon said.

Now he did turn his head; he rocked it from side to side. But he kept his eyes tightly closed, and in time the voices stopped, and he found himself in that edgy twilight that passes for sleep when you're traveling.

.   .   .

At dawn he accepted a cup of coffee, and he swallowed a vitamin pill from his bag. The other passengers looked frowsy and pale. His seatmate dragged an entire small suitcase off to the lavatory and returned all combed, but her face was puffy. Macon believed that travel causes retention of fluids. When he put his shoes on, they felt too tight, and when he went to shave he found unfamiliar pillows of flesh beneath his eyes. He was better off than most people, though, because he hadn't touched salted food or drunk any alcohol. Alcohol was definitely retained. Drink alcohol on a plane and you'd feel befuddled for days, Macon believed.

The stewardess announced what time it was in London, and there was a stir as people reset their watches. Macon adjusted the digital alarm clock in his shaving kit. The watch on his wrist—which was not digital but real time, circular—he left as it was.

They landed abruptly. It was like being recalled to the hard facts—all that friction suddenly, the gritty runway, the roaring and braking. The loudspeaker came on, purring courteous reminders. The woman next to Macon folded her afghan. "I'm so excited," she said. "I'm going to see my grandchild for the very first time." Macon smiled and told her he hoped it went well. Now that he didn't have to fear being trapped, he found her quite pleasant. Besides, she was so American-looking.

At Heathrow, there was the usual sense of some recent disaster. People rushed about distractedly, other people stood like refugees surrounded by trunks and parcels, and uniformed authorities were trying to deal with a clamor of questions. Since he didn't have to wait for his luggage, Macon sailed through the red tape far ahead of the others. Then he exchanged his currency and boarded the Underground. *I recommend the Underground for everyone except those afraid of heights, and even for them if they will avoid the following stations, which have exceptionally steep escalators . . .*

While the train racketed along, he sorted his currency into envelopes that he'd brought from home—each envelope clearly marked with a different denomination. (*No fumbling with unfamiliar coins, no peering at misleading imprints, if you separate and classify foreign money ahead of time.*) Across from him a row of faces watched. People looked different here, although he couldn't say just how. He thought they were both finer and unhealthier. A woman with a fretful baby kept saying, "Hush now, love. Hush now, love," in that clear, floating, effortless English voice. It was hot, and her forehead had a pallid shine. So did Macon's, no doubt. He slid the envelopes into his breast pocket. The train stopped and more people got on. They stood above him, clinging not to straps but to bulbs attached to flexible sticks, which Macon on his first visit had taken for some kind of microphone.

He was based in London, as usual. From there he would make brief forays into other cities, never listing more than a handful of hotels, a handful of restaurants within a tiny, easily accessible radius in each place; for his guidebooks were anything but all-inclusive. ("Plenty of other books say how to see as much of a city as possible," his boss had told him. "You should say how to see as little.") The name of Macon's hotel was the Jones Terrace. He would have preferred one of the American chain hotels, but those cost too much. The Jones Terrace was all right, though—small and well kept. He swung into action at once to make his room his own, stripping off the ugly bedspread and stuffing it into a closet, unpacking his belongings and hiding his bag. He changed clothes, rinsed the ones he'd worn and hung them in the shower stall. Then, after a wistful glance at the bed, he went out for breakfast. It was nowhere near morning back home, but breakfast was the meal that businessmen most often had to manage for themselves. He made a point of researching it thoroughly wherever he went.

He walked to the Yankee Delight, where he ordered

scrambled eggs and coffee. The service here was excellent. Coffee came at once, and his cup was kept constantly filled. The eggs didn't taste like eggs at home, but then, they never did. What was it about restaurant eggs? They had no character, no backbone. Still, he opened his guidebook and put a checkmark next to the Yankee Delight. By the end of the week, these pages would be barely legible. He'd have scratched out some names, inserted others, and scrawled notes across the margins. He always revisited past entries—every hotel and restaurant. It was tedious but his boss insisted. "Just think how it would look," Julian said, "if a reader walked into some café you'd recommended and found it taken over by vegetarians."

When he'd paid his bill, he went down the street to the New America, where he ordered more eggs and more coffee. "Decaffeinated," he added. (He was a jangle of nerves by now.) The waiter said they didn't have decaffeinated. "Oh, you don't," Macon said. After the waiter had left, Macon made a note in his guidebook.

His third stop was a restaurant called the U.S. Open, where the sausages were so dry that they might have been baked on a rooftop. It figured: The U.S. Open had been recommended by a reader. Oh, the places that readers wrote in to suggest! Macon had once (before he'd grown wiser) reserved a motel room purely on the strength of such a suggestion—somewhere in Detroit or was it Pittsburgh, some city or other, for *Accidental Tourist in America*. He had checked out again at first sight of the linens and fled across the street to a Hilton, where the doorman had rushed to meet him and seized his bag with a cry of pity as if Macon had just staggered in from the desert. Never again, Macon had vowed. He left the sausages on his plate and called for his bill.

In the afternoon (so to speak), he visited hotels. He spoke with various managers and inspected sample rooms where he tested the beds, flushed the toilets, squinted at the showerheads. Most were maintaining their standards, more or less, but something had happened to the Royal Prince. The fact was that it seemed . . . well, foreign. Dark, handsome men in slim silk suits murmured in the lobby while little brown children chased each other around the spittoons. Macon had the feeling he'd got even more hopelessly lost than usual and ended up in Cairo. Cone-shaped ladies in long black veils packed the revolving doors, spinning in from the street with shopping bags full of . . . what? He tried to imagine their purchasing stone-washed denim shorts and thigh-high boots of pink mesh—the merchandise he'd seen in most shop windows. "Er . . ." he said to the manager. How to put this? He hated to sound narrow-minded, but his readers did avoid the exotic. "Has the hotel, ah, changed ownership?" he asked. The manager seemed unusually sensitive. He drew himself up and said the Royal Prince was owned by a corporation, always had been and always would be, always the same corporation. "I see," Macon said. He left feeling dislocated.

At suppertime, he should have tried someplace formal. He had to list at least one formal restaurant in every city for entertaining clients. But tonight he wasn't up to it. Instead, he went to a café he liked called My American Cousin. The diners there had American accents, and so did some of the staff, and the hostess handed out tickets at the door with numbers on them. If your number was called on the loudspeaker you could win a free TV, or at least a framed color print of the restaurant.

Macon ordered a comforting supper of plain boiled vegetables and two lamb chops in white paper bobby socks, along with a glass of milk. The man at the next table was also on his own. He was eating a nice pork pie, and when the waitress offered him dessert he said, "Oh, now, let me see, maybe I will try some at that," in the slow, pleased, coax-me drawl of someone whose womenfolks have all his life encouraged him to put a little meat on his bones. Macon himself had the

351

gingerbread. It came with cream, just the way it used to at his grandmother's house.

By eight o'clock, according to his wristwatch, he was in bed. It was much too early, of course, but he could stretch the day only so far; the English thought it was midnight. Tomorrow he would start his whirlwind dashes through other cities. He'd pick out a few token hotels, sample a few token breakfasts. Coffee with caffeine and coffee without caffeine. Bacon underdone and overdone. Orange juice fresh and canned and frozen. More showerheads, more mattresses. Hairdryers supplied on request? 110-volt switches for electric shavers? When he fell asleep, he thought anonymous rooms were revolving past on a merry-go-round. He thought webbed canvas suitcase stands, ceiling sprinklers, and laminated lists of fire regulations approached and slid away and approached again, over and over all the rest of his days. He thought Ethan was riding a plaster camel and calling, "Catch me!" and falling, but Macon couldn't get there in time and when he reached his arms out, Ethan was gone.

It was one of Macon's bad habits to start itching to go home too early. No matter how short a stay he'd planned, partway through he would decide that he ought to leave, that he'd allowed himself far too much time, that everything truly necessary had already been accomplished—or almost everything, almost accomplished. Then the rest of his visit was spent in phone calls to travel agents and fruitless trips to airline offices and standby waits that came to nothing, so that he was forced to return to the hotel he'd just checked out of. He always promised himself this wouldn't happen again, but somehow it always did. In England, it happened on his fourth afternoon. What more was there to do? he started wondering. Hadn't he got the gist of the place?

Well, be honest: It was Saturday. He chanced to notice,

entering the date in his expense book, that at home it was Saturday morning. Sarah would be stopping by the house for the rug.

She would open the front door and smell home. She would pass through the rooms where she'd been so happy all these years. (Hadn't she been happy?) She would find the cat stretched out on the couch, long and lazy and languid, and she'd settle on the cushion next to her and think, *How could I have left?*

Unfortunately, it was summer, and the airlines were overbooked. He spent two days tracking down faint possibilities that evaporated the instant he drew close. "Anything! Get me anything! I don't have to go to New York; I'll go to Dulles. I'll go to Montreal! Chicago! Shoot, I'll go to Paris or Berlin and see if they have flights. Are there ships? How long do ships take, nowadays? What if this were an emergency? I mean my mother on her deathbed or something? Are you saying there's just no way out of this place?"

The people he dealt with were unfailingly courteous and full of chirpy good humor—really, if not for the strain of travel he believed he might actually have liked the English —but they couldn't solve his problem. In the end he had to stay on. He spent the rest of the week huddled in his room watching TV, chewing a knuckle, subsisting on nonperishable groceries and lukewarm soft drinks because he couldn't face another restaurant.

So he was first in line, naturally, at the check-in counter on the day of his departure. He had his pick of seats: window, nonsmoking. Next to him was a very young couple completely absorbed in each other, so he didn't need *Miss MacIntosh* but sat staring out at the clouds all the long, dull afternoon.

Afternoon was never his favorite time; that was the worst of these homeward flights. It was afternoon for hours and hours, through drinks and lunch and drinks again—all of which he waved away. It was afternoon when they showed the movie; the passengers had to pull their shades down. An orange light filled the plane, burdensome and thick.

Once when he'd been away on an unusually difficult trip—to Japan, where you couldn't even memorize the signs in order to find your way back to a place—Sarah had met his plane in New York. It was their fifteenth anniversary and she had wanted to surprise him. She called Becky at the travel agency to ask his flight number and then she left Ethan with her mother and flew to Kennedy, bringing with her a picnic hamper of wine and cheeses which they shared in the terminal while waiting for their plane home. Every detail of that meal remained in Macon's memory: the cheeses set out on a marble slab, the wine in stemmed crystal glasses that had somehow survived the trip. He could still taste the satiny Brie. He could still see Sarah's small, shapely hand resolutely slicing the bread.

But she didn't meet him in New York today.

She didn't even meet him in Baltimore.

He collected his car from the lot and drove into the city through a glowering twilight that seemed to promise something—a thunderstorm or heat lightning, something dramatic. Could she be waiting at home? In her striped caftan that he was so fond of? With a cool summer supper laid out on the patio table?

Careful not to take anything for granted, he stopped at a Seven-Eleven for milk. He drove to the vet's to pick up Edward. He arrived at the Meow-Bow minutes before closing time; somehow, he'd managed to lose his way. There was no one at the counter. He had to ring the service bell. A girl with a ponytail poked her head through a door, letting in a jumble of animal sounds that rose at all different pitches like an orchestra tuning up. "Yes?" she said.

"I'm here for my dog."

She came forward to open a folder that lay on the counter. "Your last name?"

354

"Leary."

"Oh," she said. "Just a minute."

Macon wondered what Edward had done wrong this time.

The girl disappeared, and a moment later the other one came out, the frizzy one. This evening she wore a V-necked black dress splashed with big pink flowers, its shoulders padded and its skirt too skimpy; and preposterously high-heeled sandals. "Well, hi there!" she said brightly. "How was your trip?"

"Oh, it was . . . where's Edward? Isn't he all right?"

"Sure, he's all right. He was so good and sweet and friendly!"

"Well, fine," Macon said.

"We just got on like a house afire. Seems he took a shine to me, I couldn't say why."

"Wonderful," Macon said. He cleared his throat. "So could I have him back, please?"

"Caroline will bring him."

"Ah."

There was a silence. The woman waited, facing him and wearing a perky smile, with her fingers laced together on the counter. She had painted her nails dark red, Macon saw, and put on a blackish lipstick that showed her mouth to be an unusually complicated shape—angular, like certain kinds of apples.

"Um," Macon said finally. "Maybe I could pay."

"Oh, yes."

She stopped smiling and peered down at the open folder. "That'll be forty-two dollars," she said.

Macon gave her a credit card. She had trouble working the embossing machine; everything had to be done with the flats of her hands, to spare her nails. She filled in the blanks in a jerky scrawl and then turned the bill in his direction. "Signature and phone," she said. She leaned over the counter to watch what he wrote. "Is that your home phone, or your business?"

"It's both. Why? What difference does it make?" he asked.

"I was just wondering," she told him. She tore off his copy, in that splay-fingered style of hers, and put the rest of the bill in a drawer. "I don't know if I mentioned before that it so happens I train dogs."

"Is that right," Macon said.

He looked toward the door where the first girl had disappeared. It always made him nervous when they took too long bringing Edward. What were they doing back there—getting rid of some evidence?

"My speciality is dogs that bite," the woman said.

"Specialty."

"Pardon?"

"Webster prefers 'specialty.' "

She gave him a blank look.

"That must be a dangerous job," Macon said politely.

"Oh, not for me! I'm not scared of a thing in this world."

There was a scuffling sound at the door behind her. Edward burst through, followed by the girl with the ponytail. Edward was giving sharp yelps and flinging himself about so joyfully that when Macon bent to pat him, he couldn't really connect.

"Now, stop that," the girl told Edward. She was trying to buckle his collar. Meanwhile, the woman behind the counter was saying, "Biters, barkers, deaf dogs, timid dogs, dogs that haven't been treated right, dogs that have learned bad habits, dogs that grew up in pet shops and don't trust human beings . . . I can handle all of those."

"Well, good," Macon said.

"Not that he would bite *me*, of course," the woman said. "He just fell in love with me, like I think I was telling you."

"I'm glad to hear it," Macon said.

"But I could train him in no time not to bite other people. You think it over and call me. Muriel, remember? Muriel Pritchett. Let me give you my card."

356

She handed him a salmon-pink business card that she seemed to have pulled out of nowhere. He had to fight his way around Edward to accept it. "I studied with a man who used to train attack dogs," she said. "This is not some amateur you're looking at."

"Well, I'll bear that in mind," Macon said. "Thank you very much."

"Or just call for no reason! Call and talk."

"Talk?"

"Sure! Talk about Edward, his problems, talk about . . . anything! Pick up the phone and just talk. Don't you ever get the urge to do that?"

"Not really," Macon said.

Then Edward gave a particularly piercing yelp, and the two of them rushed home.

Well, of course she wasn't there. He knew it the instant he stepped inside the house, when he smelled that stale hot air and heard the muffled denseness of a place with every window shut. Really he'd known it all along. He'd been fooling himself. He'd been making up fairy tales.

The cat streaked past him and escaped out the door, yowling accusingly. The dog hurtled into the dining room to roll about on the rug and get rid of the scent of the kennel. But there was no rug—only bare, linty floor, and Edward stopped short, looking foolish. Macon knew just how he felt.

He put away the milk and went upstairs to unpack. He took a shower, treading the day's dirty clothes underfoot, and prepared for bed. When he turned off the light in the bathroom, the sight of his laundry dripping over the tub reminded him of travel. Where was the real difference? *Accidental Tourist at Home*, he thought, and he slid wearily into his body bag.

4

When the phone rang, Macon dreamed it was Ethan. He dreamed Ethan was calling from camp, wondering why they'd never come to get him. "But we thought you were dead," Macon said, and Ethan said—in that clear voice of his that cracked on the high notes—"Why would you think *that*?" The phone rang again and Macon woke up. There was a thud of disappointment somewhere inside his rib cage. He understood why people said hearts "sank."

In slow motion, he reached for the receiver. "Yes," he said.

"Macon! Welcome back!"

It was Julian Edge, Macon's boss, his usual loud and sprightly self even this early in the morning. "Oh," Macon said.

"How was the trip?"

"It was okay."

"You just get in last night?"

"Yes."

"Find any super new places?"

"Well, 'super' would be putting it a bit strongly."

"So now I guess you start writing it up."

Macon said nothing.

"Just when do you figure to bring me a manuscript?" Julian asked.

"I don't know," Macon said.

"Soon, do you figure?"

"I don't know."

There was a pause.

"I guess I woke you," Julian said.

"Yes."

"Macon Leary in bed," Julian said. He made it sound like the title of something. Julian was younger than Macon and brasher, breezier, not a serious man. He seemed to enjoy pretending that Macon was some kind of character. "So anyway, can I expect it by the end of the month?"

"No," Macon said.

"Why not?"

"I'm not organized."

"Not organized! What's to organize? All you have to do is retype your old one, basically."

"There's a lot more to it than that," Macon said.

"Look. Fellow. Here it is—" Julian's voice grew fainter. He'd be drawing back to frown at his flashy gold calendar watch with the perforated leather racing band. "Here it is the third of August. I want this thing on the stands by October. That means I'd need your manuscript by August thirty-first."

"I can't do it," Macon said.

In fact, it amazed him he'd found the strength to carry on this conversation.

"August thirty-first, Macon. That's four full weeks away."

"It's not enough," Macon said.

"Not enough," Julian said. "Well. All right, then: mid-September. It's going to knock a good many things out of whack, but I'll give you till mid-September. How's that?"

"I don't know," Macon said.

The dullness of his voice interested him. He felt strangely distant from himself. Julian might have sensed this, for after another pause he said, "Hey. Pal. Are you okay?"

"I'm fine," Macon told him.

"I know you've been through a lot, pal—"

"I'm fine! Just fine! What could be wrong? All I need is time to get organized. I'll have the manuscript in by September fifteenth. Possibly earlier. Yes, very possibly earlier. Maybe the end of August. All right?"

Then he hung up.

But his study was so dim and close, and it gave off the salty, inky smell of mental fidgeting. He walked in and felt overwhelmed by his task, as if finally chaos had triumphed. He turned around and walked out again.

Maybe he couldn't get his guidebook organized, but organizing the household was another matter entirely. There was something fulfilling about that, something consoling—or more than consoling; it gave him the sense of warding off a danger. Over the next week or so, he traveled through the rooms setting up new systems. He radically rearranged all the kitchen cupboards, tossing out the little bits of things in sticky, dusty bottles that Sarah hadn't opened in years. He plugged the vacuum cleaner into a hundred-foot extension cord originally meant for lawn mowers. He went out to the yard and weeded, trimmed, pruned, clipped—stripping down, he pictured it. Up till now Sarah had done the gardening, and certain features of it came as a surprise to him. One variety of weed shot off seeds explosively the instant he touched it, a magnificent last-ditch stand, while others gave way so easily—too easily, breaking at the topmost joint so their roots remained in the ground. Such tenacity! Such genius for survival! Why couldn't human beings do as well?

He stretched a clothesline across the basement so he wouldn't have to use the dryer. Dryers were a terrible waste

360

of energy. Then he disconnected the dryer's wide, flexible exhaust tube, and he taught the cat to go in and out through the empty windowpane where the tube had exited. This meant no more litterbox. Several times a day the cat leapt soundlessly to the laundry sink, stood up long and sinewy on her hind legs, and sprang through the window.

It was a pity Edward couldn't do the same. Macon hated walking him; Edward had never been trained to heel and kept winding his leash around Macon's legs. Oh, dogs were so much trouble. Dogs ate mammoth amounts of food, too; Edward's kibble had to be lugged home from the supermarket, dragged out of the car trunk and up the steep front steps and through the house to the pantry. But for that, at least, Macon finally thought of a solution. At the foot of the old coal chute in the basement he set a plastic trash can, with a square cut out of the bottom. Then he poured the remainder of a sack of kibble into the trash can, which magically became a continuous feeder like the cat's. Next time he bought dog food, he could just drive around to the side of the house and send it rattling down the coal chute.

The only hitch was, Edward turned out to be scared of the basement. Every morning he went to the pantry where his breakfast used to be served, and he sat on his fat little haunches and whimpered. Macon had to carry him bodily down the basement stairs, staggering slightly while Edward scrabbled in his arms. Since the whole idea had been to spare Macon's trick back, he felt he'd defeated his purpose. Still, he kept trying.

Also with his back in mind, he tied the clothes basket to Ethan's old skateboard and he dropped a drawstring bag down the laundry chute at the end of a rope. This meant he never had to carry the laundry either up or down the stairs, or even across the basement. Sometimes, though—laboriously scooting the wheeled basket from the clothesline to the laundry chute, stuffing clean sheets into the bag, running upstairs to

361

haul them in by the long, stiff rope—Macon felt a twinge of embarrassment. Was it possible that this might be sort of silly?

Well, everything was silly, when you got right down to it.

The neighborhood must have learned by now that Sarah had left him. People started telephoning on ordinary week-nights and inviting him to take "potluck" with them. Macon thought at first they meant one of those arrangements where everybody brings a different pot of something and if you're lucky you end up with a balanced meal. He arrived at Bob and Sue Carney's with a bowl of macaroni and cheese. Since Sue was serving spaghetti, he didn't feel he'd been all that lucky. She set his macaroni at one end of the table and no one ate it but Delilah, the three-year-old. She had several helpings, though.

Macon hadn't expected to find the children at the table. He saw he was somebody different now, some kind of bachelor uncle who was assumed to need a glimpse of family life from time to time. But the fact was, he had never much liked other people's children. And gatherings of any sort depressed him. Physical contact with people not related to him—an arm around his shoulder, a hand on his sleeve—made him draw inward like a snail. "You know, Macon," Sue Carney said, leaning across the table to pat his wrist, "whenever you get the urge, you're welcome to drop in on us. Don't wait for an invitation."

"That's nice of you, Sue," he said. He wondered why it was that outsiders' skin felt so unreal—almost waxy, as if there were an invisible extra layer between him and them. As soon as possible, he moved his wrist.

"If you could live any way you wanted," Sarah had once told him, "I suppose you'd end up on a desert island with no other human beings."

"Why! That's not true at all," he'd said. "I'd have you, and Ethan, and my sister and brothers . . ."

"But no people. I mean, people there just by chance, people you didn't know."

"Well, no, I guess not," he'd said. "Would you?"

But of course she would—back then. Back before Ethan died. She'd always been a social person. When there was nothing else to do she'd stroll happily through a shopping mall —Macon's notion of hell, with all those strangers' shoulders brushing his. Sarah thought crowds were exciting. She liked to meet new people. She was fond of parties, even cocktail parties. You'd have to be crazy to like cocktail parties, Macon thought—those scenes of confusion she used to drag him to, where he was made to feel guilty if he managed by some fluke to get involved in a conversation of any depth. "Circulate. Circulate," Sarah would hiss, passing behind him with her drink.

That had changed during this past year. Sarah didn't like crowds anymore. She never went near a mall, hadn't made him go to any parties. They attended only quiet little dinners and she herself had not given a dinner since Ethan died. He'd asked her once, "Shouldn't we have the Smiths and Millards over? They've had us so often."

Sarah said, "Yes. You're right. Pretty soon." And then did nothing about it.

He and she had met at a party. They'd been seventeen years old. It was one of those mixer things, combining their two schools. Even at that age Macon had disliked parties, but he was secretly longing to fall in love and so he had braved this mixer but then stood off in a corner looking unconcerned, he hoped, and sipping his ginger ale. It was 1958. The rest of the world was in button-down shirts, but Macon wore a black turtleneck sweater, black slacks, and sandals. (He was passing through his poet stage.) And Sarah, a bubbly girl with a tumble of copper-brown curls and a round face, large blue eyes, a plump lower lip—she wore something pink, he remembered, that made her skin look radiant. She was ringed by

363

admiring boys. She was short and tidily made, and there was something plucky about the way her little tan calves were so firmly braced, as if she were determined that this looming flock of basketball stars and football stars would not bowl her over. Macon gave up on her at once. No, not even that—he didn't even consider her, not for a single second, but gazed beyond her to other, more attainable girls. So it had to be Sarah who made the first move. She came over to him and asked what he was acting so stuck-up about. "Stuck-up!" he said. "I'm not stuck-up."

"You sure do look it."

"No, I'm just . . . bored," he told her.

"Well, so do you want to dance, or not?"

They danced. He was so unprepared that it passed in a blur. He enjoyed it only later, back home, where he could think it over in a calmer state of mind. And thinking it over, he saw that if he hadn't looked stuck-up she never would have noticed him. He was the only boy who had not openly pursued her. He would be wise not to pursue her in the future; not to seem too eager, not to show his feelings. With Sarah you had to keep your dignity, he sensed.

Lord knows, though, keeping his dignity wasn't easy. Macon lived with his grandparents, and they believed that no one under eighteen ought to have a driver's license. (Never mind if the state of Maryland felt otherwise.) So Grandfather Leary drove Macon and Sarah on their dates. His car was a long black Buick with a velvety gray backseat on which Macon sat all by himself, for his grandfather considered it unseemly for the two of them to sit there together. "I am not your hired chauffeur," he said, "and besides, the backseat has connotations." (Much of Macon's youth was ruled by connotations.) So Macon sat alone in back and Sarah sat up front with Grandfather Leary. Her cloud of hair, seen against the glare of oncoming headlights, reminded Macon of a burning bush.

He would lean forward, clear his throat, and ask, "Um, did you finish your term paper?"

Sarah would say, "Pardon?"

"Term paper," Grandfather Leary would tell her. "Boy wants to know if you finished it."

"Oh. Yes, I finished it."

"She finished it," Grandfather Leary relayed to Macon.

"I do have ears, Grandfather."

"You want to get out and walk? Because I don't have to stand for any mouthing off. I could be home with my loved ones, not motoring around in the dark."

"Sorry, Grandfather."

Macon's only hope was silence. He sat back, still and aloof, knowing that when Sarah looked she'd see nothing but a gleam of blond hair and a blank face—the rest darkness, his black turtleneck blending into the shadows. It worked. "What do you *think* about all the time?" she asked in his ear as they two-stepped around her school gym. He only quirked a corner of his mouth, as if amused, and didn't answer.

Things weren't much different when he got his license. Things weren't much different when he went away to college, though he did give up his black turtlenecks and turn into a Princeton man, crisply, casually attired in white shirts and khakis. Separated from Sarah, he felt a constant hollowness, but in his letters he talked only about his studies. Sarah, home at Goucher, wrote back, *Don't you miss me a little? I can't go anywhere we've been for fear I'll see you looking so mysterious across the room.* She signed her letters *I love you* and he signed his *Fondly.* At night he dreamed she lay next to him, her curls making a whispery sound against his pillow, although all they'd done in real life was a lengthy amount of kissing. He wasn't sure, to tell the truth, that he could manage much more without . . . how did they put it in those days? Losing his cool. Sometimes, he was almost angry with Sarah.

He felt he'd been backed into a false position. He was forced to present this impassive front if he wanted her to love him. Oh, so much was expected of men!

She wrote she wasn't dating other people. Neither was Macon, but of course he didn't say so. He came home in the summer and worked at his grandfather's factory; Sarah worked on a tan at the neighborhood pool. Halfway through that summer, she said she wondered why he'd never asked to sleep with her. Macon thought about that and then said, levelly, that in fact he'd like to ask her now. They went to her parents' house; her parents were vacationing in Rehoboth. They climbed the stairs to her little bedroom, all white ruffles and hot sunlight baking the smell of fresh paint. "Did you bring a whatchamacallit?" Sarah asked, and Macon, unwilling to admit that he hardly knew what one looked like, barked, "No, I didn't bring a whatchamacallit, who do you think I am?"—a senseless question, if you stopped to examine it, but Sarah took it to mean that he was shocked by her, that he thought her too forward, and she said, "Well, excuse me for living!" and ran down the stairs and out of the house. It took him half an hour to find her, and longer than that to make her stop crying. Really, he said, he'd only been thinking of her welfare: In his experience, whatchamacallits weren't all that safe. He tried to sound knowledgeable and immune to passions of the moment. He suggested she visit a doctor he knew—it happened to be the doctor who treated his grandmother's Female Complaint. Sarah dried her tears and borrowed Macon's pen to write the doctor's name on the back of a chewing gum wrapper. But wouldn't the doctor refuse her? she asked. Wouldn't he say she ought to be at least engaged? Well, all right, Macon said, they would get engaged. Sarah said that would be lovely.

Their engagement lasted three years, all through college. Grandfather Leary felt the wedding should be delayed even further, till Macon was firmly settled in his place of employment; but since his place of employment would be Leary Metals, which manufactured cork-lined caps for soft drink bottles, Macon couldn't see himself concentrating on that even briefly. Besides, the rush to and from Sarah's bedroom on her mother's Red Cross days had begun to tell on them both.

So they married the spring they graduated from college, and Macon went to work at the factory while Sarah taught English at a private school. It was seven years before Ethan was born. By that time, Sarah was no longer calling Macon "mysterious." When he was quiet now it seemed to annoy her. Macon sensed this, but there was nothing he could do about it. In some odd way, he was locked inside the stand-offish self he'd assumed when he and she first met. He was frozen there. It was like that old warning of his grandmother's: Don't cross your eyes, they might get stuck that way. No matter how he tried to change his manner, Sarah continued to deal with him as if he were someone unnaturally cool-headed, someone more even in temperament than she but perhaps not quite as feeling.

He had once come upon a questionnaire that she'd filled out in a ladies' magazine—one of those "How Happy Is Your Marriage?" things—and where it said, *I believe I love my spouse more than he/she loves me,* Sarah had checked *True.* The unsettling part was that after Macon gave his automatic little snort of denial, he had wondered if it might be true after all. Somehow, his role had sunk all the way through to the heart. Even internally, by now, he was a fairly chilly man, and if you didn't count his son (who was easy, *easy;* a child is no test at all), there was not one person in his life whom he really agonized over.

When he thought about this now, it was a relief to remind himself that he did miss Sarah, after all. But then his relief seemed unfeeling too, and he groaned and shook his head and tugged his hair in great handfuls.

Some woman phoned and said, "Macon?" He could tell at once it wasn't Sarah. Sarah's voice was light and breathy; this one was rough, tough, wiry. "It's Muriel," she said.

"Muriel," he said.

"Muriel Pritchett."

"Ah, yes," he said, but he still had no clue who she was.

"From the vet's?" she asked. "Who got on so good with your dog?"

"Oh, the vet's!"

He saw her, if dimly. He saw her saying her own name, the long *u* sound and the *p* drawing up her dark red mouth.

"I was just wondering how Edward was."

Macon glanced over at Edward. The two of them were in the study, where Macon had managed to type half a page. Edward lay flat on his stomach with his legs straight out behind him—short, pudgy legs like the drumsticks of a dressed Long Island duckling. "He looks all right to me," Macon said.

"I mean, is he biting?"

"Well, not lately, but he's developed this new symptom. He gets angry if I leave the house. He starts barking and showing his teeth."

"I still think he ought to be trained."

"Oh, you know, he's four and a half and I suppose—"

"That's not too old! I could do it in no time. Tell you what, maybe I could just come around and discuss it. You and me could have a drink or something and talk about what his problems are."

"Well, I really don't think—"

"Or you could come to *my* place. I'd fix you supper."

Macon wondered how it would help Edward to be dragged to supper at some stranger's house.

"Macon? What do you say?" she asked.

"Oh, why, um . . . I think for now I'll just try to manage on my own."

"Well, I can understand that," she said. "Believe me. I've been through that stage. So what I'll do is, I'll wait for you to get in touch. You do still have my card, don't you?"

Macon said he did, although he had no idea where it had got to.

"I don't want to be pushy!" she said.

"No, well . . ." Macon said. Then he hung up and went back to his guidebook.

He was still on the introduction, and it was already the end of August. How would he meet his deadline? The back of the desk chair hit his spine in just the wrong place. The *s* key kept sticking. The typewriter tapped out audible words. "Inimitable," it said. His typing sounded just like Sarah saying "inimitable." "You in your inimitable way . . ." she told him. He gave a quick shake of his head. *Generally food in England is not as jarring as in other foreign countries. Nice cooked vegetables, things in white sauce, pudding for dessert . . . I don't know why some travelers complain about English food.*

In September, he decided to alter his system of dressing. If he wore sweat suits at home—the zipper-free kind, nothing to scratch or bind him—he could go from one shower to the next without changing clothes. The sweat suit would serve as both pajamas and day wear.

He bought a couple of them, medium gray. The first night he wore one to bed he enjoyed the feel of it, and he liked not having to dress the next morning. In fact, it occurred to him that he might as well wear the same outfit two days in a row; skip his shower on alternate evenings. Talk about saving energy! In the morning all he had to do was shave. He wondered if he ought to grow a beard.

Around noon of the second day, though, he started feeling

a little low. He was sitting at his typewriter and something made him notice his posture—stooped and sloppy. He blamed the sweat suit. He rose and went to the full-length mirror in the hall. His reflection reminded him of a patient in a mental hospital. Part of the trouble, perhaps, was his shoes—regular black tie shoes intended for dressier clothes. Should he buy sneakers? But he would hate to be mistaken for a jogger. He noticed that without a belt around his waist, he tended to let his stomach stick out. He stood up straighter. That evening when it was time to wash the first sweat suit, he used extra-hot water to shrink out some of the bagginess.

He felt much worse in the morning. It had been a warm night and he woke up sticky and cross. He couldn't face the thought of popcorn for breakfast. He laundered a load of sheets and then, in the midst of hanging them, found himself standing motionless with his head bowed, both wrists dangling over the clothesline as if he himself had been pinned there. "Buck up," he said aloud. His voice sounded creaky, out of practice.

This was his day for grocery shopping—Tuesday, when the supermarket was least crowded with other human beings. But somehow, he couldn't bring himself to get going. He dreaded all that business with the address books, the three tabbed books he shopped with. (One held data from *Consumer Reports*—the top-rated brand of bread, for instance, listed under B. In another he noted prices, and in the third he filed his coupons.) He kept having to stop and riffle through them, muttering prices under his breath, comparing house brands to cents-off name brands. Oh, everything seemed so complicated. Why bother? Why eat at all, in fact?

On the other hand, he needed milk. And Edward was low on dog food, and Helen was completely out of cat food.

He did something he'd never done before. He telephoned The Market Basket, a small, expensive grocery that delivered. And he didn't order just emergency rations. No, he called in the whole week's list. "Shall we bring this to the front or the back?" the clerk asked in her tinselly voice.

"The back," Macon said. "No, wait. Bring the perishables to the back, but put the dog food next to the coal chute."

"Coal chute," the clerk repeated, apparently writing it down.

"The coal chute at the side of the house. But not the cat food; that goes in back with the perishables."

"Well, wait now—"

"And the upstairs items at the front of the house."

"What upstairs items?"

"Toothpaste, Ivory soap, dog biscuits . . ."

"I thought you said the dog biscuits went to the coal chute."

"Not the dog biscuits, the dog *food!* It's the food that goes to the coal chute, dammit."

"Now, look here," the clerk said. "There's no call to be rude."

"Well, I'm sorry," Macon told her, "but I just want the simplest thing, it seems to me: one puny box of Milkbone biscuits up beside my bed. If I give Edward my buttered popcorn it upsets his stomach. Otherwise I wouldn't mind; it's not as if I'm hoarding it all for myself or something, but he has this sensitivity to fats and I'm the only one in the house, it's me who has to clean up if he gets sick. I'm the only one to do it; I'm all alone; it's just me; it seems everybody's just . . . fled from me, I don't know, I've lost them, I'm left standing here saying, 'Where'd they go? Where is everybody? Oh, God, what did I do that was so bad?' "

His voice was not behaving right and he hung up. He stood over the telephone rubbing his forehead. Had he given her his name? Or not. He couldn't remember. Please, please, let him not have given her his name.

He was falling apart; that much was obvious. He would have to get a grip on himself. First thing: out of this sweat suit. It was some kind of jinx. He clapped his hands together briskly, and then he climbed the stairs. In the bathroom, he yanked off the sweat suit and dropped it into the tub. Yesterday's hung from the shower curtain rod, still damp. There wasn't a chance it would dry by tonight. What a mistake! He felt like a fool. He'd come within an inch, within a hairsbreadth of turning into one of those pathetic creatures you see on the loose from time to time—unwashed, unshaven, shapeless, talking to themselves, padding along in their institutional garb.

Neatly dressed now in a white shirt and khakis, he gathered the damp sweat suit and carried it down to the basement. It would make good winter pajamas, at least. He put it in the dryer, wedged the exhaust tube in the window again, and set the dials. Better to consume a little energy than to fall into despair over a soggy sweat suit.

At the top of the basement stairs, Edward was complaining. He was hungry, but not brave enough to descend the stairs on his own. When he caught sight of Macon he lay flat, with his nose poking over the topmost step, and put on a hopeful expression. "Coward," Macon told him. He scooped Edward up in both arms and turned to lumber back down. Edward's teeth started chattering—a tickety-tick like rice in a cup. It occurred to Macon that Edward might know something he didn't. Was the basement haunted, or what? It had been weeks now, and Edward was still so frightened that sometimes, set in front of his food, he just stood there dismally and made a puddle without bothering to lift his leg. "You're being very silly, Edward," Macon told him.

Just then, an eerie howl rose from . . . where? From the basement's very air, it seemed. It continued steadily; it grew. Edward, who must have been expecting this all along, kicked off instantly with his sturdy, clawed hind legs against Macon's diaphragm. Macon felt the wind knocked out of him. Edward whomped into the wall of damp body bags on the clothesline, rebounded, and landed in the center of Macon's stomach. Macon set one foot blindly in the wheeled basket and his legs went out from under him. He stepped down hard into empty space.

He was lying on his back, on the clammy cement floor, with his left leg doubled beneath him. The sound that had set all this in motion paused for one split second and then resumed. It was clear now that it came from the dryer's exhaust tube. "Shoot," Macon said to Edward, who lay panting on top of him. "Wouldn't you think that idiot cat would know the dryer was running?"

He could see how it must have happened. Attempting to enter from outside, she'd been met by a whistling wind, but she had stubbornly continued into the tube. He pictured her eyes pressed into slits, her ears flattened back by a lint-filled gale. Wailing and protesting, she had nonetheless clung to her course. What persistence!

Macon shook Edward off and rolled over on his stomach. Even so small a movement caused him agony. He felt a lump of nausea beginning in his throat, but he rolled once more, dragging his leg behind him. With his teeth set, he reached for the door of the dryer and pulled it open. The sweat suit slowly stopped revolving. The cat stopped howling. Macon watched her bumbling, knobby shape inching backward through the tube. Just as she reached her exit, the entire tube fell out of the window and into the laundry sink, but Helen didn't fall with it. He hoped she was all right. He watched until she scurried past the other window, looking just slightly rumpled. Then he drew a breath and began the long, hard trip up the stairs for help.

5

"O h, I've erred and I have stumbled," Macon's sister sang in the kitchen, "I've been sinful and unwise . . ."

She had a tremulous soprano that sounded like an old lady's, although she was younger than Macon. You could imagine such a voice in church, some country kind of church where the women still wore flat straw hats.

> *I'm just a lucky pilgrim*
> *On the road to Paradise.*

Macon was lying on the daybed in his grandparents' sun porch. His left leg, encased in plaster from mid-thigh to instep, was not painful so much as absent. There was a constant dull, cottony numbness that made him want to pinch his own shin. Not that he could, of course. He was sealed away from himself. The hardest blow felt like a knock on the wall from a neighboring room.

Still, he felt a kind of contentment. He lay listening to his sister fix breakfast, idly scratching the cat who had made herself a nest in the blankets. "I've had trials, I've had sorrows," Rose trilled merrily, "I've had grief and sacrifice . . ."

374

Once she got the coffee started, she would come help him across the living room to the downstairs bathroom. He still found it difficult to navigate, especially on polished floors. Nowadays he marveled at all those people on crutches whom he used to take for granted. He saw them as a flock of stalky wading birds, dazzlingly competent with their sprightly hops and debonaire pivots. How did they do it?

His own crutches, so new their rubber tips were not yet scuffed, leaned against the wall. His bathrobe hung over a chair. Beneath the window was a folding card table with a wood-grained cardboard top and rickety legs. His grandparents had been dead for years, but the table remained set up as if for one of their eternal bridge games. Macon knew that on its underside was a yellowed label reading ATLAS MFG. CO., with a steel engraving of six plump, humorless men in high-collared suits standing upon a board laid across the very same table. FURNISHINGS OF DECEPTIVE DELICACY, the caption said. Macon associated the phrase with his grandmother: deceptive delicacy. Lying on the sun porch floor as a boy, he had studied her fragile legs, from which her anklebones jutted out like doorknobs. Her solid, black, chunky-heeled shoes were planted squarely a foot apart, never tapping or fidgeting.

He heard his brother Porter upstairs, whistling along with Rose's song. He knew it was Porter because Charles never whistled. There was the sound of a shower running. His sister looked through the sun porch door, with Edward peering around her and panting at Macon as if he were laughing.

"Macon? Are you awake?" Rose asked.

"I've *been* awake for hours," he told her, for there was something vague about her that caused her brothers to act put-upon and needy whenever she chanced to focus on them. She was pretty in a sober, prim way, with beige hair folded unobtrusively at the back of her neck where it wouldn't be a bother. Her figure was a very young girl's, but her clothes were spinsterly and concealing.

She wrapped him in his bathrobe and helped him stand up. Now his leg actively hurt. It seemed the pain was a matter of gravity. A throbbing ache sank slowly down the length of the bone. With Rose supporting him on one side and a crutch on the other, he hobbled out of the sun porch, through the living room with its shabby, curlicued furniture. The dog kept getting underfoot. "Maybe I could stop and rest a moment," Macon said when they passed the couch.

"It's only a little farther."

They entered the pantry. Rose opened the bathroom door and helped him inside. "Call me when you're ready," she said, closing the door after him. Macon sagged against the sink.

At breakfast, Porter was cheerily talkative while the others ate in silence. Porter was the best-looking of all the Learys—more tightly knit than Macon, his hair a brighter shade of blond. He gave an impression of vitality and direction that his brothers lacked. "Got a lot to do today," he said between mouthfuls. "That meeting with Herrin, interviews for Dave's old job, Cates flying in from Atlanta . . ."

Charles just sipped his coffee. While Porter was already dressed, Charles still wore his pajamas. He was a soft, sweet-faced man who never seemed to move; any time you looked at him he'd be watching you with his sorrowful eyes that slanted downward at the outer corners.

Rose brought the coffeepot from the stove. "Last night, Edward woke me twice asking to go out," she said. "Do you think he has some sort of kidney problem?"

"It's the adjustment," Macon said. "Adjustment to change. I wonder how he knows not to wake *me*."

Porter said, "Maybe we could rig up some sort of system. One of those little round pet doors or something."

"Edward's kind of portly for a pet door," Macon said.

"Besides," Rose said, "the yard's not fenced. We can't let him out on his own if he's not fenced in."

"A litterbox, then," Porter suggested.

"Litterbox! For a dog?"

"Why not? If it were big enough."

Macon said, "Use a bathtub. The one in the basement. No one goes there anymore."

"But who would clean it?"

"Ah."

They all looked down at Edward, who was lying at Rose's feet. He rolled his eyes at them.

"How come you have him, anyway?" Porter asked Macon.

"He was Ethan's."

"Oh. I see," Porter said. He gave a little cough. "Animals!" he said brightly. "Ever considered what they must think of us? I mean, here we come back from the grocery store with the most amazing haul—chicken, pork, half a cow. We leave at nine and we're back at ten, evidently having caught an entire herd of beasts. They must think we're the greatest hunters on earth!"

Macon leaned back in his chair with his coffee mug cupped in both hands. The sun was warming the breakfast table, and the kitchen smelled of toast. He almost wondered whether, by some devious, subconscious means, he had engineered this injury—every elaborate step leading up to it—just so he could settle down safe among the people he'd started out with.

Charles and Porter left for the factory, and Rose went upstairs and ran the vacuum cleaner. Macon, who was supposed to be typing his guidebook, struggled back to the sun porch and collapsed. Since he'd come home he'd been sleeping too much. The urge to sleep was like a great black cannonball rolling around inside his skull, making his head heavy and droopy.

On the wall at the end of the room hung a portrait of the four Leary children: Charles, Porter, Macon, and Rose, clustered in an armchair. Their grandfather had commissioned that portrait several years before they came to live with him. They were still in California with their mother—a giddy young war widow. From time to time she sent snapshots, but Grandfather Leary found those inadequate. By their very nature, he told her in his letters, photos lied. They showed what a person looked like over a fraction of a second—not over long, slow minutes, which was what you'd take to study someone in real life. In that case, said Alicia, didn't paintings lie also? They showed hours instead of minutes. It wasn't Grandfather Leary she said this to, but the artist, an elderly Californian whose name Grandfather Leary had somehow got hold of. If the artist had had a reply, Macon couldn't remember what it was.

He could remember sitting for the portrait, though, and now when he looked at it he had a very clear picture of his mother standing just outside the gilded frame in a pink kimono, watching the painting take shape while she toweled her hair dry. She had fluffy, short, brittle hair whose color she "helped along," as she put it. Her face was a type no longer seen—it wasn't just unfashionable, it had vanished altogether. How did women mold their basic forms to suit the times? Were there no more of those round chins, round foreheads, and bruised, baroque little mouths so popular in the forties?

The artist, it was obvious, found her very attractive. He kept pausing in his work to say he wished she were the subject. Alicia gave a breathless laugh and shooed away his words with one hand. Probably later she had gone out with him a few times. She was always taking up with new men, and they were always the most exciting men in the world, to hear her tell it. If they were artists, why, she had to give a party and get all her friends to buy their paintings. If they flew small planes on weekends, she had to start pilot's lessons. If they were political, there she was on street corners thrusting petitions on passersby. Her children were too young to worry about the men themselves, if there was any reason to worry. No, it was her enthusiasm that disturbed them. Her enthusiasm came in spurts, a violent zigzag of hobbies, friends, boyfriends, causes. She always seemed about to fall over the brink of something. She was always going too far. Her voice had an edge to it, as if at any moment it might break. The faster she talked and the brighter her eyes grew, the more fixedly her children stared at her, as if willing her to follow their example of steadiness and dependability. "Oh, what is it with you?" she would ask them. "Why are you such sticks?" And she would give up on them and flounce off to meet her crowd. Rose, the baby, used to wait for her return in the hall, sucking her thumb and stroking an old fur stole that Alicia never wore anymore.

Sometimes Alicia's enthusiasm turned to her children—an unsettling experience. She took them all to the circus and bought them cotton candy that none of them enjoyed. (They liked to keep themselves tidy.) She yanked them out of school and enrolled them briefly in an experimental learning community where no one wore clothes. The four of them, chilled and miserable, sat hunched in a row in the common room with their hands pressed flat between their bare knees. She dressed as a witch and went trick-or-treating with them, the most mortifying Halloween of their lives, for she got carried away as usual and cackled, croaked, scuttled up to strangers and shook her ragged broom in their faces. She started making mother-daughter outfits for herself and Rose, in strawberry pink with puffed sleeves, but stopped when the sewing machine pierced her finger and made her cry. (She was always getting hurt. It may have been because she rushed so.) Then she turned to something else, and something else, and something else. She believed in change as if it were a religion. Feeling sad? Find a new man! Creditors after you, rent due, children running fevers? Move to a new apartment! During one year, they moved so often that every day after school, Macon had to stand deliberating a while before setting out for home.

In 1950, she decided to marry an engineer who traveled around the world building bridges. "Portugal. Panama. Brazil," she told the children. "We'll finally get to see our planet." They gazed at her stonily. If they had met this man before, they had no recollection of it. Alicia said, "Aren't you excited?" Later—it may have been after he took them all out to dinner—she said she was sending them to live with their grandparents instead. "Baltimore's more suitable for children, really," she said. Did they protest? Macon couldn't remember. He recalled his childhood as a glassed-in place with grown-ups rushing past, talking at him, making changes, while he himself stayed mute. At any rate, one hot night in June Alicia put them on a plane to Baltimore. They were met by their grandparents, two thin, severe, distinguished people in dark clothes. The children approved of them at once.

After that, they saw Alicia only rarely. She would come breezing into town with an armload of flimsy gifts from tropical countries. Her print dresses struck the children as flashy; her makeup was too vivid, like a foreigner's. She seemed to find her children comical—their navy-and-white school uniforms, their perfect posture. "My God! How stodgy you've grown!" she would cry, evidently forgetting she'd thought them stodgy all along. She said they took after their father. They sensed this wasn't meant as a compliment. (When they asked what their father had been like, she looked down at her own chin and said, "Oh, Alicia, grow up.") Later, when her sons married, she seemed to see even more resemblance, for at one time or another she'd apologized to all three daughters-in-law for what they must have to put up with. Like some naughty, gleeful fairy, Macon imagined, she darted in and out of their lives leaving a trail of irresponsible remarks, apparently never considering they might be passed on. "I don't see how you stay married to the man," she'd said to Sarah. She herself was now on her fourth husband, a rock-garden architect with a white goatee.

It was true the children in the portrait seemed unrelated to her. They lacked her blue-and-gold coloring; their hair had an ashy cast and their eyes were a steely gray. They all had that distinct center groove from nose to upper lip. And never in a million years would Alicia have worn an expression so guarded and suspicious.

Uncomfortably arranged-looking, they gazed out at the viewer. The two older boys, plump Charles and trim Porter, perched on either arm of the chair in white shirts with wide, flat, open collars. Rose and Macon sat on the seat in matching playsuits. Rose appeared to be in Macon's lap, although actually she'd been settled between his knees, and Macon had the indrawn tenseness of someone placed in a physically close situation he wasn't accustomed to. His hair, like the others', slanted silkily across his forehead. His mouth was thin, almost colorless, and firmed a bit, as if he'd decided to take a stand on something. The set of that mouth echoed now in Macon's mind. He glanced at it, glanced away, glanced back. It was Ethan's mouth. Macon had spent twelve years imagining Ethan as a sort of exchange student, a visitor from the outside world, and here it turned out he'd been a Leary all along. What a peculiar thing to recognize at this late date.

He sat up sharply and reached for his trousers, which Rose had cut short across the left thigh and hemmed with tiny, even stitches.

No one else in the world had the slightest idea where he was. Not Julian, not Sarah, not anyone. Macon liked knowing that. He said as much to Rose. "It's nice to be so unconnected," he told her. "I wish things could stay that way a while."

"Why can't they?"

"Oh, well, you know, someone will call here, Sarah or someone—"

"Maybe we could just not answer the phone."

"What, let it go on ringing?"

"Why not?"

"Not answer it *any* time?"

"Most who call me are neighbors," Rose said. "They'll pop over in person if they don't get an answer. And you know the boys: Neither one of them likes dealing with telephones."

"That's true," Macon said.

Julian would come knocking on his door, planning to harangue him for letting his deadline slip past. He'd have to give up. Then Sarah would come for a soup ladle or something, and when he didn't answer she would ask the neighbors and they'd say he hadn't shown his face in some time. She would try to get in touch with his family and the telephone would ring and ring, and then she would start to worry. *What's happened?* she would wonder. *How could I have left him on his own?*

Lately, Macon had noticed he'd begun to view Sarah as a form of enemy. He'd stopped missing her and started plotting her remorsefulness. It surprised him to see how quickly he'd made the transition. Was this what two decades of marriage amounted to? He liked to imagine her self-reproaches. He composed and recomposed her apologies. He hadn't had such thoughts since he was a child, dreaming of how his mother would weep at his funeral.

In the daytime, working at the dining room table, he would hear the telephone and he'd pause, fingers at rest on the typewriter keys. One ring, two rings. Three rings. Rose would walk in with a jar of silver polish. She didn't even seem to hear. "What if that's some kind of emergency?" he would ask. Rose would say, "Hmm? Who would call *us* for an emergency?" and then she would take the silver from the buffet and spread it at the other end of the table.

382

There had always been some family member requiring Rose's care. Their grandmother had been bedridden for years before she died, and then their grandfather got so senile, and first Charles and later Porter had failed in their marriages and come back home. So she had enough right here to fill her time. Or she made it enough; for surely it couldn't be necessary to polish every piece of silver every week. Shut in the house with her all day, Macon noticed how painstakingly she planned the menus; how often she reorganized the utensil drawer; how she ironed even her brothers' socks, first separating them from the clever plastic grips she used to keep them mated in the washing machine. For Macon's lunch, she cooked a real meal and served it on regular place mats. She set out cut-glass dishes of pickles and olives that had to be returned to their bottles later on. She dolloped homemade mayonnaise into a tiny bowl.

Macon wondered if it ever occurred to her that she lived an odd sort of life—unemployed, unmarried, supported by her brothers. But what job would she be suited for? he asked himself. Although he could picture her, come to think of it, as the mainstay of some musty, antique law firm or accounting firm. Nominally a secretary, she would actually run the whole business, arranging everything just so on her employer's desk every morning and allowing no one below her or above her to overlook a single detail. Macon could use a secretary like that. Recalling the gum-chewing redhead in Julian's disastrous office, he sighed and wished the world had more Roses.

He zipped a page from his typewriter and set it face down on a stack of others. He had finished with his introduction—general instructions like *A subway is not an underground train* and *Don't say restroom, say toilet*—and he'd finished the chapter called "Trying to Eat in England." Rose had mailed those off for him yesterday. That was his new stratagem: sending his book piece by piece from this undisclosed location. "There's no return address on this," Rose told him.

"There's not meant to be," Macon said. Rose had nodded solemnly. She was the only one in the family who viewed his guidebooks as real writing. She kept a row of them in her bedroom bookcase, alphabetized by country.

In midafternoon, Rose stopped work to watch her favorite soap opera. This was something Macon didn't understand. How could she waste her time on such trash? She said it was because there was a wonderfully evil woman in it. "There are enough evil people in real life," Macon told her.

"Yes, but not wonderfully evil."

"Well, that's for sure."

"This one, you see, is so obvious. You know exactly whom to mistrust."

While she watched, she talked aloud to the characters. Macon could hear her in the dining room. "It isn't *you* he's after, sweetie," she said, and "Just you wait. Ha!"—not at all her usual style of speech. A commercial broke in, but Rose stayed transfixed where she was. Macon, meanwhile, worked on "Trying to Sleep in England," typing away in a dogged, uninspired rhythm.

When the doorbell rang, Rose didn't respond. Edward went mad, barking and scratching at the door and running back to Macon and racing again to the door. "Rose?" Macon called. She said nothing. Finally he stood up, assembled himself on his crutches, and went as quietly as possible to the hall.

Well, it wasn't Sarah. A glance through the lace curtain told him that much. He opened the door and peered out. "Yes?" he said.

It was Garner Bolt, a neighbor from home—a scrawny little gray man who had made his fortune in cleaning supplies. When he saw Macon, every line in his pert, pointed face turned upward. "There you are!" he said. It was hard to hear him over Edward, who went on barking frantically.

"Why, Garner," Macon said.

"We worried you had died."

"You did?"

Macon grabbed at Edward's collar, but missed.

"Saw the papers piling up on your lawn, mail inside your screen door, didn't know what to think."

"Well, I meant to send my sister for those," Macon said. "I broke my leg, you see."

"Now, how did you do that?"

"It's a long story."

He gave up blocking the door. "Come on in," he told Garner.

Garner took off his cap, which had a Sherwin-Williams Paint sign across the front. His jacket was part of some long-ago suit, a worn shiny brown, and his overalls were faded to white at the knees. He stepped inside, skirting the dog, and shut the door behind him. Edward's barks turned to whimpers. "My car is full of your mail," Garner said. "Brenda said I ought to bring it to your sister and ask if she knew of your whereabouts. Also I promised your friend."

"What friend?"

"Lady in pedal pushers."

"I don't know any lady in pedal pushers," Macon said. He hadn't realized pedal pushers still existed, even.

"Saw her standing on your porch, rattling your doorknob. Calling out, 'Macon? You in there?' Skinny little lady with hair. Looked to be in her twenties or so."

"Well, I can't imagine who it was."

"Squinching in and shading her eyes."

"Who could it be?"

"Tripping down the porch steps in her great tall pointy high heels."

"The dog lady," Macon said. "Jesus."

"Kind of young, ain't she?"

"I don't even know her!"

"Going round the back of the house to call out, 'Macon? Macon?' "

"I barely met her!"

"It was her that told me about the windle."

"Windle?"

"Windle to the basement, all broke out. Fall sets in and it'll turn your furnace on. Waste all kinds of energy."

"Oh. Well. Yes, I suppose it would," Macon said.

"We thought you might've been burglarized or something."

Macon led the way to the dining room. "See, what happened," he said, "I broke my leg and I came to live at my family's till I could manage for myself again."

"We didn't see no ambulance though or nothing."

"Well, I called my sister."

"Sister's a doctor?"

"Just to come and take me to the emergency room."

"When Brenda broke her hip on the missing step," Garner said, "she called the ambulance."

"Well, I called my sister."

"Brenda called the ambulance."

They seemed to be stuck.

"I guess I ought to notify the post office about my mail," Macon said finally. He lowered himself into his chair.

Garner pulled out another chair and sat down with his cap in his hands. He said, "I could just keep on bringing it."

"No, I'll have Rose notify them. Lord, all these bills must be coming due and so forth—"

"I could bring it just as easy."

"Thanks anyway."

"Why don't I bring it."

"To tell the truth," Macon said, "I'm not so sure I'll be going back there."

This hadn't occurred to him before. He placed his crutches together delicately, like a pair of chopsticks, and laid them on the floor beside his chair. "I might stay on here with my family," he said.

"And give up that fine little house?"

"It's kind of big for just one person."

Garner frowned down at his cap. He put it on his head, changed his mind, and took it off again. "Look," he said. "Back when me and Brenda were newlyweds we were awful together. Just awful. Couldn't neither one of us stand the other, I'll never know how we lasted."

"We aren't newlyweds, though," Macon said. "We've been married twenty years."

"Brenda and me did not speak to each other for very nearly every bit of nineteen and thirty-five," Garner said. "January to August, nineteen and thirty-five. New Year's Day till my summer vacation. Not a single blessed word."

Macon's attention was caught. "What," he said, "not even 'Pass the salt'? 'Open the window'?"

"Not even that."

"Well, how did you manage your daily life?"

"Mostly, she stayed over to her sister's."

"Oh, then."

"The morning my vacation began, I felt so miserable I like to died. Thought to myself, 'What am I doing, anyhow?' Called long distance to Ocean City and booked a room for two. In those days long distance was some big deal, let me tell you. Took all these operators and so forth and it cost a mint. Then I packed some clothes for me and some clothes for Brenda and went on over to her sister's house. Her sister says, 'What do *you* want?' She was the type that likes to see dissension. I walk right past her. Find Brenda in the living room, mending hose. Open my suitcase: 'Look at here. Your sun dress for dining in a seafood restaurant,' I tell her. 'Two pairs of shorts. Two blouses. Your swimsuit.' She don't even look at me. 'Your bathrobe,' I say. 'Your nightgown you wore on our honeymoon.' Acts like I'm not even there. 'Brenda,'

I tell her. I say. 'Brenda, I am nineteen years old and I'll never be nineteen again. I'll never be *alive* again. I mean this is the only life I get to go through, Brenda, so far as I know, and I've spent this great large chunk of it sitting alone in an empty apartment too proud to make up, too scared you'd say no, but even if you did say no it can't be worse than what I got now. I'm the loneliest man in the world, Brenda, so please come to Ocean City with me.' And Brenda, she lays down her mending and says, 'Well, since you ask, but it looks to me like you forgot my bathing cap.' And off we went."

He sat back triumphantly in his chair. "So," he said.

"So," Macon said.

"So you get my point."

"What point?"

"You have to let her know you need her."

"See, Garner, I think we've gone beyond little things like letting her know I—"

"Don't take this personally, Macon, but I got to level with you: There's times when you've been sort of frustrating. I'm not talking about myself, mind; *I* understand. It's just some of the others in the neighborhood, they've been put off a little. Take during your tragedy. I mean people like to offer help at occasions like that—send flowers and visit at the viewing hour and bring casseroles for after the service. Only you didn't even have a service. Held a cremation, Lord God, somewheres off in Virginia without a word to anyone and come home directly. Peg Everett tells you she's put you in her prayers and Sarah says, 'Oh, bless you, Peg,' but what do *you* say? You ask Peg if her son might care to take Ethan's bike off your hands."

Macon groaned. "Yes," he said, "I never know how to behave at these times."

"Then you mow your lawn like nothing has happened."

"The grass did keep on growing, Garner."

"We was all dying to do it for you."

"Well, thanks," Macon said, "but I enjoyed the work."

"See what I mean?"

Macon said, "Now, wait. Just to insert some logic into this discussion—"

"That's *exactly* what I mean!"

"You started out talking about Sarah. You've switched to how I disappoint the neighbors."

"What's the difference? You might not know this, Macon, but you come across as a person that charges ahead on your own somewhat. Just look at the way you walk! The way you, like, *lunge*, lope on down the street with your head running clear in front of your body. If a fellow wants to stop you and, I don't know, offer his condolences, he'd be liable to get plowed down. Now, I know you care, and you know you care, but how does it look to the others? I ask you! No wonder she up and left."

"Garner, I appreciate your thoughts on this," Macon said, "but Sarah's fully aware that I care. I'm not as tongue-tied as you like to make out. And this isn't one of those open-shut, can-this-marriage-be-saved deals, either. I mean, you're just plain goddamned *wrong*, Garner."

"Well," Garner said. He looked down at his cap, and after a moment he jammed it abruptly on his head. "I guess I'll fetch your mail in, then," he said.

"Right. Thanks."

Garner rose to his feet and shuffled out. His leaving alerted Edward, who started barking all over again. There was an empty spell during which Macon looked down at his cast and listened to the soap opera from the living room. Meanwhile Edward whined at the door and paced back and forth, clicking his toenails. Then Garner returned. "Mostly catalogs," he said, flinging his load on the table. He brought with him the smell of fresh air and dry leaves. "Brenda said we might as well not bother with the newspapers; just throw them out."

"Oh, yes, of course," Macon said.

He stood up and they shook hands. Garner's fingers were crisp and intricately shaped, like crumpled paper. "Thanks for stopping by," Macon told him.

"Any time," Garner said, looking elsewhere.

Macon said, "I didn't mean, you know—I hope I didn't sound short-tempered."

"Naw," Garner said. He lifted an arm and let it drop. "Shoot. Don't think a thing about it." Then he turned to leave.

As soon as he did, Macon thought of a flood of other things he should have mentioned. It wasn't all his fault, he wanted to say. Sarah had a little to do with it too. What Sarah needed was a rock, he wanted to say; someone who wouldn't crumble. Otherwise, why had she picked him to marry? But he held his peace and watched Garner walk out. There was something pitiable about the two sharp cords that ran down the back of Garner's neck, cupping a little ditch of mapped brown skin between them.

When his brothers came home from work, the house took on a relaxed, relieved atmosphere. Rose drew the living room curtains and lit a few soft lamps. Charles and Porter changed into sweaters. Macon started mixing his special salad dressing. He believed that if you pulverized the spices first with a marble mortar and pestle, it made all the difference. The others agreed that no one else's dressing tasted as good as Macon's. "Since you've been gone," Charles told him, "we've had to buy that bottled stuff from the grocery store." He made it sound as if Macon had been gone a few weeks or so—as if his entire marriage had been just a brief trip elsewhere.

For supper they had Rose's pot roast, a salad with Macon's dressing, and baked potatoes. Baked potatoes had always been their favorite food. They had learned to fix them as children,

390

and even after they were big enough to cook a balanced meal they used to exist solely on baked potatoes whenever Alicia left them to their own devices. There was something about the smell of a roasting Idaho that was so cozy, and also, well, *conservative*, was the way Macon put it to himself. He thought back on years and years of winter evenings: the kitchen windows black outside, the corners furry with gathering darkness, the four of them seated at the chipped enamel table meticulously filling scooped-out potato skins with butter. You let the butter melt in the skins while you mashed and seasoned the floury insides; the skins were saved till last. It was almost a ritual. He recalled that once, during one of their mother's longer absences, her friend Eliza had served them what she called potato boats—restuffed, not a bit like the genuine article. The children, with pinched, fastidious expressions, had emptied the stuffing and proceeded as usual with the skins, pretending to overlook her mistake. The skins should be crisp. They should not be salted. The pepper should be freshly ground. Paprika was acceptable, but only if it was American. Hungarian paprika had too distinctive a taste. Personally, Macon could do without paprika altogether.

While they ate, Porter discussed what to do with his children. Tomorrow was his weekly visitation night, when he would drive over to Washington, where his children lived with their mother. "The thing of it is," he said, "eating out in restaurants is so artificial. It doesn't seem like real food. And anyway, they all three have different tastes. They always argue over where to go. Someone's on a diet, someone's turned vegetarian, someone can't stand food that crunches. And I end up shouting, 'Oh, for God's sake, we're going to Such-and-Such and that's that!' So we go and everybody sulks throughout the meal."

"Maybe you should just not visit," Charles said reasonably. (He had never had children of his own.)

"Well, of course I want to visit, Charles. I just wish we had some different program. You know what would be ideal? If we could all do something with tools together. I mean like the old days before the divorce, when Danny helped me drain the hot water heater or Susan sat on a board I was sawing. If I could just drop by their house, say, and June and her husband could go to a movie or something, then the kids and I would clean the gutters, weatherstrip the windows, wrap the hot water pipes . . . Well, that husband of hers is no use at all, you can bet he lets his hot water pipes sit around naked. I'd bring my own tools, even. We'd have a fine time! Susan could fix us cocoa. Then at the end of the evening I'd pack up my tools and off I'd go, leaving the house in perfect repair. Why, June ought to jump at the chance."

"Then why not suggest it," Macon said.

"Nah. She'd never go for it. She's so impractical. I said to her last week, I said, 'You know that front porch step is loose? Springing up from its nails every time you walk on it wrong.' She said, 'Oh, Lord, yes, it's *been* that way,' as if Providence had decreed it. As if nothing could be done about it. They've got leaves in the gutter from way last winter but leaves are natural, after all; why go against nature. She's so impractical."

Porter himself was the most practical man Macon had ever known. He was the only Leary who understood money. His talent with money was what kept the family firm solvent —if just barely. It wasn't a very wealthy business. Grandfather Leary had founded it in the early part of the century as a tinware factory, and turned to bottle caps in 1915. The Bottle Cap King, he called himself, and was called in his obituary, but in fact most bottle caps were manufactured by Crown Cork and always had been; Grandfather Leary ran a distant second or third. His only son, the Bottle Cap Prince, had barely assumed his place in the firm before quitting to volunteer for World War II—a far more damaging enthusiasm, it turned out, than any of Alicia's. After he was killed the business limped along, never quite succeeding and never quite failing, till Porter bounced in straight from college and took over the money end. Money to Porter was something almost chemical—a volatile substance that reacted in various interesting ways when combined with other substances. He wasn't what you'd call mercenary; he didn't want the money for its own sake but for its intriguing possibilities, and in fact when his wife divorced him he handed over most of his property without a word of complaint.

It was Porter who ran the company, pumping in money and ideas. Charles, more mechanical, dealt with the production end. Macon had done a little of everything when he worked there, and had wasted away with boredom doing it, for there wasn't really enough to keep a third man busy. It was only for symmetry's sake that Porter kept urging him to return. "Tell you what, Macon," he said now, "why not hitch a ride down with us tomorrow and look over your old stomping ground?"

"No, thanks," Macon told him.

"Plenty of room for your crutches in back."

"Maybe some other time."

They followed Rose around while she washed the dishes. She didn't like them to help because she had her own method, she said. She moved soundlessly through the old-fashioned kitchen, replacing dishes in the high wooden cabinets. Charles took the dog out; Macon couldn't manage his crutches in the spongy backyard. And Porter pulled the kitchen shades, meanwhile lecturing Rose on how the white surfaces reflected the warmth back into the room now that the nights were cooler. Rose said, "Yes, Porter, I know all that," and lifted the salad bowl to the light and examined it a moment before she put it away.

They watched the news, dutifully, and then they went out

to the sun porch and sat at their grandparents' card table. They played something called Vaccination—a card game they'd invented as children, which had grown so convoluted over the years that no one else had the patience to learn it. In fact, more than one outsider had accused them of altering the rules to suit the circumstances. "Now, just a minute," Sarah had said, back when she'd still had hopes of figuring it out. "I thought you said aces were high."

"They are."

"So that means—"

"But not when they're drawn from the deck."

"Aha! Then why was the one that Rose drew counted high?"

"Well, she did draw it after a deuce, Sarah."

"Aces drawn after a deuce are high?"

"No, aces drawn after a number that's been drawn two times in a row just before that."

Sarah had folded her fan of cards and laid them face down —the last of the wives to give up.

Macon was in quarantine and had to donate all his cards to Rose. Rose moved her chair over next to his and played off his points while he sat back, scratching the cat behind her ears. Opposite him, in the tiny dark windowpanes, he saw their reflections—hollow-eyed and severely cheekboned, more interesting versions of themselves.

The telephone in the living room gave a nipped squeak and then a full ring. Nobody seemed to notice. Rose laid a king on Porter's queen and Porter said, "Stinker." The telephone rang again and then again. In the middle of the fourth ring, it fell silent. "Hypodermic," Rose told Porter, and she topped the king with an ace.

"You're a real stinker, Rose."

In the portrait on the end wall, the Leary children gazed out with their veiled eyes. It occurred to Macon that they were sitting in much the same positions here this evening:

394

Charles and Porter on either side of him, Rose perched in the foreground. Was there any real change? He felt a jolt of something very close to panic. Here he still was! The same as ever! *What have I gone and done?* he wondered, and he swallowed thickly and looked at his own empty hands.

6

"Help! Help! Call off your dog!"

Macon stopped typing and lifted his head. The voice came from somewhere out front, rising above a string of sharp, excited yelps. But Edward was taking a walk with Porter. This must be some other dog.

"Call him off, dammit!"

Macon rose, propping himself on his crutches, and made his way to the window. Sure enough, it was Edward. He seemed to have treed somebody in the giant magnolia to the right of the walk. He was barking so hard that he kept popping off the ground perfectly level, all four feet at once, like one of those pull toys that bounce straight up in the air when you squeeze a rubber bulb.

"Edward! Stop that!" Macon shouted.

Edward didn't stop. He might not even have heard. Macon stubbed out to the hall, opened the front door, and said, "Come here this instant!"

Edward barely skipped a beat.

It was a Saturday morning in early October, pale gray and cool. Macon felt the coolness creeping up his cut-off pants leg as he crossed the porch. When he dropped one crutch and took hold of the iron railing to descend the steps, he found the metal beaded with moisture.

He hopped over to the magnolia, leaned down precariously, and grabbed the leash that Edward was trailing. Without much effort, he reeled it in; Edward was already losing interest. Macon peered into the inky depths of the magnolia. "Who *is* that?" he asked.

"This is your employer, Macon."

"Julian?"

Julian lowered himself from one of the magnolia's weak, sprawling branches. He had a line of dirt across the front of his slacks. His white-blond hair, usually so neat it made him look like a shirt ad, stuck out at several angles. "Macon," he said, "I really hate a man with an obnoxious dog. I don't hate just the dog, I hate the man who owns him."

"Well, I'm sorry about this. I thought he was off on a walk."

"You send him on walks by himself?"

"No, no . . ."

"A dog who takes solitary strolls," Julian said. "Only Macon Leary would have one." He brushed off the sleeves of his suede blazer. Then he said, "What happened to your leg?"

"I broke it."

"Well, I see that, but how?"

"It's kind of hard to explain," Macon told him.

They started toward the house, with Edward trotting docilely alongside. Julian supported Macon as they climbed the steps. He was an athletic-looking man with a casual, sauntering style—a boater. You could tell he was a boater by his nose, which was raw across the tip even this late in the year. No one so startlingly blond, so vividly flushed in the face, should expose himself to sunburn, Macon always told him. But that was Julian for you: reckless. A dashing sailor, a speedy driver, a frequenter of singles bars, he was the kind of man who would make a purchase without consulting *Consumer*

Reports. He never seemed to have a moment's self-doubt and was proceeding into the house now as jauntily as if he'd been invited, first retrieving Macon's other crutch and then holding the door open and waving him ahead.

"How'd you find me, anyway?" Macon asked.

"Why, are you in hiding?"

"No, of course not."

Julian surveyed the entrance hall, which all at once struck Macon as slightly dowdy. The satin lampshade on the table had dozens of long vertical rents; it seemed to be rotting off its frame.

"Your neighbor told me where you were," Julian said finally.

"Oh. Garner."

"I stopped by your house when I couldn't reach you by phone. Do you know how late you're running with this guide-book?"

"Well, you can see I've had an accident," Macon said.

"Everybody's held up, waiting for the manuscript. I keep telling them I expect it momentarily, but—"

"Any moment," Macon said.

"Huh?"

"You expect it any moment."

"Yes, and all I've seen so far is two chapters mailed in with no explanation."

Julian led the way to the living room as he spoke. He selected the most comfortable chair and sat down. "Where's Sarah?" he asked.

"Who?"

"Your wife, Macon."

"Oh. Um, she and I are . . ."

Macon should have practiced saying it out loud. The word "separated" was too bald; it was something that happened to other people. He crossed to the couch and made a great busi-

398

ness of settling himself and arranging his crutches at his side. Then he said, "She's got this apartment downtown."

"You've *split?*"

Macon nodded.

"Jesus."

Edward nosed Macon's palm bossily, demanding a pat. Macon was grateful to have something to do.

"Well, Jesus, Macon, what went wrong?" Julian asked.

"Nothing!" Macon told him. His voice was a little too loud. He lowered it. "I mean, that's not something I can answer," he said.

"Oh. Excuse me."

"No, I mean . . . there *is* no answer. It turns out these things can happen for no particular reason."

"Well, you've been under a strain, you two," Julian said. "Shoot, with what happened and all . . . She'll be back, once she's gotten over it. Or not gotten *over* it of course but, you know . . ."

"Maybe so," Macon said. He felt embarrassed for Julian, who kept jiggling one Docksider. He said, "What did you think of those first two chapters?"

Julian opened his mouth to answer, but he was interrupted by the dog. Edward had flown to the hall and was barking furiously. There was a clang that Macon recognized as the sound of the front door swinging open and hitting the radiator. "Hush, now," he heard Rose tell Edward. She crossed the hall and looked into the living room.

Julian got to his feet. Macon said, "Julian Edge, this is my sister Rose. And this," he said as Charles arrived behind her, "is my brother Charles."

Neither Rose nor Charles could shake hands; they were carrying the groceries. They stood in the center of the room, hugging brown paper bags, while Julian went into what Macon thought of as his Macon Leary act. "Macon Leary with a sister! And a brother, too. Who'd have guessed it? That Macon Leary had a family just never entered my mind, somehow."

Rose gave him a polite, puzzled smile. She wasn't looking her best. She wore a long black coat that drew all the color from her face. And Charles, rumpled and out of breath, was having trouble with one of his bags. He kept trying to get a better grip on it. "Here, let me help you," Julian said. He took the bag and then peered into it. Macon was afraid he'd go off on some tangent about Macon Leary's groceries, but he didn't. He told Rose, "Yes, I do see a family resemblance."

"You're Macon's publisher," Rose said. "I remember from the address label."

"Address label?"

"I'm the one who mailed you Macon's chapters."

"Oh, yes."

"I'm supposed to send you some more, but first I have to buy nine-by-twelve envelopes. All we've got left is ten-by-thirteen. It's terrible when things don't fit precisely. They get all out of alignment."

"Ah," Julian said. He looked at her for a moment.

Macon said, "We wouldn't want to keep you, Rose."

"Oh! No," she said. She smiled at Julian, hoisted her groceries higher, and left the room. Charles retrieved his bag from Julian and slogged after her.

"The Macon Leary Nine-by-Twelve Envelope Crisis," Julian said, sitting back down.

Macon said, "Oh, Julian, drop it."

"Sorry," Julian said, sounding surprised.

There was a pause. Then Julian said, "Really I had no idea, Macon. I mean, if you'd let me know what was going on in your life . . ."

He was jiggling a Docksider again. He always seemed uneasy when he couldn't do his Macon Leary act. After Ethan died he'd avoided Macon for weeks; he'd sent a tree-sized bouquet to the house but never again mentioned Ethan's name.

"Look," he said now. "If you want another, I don't know, another month—"

Macon said, "Oh, nonsense, what's a missing wife or two, right? Ha, ha! Here, let me get what I've typed and you can check it."

"Well, if you say so," Julian said.

"After this there's only the conclusion," Macon said. He was calling over his shoulder as he made his way to the dining room, where his latest chapter lay stacked on the buffet. "The conclusion's nothing, a cinch. I'll crib from the old one, mostly."

He returned with the manuscript and handed it to Julian. Then he sat on the couch again, and Julian started reading. Meanwhile, Macon heard Porter come in the back way, where he was greeted by explosive barks from Edward. "Monster," Porter said. "Do you know how long I've been looking for you?" The phone rang over and over, unanswered. Julian looked at Macon and raised his eyebrows but made no comment.

Macon and Julian had met some dozen years ago, when Macon was still at the bottle-cap factory. He'd been casting about for other occupations at the time. He'd begun to believe he might like to work on a newspaper. But he'd had no training, not a single journalism course. So he started the only way he could think of: He contributed a free-lance article to a neighborhood weekly. His subject was a crafts fair over in Washington. *Getting there is difficult*, he wrote, *because the freeway is so blank you start feeling all lost and sad. And once you've arrived, it's worse. The streets are not like ours and don't even run at right angles.* He went on to evaluate some food he'd sampled at an outdoor booth, but found it contained a spice he wasn't used to, *something sort of cold and yellow I would almost describe as foreign,* and settled instead for a hot dog from a vendor across the street who wasn't even part of the fair. *The hot dog I can recommend,* he wrote, *though it made me a little regretful because Sarah, my wife, uses the same kind of chili sauce and I thought of home the minute I smelled it.* He also recommended the patchwork quilts, one of which had a starburst pattern like the quilt in his grandmother's room. He suggested that his readers leave the fair no later than three thirty, *since you'll be driving into Baltimore right past Lexington Market and will want to pick up your crabs before it closes.*

His article was published beneath a headline reading CRAFTS FAIR DELIGHTS, INSTRUCTS. There was a subhead under that. *Or,* it read, *I Feel So Break-Up, I Want to Go Home.* Until he saw the subhead, Macon hadn't realized what tone he'd given his piece. Then he felt silly.

But Julian Edge thought it was perfect. Julian phoned him. "You the fellow who wrote that hot dog thing in the *Watchbird?*"

"Well, yes."

"Ha!"

"Well, I don't see what's so funny," Macon said stiffly.

"Who said it was funny? It's perfect. I've got a proposition for you."

They met at the Old Bay Restaurant, where Macon's grandparents used to take the four children on their birthdays. "I can personally guarantee the crab soup," Macon said. "They haven't done a thing to it since I was nine." Julian said, "Ha!" again and rocked back in his chair. He was wearing a polo shirt and white duck trousers, and his nose was a bright shade of pink. It was summer, or maybe spring. At any rate, his boat was in the water.

"Now, here's my plan," he said over the soup. "I own this little company called the Businessman's Press. Well, little: I say little. Actually we sell coast to coast. Nothing fancy, but

402

useful, you know? Appointment pads, expense account booklets, compound interest charts, currency conversion wheels . . . And now I want to put out a guidebook for commercial travelers. Just the U.S., to begin with; maybe other countries later. We'd call it something catchy, I don't know: *Reluctant Tourist* . . . And you're the fellow to write it."

"Me?"

"I knew the minute I read your hot dog piece."

"But I hate to travel."

"I kind of guessed that," Julian said. "So do businessmen. I mean, these folks are not running around the country for the hell of it, Macon. They'd rather be home in their living rooms. So you'll be helping them pretend that's where they are."

Then he pulled a square of paper from his breast pocket and said, "What do you think?"

It was a steel engraving of an overstuffed chair. Attached to the chair's back were giant, feathered wings such as you would see on seraphim in antique Bibles. Macon blinked.

"Your logo," Julian explained. "Get it?"

"Um . . ."

"While armchair travelers dream of going places," Julian said, "traveling armchairs dream of staying put. I thought we'd use this on the cover."

"Ah!" Macon said brightly. Then he said, "But would I actually have to travel myself?"

"Well, yes."

"Oh."

"But just briefly. I'm not looking for anything encyclopedic, I'm looking for the opposite of encyclopedic. And think of the pay."

"It pays?"

"It pays a bundle."

Well, not a bundle, exactly. Still, it did make a comfortable living. It sold briskly at airport newsstands, train stations, and office supply shops. His guide to France did even better. That was part of a major promotion by an international car-rental agency—slipcased with *The Businessman's Foreign Phrase Book,* which gave the German, French, and Spanish for "We anticipate an upswing in cross-border funds." Macon, of course, was not the author of the phrase book. His only foreign language was Latin.

Now Julian restacked the pages he'd been reading. "Fine," he said. "I think we can send this through as is. What's left of the conclusion?"

"Not much."

"After this I want to start on the U.S. again."

"So soon?"

"It's been three years, Macon."

"Well, but . . ." Macon said. He gestured toward his leg. "You can see I'd have trouble traveling."

"When does your cast come off?"

"Not till the first of November at the earliest."

"So? A few weeks!"

"But it really seems to me I just did the U.S.," Macon said. A kind of fatigue fell over him. These endlessly recurring trips, Boston and Atlanta and Chicago . . . He let his head drop back on the couch.

Julian said, "Things are changing every minute, Macon. Change! It's what keeps us in the black. How far do you think we'd get selling out-of-date guidebooks?"

Macon thought of the crumbling old *Tips for the Continent* in his grandfather's library. Travelers were advised to invert a wineglass on their hotel beds, testing the sheets for damp. Ladies should seal the corks of their perfume bottles with melted candlewax before packing. Something about that book implied that tourists were all in it together, equally anxious and defenseless. Macon might almost have enjoyed a trip in those days.

Julian was preparing to go now. He stood up, and with some difficulty Macon did too. Then Edward, getting wind of a leavetaking, rushed into the living room and started barking. "Sorry!" Macon shouted above the racket. "Edward, stop it! I figure that's his sheep-herding instinct," he explained to Julian. "He hates to see anyone straying from the flock."

They moved toward the front hall, wading through a blur of dancing, yelping dog. When they reached the door, Edward blocked it. Luckily, he was still trailing his leash, so Macon gave one crutch to Julian and bent to grasp it. The instant Edward felt the tug, he turned and snarled at Macon. "Whoa!" Julian said, for Edward when he snarled was truly ugly. His fangs seemed to lengthen. He snapped at his leash with an audible click. Then he snapped at Macon's hand. Macon felt Edward's hot breath and the oddly intimate dampness of his teeth. His hand was not so much bitten as struck—slammed into with a jolt such as you'd get from an electric fence. He stepped back and dropped the leash. His other crutch clattered to the floor. The front hall seemed to be full of crutches; there was some splintery, spiky feeling to the air.

"Whoa, there!" Julian said. He spoke into a sudden silence. The dog sat back now, panting and shamefaced. "Macon? Did he get you?" Julian asked.

Macon looked down at his hand. There were four red puncture marks in the fleshy part—two in front, two in back—but no blood at all and very little pain. "I'm all right," he said.

Julian gave him his crutches, keeping one eye on Edward. "I wouldn't have a dog like that," he said. "I'd shoot him."

"He was just trying to protect me," Macon said.

"I'd call the S.P.C.A."

"Why don't you go now, Julian, while he's calm."

"Or the what's-it, dogcatcher. Tell them you want him done away with."

"Just *go*, Julian."

Julian said, "Well, fine." He opened the door and slid through it sideways, glancing back at Edward. "That is not a well dog," he said before he vanished.

Macon hobbled to the rear of the house and Edward followed, snuffling a bit and staying close to the ground. In the kitchen, Rose stood on a stepstool in front of a towering glass-fronted cupboard, accepting the groceries that Charles and Porter handed up to her. "Now I need the *n*'s, anything starting with *n*," she was saying.

"How about these noodles?" Porter asked. "N for noodles? P for pasta?"

"*E* for elbow macaroni. You might have passed those up earlier, Porter."

"Rose?" Macon said. "It seems Edward's given me a little sort of nip."

She turned, and Charles and Porter stopped work to examine the hand he held out. It was hurting him by now—a deep, stinging pain. "Oh, Macon!" Rose cried. She came down off the stepstool. "How did it happen?"

"It was an accident, that's all. But I think I need an antiseptic."

"You need a tetanus shot, too," Charles told him.

"You need to get rid of that dog," Porter said.

They looked at Edward. He grinned up at them nervously.

"He didn't mean any harm," Macon said.

"Takes off your hand at the elbow and he means no harm? You should get rid of him, I tell you."

"See, I can't," Macon said.

"Why not?"

"Well, see . . ."

They waited.

"You know I don't mind the cat," Rose said. "But Edward is so disruptive, Macon. Every day he gets more and more out of control."

406

"Maybe you could give him to someone who wants a guard dog," Charles said.

"A service station," Rose suggested. She took a roll of gauze from a drawer.

"Oh, never," Macon said. He sat where she pointed, in a chair at the kitchen table. He propped his crutches in the corner. "Edward alone in some Exxon? He'd be wretched."·

Rose swabbed Mercurochrome on his hand. It looked bruised; each puncture mark was puffing and turning blue.

"He's used to sleeping with me," Macon told her. "He's never been alone in his life."

Besides, Edward wasn't a bad dog at heart—only a little unruly. He was sympathetic and he cared about Macon and plodded after him wherever he went. There was a furrowed W on his forehead that gave him a look of concern. His large, pointed, velvety ears seemed more expressive than other dogs' ears; when he was happy they stuck straight out at either side of his head like airplane wings. His smell was unexpectedly pleasant—the sweetish smell a favorite sweater takes on when it's been folded away in a drawer unwashed.

And he'd been Ethan's.

Once upon a time Ethan had brushed him, bathed him, wrestled on the floor with him; and when Edward stopped to paw at one ear Ethan would ask, with the soberest courtesy, "Oh, may I scratch that for you?" The two of them watched daily at the window for the afternoon paper, and the instant it arrived Ethan sent Edward bounding out to fetch it—hind legs meeting front legs, heels kicking up joyfully. Edward would pause after he got the paper in his mouth and look around him, as if hoping to be noticed, and then he'd swagger back all bustling and self-important and pause again at the front hall mirror to admire the figure he cut. "Conceited," Ethan would say fondly. Ethan picked up a tennis ball to throw and Edward grew so excited that he wagged his whole hind end. Ethan took Edward outside with a soccer ball and when Edward got carried away—tearing about and shouldering the ball into a hedge and growling ferociously—Ethan's laugh rang out so high and clear, such a buoyant sound floating through the air on a summer evening.

"I just can't," Macon said.

There was a silence.

Rose wrapped gauze around his hand, so gently he hardly felt it. She tucked the end under and reached for a roll of adhesive tape. Then she said, "Maybe we could send him to obedience school."

"Obedience school is for minor things—walking to heel and things," Porter told her. "What we have here is major."

"It is not!" Macon said. "It's really nothing at all. Why, the woman at the Meow-Bow got on wonderfully with him."

"Meow-Bow?"

"Where I boarded him when I went to England. She was just crazy about him. She wanted me to let her train him."

"So call her, why don't you."

"Maybe I will," Macon said.

He wouldn't, of course. The woman had struck him as bizarre. But there was no sense going into that now.

On Sunday morning Edward tore the screen door, trying to get at an elderly neighbor who'd stopped by to borrow a wrench. On Sunday afternoon he sprang at Porter to keep him from leaving on an errand. Porter had to creep out the rear when Edward wasn't watching. "This is undignified," Porter told Macon. "When are you going to call the Kit-Kat or whatever it is?"

Macon explained that on Sundays the Meow-Bow would surely be closed.

Monday morning, when Edward went for a walk with Rose, he lunged at a passing jogger and yanked Rose off her feet. She came home with a scraped knee. She said, "Have you called the Meow-Bow yet?"

"Not quite," Macon said.

"Macon," Rose said. Her voice was very quiet. "Tell me something."

"What's that, Rose?"

"Can you explain why you're letting things go on this way?"

No, he couldn't, and that was the truth. It was getting so he was baffling even to himself. He felt infuriated by Edward's misdeeds, but somehow he viewed them as visitations of fate. There was nothing he could do about them. When Edward approached him later with a mangled belt of Porter's trailing from his mouth, all Macon said was, "Oh, Edward . . ."

He was sitting on the couch at the time, having been snagged by an especially outrageous moment in Rose's soap opera. Rose looked over at him. Her expression was odd. It wasn't disapproving; it was more like . . . He cast about for the word. Resigned. That was it. She looked at him the way she would look at, say, some hopeless wreck of a man wandering drugged on a downtown street. After all, she seemed to be thinking, there was probably not much that you could do for such a person.

"Meow-Bow Animal Hospital."

"Is, ah, Muriel there, please?"

"Hold on a minute."

He waited, braced against a cabinet. (He was using the pantry telephone.) He heard two women discussing Fluffball Cohen's rabies shot. Then Muriel picked up the receiver. "Hello?"

"Yes, this is Macon Leary. I don't know if you remember me or—"

"Oh, Macon! Hi there! How's Edward doing?"

"Well, he's getting worse."

She tsk-tsked.

"He's been attacking right and left. Snarling, biting, chewing things—"

"Did your neighbor tell you I came looking for you?"

"What? Yes, he did."

"I was right on your street, running an errand. I make a little extra money running errands. George, it's called. Don't you think that's cute?"

"Excuse me?"

"George. It's the name of my company. I stuck a flyer under your door. *Let George do it*, it says, and then it lists all the prices: meeting planes, chauffeuring, courier service, shopping . . . Gift shopping's most expensive because for that I have to use my own taste. Didn't you get my flyer? I really stopped by just to visit, though. But your neighbor said you hadn't been around."

"No, I broke my leg," Macon said.

"Oh, that's too bad."

"And I couldn't manage alone of course, so—"

"You should have called George."

"George who?"

"George my company! The one I was just telling you about."

"Oh, yes."

"Then you wouldn't have had to leave that nice house. I liked your house. Is that where you lived when you were married, too?"

"Well, yes."

"I'm surprised she agreed to give it up."

"The point is," Macon said, "I'm really at the end of my rope with Edward here, and I was wondering if you might be able to help me."

"Sure I can help!"

410

"Oh, that's wonderful," Macon said.

"I can do anything," Muriel told him. "Search and alert, search and rescue, bombs, narcotics—"

"Narcotics?"

"Guard training, attack training, poison-proofing, kennel-osis—"

"Wait, I don't even know what some of those things are," Macon said.

"I can even teach split personality."

"What's split personality?"

"Where your dog is, like, nice to you but kills all others."

"You know, I think I may be over my head here," Macon said.

"No, no! Don't say that!"

"But this is just the simplest problem. His only fault is, he wants to protect me."

"You can take protection too far," Muriel told him.

Macon tried a little joke. " 'It's a jungle out there,' he's saying. That's what he's trying to say. 'I know better than you do, Macon.' "

"Oh?" Muriel said. "You let him call you by your first name?"

"Well—"

"He needs to learn respect," she said. "Five or six times a week I'll come out, for however long it takes. I'll start with the basics; you always do that: sitting, heeling . . . My charge is five dollars a lesson. You're getting a bargain. Most I charge ten."

Macon tightened his hold on the receiver. "Then why not ten for me?" he asked.

"Oh, no! You're a friend."

He felt confused. He gave her his address and arranged a time with the nagging sense that something was slipping out of his control. "But look," he said, "about the fee, now—"

411

"See you tomorrow!" she said. She hung up.

At supper that night when he told the others, he thought they did a kind of double take. Porter said, "You actually called?" Macon said, "Yes, why not?"—acting very offhand—and so the others took their cue and dropped the subject at once.

7

"When I was a little girl," Muriel said, "I didn't like dogs at all or any other kinds of animals either. I thought they could read my mind. My folks gave me a puppy for my birthday and he would, like, cock his head, you know how they do? Cock his head and fix me with these bright round eyes and I said, 'Ooh! Get him away from me! You know I can't stand to be stared at.'"

She had a voice that wandered too far in all directions. It screeched upward; then it dropped to a raspy growl. "They had to take him back. Had to give him to a neighbor boy and buy me a whole different present, a beauty-parlor permanent which is what I'd set my heart on all along."

She and Macon were standing in the entrance hall. She still had her coat on—a bulky-shouldered, three-quarter length, nubby black affair of a type last seen in the 1940s. Edward sat in front of her as he'd been ordered. He had met her at the door with his usual display, leaping and snarling, but she'd more or less walked right through him and pointed at his rump and told him to sit. He'd gaped at her. She had reached over and poked his rear end down with a long, sharp index finger.

413

"Now you kind of cluck your tongue," she'd told Macon, demonstrating. "They get to know a cluck means praise. And when I hold my hand out—see? That means he has to stay."

Edward stayed, but a yelp erupted from him every few seconds, reminding Macon of the periodic bloops from a percolator. Muriel hadn't seemed to hear. She'd started discussing her lesson plan and then for no apparent reason had veered to her autobiography. But shouldn't Edward be allowed to get up now? How long did she expect him to sit there?

"I guess you're wondering why I'd want a permanent when this hair of mine is so frizzy," she said. "Old mop! But I'll be honest, this is not natural. My natural hair is real straight and lanky. Times I've just despaired of it. It was blond when I was a baby, can you believe that? Blond as a fairy-tale princess. People told my mother I'd look like Shirley Temple if she would just curl my hair, and so she did, she rolled my hair on orange juice tins. I had blue eyes, too, and they stayed that way for a long long time, a whole lot longer than most babies' do. People thought I'd look that way forever and they talked about me going into the movies. Seriously! My mother arranged for tap-dance school when I wasn't much more than a toddler. No one ever dreamed my hair would turn on me."

Edward moaned. Muriel looked past Macon, into the glass of a picture that hung behind him. She cupped a hand beneath the ends of her hair, as if testing its weight. "Think what it must feel like," she said, "waking up one morning and finding you've gone dark. It near about killed my mother, I can tell you. Ordinary dull old Muriel, muddy brown eyes and hair as black as dirt."

Macon sensed he was supposed to offer some argument, but he was too anxious about Edward. "Oh, well . . ." he said. Then he said, "Shouldn't we be letting him up now?"

"Up? Oh, the dog. In a minute," she said. "So anyway. The reason it's so frizzy is, I got this thing called a body perm. You ever heard of those? They're supposed to just add body, but something went wrong. You think *this* is bad! If I was to take a brush to it, my hair would spring straight out from my head. I mean absolutely straight out. Kind of like a fright wig, isn't that what you call it? So I can't even brush it. I get up in the morning and there I am, ready to go. Lord, I hate to think of the tangles."

"Maybe you could just comb it," Macon suggested.

"Hard to drag a comb *through* it. All the little teeth would break off."

"Maybe one of those thick-toothed combs that black people use."

"I know what you mean but I'd feel silly buying one."

"What for?" Macon asked. "They're just hanging there in supermarkets. It wouldn't have to be a big deal. Buy milk and bread or something and an Afro comb, no one will even think twice."

"Well, I suppose you're right," she said, but now that she'd got him involved it seemed she'd lost interest in the problem herself. She snapped her fingers over Edward's head. "Okay!" she said. Edward jumped up, barking. "That was very good," she told him.

In fact, it was so good that Macon felt a little cross. Things couldn't be that easy, he wanted to say. Edward had improved too quickly, the way a toothache will improve the moment you step into a dentist's waiting room.

Muriel slipped her purse off her shoulder and set it on the hall table. Out came a long blue leash attached to a choke chain. "He's supposed to wear this all the time," she said. "Every minute till he's trained. That way you can yank him back whenever he does something wrong. The leash is six dollars even, and the chain is two ninety-five. With tax it comes to, let's see, nine forty. You can pay me at the end of the lesson."

She slipped the choke chain over Edward's head. Then she paused to examine a fingernail. "If I break another nail I'm

415

going to scream," she said. She took a step back and pointed to Edward's rump. After a brief hesitation, he sat. Seated, he looked noble, Macon thought—chesty and solemn, nothing like his usual self. But when Muriel snapped her fingers, he jumped up as unruly as ever.

"Now you try," Muriel told Macon.

Macon accepted the leash and pointed to Edward's rump. Edward stood fast. Macon frowned and pointed more sternly. He felt foolish. Edward knew, if this woman didn't, how little authority Macon had.

"Poke him down," Muriel said.

This was going to be awkward. He propped a crutch against the radiator and bent stiffly to jab Edward with one finger. Edward sat. Macon clucked. Then he straightened and backed away, holding out his palm, but instead of staying, Edward rose and followed him. Muriel hissed between her teeth. Edward shrank down again. "He doesn't take you seriously," Muriel said.

"Well, I know that," Macon snapped.

His broken leg was starting to ache.

"In fact I didn't have so much as a kitten the whole entire time I was growing up," Muriel said. Was she just going to leave Edward sitting there? "Then a couple of years ago I saw this ad in the paper, *Make extra money in your off hours. Work as little or as much as you like.* Place was a dog-training firm that went around to people's houses. Doggie, Do, it was called. Don't you just hate that name? Reminds me of dog-do. But anyhow, I answered the ad. 'To be honest I don't like animals,' I said, but Mr. Quarles, the owner, he told me that was just as well. He told me it was people who got all mushy about them that had the most trouble."

"Well, that makes sense," Macon said, glancing at Edward. He had heard that dogs developed backaches if they were made to sit too long.

"I was just about his best pupil, it turns out. Seems I had

416

a way with animals. So then I got a job at the Meow-Bow. Before that I worked at the Rapid-Eze Copy Center and believe me, I was looking for a change. Who's the lady?"

"Lady?"

"The lady I just saw walking through the dining room."

"That's Rose."

"Is she your ex-wife? Or what."

"She's my sister."

"Oh, your sister!"

"This house belongs to her," Macon said.

"I don't live with anybody either," Muriel told him.

Macon blinked. Hadn't he just said he lived with his sister?

"Sometimes late at night when I get desperate for someone to talk to I call the time signal," Muriel said. " 'At the tone the time will be eleven . . . forty-eight. And fifty seconds.' " Her voice took on a fruity fullness. " 'At the tone the time will be eleven . . . forty-nine. Exactly.' You can release him now."

"Pardon?"

"Release your dog."

Macon snapped his fingers and Edward jumped up, yapping.

"How about you?" Muriel asked. "What do you do for a living?"

Macon said, "I write tour guides."

"Tour guides! Lucky."

"What's lucky about it?"

"Why, you must get to travel all kinds of places!"

"Oh, well, travel," Macon said.

"I'd love to travel."

"It's just red tape, mostly," Macon said.

"I've never even been on an airplane, you realize that?"

"It's red tape in motion. Ticket lines, customs lines . . . Should Edward be barking that way?"

417

Muriel gave Edward a slit-eyed look and he quieted.

"If I could go anywhere I'd go to Paris," she said.

"Paris is terrible. Everybody's impolite."

"I'd walk along the Seine, like they say in the song. 'You will find your love in Paris,'" she sang scratchily, "'if you walk along the—' I just think it sounds so romantic."

"Well, it's not," Macon said.

"I bet you don't know where to look, is all. Take me with you next time! I could show you the good parts."

Macon cleared his throat. "Actually, I have a very limited expense account," he told her. "I never even took my wife, or, um, my . . . wife."

"I was only teasing," she told him.

"Oh."

"You think I meant it?"

"Oh, no."

She grew suddenly brisk. "That will be fourteen forty, including the leash and the choke chain." Then while Macon was fumbling through his wallet she said, "You have to practice what he's learned, and no one else can practice for you. I'll come back tomorrow for the second lesson. Will eight in the morning be too early? I've got to be at the Meow-Bow at nine."

"Eight will be fine," Macon told her. He counted out fourteen dollars and all the change he had loose in his pocket —thirty-six cents.

"You can pay me the other four cents tomorrow," she said.

Then she made Edward sit and she handed the leash to Macon. "Release him when I'm gone," she said.

Macon held out his palm and stared hard into Edward's eyes, begging him to stay. Edward stayed, but he moaned when he saw Muriel leave. When Macon snapped his fingers, Edward jumped up and attacked the front door.

· · ·

All that afternoon and evening, Macon and Edward practiced. Edward learned to plop his rump down at the slightest motion of a finger. He stayed there, complaining and rolling his eyes, while Macon clucked approvingly. By suppertime, a cluck was part of the family language. Charles clucked over Rose's pork chops. Porter clucked when Macon dealt him a good hand of cards.

"Imagine a flamenco dancer with galloping consumption," Rose told Charles and Porter. "That's Edward's trainer. She talks nonstop, I don't know when she comes up for air. When she talked about her lesson plan she kept saying 'simplistic' for 'simple.' "

"I thought you were going to stay out of sight," Macon told Rose.

"Well? Did you ever see me?"

"Muriel did."

"I guess so! The way she was always peering around your back and snooping."

There were constant slamming sounds from the living room, because Edward's new leash kept catching on the rocking chair and dragging it behind him. During the course of the evening he chewed a pencil to splinters, stole a pork-chop bone from the garbage bin, and threw up on the sun porch rug; but now that he could sit on command, everyone felt more hopeful.

"When I was in high school I made nothing but A's," Muriel said. "You're surprised at that, aren't you. You think I'm kind of like, not an intellect. I know what you're thinking! You're surprised."

"No, I'm not," Macon said, although he was, actually.

"I made A's because I caught on to the trick," Muriel told him. "You think it's not a trick? There's a trick to everything; that's how you get through life."

They were in front of the house—both of them in rain-coats, for it was a damp, drippy morning. Muriel wore truncated black suede boots with witchy toes and needle heels. Her legs rose out of them like toothpicks. The leash trailed from her fingers. Supposedly, she was teaching Edward to walk right. Instead she went on talking about her schooldays.

"Some of my teachers told me I should go to college," she said. "This one in particular, well she wasn't a teacher but a librarian, I worked in the library for her, shelving books and things; she said, 'Muriel, why don't you go on to Towson State?' But I don't know . . . and now I tell my sister, 'You be thinking of college, hear? Don't drop out like I dropped out.' I've got this little sister? Claire? *Her* hair never turned. She's blond as an angel. Here's what's funny, though: she couldn't care less. Braids her hair back any old how to keep it out of her eyes. Wears raggy jeans and forgets to shave her legs. Doesn't it always work that way? My folks believe she's wonderful. She's the good one and I'm the bad one. It's not her fault, though; I don't blame Claire. People just get fixed in these certain frames of other people's opinions, don't you find that's true? Claire was always Mary in the Nativity Scene at Christmas. Boys in her grade school were always proposing, but there I was in high school and no one proposed to *me*, I can tell you. Aren't high school boys just so frustrating? I mean they'd invite me out and all, like to drive-in movies and things, and they'd act so tense and secret, sneaking one arm around my shoulder inch by inch like they thought I wouldn't notice and then dropping a hand down, you know how they do, lower and lower while all the time staring straight ahead at the movie like it was the most fascinating spectacle they'd ever seen in their lives. You just had to feel sorry for them. But then Monday morning there they were like nothing had taken place, real boisterous and horsing around with their friends and nudging each other when I walked past but not so much as saying hello to me. You think that didn't hurt my feelings? Not one boy in all that time treated me like a steady girlfriend. They'd ask me out on Saturday night and expect me to be so nice to them, but you think they ever ate lunch with me next Monday in the school cafeteria, or walked me from class to class?"

She glanced down at Edward. Abruptly, she slapped her hip; her black vinyl raincoat made a buckling sound. "That's the 'heel' command," she told Macon. She started walking. Edward followed uncertainly. Macon stayed behind. It had been hard enough getting down the front porch steps.

"He's supposed to match his pace to anything," she called back. "Slow, fast, anything I do." She speeded up. When Edward crossed in front of her, she walked right into him. When he dawdled, she yanked his leash. She tip-tapped briskly eastward, her coat a stiff, swaying triangle beneath the smaller triangle of her hair blowing back. Macon waited, ankle-deep in wet leaves.

On the return trip, Edward kept close to Muriel's left side. "I think he's got the hang of it," she called. She arrived in front of Macon and offered him the leash. "Now you."

He attempted to slap his hip—which was difficult, on crutches. Then he set off. He was agonizingly slow and Edward kept pulling ahead. "Yank that leash!" Muriel said, clicking along behind. "He knows what he's supposed to do. Contrary thing."

Edward fell into step, finally, although he gazed off in a bored, lofty way. "Don't forget to cluck," Muriel said. "Every little minute, you have to praise him." Her heels made a scraping sound behind them. "Once I worked with this dog that had never in her life been housebroken. Two years old and not one bit housebroken and the owners were losing their minds. First I can't figure it out; then it comes to me. That dog thought she wasn't supposed to piddle *any*place, not indoors or outdoors, either one. See, no one had ever praised her when she did it right. Did you ever hear of such a thing?

I had to catch her peeing outdoors which wasn't easy, believe me, because she was all the time ashamed and trying to hide it, and then I praised her to bits and after a while she caught on."

They reached the corner. "Now, when you stop, he has to sit," she said.

"But how will I practice?" Macon asked.

"What do you mean?"

"I'm on these crutches."

"So? It's good exercise for your leg," she said. She didn't ask how the leg had been broken. Come to think of it, there was something impervious about her, in spite of all her interest in his private life. She said, "Practice lots, ten minutes a session."

"Ten minutes!"

"Now let's start back."

She led the way, her angular, sashaying walk broken by the jolt of her sharp heels. Macon and Edward followed. When they reached the house, she asked what time it was. "Eight fifty," Macon said severely. He mistrusted women who wore no watches.

"I have to get going. That will be five dollars, please, and the four cents you owe me from yesterday."

He gave her the money and she stuffed it in her raincoat pocket. "Next time, I'll stay longer and talk," she said. "That's a promise." She trilled her fingers at him, and then she clicked off toward a car that was parked down the street—an aged, gray, boatlike sedan polished to a high shine. When she slid in and slammed the door behind her, there was a sound like falling beer cans. The engine twanged and rattled before it took hold. Macon shook his head, and he and Edward returned to the house.

Between Wednesday and Thursday, Macon spent what seemed a lifetime struggling up and down Dempsey Road

422

beside Edward. His armpits developed a permanent ache. There was a vertical seam of pain in his thigh. This made no sense; it should have been in the shin. He wondered if something had gone wrong—if the break had been set improperly, for instance, so that some unusual strain was being placed upon the thighbone. Maybe he'd have to go back to the hospital and get his leg rebroken, probably under general anesthesia with all its horrifying complications; and then he'd spend months in traction and perhaps walk the rest of his life with a limp. He imagined himself tilting across intersections with a grotesque, lopsided gait. Sarah, driving past, would screech to a halt. "Macon?" She would roll down her window. "Macon, what *happened?*"

He would raise one arm and let it flop and totter away from her.

Or tell her, "I'm surprised you care enough to inquire."

No, just totter away.

Most likely these little spells of self-pity (an emotion he despised ordinarily) were caused by sheer physical exhaustion. How had he got himself into this? Slapping his haunch was the first problem; then summoning his balance to jerk the leash when Edward fell out of step, and staying constantly alert for any squirrel or pedestrian. "Sss!" he kept saying, and "Cluck-cluck!" and "Sss!" again. He supposed passersby must think he was crazy. Edward loped beside him, occasionally yawning, looking everywhere for bikers. Bikers were his special delight. Whenever he saw one, the hair between his shoulders stood on end and he lunged forward. Macon felt like a man on a tightrope that was suddenly set swinging.

At this uneven, lurching pace, he saw much more than he would have otherwise. He had a lengthy view of every bush and desiccated flower bed. He memorized eruptions in the sidewalk that might trip him. It was an old people's street, and not in the best of repair. The neighbors spent their days telephoning back and forth amongst themselves, checking to see that no one had suffered a stroke alone on the stairs or a heart attack in the bathroom, a broken hip, blocked windpipe, dizzy spell over the stove with every burner alight. Some would set out for a walk and find themselves hours later in the middle of the street, wondering where they'd been headed. Some would start fixing a bite to eat at noon, a soft-boiled egg or a cup of tea, and by sundown would still be puttering in their kitchen, fumbling for the salt and forgetting how the toaster worked. Macon knew all this through his sister, who was called upon by neighbors in distress. "Rose, dear! Rose, dear!" they would quaver, and they'd stumble into her yard waving an overdue bill, an alarming letter, a bottle of pills with a childproof top.

In the evening, taking Edward for his last walk, Macon glanced in windows and saw people slumped in flowered armchairs, lit blue and shivery by their TV sets. The Orioles were winning the second game of the World Series, but these people seemed to be staring at their own thoughts instead. Macon imagined they were somehow dragging him down, causing him to walk heavily, to slouch, to grow short of breath. Even the dog seemed plodding and discouraged.

And when he returned to the house, the others were suffering one of their fits of indecisiveness. Was it better to lower the thermostat at night, or not? Wouldn't the furnace have to work harder if it were lowered? Hadn't Porter read that someplace? They debated back and forth, settling it and then beginning again. Why! Macon thought. They were not so very different from their neighbors. They were growing old themselves. He'd been putting in his own two bits (by all means, lower the thermostat), but now his voice trailed off, and he said no more.

That night, he dreamed he was parked near Lake Roland in his grandfather's '57 Buick. He was sitting in the dark and some girl was sitting next to him. He didn't know her, but the bitter smell of her perfume seemed familiar, and the rustle of her skirt when she moved closer. He turned and looked at her. It was Muriel. He drew a breath to ask what she was doing here, but she put a finger to his lips and stopped him. She moved closer still. She took his keys from him and set them on the dashboard. Gazing steadily into his face, she unbuckled his belt and slipped a cool, knowing hand down inside his trousers.

He woke astonished and embarrassed, and sat bolt upright in his bed.

"Everybody always asks me, 'What is *your* dog like?' " Muriel said. " 'I bet he's a model of good behavior,' they tell me. But you want to hear something funny? I don't own a dog. In fact, the one time I had one around, he ran off. That was Norman's dog, Spook. My ex-husband's. First night we were married, Spook ran off to Norman's mom's. I think he hated me."

"Oh, surely not," Macon said.

"He hated me. I could tell."

They were outdoors again, preparing to put Edward through his paces. By now, Macon had adjusted to the rhythm of these lessons. He waited, gripping Edward's leash. Muriel said, "It was just like one of those Walt Disney movies. You know: where the dog walks all the way to the Yukon or something. Except Spook only walked to Timonium. Me and Norman had him downtown in our apartment, and Spook took off and traveled the whole however many miles it was back to Norman's mom's house in Timonium. His mom calls up: 'When did you drop Spook off?' 'What're you talking about?' Norman asks her."

She changed her voice to match each character. Macon heard the thin whine of Norman's mother, the stammering boyishness of Norman himself. He remembered last night's dream and felt embarrassed all over again. He looked at her directly, hoping for flaws, and found them in abundance—a

425

long, narrow nose, and sallow skin, and two freckled knobs of collarbone that promised an unluxurious body.

"Seems his mom woke up in the morning," she was saying, "and there was Spook, sitting on the doorstep. But that was the first we realized he was missing. Norman goes, 'I don't know what got into him. He never ran off before.' And gives me this doubtful kind of look. I could tell he wondered if it might be my fault. Maybe he thought it was a omen or something. We were awful young to get married. I can see that now. I was seventeen. He was eighteen—an only child. His mother's pet. Widowed mother. He had this fresh pink face like a girl's and the shortest hair of any boy in my school and he buttoned his shirt collars all the way to the neck. Moved in from Parkville the end of junior year. Caught sight of me in my strapless sun dress and goggled at me all through every class; other boys teased him but he didn't pay any mind. He was just so . . . innocent, you know? He made me feel like I had powers. There he was following me around the halls with his arms full of books and I'd say, 'Norman? You want to eat lunch with me?' and he'd blush and say, 'Oh, why, uh, you serious?' He didn't even know how to drive, but I told him if he got his license I'd go out with him. 'We could ride to someplace quiet and talk and be alone,' I'd say, 'you know what I mean?' Oh, I was bad. I don't know what was wrong with me, back then. He got his license in no time flat and came for me in his mother's Chevy, which incidentally she happened to have purchased from my father, who was a salesman for Ruggles Chevrolet. We found that out at the wedding. Got married the fall of senior year, he was just dying to marry me so what could I say? and at the wedding my daddy goes to Norman's mom, 'Why, I believe I sold you a car not long ago,' but she was too busy crying to take much notice. That woman carried on like marriage was a fate worse than death. Then when Spook runs off to her house she tells us, 'I suppose I'd best keep him, it's clear as day he don't

426

like it there with you-all.' With *me,* is what she meant. She held it against me I took her son away. She claimed I ruined his chances; she wanted him to get his diploma. But I never kept him from getting his diploma. He was the one who said he might as well drop out; said why bother staying in school when he could make a fine living on floors."

"On what?" Macon asked.

"Floors. Sanding floors. His uncle was Pritchett Refinishing. Norman went into the business as soon as we got married and his mom was always talking about the waste. She said he could have been an accountant or something, but I don't know who she thought she was kidding. He never mentioned accounting to *me.*"

She pulled a dog hair off her coat sleeve, examined it, and flicked it away. "So let's see him," she said.

"Pardon?"

"Let's see him heel."

Macon slapped his hip and started off, with Edward lagging just a bit behind. When Macon stopped, Edward stopped too and sat down. Macon was pleasantly surprised, but Muriel said, "He's not sitting."

"What? What do you call it, then?"

"He's keeping his rear end about two inches off the ground. Trying to see what he can get away with."

"Oh, Edward," Macon said sadly.

He pivoted and returned. "Well, you'll have to work on that," Muriel said. "But meantime, we'll go on to the downstay. Let's try it in the house."

Macon worried they'd meet up with Rose, but she was nowhere to be seen. The front hall smelled of radiator dust. The clock in the living room was striking the half hour.

"This is where we start on Edward's real problem," Muriel said. "Getting him to lie down and stay, so he won't all the time be jumping at the door."

She showed him the command: two taps of the foot. Her

427

boot made a crisp sound. When Edward didn't respond, she bent and pulled his forepaws out from under him. Then she let him up and went through it again, several times over. Edward made no progress. When she tapped her foot, he panted and looked elsewhere. "Stubborn," Muriel told him. "You're just as stubborn as they come." She said to Macon, "A lot of dogs will act like this. They hate to lie down; I don't know why. Now you."

Macon tapped his foot. Edward seemed fascinated by something off to his left.

"Grab his paws," Muriel said.

"On crutches?"

"Sure."

Macon sighed and propped his crutches in the corner. He lowered himself to the floor with his cast in front of him, took Edward's paws and forced him down. Edward rumbled threateningly, but in the end he submitted. To get up again, Macon had to hold onto the lamp table. "This is really very difficult," he said, but Muriel said, "Listen, I've taught a man with no legs at all."

"You have?" Macon said. He pictured a legless man dragging along the sidewalk with some vicious breed of dog, Muriel standing by unconcerned and checking her manicure. "I don't suppose *you* ever broke a leg," he accused her. "Getting around is harder than it looks."

"I broke an arm once," Muriel said.

"An arm is no comparison."

"I did it training dogs, in fact. Got knocked off a porch by a Doberman pinscher."

"A Doberman!"

"Came to to find him standing over me, showing all his teeth. Well, I thought of what they said at Doggie, Do: Only one of you can be boss. So I tell him, 'Absolutely not.' Those were the first words that came to me—what my mother used to say when she wasn't going to let me get away with some-

428

thing. 'Absolutely not,' I tell him, and my right arm is broken so I hold out my left, hold out my palm and stare into his eyes—they can't stand for you to meet their eyes—and get to my feet real slow. And durned if that dog doesn't settle right back on his haunches."

"Good Lord," Macon said.

"I've had a cocker spaniel fly directly at my throat. Meanest thing you ever saw. Had a German shepherd take my ankle in his teeth. Then he let it go."

She lifted a foot and rotated it. Her ankle was about the thickness of a pencil.

"Have you ever met with a failure?" Macon asked her. "Some dog you just gave up on?"

"Not a one," she said. "And Edward's not about to be the first."

But Edward seemed to think otherwise. Muriel worked with him another half hour, and although he would stay once he was down, he flatly refused to lie down on his own. Each time, he had to be forced. "Never mind," Muriel said. "This is the way most of them do. I bet tomorrow he'll be just as stubborn, so I'm going to skip a day. You keep practicing, and I'll be back this same time Saturday."

Then she told Edward to stay, and she accepted her money and slipped out the door. Observing Edward's erect, resisting posture, Macon felt discouraged. Why hire a trainer at all, if she left him to do the training? "Oh, I don't know, I don't know," he said. Edward gave a sigh and walked off, although he hadn't been released.

All that afternoon and evening, Edward refused to lie down. Macon wheedled, threatened, cajoled; Edward muttered ominously and stood firm. Rose and the boys edged around the two of them, politely averting their eyes as if they'd stumbled on some private quarrel.

Then the next morning, Edward charged the mailman.

Macon managed to grab the leash, but it raised some doubts in his mind. What did all this sitting and heeling have to do with Edward's real problem? "I should just ship you off to the pound," he told Edward. He tapped his foot twice. Edward did not lie down.

In the afternoon, Macon called the Meow-Bow. "May I speak to Muriel, please?" he asked. He couldn't think of her last name.

"Muriel's not working today," a girl told him.

"Oh, I see."

"Her little boy is sick."

He hadn't known she had a little boy. He felt some inner click of adjustment; she was a slightly different person from the one he'd imagined. "Well," he said, "this is Macon Leary. I guess I'll talk to her tomorrow."

"Oh, Mr. Leary. You want to call her at home?"

"No, that's all right."

"I can give you her number if you want to call her at home."

"I'll just talk to her tomorrow. Thank you."

Rose had an errand downtown, so she agreed to drop him off at the Businessman's Press. He wanted to deliver the rest of his guidebook. Stretched across the backseat with his crutches, he gazed at the passing scenery: antique office buildings, tasteful restaurants, health food stores and florists' shops, all peculiarly hard-edged and vivid in the light of a brilliant October afternoon. Rose perched behind the wheel and drove at a steady, slow pace that was almost hypnotic. She wore a little round basin-shaped hat with ribbons down the back. It made her look prim and Sunday schoolish.

One of the qualities that all four Leary children shared was a total inability to find their way around. It was a kind of dyslexia, Macon believed—a geographic dyslexia. None of them ever stepped outside without obsessively noting all avail-

430

able landmarks, clinging to a fixed and desperate mental map of the neighborhood. Back home, Macon had kept a stack of index cards giving detailed directions to the houses of his friends—even friends he'd known for decades. And it used to be that whenever Ethan met a new boy, Macon's first anxious question was, "Where exactly does he live, do you know?" Ethan had had a tendency to form inconvenient alliances. He couldn't just hang out with the boy next door; oh, no, it had to be someone who lived way beyond the Beltway. What did Ethan care? *He* had no trouble navigating. This was because he'd lived all his life in one house, was Macon's theory; while a person who'd been moved around a great deal never acquired a fixed point of reference but wandered forever in a fog—adrift upon the planet, helpless, praying that just by luck he might stumble across his destination.

At any rate, Rose and Macon got lost. Rose knew where she wanted to go—a shop that sold a special furniture oil—and Macon had visited Julian's office a hundred times; but even so, they drove in circles till Macon noticed a familiar steeple. "Stop! Turn left," he said. Rose pulled up where he directed. Macon struggled out. "Will you be all right?" he asked Rose. "Do you think you can find your way back to pick me up?"

"I hope so."

"Look for the steeple, remember."

She nodded and drove away.

Macon swung up three granite steps to the brick mansion that housed the Businessman's Press. The door was made of polished, golden wood. The floor inside was tiled with tiny black and white hexagons, just uneven enough to give purchase to Macon's crutches.

This wasn't an ordinary office. The secretary typed in a back room while Julian, who couldn't stand being alone, sat out front. He was talking on a red telephone, lounging behind a desk that was laden with a clutter of advertisements, pamphlets, unpaid bills, unanswered letters, empty Chinese carry-out cartons, and Perrier bottles. The walls were covered with sailing charts. The bookshelves held few books but a great many antique brass mariners' instruments that probably didn't even work anymore. Anybody with eyes could see that Julian's heart was not in the Businessman's Press but out on the Chesapeake Bay someplace. This was to Macon's advantage, he figured. Surely no one else would have continued backing his series, with its staggering expenses and its constant need for updating.

"Rita's bringing croissants," Julian said into the phone. "Joe is making his quiche." Then he caught sight of Macon. "Macon!" he said. "Stefanie, I'll get back to you." He hung up. "How's the leg? Here, have a seat."

He dumped a stack of yachting magazines off a chair. Macon sat down and handed over his folder. "Here's the rest of the material on England," he said.

"Well, finally!"

"This edition as I see it is going to run about ten or twelve pages longer than the last one," Macon said. "It's adding the business *women* that does it—listing which hotels offer elevator escorts, which ones serve drinks in the lobbies . . . I think I ought to be paid more."

"I'll talk it over with Marvin," Julian said, flipping through the manuscript.

Macon sighed. Julian spent money like water but Marvin was more cautious.

"So now you're on the U.S. again," Julian said.

"Well, if you say so."

"I hope it's not going to take you long."

"I can only go so fast," Macon said. "The U.S. has more cities."

"Yes, I realize that. In fact I might print this edition in sections: northeast, mid-Atlantic, and so forth; I don't know . . ." But then he changed the subject. (He had a rather

432

skittery mind.) "Did I tell you my new idea? Doctor friend of mine is looking into it: *Accidental Tourist in Poor Health.* A list of American-trained doctors and dentists in every foreign capital, plus maybe some suggestions for basic medical supplies: aspirin, Merck Manual—"

"Oh, not a Merck Manual away from home!" Macon said. "Every hangnail could be cancer, when you're reading a Merck Manual."

"Well, I'll make a note of that," Julian said (without so much as lifting a pencil). "Aren't you going to ask me to autograph your cast? It's so white."

"I like it white," Macon said. "I polish it with shoe polish."

"I didn't realize you could do that."

"I use the liquid kind. It's the brand with a nurse's face on the label, if you ever need to know."

"*Accidental Tourist on Crutches,*" Julian said, and he rocked back happily in his chair.

Macon could tell he was about to start his Macon Leary act. He got hastily to his feet and said, "Well, I guess I'll be going."

"So soon? Why don't we have a drink?"

"No, thanks, I can't. My sister's picking me up as soon as she gets done with her errand."

"Ah," Julian said. "What kind of errand?"

Macon looked at him suspiciously.

"Well? Dry cleaner's? Shoe repair?"

"Just an ordinary errand, Julian. Nothing special."

"Hardware store? Pharmacy?"

"No."

"So what is it?"

"Uh . . . she had to buy Furniture Food."

Julian's chair rocked so far back, Macon thought he was going to tip over. He wished he would, in fact. "Macon, do me a favor," Julian said. "Couldn't you just once invite me to a family dinner?"

"We're really not much for socializing," Macon told him.

"It wouldn't have to be fancy. Just whatever you eat normally. What *do* you eat normally? Or I'll bring the meal myself. You could lock the dog up . . . what's his name again?"

"Edward."

"Edward. Ha! And I'll come spend the evening."

"Oh, well," Macon said vaguely. He arranged himself on his crutches.

"Why don't I step outside and wait with you."

"I'd really rather you didn't," Macon said.

He couldn't bear for Julian to see his sister's little basin hat.

He pegged out to the curb and stood there, gazing in the direction Rose should be coming from. He supposed she was lost again. The cold was already creeping through the stretched-out sock he wore over his cast.

The trouble was, he decided, Julian had never had anything happen to him. His ruddy, cheerful face was unscarred by anything but sunburn; his only interest was a ridiculously inefficient form of transportation. His brief marriage had ended amicably. He had no children. Macon didn't want to sound prejudiced, but he couldn't help feeling that people who had no children had never truly grown up. They weren't entirely . . . real, he felt.

Unexpectedly, he pictured Muriel after the Doberman had knocked her off the porch. Her arm hung lifeless; he knew the leaden look a broken limb takes on. But Muriel ignored it; she didn't even glance at it. Smudged and disheveled and battered, she held her other hand up. "Absolutely not," she said.

She arrived the next morning with a gauzy bouffant scarf swelling over her hair, her hands thrust deep in her coat pockets. Edward danced around her. She pointed to his rump. He sat, and she bent to pick up his leash.

"How's your little boy?" Macon asked her.

She looked over at him. "What?" she said.

"Wasn't he sick?"

"Who told you that?"

"Someone at the vet's, when I phoned."

She went on looking at him.

"What was it? The flu?" he asked.

"Oh, yes, probably," she said after a moment. "Some little stomach thing."

"It's that time of year, I guess."

"How come you phoned?" she asked him.

"I wanted to know why Edward wouldn't lie down."

She turned her gaze toward Edward. She wound the leash around her hand and considered him.

"I tap my foot but he never obeys me," Macon said. "Something's wrong."

"I told you he'd be stubborn about it."

"Yes, but I've been practicing two days now and he's not making any—"

"What do you expect? You think I'm magical or something? Why blame me?"

"Oh, I'm not blaming—"

"You most certainly are. You tell me something's wrong, you call me on the phone—"

"I just wanted to—"

"You think it's weird I didn't mention Alexander, don't you?"

"Alexander?"

"You think I'm some kind of unnatural mother."

"What? No, wait a minute—"

"You're not going to give me another thought, are you, now you know I've got a kid. You're like, 'Oh, forget it, no point getting involved in *that*,' and then you wonder why I didn't tell you about him right off. Well, isn't it obvious? Don't you see what happens when I do?"

Macon wasn't quite following her logic, perhaps because he was distracted by Edward. The shriller Muriel's voice grew, the stiffer Edward's hair stood up on the back of his neck. A bad sign. A very bad sign. Edward's lip was slowly curling. Gradually, at first almost soundlessly, he began a low growl.

Muriel glanced at him and stopped speaking. She didn't seem alarmed. She merely tapped her foot twice. But Edward not only failed to lie down; he rose from his sitting position. Now he had a distinct, electrified hump between his shoulders. He seemed to have altered his basic shape. His ears were flattened against his skull.

"Down," Muriel said levelly.

With a bellow, Edward sprang straight at her face. Every tooth was bare and gleaming. His lips were drawn back in a horrible grimace and flecks of white foam flew from his mouth. Muriel instantly raised the leash. She jerked it upward with both fists and lifted Edward completely off the floor. He stopped barking. He started making gargling sounds.

"He's choking," Macon said.

Edward's throat gave an odd sort of click.

"Stop it. It's enough! You're choking him!"

Still, she let him hang. Now Edward's eyes rolled back in their sockets. Macon grabbed at Muriel's shoulder but found himself with a handful of coat, bobbled and irregular like something alive. He shook it, anyhow. Muriel lowered Edward to the floor. He landed in a boneless heap, his legs crumpling beneath him and his head flopping over. Macon crouched at his side. "Edward? Edward? Oh, God, he's dead!"

Edward raised his head and feebly licked his lips.

"See that? When they lick their lips it's a sign they're giving in," Muriel said cheerfully. "Doggie, Do taught me that."

Macon stood up. He was shaking.

"When they lick their lips it's good but when they put a

436

foot on top of your foot it's bad," Muriel said. "Sounds like a secret language, just about, doesn't it?"

"Don't you ever, ever do that again," Macon told her.

"Huh?"

"In fact, don't even bother coming again."

There was a startled silence.

"Well, fine," Muriel said, tightening her scarf. "If that's the way you feel, just fine and dandy." She stepped neatly around Edward and opened the front door. "You want a dog you can't handle? Fine with me."

"I'd rather a barking dog than a damaged, timid dog," Macon said.

"You want a dog that bites all your friends? Scars neighbor kids for life? Gets you into lawsuits? You want a dog that hates the whole world? Evil, nasty, *angry* dog? That kills the whole world?"

She slipped out the screen door and closed it behind her. Then she looked through the screen directly into Macon's eyes. "Why, yes, I guess you do," she said.

From the hall floor, Edward gave a moan and watched her walk away.

437

8

Now the days were shorter and colder, and the trees emptied oceans of leaves on the lawn but remained, somehow, as full as ever, so you'd finish raking and look upward to see a great wash of orange and yellow just waiting to cover the grass again the minute your back was turned. Charles and Porter drove over to Macon's house and raked there as well, and lit the pilot light in the furnace and repaired the basement window. They reported that everything seemed fine. Macon heard the news without much interest. Next week he'd be out of his cast, but no one asked when he was moving back home.

Each morning he and Edward practiced heeling. They would trudge the length of the block, with Edward matching Macon's gait so perfectly that he looked crippled himself. When they met passersby now he muttered but he didn't attack. "See there?" Macon wanted to tell someone. Bikers were another issue, but Macon had confidence they would solve that problem too, eventually.

He would make Edward sit and then he'd draw back, holding out a palm. Edward waited. Oh, he wasn't such a bad dog! Macon wished he could change the gestures of command—the palm, the pointed finger, all vestiges of that heartless trainer—but he supposed it was too late. He tapped his foot. Edward growled. "Dear one," Macon said, dropping heavily beside him. "Won't you please consider lying down?" Edward looked away. Macon stroked the soft wide space between his ears. "Ah, well, maybe tomorrow," he said.

His family was not so hopeful. "What about when you start traveling again?" Rose asked. "You're not leaving him with me. I wouldn't know how to handle him."

Macon told her they would get to that when they got to it.

It was hard for him to imagine resuming his travels. Sometimes he wished he could stay in his cast forever. In fact, he wished it covered him from head to foot. People would thump faintly on his chest. They'd peer through his eyeholes. "Macon? You in there?" Maybe he was, maybe he wasn't. No one would ever know.

One evening just after supper, Julian stopped by with a stack of papers. Macon had to slam Edward into the pantry before he opened the door. "Here you are!" Julian said, strolling past him. He wore corduroys and looked rugged and healthy. "I've been phoning you for three days straight. That dog sounds awfully close by, don't you think?"

"He's in the pantry," Macon said.

"Well, I've brought you some materials, Macon—mostly on New York. We've got a lot of suggestions for New York."

Macon groaned. Julian set his papers on the couch and looked around him. "Where are the others?" he asked.

"Oh, here and there," Macon said vaguely, but just then Rose appeared, and Charles was close behind.

"I hope I'm not interfering with supper," Julian told them.

"No, no," Rose said.

"We've finished," Macon said triumphantly.

Julian's face fell. "Really?" he said. "What time do you eat, anyhow?"

Macon didn't answer that. (They ate at five thirty. Julian would laugh.)

Rose said, "But we haven't had our coffee. Wouldn't you like some coffee?"

"I'd love some."

"It seems a little silly," Macon said, "if you haven't eaten."

"Well, yes," Julian said, "I suppose it does, Macon, to someone like you. But for me, home-brewed coffee is a real treat. All the people in my apartment building eat out, and there's nothing in any of the kitchens but a couple cans of peanuts and some diet soda."

"What kind of place *is* that?" Rose asked.

"It's the Calvert Arms—a singles building. Everybody's single."

"Oh! What an interesting idea."

"Well, not really," Julian said gloomily. "Not after a while. I started out enjoying it but now I think it's getting me down. Sometimes I wish for the good old-fashioned way of doing things, with children and families and old people like normal buildings have."

"Well, of course you do," Rose told him. "I'm going to get you some nice hot coffee."

She left, and the others sat down. "So. Are you three all there is?" Julian asked.

Macon refused to answer, but Charles said, "Oh, no, there's Porter too."

"Porter? Where is Porter?"

"Um, we're not too sure."

"*Missing?*"

"He went to a hardware store and we think he got lost."

"Good grief, when did this happen?"

"A little while before supper."

"Supper. You mean today."

"He's just running an errand," Macon said. "Not lost in any permanent sense."

440

"Where was the store?"

"Someplace on Howard Street," Charles said. "Rose needed hinges."

"He got lost on Howard Street?"

Macon stood up. "I'll go help Rose," he said.

Rose was setting their grandmother's clear glass coffee mugs on a silver tray. "I hope he doesn't take sugar," she said. "The sugarbowl is empty and Edward's in the pantry where I keep the bag."

"I wouldn't worry about it."

"Maybe you could go to the pantry and get it for me."

"Oh, just give him his coffee straight and tell him to take it or leave it."

"Why, Macon! This is your employer!"

"He's only here because he hopes we'll do something eccentric," Macon told her. "He has this one-sided notion of us. I just pray none of us says anything unconventional around him, are you listening?"

"What would we say?" Rose asked. "We're the most conventional people I know."

This was perfectly true, and yet in some odd way it wasn't. Macon couldn't explain it. He sighed and followed her out of the kitchen.

In the living room, Charles was doggedly debating whether they should answer the phone in case it rang, in case it might be Porter, in case he needed them to consult a map. "Chances are, though, he wouldn't bother calling," he decided, "because he knows we wouldn't answer. Or he thinks we wouldn't answer. Or I don't know, maybe he figures we would answer even so, because we're worried."

"Do you always give this much thought to your phone calls?" Julian asked.

Macon said, "Have some coffee, Julian. Try it black."

"Why, thank you," Julian said. He accepted a mug and studied the inscription that arched across it. "CENTURY OF

441

PROGRESS 1933," he read off. He grinned and raised the mug in a toast. "To progress," he said.

"Progress," Rose and Charles echoed. Macon scowled.

Julian said, "What do you do for a living, Charles?"

"I make bottle caps."

"Bottle caps! Is that a fact!"

"Oh, well, it's no big thing," Charles said. "I mean it's not half as exciting as it sounds, really."

"And Rose? Do you work?"

"Yes, I do," Rose said, in the brave, forthright style of someone being interviewed. "I work at home; I keep house for the boys. Also I take care of a lot of the neighbors. They're mostly old and they need me to read their prescriptions and repair their plumbing and such."

"You repair their plumbing?" Julian asked.

The telephone rang. The others stiffened.

"What do you think?" Rose asked Macon.

"Um . . ."

"But he knows we wouldn't answer," Charles told them.

"Yes, he'd surely call a neighbor instead."

"On the other hand . . ." Charles said.

"On the other hand," Macon said.

It was Julian's face that decided him—Julian's pleased, perked expression. Macon reached over to the end table and picked up the receiver. "Leary," he said.

"Macon?"

It was Sarah.

Macon shot a glance at the others and turned his back to them. "Yes," he said.

"Well, finally," she said. Her voice seemed oddly flat and concrete. All at once he saw her clearly: She wore one of his cast-off shirts and she sat hugging her bare knees. "I've been trying to get in touch with you at home," she said. "Then it occurred to me you might be having supper with your family."

"Is something wrong?" he asked.

442

He was nearly whispering. Maybe Rose understood, from that, who it was, for she suddenly began an animated conversation with the others. Sarah said, "What? I can't hear you."

"Is everything all right?"

"Who's that talking?"

"Julian's here."

"Oh, Julian! Give him my love. How's Sukie?"

"Sukie?"

"His boat, Macon."

"It's fine," he said. Or should he have said "she"? For all he knew, *Sukie* was at the bottom of the Chesapeake.

"I called because I thought we should talk," Sarah said. "I was hoping we could meet for supper some night."

"Oh. Well. Yes, we could do that," Macon said.

"Would tomorrow be all right?"

"Certainly."

"What restaurant?"

"Well, why not the Old Bay," Macon said.

"The Old Bay. Of course," Sarah said. She either sighed or laughed, he wasn't sure which.

"It's only because you could walk there," he told her. "That's the only reason I suggested it."

"Yes, well, let's see. You like to eat early; shall we say six o'clock?"

"Six will be fine," he said.

When he hung up, he found Rose embarked on a discussion of the English language. She pretended not to notice he had rejoined them. It was shocking, she was saying, how sloppy everyday speech had become. How the world seemed bound and determined to say "*the* hoi polloi," a clear redundancy in view of the fact that "hoi" was an article. How "chauvinist" had come to be a shorthand term for "male chauvinist," its original meaning sadly lost to common knowledge. It was incredible, Charles chimed in, that a female movie star traveled "incognito" when any fool should know

443

she was "incognita" instead. Julian appeared to share their indignation. It was more incredible still, he said, how everyone slung around the word "incredible" when really there was very little on earth that truly defied credibility. "Credence," Macon corrected him, but Rose rushed in as if Macon hadn't spoken. "Oh, I know just what you mean," she told Julian. "Words are getting devalued, isn't that right?" She tugged handfuls of her gray tube skirt over her knees in a childlike gesture. You would think she had never been warned that outsiders were not to be trusted.

To enter the Old Bay Restaurant, Macon had to climb a set of steps. Before he broke his leg he hadn't even noticed those steps existed—let alone that they were made of smooth, un-blemished marble, so that his crutches kept threatening to slide out from under him. Then he had to fight the heavy front door, hurrying a bit because Rose had taken a wrong turn driving him down and it was already five after six.

The foyer was dark as night. The dining room beyond was only slightly brighter, lit by netted candles on the tables. Macon peered into the gloom. "I'm meeting someone," he told the hostess. "Is she here yet?"

"Not as I know of, hon."

She led him past a tankful of sluggish lobsters, past two old ladies in churchy hats sipping pale pink drinks, past a whole field of empty tables. It was too early for anyone else to be eating; all the other customers were still in the bar. The tables stood very close together, their linens brushing the floor, and Macon had visions of catching a crutch on a tablecloth and dragging the whole thing after him, candle included. The maroon floral carpet would burst into flames. His grand-father's favorite restaurant—his great-grandfather's too, quite possibly—would be reduced to a heap of charred metal crab pots. "Miss! Slow down!" he called, but the hostess strode on,

444

muscular and athletic in her off-the-shoulder square-dance dress and sturdy white crepe-soled shoes.

She put him in a corner, which was lucky because it gave him a place to lean his crutches. But just as he was matching them up and preparing to set them aside, she said, "I'll take those for you, darlin'."

"Oh, they'll be fine here."

"I need to check them up front, sweetheart. It's a rule."

"You have a rule about crutches?"

"They might trip the other customers, honeybunch."

This was unlikely, since the two other customers were clear across the room, but Macon handed his crutches over. Come to think of it, he might be better off without them. Then Sarah wouldn't get the impression (at least at first glance) that he'd fallen apart in her absence.

As soon as he was alone he tugged each shirt cuff till a quarter-inch of white showed. He was wearing his gray tweed suit coat with gray flannel trousers—an old pair of trousers, so it hadn't mattered if he cut one leg off. Charles had fetched them from home and Rose had hemmed them, and she'd also trimmed his hair. Porter had lent him his best striped tie. They had all been so discreetly helpful that Macon had felt sad, for some reason.

The hostess reappeared in the doorway, followed by Sarah. Macon had an instant of stunned recognition; it was something like accidentally glimpsing his own reflection in a mirror. Her halo of curls, the way her coat fell around her in soft folds, her firm, springy walk in trim pumps with wineglass heels—how had he forgotten all that?

He half stood. Would she kiss him? Or just, God forbid, coolly shake hands. But no, she did neither; she did something much worse. She came around the table and pressed her cheek to his briefly, as if they were mere acquaintances meeting at a cocktail party.

"Hello, Macon," she said.

He waved her speechlessly into the chair across from his. He sat again, with some effort.

"What happened to your leg?" she asked.

"I had a kind of . . . fall."

"Is it broken?"

He nodded.

"And what did you do to your hand?"

He held it up to examine it. "Well, it's a sort of dog bite. But it's nearly healed by now."

"I meant the other one."

The other one had a band of gauze around the knuckles. "Oh, that," he said. "It's just a scrape. I've been helping Rose build a cat door."

She studied him.

"But I'm all right!" he told her. "In fact the cast is almost comfortable. Almost familiar! I'm wondering if I broke a leg once before in some previous incarnation."

Their waitress asked, "Can I bring you something from the bar?"

She was standing over them, pad and pencil poised. Sarah started flipping hastily through the menu, so Macon said, "A dry sherry, please." Then he and the waitress turned back to Sarah. "Oh, my," Sarah said. "Let me see. Well, how about a Rob Roy. Yes, a Rob Roy would be nice, with extra cherries."

That was something else he'd forgotten—how she loved to order complicated drinks in restaurants. He felt the corners of his mouth twitching upward.

"So," Sarah said when the waitress had gone. "Why would Rose be building a cat door? I thought they didn't have any pets."

"No, this is for our cat. Helen. Helen and I have been staying there."

"What for?"

"Well, because of my leg."

446

Sarah said nothing.

"I mean, can you see me managing those steps at home?" Macon asked her. "Taking Edward for walks? Lugging the trash cans out?"

But she was busy shucking off her coat. Beneath it she wore a gathered wool dress in an indeterminate color. (The candlelight turned everything to shades of sepia, like an old-fashioned photograph.) Macon had time to wonder if he'd given her the wrong idea. It sounded, perhaps, as if he were complaining—as if he were reproaching her for leaving him alone.

"But really," he said, "I've been getting along wonderfully."

"Good," Sarah said, and she smiled at him and went back to her menu.

Their drinks were set before them on little cardboard disks embossed with crabs. The waitress said, "Ready to order, dearies?"

"Well," Sarah said, "I think I'll have the hot antipasto and the beef Pierre."

The waitress, looking startled, peered over Sarah's shoulder at the menu. (Sarah had never seemed to realize what the Old Bay Restaurant was all about.) "Here," Sarah said, pointing, "and here."

"If you say so," the waitress said, writing it down.

"I'll just have the, you know," Macon said. "Crab soup, shrimp salad platter . . ." He handed back his menu. "Sarah, do you want wine?"

"No, thank you."

When they were alone again, she said, "How long have you been at your family's?"

"Since September," Macon said.

"September! Your leg's been broken all that time?"

He nodded and took a sip of his drink. "Tomorrow I get the cast off," he said.

447

"And is Edward over there too?"

He nodded again.

"Was it Edward who bit your hand?"

"Well, yes."

He wondered if she'd act like the others, urge him to call the S.P.C.A.; but instead she meditatively plucked a cherry off the plastic sword from her drink. "I guess he's been upset," she said.

"Yes, he has, in fact," Macon said. "He's not himself at all."

"Poor Edward."

"He's getting kind of out of control, to tell the truth."

"He always did have a sensitivity to change," Sarah said.

Macon took heart. "Actually, he's been attacking right and left," he told her. "I had to hire a special trainer. But she was too harsh; let's face it, she was brutal. She nearly strangled him when he tried to bite her."

"Ridiculous," Sarah said. "He was only frightened. When Edward's frightened he attacks; that's just the way he is. There's no point scaring him more."

Macon felt a sudden rush of love.

Oh, he'd raged at her and hated her and entirely forgotten her, at different times. He'd had moments when he imagined he'd never cared for her to begin with; only went after her because everybody else had. But the fact was, she was his oldest friend. The two of them had been through things that no one else in the world knew of. She was embedded in his life. It was much too late to root her out.

"What he wants," she was saying, "is a sense of routine. That's all he needs: reassurance."

"Sarah," he said, "it's been awful living apart."

She looked at him. Some trick of light made her eyes appear a darker blue, almost black.

"Hasn't it?" he said.

She lowered her glass. She said, "I asked you here for a reason, Macon."

He could tell it was something he didn't want to hear.

She said, "We need to spell out the details of our separation."

"We've been separated; what's to spell out?" he asked.

"I meant in a legal way."

"Legal. I see."

"Now, according to the state of Maryland—"

"I think you ought to come home."

Their first course arrived, placed before them by a hand that, as far as Macon was concerned, was not attached to a body. Condiment bottles were shifted needlessly; a metal stand full of sugar packets was moved a half-inch over. "Anything else?" the waitress asked.

"No!" Macon said. "Thank you."

She left.

He said, "Sarah?"

"It's not possible," she told him.

She was sliding a single pearl up and down the chain at her throat. He had given her that pearl when they were courting. Was there any significance in her wearing it this evening? Or maybe she cared so little now, it hadn't even occurred to her to leave it off. Yes, that was more likely.

"Listen," he said. "Don't say no before you hear me out. Have you ever considered we might have another baby?"

He had shocked her, he saw; she drew in a breath. (He had shocked himself.)

"Why not?" he asked her. "We're not too old."

"Oh, Macon."

"This time, it would be easy," he said. "It wouldn't take us seven years again; I bet you'd get pregnant in no time!" He leaned toward her, straining to make her see it: Sarah blossoming in that luscious pink maternity smock she used

449

to wear. But oddly enough, what flashed across his mind instead was the memory of those first seven years—their disappointment each month. It had seemed to Macon back then (though of course it was pure superstition) that their failures were a sign of something deeper, some essential incompatibility. They had missed connections in the most basic and literal sense. When she finally got pregnant, he had felt not only relieved but guilty, as if they had succeeded in putting something over on someone.

He pushed these thoughts back down. "I realize," he said, "that it wouldn't be Ethan. I realize we can't replace him. But—"

"No," Sarah said.

Her eyes were very steady. He knew that look. She'd never change her mind.

Macon started on his soup. It was the best crab soup in Baltimore, but unfortunately the spices had a tendency to make his nose run. He hoped Sarah wouldn't think he was crying.

"I'm sorry," she said more gently. "But it would never work."

He said, "All right, forget that. It was crazy, right? Crazy notion. By the time that baby was twenty we'd be . . . Aren't you going to eat?"

She glanced down at her plate. Then she picked up a fork.

"Suppose I did this," Macon said. "Suppose I packed a suitcase with your clothes and knocked on your door and said, 'Come on, we're going to Ocean City. We've wasted long enough.' "

She stared, an artichoke heart raised halfway to her mouth.

"Ocean City?" she said. "You hate Ocean City!"

"Yes, but I meant—"

"You always said it was way too crowded."

"Yes, but—"

450

"And what clothes could you be talking about? They're all in my apartment."

"It was only a manner of speaking," Macon said.

"Really, Macon," she told him. "You don't even communicate when you communicate."

"Oh, *communicate*," he said. (His least favorite word.) "All I'm saying is, I think we ought to start over."

"I am starting over," she said. She returned the artichoke heart to her plate. "I'm doing everything I can to start over," she said, "but that doesn't mean I want to live the same life twice. I'm trying to branch off in new directions. I'm taking some courses. I'm even dating, a little."

"Dating?"

"I've been going out with this physician."

There was a pause.

Macon said, "Why not just call him a doctor."

Sarah briefly closed her eyes.

"Look," she said. "I know this is hard for you. It's hard for both of us. But we really didn't have much left, don't you see? Look who you turned to when you broke your leg: your sister Rose! You didn't even let me know, and you do have my telephone number."

"If I'd turned to you instead," he said, "would you have come?"

"Well . . . but at least you could have asked. But no, you called on your family. You're closer to them than you ever were to me."

"That's not true," Macon said. "Or rather, it's true but it's not the point. I mean, in one sense, of course we're closer; we're blood relations."

"Playing that ridiculous card game no one else can fathom," Sarah said. "Plotting your little household projects, Rose with her crescent wrench and her soldering gun. Cruising hardware stores like other people cruise boutiques."

"As other people cruise boutiques," Macon said. And then regretted it.

"Picking apart people's English," Sarah said. "Hauling forth the dictionary at every opportunity. Quibbling over *method*. The kind of family that always fastens their seatbelts."

"For God's sake, Sarah, what's wrong with fastening your seatbelt?"

"They always go to one restaurant, the one their grandparents went to before them, and even there they have to rearrange the silver and set things up so they're sitting around the table the same way they sit at home. They dither and deliberate, can't so much as close a curtain without this group discussion back and forth, to and fro, all the pros and cons. 'Well if we leave it open it will be so hot but if we close it things will get musty . . .' They have to have their six glasses of water every day. Their precious baked potatoes every night. They don't believe in ballpoint pens or electric typewriters or automatic transmissions. They don't believe in hello and good-bye."

"Hello? Good-bye?" Macon said.

"Just watch yourself some time! People walk in and you just, oh, register it with your eyes; people leave and you just look away quickly. You don't admit to comings and goings. And the best house in the world might come on the market, but you can't buy it because you've ordered these address labels for the old house, a thousand five hundred gummed labels, and you have to use them up before you move."

"That wasn't me, it was Charles," Macon said.

"Yes, but it could have been you. And his wife divorced him for it, and I don't blame her."

"And now you're about to do the same damn thing," Macon said. "Ruin twenty years of marriage over whether I fasten my seatbelt."

"They were ruined long ago, believe me," Sarah said.

Macon laid down his spoon. He forced himself to take a deep breath.

"Sarah," he said. "We're getting away from the point."

After a silence, Sarah said, "Yes, I guess we are."

"It's what happened to Ethan that ruined us," Macon told her.

She set an elbow on the table and covered her eyes.

"But it wouldn't have to," he said. "Why, some people, a thing like this brings them closer together. How come we're letting it part us?"

The waitress said, "Is everything all right?"

Sarah sat up straighter and started rummaging through her purse.

"Yes, certainly," Macon said.

The waitress was carrying a tray with their main dishes. She cast a doubtful look at Sarah's antipasto. "Isn't she going to eat that, or what?" she asked Macon.

"No, I guess, um, maybe not."

"Didn't she like it?"

"She liked it fine. Take it away."

The waitress bustled around the table in an offended silence. Sarah put aside her purse. She looked down at her meal, which was something brown and gluey.

"You're welcome to half my shrimp salad," Macon told her when the waitress had gone.

She shook her head. Her eyes were deep with tears, but they hadn't spilled over.

"Macon," she said, "ever since Ethan died I've had to admit that people are basically bad. Evil, Macon. So evil they would take a twelve-year-old boy and shoot him through the skull for no reason. I read a paper now and I despair; I've given up watching the news on TV. There's so much wickedness, children setting other children on fire and grown men throwing babies out second-story windows, rape and torture and terrorism, old people beaten and robbed, men in our very own

453

government willing to blow up the world, indifference and greed and instant anger on every street corner. I look at my students and they're so ordinary, but they're exactly like the boy who killed Ethan. If it hadn't said beneath that boy's picture what he'd been arrested for, wouldn't you think he was just anyone? Someone who'd made the basketball team or won a college scholarship? You can't believe in a soul. Last spring, Macon, I didn't tell you this, I was cutting back our hedge and I saw the bird feeder had been stolen out of the crape myrtle tree. Someone will even steal food from little birds! And I just, I don't know, went kind of crazy and attacked the crape myrtle. Cut it all up, ripped off branches, slashed it with my pruning shears . . ."

Tears were running down her face now. She leaned across the table and said, "There are times when I haven't been sure I could—I don't want to sound melodramatic but—Macon, I haven't been sure I could live in this kind of a world anymore."

Macon felt he had to be terribly careful. He had to choose exactly the right words. He cleared his throat and said, "Yes, um, I see what you mean but . . ." He cleared his throat again. "It's true," he said, "what you say about human beings. I'm not trying to argue. But tell me this, Sarah: Why would that cause you to leave me?"

She crumpled up her napkin and dabbed at her nose. She said, "Because I *knew* you wouldn't try to argue. You've believed all along they were evil."

"Well, so—"

"This whole last year I felt myself retreating. Withdrawing. I could feel myself shrinking. I stayed away from crowds, I didn't go to parties, I didn't ask our friends in. When you and I went to the beach in the summer I lay on my blanket with all those people around me, their squawking radios and their gossip and their quarrels, and I thought, 'Ugh, they're so depressing. They're so unlikable. So vile, really.' I felt my-

454

self shrinking away from them. Just like you do, Macon—just *as* you do; sorry. Just as you have always done. I felt I was turning into a Leary."

Macon tried for a lighter tone. He said, "Well, there are worse disasters than that, I guess."

She didn't smile. She said, "I can't afford it."

"Afford?"

"I'm forty-two years old. I don't have enough time left to waste it holing up in my shell. So I've taken action. I've cut myself loose. I live in this apartment you'd hate, all clutter. I've made a whole bunch of new friends, and you wouldn't like them much either, I guess. I'm studying with a sculptor. I always did want to be an artist, only teaching seemed more sensible. That's how you would think: sensible. You're so quick to be sensible, Macon, that you've given up on just about everything."

"What have I given up on?"

She refolded the napkin and blotted her eyes. An appealing blur of mascara shadowed the skin beneath them. She said, "Remember Betty Grand?"

"No."

"Betty Grand, she went to my school. You used to like her before you met me."

"I never liked anyone on earth before I met you," Macon said.

"You liked Betty Grand, Macon. You told me so when we first went out. You asked me if I knew her. You said you used to think she was pretty and you'd invited her to a ball game but she turned you down. You told me you'd changed your mind about her being pretty. Her gums showed any time she smiled, you said."

Macon still didn't remember, but he said, "Well? So?"

"Everything that might touch you or upset you or disrupt you, you've given up without a murmur and done without, said you never wanted it anyhow."

455

"I suppose I would have done better if I'd gone on pining for Betty Grand all my life."

"Well, you would have shown some feeling, at least."

"I do show feeling, Sarah. I'm sitting here with you, am I not? You don't see me giving up on *you*."

She chose not to hear this. "And when Ethan died," she said, "you peeled every single Wacky Pack sticker off his bedroom door. You emptied his closet and his bureau as if you couldn't be rid of him soon enough. You kept offering people his junk in the basement, stilts and sleds and skateboards, and you couldn't understand why they didn't accept them. 'I hate to see stuff sitting there useless,' you said. Macon, I know you loved him but I can't help thinking you didn't love him as much as I did, you're not so torn apart by his going. I know you mourned him but there's something so what-do-you-call, so muffled about the way you experience things, I mean love or grief or anything; it's like you're trying to slip through life unchanged. Don't you see why I had to get out?"

"Sarah, I'm not muffled. I . . . endure. I'm trying to endure, I'm standing fast, I'm holding steady."

"If you really think that," Sarah said, "then you're fooling yourself. You're not holding steady; you're ossified. You're encased. You're like something in a capsule. You're a dried-up kernel of a man that nothing really penetrates. Oh, Macon, it's not by chance you write those silly books telling people how to take trips without a jolt. That traveling armchair isn't just your logo; it's you."

"No, it's not," Macon said. "It's not!"

Sarah pulled her coat on, making a sloppy job of it. One corner of her collar was tucked inside. "So anyway," she said. "This is what I wanted to tell you: I'm having John Albright send you a letter."

"Who's John Albright?"

"He's an attorney."

"Oh," Macon said.

456

It was at least a full minute before he thought to say, "I guess you must mean a lawyer."

Sarah collected her purse, stood up, and walked out.

Macon made his way conscientiously through his shrimp salad. He ate his cole slaw for the vitamin C. Then he finished every last one of his potato chips, although he knew his tongue would feel shriveled the following morning.

Once when Ethan was little, not more than two or three, he had run out into the street after a ball. Macon had been too far away to stop him. All he could do was shout, "No!" and then watch, frozen with horror, as a pickup truck came barreling around the curve. In that instant, he released his claim. In one split second he adjusted to a future that held no Ethan—an immeasurably bleaker place but also, by way of compensation, plainer and simpler, free of the problems a small child trails along with him, the endless demands and the mess and the contests for his mother's attention. Then the truck stopped short and Ethan retrieved his ball, and Macon's knees went weak with relief. But he remembered forever after how quickly he had adjusted. He wondered, sometimes, if that first adjustment had somehow stuck, making what happened to Ethan later less of a shock than it might have been. But if people didn't adjust, how could they bear to go on?

He called for his bill and paid it. "Was there something wrong?" the waitress asked. "Did your friend not like her meal? She could always have sent it back, hon. We always let you send it back."

"I know that," Macon said.

"Maybe it was too spicy for her."

"It was fine," he said. "Could I have my crutches, please?"

She went off to get them, shaking her head.

He would have to locate a taxi. He'd made no arrangements for Rose to pick him up. Secretly, he'd been hoping to go home with Sarah. Now that hope seemed pathetic. He looked around the dining room and saw that most of the tables were filled, and that every person had someone else to eat with. Only Macon sat alone. He kept very erect and dignified but inside, he knew, he was crumbling. And when the waitress brought him his crutches and he stood to leave, it seemed appropriate that he had to walk nearly doubled, his chin sunk low on his chest and his elbows jutting out awkwardly like the wings of a baby bird. People stared at him as he passed. Some snickered. Was his foolishness so obvious? He passed the two churchy old ladies and one of them tugged at his sleeve. "Sir? Sir?"

He came to a stop.

"I suspect they may have given you my crutches," she said.

He looked down at the crutches. They were, of course, not his. They were diminutive—hardly more than child-sized. Any other time he would have grasped the situation right off, but today it had somehow escaped him. Any other time he would have swung into action—called for the manager, pointed out the restaurant's lack of concern for the handicapped. Today he only stood hanging his head, waiting for someone to help him.

9

Back when Grandfather Leary's mind first began to wander, no one had guessed what was happening. He was such an upright, firm old man. He was all sharp edges. Definite. "Listen," he told Macon, "by June the twelfth I'll need my passport from the safe deposit box. I'm setting sail for Lassaque."

"Lassaque, Grandfather?"

"If I like it I may just stay there."

"But where is Lassaque?"

"It's an island off the coast of Bolivia."

"Ah," Macon said. And then, "Well, wait a minute . . ."

"It interests me because the Lassaquans have no written language. In fact if you bring any reading matter they confiscate it. They say it's black magic."

"But I don't think Bolivia *has* a coast," Macon said.

"They don't even allow, say, a checkbook with your name on it. Before you go ashore you have to soak the label off your deodorant. You have to get your money changed into little colored wafers."

"Grandfather, is this a joke?"

"A joke! Look it up if you don't believe me." Grandfather

Leary checked his steel pocket watch, then wound it with an assured, back-and-forth motion. "An intriguing effect of their illiteracy," he said, "is their reverence for the elderly. This is because the Lassaquans' knowledge doesn't come from books but from living; so they hang on every word from those who have lived the longest."

"I see," Macon said, for now he thought he did see. "We hang on your words, too," he said.

"That may be so," his grandfather told him, "but I still intend to see Lassaque before it's corrupted."

Macon was silent a moment. Then he went over to the bookcase and selected a volume from his grandfather's set of faded brown encyclopedias. "Give it here," his grandfather said, holding out both hands. He took the book greedily and started riffling through the pages. A smell of mold floated up. "Laski," he muttered, "Lassalle, Lassaw . . ." He lowered the book and frowned. "I don't . . ." he said. He returned to the book. "Lassalle, Lassaw . . ."

He looked confused, almost frightened. His face all at once collapsed—a phenomenon that had startled Macon on several occasions lately. "I don't understand," he whispered to Macon. "I don't understand."

"Well," Macon said, "maybe it was a dream. Maybe it was one of those dreams that seem real."

"Macon, this was no dream. I know the place. I've bought my ticket. I'm sailing June the twelfth."

Macon felt a strange coldness creeping down his back.

Then his grandfather became an inventor—spoke of various projects he was tinkering with, he said, in his basement. He would sit in his red leather armchair, his suit and white shirt immaculate, his black dress shoes polished to a glare, his carefully kept hands folded in his lap, and he would announce that he'd just finished welding together a motorcycle that would pull a plow. He would earnestly discuss crankshafts and cotter pins, while Macon—though terribly distressed—had to fight down a bubble of laughter at the thought of some leather-booted Hell's Angel grinding away at a wheatfield. "If I could just get the kinks ironed out," his grandfather said, "I'd have my fortune made. We'll all be rich." For he seemed to believe he was poor again, struggling to earn his way in the world. His motorized radio that followed you from room to room, his floating telephone, his car that came when you called it—wouldn't there be some application for those? Wouldn't the right person pay an arm and a leg?

Having sat out on the porch for one entire June morning, studiously pinching the creases of his trousers, he announced that he had perfected a new type of hybrid: flowers that closed in the presence of tears. "Florists will be mobbing me," he said. "Think of the dramatic effect at funerals!" He was working next on a cross between basil and tomatoes. He said the spaghetti-sauce companies would make him a wealthy man.

By then, all three of his grandsons had left home and his wife had died; so Rose alone took care of him. Her brothers began to worry about her. They took to dropping by more and more often. Then Rose said, "You don't have to do this, you know."

They said, "What? Do what? What are you talking about?" And other such things.

"If you're coming so often on account of Grandfather, it's not necessary. I'm managing fine, and so is he. He's very happy."

"Happy!"

"I honestly believe," Rose said, "that he's having the richest and most . . . colorful, really, time of his life. I'll bet even when he was young, he never enjoyed himself this much."

They saw what she meant. Macon felt almost envious, once he thought about it. And later, when that period was over, he was sorry it had been so short. For their grandfather soon passed to pointless, disconnected mumbles, and then to a staring silence, and at last he died.

Early Wednesday morning, Macon dreamed Grandfather Leary woke him and asked where the center punch was. "What are you talking about?" Macon said. "I never had your center punch."

"Oh, Macon," his grandfather said sadly, "can't you tell that I'm not saying what I mean?"

"What do you mean, then?"

"You've lost the center of your *life*, Macon."

"Yes, I know that," Macon said, and it seemed that Ethan stood just slightly to the left, his bright head nearly level with the old man's.

But his grandfather said, "No, no," and made an impatient, shaking-off gesture and went over to the bureau. (In this dream, Macon was not in the sun porch but upstairs in his boyhood bedroom, with the bureau whose cut-glass knobs Rose had stolen long ago to use as dishes for her dolls.) "It's Sarah I mean," his grandfather said, picking up a hairbrush. "Where is Sarah?"

"She's left me, Grandfather."

"Why, Sarah's the best of all of us!" his grandfather said. "You want to sit in this old house and rot, boy? It's time we started digging out! How long are we going to stay fixed here?"

Macon opened his eyes. It wasn't morning yet. The sun porch was fuzzy as blotting paper.

There was still a sense of his grandfather in the air. His little shaking-off gesture was one that Macon had forgotten entirely; it had reappeared on its own. But Grandfather Leary would never have said in real life what he'd said in the dream. He had liked Sarah well enough, but he seemed to view wives as extraneous, and he'd attended each of his grandsons' weddings with a resigned and tolerant expression. He wouldn't have thought of any woman as a "center." Except, perhaps,

462

Macon thought suddenly, his own wife, Grandmother Leary. After whose death—why, yes, immediately after—his mind had first begun to wander.

Macon lay awake till dawn. It was a relief to hear the first stirrings overhead. Then he got up and shaved and dressed and sent Edward out for the paper. By the time Rose came downstairs, he had started the coffee perking. This seemed to make her anxious. "Did you use the morning beans or the evening beans?" she asked.

"The morning beans," he assured her. "Everything's under control."

She moved around the kitchen raising shades, setting the table, opening a carton of eggs. "So today's the day you get your cast off," she said.

"Looks that way."

"And this afternoon's your New York trip."

"Oh, well . . ." he said vaguely, and then he asked if she wanted a bacon coupon he'd spotted in the paper.

She persisted: "Isn't it this afternoon you're going?"

"Well, yes."

The fact of the matter was, he was leaving for New York without having made any arrangements for Edward. The old place wouldn't accept him, the new place had that Muriel woman . . . and in Macon's opinion, Edward was best off at home with the family. Rose, no doubt, would disagree. He held his breath, but Rose started humming "Clementine" and breaking eggs into a skillet.

At nine o'clock, in an office down on St. Paul Street, the doctor removed Macon's cast with a tiny, purring electric saw. Macon's leg emerged dead-white and wrinkled and ugly. When he stood up, his ankle wobbled. He still had a limp. Also, he'd forgotten to bring different trousers and he was forced to parade back through the other patients in his one-legged summer khakis, exposing his repulsive-looking shin. He wondered if he'd ever return to his old, unbroken self.

Driving him home, Rose finally thought to ask where he planned to board Edward. "Why, I'm leaving him with you," Macon said, acting surprised.

"With me? Oh, Macon, you know how out of hand he gets."

"What could happen in such a short time? I'll be home by tomorrow night. If worst comes to worst you could lock him in the pantry; toss him some kibble now and then till I get back."

"I don't like this at all," Rose said.

"It's visitors that set him off. It's not as if you're expecting any visitors."

"Oh, no," she said, and then she let the subject drop, thank heaven. He'd been fearing more of a battle.

He took a shower, and he dressed in his traveling suit. Then he had an early lunch. Just before noon Rose drove him down to the railroad station, since he didn't yet trust his clutch foot. When he stepped from the car, his leg threatened to buckle. "Wait!" he said to Rose, who was handing his bag out after him. "Do you suppose I'm up to this?"

"I'm sure you are," she said, without giving it anywhere near enough thought. She pulled the passenger door shut, waved at him, and drove off.

In the period since Macon's last train trip, something wonderful had happened to the railroad station. A skylight in shades of watery blue arched gently overhead. Pale globe lamps hung from brass hooks. The carpenters' partitions that had divided the waiting room for so long had disappeared, revealing polished wooden benches. Macon stood bewildered at the brand-new, gleaming ticket window. Maybe, he thought, travel was not so bad. Maybe he'd got it all wrong. He felt a little sprig of hopefulness beginning.

But immediately afterward, limping toward his gate, he was overcome by the lost feeling that always plagued him on these trips. He envisioned himself as a stark Figure 1 in a throng of 2's and 3's. Look at that group at the Information counter, those confident young people with their knapsacks and sleeping bags. Look at the family occupying one entire bench, their four little daughters so dressed up, so stiff in new plaid coats and ribboned hats, you just knew they'd be met by grandparents at the other end of the line. Even those sitting alone—the old woman with the corsage, the blonde with her expensive leather luggage—gave the impression of belonging to someone.

He sat down on a bench. A southbound train was announced and half the crowd went off to catch it, followed by the inevitable breathless, disheveled woman galloping through some time later with far too many bags and parcels. Arriving passengers began to straggle up the stairs. They wore the dazed expressions of people who had been elsewhere till just this instant. A woman was greeted by a man holding a baby; he kissed her and passed her the baby at once, as if it were a package he'd been finding unusually heavy. A young girl in jeans, reaching the top of the stairs, caught sight of another girl in jeans and threw her arms around her and started crying. Macon watched, pretending not to, inventing explanations. (She was home for their mother's funeral? Her elopement hadn't worked out?)

Now his own train was called, so he picked up his bag and limped behind the family with all the daughters. At the bottom of the stairs a gust of cold, fresh air hit him. Wind always seemed to be howling down these platforms, no matter what the weather elsewhere. The smallest of the daughters had to have her coat buttoned. The train came into view, slowly assembling itself around a pinpoint of yellow light.

Most of the cars were full, it turned out. Macon gave up trying to find a completely empty seat and settled next to a plump young man with a briefcase. Just to be on the safe side, he unpacked *Miss MacIntosh*.

The train lurched forward and then changed its mind and

465

then lurched forward again and took off. Macon imagined he could feel little scabs of rust on the tracks; it wasn't a very smooth ride. He watched the sights of home rush toward him and disappear—a tumble of row houses, faded vacant lots, laundry hanging rigid in the cold.

"Gum?" his seatmate asked.

Macon said, "No, thanks," and quickly opened his book.

When they'd been traveling an hour or so, he felt his lids grow heavy. He let his head fall back. He thought he was only resting his eyes, but he must have gone to sleep. The next thing he knew, the conductor was announcing Philadelphia. Macon jerked and sat up straight and caught his book just before it slid off his lap.

His seatmate was doing some kind of paperwork, using his briefcase as a desk. A businessman, obviously—one of the people Macon wrote his guides for. Funny, Macon never pictured his readers. What did businessmen do, exactly? This one was jotting notes on index cards, referring now and then to a booklet full of graphs. One graph showed little black trucks marching across the page—four trucks, seven trucks, three and a half trucks. Macon thought the half-truck looked deformed and pitiable.

Just before they arrived, he used the restroom at the rear of the car—not ideal, but more homey than anything he'd find in New York. He went back to his seat and packed *Miss MacIntosh*. "Going to be cold there," his seatmate told him.

"I imagine so," Macon said.

"Weather report says cold and windy."

Macon didn't answer.

He believed in traveling without an overcoat—just one more thing to carry—but he wore a thermal undershirt and long johns. Cold was the least of his worries.

In New York the passengers scattered instantly. Macon thought of a seed pod bursting open. He refused to be rushed and made his way methodically through the crowd, up a set of clanking, dark stairs, and through another crowd that seemed more extreme than the one he had left down below. Goodness, where did these women get their clothes? One wore a bushy fur tepee and leopardskin boots. One wore an olive-drab coverall exactly like an auto mechanic's except that it was made of leather. Macon took a firmer grip on his bag and pushed through the door to the street, where car horns blasted insistently and the air smelled gray and sharp, like the interior of a dead chimney. In his opinion, New York was a foreign city. He was forever taken aback by its pervasive atmosphere of purposefulness—the tight focus of its drivers, the brisk intensity of its pedestrians drilling their way through all obstacles without a glance to either side.

He hailed a cab, slid across the worn, slippery seat, and gave the address of his hotel. The driver started talking at once about his daughter. "I mean she's thirteen years old," he said, nosing out into traffic, "and got three sets of holes in her ears and an earring in each hole, and now she wants to get another set punched up toward the top. Thirteen years old!" He either had or had not heard the address. At any rate, he was driving along. "I wasn't even in favor of the first set of holes," he said. "I told her, 'What; you don't read Ann Landers?' Ann Landers says piercing your ears is mutilating your body. Was it Ann Landers? I think it was Ann Landers. You might as well wear a ring through your nose like the Africans, right? I told my daughter that. She says, 'So? What's wrong with a ring through my nose? Maybe that's what I'll get next.' I wouldn't put it past her, either. I would not put it past her. Now this fourth set goes through cartilage and most of these ear-piercing places won't do that; so you see how crazy it is. Cartilage is a whole different ball game. It's not like your earlobe, all spongy."

Macon had the feeling he wasn't fully visible. He was listening to a man who was talking to himself, who may have been talking before he got in and might possibly go on talking after he got out. Or was he present in this cab at all? Such thoughts often attacked while he was traveling. In desperation, he said, "Um—"

The driver stopped speaking, surprisingly enough. The back of his neck took on an alert look. Macon had to continue. He said, "Tell her something scary."

"Like what?"

"Like . . . tell her you know a girl whose ears dropped off."

"She'd never go for that."

"Make it scientific. Say if you puncture cartilage, it will wither right away."

"Hmm," the driver said. He honked his horn at a produce truck.

" 'Imagine how you'd feel,' tell her, 'having to wear the same hairstyle forever. Covering up your withered ears.' "

"Think she'd believe me?"

"Why not?" Macon asked. And then, after a pause, "In fact, it may be true. Do you suppose I could have read it someplace?"

"Well, now, maybe you did," the driver said. "There's this sort of familiar ring to it."

"I might even have seen a photograph," Macon said. "Somebody's ears, shriveled. All shrunken."

"Wrinkly, like," the driver agreed.

Macon said, "Like two dried apricots."

"Christ! I'll tell her."

The taxi stopped in front of Macon's hotel. Macon paid the fare and said, as he slid out, "I hope it works."

"Sure it will," the driver said, "till next time. Till she wants a nose ring or something."

"Noses are cartilage too, remember! Noses can wither too!"

The driver waved and pulled into traffic again.

After Macon had claimed his room, he took a subway to the Buford Hotel. An electronics salesman had written to

468

suggest it; the Buford rented small apartments, by the day or the week, to businessmen. The manager, a Mr. Aggers, turned out to be a short, round man who walked with a limp exactly like Macon's. Macon thought they must look very odd together, crossing the lobby to the elevators. "Most of our apartments are owned by corporations," Mr. Aggers said. He pressed the "Up" button. "Companies who send their men to the city regularly will often find it cheaper to buy their own places. Then those weeks the apartments are empty, they look to me to find other tenants, help defray the costs."

Macon made a note of this in the margin of his guidebook. Using an infinitesimal script, he also noted the decor of the lobby, which reminded him of some old-fashioned men's club. On the massive, claw-footed table between the two elevators stood a yard-high naked lady in brass, trailing brass draperies and standing on brass clouds, holding aloft a small, dusty light bulb with a frayed electric cord dangling from it. The elevator, when it arrived, had dim floral carpeting and paneled walls.

"May I ask," Mr. Aggers said, "whether you personally write the Accidental Tourist series?"

"Yes, I do," Macon told him.

"Well!" Mr. Aggers said. "This is a real honor, then. We keep your books in the lobby for our guests. But I don't know, I somehow pictured you looking a little different."

"How did you think I would look?" Macon asked.

"Well, maybe not quite so tall. Maybe a bit, well, heavier. More . . . upholstered."

"I see," Macon said.

The elevator had stopped by now but it took its time sliding open. Then Mr. Aggers led Macon down a hall. A woman with a laundry cart stood aside to let them pass. "Here we are," Mr. Aggers said. He unlocked a door and turned on a light.

Macon walked into an apartment that could have come straight from the 1950s. There was a square sofa with metallic

469

threads in its fabric, a chrome-trimmed dinette set, and in the bedroom a double bed whose headboard was quilted in cream-colored vinyl. He tested the mattress. He took off his shoes, lay down, and thought a while. Mr. Aggers stood above him with his fingers laced. "Hmm," Macon said. He sat up and put his shoes back on. Then he went into the bathroom, where the toilet bore a white strip reading SANITIZED. "I've never understood these things," he said. "Why should it reassure me to know they've glued a paper band across my toilet seat?" Mr. Aggers made a helpless gesture with both hands. Macon drew aside a shower curtain printed with pink and blue fish, and he inspected the tub. It looked clean enough, although there was a rust stain leading down from the faucet.

In the kitchenette he found a single saucepan, two faded plastic plates and mugs, and an entire shelf of highball glasses. "Usually our guests don't cook much," Mr. Aggers explained, "but they might have their associates in for drinks." Macon nodded. He was faced with a familiar problem, here: the narrow line between "comfortable" and "tacky." In fact, sometimes comfortable *was* tacky. He opened the refrigerator, a little undercounter affair. The ice trays in the freezing compartment were exactly the same kind of trays—scummy aqua plastic, heavily scratched—that Rose had back in Baltimore.

"You have to admit it's well stocked," Mr. Aggers said. "See? An apron in the kitchen drawer. My wife's idea. Protects their suits."

"Yes, very nice," Macon said.

"It's just like home away from home; that's how I like to think of it."

"Oh, well, home," Macon said. "Nothing's *home*, really."

"Why? What's missing?" Mr. Aggers asked. He had very pale, fine-grained skin that took on a shine when he was anxious. "What more would you like to see added?"

470

"To tell the truth," Macon said, "I've always thought a hotel ought to offer optional small animals."

"Animals?"

"I mean a cat to sleep on your bed at night, or a dog of some kind to act pleased when you come in. You ever notice how a hotel room feels so lifeless?"

"Yes, but—well, I don't see how I could—there are surely health regulations or something . . . complications, paperwork, feeding all those different . . . and allergies, of course, many guests have—"

"Oh, I understand, I understand," Macon said. In the margin of his guidebook he was noting the number of wastebaskets: four. Excellent. "No," he said, "it doesn't seem that people ever take me up on that."

"Will you recommend us anyway?"

"Certainly," Macon said, and he closed his guidebook and asked for a list of the rates.

The rest of the afternoon he spent in hotels that he'd covered before. He visited managers in their offices, took brief guided tours to see that nothing had slid into ruin, and listened to talk of rising costs and remodeling plans and new, improved conference settings. Then he returned to his room and switched on the evening news. The world was doing poorly; but watching this unfamiliar TV set, propping his aching leg and braced in this chair that seemed designed for someone else's body, Macon had the feeling that none of the wars and famines he saw were real. They were more like, oh, staged. He turned off the set and went downstairs to hail a cab.

At Julian's suggestion, he was dining on the very top of an impossibly tall building. (Julian had a fondness for restaurants with gimmicks, Macon had noticed. He wasn't happy unless a place revolved, or floated, or could be reached only by catwalk.) "Imagine," Julian had said, "the effect on your

471

out-of-town client. Yes, he'd have to be from out of town; I don't suppose a native New Yorker . . ." Macon had snorted. Now the cabdriver snorted, too. "Cup of coffee there will cost you five bucks," he told Macon.

"It figures."

"You're better off at one of those little Frenchy places."

"That's for tomorrow. *In*-town clients."

The taxi coasted down streets that grew darker and more silent, leading away from the crowds. Macon peered out of his window. He saw a lone man huddled in a doorway, wrapped in a long coat. Wisps of steam drifted up from manhole covers. All the shops were locked behind iron grilles.

At the end of the darkest street of all, the taxi stopped. The driver gave another snort, and Macon paid his fare and stepped out. He wasn't prepared for the wind, which rushed up against him like a great flat sheet of something. He hurried across the sidewalk, or was propelled, while his trousers twisted and flapped about his legs. Just before entering the building, he thought to look up. He looked up and up and up, and finally he saw a faint white pinnacle dwindling into a deep, black, starless sky eerily far away. He thought of once long ago when Ethan, visiting the zoo as a toddler, had paused in front of an elephant and raised his face in astonishment and fallen over backwards.

Inside, everything was streaky pink marble and acres of textureless carpeting. An elevator the size of a room stood open, half filled with people, and Macon stepped in and took his place between two women in silks and diamonds. Their perfume was almost visible. He imagined he could see it rippling the air.

Have chewing gum handy, he wrote in his guidebook as the elevator shot upward. His ears were popping. There was a dense, unresonant stillness that made the women's voices sound tinny. He tucked his guidebook in his pocket and glanced at the numbers flashing overhead. They progressed by tens: forty, fifty, sixty . . . One of the men said they'd have to bring Harold sometime—remember Harold when he got so scared on the ski lift?—and everyone laughed.

The elevator gave a sort of lilt and the door slid open without a sound. A girl in a white trouser suit directed them down a corridor, into a spacious darkness flickering with candles. Great black windows encircled the room from floor to ceiling, but Macon was taken to a table without a view. Lone diners, he supposed, were an embarrassment here. He might be the first they'd ever had. The array of silver at his single place could easily serve a family of four.

His waiter, far better dressed than Macon, handed him a menu and asked what he wanted to drink. "Dry sherry, please," Macon said. The minute the waiter left, Macon folded his menu in two and sat on it. Then he looked around at his neighbors. Everyone seemed to be celebrating something. A man and a pregnant woman held hands and smiled across the moony glow of their candle. A boisterous group to his left toasted the same man over and over.

The waiter returned, balancing a sherry neatly on a tray. "Very good," Macon said. "And now perhaps a menu."

"Menu? Didn't I give you one?"

"There could have been an oversight," he said, not exactly lying.

A second menu was brought and opened with a flourish before him. Macon sipped his sherry and considered the prices. Astronomical. He decided, as usual, to eat what he thought his readers might eat—not the quenelles or the sweetbreads but the steak, medium rare. After he'd given his order, he rose and slid his chair in and took his sherry over to a window.

All of a sudden, he thought he had died.

He saw the city spread far below like a glittering golden ocean, the streets tiny ribbons of light, the planet curving away at the edges, the sky a purple hollow extending to infinity. It wasn't the height; it was the distance. It was his vast, lonely distance from everyone who mattered. Ethan, with his bouncy walk—how would he ever know that his father had come to be trapped in this spire in the heavens? How would Sarah know, lazily tanning herself in the sunshine? For he did believe the sun could be shining wherever she was at this moment; she was so removed from him. He thought of his sister and brothers going about their business, playing their evening card game, unaware of how far behind he'd left them. He was too far gone to return. He would never, ever get back. He had somehow traveled to a point completely isolated from everyone else in the universe, and nothing was real but his own angular hand clenched around the sherry glass.

He dropped the glass, causing a meaningless little flurry of voices, and he spun around and ran lopsidedly across the room and out the door. But there was that endless corridor, and he couldn't manage the trip. He took a right turn instead. He passed a telephone alcove and stumbled into a restroom—yes, a men's room, luckily. More marble, mirrors, white enamel. He thought he was going to throw up, but when he entered one of the cubicles the sick feeling left his stomach and floated to his head. He noticed how light his brain felt. He stood above the toilet pressing his temples. It occurred to him to wonder how many feet of pipe a toilet at this altitude required.

He heard someone else come in, coughing. A cubicle door slammed shut. He opened his own door a crack and looked out. The impersonal lushness of the room made him think of science-fiction movies.

Well, this difficulty probably happened here often, didn't it? Or maybe not this difficulty exactly but others like it—people with a fear of heights, say, going into a panic, having to call upon . . . whom? The waiter? The girl who met the elevator?

He ventured cautiously out of the cubicle, then out of the restroom altogether, and he nearly bumped into a woman in

474

the telephone alcove. She wore yards and yards of pale chiffon. She was just hanging up the phone, and she gathered her skirts around her and moved languidly, gracefully toward the dining room. *Excuse me, ma'am, I wonder if you would be so kind as to, um . . .* But the only request that came to mind rose up from his earliest childhood: *Carry me!*

The woman's little sequined evening purse was the last of her to go, trailed behind her in one white hand as she disappeared into the darkness of the restaurant.

He stepped over to the telephone and lifted the receiver. It was cool to the touch; she hadn't talked long. He fumbled through his pockets, found coins and dropped them in. But there was no one he could contact. He didn't know a soul in all New York. Instead he called home, miraculously summoning up his credit card number. He worried his family would let the phone ring—it was a habit, by now—but Charles answered. "Leary."

"Charles?"

"Macon!" Charles said, unusually animated.

"Charles, I'm up on top of this building and a sort of . . . silly thing has happened. Listen: You've got to get me out of here."

"*You* out! What are you talking about? You've got to get *me* out!"

"Pardon?"

"I'm shut in the pantry; your dog has me cornered."

"Oh. Well, I'm sorry, but . . . Charles, it's like some kind of illness. I don't think I can manage the elevator and I doubt I could manage a stairway either and—"

"Macon, do you hear that barking? That's Edward. Edward has me treed, I tell you, and you have to come home this instant."

"But I'm in New York! I'm up on top of this building and I can't get down!"

"Every time I open the door he comes roaring over and I

475

slam the door and he attacks it, he must have clawed halfway through it by now."

Macon made himself take a deep breath. He said, "Charles, could I speak to Rose?"

"She's out."

"Oh."

"How do you think I got into this?" Charles asked. "Julian came to take her to dinner and—"

"Julian?"

"Isn't that his name?"

"Julian my *boss*?"

"Yes, and Edward went into one of his fits; so Rose said, 'Quick, shut him in the pantry.' So I grabbed his leash and he turned on me and nearly took my hand off. So I shut myself in the pantry instead and Rose must have left by then so—"

"Isn't Porter there?"

"It's his visitation night."

Macon imagined how safe the pantry must feel, with Rose's jams lined up in alphabetical order and the black dial telephone so ancient that the number on its face was still the old Tuxedo exchange. What he wouldn't give to be there!

Now he had a new symptom. His chest had developed a flutter that bore no resemblance to a normal heartbeat.

"If you don't get me out of this I'm going to call for the police to come shoot him," Charles said.

"No! Don't do that!"

"I can't just sit here waiting for him to break through."

"He won't break through. You could open the door and walk right past him. Believe me, Charles. Please: I'm up on top of this building and—"

"Maybe you don't know that I'm prone to claustrophobia," Charles said.

One possibility, Macon decided, was to tell the restaurant people he was having a coronary. A coronary was so respectable. They would send for an ambulance and he would be, yes, carried—just what he needed. Or he wouldn't have to be carried but only touched, a mere human touch upon his arm, a hand on his shoulder, something to put him back in connection with the rest of the world. He hadn't felt another person's touch in so long.

"I'll tell them about the key in the mailbox so they won't have to break down the door," Charles said.

"What? Who?"

"The police, and I'll tell them to—Macon, I'm sorry but you knew that dog would have to be done away with sooner or later."

"Don't do it!" Macon shouted.

A man emerging from the restroom glanced in his direction.

Macon lowered his voice and said, "He was Ethan's."

"Does that mean he's allowed to tear my throat out?"

"Listen. Let's not be hasty. Let's think this through. Now, I'm going to . . . I'm going to telephone Sarah. I'm going to ask her to come over and take charge of Edward. Are you listening, Charles?"

"But what if he attacks her too?" Charles asked.

"He won't, believe me. Now, don't do anything till she comes, you understand? Don't do anything hasty."

"Well . . ." Charles said doubtfully.

Macon hung up and took his wallet from his pocket. He rummaged through the business cards and torn-off snippets of paper, some of them yellow with age, that he kept in the secret compartment. When he found Sarah's number he punched it in with a trembling finger and held his breath. *Sarah*, he would say, *I'm up on top of this building and—*

She didn't answer.

That possibility hadn't occurred to him. He listened to her phone ring. What now? What on earth now?

Finally he hung up. He sifted despairingly through the

477

other numbers in his wallet—dentist, pharmacist, animal trainer . . .

Animal trainer?

He thought at first of someone from a circus—a brawny man in satin tights. Then he saw the name: Muriel Pritchett. The card was handwritten, even hand-cut, crookedly snipped from a larger piece of paper.

He called her. She answered at once. "*Hel*-lo," roughly, like a weary barmaid.

"Muriel? It's Macon Leary," he told her.

"Oh! How you doing?"

"I'm fine. Or, rather . . . See, the trouble is, Edward's got my brother cornered in the pantry, overreacting, Charles I mean, he always overreacts, and here I am on top of this building in New York and I'm having this kind of, um, disturbance, you know? I was looking down at the city and it was miles away, miles, I can't describe to you how—"

"Let's make sure I've got this right," Muriel said. "Edward's in your pantry—"

Macon collected himself. He said, "Edward's *outside* the pantry, barking. My brother's inside. He says he's going to call the police and tell them to come shoot Edward."

"Well, what a dumb fool idea."

"Yes!" Macon said. "So I thought if you could go over and get the key from the mailbox, it's lying on the bottom of the mailbox—"

"I'll go right away."

"Oh, wonderful."

"So good-bye for now, Macon."

"Well, but also—" he said.

She waited.

"See, I'm up on top of this building," he said, "and I don't know what it is but something has scared the hell out of me."

478

"Oh, Lord, I'd be scared too after I went and saw *Towering Inferno*."

"No, no, it's nothing like that, fire or heights—"

"Did you see *Towering Inferno*? Boy, after that you couldn't get me past jumping level in any building. I think people who go up in skyscrapers are just plain brave. I mean if you think about it, Macon, you *have* to be brave to be standing where you are right now."

"Oh, well, not so brave as all that," Macon said.

"No, I'm serious."

"You're making too much out of it. It's nothing, really."

"You just say that because you don't realize what you went through before you stepped into the elevator. See, underneath you said, 'Okay. I'll trust it.' That's what everyone does; I bet it's what they do on airplanes, too. 'This is dangerous as all get-out but what the hay,' they say, 'let's fling ourselves out on thin air and trust it.' Why, you ought to be walking around that building so amazed and proud of yourself!"

Macon gave a small, dry laugh and gripped the receiver more tightly.

"Now, here's what I'm going to do," she said. "I'm going to go get Edward and take him to the Meow-Bow. It doesn't sound to me like your brother is much use with him. Then when you get back from your trip, we need to talk about his training. I mean, things just can't go on this way, Macon."

"No, they can't. You're right. They can't," Macon said.

"I mean this is ridiculous."

"You're absolutely right."

"See you, then. Bye."

"Well, wait!" he said.

But she was gone.

After he hung up, he turned and saw the latest arrivals just heading toward him from the elevator. First came three men, and then three women in long gowns. Behind them was a

479

couple who couldn't be past their teens. The boy's wrist bones stuck out of the sleeves of his suit. The girl's dress was clumsy and touching, her small chin obscured by a monstrous orchid.

Halfway down the corridor, the boy and girl stopped to gaze around them. They looked at the ceiling, and then at the floor. Then they looked at each other. The boy said, "Hoo!" and grabbed both the girl's hands, and they stood there a moment, laughing, before they went into the restaurant.

Macon followed them. He felt soothed and tired and terribly hungry. It was good to find the waiter just setting his food in place when he sank back into his seat.

10

I 'll be honest," Muriel said, "my baby was not exactly planned for. I mean we weren't exactly even married yet, if you want to know the truth. If you want to know the truth the baby was the reason we got married in the first place, but I did tell Norman he didn't have to go through with it if he didn't want to. It's not like I pushed him into it or anything."

She looked past Macon at Edward, who lay prone on the front hall rug. He'd had to be forced into position, but at least he was staying put.

"Notice I let him move around some, as long as he stays down," she said. "Now I'm going to turn my back, and you watch how he does."

She wandered into the living room. She lifted a vase from a table and examined its underside. "So anyhow," she said, "we went ahead and got married, with everybody acting like it was the world's biggest tragedy. My folks really never got over it. My mom said, 'Well, I always knew this was going to happen. Back when you were hanging out with Dana Scully and them, one or another of them no-count boys always honking out front for you, didn't I tell you this was going to happen?' We had a little bitty wedding at my folks' church, and we didn't take a honeymoon trip but went straight to our apartment and next day Norman started work at his uncle's. He just settled right into being married—shopping with me for groceries and picking out curtains and such. Oh, you know, sometimes I get to thinking what kids we were. It was almost like playing house! It was pretend! The candles I lit at suppertime, flowers on the table, Norman calling me 'hon' and bringing his plate to the sink for me to wash. And then all at once it turned serious. Here I've got this little boy now, this great big seven-year-old boy with his clompy leather shoes, and it wasn't playing house after all. It was for real, all along, and we just didn't know it."

She sat on the couch and raised one foot in front of her. She turned it admiringly this way and that. Her stocking bagged at the ankle.

"What is Edward up to?" she asked.

Macon said, "He's still lying down."

"Pretty soon he'll do that for three hours straight."

"Three *hours*?"

"Easy."

"Isn't that sort of cruel?"

"I thought you promised not to talk like that," she told him.

"Right. Sorry," Macon said.

"Maybe tomorrow he'll lie down on his own."

"You think so?"

"If you practice. If you don't give in. If you don't go all softhearted."

Then she stood up and came over to Macon. She patted his arm. "But never mind," she told him. "*I* think softhearted men are sweet."

Macon backed away. He just missed stepping on Edward.

It was getting close to Thanksgiving, and the Learys were debating as usual about Thanksgiving dinner. The fact was, none of them cared for turkey. Still, Rose said, it didn't seem right to serve anything else. It would just feel wrong. Her brothers pointed out that she'd have to wake up at five a.m. to put a turkey in the oven. But it was she who'd be doing it, Rose said. It wouldn't be troubling *them* any.

Then it began to seem she had had an ulterior motive, for as soon as they settled on turkey she announced that she might just invite Julian Edge. Poor Julian, she said, had no close family living nearby, and he and his neighbors gathered forlornly at holidays, each bringing his or her specialty. Thanksgiving dinner last year had been a vegetarian pasta casserole and goat cheese on grape leaves and kiwi tarts. The least she could do was offer him a normal family dinner.

"What!" Macon said, acting surprised and disapproving, but unfortunately, it wasn't that much of a surprise. Oh, Julian was up to something, all right. But what could it be? Whenever Rose came down the stairs in her best dress and two spots of rouge, whenever she asked Macon to shut Edward in the pantry because Julian would be stopping by to take her this place or that—well, Macon had a very strong urge to let Edward accidentally break loose. He made a point of meeting Julian at the door, eyeing him for a long, silent moment before calling Rose. But Julian behaved; no glint of irony betrayed him. He was respectful with Rose, almost shy, and hovered clumsily when he ushered her out the door. Or was that the irony? His Rose Leary act. Macon didn't like the looks of this.

Then it turned out that Porter's children would be coming for Thanksgiving too. They usually came at Christmas instead, but wanted to trade off this year due to some complication with their grandparents on their stepfather's side. So really, Rose said, wasn't it good they were having turkey? Children were such traditionalists. She set to work baking pumpkin pies. "We gather together," she sang, "to ask the Lord's blessing . . ." Macon looked up from the sheaf of stolen menus he was spreading across the kitchen table. There was a note of gaiety in her voice that made him uneasy. He wondered if she had any mistaken ideas about Julian—if, for instance, she hoped for some kind of romance. But Rose was so plain and sensible in her long white apron. She reminded him of Emily Dickinson; hadn't Emily Dickinson also baked for her nieces and nephews? Surely there was no need for concern.

"My son's name is Alexander," Muriel said. "Did I tell you that? I named him Alexander because I thought it sounded high-class. He was never an easy baby. For starters something went wrong while I was carrying him and they had to do a Caesarean and take him out early and I got all these complications and can't ever have any more children. And then Alexander was so teeny he didn't even look like a human, more like a big-headed newborn kitten, and he had to stay in an incubator forever, just about, and nearly died. Norman said, 'When's it going to look like other babies?' He always called Alexander 'it.' I adjusted better; I mean pretty soon it seemed to me that that was what a baby *ought* to look like, and I hung around the hospital nursery but Norman wouldn't go near him, he said it made him too nervous."

Edward whimpered. He was just barely lying down—his haunches braced, his claws digging into the carpet. But Muriel gave no sign she had noticed.

"Maybe you and Alexander should get together some time," she told Macon.

"Oh, I, ah . . ." Macon said.

"He doesn't have enough men in his life."

"Well, but—"

"He's supposed to see men a lot; it's supposed to show him how to act. Maybe the three of us could go to a movie. Don't you ever go to movies?"

"No, I don't," Macon said truthfully. "I haven't been to a movie in months. I really don't care for movies. They make everything seem so close up."

484

"Or just out to a McDonald's, maybe."

"I don't think so," Macon said.

Porter's children arrived the evening before Thanksgiving, traveling by car because Danny, the oldest, had just got his driver's license. That worried Porter considerably. He paced the floor from the first moment they could be expected. "I don't know where June's brain is," he said. "Letting a sixteen-year-old boy drive all the way from Washington the first week he has his license! With his two little sisters in the car! I don't know how her mind works."

To make it worse, the children were almost an hour late. When Porter finally saw their headlights, he rushed out the door and down the steps well ahead of the others. "What kept you?" he cried.

Danny unfurled himself from the car with exaggerated nonchalance, yawning and stretching, and shook Porter's hand as a kind of afterthought while turning to study his tires. He was as tall as Porter now but very thin, with his mother's dark coloring. Behind him came Susan, fourteen—just a few months older than Ethan would have been. It was lucky she was so different from Ethan, with her cap of black curls and her rosy cheeks. This evening she wore jeans and hiking boots and one of those thick down jackets that made young people look so bulky and graceless. Then last came Liberty. What a name, Macon always thought. It was an invention of her mother's— a flighty woman who had run away from Porter with a hippie stereo salesman eight and a half years ago and discovered immediately afterward that she was two months pregnant. Ironically, Liberty was the one who looked most like Porter. She had fair, straight hair and a chiseled face and she was dressed in a little tailored coat. "Danny got lost," she said severely. "What a dummy." She kissed Porter and her aunt and uncles, but Susan wandered past them in a way that let everyone know she had outgrown all that.

"Oh, isn't this nice?" Rose said. "Aren't we going to have a wonderful Thanksgiving?" She stood on the sidewalk wrapping her hands in her apron, perhaps to stop herself from reaching out to Danny as he slouched toward the house. It was dusk, and Macon, happening to glance around, saw the grown-ups as pale gray wraiths—four middle-aged unmarried relatives yearning after the young folks.

For supper they had carry-out pizza, intended to please the children, but Macon kept smelling turkey. He thought at first it was his imagination. Then he noticed Danny sniffing the air. "Turkey? Already?" Danny asked his aunt.

"I'm trying this new method," she said. "It's supposed to save energy. You set your oven extremely low and cook your meat all night."

"Weird."

After supper they watched TV—the children had never seemed to warm to cards—and then they went to bed. But in the middle of the night, Macon woke with a start and gave serious thought to that turkey. She was cooking it till tomorrow? At an extremely low temperature? What temperature was that, exactly?

He was sleeping in his old room, now that his leg had mended. Eventually he nudged the cat off his chest and got up. He made his way downstairs in the dark, and he crossed the icy kitchen linoleum and turned on the little light above the stove. One hundred and forty degrees, the oven dial read. "Certain death," he told Edward, who had tagged along behind him. Then Charles walked in, wearing large, floppy pajamas. He peered at the dial and sighed. "Not only that," he said, "but this is a *stuffed* turkey."

"Wonderful."

"Two quarts of stuffing. I heard her say so."

"Two quarts of teeming, swarming bacteria."

"Unless there's something more to this method we don't understand."

486

"We'll ask her in the morning," Macon said, and they went back to bed.

In the morning, Macon came down to find Rose serving pancakes to the children. He said, "Rose, what exactly is it you're doing to this turkey?"

"I told you: slow heat. Jam, Danny, or syrup?"

"Is that *it*?" Macon asked.

"You're dripping," Rose said to Liberty. "What, Macon? See, I read an article about slow-cooked beef and I thought, well, if it works with beef it must work with turkey too so I—"

"It might work with beef but it will murder us with turkey," Macon told her.

"But at the end I'm going to raise the temperature!"

"You'd have to raise it mighty high. You'd have to autoclave the thing."

"You'd have to expose it to a nuclear flash," Danny said cheerfully.

Rose said, "Well, you're both just plain wrong. Who's the cook here, anyhow? I say it's going to be delicious."

Maybe it was, but it certainly didn't look it. By dinnertime the breast had caved in and the skin was all dry and dull. Rose entered the dining room holding the turkey high as if in triumph, but the only people who looked impressed were those who didn't know its history—Julian and Mrs. Barrett, one of Rose's old people. Julian said, "Ah!" and Mrs. Barrett beamed. "I just wish my neighbors could see this," Julian said. He wore a brass-buttoned navy blazer, and he seemed to have polished his face.

"Well, there may be a little problem here," Macon said.

Rose set the turkey down and glared at him.

"Of course, the rest of the meal is excellent," he said. "Why, we could fill up on the vegetables alone! In fact I think I'll do that. But the turkey . . ."

"It's pure poison," Danny finished for him.

Julian said, "Come again?" but Mrs. Barrett just smiled harder.

"We think it may have been cooked at a slightly inadequate temperature," Macon explained.

"It was not!" Rose said. "It's perfectly good."

"Maybe you'd rather just stick to the side dishes," Macon told Mrs. Barrett. He was worried she might be deaf.

But she must have heard, for she said, "Why, perhaps I will," never losing her smile. "I don't have much of an appetite anyhow," she said.

"And I'm a vegetarian," Susan said.

"So am I," Danny said suddenly.

"Oh, Macon, how could you do this?" Rose asked. "My lovely turkey! All that work!"

"I think it looks delicious," Julian said.

"Yes," Porter told him, "but you don't know about the other times."

"Other times?"

"Those were just bad luck," Rose said.

"Why, of course!" Porter said. "Or economy. You don't like to throw things away; I can understand that! Pork that's been sitting too long, or chicken salad left out all night . . ."

Rose sat down. Tears were glazing her eyes. "Oh," she said, "you're all so mean! You don't fool me for an instant; I know why you're doing this. You want to make me look bad in front of Julian."

"Julian?"

Julian seemed distressed. He took a handkerchief from his breast pocket but then went on holding it.

"You want to drive him off! You three wasted your chances and now you want me to waste mine, but I won't do it. I can see what's what! Just listen to any song on the radio; look at any soap opera. *Love* is what it's all about. On soap operas everything revolves around love. A new person comes to town

488

and right away the question is, who's he going to love? Who's going to love him back? Who'll lose her mind with jealousy? Who's going to ruin her life? And you want to make me miss it!"

"Well, goodness," Macon said, trying to sort this out.

"You know perfectly well there's nothing wrong with that turkey. You just don't want me to stop cooking for you and taking care of this house, you don't want Julian to fall in love with me."

"Do what?"

But she scraped her chair back and ran from the room. Julian sat there with his mouth open.

"Don't you dare laugh," Macon told him.

Julian just went on gaping.

"Don't even consider it."

Julian swallowed. He said, "Do you think I ought to go after her?"

"No," Macon said.

"But she seems so—"

"She's fine! She's perfectly fine."

"Oh."

"Now, who wants a baked potato?"

There was a kind of murmur around the table; everyone looked unhappy. "That poor, dear girl," Mrs. Barrett said. "I feel just awful."

"Me too," Susan said.

"Julian?" Macon asked, clanging a spoon. "Potato?"

"I'll take the turkey," Julian said firmly.

At that moment, Macon almost liked the man.

"It was having the baby that broke our marriage up," Muriel said. "When you think about it, that's funny. First we got married on account of the baby and then we got divorced on account of the baby, and in between, the baby was what we

489

argued about. Norman couldn't understand why I was all the time at the hospital visiting Alexander. 'It doesn't know you're there, so why go?' he said. I'd go early in the morning and just hang around, the nurses were as nice as could be about it, and I'd stay till night. Norman said, 'Muriel, won't we ever get our ordinary life back?' Well, you can see his point, I guess. It's like I only had room in my mind for Alexander. And he was in the hospital for months, for really months; there was everything in this world wrong with him. You should have seen our medical bills. We only had partial insurance and there were these bills running up, thousands and thousands of dollars. Finally I took a job at the hospital. I asked if I could work in the nursery but they said no, so I got a kind of, more like a maid's job, cleaning patients' rooms and so forth. Emptying trash cans, wet-mopping floors . . ."

She and Macon were walking along Dempsey Road with Edward, hoping to run into a biker. Muriel held the leash. If a biker came, she said, and Edward lunged or gave so much as the smallest yip, she was going to yank him so hard he wouldn't know what hit him. She warned Macon of that before they started out. She said he'd better not object because this was for Edward's own good. Macon hoped he'd be able to remember that when the time came.

It was the Friday after Thanksgiving and there'd been a light snow earlier, but the air didn't have a real bite to it yet and the sidewalks were merely damp. The sky seemed to begin about two feet above their heads.

"This one patient, Mrs. Brimm, she took a liking to me," Muriel said. "She said I was the only person who ever bothered talking to her. I'd come in and tell her about Alexander. I'd tell her what the doctors said, how they didn't give him much of a chance and some had even wondered if we *wanted* a chance, what with all that might be wrong with him. I'd tell her about me and Norman and the way he was acting, and she said it sounded exactly like a story in a magazine. When they let her go home she wanted me to come with her, take a job looking out for her, but I couldn't on account of Alexander."

A biker appeared at the end of the street, a girl with a Baskin-Robbins uniform bunching below her jacket. Edward perked his ears up. "Now, act like we expect no trouble," Muriel told Macon. "Just go along, go along, don't even look in Edward's direction."

The girl skimmed toward them—a little slip of a person with a tiny, serious face. When she passed, she gave off a definite smell of chocolate ice cream. Edward sniffed the breeze but marched on.

"Oh, Edward, that was wonderful!" Macon told him.

Muriel just clucked. She seemed to take his good behavior for granted.

"So anyhow," she said. "They finally did let Alexander come home. But he was still no bigger than a minute. All wrinkles like a little old man. Cried like a kitten would cry. Struggled for every breath. And *Norman* was no help. I think he was jealous. He got this kind of stubborn look whenever I had to do something, go warm a bottle or something. He'd say, 'Where you off to? Don't you want to watch the end of this program?' I'd be hanging over the crib watching Alexander fight for air, and Norman would call, 'Muriel? Commercial's just about over!' Then next thing I knew, there was his mother standing on my doorstep saying it wasn't his baby anyhow."

"What? Well, of all things!" Macon said.

"Can you believe it? Standing on my doorstep looking so pleased with herself. 'Not his baby!' I said. 'Whose, then?' 'Well, that I couldn't say,' she said, 'and I doubt if you could either. But I can tell you this much: If you don't give my son a divorce and release all financial claims on him, I will personally produce Dana Scully and his friends in a court of law and they will swear you're a known tramp and that baby could be

491

any one of theirs. Clearly it's not Norman's; Norman was a *darling* baby.' Well. I waited till Norman got home from work and I said, 'Do you know what your mother told me?' Then I saw by his face that he did. I saw she must have been talking behind my back for who knows how long, putting these suspicions in his head. I said, 'Norman?' He just stuttered around. I said, 'Norman, she's lying, it's not true, I wasn't going with those boys when I met you! That's all in the past!' He said, 'I don't know what to think.' I said, 'Please!' He said, 'I don't know.' He went out to the kitchen and started fixing this screen I'd been nagging him about, window screen halfway out of its frame, even though supper was already on the table. I'd made him this special supper. I followed after him. I said, 'Norman. Dana and them are from way, way back. That baby couldn't be theirs.' He pushed up on one side of the screen and it wouldn't go, and he pushed up on the other side and it cut his hand, and all at once he started crying and wrenched the whole thing out of the window and threw it as far as he could. And next day his mother came to help him pack his clothes and he left me."

"Good Lord," Macon said. He felt shocked, as if he'd known Norman personally.

"So I thought about what to do. I knew I couldn't go back to my folks. Finally I phoned Mrs. Brimm and asked if she still wanted me to come take care of her, and she said yes, she did; the woman she had wasn't any use at all. So I said I would do it for room and board if I could bring the baby and she said yes, that would be fine. She had this little row house downtown and there was an extra bedroom where me and Alexander could sleep. And that's how I managed to keep us going."

They were several blocks from home now, but she didn't suggest turning back. She held the leash loosely and Edward strutted next to her, matching her pace. "I was lucky, wasn't I," she said. "If it wasn't for Mrs. Brimm I don't know what

492

I'd have done. And it's not like it was all that much work. Just keeping the house straight, fixing her a bite to eat, helping her get around. She was crippled up with arthritis but just as spunky! It's not like I really had to nurse her."

She slowed and then came to a stop. Edward, with a martyred sigh, sat down at her left heel. "When you think about it, it's funny," she said. "All that time Alexander was in the hospital seemed so awful, seemed it would go on forever, but now when I look back, I almost miss it. I mean there was something cozy about it, now that I recall. I think about those nurses gossiping at the nurses' station and those rows of little babies sleeping. It was winter and sometimes I'd stand at a window and look out and I'd feel happy to be warm and safe. I'd look down at the emergency room entrance and watch the ambulances coming in. You ever wonder what a Martian might think if he happened to land near an emergency room? He'd see an ambulance whizzing in and everybody running out to meet it, tearing the doors open, grabbing up the stretcher, scurrying along with it. 'Why,' he'd say, 'what a helpful planet, what kind and helpful creatures.' He'd never guess we're not always that way; that we had to, oh, put aside our natural selves to do it. 'What a helpful race of beings,' a Martian would say. Don't you think so?"

She looked up at Macon then. Macon experienced a sudden twist in his chest. He felt there was something he needed to do, some kind of connection he wanted to make, and when she raised her face he bent and kissed her chapped, harsh lips even though that wasn't the connection he'd intended. Her fist with the leash in it was caught between them like a stone. There was something insistent about her—pressing. Macon drew back. "Well . . ." he said.

She went on looking up at him.

"Sorry," he said.

Then they turned around and walked Edward home.

Danny spent the holiday practicing his parallel parking, tirelessly wheeling his mother's car back and forth in front of the house. And Liberty baked cookies with Rose. But Susan had nothing to do, Rose said, and since Macon was planning a trip to Philadelphia, wouldn't he consider taking her along? "It's only hotels and restaurants," Macon said. "And I'm cramming it into one day, leaving at crack of dawn and coming back late at night—"

"She'll be company for you," Rose told him.

However, Susan went to sleep when the train was hardly out of Baltimore, and she stayed asleep for the entire ride, sunk into her jacket like a little puffed-up bird roosting on a branch. Macon sat next to her with a rock magazine he'd found rolled up in one of her pockets. He saw that the Police were experiencing personality conflicts, that David Bowie worried about mental illness, that Billy Idol's black shirt appeared to have been ripped halfway off his body. Evidently these people led very difficult lives; he had no idea who they were. He rolled the magazine up again and replaced it in Susan's pocket.

If Ethan were alive, would he be sitting where Susan was? He hadn't traveled with Macon as a rule. The overseas trips were too expensive, the domestic trips too dull. Once he'd gone with Macon to New York, and he'd developed stomach pains that resembled appendicitis. Macon could still recall his frantic search for a doctor, his own stomach clenching in sympathy, and his relief when they were told it was nothing but too many breakfasts. He hadn't taken Ethan anywhere else after that. Only to Bethany Beach every summer, and that was not so much a trip as a kind of relocation of home base, with Sarah sunbathing and Ethan joining other Baltimore boys, also relocated, and Macon happily tightening all the doorknobs in their rented cottage or unsticking the windows or—one blissful year—solving a knotty problem he'd discovered in the plumbing.

494

In Philadelphia, Susan came grumpily awake and staggered off the train ahead of him. She complained about the railroad station. "It's way too big," she said. "The loudspeakers echo so you can't hear what they're saying. Baltimore's station is better."

"Yes, you're absolutely right," Macon said.

They went for breakfast to a café he knew well, which unfortunately seemed to have fallen upon hard times. Little chips of ceiling plaster kept dropping into his coffee. He crossed the name out of his guidebook. Next they went to a place that a reader had suggested, and Susan had walnut waffles. She said they were excellent. "Are you going to quote me on this?" she asked. "Will you put my name in your book and say I recommended the waffles?"

"It's not that kind of a book," he told her.

"Call me your companion. That's what restaurant critics do. 'My companion, Susan Leary, pronounced the waffles remarkable.'"

Macon laughed and signaled for their bill.

After their fourth breakfast, they started on hotels. Susan found these less enjoyable, though Macon kept trying to involve her. He told a manager, "My companion here is the expert on bathrooms." But Susan just opened a medicine cabinet, yawned, and said, "All they have is Camay."

"What's wrong with that?"

"When Mama came back from her honeymoon she brought us perfumed designer soap from her hotel. One bar for me and one for Danny, in little plastic boxes with drainage racks."

"I think Camay is fine," Macon told the manager, who was looking worried.

Late in the afternoon Susan started feeling peckish again; so they had two more breakfasts. Then they went to Independence Hall. (Macon felt they should do something educational.) "You can tell your civics teacher," he said. She rolled her eyes and said, "Social studies."

495

"Whatever."

The weather was cold, and the interior of the hall was chilly and bleak. Macon noticed Susan gaping vacantly at the guide, who wasn't making his spiel very exciting; so he leaned over and whispered, "Imagine. George Washington sat in that very chair."

"I'm not really into George Washington, Uncle Macon."

"Human beings can only go 'into' houses, cars, and coffins, Susan."

"Huh?"

"Never mind."

They followed the crowd upstairs, through other rooms, but Susan had plainly exhausted her supply of good humor. "If it weren't for what was decided in this building," Macon told her, "you and I might very well be living under a dictatorship."

"We are anyhow," she said.

"Pardon?"

"You really think that you and me have any power?"

"You and I, honey."

"It's just free speech, that's all we've got. We can say whatever we like, then the government goes on and does exactly what it pleases. You call that democracy? It's like we're on a ship, headed someplace terrible, and somebody else is steering and the passengers can't jump off."

"Why don't we go get some supper," Macon said. He was feeling a little depressed.

He took her to an old-fashioned inn a few streets over. It wasn't even dark yet, and they were the first customers. A woman in a Colonial gown told them they'd have to wait a few minutes. She led them into a small, snug room with a fireplace, and a waitress offered them their choice of buttered rum or hot spiked cider. "I'll have buttered rum," Susan said, shucking off her jacket.

Macon said, "Uh, Susan."

She glared at him.

496

"Oh, well, make that two," he told the waitress. He supposed a little toddy couldn't do much harm.

But it must have been an exceptionally strong toddy—either that, or Susan had an exceptionally weak head for alcohol. At any rate, after two small sips she leaned toward him in an unbalanced way. "This is sort of fun!" she said. "You know, Uncle Macon, I like you much better than I thought I did."

"Why, thank you."

"I used to think you were kind of finicky. Ethan used to make us laugh, pointing to your artichoke plate."

"My artichoke plate."

She pressed her fingertips to her mouth. "I'm sorry," she said.

"For what?"

"I didn't mean to talk about him."

"You can talk about him."

"I don't want to," she said.

She gazed off across the room. Macon, following her eyes, found only a harpsichord. He looked back at her and saw her chin trembling.

It had never occurred to him that Ethan's cousins missed him too.

After a minute, Susan picked her mug up and took several large swallows. She wiped her nose with the back of her hand. "Hot," she explained. It was true she seemed to have recovered herself.

Macon said, "What was funny about my artichoke plate?"

"Oh, nothing."

"I won't be hurt. What was funny?"

"Well, it looked like geometry class. Every leaf laid out in such a perfect circle when you'd finished."

"I see."

"He was laughing *with* you, not at you," Susan said, peering anxiously into his face.

"Well, since I wasn't laughing myself, that statement seems

inaccurate. But if you mean he wasn't laughing unkindly, I believe you."

She sighed and drank some more of her rum.

"Nobody talks about him," Macon said. "None of you mentions his name."

"We do when you're not around," Susan said.

"You do?"

"We talk about what he'd think, you know. Like when Danny got his license, or when I had a date for the Halloween Ball. I mean we used to make so much fun of the grown-ups. And Ethan was the funniest one; he could always get us to laugh. Then here we are, growing up ourselves. We wonder what Ethan would think of us, if he could come back and see us. We wonder if he'd laugh at *us*. Or if he'd feel . . . left out. Like we had moved on and left him behind."

The woman in the Colonial gown came to show them to their table. Macon brought his drink; Susan had already finished hers. She was a bit unsteady on her feet. When their waitress asked them if they'd like a wine list, Susan gave Macon a bright-eyed look but Macon said, "No," very firmly. "I think we ought to start with soup," he said. He had some idea soup was sobering.

But Susan talked in a reckless, headlong way all through the soup course, and the main course, and the two desserts she hadn't been able to decide between, and the strong black coffee that he pressed upon her afterward. She talked about a boy she liked who either liked her back or else preferred someone named Sissy Pace. She talked about the Halloween Ball where this really juvenile eighth-grader had thrown up all over the stereo. She said that when Danny was eighteen, the three of them were moving to their own apartment because now that their mother was expecting (which Macon hadn't known), she wouldn't even realize they were gone. "That's not true," Macon told her. "Your mother would feel terrible if you left." Susan propped her cheek on her fist in a sort of slipshod man-

498

ner and said that she wasn't born yesterday. Her hair had grown wilder through the evening, giving her an electrified appearance. Macon found it difficult to stuff her into her jacket, and he had to hold her up more or less by the back of her collar while they were waiting for a taxi.

In the railroad station she got a confused, squinty look, and once they were on the train she fell asleep with her head against the window. In Baltimore, when he woke her, she said, "You don't think he's mad at us, do you, Uncle Macon?"

"Who's that?"

"You think he's mad we're starting to forget him?"

"Oh, no, honey. I'm sure he's not."

She slept in the car all the way from the station, and he drove very gently so as not to wake her. When they got home, Rose said it looked as if he'd worn the poor child right down to a frazzle.

"You want your dog to mind you in every situation," Muriel said. "Even out in public. You want to leave him outside a public place and come back to find him waiting. That's what we'll work on this morning. We'll start with him waiting right on your own front porch. Then next lesson we'll go on to shops and things."

She picked up the leash and they stepped out the door. It was raining, but the porch roof kept them dry. Macon said, "Hold on a minute, I want to show you something."

"What's that?"

He tapped his foot twice. Edward looked uncomfortable; he gazed off toward the street and gave a sort of cough. Then slowly, slowly, one forepaw crumpled. Then the other. He lowered himself by degrees until he was lying down.

"Well! Good dog!" Muriel said. She clucked her tongue.

Edward flattened his ears back for a pat.

"I worked on him most of yesterday," Macon said. "It was Sunday and I had nothing to do. And then my brother's kids were getting ready to leave and Edward was growling the way he usually does; so I tapped my foot and down he went."

"I'm proud of both of you."

She told Edward, "Stay," holding out a hand. She backed into the house again. "Now, Macon, you come in too."

They closed the front door. Muriel tweaked the lace curtain and peered out. "Well, he's staying so far," she announced.

She turned her back to the door. She checked her fingernails and said, "Tsk!" Tiny beads of rain trickled down her raincoat, and her hair—reacting to the damp—stood out in corkscrews. "Someday I'm going to get me a professional manicure," she said.

Macon tried to see around her; he wasn't sure that Edward would stay put.

"Have you ever been to a manicurist?" she asked.

"Me? Goodness, no."

"Well, some men go."

"Not me."

"I'd like just once to get everything done professional. Nails, skin . . . My girlfriend goes to this place where they vacuum your skin. They just vacuum all your pores, she says. I'd like to go there sometime. And I'd like to have my colors done. What colors look good on me? What don't? What brings out the best in me?"

She looked up at him. All at once, Macon got the feeling she had not been talking about colors at all but something else. It seemed she used words as a sort of background music. He took a step away from her. She said, "You didn't have to apologize, the other day."

"Apologize?"

Although he knew exactly what she was referring to.

She seemed to guess that. She didn't explain herself.

"Um, I don't remember if I ever made this clear," Macon said, "but I'm not even legally divorced yet."

500

"So?"

"I'm just, what do you call. Separated."

"Well? So?"

He wanted to say, *Muriel, forgive me, but since my son died, sex has . . . turned.* (As milk turns; that was how he thought of it. As milk will alter its basic nature and turn sour.) *I really don't think of it anymore. I honestly don't. I can't imagine anymore what all that fuss was about. Now it seems pathetic.*

But what he said was, "I'm worried the mailman's going to come."

She looked at him for a moment longer, and then she opened the door for Edward.

Rose was knitting Julian a pullover sweater for Christmas. "Already?" Macon asked. "We've barely got past Thanksgiving."

"Yes, but this is a really hard pattern and I want to do it right."

Macon watched her needles flashing. "Actually," he said, "have you ever noticed that Julian wears cardigans?"

"Yes, I guess he does," she said.

But she went on knitting her pullover.

It was a heathery gray wool, what he believed they called Ragg wool. Macon and both his brothers had sweaters that color. But Julian wore crayon colors or navy blue. Julian dressed like a golfer. "He tends toward the V-necked look," Macon said to Rose.

"That doesn't mean he wouldn't wear a crew neck if he had one."

"Look," Macon said. "I guess what I'm getting at—"

Rose's needles clicked serenely.

"He's really kind of a playboy," he said. "I don't know if you realize that. And besides, he's younger."

"Two years," she said.

"But he's got a younger, I don't know, style of living. Singles apartments and so on."

"He says he's tired of all that."

"Oh, Lord."

"He says he likes homeyness. He appreciates my cooking. He can't believe I'm knitting him a sweater."

"No, I guess not," Macon said grimly.

"Don't try to spoil this, Macon."

"Sweetheart, I only want to protect you. It's wrong, you know, what you said at Thanksgiving. Love is *not* what it's all about. There are other things to consider besides, all kinds of other issues."

"He ate my turkey and did not get sick. Two big helpings," Rose said.

Macon groaned and tore at a handful of his hair.

"First we try him on a real quiet street," Muriel said. "Someplace public, but not too busy. Some out-of-the-way little store or something."

She was driving her long gray boat of a car. Macon sat in front beside her, and Edward sat in back, his ears out horizontal with joy. Edward was always happy to be invited for a car ride, though very soon he'd turn cranky. ("How much *longer*?" you could almost hear him whine.) It was lucky they weren't going far.

"I got this car on account of its big old trunk," Muriel said. She slung it dashingly around a corner. "I needed it for my errand business. Guess how much it cost?"

"Um . . ."

"Only two hundred dollars. That's because it needed work, but I took it to this boy down the street from where I live. I said, 'Here's the deal. You fix my car up, I let you have the use of it three nights a week and all day Sunday.' Wasn't that a good idea?"

502

"Very inventive," Macon said.

"I've *had* to be inventive. It's been scrape and scrounge, nail and knuckle, ever since Norman left me," she said. She had pulled into a space in front of a little shopping center, but she made no move to get out of the car. "I've lain awake, oh, many a night, thinking up ways to earn money. It was bad enough when room and board came free, but after Mrs. Brimm died it was worse; her house passed on to her son and I had to pay him rent. Her son's an old skinflint. Always wanting to jack up the price. I said, 'How's about this? You leave the rent where it is and I won't trouble you with maintenance. I'll tend to it all myself,' I said. 'Think of the headaches you'll save.' So he agreed and now you should see what I have to deal with, things go wrong and I can't fix them and so we just live with them. Leaky roof, stopped-up sink, faucet dripping hot water so my gas bill's out of this world, but at least I've kept the rent down. And I've got about fifty jobs, if you count them all up. You could say I'm lucky; I'm good at spotting a chance. Like those lessons at Doggie, Do, or another time a course in massage at the Y. The massage turned out to be a dud, seems you have to have a license and all like that, but I will say Doggie, Do paid off. And also I'm trying to start this research service; that's on account of all I picked up helping the school librarian. Wrote out these little pink cards I passed around at Towson State: We-Search Research. Xeroxed these flyers and mailed them to every Maryland name in the *Writer's Directory. Men and Women of Letters!* I said. *Do you want a long slow illness that will effectively kill off a character without unsightly disfigurement?* So far no one's answered but I'm still hoping. Twice now I've paid for an entire Ocean City vacation just by going up and down the beach offering folks these box lunches me and Alexander fixed in our motel room every morning. We lug them in Alexander's red wagon; I call out, 'Cold drinks! Sandwiches! Step right up!' And this is not even counting the regular jobs, like the Meow-Bow or before that the Rapid-Eze. Tiresome old Rapid-Eze; they did let me bring Alexander but it was nothing but copying documents and tedious things like that, canceled checks and invoices, little chits of things. I've never been so disinterested."

Macon stirred and said, "Don't you mean uninterested?"

"Exactly. Wouldn't you be? Copies of letters, copies of exams, copies of articles on how to shop for a mortgage. Knitting instructions, crochet instructions, all rolling out of the machine real slow and stately like they're such a big deal. Finally I quit. When I got my training at Doggie, Do I said, 'I quit. I've had it!' Why don't we try the grocery."

Macon felt confused for a second. Then he said, "Oh. All right."

"You go into the grocery, put Edward on a down-stay outside. I'll wait here in the car and see if he behaves."

"All right."

He climbed from the car and opened the back door for Edward. He led him over to the grocery. He tapped his foot twice. Edward looked distressed, but he lay down. Was this humane, when the sidewalk was still so wet? Reluctantly, Macon stepped into the store. It had the old-fashioned smell of brown paper bags. When he looked back out, Edward's expression was heartbreaking. He wore a puzzled, anxious smile and he was watching the door intently.

Macon cruised an aisle full of fruits and vegetables. He picked up an apple and considered it and set it down again. Then he went back outside. Edward was still in place. Muriel had emerged from her car and was leaning against the fender, making faces into a brown plastic compact. "Give him lots of praise!" she called, snapping the compact shut. Macon clucked and patted Edward's head.

They went next door to the drugstore. "This time we'll both go in," Muriel said.

"Is that safe?"

504

"We'll have to try it sooner or later."

They strolled the length of the hair care aisle, all the way back to cosmetics, where Muriel stopped to try on a lipstick. Macon imagined Edward yawning and getting up and leaving. Muriel said, "Too pink." She took a tissue from her purse and rubbed the pink off. Her own lipstick stayed on, as if it were not merely a 1940s color but a 1940s formula—that glossless, cakey substance that used to cling to pillowcases, napkins, and the rims of coffee cups. She said, "What are you doing for dinner tomorrow night?"

"For—?"

"Come and eat at my house."

He blinked.

"Come on. We'll have fun."

"Um . . ."

"Just for dinner, you and me and Alexander. Say six o'clock. Number Sixteen Singleton Street. Know where that is?"

"Oh, well, I don't believe I'm free then," Macon said.

"Think it over a while," she told him.

They went outside. Edward was still there but he was standing up, bristling in the direction of a Chesapeake Bay retriever almost a full block away. "Shoot," Muriel said. "Just when I thought we were getting someplace." She made him lie down again. Then she released him and the three of them walked on. Macon was wondering how soon he could decently say that he had thought it over now and remembered he definitely had an invitation elsewhere. They rounded a corner. "Oh, look, a thrift shop!" Muriel said. "My biggest weakness." She tapped her foot at Edward. "This time, I'll go in," she said. "I want to see what they have. You step back a bit and watch he doesn't stand up like before."

She went inside the thrift shop while Macon waited, skulking around the parking meters. Edward knew he was there, though. He kept turning his head and giving Macon beseeching looks.

Macon saw Muriel at the front of the shop, picking up and setting down little gilded cups without saucers, chipped green glass florists' vases, ugly tin brooches as big as ashtrays. Then he saw her dimly in the back where the clothes were. She drifted into sight and out again like a fish in dark water. She appeared all at once in the doorway, holding up a hat. "Macon? What do you think?" she called. It was a dusty beige turban with a jewel pinned to its center, a great false topaz like an eye.

"Very interesting," Macon said. He was starting to feel the cold.

Muriel vanished again, and Edward sighed and settled his chin on his paws.

A teenaged girl walked past—a gypsy kind of girl with layers of flouncy skirts and a purple satin knapsack plastered all over with Grateful Dead emblems. Edward tensed. He watched every step she took; he rearranged his position to watch after her as she left. But he said nothing, and Macon—tensed himself—felt relieved but also a little let down. He'd been prepared to leap into action. All at once the silence seemed unusually deep; no other people passed. He experienced one of those hallucinations of sound that he sometimes got on planes or trains. He heard Muriel's voice, gritty and thin, rattling along. "At the tone the time will be . . ." she said, and then she sang, "You will find your love in . . ." and then she shouted, "Cold drinks! Sandwiches! Step right up!" It seemed she had webbed his mind with her stories, wound him in slender steely threads from her life—her Shirley Temple childhood, unsavory girlhood, Norman flinging the screen out the window, Alexander mewing like a newborn kitten, Muriel wheeling on Doberman pinschers and scattering her salmon-pink business cards and galloping down the beach, all spiky limbs and flying hair, hauling a little red wagon full of lunches.

Then she stepped out of the thrift shop. "It was way too expensive," she told Macon. "Good dog," she said, and she snapped her fingers to let Edward up. "Now one more test." She was heading back toward her car. "We want to try both of us going in again. We'll do it down at the doctor's."

"What doctor's?"

"Dr. Snell's. I've got to pick up Alexander; I want to return him to school after I drop you off."

"Will that take long?"

"Oh, no."

They drove south, with the engine knocking in a way that Macon hadn't noticed the first time. In front of a building on Cold Spring Lane, Muriel parked and got out. Macon and Edward followed her. "Now, I don't know if he's ready or not," she said. "But all the better if he's not; gives Edward practice."

"I thought you said this wouldn't take long."

She didn't seem to hear him.

They left Edward on the stoop and went into the waiting room. The receptionist was a gray-haired woman with sequined glasses dangling from a chain of fake scarabs. Muriel asked her, "Is Alexander through yet?"

"Any minute, hon."

Muriel found a magazine and sat down but Macon remained standing. He raised one of the slats of the venetian blind to check on Edward. A man in a nearby chair glanced over at him suspiciously. Macon felt like someone from a gangster movie—one of those shady characters who twitches back a curtain to make sure the coast is clear. He dropped the blind. Muriel was reading an article called "Put on the New Sultry, Shadowed Eyes!" There were pictures of different models looking malevolent.

"How old did you say Alexander was?" Macon asked.

She glanced up. Her own eyes, untouched by cosmetics, were disquietingly naked compared to those in the magazine.

"He's seven," she said.

Seven.

Seven was when Ethan had learned to ride a bicycle.

Macon was visited by one of those memories that dent the skin, that strain the muscles. He felt the seat of Ethan's bike pressing into his hand—the curled-under edge at the rear that you hold onto when you're trying to keep a bicycle upright. He felt the sidewalk slapping against his soles as he ran. He felt himself let go, slow to a walk, stop with his hands on his hips to call out, "You've got her now! You've got her!" And Ethan rode away from him, strong and proud and straight-backed, his hair picking up the light till he passed beneath an oak tree.

Macon sat down next to Muriel. She looked over and said, "Have you thought?"

"Hmm?"

"Have you given any thought to coming to dinner?"

"Oh," he said. And then he said, "Well, I could come. If it's only for dinner."

"What else would it be for?" she asked. She smiled at him and tossed her hair back.

The receptionist said, "*Here* he is."

She was talking about a small, white, sickly boy with a shaved-looking skull. He didn't appear to have quite enough skin for his face; his skin was stretched, his mouth was stretched to an unattractive width, and every bone and blade of cartilage made its presence known. His eyes were light blue and lashless, bulging slightly, rimmed with pink, magnified behind large, watery spectacles whose clear frames had an unfortunate pinkish cast themselves. He wore a carefully coordinated shirt-and-slacks set such as only a mother would choose.

"How'd it go?" Muriel asked him.

"Okay."

"Sweetie, this is Macon. Can you say hi? I've been training his dog."

Macon stood up and held out his hand. After a moment, Alexander responded. His fingers felt like a collection of wilted

508

stringbeans. He took his hand away again and told his mother, "You have to make another appointment."

"Sure thing."

She went over to the receptionist, leaving Macon and Alexander standing there. Macon felt there was nothing on earth he could talk about with this child. He brushed a leaf off his sleeve. He pulled his cuffs down. He said, "You're pretty young to be at the doctor's without your mother."

Alexander didn't answer, but Muriel—waiting for the receptionist to flip through her calendar—turned and answered for him. "He's used to it," she said, "because he's had to go so often. He's got these allergies."

"I see," Macon said.

Yes, he was just the type for allergies.

"He's allergic to shellfish, milk, fruits of all kinds, wheat, eggs, and most vegetables," Muriel said. She accepted a card from the receptionist and dropped it into her purse. She said as they were walking out, "He's allergic to dust and pollen and paint, and there's some belief he's allergic to air. Whenever he's outside a long time he gets these bumps on any uncovered parts of his body."

She clucked at Edward and snapped her fingers. Edward jumped up, barking. "Don't pat him," she told Alexander. "You don't know what dog fur will do to you."

They got into her car. Macon sat in back so Alexander could take the front seat, as far from Edward as possible. They had to drive with all the windows down so Alexander wouldn't start wheezing. Over the rush of wind, Muriel called, "He's subject to asthma, eczema, and nosebleeds. He has to get these shots all the time. If a bee ever stings him and he hasn't had his shots he could be dead in half an hour."

Alexander turned his head slowly and gazed at Macon. His expression was prim and censorious.

When they drew up in front of the house, Muriel said,

"Well, let's see now. I'm on full time at the Meow-Bow tomorrow . . ." She ran a hand through her hair, which was scratchy, rough, disorganized. "So I guess I won't see you till dinner," she said.

Macon couldn't think of any way to tell her this, but the fact was that he would never be able to make that dinner. He missed his wife. He missed his son. They were the only people who seemed real to him. There was no point looking for substitutes.

11

Muriel Pritchett, was how she was listed. Brave and cocky: no timorous initials for Muriel. Macon circled the number. He figured now was the time to call. It was nine in the evening. Alexander would have gone to bed. He lifted the receiver.

But what would he say?

Best to be straightforward, of course, much less hurtful; hadn't Grandmother Leary always told them so? *Muriel, last year my son died and I don't seem to . . . Muriel, this has nothing to do with you personally but really I have no . . .*

Muriel, I can't. I just can't.

It seemed his voice had rusted over. He held the receiver to his ear but great, sharp clots of rust were sticking in his throat.

He had never actually said out loud that Ethan was dead. He hadn't needed to; it was in the papers (page three, page five), and then friends had told other friends, and Sarah got on the phone . . . So somehow, he had never spoken the words. How would he do it now? Or maybe he could make Muriel do it. *Finish this sentence, please: I did have a son but he ——.* "He what?" she would ask. "He went to live with your wife?

511

He ran away? He died?" Macon would nod. "But *how* did he die? Was it cancer? Was it a car wreck? Was it a nineteen-year-old with a pistol in a Burger Bonanza restaurant?"

He hung up.

He went to ask Rose for notepaper and she gave him some from her desk. He took it to the dining room table, sat down, and uncapped his fountain pen. *Dear Muriel*, he wrote. And stared at the page a while.

Funny sort of name.

Who would think of calling a little newborn baby Muriel?

He examined his pen. It was a Parker, a swirly tortoiseshell lacquer with a complicated gold nib that he liked the looks of. He examined Rose's stationery. Cream colored. Deckle edged. Deckle! What an odd word.

Well.

Dear Muriel.

I am very sorry, he wrote, *but I won't be able to have dinner with you after all. Something has come up.* He signed it, *Regretfully, Macon.*

Grandmother Leary would not have approved.

He sealed the envelope and tucked it in his shirt pocket. Then he went to the kitchen where Rose kept a giant city map thumbtacked to the wall.

Driving through the labyrinth of littered, cracked, dark streets in the south of the city, Macon wondered how Muriel could feel safe living here. There were too many murky alleys and stairwells full of rubbish and doorways lined with tattered shreds of posters. The gridded shops with their ineptly lettered signs offered services that had a sleazy ring to them: CHECKS CASHED NO QUESTIONS, TINY BUBBA'S INCOME TAX, SAME DAY AUTO RECOLORING. Even this late on a cold November night, clusters of people lurked in the shadows—young men drinking out of brown paper bags, middle-aged women arguing under a movie marquee that read CLOSED.

512

He turned onto Singleton and found a block of row houses that gave a sense of having been skimped on. The roofs were flat, the windows flush and lacking depth. There was nothing to spare, no excess material for overhangs or decorative moldings, no generosity. Most were covered in formstone, but the bricks of Number 16 had been painted a rubbery maroon. An orange bugproof bulb glowed dimly above the front stoop.

He got out of the car and climbed the steps. He opened the screen door, which was made of pitted aluminum. It clattered in a cheap way and the hinges shrieked. He winced. He took the letter from his pocket and bent down.

"I've got a double-barreled shotgun," Muriel said from inside the house, "and I'm aiming it exactly where your head is."

He straightened sharply. His heart started pounding. (Her voice sounded level and accurate—like her shotgun, he imagined.) He said, "It's Macon."

"Macon?"

The latch clicked and the inner door opened several inches. He saw a sliver of Muriel in a dark-colored robe. She said, "Macon! What are you doing here?"

He gave her the letter.

She took it and opened it, using both hands. (There wasn't a trace of a shotgun.) She read it and looked up at him.

He saw he had done it all wrong.

"Last year," he said, "I lost . . . I experienced a . . . loss, yes, I lost my . . ."

She went on looking into his face.

"I lost my son," Macon said. "He was just . . . he went to a hamburger joint and then . . . someone came, a holdup man, and shot him. I can't go to dinner with people! I can't talk to their little boys! You have to stop asking me. I don't mean to hurt your feelings but I'm just not up to this, do you hear?"

She took one of his wrists very gently and she drew him into the house, still not fully opening the door, so that he had

513

a sense of slipping through something, of narrowly evading something. She closed the door behind him. She put her arms around him and hugged him.

"Every day I tell myself it's time to be getting over this," he said into the space above her head. "I know that people expect it of me. They used to offer their sympathy but now they don't; they don't even mention his name. They think it's time my life moved on. But if anything, I'm getting worse. The first year was like a bad dream—I was clear to his bedroom door in the morning before I remembered he wasn't there to be wakened. But this second year is real. I've stopped going to his door. I've sometimes let a whole day pass by without thinking about him. That absence is more terrible than the first, in a way. And you'd suppose I would turn to Sarah but no, we only do each other harm. I believe that Sarah thinks I could have prevented what happened, somehow—she's so used to my arranging her life. I wonder if all this has only brought out the truth about us—how far apart we are. I'm afraid we got married *because* we were far apart. And now I'm far from everyone; I don't have any friends anymore and everyone looks trivial and foolish and not related to me."

She drew him through a living room where shadows loomed above a single beaded lamp, and a magazine lay face down on a lumpy couch. She led him up a stairway and across a hall and into a bedroom with an iron bedstead and a varnished orange bureau.

"No," he said, "wait. This is not what I want."

"Just sleep," she told him. "Lie down and sleep."

That seemed reasonable.

She removed his duffel coat and hung it on a hook in a closet curtained with a length of flowered sheeting. She knelt and untied his shoes. He stepped out of them obediently. She rose to unbutton his shirt and he stood passive with his hands at his sides. She hung his trousers over a chair back. He

514

dropped onto the bed in his underwear and she covered him with a thin, withered quilt that smelled of bacon grease.

Next he heard her moving through the rest of the house, snapping off lights, running water, murmuring something in another room. She returned to the bedroom and stood in front of the bureau. Earrings clinked into a dish. Her robe was old, shattered silk, the color of sherry. It tied at the waist with a twisted cord and the elbows were clumsily darned. She switched off the lamp. Then she came over to the bed and lifted the quilt and slid under it. He wasn't surprised when she pressed against him. "I just want to sleep," he told her. But there were those folds of silk. He felt how cool and fluid the silk was. He put a hand on her hip and felt the two layers of her, cool over warm. He said, "Will you take this off?"

She shook her head. "I'm bashful," she whispered, but immediately afterward, as if to deny that, she put her mouth on his mouth and wound herself around him.

In the night he heard a child cough, and he swam up protestingly through layers of dreams to answer. But he was in a room with one tall blue window, and the child was not Ethan. He turned over and found Muriel. She sighed in her sleep and lifted his hand and placed it upon her stomach. The robe had fallen open; he felt smooth skin, and then a corrugated ridge of flesh jutting across her abdomen. The Caesarean, he thought. And it seemed to him, as he sank back into his dreams, that she had as good as spoken aloud. *About your son*, she seemed to be saying: *Just put your hand here. I'm scarred, too. We're all scarred. You are not the only one.*

12

I don't understand you," Rose told Macon. "First you say yes, you'll be here all afternoon, and then you say you won't. How can I plan when you're so disorganized?"

She was folding linen napkins and stacking them on the table, preparing her annual tea for the old people. Macon said, "Sorry, Rose, I didn't think it would matter that much."

"Last night you said you'd want supper and then you weren't here to eat it. Three separate mornings these past two weeks I go to call you for breakfast and I find you haven't slept in your bed. Don't you think I worry? Anything might have happened."

"Well, I said I was sorry."

Rose smoothed the stack of napkins.

"Time creeps up on me," he told her. "You know how it is. I mean I don't intend to go out at all, to begin with, but then I think, 'Oh, maybe for a little while,' and next thing I know it's so late, much too late to be driving, and I think to myself, 'Well . . .' "

Rose turned away quickly and went over to the buffet. She started counting spoons. "I'm not asking about your private life," she said.

516

"I thought in a sense you were."

"I just need to know how much food to cook, that's all."

"I wouldn't blame you for being curious," he said.

"I just need to know how many breakfasts to fix."

"You think I don't notice you three? Whenever she's here giving Edward his lesson, everyone starts coming out of the woodwork. Edging through the living room—'Just looking for the pliers! Don't mind me!' Sweeping the entire front porch the minute we take Edward out for a walk."

"Could I help it if the porch was dirty?"

"Well, I'll tell you what," he said. "Tomorrow night I'll definitely be here for supper. That's a promise. You can count on it."

"I'm not asking you to stay if you don't want to," she told him.

"Of course I want to! It's just this evening I'll be out," he said, "but not late, I'm sure of that. Why, I bet I'll be home before ten!"

Although even as he spoke, he heard how false and shallow he sounded, and he saw how Rose lowered her eyes.

He bought a large combination pizza and drove downtown with it. The smell made him so hungry that he kept snitching bits off the top at every stoplight—coins of pepperoni, crescents of mushroom. His fingers got all sticky and he couldn't find his handkerchief. Pretty soon the steering wheel was sticky too. Humming to himself, he drove past tire stores, liquor stores, discount shoe stores, the Hot-Tonight Novelty Company. He took a shortcut through an alley and jounced between a double row of backyards—tiny rectangles crammed with swing sets and rusted auto parts and stunted, frozen bushes. He turned onto Singleton and drew up behind a pickup truck full of moldy rolls of carpet.

The next-door neighbor's twin daughters were perched on their front stoop—flashy sixteen-year-olds in jeans as tight as

517

sausage casings. It was too cold to sit outside, but that never stopped them. "Hey there, Macon," they singsonged.

"How are you, girls."

"You going to see Muriel?"

"I thought I might."

He climbed Muriel's steps, holding the pizza level, and knocked on the door. Debbie and Dorrie continued to watch him. He flashed them a broad smile. They sometimes baby-sat with Alexander; he had to be nice to them. Half the neighborhood sat with Alexander, it seemed. He still felt confused by Muriel's network of arrangements.

It was Alexander who opened the door. "Pizza man!" Macon told him.

"Mama's on the phone," Alexander said flatly. He turned away and wandered back to the couch, adjusting his glasses on his nose. Evidently he was watching TV.

"Extra-large combination, no anchovies," Macon said.

"I'm allergic to pizza."

"What part of it?"

"Huh?"

"What part are you allergic to? The pepperoni? Sausage? Mushrooms? We could take those off."

"All of it," Alexander said.

"You can't be allergic to all of it."

"Well, I am."

Macon went on into the kitchen. Muriel stood with her back to him, talking on the phone with her mother. He could tell it was her mother because of Muriel's high, sad, querulous tone. "Aren't you going to ask how Alexander is? Don't you want to know about his rash? I ask after *your* health, why don't you ask about ours?"

He stepped up behind her soundlessly. "You didn't even ask what happened with his eye doctor," she said, "and here I was so worried about it. I swear sometimes you'd think he

518

wasn't your grandson! That time I sprained my ankle falling off my shoes and called to see if you'd look after him, what did you say? Said, 'Now let me get this straight. You want me to come all the way down to your house.' You'd think Alexander was nothing to do with you!"

Macon presented himself in front of her, holding out the pizza. "Ta-da!" he whispered. She looked up at him and gave that perky smile of hers—an ornate, Victorian V.

"Ma," she said, "I'm going now! Macon's here!"

It had been a long, long time since anyone made such an event of his arrival.

He went to Julian's office on a Monday afternoon and handed over what he'd done on the U.S. guidebook. "That wraps up the Northeast," he said. "I guess next I'll start on the South."

"Well, good," Julian told him. He was bent over behind his desk, rummaging through a drawer. "Excellent. Like to show you something, Macon. Now, where in hell—ah."

He straightened, with his face flushed. He gave Macon a tiny blue velvet box. "Your sister's Christmas present," he said.

Macon raised the lid. Inside, on a bed of white satin, was a diamond ring. He looked at Julian.

"What is it?" he asked.

"What *is* it?"

"I mean, is this a . . . what you would call, dinner ring? Or is it meant to be, rather . . ."

"It's an engagement ring, Macon."

"Engagement?"

"I want to marry her."

"You want to marry Rose?"

"What's so odd about that?"

"Well, I—" Macon said.

"If she'll agree to it, that is."

"What, you haven't asked her yet?"

"I'll ask her at Christmas, when I give her the ring. I want to do this properly. Old-fashioned. Do you think she'll have me?"

"Well, I really couldn't say," Macon said. Unfortunately, he was sure she would, but he'd be damned if he'd tell Julian that.

"She's got to," Julian said. "I am thirty-six years old, Macon, but I tell you, I feel like a schoolboy about that woman. She's everything those girls in my apartment building are not. She's so . . . true. Want to know something? I've never even slept with her."

"Well, I don't care to hear about that," Macon said hastily.

"I want us to have a real wedding night," Julian told him. "I want to do everything right. I want to join a real family. God, Macon, isn't it amazing how two separate lives can link up together? I mean two *differentnesses*? What do you think of the ring?"

Macon said, "It's okay." He looked down at it. Then he said, "It's very nice, Julian," and he closed the box gently and handed it back.

"Now, this is not your ordinary airplane," Macon told Muriel. "I wouldn't want you to get the wrong idea. This is what they call a commuter plane. It's something a businessman would take, say, to hop to the nearest city for a day and make a few sales and hop back again."

The plane he was referring to—a little fifteen-seater that resembled a mosquito or a gnat—stood just outside the door of the commuters' waiting room. A girl in a parka was loading it with baggage. A boy was checking something on the wings. This appeared to be an airline run by teenagers. Even the pilot was a teenager, it seemed to Macon. He entered the waiting room, carrying a clipboard. He read off a list of names. "Marshall? Noble? Albright?" One by one the passengers stepped forward—just eight or ten of them. To each the pilot said, "Hey, how you doing." He let his eyes rest longest on Muriel. Either he found her the most attractive or else he was struck by her outfit. She wore her highest heels, black stockings spattered with black net roses, and a flippy little fuchsia dress under a short fat coat that she referred to as her "fun fur." Her hair was caught all to one side in a great bloom of frizz, and there was a silvery dust of some kind on her eyelids. Macon knew she'd overdone it, but at the same time he liked her considering this such an occasion.

The pilot propped open the door and they followed him outside, across a stretch of concrete, and up two rickety steps into the plane. Macon had to bend almost double as he walked down the aisle. They threaded between two rows of single seats, each seat as spindly as a folding chair. They found spaces across from each other and settled in. Other passengers struggled through, puffing and bumping into things. Last came the copilot, who had round, soft, baby cheeks and carried a can of Diet Pepsi. He slammed the door shut behind him and went up front to the controls. Not so much as a curtain hid the cockpit. Macon could lean out into the aisle and see the banks of knobs and gauges, the pilot positioning his headset, the copilot taking a final swig and setting his empty can on the floor.

"Now, on a bigger plane," Macon called to Muriel as the engines roared up, "you'd hardly feel the takeoff. But here you'd better brace yourself."

Muriel nodded, wide-eyed, gripping the seat ahead of her. "What's that light that's blinking in front of the pilot?" she asked.

"I don't know."

"What's that little needle that keeps sweeping round and round?"

"I don't know."

521

He felt he'd disappointed her. "I'm used to jets, not these toys," he told her. She nodded again, accepting that. It occurred to Macon that he was really a very worldly and well-traveled man.

The plane started taxiing. Every pebble on the runway jolted it; every jolt sent a series of creaks through the framework. They gathered speed. The crew, suddenly grave and professional, made complicated adjustments to their instruments. The wheels left the ground. "Oh!" Muriel said, and she turned to Macon with her face all lit up.

"We're off," he told her.

"I'm flying!"

They rose—with some effort, Macon felt—over the fields surrounding the airport, over a stand of trees and a grid of houses. Above-ground swimming pools dotted backyards here and there like pale blue thumbtacks. Muriel pressed so close to her window that she left a circle of mist on the glass. "Oh, look!" she said to Macon, and then she said something else that he couldn't hear. The engines on this plane were loud and harsh, and the Pepsi can was rolling around with a clattering sound, and also the pilot was bellowing to the copilot, saying something about his refrigerator. "So I wake up in the middle of the night," he was shouting, "damn thing's thudding and thumping—"

Muriel said, "Wouldn't Alexander enjoy this!"

Macon hadn't seen Alexander enjoying anything yet, but he said dutifully, "We'll have to bring him sometime."

"We'll have to take just lots of trips! France and Spain and Switzerland . . ."

"Well," Macon said, "there's the little matter of money."

"Just America, then. California, Florida . . ."

California and Florida took money too, Macon should have said (and Florida wasn't even given space in his guidebook), but for the moment, he was borne along by her vision of things. "Look!" she said, and she pointed to something.

Macon leaned across the aisle to see what she meant. This airplane flew so low that it might have been following road signs; he had an intimate view of farmlands, woodlands, roofs of houses. It came to him very suddenly that every little roof concealed actual lives. Well, of course he'd known that, but all at once it took his breath away. He saw how real those lives were to the people who lived them—how intense and private and absorbing. He stared past Muriel with his mouth open. Whatever she had wanted him to look at must be long past by now, but still he went on gazing out her window.

Porter and the others were talking money. Or Porter was talking money and the others were half listening. Porter was planning ahead for income taxes. He was interested in something called a chicken straddle. "The way it works," he said, "you invest in baby chicks right now, before the end of the year. Deduct the cost of feed and such. Then sell the grown hens in January and collect the profit."

Rose wrinkled her forehead. She said, "But chickens are so prone to colds. Or would you call it distemper. And December and January aren't usually all that warm here."

"They wouldn't be here in Baltimore, Rose. God knows where they'd be. I mean these are not chickens you actually see; they're a way to manage our taxes."

"Well, I don't know," Charles said. "I hate to get involved in things someone else would be handling. It's someone else's word those chickens even exist."

"You people have no imagination," Porter said.

The four of them stood around the card table in the sun porch, helping Rose with her Christmas present for Liberty. She had constructed an addition to Liberty's dollhouse—a garage with a guest apartment above it. The garage was convincingly untidy. Miniature wood chips littered the floor around a stack of twig-sized fire logs, and a coil of green wire made a perfect garden hose. Now they were working on the upstairs. Rose was stuffing an armchair cushion no bigger than an aspirin. Charles was cutting a sheet of wallpaper from a sample book. Porter was drilling holes for the curtain rods. There was hardly elbow room; so Macon, who had just come in with Edward, stood back and merely watched.

"Besides," Charles said, "chickens are really not, I don't know, very classy animals. I would hate to go round saying I'm a chicken magnate."

"You don't even have to mention the fact," Porter said.

"*Beef* magnate, now; that I wouldn't mind. Beef has more of a ring to it."

"They're not offering a straddle for beef, Charles."

Macon picked up some color photos that sat beside the wallpaper book. The top photo showed a window in a room he didn't recognize—a white-framed window with louvered shutters closed across its lower half. The next was a group portrait. Four people—blurry, out of focus—stood in a line in front of a couch. The woman wore an apron, the men wore black suits. There was something artificial about their posture. They were lined up too precisely; none of them touched the others. "Who *are* these people?" Macon asked.

Rose glanced over. "That's the family from Liberty's dollhouse," she said.

"Oh."

"Her mother sent me those pictures."

"It's a family with nothing but grown-ups?" he asked.

"One's a boy; you just can't tell. And one's a grandpa or a butler; June says Liberty switches him back and forth."

Macon laid the photos aside without looking at the rest of them. He knelt to pat Edward. "A cattle straddle," Charles was saying thoughtfully. Macon suddenly wished he were at Muriel's. He wrapped his arms around Edward and imagined he smelled her sharp perfume deep in Edward's fur.

. . .

524

Oh, above all else he was an orderly man. He was happiest with a regular scheme of things. He tended to eat the same meals over and over and to wear the same clothes; to drop off his cleaning on a certain set day and to pay all his bills on another. The teller who helped him on his first trip to a bank was the teller he went to forever after, even if she proved not to be efficient, even if the next teller's line was shorter. There was no room in his life for anyone as unpredictable as Muriel. Or as extreme. Or as . . . well, unlikable, sometimes.

Her youthfulness was not appealing but unsettling. She barely remembered Vietnam and had no idea where she'd been when Kennedy was shot. She made him anxious about his own age, which had not previously troubled him. He realized how stiffly he walked after he had been sitting in one position too long; how he favored his back, always expecting it to go out on him again; how once was plenty whenever they made love.

And she talked so much—almost ceaselessly; while Macon was the kind of man to whom silence was better than music. ("Listen! They're playing my song," he used to say when Sarah switched the radio off.) She talked about blushers, straighteners, cellulite, hemlines, winter skin. She was interested in the appearance of things, only the appearance: in lipstick shades and nail wrapping and facial masques and split ends. Once, on one of her more attractive days, he told her she was looking very nice, and she grew so flustered that she stumbled over a curb. She asked if that was because she had tied her hair back; and was it the hair itself or the ribbon; or rather the color of the ribbon, which she'd feared might be just a little too bright and set off the tone of her complexion wrong. And didn't he think her hair was hopeless, kerblamming out the way it did in the slightest bit of humidity? Till he was sorry he had ever brought it up. Well, not sorry, exactly, but tired. Exhausted.

Yet she could raise her chin sometimes and pierce his mind like a blade. Certain images of her at certain random, insignificant moments would flash before him: Muriel at her kitchen table, ankles twined around her chair rungs, filling out a contest form for an all-expense-paid tour of Hollywood. Muriel telling her mirror, "I look like the wrath of God"—a kind of ritual of leavetaking. Muriel doing the dishes in her big pink rubber gloves with the crimson fingernails, raising a soapy plate and trailing it airily over to the rinse water and belting out one of her favorite songs—"War Is Hell on the Home Front Too" or "I Wonder If God Likes Country Music." (Certainly *she* liked country music—long, complaining ballads about the rocky road of life, the cold gray walls of prison, the sleazy, greasy heart of a two-faced man.) And Muriel at the hospital window, as he'd never actually seen her, holding a mop and gazing down at the injured coming in.

Then he knew that what mattered was the pattern of her life; that although he did not love her he loved the surprise of her, and also the surprise of himself when he was with her. In the foreign country that was Singleton Street he was an entirely different person. This person had never been suspected of narrowness, never been accused of chilliness; in fact, was mocked for his soft heart. And was anything but orderly.

"Why don't you come to my folks' house for Christmas dinner?" she asked him.

Macon was in her kitchen at the time. He was crouched beneath the sink, turning off a valve. For a moment he didn't answer; then he emerged and said, "Your folks?"

"For Christmas dinner."

"Oh, well, I don't know," he said.

"Come on, Macon, please say yes! I want you to meet them. Ma thinks I'm making you up. 'You made him up,' she says. You know how she is."

Yes, Macon did know, at least from second hand, and he could just imagine what that dinner would be like. Booby-trapped. Full of hidden digs and hurt feelings. The fact was, he just didn't want to get involved.

So instead of answering, he turned his attention to Alexander. He was trying to teach Alexander how to fix a faucet. "Now," he said, "you see I shut the valve off. What did I do that for?"

All he got was a glassy pale stare. This was Macon's idea, not Alexander's. Alexander had been hauled away from the TV like a sack of stones, plunked on a kitchen chair, and instructed to watch closely. "Oh," Muriel said, "I'm not so sure about this. He's not so very strong."

"You don't have to be Tarzan to fix a kitchen faucet, Muriel."

"Well, no, but I don't know . . ."

Sometimes Macon wondered if Alexander's ailments were all in Muriel's head.

"Why did I shut off the valve, Alexander?" he asked.

Alexander said, "Why."

"You tell me."

"You tell *me*."

"No, you," Macon said firmly.

There was a bad moment or two in which it seemed that Alexander might keep up that stare of his forever. He sat C-shaped in his chair, chin on one hand, eyes expressionless. The shins emerging from his trousers were thin as Tinkertoys, and his brown school shoes seemed very large and heavy. Finally he said, "So the water won't whoosh all over."

"Right."

Macon was careful not to make too much of his victory.

"Now, this leak is not from the spout, but from the handle," he said. "So you want to take the handle apart and replace the packing. First you unscrew the top screw. Let's see you do it."

"Me?"

527

Macon nodded and offered him the screwdriver.

"I don't want to," Alexander said.

"Let him just watch," Muriel suggested.

"If he just watches he won't know how to fix the one in the bathtub, and I'm going to ask him to manage that without me."

Alexander took the screwdriver, in one of those small, stingy gestures of his that occupied a minimum of space. He inched off the chair and came over to the sink. Macon pulled another chair up close and Alexander climbed onto it. Then there was the problem of fitting the screwdriver into the slot of the screw. It took him forever. He had tiny fingers, each tipped with a little pink pad above painfully bitten nails. He concentrated, his glasses slipping down on his nose. Always a mouth-breather, he was biting his tongue now and panting slightly.

"Wonderful," Macon said when the screwdriver finally connected.

At each infinitesimal turn, though, it slipped and had to be repositioned. Macon's stomach muscles felt tight. Muriel, for once, was silent, and her silence was strained and anxious.

Then, "Ah!" Macon said. The screw had loosened enough so that Alexander could twist it by hand. He managed that part fairly easily. He even removed the faucet without being told. "Very good," Macon said. "I believe you may have natural talents."

Muriel relaxed. Leaning back against the counter, she said, "My folks have their Christmas dinner in the daytime. I mean it's not at noon but it's not at night either, it's more like mid-afternoon, or this year it's really late afternoon because I've got the morning shift at the Meow-Bow and—"

"Look at this," Macon told Alexander. "See that gunk? That's old, rotted packing. So take it away. Right. Now here's the new packing. You wind it around, wind even a little more than you need. Let's see you wind it around."

Alexander wrapped the thread. His fingers turned white with the effort. Muriel said, "Usually we have a goose. My daddy brings a goose from the Eastern Shore. Or don't you care for goose. Would you rather just a turkey? A duck? What are you used to eating, Macon?"

Macon said, "Oh, well . . ." and was saved by Alexander. Alexander turned, having reassembled the faucet without any help, and said, "Now what?"

"Now make sure the screw is well in."

Alexander resumed his struggles with the screwdriver. Muriel said, "Maybe you'd rather a good hunk of beef. I know some men are like that. They think poultry is kind of pansy. Is that how you think too? You can tell me! I won't mind! My folks won't mind!"

"Oh, um, Muriel . . ."

"Now what," Alexander ordered.

"Why, now we turn the water back on and see what kind of job you've done."

Macon crouched beneath the sink and showed him where the valve was. Alexander reached past him and twisted it, grunting. Wasn't it odd, Macon thought, how little boys all had that same slightly green smell, like a cedar closet. He rose and turned on the faucet. No leak. "Look at that!" he told Alexander. "You've solved the problem."

Alexander fought to hold a grin back.

"Will you know how to do it the next time?"

He nodded.

"Now when you're grown," Macon said, "you can fix the faucets for your wife."

Alexander's face squinched up with amusement at the thought.

" 'Step back, dearie,' you can say. 'Just let me see to this.' "

Alexander said, "Tssh!"—his face like a little drawstring purse.

" 'Let a real *man* take care of this,' you can tell her."

"Tssh! Tssh!"

"Macon? Are you coming to my folks', or aren't you?" Muriel asked.

It seemed unreasonable to say he wasn't. Somehow or other, he had got himself involved already.

13

Muriel's parents lived out in Timonium, in a development called Foxhunt Acres. Muriel had to show Macon the way. It was the coldest Christmas Day either of them could remember, but they drove with the windows slightly open so that Alexander, riding in back, would not be bothered by the dog hair. The radio was tuned to Muriel's favorite station. Connie Francis was singing "Baby's First Christmas."

"You warm enough?" Muriel asked Alexander. "You doing okay?"

Alexander must have nodded.

"You feel like you're wheezing at all?"

"Nope."

"No, ma'am," she corrected him.

Sarah used to do that, too, Macon remembered—give their son a crash course in manners any time they set out to visit her mother.

Muriel said, "Once I was riding Alexander uptown on some errands for George? My company? And I'd had these two cats in the car just the day before? And I didn't think a thing about it, clean forgot to vacuum like I usually do, and all at once I turn around and Alexander's stretched across the seat, flat out."

"I wasn't flat *out*," Alexander said.

"You were just as good as."

"I was only laying down so I wouldn't need so much air."

"See there?" Muriel said to Macon.

They were traveling up York Road now, past body shops and fast food outlets all closed and bleak. Macon had never seen this road so empty. He overtook a van and then a taxicab; nothing else. Swags of Christmas greens hung stiffly above a used car lot.

"He can get shots, though," Muriel said.

"Shots?"

"He can get shots to keep him from wheezing."

"Then why doesn't he?"

"Well, if Edward was to move in I guess that's what we'd do."

"Edward?"

"I mean if, you know. If you moved in on a permanent basis and Edward came too."

"Oh," Macon said.

Brenda Lee was singing "I'm Gonna Lasso Santa Claus." Muriel hummed along, tipping her head perkily left and right to keep time.

"Would you ever think of doing that?" she asked him finally.

"Doing what?" he said, pretending not to know.

"Would you ever think of moving in with us?"

"Oh, um . . ."

"Or we could move in with you," she said. "Either way you preferred."

"With me? But my sister and my—"

"I'm talking about *your* house."

"Oh. My house."

His house swam up before him—small and dim and aban-

532

doned, hunkered beneath the oak trees like a woodchopper's cottage in a fairy tale. Muriel glanced at his face and then said, quickly, "I could understand if you didn't want to go back there."

"It's not that," he said. He cleared his throat. He said, "It's just that I haven't given it much thought."

"Oh, I understand!"

"Not yet, at least."

"You don't have to explain!"

She pointed out where to turn, and they started down a winding road. The eating places grew sparser and shabbier. There were scratchy little trees, frozen fields, a whole village of different-sized mailboxes bristling at the end of a driveway.

Every time the car jounced, something rattled on the backseat. That was Macon's Christmas present to Alexander—a kit full of tools that were undersized but real, with solid wooden handles. Macon had hunted those tools down one by one. He had rearranged them in their compartments a dozen times at least, like a miser counting his money.

They passed a segment of rickrack fence that was dissolving back into the ground. Muriel said, "What is *your* family doing today?"

"Oh, nothing much."

"Having a big Christmas dinner?"

"No, Rose has gone to Julian's. Charles and Porter are, I don't know, I think they said something about caulking the second-floor bathtub."

"Oh, the poor things! They should have come with us to my folks'."

Macon smiled, picturing that.

He turned where she directed, into a meadow dotted with houses. All were built to the same general plan—brick with half-stories of aluminum siding above. The streets were named for trees that weren't there, Birch Lane and Elm Court and Apple Blossom Way. Muriel had him make a right onto Apple

Blossom Way. He pulled up behind a station wagon. A girl burst out of the house—a chunky, pretty teenager in blue jeans and a long yellow ponytail. "Claire!" Alexander shouted, bouncing in his seat.

"That's my sister," Muriel told Macon.

"Ah."

"Do you think she's good-looking?"

"Yes, she's very good-looking."

Claire had the car door open by now and was hoisting Alexander into her arms. "How's my fellow?" she was asking. "What did Santa Claus bring you?" She was so unlike Muriel that you'd never guess they were sisters. Her face was almost square, and her skin was golden, and by present-day standards she was probably ten pounds overweight. After she'd set Alexander down, she stuffed her hands awkwardly into the back pockets of her jeans. "So anyhow," she told Macon and Muriel. "Merry Christmas, and all that."

"Look," Muriel said, flashing a wristwatch. "See what Macon gave me."

"What'd you give him?"

"A key tag from a thrift shop. Antique."

"Oh."

With her house key attached, Muriel had neglected to say.

Macon unloaded things from the trunk—Muriel's presents for her family, along with his hostess gift—and Alexander took his toolbox from the backseat. They followed Claire across the yard. Muriel was anxiously feeling her hair as she walked. "You ought to see what Daddy gave Ma," Claire told her. "Gave her a microwave oven. Ma says she's scared to death of it. 'I just know I'll get radiation,' she says. We're worried she won't use it."

The door was held open for them by a small, skinny, gray woman in an aqua pantsuit. "Ma, this is Macon," Muriel said. "Macon, this is my mother."

Mrs. Dugan studied him, pursing her lips. Lines radiated

534

from the corners of her mouth like cat whiskers. "Pleased to meet you," she said finally.

"Merry Christmas, Mrs. Dugan," Macon said. He handed her his gift—a bottle of cranberry liqueur with a ribbon tied around it. She studied that, too.

"Just put the rest of those things under the tree," Muriel told Macon. "Ma, aren't you going to say hello to your grandson?"

Mrs. Dugan glanced briefly at Alexander. He must not have expected anything more; he was already wandering over to the Christmas tree. Unrelated objects sat beneath it—a smoke detector, an electric drill, a makeup mirror encircled with light bulbs. Macon laid Muriel's packages next to them, and then he removed his coat and draped it across the arm of a white satin couch. Fully a third of the couch was occupied by the microwave oven, still jauntily decorated with a large red bow. "Look at my new microwave," Mrs. Dugan said. "If that's not just the weirdest durn thing I ever laid eyes on." She cleared a crumple of gift wrap off an armchair and waved Macon into it.

"Something certainly smells good," he said.

"Goose," she told him. "Boyd went and shot me a goose."

She sat down next to the oven. Claire was on the floor with Alexander, helping him open a package. Muriel, still in her coat, scanned a row of books on a shelf. "Ma—" she said. "No, never mind, I found it." She came over to Macon with a photo album, the modern kind with clear plastic pages. "Look here," she said, perching on the arm of his chair. "Pictures of me when I was little."

"Why not take off your coat and stay a while," Mrs. Dugan told her.

"Me at six months. Me in my stroller. Me and my first birthday cake."

They were color photos, shiny, the reds a little too blue. (Macon's own baby pictures were black-and-white, which was all that was generally available back then.) Each showed her to be a chubby, giggling blonde, usually with her hair fixed in some coquettish style—tied in a sprig at the top of her head, or in double ponytails so highly placed they looked like puppy ears. At first the stages of her life passed slowly—it took her three full pages to learn to walk—but then they speeded up. "Me at two. Me at five. Me when I was seven and a half." The chubby blonde turned thin and dark and sober and then vanished altogether, replaced by the infant Claire. Muriel said, "Oh, well," and snapped the album shut just midway through. "Wait," Macon told her. He had an urge to see her at her worst, at her most outlandish, hanging out with motorcycle gangs. But when he took the album away from her and flipped to the very last pages, they were blank.

Mr. Dugan wandered in—a fair, freckled man in a plaid flannel shirt—and gave Macon a callused hand to shake and then wandered out again, mumbling something about the basement. "He's fretting over the pipes," Mrs. Dugan explained. "Last night it got down below zero, did you know that? He's worried the pipes'll freeze."

"Oh, could I help?" Macon asked, perking up.

"Now, you just sit right where you are, Mr. Leary."

"Macon," he said.

"Macon. And you can call me Mother Dugan."

"Um . . ."

"Muriel tells me you're separated, Macon."

"Well, yes, I am."

"Do you think it's going to take?"

"Pardon?"

"I mean you're not just leading this child around Robin Hood's barn now, are you?"

"Ma, quit that," Muriel said.

"Well, I wouldn't have to ask, Muriel, if you had ever showed the least bit of common sense on your own. I mean face it, you don't have such a great track record."

"She's just worried for me," Muriel told Macon.

536

"Well, of course," he said.

"This girl was not but thirteen years old," Mrs. Dugan said, "when all at once it seemed boys of the very slipperiest character just came crawling out of the woodwork. I haven't had a good night's sleep since."

"Well, I don't know why not," Muriel told her. "That was years and years ago."

"Seemed every time we turned around, off she'd gone to the Surf'n'Turf or the Torch Club or the Hi-Times Lounge on Highway Forty."

"Ma, will you please open up you and Daddy's Christmas present?"

"Oh, did you bring us a present?"

Muriel rose to fetch it from under the tree, where Claire sat with Alexander. She was helping him set up some little cardboard figures. "This one goes on the green. This one goes on the blue," she said. Alexander jittered next to her, impatient to take over.

"Claire was the one who picked that game for him," Mrs. Dugan said, accepting the package Muriel handed her. "I thought it was too advanced, myself."

"It is not," Muriel said (although she hadn't even glanced at it). She returned to Macon's chair. "Alexander's just as smart as a tack. He'll catch on in no time."

"Nobody said he wasn't smart, Muriel. You don't have to take offense at every little thing a person says."

"Will you just open your present?"

But Mrs. Dugan proceeded at her own pace. She took off the ribbon and laid it in a box on the coffee table. "Your daddy has a bit of cash for your Christmas," she told Muriel. "Remind him before you go." She examined the wrapping. "Will you look at that! Teeny little Rudolph the Red-nosed Reindeers all over it. Real aluminum foil for their noses. I don't know why you couldn't just use tissue like I do."

"I wanted it to be special," Muriel told her.

Mrs. Dugan took off the paper, folded it, and laid it aside. Her gift was something in a gilded frame. "Well, isn't that nice," she said finally. She turned it toward Macon. It was a picture of Muriel and Alexander—a studio portrait in dreamy pastels, the lighting so even that it seemed to be coming from no particular place at all. Muriel was seated and Alexander stood beside her, one hand resting delicately upon her shoulder. Neither of them smiled. They looked wary and uncertain, and very much alone.

Macon said, "It's beautiful."

Mrs. Dugan only grunted and leaned forward to lay the photo beside the box of ribbons.

Dinner was an industrious affair, with everyone working away at the food—goose, cranberry relish, two kinds of potatoes, and three kinds of vegetables. Mr. Dugan remained spookily quiet, although Macon offered him several openers about the basement plumbing. Muriel devoted herself to Alexander. "There's bread in that stuffing, Alexander. Put it back this instant. You want your allergy to start up? I wouldn't trust that relish, either."

"Oh, for Lord's sake, let him be," Mrs. Dugan said.

"You wouldn't say that if it was you he kept awake at night with itchy rashes."

"Half the time I believe you bring on those rashes yourself with all your talk," Mrs. Dugan said.

"That just shows how much you know about it."

Macon had a sudden feeling of dislocation. What would Sarah say if she could see him here? He imagined her amused, ironic expression. Rose and his brothers would just look baffled. Julian would say, "Ha! *Accidental Tourist in Timonium.*"

Mrs. Dugan brought out three different pies, and Claire scurried around with the coffeepot. Over her jeans now she wore an embroidered dirndl skirt—her gift from Muriel,

538

purchased last week at Value Village. Her layers of clothing reminded Macon of some native costume. "What about the liqueur?" she asked her mother. "Shall I set out Macon's liqueur?"

"Maybe he wants you to call him Mr. Leary, hon."

"No, please, Macon's fine," he said.

He supposed there'd been a lot of discussion about his age. Oh, no doubt about it: He was too old, he was too tall, he was too dressed up in his suit and tie.

Mrs. Dugan said the liqueur was just about the best thing she'd ever drunk. Macon himself found it similar to the fluoride mixture his dentist coated his teeth with; he'd envisioned something different. Mr. Dugan said, "Well, these sweet-tasting, pretty-colored drinks are all very well for the ladies, but personally I favor a little sipping whiskey, don't you, Macon?" and he rose and brought back a fifth of Jack Daniel's and two shot glasses. The mere weight of the bottle in his hand seemed to loosen his tongue. "So!" he said, sitting down. "What you driving these days, Macon?"

"Driving? Oh, um, a Toyota."

Mr. Dugan frowned. Claire giggled. "Daddy hates and despises foreign cars," she told Macon.

"What is it, you don't believe in buying American?" Mr. Dugan asked him.

"Well, as a matter of fact—"

As a matter of fact his wife drove a Ford, he'd been going to say, but he changed his mind. He took the glass that Mr. Dugan held out to him. "I did once have a Rambler," he said.

"You want to try a Chevy, Macon. Want to come to the showroom sometime and let me show you a Chevy. What's your preference? Family-size? Compact?"

"Well, compact, I guess, but—"

"I'll tell you one thing: There is no way on earth you're going to get me to sell you a *sub*compact. No sir, you can beg and you can whine, you can get down on bended knee, I won't sell you one of those deathtraps folks are so set on buying nowadays. I tell my customers, I say, 'You think I got no principles? You're looking here before you at a man of principle,' I tell them, and I say, 'You want a subcompact you better go to Ed Mackenzie there. He'll sell you one without a thought. What does he care? But I'm a man of principle.' Why, Muriel here near about lost her life in one of them things."

"Oh, Daddy, I did not," Muriel said.

"Came a lot closer than I'd like to get."

"I walked away without a scratch."

"Car looked like a little stove-in sardine can."

"Worst thing I got was a run in my stocking."

"Muriel was taking a lift from Dr. Kane at the Meow-Bow," Mr. Dugan told Macon, "one day when her car was out of whack, and some durn fool woman driver swung directly into their path. See, she was hanging a left when—"

"Let me tell it," Mrs. Dugan said. She leaned toward Macon, gripping the wineglass that held her liqueur. "I was just coming in from the grocery store, carrying these few odds and ends I needed for Claire's school lunches. That child eats more than some grown men I know. Phone rings. I drop everything and go to answer. Man says, 'Mrs. Dugan?' I say, 'Yes.' Man says, 'Mrs. Dugan, this is the Baltimore City Police and I'm calling about your daughter Muriel.' I think, 'Oh, my God.' Right away my heart starts up and I have to find someplace to sit. Still have my coat on, rain scarf tied around my head so I couldn't even hear all that good but I never thought to take it off, that's how flustered I was. It was one of those hard rainy days like someone is purposely heaving buckets of water at you. I think, 'Oh, my God, now what has Muriel gone and—' "

"Lillian, you are getting way off the subject here," Mr. Dugan said.

"How can you say that? I'm telling him about Muriel's accident."

"He don't want to hear every little oh-my-God, he wants to know why he can't have a subcompact. Lady hangs a left smack in front of Dr. Kane's little car," Mr. Dugan told Macon, "and he has no choice but to ram her. He had the right of way. Want to know what happened? His little car is totaled. Little bitty Pinto. Lady's big old Chrysler barely dents its fender. Now tell me you still want a subcompact."

"But I didn't—"

"And the other thing is that Dr. Kane never, ever offered her another ride home, even after he got a new car," Mrs. Dugan said.

"Well, I don't exactly live in his neighborhood, Ma."

"He's a bachelor," Mrs. Dugan told Macon. "Have you met him? Real good-looking, Muriel says. First day on the job she says, 'Guess what, Ma.' Calls me on the phone. 'Guess what, my boss is single and he's real good-looking, a professional man, the other girls tell me he isn't even engaged.' Then he offers her that one lift home and they go and have an accident and he never offers again. Even when she lets him know she don't have her car some days, he never offers again."

"He does live clear up in Towson," Muriel said.

"I believe he thinks you're bad luck."

"He lives up in Towson and I live down on Singleton Street! What do you expect?"

"Next he got a Mercedes sports car," Claire put in.

"Well, sports cars," Mr. Dugan said. "We don't even talk about those."

Alexander said, "Can I be excused now?"

"I really had high hopes for Dr. Kane," Mrs. Dugan said sadly.

"Oh, quit it, Ma."

"You did, too! You said you did!"

"Why don't you just hush up and drink your drink."

Mrs. Dugan shook her head, but she took another sip of liqueur.

They left in the early evening, when the last light had faded and the air seemed crystallized with cold. Claire stood in the doorway singing out, "Come back soon! Thanks for the skirt! Merry Christmas!" Mrs. Dugan shivered next to her, a sweater draped over her shoulders. Mr. Dugan merely lifted an arm and disappeared—presumably to check on the basement again.

Traffic was heavier now. Headlights glowed like little white smudges. The radio—having given up on Christmas for another year—played "I Cut My Fingers on the Pieces of Your Broken Heart," and the toolbox rattled companionably in the backseat.

"Macon? Are you mad?" Muriel asked.

"Mad?"

"Are you mad at me?"

"Why, no."

She glanced back at Alexander and said no more.

It was night when they reached Singleton Street. The Butler twins, bundled into identical lavender jackets, stood talking with two boys on the curb. Macon parked and opened the back door for Alexander, who had fallen asleep with his chin on his chest. He gathered him up and carried him into the house. In the living room, Muriel set down her own burdens—the toolbox, Alexander's new game, and a pie Mrs. Dugan had pressed on them—and followed Macon up the stairs. Macon walked sideways to keep Alexander's feet from banging into the wall. They went into the smaller of the bedrooms and he laid Alexander on the bed. "I know what you must be thinking," Muriel said. She took Alexander's shoes off. "You're thinking, 'Oh, now I see, this Muriel was just on the lookout for anybody in trousers.' Aren't you."

Macon didn't answer. (He worried they'd wake Alexander.)

"I know what you're thinking!"

542

She tucked Alexander in. Turned off the light. They started back downstairs. "But that's not the way it was; I swear it," she said. "Oh, of course since he was single the possibility did cross my mind. Who would I be kidding if I said it didn't? I'm all alone, raising a kid. Scrounging for money. Of course it crossed my mind!"

"Well, of course," Macon said mildly.

"But it wasn't like she made it sound," Muriel told him.

She clattered after him across the living room. When he sat on the couch she sat next to him, still in her coat. "Are you going to stay?" she asked.

"If you're not too sleepy."

Instead of answering, she tipped her head back against the couch. "I meant are you giving up on me. I meant did you want to stop seeing me."

"Why would I want to stop seeing you?"

"After how bad she made me look."

"You didn't look bad."

"Oh, no?"

When she was tired, her skin seemed to tighten over her bones. She pressed her fingertips to her eyelids.

"Last Christmas," Macon said, "was the first one we had without Ethan. It was very hard to get through."

He often found himself talking with her about Ethan. It felt good to say his name out loud.

"We didn't know how to have a childless Christmas anymore," he said. "I thought, 'Well, after all, we managed before we had him, didn't we?' But in fact I couldn't remember how. It seemed to me we'd *always* had him; it's so unthinkable once you've got children that they ever didn't exist. I've noticed: I look back to when I was a boy, and it seems to me that Ethan was somehow there even then; just not yet visible, or something. So anyway. I decided what I should do was get Sarah a whole flood of presents, and I went out to Hutzler's the day before Christmas and bought all this junk—closet organizers and such. And Sarah: She went to the other extreme. She didn't buy anything. So there we were, each of us feeling we'd done it all wrong, acted inappropriately, but also that the other had done wrong; I don't know. It was a terrible Christmas."

He smoothed Muriel's hair off her forehead. "This one was better," he said.

She opened her eyes and studied him a moment. Then she slipped her hand in her pocket, came up with something and held it toward him—palming it, like a secret. "For you," she said.

"For me?"

"I'd like you to have it."

It was a snapshot stolen from her family album: Muriel as a toddler, clambering out of a wading pool.

She meant, he supposed, to give him the best of her. And so she had. But the best of her was not that child's Shirley Temple hairdo. It was her fierceness—her spiky, pugnacious fierceness as she fought her way toward the camera with her chin set awry and her eyes bright slits of determination. He thanked her. He said he would keep it forever.

14

You would have to say that he was living with
her now. He began to spend all his time at her house, to
contribute toward her rent and her groceries. He kept his
shaving things in her bathroom and squeezed his clothes
among the dresses in her closet. But there wasn't one particular point at which he made the shift. No, this was a matter
of day by day. First there was that long Christmas vacation
when Alexander was home alone; so why shouldn't Macon
stay on with him once he'd spent the night there? And why
not fetch his typewriter and work at the kitchen table? And
then why not remain for supper, and after that for bed?

Though if you needed to put a date on it, you might say
he truly moved in the afternoon he moved Edward in. He'd
just got back from a business trip—an exhausting blitz of five
southern cities, not one of which was any warmer than Baltimore—and he stopped by Rose's house to check the animals.
The cat was fine, Rose said. (She had to speak above Edward's yelps; he was frantic with joy and relief.) The cat had
probably not noticed Macon was missing. But Edward, well
. . . "He spends a lot of time sitting in the hall," she said,

"staring at the door. He keeps his head cocked and he waits for you to come back."

That did it. He brought Edward with him when he returned to Singleton Street.

"What do you think?" he asked Muriel. "Could we keep him just a day or two? See if Alexander can take it, without any shots?"

"I can take it!" Alexander said. "It's cats that get to me; not dogs."

Muriel looked doubtful, but she said they could give it a try.

Meanwhile, Edward darted madly all over the house snuffling into corners and under furniture. Then he sat in front of Muriel and grinned up at her. He reminded Macon of a schoolboy with a crush on his teacher; all his fantasies were realized, here he was at last.

For the first few hours they tried to keep him in a separate part of the house, which of course was hopeless. He had to follow Macon wherever he went, and also he developed an immediate interest in Alexander. Lacking a ball, he kept dropping small objects at Alexander's feet and then stepping back to look expectantly into his face. "He wants to play fetch," Macon explained. Alexander picked up a matchbook and tossed it, angling his arm behind him in a prissy way. While Edward went tearing after it, Macon made a mental note to buy a ball first thing in the morning and teach Alexander how to throw.

Alexander watched TV and Edward snoozed on the couch beside him, curled like a little blond cashew nut with a squinty, blissful expression on his face. Alexander hugged him and buried his face in Edward's ruff. "Watch it," Macon told him. He had no idea what to do if Alexander started wheezing. But Alexander didn't wheeze. By bedtime he just had a stuffy nose, and he usually had that anyhow.

. . .

546

Macon liked to believe that Alexander didn't know he and Muriel slept together. "Well, that's just plain ridiculous," Muriel said. "Where does he imagine you spend the night—on the living room couch?"

"Maybe," he said. "I'm sure he has some explanation. Or maybe he doesn't. All I'm saying is, we shouldn't hit him in the face with it. Let him think what he wants to think."

So every morning, Macon rose and dressed before Alexander woke. He started fixing breakfast and then roused him. "Seven o'clock! Time to get up! Go call your mother, will you?" In the past, he learned, Muriel had often stayed in bed while Alexander woke on his own and got ready for school. Sometimes he left the house while she was still asleep. Macon thought that was shocking. Now he made a full breakfast, and he insisted that Muriel sit at the table with them. Muriel claimed breakfast made her sick to her stomach. Alexander said it made him sick, too, but Macon said that was just too bad. "Ninety-eight percent of all A students eat eggs in the morning," he said (making it up as he went along). "Ninety-nine percent drink milk." He untied his apron and sat down. "Are you listening, Alexander?"

"I'll throw up if I drink milk."

"That's all in your head."

"Tell him, Mama!"

"He throws up," Muriel said gloomily. She sat hunched at the table in her long silk robe, resting her chin on one hand. "It's something to do with enzymes," she said. She yawned. Her hair, growing out of its permanent at last, hung down her back in even ripples like the crimps on a bobby pin.

Alexander walked to school with Buddy and Sissy Ebbetts, two tough-looking older children from across the street. Muriel either went back to bed or dressed and left for one or another of her jobs, depending on what day it was. Then Macon did the breakfast dishes and took Edward out. They didn't go far; it was much too cold. The few people they encountered

547

walked rapidly, with jerky steps, like characters in a silent film. They knew Macon by sight now and would allow their eyes to flick over his face as they passed—a gesture like a nod —but they didn't speak. Edward ignored them. Other dogs could come up and sniff him and he wouldn't even break stride. Mr. Marcusi, unloading crates outside Marcusi's Grocery, would pause to say, "Well, hey there, stubby. Hey there, tub of lard." Edward, smugly oblivious, marched on. "Weirdest animal I ever saw," Mr. Marcusi called after Macon. "Looks like something that was badly drawn." Macon always laughed.

He was beginning to feel easier here. Singleton Street still unnerved him with its poverty and its ugliness, but it no longer seemed so dangerous. He saw that the hoodlums in front of the Cheery Moments Carry-Out were pathetically young and shabby—their lips chapped, their sparse whiskers ineptly shaved, an uncertain, unformed look around their eyes. He saw that once the men had gone off to work, the women emerged full of good intentions and swept their front walks, picked up the beer cans and potato chip bags, even rolled back their coat sleeves and scrubbed their stoops on the coldest days of the year. Children raced past like so many scraps of paper blowing in the wind—mittens mismatched, noses running—and some woman would brace herself on her broom to call, "You there! I see you! Don't think I don't know you're skipping school!" For this street was always backsliding, Macon saw, always falling behind, but was caught just in time by these women with their carrying voices and their pushy jaws.

Returning to Muriel's house, he would warm himself with a cup of coffee. He would set his typewriter on the kitchen table and sit down with his notes and brochures. The window next to the table had large, cloudy panes that rattled whenever the wind blew. Something about the rattling sound reminded him of train travel. *The airport in Atlanta must have ten miles of corridors,* he typed, and then a gust shook the panes and he had an eerie sensation of movement, as if the cracked linoleum floor were skating out from under him.

He would telephone hotels, motels, Departments of Commerce, and his travel agent, arranging future trips. He would note these arrangements in the datebook that Julian gave him every Christmas—a Businessman's Press product, spiral-bound. In the back were various handy reference charts that he liked to thumb through. The birthstone for January was a garnet; for February, an amethyst. One square mile equaled 2.59 square kilometers. The proper gift for a first anniversary was paper. He would ponder these facts dreamily. It seemed to him that the world was full of equations; that there must be an answer for everything, if only you knew how to set forth the questions.

Then it was lunchtime, and he would put away his work and make himself a sandwich or heat a can of soup, let Edward have a quick run in the tiny backyard. After that he liked to putter around the house a bit. There was so much that needed fixing! And all of it somebody else's, not his concern, so he could approach it lightheartedly. He whistled while he probed the depth of a crack. He hummed as he toured the basement, shaking his head at the disarray. Upstairs he found a three-legged bureau leaning on a can of tomatoes, and he told Edward, "Scandalous!" in a tone of satisfaction.

It occurred to him—as he oiled a hinge, as he tightened a doorknob—that the house reflected amazingly little of Muriel. She must have lived here six or seven years by now, but still the place had an air of transience. Her belongings seemed hastily placed, superimposed, not really much to do with her. This was a disappointment, for Macon was conscious while he worked of his intense curiosity about her inner workings. Sanding a drawer, he cast a guilty eye upon its contents but found only fringed shawls and yellowed net gloves from the forties—clues to other people's lives, not hers.

But what was it he wanted to know? She was an open book, would tell him anything—more than he felt comfortable with. Nor did she attempt to hide her true nature, which was certainly far from perfect. It emerged that she had a nasty temper, a shrewish tongue, and a tendency to fall into spells of self-disgust from which no one could rouse her for hours. She was inconsistent with Alexander to the point of pure craziness—one minute overprotective, the next minute callous and offhand. She was obviously intelligent, but she counteracted that with the most global case of superstition Macon had ever witnessed. Hardly a day passed when she didn't tell him some dream in exhaustive detail and then sift through it for omens. (A dream of white ships on a purple sea came true the very next morning, she claimed, when a door-to-door salesman showed up in a purple sweater patterned with little white boats. "The very same purple! Same shape of ship!" Macon only wondered what kind of salesman would wear such clothing.) She believed in horoscopes and tarot cards and Ouija boards. Her magic number was seventeen. In a previous incarnation she'd been a fashion designer, and she swore she could recall at least one of her deaths. ("We think she's passed on," they told the doctor as he entered, and the doctor unwound his muffler.) She was religious in a blurry, nondenominational way and had no doubt whatsoever that God was looking after her personally—ironic, it seemed to Macon, in view of how she'd had to fight for every little thing she wanted.

He knew all this and yet, finding a folded sheet of paper on the counter, he opened it and devoured her lurching scrawl as if she were a stranger. *Pretzels. Pantyhose. Dentist*, he read. *Pick up Mrs. Arnold's laundry.*

No, not that. Not that.

Then it was three o'clock and Alexander was home from school, letting himself in with a key that he wore on a shoelace around his neck. "Macon?" he'd call tentatively. "Is that you out there?" He was scared of burglars. Macon said, "It's me." Edward leapt up and went running for his ball. "How was your day?" Macon always asked.

"Oh, okay."

But Macon had the feeling that school never went very well for Alexander. He came out of it with his face more pinched than ever, his glasses thick with fingerprints. He reminded Macon of a homework paper that had been erased and rewritten too many times. His clothes, on the other hand, were as neat as when he'd left in the morning. Oh, those clothes! Spotless polo shirts with a restrained brown pinstripe, matching brown trousers gathered bulkily around his waist with a heavy leather belt. Shiny brown shoes. Blinding white socks. Didn't he ever play? Didn't kids have recess anymore?

Macon gave him a snack: milk and cookies. (Alexander drank milk in the afternoons without complaint.) Then he helped him with his schoolwork. It was the simplest sort— arithmetic sums and reading questions. "Why did Joe need the dime? Where was Joe's daddy?"

"Umm . . ." Alexander said. Blue veins pulsed in his temples.

He was not a stupid child but he was limited, Macon felt. Limited. Even his walk was constricted. Even his smile never dared to venture beyond two invisible boundaries in the center of his face. Not that he was smiling now. He was wrinkling his forehead, raising his eyes fearfully to Macon.

"Take your time," Macon told him. "There's no hurry."

"But I can't! I don't know! I don't know!"

"You remember Joe," Macon said patiently.

"I don't think I do!"

Sometimes Macon stuck with it, sometimes he simply dropped it. After all, Alexander had managed without him up till now, hadn't he? There was a peculiar kind of luxury here: Alexander was not his own child. Macon felt linked to him in all sorts of complicated ways, but not in that inseparable, inevitable way that he'd been linked to Ethan. He could still draw back from Alexander; he could still give up on him. "Oh, well," he could say, "talk it over with your teacher tomorrow." And then his thoughts could wander off again.

The difference was, he realized, that he was not held responsible here. It was a great relief to know that.

When Muriel came home she brought fresh air and bustle and excitement. "Is it ever cold! Is it ever windy! Radio says three below zero tonight. Edward, down, this minute. Who wants lemon pie for dessert? Here's what happened: I had to go shopping for Mrs. Quick. First I had to buy linens for her daughter who's getting married, then I had to take them back because they were all the wrong color, her daughter didn't want pastel but white and told her mother plain as day, she said . . . and then I had to pick up pastries for the bridesmaids' party and when Mrs. Quick sees the lemon pie she says, 'Oh, no, not lemon! Not that tacky lemon that always tastes like Kool-Aid!' I'm like, 'Mrs. Quick, you don't have any business telling me what is tacky. This is a fresh-baked, lemon meringue pie without a trace of artificial . . .' So anyway, to make a long story short, she said to take it home to my little boy. 'Well, for your information I'm certain he can't eat it,' I say. 'Chances are he's allergic.' But I took it."

She ranged around the kitchen putting together a supper—BLTs, usually, and vegetables from a can. Sometimes things were not where she expected (Macon's doing—he couldn't resist reorganizing), but she adapted cheerfully. While the bacon sputtered in the skillet she usually phoned her mother and went over all she'd just told Macon and Alexander. "But the daughter wanted white and . . . 'Oh, not that tacky lemon pie!' she says . . ."

If Mrs. Dugan couldn't come to the phone (which was often the case), Muriel talked to Claire instead. Evidently Claire was having troubles at home. "Tell them!" Muriel

552

counseled her. "Just tell them! Tell them you won't stand for it." Cradling the receiver against her shoulder, she opened a drawer and took out knives and forks. "Why should they have to know every little thing you do? It doesn't *matter* that you're not up to anything, Claire. Tell them, 'I'm seventeen years old and it's none of your affair anymore if I'm up to anything or not. I'm just about a grown woman,' tell them."

But later, if Mrs. Dugan finally came to the phone, Muriel herself sounded like a child. "Ma? What kept you? You can't say a couple of words to your daughter just because your favorite song is playing on the radio? 'Lara's Theme' is more important than flesh and blood?"

Even after Muriel hung up, she seldom really focused on dinner. Her girlfriend might drop by and stay to watch them eat—a fat young woman named Bernice who worked for the Gas and Electric Company. Or neighbors would knock on the kitchen door and walk right in. "Muriel, do you happen to have a coupon for support hose? Young and slim as *you* are, I know you wouldn't need it yourself." "Muriel, Saturday morning I got to go to the clinic for my teeth, any chance of you giving me a lift?" Muriel was an oddity on this street—a woman with a car of her own—and they knew by heart her elaborate arrangement with the boy who did her repairs. Sundays, when Dominick had the car all day, nobody troubled her; but as soon as Monday rolled around they'd be lining up with their requests. "Doctor wants me to come in and show him my . . ." "I promised I'd take my kids to the . . ."

If Muriel couldn't do it, they never thought to ask Macon instead. Macon was still an outsider; they shot him quick glances but pretended not to notice he was listening. Even Bernice was bashful with him, and she avoided using his name.

By the time the lottery number was announced on TV, everyone would have left. That was what mattered here, Macon had discovered: the television schedule. The news could be missed but the lottery drawing could not; nor could "Evening Magazine" or any of the action shows that followed. Alexander watched these shows but Muriel didn't, although she claimed to. She sat on the couch in front of the set and talked, or painted her nails, or read some article or other. "Look here! 'How to Increase Your Bustline.' "

"You don't want to increase your bustline," Macon told her.

" 'Thicker, More Luxurious Eyelashes in Just Sixty Days.' "

"You don't want thicker eyelashes."

He felt content with everything exactly the way it was. He seemed to be suspended, his life on hold.

And later, taking Edward for his final outing, he liked the feeling of the neighborhood at night. This far downtown the sky was too pale for stars; it was pearly and opaque. The buildings were muffled dark shapes. Faint sounds threaded out of them—music, rifle shots, the whinnying of horses. Macon looked up at Alexander's window and saw Muriel unfolding a blanket, as delicate and distinct as a silhouette cut from black paper.

One Wednesday there was a heavy snowstorm, starting in the morning and continuing through the day. Snow fell in clumps like white woolen mittens. It wiped out the dirty tatters of snow from earlier storms; it softened the street's harsh angles and hid the trash cans under cottony domes. Even the women who swept their stoops hourly could not keep pace with it, and toward evening they gave up and went inside. All night the city glowed lilac. It was absolutely silent.

The next morning, Macon woke late. Muriel's side of the bed was empty, but her radio was still playing. A tired-sounding announcer was reading out cancellations. Schools were closed, factories were closed, Meals on Wheels was not running. Macon was impressed by the number of activities that people had been planning for just this one day—the luncheons and lectures and protest meetings. What energy, what spirit! He felt almost proud, though he hadn't been going to attend any of these affairs himself.

Then he realized he was hearing voices downstairs. Alexander must be awake, and here he was, trapped in Muriel's bedroom.

He dressed stealthily, making sure the coast was clear before crossing the hall to the bathroom. He tried not to creak the floorboards as he descended the stairs. The living room was unnaturally bright, reflecting the snow outside. The couch was opened, a mass of sheets and blankets; Claire had slept over the last few nights. Macon followed the voices into the kitchen. He found Alexander eating pancakes, Claire at the stove making more, Muriel curled in her usual morning gloom above her coffee cup. Just inside the back door Bernice stood dripping snow, swathed in various enormous plaids. "So anyhow," Claire was telling Bernice, "Ma says, 'Claire, who was that boy you drove up with?' I said, 'That was no boy, that was Josie Tapp with her new punk haircut,' and Ma says, 'Expect me to believe a cock-and-bull story like that!' So I say, 'I've had enough of this! Grillings! Curfews! Suspicions!' And I leave and catch a bus down here."

"They're just worried you'll turn out like Muriel did," Bernice told her.

"But Josie Tapp! I mean God Almighty!"

There was a general shifting motion in Macon's direction. Claire said, "Hey there, Macon. Want some pancakes?"

"Just a glass of milk, thanks."

"They're nice and hot."

"Macon thinks sugar on an empty stomach causes ulcers," Muriel said. She wrapped both hands around her cup.

Bernice said, "Well, *I'm* not saying no," and she crossed the kitchen to pull out a chair. Her boots left pads of snow with each step. Edward toddled after her, licking them up. "You and me ought to build a snowman," Bernice told Alexander. "Snow must be four feet deep out there."

"Have the streets been cleared?" Macon asked.

"Are you kidding?"

"They couldn't even get through with the newspaper," Alexander told him. "Edward's about to lose his mind wondering where it's got to."

"And there's cars abandoned all over the city. Radio says nobody's going anywhere at all."

But Bernice had hardly spoken when Edward wheeled toward the back door and started barking. A figure loomed outside. "Who's that?" Bernice asked.

Muriel tapped her foot at Edward. He lay down but kept on barking, and Macon opened the door. He found himself face to face with his brother Charles—unusually rugged-looking in a visored cap with earflaps. "Charles?" Macon said. "What are you doing here?"

Charles stepped in, bringing with him the fresh, expectant smell of new snow. Edward's yelps changed to welcoming whines. "I came to pick you up," Charles said. "Couldn't reach you on the phone."

"Pick me up for what?"

"Your neighbor Garner Bolt called and said pipes or something have burst in your house, water all over everything. I've been trying to get you since early morning but your line was always busy."

"That was me," Claire said, setting down a platter of pancakes. "I took the receiver off the hook so my folks wouldn't call me up and nag me."

"This is Muriel's sister, Claire," Macon said, "and that's Alexander and that's Bernice Tilghman. My brother Charles."

Charles looked confused.

Come to think of it, this wasn't an easy group to sort out. Claire was her usual mingled self—rosebud bathrobe over

556

faded jeans, fringed moccasin boots that laced to her knees. Bernice could have been a lumberjack. Alexander was neat and polished, while Muriel in her slinky silk robe was barely decent. Also, the kitchen was so small that there seemed to be more people than there actually were. And Claire was waving her spatula, spangling the air with drops of grease. "Pancakes?" she asked Charles. "Orange juice? Coffee?"

"No, thank you," Charles said. "I really have to be—"

"I bet you want milk," Muriel said. She got to her feet, fortunately remembering to clutch her robe together. "I bet you don't want sugar on an empty stomach."

"No, really I—"

"It won't be any trouble!" She was taking the carton from the refrigerator. "How'd you get here, anyways?"

"I drove."

"I thought the streets were blocked."

"They weren't so bad," Charles said, accepting a glass of milk. "*Finding* the place was the hard part." He told Macon, "I looked it up on the map but evidently I was mizzled."

"Mizzled?" Muriel asked.

"He was misled," Macon explained. "What did Garner say, exactly, Charles?"

"He said he saw water running down the inside of your living room window. He looked in and saw the ceiling dripping. Could have been that way for weeks, he said; you know that cold spell we had over Christmas."

"Doesn't sound good," Macon said.

He went to the closet for his coat. When he came back, Muriel was saying, "Now that you don't have an empty stomach, Charles, won't you try some of Claire's pancakes?"

"I've had half a dozen," Bernice told him. "They don't call me Big-Ass Bernice for nothing."

Charles said, "Uh, well—" and gave Macon a helpless look.

"We have to be going," Macon told the others. "Charles, are you parked in back?"

557

"No, in front. Then I went around back because I couldn't get the doorbell to work."

There was a reserved, disapproving note in Charles's voice when he said this, but Macon just said airily, "Oh, yes! Place is a wreck." He led the way toward the front of the house. He felt like someone demonstrating how well he got on with the natives.

They pushed open the door with some difficulty and floundered down steps so deeply buried that both men more or less fell the length of them, trusting that they would be cushioned. The sunlight sparked and flashed. They waded toward the street, Macon's shoes quickly filling with snow—a refreshing sharpness that almost instantly turned painful.

"I guess we'd better take both cars," he told Charles.

"How come?"

"Well, you don't want to have to drive all the way back down here."

"But if we take just one, then one of us can drive and one can push if we get stuck."

"Let's take mine, then."

"But mine's already cleared and dug out."

"But with mine I could drop you off home and save you the trip back down."

"But that leaves my car stranded on Singleton Street."

"We could get it to you after they plowed."

"And *my* car has its engine warmed!" Charles said.

Was this how they had sounded, all these years? Macon gave a short laugh, but Charles waited intently for his answer. "Fine, we'll take yours," Macon told him. They climbed into Charles's VW.

It was true there were a lot of abandoned cars. They sat in no particular pattern, featureless white mounds turned this way and that, so the street resembled a river of drifting boats. Charles dodged expertly between them. He kept a slow, steady

558

speed and talked about Rose's wedding. "We told her April was too iffy. Better wait, we told her, if she's so set on an outdoor service. But Rose said no, she'll take her chances. She's sure the weather will be perfect."

A snow-covered jeep in front of them, the only moving vehicle they'd yet encountered, suddenly slurred to one side. Charles passed it smoothly in a long, shallow arc. Mason said, "Where will they live, anyhow?"

"Why, at Julian's, I suppose."

"In a singles building?"

"No, he's got another place now, an apartment near the Belvedere."

"I see," Macon said. But he had trouble picturing Rose in an apartment—or anywhere, for that matter, if it wasn't her grandparents' house with its egg-and-dart moldings and heavily draped windows.

All through the city people were digging out—tunneling toward their parked cars, scraping off their windshields, shoveling sidewalks. There was something holidaylike about them; they waved to each other and called back and forth. One man, having cleared not only his walk but a section of the street as well, was doing a little soft-shoe dance on the wet concrete, and when Charles and Macon drove through he stopped to shout, "What are you, crazy? Traveling around in this?"

"I must say you're remarkably calm in view of the situation," Charles told Macon.

"What situation?"

"Your house, I mean. Water pouring through the ceiling for who knows how long."

"Oh, that," Macon said. Yes, at one time he'd have been very upset about that.

By now they were high on North Charles Street, which the plows had already cleared. Macon was struck by the spaciousness here—the buildings set far apart, wide lawns sloping

559

between them. He had never noticed that before. He sat forward to gaze at the side streets. They were still completely white. And just a few blocks over, when Charles turned into Macon's neighborhood, they saw a young girl on skis.

His house looked the same as ever, though slightly dingy in comparison with the snow. They sat in the car a moment studying it, and then Macon said, "Well, here goes, I guess," and they climbed out. They could see where Garner Bolt had waded through the yard; they saw the scalloping of footprints where he'd stepped closer to peer in a window. But the sidewalk bore no tracks at all, and Macon found it difficult in his smooth-soled shoes.

The instant he unlocked the door, they heard the water. The living room was filled with a cool, steady, dripping sound, like a greenhouse after the plants have been sprayed. Charles, who was the first to enter, said, "Oh, my God." Macon stopped dead in the hallway behind him.

Apparently an upstairs pipe (in that cold little bathroom off Ethan's old room, Macon would bet) had frozen and burst, heaven only knew how long ago, and the water had run and run until it saturated the ceiling and started coming through the plaster. All over the room it was raining. Chunks of plaster had fallen on the furniture, turning it white and splotchy. The floorboards were mottled. The rug, when Macon stepped on it, squelched beneath his feet. He marveled at the thoroughness of the destruction; not a detail had been overlooked. Every ashtray was full of wet flakes and every magazine was sodden. There was a gray smell rising from the upholstery.

"What are you going to *do*?" Charles breathed.

Macon pulled himself together. "Why, turn off the water main, of course," he said.

"But your living room!"

Macon didn't answer. His living room was . . . appropriate, was what he wanted to say. Even more appropriate if it had

560

been washed away entirely. (He imagined the house under twelve feet of water, uncannily clear, like a castle at the bottom of a goldfish bowl.)

He went down to the basement and shut off the valve, and then he checked the laundry sink. It was dry. Ordinarily he let the tap run all winter long, a slender stream to keep the pipes from freezing, but this year he hadn't thought of it and neither had his brothers, evidently, when they came to light the furnace.

"Oh, this is terrible, just terrible," Charles was saying when Macon came back upstairs. But he was in the kitchen now, where there wasn't any problem. He was opening and shutting cabinet doors. "Terrible. Terrible."

Macon had no idea what he was going on about. He said, "Just let me find my boots and we can leave."

"Leave?"

He thought his boots must be in his closet. He went upstairs to the bedroom. Everything here was so dreary—the naked mattress with its body bag, the dusty mirror, the brittle yellow newspaper folded on the nightstand. He bent to root through the objects on the closet floor. There were his boots, all right, along with some wire hangers and a little booklet of some sort. A *Gardener's Diary, 1976*. He flipped through it. *First lawn-mowing of the spring,* Sarah had written in her compact script. *Forsythia still in bloom.* Macon closed the diary and smoothed the cover and laid it aside.

Boots in hand, he went back downstairs. Charles had returned to the living room; he was wringing out cushions. "Never mind those," Macon said. "They'll just get wet again."

"Will your insurance cover this?"

"I suppose so."

"What would they call it? Flood damage? Weather damage?"

"I don't know. Let's get going."

"You should phone our contractor, Macon. Remember the man who took care of our porch?"

"Nobody lives here anyhow," Macon said.

Charles straightened, still holding a cushion. "What's that supposed to mean?" he asked.

"Mean?"

"Are you saying you'll just let this stay?"

"Probably," Macon told him.

"All soaked and ruined? Nothing done?"

"Oh, well," Macon said, waving a hand. "Come along, Charles."

But Charles hung back, still gazing around the living room. "Terrible. Even the curtains are dripping. Sarah will feel just terrible."

"I doubt she'll give it a thought," Macon said.

He paused on the porch to pull his boots on. They were old and stiff, the kind with metal clasps. He tucked his wet trouser cuffs inside them and then led the way to the street.

Once they were settled in the car, Charles didn't start the engine but sat there, key in hand, and looked soberly at Macon. "I think it's time we had a talk," he said.

"What about?"

"I'd like to know what you think you're up to with this Muriel person."

"Is that what you call her? 'This Muriel person'?"

"No one else will tell you," Charles said. "They say it's none of their business. But I can't just stand by and watch, Macon. I have to say what I think. How old are you—forty-two? Forty-three now? And she is . . . but more than that, she's not your type of woman."

"You don't even know her!"

"I know her type."

"I have to be getting home now, Charles."

Charles looked down at his key. Then he started the car

and pulled into the street, but he didn't drop the subject. "She's some kind of symptom, Macon! You're not yourself these days and this Muriel person's a symptom. Everybody says so."

"I'm more myself than I've been my whole life long," Macon told him.

"What kind of remark is that? It doesn't even make sense!"

"And who is 'everybody,' anyway?"

"Why, Porter, Rose, me . . ."

"All such experts."

"We're just worried for you, Macon."

"Could we switch to some other topic?"

"I had to tell you what I thought," Charles said.

"Well, fine. You've told me."

But Charles didn't look satisfied.

The car wallowed back through the slush, with ribbons of bright water trickling down the windshield from the roof. Then out on the main road, it picked up speed. "Hate to think what all that salt is doing to your underbody," Macon said.

Charles said, "I never told you this before, but it's my opinion sex is overrated."

Macon looked at him.

"Oh, when I was in my teens I was as interested as anyone," Charles said. "I mean it occupied my thoughts for every waking moment and all that. But that was just the *idea* of sex, you know? Somehow, the real thing was less . . . I don't mean I'm opposed to it, but it's just not all I expected. For one thing, it's rather messy. And then the weather is such a problem."

"Weather," Macon said.

"When it's cold you hate to take your clothes off. When it's hot you're both so sticky. And in Baltimore, it does always seem to be either too cold or too hot."

"Maybe you ought to consider a change of climate," Macon said. He was beginning to enjoy himself. "Do you suppose anyone's done a survey? City by city? Maybe the Business-man's Press could put out some sort of pamphlet."

"And besides it often leads to children," Charles said. "I never really cared much for children. They strike me as dis-ruptive."

"Well, if that's why you brought this up, forget it," Macon said. "Muriel can't have any more."

Charles gave a little cough. "That's good to hear," he said, "but it's not why I brought it up. I believe what I was trying to say is, I just don't think sex is important enough to ruin your life for."

"So? Who's ruining his life?"

"Macon, face it. She's not worth it."

"How can you possibly know that?"

"Can you tell me one unique thing about her?" Charles asked. "I mean one really special quality, Macon, not some-thing sloppy like 'She appreciates me' or 'She listens . . .'"

She looks out hospital windows and imagines how the Martians would see us, Macon wanted to say. But Charles wouldn't understand that, so instead he said, "I'm not such a bargain myself, in case you haven't noticed. I'm kind of, you could say, damaged merchandise. Somebody ought to warn *her* away from *me*, when you get right down to it."

"That's not true. That's not true at all. As a matter of fact, I imagine her people are congratulating her on her catch."

"Her catch!"

"Someone to support her. Anyone," Charles said. "She'd be lucky to find anyone. Why, she doesn't even speak proper English! She lives in that slummy house, she dresses like some kind of bag lady, she's got that little boy who appears to have hookworm or something—"

"Charles, just shut the hell up," Macon said.

Charles closed his mouth.

They had reached Muriel's neighborhood by now. They

were driving past the stationery factory with its tangled wire fence like old bedsprings. Charles took a wrong turn. "Let's see, now," he said, "where do I . . ."

Macon didn't offer to help.

"Am I heading in the right direction? Or not. Somehow I don't seem to . . ."

They were two short blocks from Singleton Street, but Macon hoped Charles would drive in circles forever. "Lots of luck," he said, and he opened the door and hopped out.

"Macon?"

Macon waved and ducked down an alley.

Freedom! Sunlight glinting off blinding white drifts, and children riding sleds and TV trays. Cleared parking spaces guarded with lawn chairs. Throngs of hopeful boys with shovels. And then Muriel's house with its walk still deep in snow, its small rooms smelling of pancakes, its cozy mix of women lounging about in the kitchen. They were drinking cocoa now. Bernice was braiding Claire's hair. Alexander was painting a picture. Muriel kissed Macon hello and squealed at his cold cheeks. "Come in and get warm! Have some cocoa! Look at Alexander's picture," she said. "Don't you love it? Isn't he something? He's a regular da Vinci."

"Leonardo," Macon said.

"What?"

"Not da Vinci. For God's sake. It's Leonardo," he told her. Then he stamped upstairs to change out of his clammy trousers.

15

"I'm sorry I'm so fat," Macon's seatmate said.

Macon said, "Oh, er, ah—"

"I know I'm using more than my share of space," the man told him. "Do you think I'm not aware of that? Every trip I take, I have to ask the stewardess for a seatbelt extender. I have to balance my lunch on my knees because the tray can't unfold in front of me. Really I ought to purchase two seats but I'm not a wealthy man. I ought to purchase two tickets and not spread all over my fellow passengers."

"Oh, you're not spreading all over me," Macon said.

This was because he was very nearly sitting in the aisle, with his knees jutting out to the side so that every passing stewardess ruffled the pages of *Miss MacIntosh*. But he couldn't help feeling touched by the man's great, shiny, despairing face, which was as round as a baby's. "Name's Lucas Loomis," the man said, holding out a hand. When Macon shook it, he was reminded of risen bread dough.

"Macon Leary," Macon told him.

"The stupid thing is," Lucas Loomis said, "I travel for a living."

566

"Do you."

"I demonstrate software to computer stores. I'm sitting in an airplane seat six days out of seven sometimes."

"Well, none of us finds them all that roomy," Macon said.

"What do you do, Mr. Leary?"

"I write guidebooks," Macon said.

"Is that so? What kind?"

"Oh, guides for businessmen. People just like you, I guess."

"*Accidental Tourist*," Mr. Loomis said instantly.

"Why, yes."

"Really? Am I right? Well, what do you know," Mr. Loomis said. "Look at this." He took hold of his own lapels, which sat so far in front of him that his arms seemed too short to reach them. "Gray suit," he told Macon. "Just what you recommend. Appropriate for all occasions." He pointed to the bag at his feet. "See my luggage? Carry-on. Change of underwear, clean shirt, packet of detergent powder."

"Well, good," Macon said. This had never happened to him before.

"You're my hero!" Mr. Loomis told him. "You've improved my trips a hundred percent. You're the one who told me about those springy items that turn into clotheslines."

"Oh, well, you could have run across those in any drugstore," Macon said.

"I've stopped relying on hotel laundries; I hardly need to venture into the streets anymore. I tell my wife, I say, you just ask her, I tell her often, I say, 'Going with the *Accidental Tourist* is like going in a capsule, a cocoon. Don't forget to pack my *Accidental Tourist*!' I tell her."

"Well, this is very nice to hear," Macon said.

"Times I've flown clear to Oregon and hardly knew I'd left Baltimore."

"Excellent."

There was a pause.

"Although," Macon said, "lately I've been wondering."

Mr. Loomis had to turn his entire body to look at him, like someone encased in a hooded parka.

"I mean," Macon said, "I've been out along the West Coast. Updating my U.S. edition. And of course I've covered the West Coast before, Los Angeles and all that; Lord, yes, I knew the place as a child; but this was the first I'd seen of San Francisco. My publisher wanted me to add it in. Have you been to San Francisco?"

"That's where we just now got on the plane," Mr. Loomis reminded him.

"San Francisco is certainly, um, beautiful," Macon said.

Mr. Loomis thought that over.

"Well, so is Baltimore too, of course," Macon said hastily. "Oh, no place on earth like Baltimore! But San Francisco, well, I mean it struck me as, I don't know . . ."

"I was born and raised in Baltimore, myself," Mr. Loomis said. "Wouldn't live anywhere else for the world."

"No, of course not," Macon said. "I just meant—"

"Couldn't pay me to leave it."

"No, me either."

"You a Baltimore man?"

"Yes, certainly."

"No place like it."

"Certainly isn't," Macon said.

But a picture came to his mind of San Francisco floating on mist like the Emerald City, viewed from one of those streets so high and steep that you really could hang your head over and hear the wind blow.

He'd left Baltimore on a sleety day with ice coating the airport runways, and he hadn't been gone all that long; but when he returned it was spring. The sun was shining and the trees were tipped with green. It was still fairly cool but he drove

568

with his windows down. The breeze smelled exactly like Vouvray—flowery, with a hint of mothballs underneath.

On Singleton Street, crocuses were poking through the hard squares of dirt in front of basement windows. Rugs and bedspreads flapped in backyards. A whole cache of babies had surfaced. They cruised imperiously in their strollers, propelled by their mothers or by pairs of grandmothers. Old people sat out on the sidewalk in beach chairs and wheelchairs, and groups of men stood about on corners, their hands in their pockets and their posture elaborately casual—the unemployed, Macon imagined, emerging from the darkened living rooms where they'd spent the winter watching TV. He caught snatches of their conversation:

"What's going down, man?"

"Nothing much."

"What you been up to?"

"Not a whole lot."

He parked in front of Muriel's house, where Dominick Saddler was working on Muriel's car. The hood was open and Dominick was deep in its innards; all Macon saw was his jeans and his gigantic, ragged sneakers, a band of bare flesh showing above his cowhide belt. On either side of him stood the Butler twins, talking away a mile a minute. "So she says to us we're grounded—"

"Can't go out with no one till Friday—"

"Takes away our fake i.d.'s—"

"Won't let us answer the phone—"

"We march upstairs and slam our bedroom door, like, just a little slam to let her know what we think of her—"

"And up she comes with a screwdriver and takes our door off its hinges!"

"Hmm," Dominick said.

Macon rested his bag on the hood and peered down into the engine. "Car acting up again?" he asked.

569

The Butler twins said, "Hey there, Macon," and Dominick straightened and wiped his forehead with the back of his hand. He was a dark, good-looking boy whose bulging muscles made Macon feel inadequate. "Damn thing keeps stalling out," he said.

"How'd Muriel get to work?"

"Had to take the bus."

Macon was hoping to hear she'd stayed home.

He climbed the steps and unlocked the front door. Just inside, Edward greeted him, squeaking and doing back flips and trying to hold still long enough to be petted. Macon walked through the rest of the house. Clearly, everyone had left in a hurry. The sofa was opened out. (Claire must have had another fight with her folks.) The kitchen table was littered with dishes and no one had put the cream away. Macon did that. Then he took his bag upstairs. Muriel's bed was unmade and her robe was slung across a chair. There was a snarl of hair in the pin tray on her bureau. He picked it up between thumb and index finger and dropped it into the wastebasket. It occurred to him (not for the first time) that the world was divided sharply down the middle: Some lived careful lives and some lived careless lives, and everything that happened could be explained by the difference between them. But he could not have said, not in a million years, why he was so moved by the sight of Muriel's thin quilt trailing across the floor where she must have dragged it when she rose in the morning.

It wasn't quite time for Alexander to come home from school, so he thought he would walk the dog. He put Edward on his leash and let himself out the front door. When he passed the Butler twins again they said, "Hey, there, Macon," singsong as ever, while Dominick cursed and reached for a wrench.

The men standing on the corner were discussing a rumor of jobs in Texas. Someone's brother-in-law had found work there. Macon passed with his head lowered, feeling uncomfortably privileged. He skirted a welcome mat that had been scrubbed and set out to dry on the pavement. The women here took spring cleaning seriously, he saw. They shook their dust mops out of upstairs windows; they sat on their sills to polish the panes with crumpled sheets of newspapers. They staggered between houses with borrowed vacuum cleaners, rug machines, and gallon jugs of upholstery shampoo. Macon rounded the block and started home, having paused to let Edward pee against a maple sapling.

Just as he was approaching Singleton Street, whom should he see but Alexander scurrying up ahead. There was no mistaking that stiff little figure with the clumsy backpack. "Wait!" Alexander was crying. "Wait for me!" The Ebbetts children, some distance away, turned and called something back. Macon couldn't hear what they said but he knew the tone, all right—that high, mocking chant. "Nyah-nyah-nyah-NYAH-nyah!" Alexander started running, stumbling over his own shoes. Behind him came another group, two older boys and a girl with red hair, and they began jeering too. Alexander wheeled and looked at them. His face was somehow smaller than usual. "Go," Macon told Edward, and he dropped the leash. Edward didn't need any urging. His ears had perked at the sound of Alexander's voice, and now he hurtled after him. The three older children scattered as he flew through them, barking. He drew up short in front of Alexander, and Alexander knelt to hug his neck.

When Macon arrived, he said, "Are you all right?"

Alexander nodded and got to his feet.

"What was that all about?" Macon asked him.

Alexander said, "Nothing."

But when they started walking again, he slipped his hand into Macon's.

Those cool little fingers were so distinct, so particular, so full of character. Macon tightened his grip and felt a pleasant kind of sorrow sweeping through him. Oh, his life had regained all its old perils. He was forced to worry once again about nuclear war and the future of the planet. He often had the same secret, guilty thought that had come to him after Ethan was born: *From this time on I can never be completely happy.*

Not that he was before, of course.

Macon's U.S. edition was going to be five separate pamphlets now, divided geographically, slipcased together so you had to buy all five even if you needed only one. Macon thought this was immoral. He said so when Julian stopped by for the West Coast material. "What's immoral about it?" Julian asked. He wasn't really paying attention; Macon could see that. He was filing mental notes on Muriel's household, no doubt the real purpose of this unannounced, unnecessary visit. Even though he'd already collected his material, he was wandering around the living room in an abstracted way, first examining a framed school photo of Alexander and then a beaded moccasin that Claire had left on the couch. It was Saturday and the others were in the kitchen, but Macon had no intention of letting Julian meet them.

"It's always immoral to force a person to buy something he doesn't want," Macon said. "If he only wants the Midwest, he shouldn't have to buy New England too, for heaven's sake."

Julian said, "Is that your friend I hear out there? Is it Muriel?"

"Yes, I suppose it is," Macon said.

"Aren't you going to introduce us?"

"She's busy."

"I'd really like to meet her."

"Why? Hasn't Rose given you a full report?"

"Macon," Julian said, "I'm soon going to be a relative of yours."

572

"Ah, God."

"It's only natural I'm interested in knowing her."

Macon said nothing.

"Besides," Julian told him, "I want to invite her to the wedding."

"You do?"

"So can I talk to her?"

"Oh. Well. I guess so."

Macon led the way to the kitchen. He felt he'd made a mistake—that having acted so thorny, he'd caused this meeting to seem more important than it was. But Julian, as it happened, was breezy and offhand. "Hello, ladies," he said.

They looked up—Muriel, Claire, and Bernice, seated around a sheaf of notebook paper. Macon reeled their names off rapidly but got stuck on Julian's. "Julian, ah, Edge, my . . ."

"Future brother-in-law," Julian said.

"My boss."

"I've come to invite you to the wedding, Muriel. Also your little boy, if—where's your little boy?"

"He's out walking the dog," Muriel said. "But he's not too good in churches."

"This'll be a garden wedding."

"Well, maybe, then, I don't know . . ."

Muriel was wearing what she called her "paratrooper look" —a coverall from Sunny's Surplus—and her hair was concealed beneath a wildly patterned silk turban. A ballpoint pen mark slashed across one cheekbone. "We're entering this contest," she told Julian. "Write a country-music song and win a trip for two to Nashville. We're working on it all together. We're going to call it 'Happier Days.' "

"Hasn't that already been written?"

"Oh, I hope not. You know how they always have these photographs of couples in magazines? 'Mick Jagger and Bianca, in happier days.' 'Richard Burton and Liz Taylor, in—' "

"Yes, I get it."

"So this man is talking about his ex-wife. 'I knew her in another time and place . . .' "

She sang it right out, in her thin, scratchy voice that gave a sense of distance, like a used-up phonograph record:

> *When we kissed in the rain,*
> *When we shared every pain,*
> *When we both enjoyed happier days.*

"Very catchy," Julian said, "but I don't know about 'shared every pain.' "

"What's wrong with it?"

"I mean, in happier days they had pain?"

"He's right," Bernice told Muriel.

"Rain, brain, drain," Julian reflected. " 'When our lives were more sane,' 'When we used to raise Cain . . .' "

"Let it be, why don't you," Macon told him.

" 'When I hadn't met Jane,' 'When she didn't know Wayne . . .' "

"Wait!" Bernice said, scribbling furiously.

"I may have tapped some hidden talent here," Julian told Macon.

"I'll see you to the door," Macon said.

" 'When our love had no stain,' 'When she wasn't inane . . .' " Julian said, trailing Macon through the living room. "Don't forget the wedding!" he called back. He told Macon, "If she wins, you could cover Nashville free for your next U.S. edition."

"I think she's planning on taking Bernice," Macon told him.

" 'When we guzzled champagne . . .' " Julian mused.

"I'll be in touch," Macon said, "as soon as I start on the Canada guide."

"Canada! Aren't you coming to the wedding?"

"Well, that too, of course," Macon said, opening the door.

574

"Wait a minute, Macon. What's your hurry? Wait, I want to show you something."

Julian set down the West Coast material to search his pockets. He pulled out a shiny, colored advertisement. "Hawaii," he said.

"Well, I certainly see no point in covering—"

"Not for you; for me! For our honeymoon. I'm taking Rose."

"Oh, I see."

"Look," Julian said. He unfolded the ad. It turned out to be a map—one of those useless maps that Macon detested, with outsized, whimsical drawings of pineapples, palm trees, and hula dancers crowding the apple-green islands. "I got this from The Travel People Incorporated. Have you heard of them? Are they reliable? They suggested a hotel over here on . . ." He drew a forefinger across the page, hunting down the hotel.

"I know nothing at all about Hawaii," Macon said.

"Somewhere here . . ." Julian said. Then he gave up, perhaps just at that moment hearing what Macon had told him, and refolded the map. "She may be exactly what you need," he said.

"Pardon?"

"This Muriel person."

"Why does everyone call her—"

"She's not so bad! I don't think your family understands how you're feeling."

"No, they don't. They really don't," Macon said. He was surprised that it was Julian, of all people, who saw that.

Although Julian's parting words were, " 'When we stuffed on chow mein . . .' "

Macon shut the door firmly behind him.

He decided to buy Alexander some different clothes. "How would you like some blue jeans?" he asked. "How would you

575

like some work shirts? How would you like a cowboy belt with 'Budweiser Beer' on the buckle?"

"You serious?"

"Would you wear that kind of thing?"

"Yes! I would! I promise!"

"Then let's go shopping."

"Is Mama coming?"

"We'll surprise her."

Alexander put on his spring jacket—a navy polyester blazer that Muriel had just paid a small fortune for. Macon didn't know if she would approve of jeans, which was why he'd waited till she was off buying curtains for a woman in Guilford.

The store he drove to was a Western-wear place where he used to take Ethan. It hadn't changed a bit. Its wooden floorboards creaked, its aisles smelled of leather and new denim. He steered Alexander to the boys' department, where he spun a rack of shirts. How many times had he done this before? It wasn't even painful. Only disorienting, in a way, to see that everything continued no matter what. The student jeans were still stacked according to waist and inseam. The horsey tie pins were still arrayed behind glass. Ethan was dead and gone but Macon was still holding up shirts and asking, "This one? This one? This one?"

"What I'd really like is T-shirts," Alexander said.

"T-shirts. Ah."

"The kind with a sort of stretched-out neck. And jeans with raggedy bottoms."

"Well, that you have to do for yourself," Macon said. "You have to break them in."

"I don't want to look new."

"Tell you what. Everything we buy, we'll wash about twenty times before you wear it."

"But nothing *pre*washed," Alexander said.

"No, no."

576

"Only nerds wear prewashed."

"Right."

Alexander chose several T-shirts, purposely too big, along with an assortment of jeans because he wasn't sure of his size. Then he went off to try everything on. "Shall I come with you?" Macon asked.

"I can do it myself."

"Oh. All right."

That was familiar, too.

Alexander disappeared into one of the stalls and Macon went on a tour of the men's department. He tried on a leather cowboy hat but took it off immediately. Then he went back to the stall. "Alexander?"

"Huh?"

"How's it going?"

"Okay."

In the space below the door, Macon saw Alexander's shoes and his trouser cuffs. Evidently he hadn't got around to putting on the jeans yet.

Someone said, "Macon?"

He turned and found a woman in a trim blond pageboy, her wrap skirt printed with little blue whales. "Yes," he said.

"Laurel Canfield. Scott's mother, remember?"

"Of course," Macon said, shaking her hand. Now he caught sight of Scott, who had been in Ethan's class at school —an unexpectedly tall, gawky boy lurking at his mother's elbow with an armload of athletic socks. "Why, Scott. Nice to see you," Macon said.

Scott flushed and said nothing. Laurel Canfield said, "It's nice to see *you*. Are you doing your spring shopping?"

"Oh, well, ah—"

He looked toward the stall. Now Alexander's trousers were slumped around his ankles. "I'm helping the son of a friend," he explained.

"We've just been buying out the sock department."

"Yes, I see you have."

"Seems every other week I find Scott's run through his socks again; you know how they are at this age—"

She stopped herself. She looked horrified. She said, "Or, rather . . ."

"Yes, certainly!" Macon said. "Amazing, isn't it?" He felt so embarrassed for her that he was pleased, at first, to see another familiar face behind her. Then he realized whose it was. There stood his mother-in-law. "Why!" he said. Was she still Mother Sidey? *Mrs.* Sidey? Who, for God's sake?

Luckily, it turned out that Laurel Canfield knew her too. "Paula Sidey," she said. "I haven't seen you since last year's Hunt Cup."

"Yes, I've been away," Mrs. Sidey told her, and then she dropped her lids somewhat, as if drawing a curtain, before saying, "Macon."

"How are you?" Macon said.

She was flawlessly groomed, industriously tended—a blue-haired woman in tailored slacks and a turtleneck. He used to worry that Sarah would age the same way, develop the same brittle carapace, but now he found himself admiring Mrs. Sidey's resolve. "You're looking well," he told her.

"Thank you," she said, touching her hairdo. "I suppose you're here for your spring wardrobe."

"Oh, Macon's helping a friend!" Laurel Canfield caroled. She was so chirpy, all of a sudden, that Macon suspected she'd just now recalled Mrs. Sidey's relationship to him. She looked toward Alexander's stall. Alexander was in his socks now. One sock rose and vanished, stepping into a flood of blue denim. "Isn't shopping for boys so difficult?" she said.

"I wouldn't know," Mrs. Sidey said. "I never had one. I'm here for the denim skirts."

"Oh, the skirts, well, I notice they're offering a—"

"What friend are you helping to buy for?" Mrs. Sidey asked Macon.

Macon didn't know what to tell her. He looked toward the stall. If only Alexander would just stay hidden forever, he thought. How to explain this scrawny little waif, this poor excuse of a child who could never hold a candle to the real child?

Contrary as always, Alexander chose that moment to step forth.

He wore an oversized T-shirt that slipped a bit off one shoulder, as if he'd just emerged from some rough-and-tumble game. His jeans were comfortably baggy. His face, Macon saw, had somehow filled out in the past few weeks without anybody's noticing; and his hair—which Macon had started cutting at home—had lost that shaved prickliness and grown thick and floppy.

"I look *wonderful!*" Alexander said.

Macon turned to the women and said, "Actually, I find shopping for boys is a pleasure."

16

There is no sound more peaceful than rain on the roof, if you're safe asleep in someone else's house. Macon heard the soft pattering; he heard Muriel get up to close a window. She crossed his vision like the gleam of headlights crossing a ceiling, white and slim and watery in a large plain slip from Goodwill Industries. She shut the window and the stillness dropped over him and he went back to sleep.

But in the morning his first thought was, *Oh, no! Rain! On Rose's wedding day!*

He got up, careful not to wake Muriel, and looked out. The sky was bright but flat, the color of oyster shells—not a good sign. The scrawny little dogwood in back was dripping from every twig and bud. Next door, Mr. Butler's ancient heap of scrap lumber had grown several shades darker.

Macon went downstairs, tiptoeing through the living room where Claire lay snoring in a tangle of blankets. He fixed a pot of coffee and then called Rose on the kitchen phone. She answered instantly, wide awake. "Are you moving the wedding indoors?" he asked her.

"We've got too many guests to move it indoors."

"Why? How many are coming?"

"Everyone we've ever known."

"Good grief, Rose."

"Never mind, it will clear."

"But the grass is all wet!"

"Wear galoshes," she told him. She hung up.

Since she'd met Julian she'd grown so airy, Macon thought. So flippant. Lacking in depth.

She was right about the weather, though. By afternoon there was a weak, pale sun. Muriel decided to wear the short-sleeved dress she'd planned on, but maybe with a shawl tossed over her shoulders. She wanted Alexander to put on a suit—he did have one, complete with waistcoat. He protested, though, and so did Macon. "Jeans and a good white shirt. That's plenty," Macon told her.

"Well, if you're sure."

Lately, she'd been deferring to him about Alexander. She had finally given in on the question of sneakers and she'd stopped policing his diet. Contrary to her predictions, Alexander's arches did not fall flat and he was not overtaken by raging eczema. At worst, he suffered a mild skin rash now and then.

The wedding was set for three o'clock. Around two thirty they started out, proceeding self-consciously toward Macon's car. It was a Saturday and no one else in the neighborhood was so dressed up. Mr. Butler was standing on a ladder with a hammer and a sack of nails. Rafe Daggett was taking his van apart. The Indian woman was hosing down a glowing thread-bare carpet that she'd spread across the sidewalk, and then she turned off the water and lifted the hem of her sari and stamped around so the carpet radiated little bursts of droplets. Every passing car, it seemed, labored under a top-heavy burden of mattresses and patio furniture, reminding Macon of those ants who scuttle back to their nests with loads four times their own size.

"I think I'm supposed to be the best man," Macon told Muriel after he'd started driving.

"You didn't mention that!"

"And Charles is giving her away."

"It's a real wedding, then," Muriel said. "Not just two people standing up together."

"That's what Rose said she wanted."

"I wouldn't do it like that at all," Muriel said. She glanced toward the rear and said, "Alexander, quit kicking my seat. You're about to drive me crazy. No," she said, facing forward, "if I was to marry, know what I'd do? Never tell a soul. Act like I'd been married for years. Slip off somewheres to a justice of the peace and come back like nothing had happened and make out like I'd been married all along."

"This is Rose's first time, though," Macon told her.

"Yes, but even so, people can say, 'It sure *took* you long enough.' I can hear my mother now; that's what she'd say for certain. 'Sure *took* you long enough. I thought you'd never get around to it,' is what she'd say. If I was ever to marry."

Macon braked for a traffic light.

"If I was ever to decide to marry," Muriel said.

He glanced over at her and was struck by how pretty she looked, with the color high in her cheeks and the splashy shawl flung around her shoulders. Her spike-heeled shoes had narrow, shiny ankle straps. He never could figure out why ankle straps were so seductive.

The first person they saw when they arrived was Macon's mother. For some reason it hadn't occurred to Macon that Alicia would be invited to her daughter's wedding, and when she opened the front door it took him a second to place her. She was looking so different, for one thing. She had dyed her hair a dark tomato red. She wore a long white caftan trimmed with vibrant bands of satin, and when she reached up to hug him a whole culvert of metal bangles clattered and slid down her left arm. "Macon, dear!" she said. She smelled of bruised gardenias. "And who may this be?" she asked, peering past him.

"Oh, um, I'd like you to meet Muriel Pritchett. And Alexander, her son."

"Really?"

A politely inquisitive look remained on her face. Evidently no one had filled her in. (Or else she hadn't bothered to listen.) "Well, since I seem to be the maître d'," she said, "I'll show you out back where the bride and groom are."

"Rose is not in hiding?"

"No, she says she doesn't see the logic in missing her own wedding," Alicia said, leading them toward the rear of the house. "Muriel, have you known Macon long?"

"Oh, kind of."

"He's very stuffy," Alicia said confidingly. "All my children are. They get it from the Leary side."

"I think he's nice," Muriel said.

"Oh, *nice*, yes. All very well and good," Alicia said, throwing Macon a look he couldn't read. She had linked arms with Muriel; she was always so physical. The trim on her caftan nearly matched Muriel's shawl. Macon had a sudden appalling thought: Maybe in his middle age he was starting to choose his mother's style of person, as if concluding that Alicia—silly, vain, annoying woman—might have the right answers after all. But no. He put the thought away from him. And Muriel slipped free of Alicia's arm. "Alexander? Coming?" she asked.

They stepped through the double doors of the sun porch. The backyard was full of pastels—Rose's old ladies in pale dresses, daffodils set everywhere in buckets, forsythia in full bloom along the alley. Dr. Grauer, Rose's minister, stepped forward and shook Macon's hand. "Aha! The best man," he said, and behind him came Julian in black—not his color. His nose was peeling. It must be boating season again. He put a gold ring in Macon's palm and said, "Like for you to have this." For a moment Macon imagined he was really meant to *have* it. Then he said, "Oh, yes, the ring," and dropped it in his pocket.

"I can't believe I'm finally getting a son-in-law," Alicia told Julian. "All I've ever had is daughter-in-laws."

"Daughters," Macon said automatically.

"No, daughter-in-laws."

"*Daughters*-in-law, Mother."

"And didn't manage to keep them long, either," Alicia said.

When Macon was small, he used to worry that his mother was teaching him the wrong names for things. "They call this corduroy," she'd said, buttoning his new coat, and he had thought, *But do they really?* Funny word, in fact, corduroy. Very suspicious. How could he be sure that other people weren't speaking a whole different language out there? He'd examined his mother distrustfully—her foolish fluff of curls and her flickery, unsteady eyes.

Now here came Porter's children, the three of them sticking close together; and behind them June, their mother. Wasn't it unusual to invite your brother's ex-wife to your wedding? Particularly when she was big as a barn with another man's baby. But she seemed to be enjoying herself. She pecked Macon on the cheek and cocked her head appraisingly at Muriel. "Kids, this is Alexander," Macon said. He was hoping against hope that they'd all just fall in together somehow and be friends, which of course didn't happen. Porter's children eyed Alexander sullenly and said nothing. Alexander knotted his fists in his pockets. June told Julian, "Your bride is looking just radiant," and Julian said, "Yes, isn't she," but when Macon located Rose he thought she looked tense and frayed, as most brides do if people would only admit it. She wore a white dress, mid-calf length but very simple, and a little puff of lace or net or something on her head. She was talking to their hardware man. And yes, there was the girl who

584

cashed their checks at the Mercantile Bank, and over next to Charles was the family dentist. Macon thought of *Mary Poppins*—those late-night adventures he used to read to Ethan, where all the tradespeople showed up behaving nothing like their daytime selves.

"I'm not sure if there's been any research on this," Charles was telling the dentist, "but have you ever tried polishing your teeth with a T-shirt after flossing?"

"Er . . ."

"A plain cotton T-shirt. One hundred percent cotton. I think you're going to be impressed when I have my next checkup. See, my theory is—"

Muriel and June were discussing Caesareans. Julian was asking Alicia if she'd ever sailed the Intracoastal Waterway. Mrs. Barrett was telling the mailman that Leary Metals used to make the handsomest stamped tin ceilings in Baltimore.

And Sarah was talking to Macon about the weather.

"Yes, I worried when it rained last night," Macon said. Or he said something; something or other . . .

He was looking at Sarah. Really he was consuming her: her burnished curls and her round, sweet face, and the dusting of powder on the down along her jawline.

"How have you been, Macon?" she asked him.

"I've been all right."

"Are you pleased about the wedding?"

"Well," he said, "I am if Rose is, I guess. Though I can't help feeling . . . well, Julian. You know."

"Yes, I know. But there's more to him than you think. He might be a very good choice."

When she stood in this kind of sunlight her eyes were so clear that it seemed you could see to the backs of them. He knew that from long ago. They might have been his own eyes; they were so familiar. He said, "How have *you* been?"

"I've been fine."

"Well. Good."

"I know that you're living with someone," she told him in a steady voice.

"Ah! Yes, actually I . . . yes. I am."

She knew who it was, too, because she looked past him then at Muriel and Alexander. But all she said was, "Rose told me when she invited me."

He said, "How about you?"

"Me?"

"Are you living with anyone?"

"Not really."

Rose came over and touched their arms, which was unlike her. "We're ready now," she said. She told Macon, "Sarah's my matron of honor, did I happen to mention that?"

"No, you didn't," Macon said.

Then he and Sarah followed her to a spot beneath a tulip tree, where Julian and Dr. Grauer were waiting. There was some kind of makeshift altar there—some little table or something covered with a cloth; Macon didn't pay much attention. He stood beside the minister and fingered the ring in his pocket. Sarah stood across from him, looking gravely into his face.

It all felt so natural.

17

Muriel said, "I never told you this, but a while before I met you I was dating somebody else."

"Oh? Who was that?" Macon asked.

"He was a customer at the Rapid-Eze Copy Center. He brought me his divorce papers to copy and we started having this conversation and ended up going out together. His divorce was awful. Really messy. His wife had been two-timing him. He said he didn't think he could ever trust a woman again. It was months before he would spend the night, even; he didn't like going to sleep when a woman was in the same room. But bit by bit I changed all that. He relaxed. He got to be a whole different man. Moved in with me and took over the bills, paid off all I still owed Alexander's doctor. We started talking about getting married. Then he met an airline stewardess and eloped with her within the week."

"I see," Macon said.

"It was like I had, you know, cured him, just so he could elope with another woman."

"Well," he said.

"You wouldn't do anything like that, would you, Macon?"

"Who, me?"

"Would you elope with someone else? Would you see someone else behind my back?"

"Oh, Muriel, of course not," he told her.

"Would you leave me and go home to your wife?"

"What are you talking about?"

"Would you?"

"Don't be silly," he said.

She cocked her head and considered him. Her eyes were alert and bright and knowing, like the eyes of some small animal.

It was a rainy Tuesday morning and Edward, who was squeamish about rain, insisted he didn't need to go out, but Macon took him anyway. While he was waiting in the backyard beneath his umbrella, he saw a young couple walking down the alley. They caught his attention because they walked so slowly, as if they didn't realize they were getting wet. The boy was tall and frail, in ragged jeans and a soft white shirt. The girl wore a flat straw hat with ribbons down the back and a longish, limp cotton dress. They swung hands, looking only at each other. They came upon a tricycle and they separated to walk around it; only instead of simply walking the girl did a little sort of dance step, spinning her skirt out, and the boy spun too and laughed and took her hand again.

Edward finally, finally peed, and Macon followed him back into the house. He set his umbrella in the kitchen sink and squatted to dry Edward off with an old beach towel. He rubbed briskly at first, and then more slowly. Then he stopped but remained on the floor, the towel bunched in his hands, the tin-can smell of wet dog rising all around him.

When he'd asked Sarah whether she was living with anyone, and Sarah had said, "Not really," what exactly had she meant by that?

.   .   .

588

The rain stopped and they put Edward on his leash and went out shopping. Muriel needed bedroom slippers with feathers on them. "Red. High-heeled. Pointy-toed," she said.

"Goodness. Whatever for?" Macon asked her.

"I want to clop around the house in them on Sunday mornings. Can't you just see it? I wish I smoked cigarettes. I wish Alexander wasn't allergic to smoke."

Yes, he could see it, as a matter of fact. "In your black-and-gold kimono," he said.

"Exactly."

"But I don't believe they sell those feathered slippers anymore."

"In thrift shops they do."

"Oh. Right."

Lately, Macon had begun to like thrift shops himself. In the usual sea of plastic he had found, so far, a folding box-wood carpenter's rule, an ingenious wheeled cookie cutter that left no waste space between cookies, and a miniature brass level for Alexander's toolbox.

The air outside was warm and watery. Mrs. Butler was propping up the squashed geraniums that flopped in the white-washed tire in her yard. Mrs. Patel—out of her luminous sari for once, clumsy and unromantic in tight, bulgy Calvin Klein jeans—was sweeping the puddles off her front steps. And Mrs. Saddler stood in front of the hardware store waiting for it to open. "I don't guess you'd have seen Dominick," she said to Muriel.

"Not lately."

"Last night he never came home," Mrs. Saddler said. "That boy just worries the daylights out of me. He's not what you would call bad," she told Macon, "but he's worrisome, know what I mean? When he's at home he's so much at home, those big noisy boots all over the place, but then when he's away he's so much away. You wouldn't believe how the house feels: just empty. Just echoing."

"He'll be back," Muriel said. "Tonight's his turn to have the car."

"Oh, and when he's out with the car it's worst of all," Mrs. Saddler said. "Then every siren I hear, I wonder if it's Dommie. I know how he screeches round corners! I know those fast girls he goes out with!"

They left her still standing there, distractedly fingering her coin purse, although the hardware-store owner had unlocked his door by now and was cranking down his awnings.

Outside a shop called Re-Runs, they ordered Edward to stay. He obeyed, looking put upon, while they went in. Muriel sifted through stacks of curled, brittle shoes that had hardened into the shapes of other people's feet. She shucked off her own shoes and stepped into a pair of silver evening sandals. "What do you think?" she asked Macon.

"I thought you were looking for slippers."

"But what do you think of these?"

"I can live without them," he said.

He was feeling bored because Re-Runs carried nothing but clothes.

Muriel abandoned the shoes and they went next door to Garage Sale Incorporated. Macon tried to invent a need for a rusty metal Rolodex file he found in a heap of tire chains. Could he use it for his guidebooks in some way? And make it tax-deductible. Muriel picked up a tan vinyl suitcase with rounded edges; it reminded Macon of a partly sucked caramel. "Should I get this?" she asked.

"I thought you wanted slippers."

"But for travel."

"Since when do you travel?"

"I know where you're going next," she said. She came closer to him, both hands clutching the suitcase handle. She looked like a very young girl at a bus stop, say, or out hitching a ride on the highway. "I wanted to ask if I could come with you."

590

"To Canada?"

"I mean the next place after that. France."

He set down the Rolodex. (Mention of France always depressed him.)

"Julian *said*!" she reminded him. "He said it's getting to be time to go to France again."

"You know I can't afford to bring you."

Muriel replaced the suitcase and they left the shop. "But just this once," she said, hurrying along beside him. "It wouldn't cost much!"

Macon retrieved Edward's leash and motioned him up. "It would cost a mint," he said, "not to mention that you'd have to miss work."

"No, I wouldn't. I've quit."

He looked over at her. "Quit?"

"Well, at the Meow-Bow. Then things like George and the dog training I'll just rearrange; if I was to travel I could just—"

"You quit the Meow-Bow?"

"So what?"

He couldn't explain the sudden weight that fell on him.

"It's not like it really paid much," Muriel said. "And you do buy most of the groceries now and help me with the rent and all; it's not like I needed the money. Besides, it took so much time! Time I could spend with you and Alexander! Why, I was coming home nights literally dead with exhaustion, Macon."

They passed Methylene's Beauty Salon, an insurance agency, a paint-stripping shop. Edward gave an interested glance at a large, jowly tomcat basking on the hood of a pickup.

"Figuratively," Macon said.

"Huh?"

"You were *figuratively* dead with exhaustion. Jesus, Muriel, you're so imprecise. You're so sloppy. And how could you quit

591

your job like that? How could you just assume like that? You never even warned me!"

"Oh, don't make such a big deal about it," Muriel said.

They arrived at her favorite shop—a nameless little hole in the wall with a tumble of dusty hats in the window. Muriel started through the door but Macon stayed where he was. "Aren't you coming in?" she asked him.

"I'll wait here."

"But it's the place with all the gadgets!"

He said nothing. She sighed and disappeared.

Seeing her go was like shucking off a great, dragging burden.

He squatted to scratch behind Edward's ears, and then he rose and studied a sun-bleached election poster as if it held some fascinating coded message. Two black women passed him, pulling wire carts full of laundry. "It was just as warm as this selfsame day I'm speaking to you but she wore a very very fur coat . . ."

"May-con."

He turned toward the door of the shop.

"Oh, Maay-con!"

He saw a mitten, one of those children's mittens designed to look like a puppet. The palm was a red felt mouth that widened to squeak, "Macon, *please* don't be angry with Muriel."

Macon groaned.

"Come into this nice store with her," the puppet urged.

"Muriel, I think Edward's getting restless now."

"There's lots of things to buy here! Pliers and wrenches and T-squares . . . There's a silent hammer."

"What?"

"A hammer that doesn't make a sound. You can pound in nails in the dead of night."

"Listen—" Macon said.

"There's a magnifying glass all cracked and broken, and

when you look at broken things through the lens you'd swear they'd turned whole again."

"Really, Muriel."

"I'm not Muriel! I'm Mitchell Mitten! Macon, don't you know Muriel can always take care of herself?" the puppet asked him. "Don't you know she could find another job tomorrow, if she wanted? So come inside! Come along! There's a pocketknife here with its own whetstone blade."

"Oh, for Lord's sake," Macon said.

But he gave a grudging little laugh.

And went on inside.

Over the next few days she kept bringing up France again and again. She sent him an anonymous letter pasted together from magazine print: *Don't FoRget tO BUY plANe Ticket for MuRiel.* (And the telltale magazine—with little blocks clipped out of its pages—still lay on the kitchen table.) She asked him to get her her keys from her purse and when he opened her purse he found photographs, two slick colored squares on thin paper showing Muriel's eyes at half mast. Passport photos, plainly. She must have meant for him to see them; she was watching him so intently. But all he did was drop her keys in her palm without comment.

He had to admire her. Had he ever known such a fighter? He went grocery shopping with her unusually late one evening, and just as they were crossing a shadowed area a boy stepped forth from a doorway. "Give over all what you have in your purse," he told Muriel. Macon was caught off guard; the boy was hardly more than a child. He froze, hugging the sack of groceries. But Muriel said, "The hell I will!" and swung her purse around by its strap and clipped the boy in the jaw. He lifted a hand to his face. "You get on home this instant or you'll be sorry you were ever born," Muriel told him. He slunk away, looking back at her with a puzzled expression.

When Macon had caught his breath again, he told Muriel

she was a fool. "He might have had a gun, for all you knew," he said. "Anything might have happened! Kids show less mercy than grown-ups; you can see that any day in the papers."

"Well, it turned out fine, didn't it?" Muriel asked. "What are you so mad at?"

He wasn't sure. He supposed he might be mad at himself. He had done nothing to protect her, nothing strong or chivalrous. He hadn't thought as fast as she had or thought at all, in fact. While Muriel . . . why, Muriel hadn't even seemed surprised. She might have strolled down that street expecting a neighbor here, a stray dog there, a holdup just beyond—all equally part of life. He felt awed by her, and diminished. Muriel just walked on, humming "Great Speckled Bird" as if nothing particular had happened.

"I don't think Alexander's getting a proper education," he said to her one evening.

"Oh, he's okay."

"I asked him to figure what change they'd give back when we bought the milk today, and he didn't have the faintest idea. He didn't even know he'd have to subtract."

"Well, he's only in second grade," Muriel said.

"I think he ought to switch to a private school."

"Private schools cost money."

"So? I'll pay."

She stopped flipping the bacon and looked over at him. "What are you saying?" she asked.

"Pardon?"

"What are you saying, Macon? Are you saying you're committed?"

Macon cleared his throat. He said, "Committed."

"Alexander's got ten more years of school ahead of him. Are you saying you'll be around for all ten years?"

"Um . . ."

594

"I can't just put him in a school and take him out again with every passing whim of yours."

He was silent.

"Just tell me this much," she said. "Do you picture us getting married sometime? I mean when your divorce comes through?"

He said, "Oh, well, marriage, Muriel . . ."

"You don't, do you. You don't know *what* you want. One minute you like me and the next you don't. One minute you're ashamed to be seen with me and the next you think I'm the best thing that ever happened to you."

He stared at her. He had never guessed that she read him so clearly.

"You think you can just drift along like this, day by day, no plans," she said. "Maybe tomorrow you'll be here, maybe you won't. Maybe you'll just go on back to Sarah. Oh yes! I saw you at Rose's wedding. Don't think I didn't see how you and Sarah looked at each other."

Macon said, "All I'm saying is—"

"All *I'm* saying," Muriel told him, "is take care what you promise my son. Don't go making him promises you don't intend to keep."

"But I just want him to learn to subtract!" he said.

She didn't answer, and so the last word rang in the air for moments afterward. Subtract. A flat, sharp, empty sound that dampened Macon's spirits.

At supper she was too quiet; even Alexander was quiet, and excused himself the minute he'd finished his BLT. Macon, though, hung around the kitchen. Muriel was running a sink-ful of water. He said, "Shall I dry?" Without any sort of warning, she whirled and flung a wet sponge in his face. Macon said, "Muriel?"

"Just get out!" she shouted, tears spiking her lashes, and she turned away again and plunged her hands into water so hot that it steamed. Macon retreated. He went into the living room where Alexander was watching TV, and Alexander moved over on the couch to give him space. He didn't say anything, but Macon could tell he'd heard from the way he tensed at each clatter in the kitchen. After a while the clatters died down. Macon and Alexander looked at each other. There was a silence; a single murmuring voice. Macon rose and returned to the kitchen, walking more quietly than usual and keeping a weather eye out, the way a cat creeps back after it's been dumped from someone's lap.

Muriel was talking on the phone with her mother. Her voice was gay and chirpy but just a shade thicker than usual, as if she were recovering from a cold. "So anyhow," she said, "I ask what kind of trouble her dog is giving her and the lady's like, 'Oh, no trouble,' so I ask her, 'Well, what's his problem, then?' and the lady's like, 'No real problem.' I say, 'Ma'am. You must have called me here for some reason.' She says, 'Oh. Well. That.' She says, 'Actually,' she says, 'I was wondering about when he makes.' I say, 'Makes?' She says, 'Yes, when he makes number one. He makes like little girl dogs do, he doesn't lift his leg.' I say to her, 'Now let me see if I've got this straight. You have called me here to teach your dog to lift his leg when he tinkles.' "

Her free hand kept flying out while she talked, as if she imagined her mother could see her. Macon came up behind her and put his arms around her, and she leaned back against him. "Oh, there's never a dull moment, I tell you," she said into the phone.

That night he dreamed he was traveling in a foreign country, only it seemed to be a medley of all the countries he'd ever been to and even some he hadn't. The sterile vast spaces of Charles de Gaulle airport chittered with those tiny birds he'd seen inside the terminal at Brussels; and when he stepped outdoors he was in Julian's green map of Hawaii with native dancers, oversized, swaying near the dots that marked various

596

tourist attractions. Meanwhile his own voice, neutral and monotonous, murmured steadily: *In Germany the commercial traveler must be punctual for all appointments, in Switzerland he should be five minutes early, in Italy delays of several hours are not uncommon . . .*

He woke. It was pitch dark, but through the open window he heard distant laughter, a strain of music, faint cheers as if some sort of game were going on. He squinted at the clock radio: three thirty. Who would be playing a game at this hour? And on this street—this worn, sad street where nothing went right for anyone, where the men had dead-end jobs or none at all and the women were running to fat and the children were turning out badly. But another cheer went up, and someone sang a line from a song. Macon found himself smiling. He turned toward Muriel and closed his eyes; he slept dreamlessly the rest of the night.

The mailman rang the doorbell and presented a long, tube-shaped package addressed to Macon. "What's this?" Macon asked. He returned to the living room, frowning down at the label. Muriel was reading a paperback book called *Beauty Tips from the Stars.* She glanced up and said, "Why not open it and find out."

"Oh? Is this some of your doing?"

She only turned a page.

Another plea for the France trip, he supposed. He pulled off the tape on one end and shook the package till a cylinder of glossy paper slid out. When he unrolled it, he found a full-color photo of two puppies in a basket, with DR. MACK'S PET-VITES above it and a calendar for January below it.

"I don't understand," he said to Muriel.

She turned another page.

"Why would you send me a calendar for a year that's half gone?"

"Maybe there's something written on it," she told him.

597

He flipped through February, March, April. Nothing there. May. Then June: a scribble of red ink across a Saturday. "*Wedding*," he read out. "Wedding? Whose wedding?"

"Ours?" she asked him.

"Oh, Muriel . . ."

"You'll be separated a year then, Macon. You'll be able to get your divorce."

"But, Muriel—"

"I always did want to have a June wedding."

"Muriel, please, I'm not ready for this! I don't think I ever will be. I mean I don't think marriage ought to be as common as it is; I really believe it ought to be the exception to the rule; oh, perfect couples could marry, maybe, but who's a perfect couple?"

"You and Sarah, I suppose," Muriel said.

The name brought Sarah's calm face, round as a daisy.

"No, no . . ." he said weakly.

"You're so selfish!" Muriel shouted. "You're so self-centered! You've got all these fancy reasons for never doing a single thing I want!"

Then she flung down her book and ran upstairs.

Macon heard the cautious, mouselike sounds of Alexander as he tiptoed around the kitchen fixing himself a snack.

Muriel's sister Claire arrived on the doorstep with a suitcase spilling clothes and her eyes pink with tears. "I'm never speaking to Ma again," she told them. She pushed past them into the house. "You want to know what happened? Well, I've been dating this guy, see: Claude McEwen. Only I didn't let on to Ma, you know how she's scared I'll turn out like Muriel did, and so last night when he came for me I jumped into his car and she happened to catch sight of me from the window, noticed he had a bumper sticker reading EDGEWOOD. That's because he used to go to a high school called Edgewood Prep in Delaware, but Ma thought it was Edgewood Arsenal and therefore he must be an Army man. So anyhow, this morning I get up and there she is fit to be tied, says, 'I know what you've been up to! Out all hours last night with the General!' and I say, 'Who? The what?' but there's never any stopping her once she gets started. She tells me I'm grounded for life and can't ever see the General again or she'll have him hauled up for court-martial and all his stars ripped off his uniform, so quick as a wink I pack up my clothes . . ."

Macon, listening absently while Edward sighed at his feet, had a sudden view of his life as rich and full and astonishing. He would have liked to show it off to someone. He wanted to sweep out an arm and say, "See?"

But the person he would have liked to show it to was Sarah.

Rose and Julian were back from their honeymoon; they were giving a family supper and Macon and Muriel were invited. Macon bought a bottle of very good wine as a hostess gift. He set the bottle on the counter, and Muriel came along and said, "What's this?"

"It's wine for Rose and Julian."

"Thirty-six dollars and ninety-nine cents!" she said, examining the sticker.

"Yes, well, it's French."

"I didn't know a wine *could* cost thirty-six ninety-nine."

"I figured since, you know, this'll be our first visit to their apartment . . ."

"You sure do think a lot of your family," Muriel said.

"Yes, of course."

"You never bought *me* any wine."

"I didn't know you wanted any; you told me it makes your teeth feel rough."

She didn't argue with that.

Later that day he happened to notice that the bottle had

599

been moved. And was opened. And was half emptied. The cork lay beside it, still impaled on the corkscrew. A cloudy little juice glass gave off the smell of grapes. Macon called, "Muriel?"

"What," she answered from the living room.

He went to the living room doorway. She was watching a ball game with Alexander. He said, "Muriel, have you been drinking that wine I bought?"

"Yes."

He said, "Why, Muriel?"

"Oh, I just had this irresistible urge to try it out," she said. Then she looked at him with slitted eyes, tilting her chin. He felt she was challenging him to take some action, but he said nothing. He picked up his car keys and went out to buy another bottle.

Macon felt shy about attending this dinner, as if Rose had turned into a stranger. He took longer than usual dressing, unable to decide between two shirts, and Muriel seemed to be having some trouble too. She kept putting on outfits and taking them off; brightly colored fabrics began to mount on the bed and on the floor all around it. "Oh, Lord, I wish I was just a totally nother person," she sighed. Macon, concentrating on tying his tie, said nothing. Her baby photo grinned out at him from the frame of the mirror. He happened to notice the date on the border: AUG 60. Nineteen sixty.

When Muriel was two years old, Macon and Sarah were already engaged to be married.

Downstairs, Dominick Saddler was sitting on the couch with Alexander. "Now this here is your paste wax," he was saying. He held up a can. "You never want to polish a car with anything but paste wax. And here we have a diaper. Diapers make real good rags because they don't shed hardly no lint. I generally buy a dozen at a time from Sears and Roebuck. And chamois skins: well, you know chamois skins. So what you do

600

is, you get yourself these here supplies and a case of good beer and a girl, and you head on out to Loch Raven. Then you park in the sun and you take off your shirt and you and the girl start to polishing. Ain't no sweeter way that I know of to use up a spring afternoon."

Dominick's version of a bedtime story, Macon supposed. He was baby-sitting tonight. (The Butler twins had dates, and Claire was out with the General. As everybody referred to him now.) In payment, Muriel's car would be Dominick's to use for a week; mere money would never have persuaded him. He slouched next to Alexander with the diaper spread over one knee, muscles bulging under a T-shirt that read WEEKEND WARRIOR. A Greek sailor cap was tipped back on his head with a Judas Priest button pinned above the visor. Alexander looked enthralled.

Muriel came tapping down the stairs; she arrived craning her neck to see if her slip showed. "Is this outfit okay?" she asked Macon.

"It's very nice," he said, which was true, although it was also totally unlike her. Evidently, she had decided to take Rose for her model. She had pulled her hair back in a low bun and she wore a slim gray dress with shoulder pads. Only her spike-heeled sandals seemed her own; probably she didn't possess any shoes so sensible as Rose's schoolgirl flats. "I want you to tell me if there's anything not right," she said to Macon. "Anything you think is tacky."

"Not a thing," Macon assured her.

She kissed Alexander, leaving a dark red mark on his cheek. She made one last survey in the mirror beside the front door, meanwhile calling, "Don't let him stay up too late, now, Dommie; don't let him watch anything scary on TV—"

Macon said, "*Muriel.*"

"I look like the wrath of God."

The Leary children had been raised to believe that when

an invitation involved a meal, the guests should arrive exactly on time. Never mind that they often caught their hostess in curlers; they went on doing what they were taught. So Macon pressed the buzzer in the lobby at precisely six twenty-seven, and Porter and Charles joined them in front of the elevator. They both told Muriel it was nice to see her. Then they rode upward in a gloomy silence, eyes fixed on the numbers over the door. Charles carried a potted jade tree, Porter another bottle of wine.

"Isn't this exciting?" Muriel said. "We're their first invited guests."

"At home now we'd be watching the CBS Evening News," Charles told her.

Muriel couldn't seem to think of any answer to that.

By six thirty sharp they were ringing the doorbell, standing in a hushed corridor carpeted in off-white. Rose opened the door and called, "They're here!" and set her face lightly against each of theirs. She wore Grandmother Leary's lace-trimmed company apron and she smelled of lavender soap, the same as always.

But there was a strip of peeling sunburn across the bridge of her nose.

Julian, natty and casual in a navy turtleneck and white slacks (when it wasn't yet Memorial Day), fixed the drinks while Rose retreated to the kitchen. This was one of those ultra-modern apartments where the rooms all swam into each other, so they could see her flitting back and forth. Julian passed around snapshots of Hawaii. Either he had used inferior film or else Hawaii was a very different place from Baltimore, because some of the colors were wrong. The trees appeared to be blue. In most of the photos Rose stood in front of flower beds or flowering shrubs, wearing a white sleeveless dress Macon had never seen before, hugging her arms and smiling too broadly so that she looked older than she was. "I tell Rose you'd think she went on our honeymoon by herself," Julian said. "I'm the one who took the pictures because Rose never did learn how to work my camera."

"She didn't?" Macon asked.

"It was one of those German models with all the buttons."

"She couldn't figure out the buttons?"

"I tell her, 'People will think I wasn't even there.'"

"Why, Rose could have taken that camera apart and put it together twice over," Macon said.

"No, this was one of those German models with—"

"It wasn't very logically constructed," Rose called from the kitchen.

"Ah," Macon said, sitting back.

She entered the room with a tray and placed it on the glass coffee table. Then she knelt and began to spread pâté on little crackers. There was some change in the way she moved, Macon noticed. She was more graceful, but also more self-conscious. She offered the pâté first to Muriel, then to each of her brothers, last to Julian. "In Hawaii I started learning to sail," she said. She pronounced the two *i*'s in "Hawaii" separately; Macon thought it sounded affected. "Now I'm going to practice out on the Bay."

"She's trying to find her sea legs," Julian said. "She tends to feel motion-sick."

Macon bit into his cracker. The pâté was something familiar. It was rough in texture but delicate in taste; there was a kind of melting flavor that he believed came from adding a great amount of butter. The recipe was Sarah's. He sat very still, not chewing. He was flooded by a subtle blend of tarragon and cream and home.

"Oh, I know just what you're going through," Muriel said to Rose. "All I have to do is look at a boat and I get nauseous."

Macon swallowed and gazed down at the carpet between his feet. He waited for someone to correct her, but nobody did. That was even worse.

.   .   .

603

In bed she said, "You wouldn't ever leave me, would you? Would you ever think of leaving me? You won't be like the others, will you? Will you promise not to leave me?"

"Yes, yes," he said, floating in and out of dreams.

"You do take me seriously, don't you? Don't you?"

"Oh, Muriel, for pity's sake . . ." he said.

But later, when she turned in her sleep and moved away from him, his feet followed hers of their own accord to the other side of the bed.

18

Macon was sitting in a hotel room in Winnipeg, Manitoba, when the phone rang. Actually it took him a second to realize it was the phone. He happened to be having a very good time with a mysterious object he'd just discovered —an ivory-painted metal cylinder affixed to the wall above the bed. He'd never noticed such a thing before, although he'd stayed in this hotel on two previous trips. When he touched the cylinder to see what it was, it rotated, disappearing into the wall, while from within the wall a light bulb swung out already lit. At the same moment, the phone rang. Macon experienced an instant of confusion during which he imagined it was the cylinder that was ringing. Then he saw the telephone on the nightstand. Still he was confused. No one had his number, so far as he knew.

He picked up the receiver and said, "Yes?"

"Macon."

His heart lurched. He said, "Sarah?"

"Have I caught you at a bad time?"

"No, no . . . How did you know where I was?"

"Well, Julian thought you'd be in either Toronto or Winnipeg by now," she said, "so I looked in your last guidebook, and I knew the hotels where you discussed night noises were the ones where you stayed yourself, so . . ."

"Is anything wrong?" he asked.

"No, I just needed a favor. Would it be all right with you if I moved back into our house?"

"Um—"

"Just as a place to stay," she said hastily. "Just for a little while. My lease runs out at the end of the month and I can't find a new apartment."

"But the house is a mess," he told her.

"Oh, I'll take care of that."

"No, I mean something happened to it over the winter, pipes burst or something, ceiling came down—"

"Yes, I know."

"You do?"

"Your brothers told me."

"My brothers?"

"I went to ask them your whereabouts when they wouldn't answer their phone. And Rose said she'd been over to the house herself and—"

"You went to Rose's, too?"

"No, Rose was at your brothers'."

"Oh."

"She's living there for a while."

"I see," he said. Then he said, "She's what?"

"Well, June has had her baby," Sarah said, "so she asked Porter to keep the children a while."

"But what does that have to do with Rose?" he said. "Does Rose imagine Porter can't open a tin of soup for them? And how come June sent them away?"

"Oh, you know June, she always was kind of a birdbrain."

She sounded like her old self, when she said that. Up till now there'd been something careful about her voice, something wary and ready to retreat, but now a certain chuckly,

606

confiding quality emerged. Macon leaned back against his pillow.

"She told the children she needs time to bond," Sarah said.

"Time to what?"

"She and her husband need to bond with the baby."

"Good grief," Macon said.

"When Rose heard that, she told Porter she was coming home. Anyhow she didn't think the boys were eating right, Porter and Charles; and also there's a crack in the side of the house and she wanted to get it patched before it spreads."

"What kind of crack?" Macon asked.

"Some little crack in the masonry; I don't know. When the rain comes from a certain direction water seeps in above the kitchen ceiling, Rose says, and Porter and Charles were planning to fix it but they couldn't agree on the best way to do it."

Macon slipped out of his shoes and hoisted his feet up onto the bed. He said, "So is Julian living alone now, or what?"

"Yes, but she brings him casseroles," Sarah said. Then she said, "Have you thought about it, Macon?"

His heart gave another lurch. He said, "Have I thought about what?"

"About my using the house."

"Oh. Well. It's fine with me, but I don't believe you realize the extent of the damage."

"But we'd have to fix that anyway, if we were to sell it. So here's what I was thinking: I could pay for the repairs myself —anything the insurance doesn't cover—with what I'd ordinarily use for rent. Does that seem fair to you?"

"Yes, of course," Macon said.

"And maybe I'll get someone to clean the upholstery," she said.

"Yes."

"And the rugs."

"Yes."

After all these years, he knew when she was leading up to

something. He recognized that distracted tone that meant she was bracing herself for what she really wanted to say.

"Incidentally," she said, "the papers came through from the lawyer."

"Ah."

"The final arrangements. You know. Things I have to sign."

"Yes."

"It was kind of a shock."

He said nothing.

"I mean of course I knew they were coming; it's been nearly a year; in fact he called ahead and told me they were coming, but when I saw them in black and white they just seemed so brisk. They didn't take into account the feelings of the thing. I guess I wasn't expecting that."

Macon had a sense of some danger approaching, something he couldn't handle. He said, "Ah! Yes! Certainly! That seems a natural reaction. So anyway, good luck with the house, Sarah."

He hung up quickly.

His seatmate on the flight to Edmonton was a woman who was scared of flying. He knew that before the plane had left the ground, before he'd looked in her direction. He was gazing out the window, keeping to himself as usual, and he heard her swallowing repeatedly. She kept tightening and releasing her grasp on the armrests and he could feel that, too. Finally he turned to see who this was. A pair of pouched eyes met his. A very old, baggy woman in a flowered dress was staring at him intently, had perhaps been willing him to turn. "Do you think this plane is safe," she said flatly, not exactly asking.

"It's perfectly safe," he told her.

"Then why have all these signs about. Oxygen. Life vests. Emergency exits. They're clearly expecting the worst."

"That's just federal regulations," Macon said.

Then he started thinking about the word "federal." In

608

Canada, would it apply? He frowned at the seat ahead of him, considering. Finally he said, "*Government* regulations." When he checked the old woman's expression to see if this made any better sense to her, he discovered that she must have been staring at him all this time. Her face lunged toward him, gray and desperate. He began to worry about her. "Would you like a glass of sherry?" he asked.

"They don't give us sherry till we're airborne. By then it's much too late."

"Just a minute," he said.

He bent to unzip his bag, and from his shaving kit he took a plastic travel flask. This was something he always packed, in case of sleepless nights. He had never used it, though—not because he'd never had a sleepless night but because he'd gone on saving it for some occasion even worse than whatever the current one was, something that never quite arrived. Like his other emergency supplies (the matchbook-sized sewing kit, the tiny white Lomotil tablet), this flask was being hoarded for the *real* emergency. In fact, its metal lid had grown rusty inside, as he discovered when he unscrewed it. "I'm afraid this may have . . . turned a bit, or whatever sherry does," he told the old woman. She didn't answer but continued staring into his eyes. He poured the sherry into the lid, which was meant to double as a cup. Meanwhile the plane gave a creak and started moving down the runway. The old woman drank off the sherry and handed him the cup. He understood that she was not returning it for good. He refilled it. She drank that more slowly and then let her head tip back against her seat.

"Better?" he asked her.

"My name is Mrs. Daniel Bunn," she told him.

He thought it was her way of saying she was herself again —her formal, dignified self. "How do you do," he said. "I'm Macon Leary."

"I know it's foolish, Mr. Leary," she said, "but a drink does give the illusion one is doing something to cope, does it not."

609

"Absolutely," Macon said.

He wasn't convinced, though, that she was coping all that well. As the plane gathered speed, her free hand tightened on the armrest. Her other hand—the one closest to him, clutching the cup—grew white around the nails. All at once the cup popped up in the air, squeezed out of her grip. Macon caught it nimbly and said, "Whoa there!" and screwed it onto the flask. Then he replaced the flask in his bag. "Once we're off the ground—" he said.

But a glance at her face stopped him. She was swallowing again. The plane was beginning to rise now—the nose was lifting off—and she was pressed back against her seat. She seemed flattened. "Mrs. Bunn?" Macon said. He was scared she was having a heart attack.

Instead of answering, she turned toward him and crumpled onto his shoulder. He put an arm around her. "Never mind," he said. "Goodness. You'll be all right. Never mind."

The plane continued slanting backward. When the landing gear retracted (groaning), Macon felt the shudder through Mrs. Bunn's body. Her hair smelled like freshly ironed tea cloths. Her back was large and boneless, a mounded shape like the back of a whale.

He was impressed that someone so old still wanted so fiercely to live.

Then the plane leveled off and she pulled herself together —straightening and drawing away from him, brushing at the teardrops that lay in the folds beneath her eyes. She was full of folds, wide and plain and sagging, but valiantly wore two pearl buttons in her long, spongy earlobes and maintained a coat of brave red lipstick on a mouth so wrinkled that it didn't even have a clear outline.

He asked, "Are you all right?"

"Yes, and I apologize a thousand times," she said. And she patted the brooch at her throat.

When the drink cart came he ordered her another sherry, which he insisted on paying for, and he ordered one for himself as well, even though he didn't plan to drink it. He thought it might be needed for Mrs. Bunn. He was right, as things turned out, because their flight was unusually rough. The seatbelt sign stayed lit the whole way, and the plane bounced and grated as if rolling over gravel. Every now and then it dropped sharply and Mrs. Bunn winced, but she went on taking tiny sips of sherry. "This is nothing," Macon told her. "I've been in much worse than this." He told her how to give with the bumps. "It's like traveling on a boat," he said. "Or on wheels, on roller skates. You keep your knees loose. You bend. Do you understand what I'm saying? You go along with it. You ride it out."

Mrs. Bunn said she'd certainly try.

Not only was the air unsteady, but also little things kept going wrong inside the plane. The drink cart raced away from the stewardess every time she let go of it. Mrs. Bunn's tray fell into her lap twice without warning. At each new mishap Macon laughed and said, "Ah, me," and shook his head. "Oh, not again," he said. Mrs. Bunn's eyes remained fixed on his face, as if Macon were her only hope. Once there was a bang and she jumped; the door to the cockpit had flung itself open for no good reason. "What? What?" she said, but Macon pointed out that now she could see for herself how unconcerned the pilot was. They were close enough to the front so she could even hear what the pilot was talking about; he was shouting some question to the copilot, asking why any ten-year-old girl with half a grain of sense would wear a metal nightbrace in a sauna room. "You call that a worried man?" Macon asked Mrs. Bunn. "You think a man about to bail out of his plane would be discussing orthodontia?"

"Bail out!" Mrs. Bunn said. "Oh, my, I never thought of that!"

Macon laughed again.

He was reminded of a trip he'd taken alone as a boy, touring colleges. Heady with his new independence, he had lied to the man sitting next to him and said he came from Kenya, where his father led safaris. In the same way he was lying now, presenting himself to Mrs. Bunn as this merry, tolerant person.

But after they had landed (with Mrs. Bunn hardly flinching, bolstered by all those sherries), and she had gone off with her grown daughter, a very small child ran headlong into Macon's kneecap. This child was followed by another and another, all more or less the same size—some kind of nursery school, Macon supposed, visiting the airport on a field trip—and each child, as if powerless to veer from the course the first had set, careened off Macon's knees and said, "Oops!" The call ran down the line like little bird cries—"Oops!" "Oops!" "Oops!"—while behind the children, a harassed-looking woman clapped a hand to her cheek. "Sorry," she said to Macon, and he said, "No harm done."

Only later, when he passed a mirror and noticed the grin on his face, did he realize that, in fact, he might not have been lying to Mrs. Bunn after all.

"The plumber says it won't be hard to fix," Sarah told him. "He says it *looks* bad but really just one pipe is cracked."

"Well, good," Macon said.

He was not as surprised this time by her call, of course, but he did feel there was something disconcerting about it—standing in an Edmonton hotel room on a weekday afternoon, listening to Sarah's voice at the other end of the line.

"I went over there this morning and straightened up a little," she said. "Everything's so disorganized."

"Disorganized?"

"Why are some of the sheets sewn in half? And the popcorn popper's in the bedroom. Were you eating popcorn in the bedroom?"

"I guess I must have been," he said.

He was near an open window, and he could look out upon a strangely beautiful landscape: an expanse of mathematical flatness, with straight-edged buildings rising in the distance like a child's toy blocks on a rug. It was difficult, in these surroundings, to remember why he'd had a popcorn popper in the bedroom.

"So how's the weather there?" Sarah asked.

"Kind of gray."

"Here it's sunny. Sunny and humid."

"Well, it's certainly not humid here," he told her. "The air's so dry that rain disappears before it hits the ground."

"Really? Then how can you tell it's raining?"

"You can see it above the plains," he said. "It looks like stripes that just fade away about halfway down from the sky."

"I wish I were there to watch it with you," Sarah said.

Macon swallowed.

Gazing out of the window, he all at once recalled Ethan as an infant. Ethan used to cry unless he was tightly wrapped in a blanket; the pediatrician had explained that new babies have a fear of flying apart. Macon had not been able to imagine that at the time, but now he had no trouble. He could picture himself separating, falling into pieces, his head floating away with terrifying swiftness in the eerie green air of Alberta.

In Vancouver she asked if the rain vanished there as well. "No," he said.

"No?"

"No, it rains in Vancouver."

It was raining this minute—a gentle night rain. He could hear it but not see it, except for the cone of illuminated drops spilling beneath a street lamp just outside his hotel room. You could almost suppose it was the lamp itself that was raining.

"Well, I've moved back into the house," she said. "Mostly I just stay upstairs. The cat and I: We camp in the bedroom. Creep downstairs for meals."

"What cat is that?" he asked.

"Helen."

"Oh, yes."

"I went and picked her up at Rose's. I needed company. You wouldn't believe how lonely it is."

Yes, he would believe it, he could have said. But didn't.

So here they were in their same old positions, he could have said: He had won her attention only by withdrawing. He wasn't surprised when she said, "Macon? Do you . . . What's her name? The person you live with?"

"Muriel," he said.

Which she knew before she asked, he suspected.

"Do you plan on staying with Muriel forever?"

"I really couldn't say," he said.

He was noticing how oddly the name hung in this starchy, old-fashioned hotel room. Muriel. Such a peculiar sound. So unfamiliar, suddenly.

On the flight back, his seatmate was an attractive young woman in a tailored suit. She spread the contents of her brief-case on her folding tray, and she riffled through computer printout sheets with her perfectly manicured hands. Then she asked Macon if he had a pen she might borrow. This struck him as amusing—her true colors shining out from beneath her businesslike exterior. However, his only pen was a fountain pen that he didn't like lending, so he said no. She seemed relieved; she cheerfully repacked all she'd taken from her briefcase. "I could have sworn I swiped a ballpoint from my last hotel," she said, "but maybe that was the one before this one; you know how they all run together in your mind."

"You must do a lot of traveling," Macon said politely.

"Do I! Some mornings when I wake up I have to check my hotel stationery just to find out what city I'm in."

"That's terrible."

"Oh, I like it," she said, bending to slip her briefcase under

614

her seat. "It's the only time I can relax anymore. When I come home I'm all nervous, can't sit still. I prefer to be a . . . moving target, you could say."

Macon thought of something he'd once read about heroin: how it's not a pleasure, really, but it so completely alters the users' body chemistry that they're forced to go on once they've started.

He turned down drinks and dinner, and so did his seat-mate; she rolled her suit jacket expertly into a pillow and went to sleep. Macon got out *Miss MacIntosh* and stared at a single page for a while. The top line began with *brows bristling, her hair streaked with white.* He studied the words so long that he almost wondered if they *were* words; the whole English language seemed chunky and brittle. "Ladies and gentlemen," the loudspeaker said, "we will be starting our descent . . ." and the word "descent" struck him as an invention, some new euphemism concocted by the airlines.

After they landed in Baltimore, he took a shuttle bus to the parking lot and retrieved his car. It was late evening here and the sky was pale and radiant above the city. As he drove he continued to see the words from *Miss MacIntosh.* He continued to hear the stewardess's gliding voice: *complimentary beverages* and *the captain has asked us* and *trays in an upright position.* He considered switching on the radio but he didn't know what station it was set to. Maybe it was Muriel's country music station. This possibility made him feel weary; he felt he wouldn't have the strength to press the buttons, and so he drove in silence.

He came to Singleton Street and flicked his signal on but didn't turn. After a while the signal clicked off on its own. He rode on through the city, up Charles Street, into his old neighborhood. He parked and cut the engine and sat looking at the house. The downstairs windows were dark. The upstairs windows were softly glowing. Evidently, he had come home.

19

Macon and Sarah needed to buy a new couch. They set aside a Saturday for it—actually just half a Saturday, because Sarah had a class to attend in the afternoon. At breakfast, she flipped through an interior decorating book so they could get a head start on their decision. "I'm beginning to think along the lines of something flowered," she told Macon. "We've never had a flowered couch before. Or would that be too frilly?"

"Well, I don't know. I wonder about winter," Macon said.

"Winter?"

"I mean right now in the middle of June a flowered couch looks fine, but it might seem out of place in December."

"So you prefer something in a solid," Sarah said.

"Well, I don't know."

"Or maybe stripes."

"I'm not sure."

"I know you don't like plaids."

"No."

"How do you feel about tweeds?"

"Tweeds," Macon said, considering.

Sarah handed over the book and started loading the dishwasher.

Macon studied pictures of angular modern couches, cozy chintz-covered couches, and period reproduction couches covered in complex fabrics. He took the book to the living room and squinted at the spot where the couch would be sitting. The old one, which had turned out to be too waterlogged to salvage, had been carted away, along with both armchairs. Now there was just a long blank wall, with the freshly plastered ceiling glaring above it. Macon observed that a room without furniture has a utilitarian feeling, as if it were merely a container. Or a vehicle. Yes, a vehicle: He had a sense of himself speeding through the universe as he stood there.

While Sarah got dressed, Macon took the dog out. It was a warm, golden morning. Neighbors were trimming their grass and weeding their flower beds. They nodded as Macon walked past. He had not been back long enough for them to feel at ease yet; there was something a little too formal about their greetings. Or maybe he was imagining that. He made an effort to remind them of how many years he had lived here: "I've always liked those tulips of yours!" and "Still got that nice hand mower, I see!" Edward marched beside him with a busybody waggle of his hind end.

In movies and such, people who made important changes in their lives accomplished them and were done with it. They walked out and never returned; or they married and lived happily ever after. In real life, things weren't so clean-cut. Macon, for instance, had had to go down to Muriel's and retrieve this dog, once he'd decided to move back home. He had had to collect his clothing and pack up his typewriter while Muriel watched in silence with her accusing, reproaching eyes. Then there were all kinds of other belongings that he discovered too late he'd forgotten—clothes that had been in the wash at the time, and his favorite dictionary, and the extra-large pottery mug he liked to drink his coffee from. But of course he couldn't go back for them. He had to abandon them —messy, trailing strings of himself cluttering his leavetaking.

By the time he and Edward returned from their outing, Sarah was waiting in the front yard. She wore a yellow dress that made her tan glow; she looked very pretty. "I was just wondering about the azaleas," she told Macon. "Weren't we supposed to feed them in the spring?"

"Well, probably," Macon said, "but they seem all right to me."

"In April, I think," she said. "Or maybe May. No one was here to do it."

Macon veered away from that. He preferred to pretend that their lives had been going on as usual. "Never mind, Rose has whole sacks of fertilizer," he said. "We'll pick up some from her while we're out."

"No one was here to seed the lawn, either."

"The lawn looks fine," he said, more forcefully than he'd meant to.

They shut Edward in the house and climbed into Macon's car. Sarah had brought along a newspaper because there were several furniture ads. "Modern Homewares," she read off. "But that's all the way down on Pratt Street."

"Might as well give it a try," Macon said. Pratt was one of the few streets he knew how to find.

After they left their neighborhood, with its trees arching overhead, the car grew hotter and Macon rolled his window down. Sarah lifted her face to the sunlight. "Be a good day to go to the pool," she said.

"Well, if we have time. I was thinking of asking you to lunch."

"Oh, where?"

"Anywhere you like. Your choice."

"Aren't you nice," she said.

618

Macon drove past two unshaven men talking on a corner. Sarah locked her door. Macon thought of what the men would be saying: "What's coming down, man?" "Not all that much."

The sidewalks grew more crowded. Women lugged string-handled shopping bags, an old man dragged a grocery cart, and a girl in a faded dress leaned her head against a bus stop sign.

At Modern Homewares, huge paper banners covered the plate glass windows. SPECIAL FOR FATHER'S DAY! they read. Sarah hadn't mentioned that this was a Father's Day sale. Macon made a point of mentioning it himself, to show it didn't bother him. Taking her arm as they entered, he said, "Isn't that typical. Father's Day! They'll capitalize on any-thing."

Sarah looked away from him and said, "All they seem to have is beds."

"I suppose it began with reclining chairs," Macon said. "A Barcalounger for Dad, and next thing you know it's a whole dinette set."

"Could we see your couches," Sarah told a salesman firmly.

The couches were all of the straight-backed, Danish sort, which was fine with Macon. He didn't really care. Sarah said, "What do you think? Legs? Or flush with the floor."

"It's all the same to me," he said. He sat down heavily on something covered in leather.

Sarah chose a long, low couch that opened into a queen-sized bed. "Macon? What do you say?" she asked. "Do you like what you're sitting on better?"

"No, no," he said.

"Well, what do you think of this one?"

"It's fine."

"Don't you have any opinion?"

"I just gave you my opinion, Sarah."

Sarah sighed and asked the salesman if he offered same-day delivery.

They'd been so efficient about picking out the couch that time remained for other errands as well. First they drove to Hutzler's and bought queen-sized sheets. Then they checked the furniture department for armchairs; there was a Father's Day sale there, too. "Maybe we're on a roll," Sarah told Macon. But they weren't as lucky with the armchairs; nothing looked just right. Not to Macon, at least. He gave up trying and stood watching a kiddie show on a row of television sets.

After Hutzler's they went to get fertilizer from Rose, but Macon braked on the way and said, "Wait! There's my bank." It had come upon him unexpectedly—the branch where he rented a safe deposit box. "I need my passport for the France trip," he told Sarah. "Might as well pick it up while I'm here."

Sarah said she'd just wait in the car.

He had to stand in line; two elderly women were ahead of him. They were checking out their jewels for Saturday night, he liked to imagine. Or clipping their coupons—whatever coupons were. While he stood there he kept feeling the presence of someone behind him. For some reason he didn't want to turn and find out who it was. He just kept staring ahead, every now and then glancing at his watch in a businesslike way. This person breathed very gently and smelled like flowers— bitter, real-life flowers, not the kind in perfume bottles. But when he finally squared his shoulders and looked around, he found only another stranger waiting for her jewels.

It wasn't true that Muriel had watched in silence as he packed. Actually, she had spoken. She had said, "Macon? Are you really doing this? Do you mean to tell me you can just use a person up and then move on? You think I'm some kind of . . . bottle of something you don't have any further need for? Is that how you see me, Macon?"

His turn for the vault had arrived, and he followed a girl in a miniskirt across a carpeted area, into the windowless cubicle lined with drawers. "I won't need to take my box to the other room," he told the girl. "I just want to get one thing."

She gave him his card to sign and accepted his key. After she had unlocked his box she stood back, scrutinizing her nails, while he rummaged through various papers for his passport. Then he turned to tell her he was finished, but all at once he was so moved by her tact in looking elsewhere, by the delicacy that people could come up with on their own (for surely it wouldn't have been written into the bank's instructions) . . . Well, he must be going soft in the head. It was the weather or something; it was the season or something; he had not been sleeping well. He said, "Thank you very much," and took back his key and left.

At his grandfather's house, Rose was out front pruning the hedge. Her gardening smock was an enormous gray workshirt inherited from Charles. When she saw their car pull up she straightened and waved. Then she went on pruning while they consulted her about fertilizers. "For azaleas and what else do you have, andromeda, acid-loving plants . . ." she mused.

Sarah said, "Where are the children today?"

"Children?"

"Your nephew and nieces."

"Oh, they went home to their mother."

Sarah said, "I just assumed, since you hadn't moved back with Julian . . ."

"Well, not yet, of course," Rose said.

Macon, anxious to guard her privacy, murmured, "No, of course not," practically at the same moment, but Sarah said, "Why? What's keeping you?"

"Oh, Sarah, you wouldn't believe what a state I found the boys in when I came back here," Rose said. "They were living in their pajamas so as not to have too much laundry. They were eating gorp for their suppers."

"I'm not even going to ask what gorp is," Sarah said.

"It's a mixture of wheat germ and nuts and dried—"

"But what about your apartment, Rose? What about Julian?"

"Oh, you know, I kept losing that apartment every time I turned around," Rose said vaguely. "I'd head one block east to the grocery store and then turn west to get back again and I'd always be wrong; always. The apartment building would have worked over to the east somehow; I don't know how."

There was a silence. Finally Macon said, "Well, if you could get us some of that fertilizer, Rose . . ."

"Certainly," she said. And she went off to the toolshed.

They had lunch at the Old Bay Restaurant—Sarah's idea. Macon said, "Are you sure?" and Sarah said, "Why wouldn't I be?"

"But you always tell me it's boring," Macon said.

"There are worse things than boring, I've decided."

He didn't think that was much of a recommendation, but he went along with it.

The restaurant was full, even though it was barely noon, and they had to wait a few minutes to be seated. Macon stood by the hostess's podium trying to adjust to the dimness. He surveyed the other diners and found something odd about them. They were not the usual Old Bay crowd—middle-aged, one face much like the next—but an assortment of particular and unusual individuals. He saw a priest offering a toast to a woman in a tennis dress, and a smartly suited woman with a young man in an orange gauze robe, and two cheerful school-girls loading all their potato chips onto the plate of a small boy. From where he stood Macon couldn't hear what any of these people were saying; he had to guess. "Maybe the woman wants to join a convent," he told Sarah, "and the priest is trying to discourage her."

"Pardon?"

"He's pointing out that sorting her husband's socks can be equally whatever-he'd-call-it, equally holy. And the young man in gauze, well . . ."

"The young man in gauze is Ashley Demming," Sarah said.

622

"You know Ashley. Peter and Lindy Demming's son. My, he's aged poor Lindy twenty years in the last six months, hasn't he? I don't think they're ever going to get over this."

"Ah, well," Macon said.

Then they were shown to a table.

Sarah ordered something called a White Lady and Macon ordered a sherry. With their meal they had a bottle of wine. Macon wasn't used to drinking in the daytime; he grew a little muzzy. So did Sarah, evidently, for she drifted off in the middle of a sentence about upholstery fabrics. She touched his hand, which was lying on the tablecloth. "We ought to do this more often," she said.

"Yes, we ought to."

"You know what I missed most when we were separated? The little, habitual things. The Saturday errands. Going to Eddie's for coffee beans. Even things that used to seem tiresome, like the way you'd take forever in the hardware store."

When he folded her hand into a fist it was round, like a bird. It had no sharp angles.

"I'm not sure if you know this," she said, "but for a while I was seeing another man."

"Well, fine; whatever; eat your salad," he told her.

"No, I want to say it, Macon. He was just getting over the death of his wife, and I was getting over things too so of course . . . Well, we started out very slowly, we started as friends, but then he began talking about getting married someday. After we'd given ourselves some time, he meant. In fact I think he really loved me. He took it hard when I told you'd moved back."

She looked straight at Macon when she said that, her eyes a sudden blue flash. He nodded.

"But there were these things I had trouble with," she said. "I mean good things; qualities I'd always wished for. He was a very dashing driver, for instance. Not unsafe; just dashing. At first, I liked that. Then bit by bit it began to feel wrong.

'Double-check your rearview mirror!' I wanted to tell him. 'Fasten your seatbelt! Inch past stop signs the way my husband does!' He never examined a restaurant bill before he paid it— shoot, he didn't even take his credit card receipt when he walked away from a table—and I thought of all the times I sat stewing while you totted up every little item. I thought, 'Why do I miss that? It's perverse!' "

Like "eck cetera," Macon thought.

Like Muriel saying, "eck cetera." And Macon wincing.

And the emptiness now, the thinness, when he heard it pronounced correctly.

He stroked the dimpled peaks that were Sarah's knuckles.

"Macon, I think that after a certain age people just don't have a choice," Sarah said. "You're who I'm with. It's too late for me to change. I've used up too much of my life now."

You mean to tell me you can just use a person up and then move on? Muriel had asked.

Evidently so, was the answer. For even if he had stayed with Muriel, then wouldn't Sarah have been left behind?

"After a certain age," he told Sarah, "it seems to me you can only choose what to lose."

"What?" she said.

"I mean there's going to be something you have to give up, whichever way you cut it."

"Well, of course," she said.

He supposed she'd always known that.

They finished their meal but they didn't order coffee because they were running late. Sarah had her class; she was studying with a sculptor on Saturdays. Macon called for the bill and paid it, self-consciously totaling it first. Then they stepped out into the sunshine. "What a pretty day," Sarah said. "It makes me want to play hooky."

"Why don't you?" Macon asked. If she didn't go to class, he wouldn't have to work on his guidebook.

But she said, "I can't disappoint Mr. Armistead."

624

They drove home, and she changed into a sweat suit and set off again. Macon carried in the fertilizer, which Rose had poured into a bucket. It was something shredded that had no smell—or only a harsh, chemical smell, nothing like the truckloads of manure the men used to bring for his grandmother's camellias. He set it on the pantry floor and then he took the dog out. Then he made himself a cup of coffee to clear his head. He drank it at the kitchen sink, staring into the yard. The cat rubbed against his ankles and purred. The clock over the stove ticked steadily. There was no other sound.

When the telephone rang, he was glad. He let it ring twice before he answered so as not to seem overeager. Then he picked up the receiver and said, "Hello?"

"Mr. Leary?"

"Yes!"

"This is Mrs. Morton calling, at Merkle Appliance Store. Are you aware that the maintenance policy on your hot water heater expires at the end of the month?"

"No, I hadn't realized," Macon said.

"You had a two-year policy at a cost of thirty-nine eighty-eight. Now to renew it for another two years the cost of course would be slightly higher since your hot water heater is older."

"Well, that makes sense," Macon said. "Gosh! How old *is* that thing by now?"

"Let's see. You purchased it three years ago this July."

"Well, I'd certainly like to keep the maintenance policy."

"Wonderful. I'll send you a new contract then, Mr. Leary, and thank you for—"

"And would that still include replacement of the tank?" Macon asked.

"Oh, yes. Every part is covered."

"And they'd still do the yearly checkups."

"Why, yes."

"I've always liked that. A lot of the other stores don't offer it; I remember from when I was shopping around."

"So I'll send you the contract, Mr.—"

"But I would have to arrange for the checkup myself, as I recall."

"Yes, the customer schedules the checkup."

"Maybe I'll just schedule it now. Could I do that?"

"That's a whole different department, Mr. Leary. I'll mail you out the contract and you can read all about it. Bye bye."

She hung up.

Macon hung up too.

He thought a while.

He had an urge to go on talking; anyone would do. But he couldn't think what number to dial. Finally he called the time lady. She answered before the first ring was completed. (*She* had no worries about seeming overeager.) "At the tone," she said, "the time will be one . . . forty-nine. And ten seconds." What a voice. So melodious, so well modulated. "At the tone the time will be one . . . forty-nine. And twenty seconds."

He listened for over a minute, and then the call was cut off. The line clicked and the dial tone started. This made him feel rebuffed, although he knew he was being foolish. He bent to pat the cat. The cat allowed it briefly before walking away.

There was nothing to do but sit down at his typewriter.

He was behind schedule with this guidebook. Next week he was supposed to start on France, and he still hadn't finished the conclusion to the Canada book. He blamed it on the season. Who could sit alone indoors when everything outside was blooming? *Travelers should be forewarned*, he typed, but then he fell to admiring a spray of white azaleas that trembled on the ledge of his open window. A bee crawled among the blossoms, buzzing. He hadn't known the bees were out yet. Did Muriel know? Would she recall what a single bee could do to Alexander?

. . . *should be forewarned*, he read over, but his concentration was shot now.

626

She was so careless, so unthinking; how could he have put up with her? That unsanitary habit she had of licking her finger before she turned a magazine page; her tendency to use the word "enormity" as if it referred to size. There wasn't a chance in this world that she'd remember about bee stings.

He reached for the phone on his desk and dialed her number. "Muriel?"

"What," she said flatly.

"This is Macon."

"Yes, I know."

He paused. He said, "Um, it's bee season, Muriel."

"So?"

"I wasn't sure you were aware. I mean summer just creeps up, *I* know how summer creeps up, and I was wondering if you'd thought about Alexander's shots."

"Don't you believe I can manage that much for myself?" she screeched.

"Oh. Well."

"What do you think I am, some sort of ninny? Don't you think I know the simplest dumbest thing?"

"Well, I wasn't sure, you see, that—"

"A fine one you are! Ditch that child without a word of farewell and then call me up on the telephone to see if I'm raising him right!"

"I just wanted to—"

"Criticize, criticize! Tell me Oodles of Noodles is not a balanced meal and then go off and desert him and then have the nerve to call me up and tell me I'm not a good mother!"

"No, wait, Muriel—"

"Dominick is dead," she said.

"What?"

"Not that you would care. He died."

Macon noticed how the sounds in the room had stopped. "Dominick Saddler?" he asked.

"It was his night to take my car and he went to a party in Cockeysville and coming home he crashed into a guardrail."

"Oh, no."

"The girl he had with him didn't get so much as a scratch."

"But Dominick . . ." Macon said, because he didn't believe it yet.

"But Dominick died instantly."

"Oh, my Lord."

He saw Dominick on the couch with Alexander, holding aloft a can of paste wax.

"Want to hear something awful? My car will be just fine," Muriel said. "Straighten the front end and it'll run good as ever."

Macon rested his head in his hand.

"I have to go now and sit with Mrs. Saddler in the funeral home," she said.

"Is there something I can do?"

"No," she said, and then, spitefully, "How could *you* be any help?"

"I could stay with Alexander, maybe."

"Alexander's got people of our own to stay with him," she said.

The doorbell rang, and Edward started barking. Macon heard him in the front hall.

"Well, I'll say good-bye now," Muriel said. "Sounds like you have company."

"Never mind that."

"I'll let you get back to your *life*," she said. "So long."

He kept the receiver to his ear a moment, but she had hung up.

He went out to the hall and tapped his foot at Edward. "Down!" he said. Edward lay down, the hump on his back still bristling. Macon opened the door and found a boy with a clipboard.

"Modern Homewares," the boy told him.

"Oh. The couch."

While the couch was being unloaded, Macon shut Edward in the kitchen. Then he returned to the hall and watched the couch lumbering toward him, borne by the first boy and another, just slightly older, who had an eagle tattooed on his forearm. Macon thought of Dominick Saddler's muscular, corded arms grappling beneath the hood of Muriel's car. The first boy spat as he approached the house, but Macon saw how young and benign his face was. "Aw, man," the second one said, stumbling over the doorstep.

Macon said, "That's all right," and gave them each a five-dollar bill when they'd placed the couch where he directed.

After they'd gone he sat down on the couch, which still had some sort of cellophane covering. He rubbed his hands on his knees. Edward barked in the kitchen. Helen padded in softly, stopped still, eyed the couch, and continued through the room with an offended air. Macon went on sitting.

When Ethan died, the police had asked Macon to identify the body. But Sarah, they suggested, might prefer to wait outside. Yes, Sarah had said; she would. She had taken a seat on a molded beige chair in the hallway. Then she'd looked up at Macon and said, "Can you do this?"

"Yes," he'd told her, evenly. He had felt he was barely breathing; he was keeping himself very level, with most of the air emptied out of his lungs.

He had followed a man into a room. It was not as bad as it could have been because someone had folded a wad of toweling under the back of Ethan's head to hide the damage. Also it wasn't Ethan. Not the real Ethan. Odd how clear it suddenly became, once a person had died, that the body was the very least of him. This was simply an untenanted shell, although it bore a distant resemblance to Ethan—the same groove down the upper lip, same cowlick over the forehead. Macon had a sensation like pressing against a blank wall, willing with all his being something that could never happen: *Please, please come back inside.* But finally he said, "Yes. That is my son."

He'd returned to Sarah and given her a nod. Sarah had risen and put her arms around him. Later, when they were alone in their motel, she'd asked him what he had seen. "Not really much of anything, sweetheart," he had told her. She kept at him. Was Ethan . . . well, hurt-looking? Scared? He said, "No, he was nothing." He said, "Let me get you some tea."

"I don't want tea, I want to hear!" she'd said. "What are you hiding?" He had the impression she was blaming him for something. Over the next few weeks it seemed she grew to hold him responsible, like a bearer of bad tidings—the only one who could say for a fact that Ethan had truly died. She made several references to Macon's chilliness, to his appalling calm that night in the hospital morgue. Twice she expressed some doubt as to whether, in fact, he was really capable of distinguishing Ethan from some similar boy. In fact, that may not have been Ethan at all. It may have been somebody else who had died. She should have ascertained for herself. She was the mother, after all; she knew her child far better; what did Macon know?

Macon said, "Sarah. Listen. I will tell you as much as I can. He was very pale and still. You wouldn't believe how still. He didn't have any expression. His eyes were closed. There was nothing bloody or gruesome, just a sense of . . . futility. I mean I wondered what the purpose had been. His arms were down by his sides and I thought about last spring when he started lifting weights. I thought, 'Is this what it comes to? Lift weights and take vitamins and build yourself up and then— nothing?' "

He hadn't been prepared for Sarah's response. "So what are you saying?" she asked him. "We die in the end, so why bother to live in the first place? Is that what you're saying?"

"No—" he said.

"It all comes down to a question of economy?" she asked.

"No, Sarah. Wait," he had said.

Thinking back on that conversation now, he began to believe that people could, in fact, be used up—could use each other up, could be of no further help to each other and maybe even do harm to each other. He began to think that who you are when you're with somebody may matter more than whether you love her.

Lord knows how long he sat there.

Edward had been barking in the kitchen all this time, but now he went into a frenzy. Somebody must have knocked. Macon rose and went to the front of the house, where he found Julian standing on the porch with a file folder. "Oh. It's you," Macon said.

"What's all that barking I hear?"

"Don't worry, he's shut in the kitchen. Come on in."

He held the screen door open and Julian stepped inside. "Thought I'd bring you the material for Paris," Julian said.

"I see," Macon said. But he suspected he was really here for some other reason. Probably hoping to hurry the Canada book. "Well, I was just this minute touching up my conclusion," he said, leading the way to the living room. And then, hastily, "Few details here and there I'm not entirely happy with; may be a little while yet . . ."

Julian didn't seem to be listening. He sat down on the cellophane that covered the couch. He tossed the folder aside and said, "Have you seen Rose lately?"

"Yes, we were over there just this morning."

"Do you think she's not coming back?"

Macon hadn't expected him to be so direct. In fact, Rose's situation had begun to look like one of those permanent irregularities that couples never refer to. "Oh, well," he told Julian, "you know how it is. She's worried about the boys. They're eating glop or something."

"Those are not boys, Macon. They're men in their forties."

Macon stroked his chin.

"I'm afraid she's left me," Julian said.

"Oh, now, you can't be sure of that."

"And not even for a decent reason!" Julian said. "Or for any reason. I mean our marriage was working out fine; that much I can swear to. But she'd worn herself a groove or something in that house of hers, and she couldn't help swerving back into it. At least, I can't think of any other explanation."

"Well, it sounds about right," Macon told him.

"I went to see her two days ago," Julian said, "but she was out. I was standing in the yard wondering where she'd got to when who should drive past but Rose in person, with her car stuffed full of old ladies. All the windows packed with these little old faces and feathered hats. I shouted after her, I said, 'Rose! Wait!' but she didn't hear me and she drove on by. Then just at the last minute she caught sight of me, I guess, and she turned and stared, and I got the funniest feeling, like the car was driving *her*—like she was just gliding past helpless and couldn't do a thing but send me one long look before she disappeared."

Macon said, "Why don't you give her a job, Julian."

"Job?"

"Why don't you show her that office of yours. That filing system you never get sorted, that secretary chewing her gum and forgetting whose appointment is when. Don't you think Rose could take all that in hand?"

"Well, sure, but—"

"Call her up and tell her your business is going to pieces. Ask if she could just come in and get things organized, get things under control. Put it that way. Use those words. *Get things under control*, tell her. Then sit back and wait."

Julian thought that over.

"But of course, what do I know," Macon said.

"No, you're right."

632

"Now let's see your folder."

"You're absolutely right," Julian said.

"Look at this!" Macon said. He held up the topmost letter. "Why do you bother me with this? *I just wanted to appraise you folks of a wonderful little hotel in . . .* A man who says he wants to 'appraise' us, do you really suppose he'd know a good hotel when he saw one?"

"Macon," Julian said.

"The whole damn language has been slaughtered," Macon said.

"Macon, I know you feel I'm crass and brash."

This took Macon a moment to answer, only partly because he first heard it as "crash and brass." "Oh," he said. "Why, no, Julian, not at—"

"But I just want to say this, Macon. I care about that sister of yours more than anything else in the world. It's not just Rose, it's the whole way she lives, that house and those turkey dinners and those evening card games. And I care about you, too, Macon. Why, you're my best friend! At least, I hope so."

"Oh, why, ah—" Macon said.

Julian rose and shook his hand, mangling all the bones inside, and clapped him on the shoulder and left.

Sarah came home at five thirty. She found Macon standing at the kitchen sink with yet another cup of coffee. "Did the couch get here?" she asked him.

"All safe and sound."

"Oh, good! Let's see it."

She went into the living room, leaving tracks of gray dust that Macon supposed was clay or granite. There was dust in her hair, even. She squinted at the couch and said, "What do you think?"

"Seems fine to me," he said.

"Honestly, Macon. I don't know what's come over you; you used to be downright finicky."

"It's fine, Sarah. It looks very nice."

She stripped off the cellophane and stood back, arms full of crackling light. "We ought to see how it opens out," she said.

While she was stuffing the cellophane into the wastebasket, Macon pulled at the canvas strap that turned the couch into a bed. It made him think of Muriel's house. The strap's familiar graininess reminded him of all the times Muriel's sister had slept over, and when the mattress slid forth he saw the gleam of Claire's tangled golden hair.

"Maybe we should put on the sheets, now that we've got it open," Sarah said. She brought the sack of linens from the front hall. With Macon positioned at the other side of the couch, she floated a sheet above the mattress and then bustled up and down, tucking it in. Macon helped, but he wasn't as fast as Sarah. The clay dust or whatever it was had worked itself into the seams of her knuckles, he saw. There was something appealing about her small, brown, creased hands against the white percale. He said, "Let's give the bed a trial run."

Sarah didn't understand at first. She looked up from unfolding the second sheet and said, "Trial run?"

But she allowed him to take the sheet away and slip her sweat shirt over her head.

Making love to Sarah was comfortable and soothing. After all their years together, her body was so well known to him that he couldn't always tell the difference between what he was feeling and what she was feeling. But wasn't it sad that they hadn't the slightest uneasiness about anyone's walking in on them? They were so alone. He nestled his face in her warm, dusty neck and wondered if she shared that feeling as well—if she sensed all the empty air in the house. But he would never ask.

While Sarah took a shower, he shaved. They were supposed to go to Bob and Sue Carney's for supper. When he came out of

634

the bathroom Sarah was standing in front of the bureau, screwing on little gold earrings. (She was the only woman Macon knew of who didn't have pierced ears.) He thought Renoir could have painted her: Sarah in her slip with her head cocked slightly, plump tanned arms upraised. "I'm really not in the mood to go out," she said.

"Me neither," Macon said, opening his closet door.

"I'd be just as content to stay home with a book."

He pulled a shirt off a hanger.

"Macon," she said.

"Hmm."

"You never asked me if I slept with anyone while we were separated."

Macon paused, halfway into one sleeve.

"Don't you want to know?" she asked him.

"No," he said.

He put on the shirt and buttoned the cuffs.

"I would think you'd wonder."

"Well, I don't," he said.

"The trouble with you is, Macon—"

It was astonishing, the instantaneous flare of anger he felt. "Sarah," he said, "don't even start. By God, if that doesn't sum up every single thing that's wrong with being married. 'The trouble with you is, Macon—' and, 'I know you better than you know yourself, Macon—' "

"The trouble with you is," she continued steadily, "you think people should stay in their own sealed packages. You don't believe in opening up. You don't believe in trading back and forth."

"I certainly don't," Macon said, buttoning his shirt front.

"You know what you remind me of? That telegram Harpo Marx sent his brothers: *No message. Harpo.*"

That made him grin. Sarah said, "You *would* think it was funny."

"Well? Isn't it?"

635

"It isn't at all! It's sad! It's infuriating! It would be infuriating to go to your door and sign for that telegram and tear it open and find no message!"

He took a tie from the rack in his closet.

"For your information," she said, "I didn't sleep with anyone the whole entire time."

He felt she'd won some kind of contest. He pretended he hadn't heard her.

Bob and Sue had invited just neighbors—the Bidwells and a new young couple Macon hadn't met before. Macon stuck mainly to the new couple because with them, he had no history. When they asked if he had children, he said, "No." He asked if they had any children.

"No," Brad Frederick said.

"Ah."

Brad's wife was in transit between girlhood and womanhood. She wore her stiff navy blue dress and large white shoes as if they belonged to her mother. Brad himself was still a boy. When they all went out back to watch the barbecue, Brad found a Frisbee in the bushes and flung it to little Delilah Carney. His white polo shirt pulled loose from his trousers. Dominick Saddler came to Macon's mind like a deep, hard punch. He remembered how, after his grandfather died, the sight of any old person could make his eyes fill with tears. Lord, if he wasn't careful he could end up feeling sorry for the whole human race. "Throw that thing here," he said briskly to Delilah, and he set aside his sherry and held out a hand for the Frisbee. Before long they had a real game going—all the guests joining in except Brad's wife, who was still too close to childhood to risk getting stuck there on a visit back.

At supper, Sue Carney seated Macon at her right. She put a hand on his and said it was wonderful that he and Sarah had worked things out. "Well, thank you," Macon said. "Gosh, you make a really good salad, Sue."

636

"We all have our ups and downs," she said. For a second, he thought she meant her salads weren't consistently successful. "I'll be honest," she told him, "there've been times when I have wondered if Bob and I would make it. There's times I feel we're just hanging in there, you know what I mean? Times I say, 'Hi, honey, how was your day?' but inside I'm feeling like a Gold Star mother."

Macon turned the stem of his glass and tried to think what step he'd missed in her logic.

"Like someone who's suffered a loss in a war," she said, "and then forever afterward she has to go on supporting the war; she has to support it louder than anyone else, because otherwise she'd be admitting the loss was for no purpose."

"Um . . ."

"But that's just a passing mood," she said.

"Well, naturally," Macon said.

He and Sarah walked home through air as heavy as water. It was eleven o'clock and the teenagers who had eleven o'clock curfews were just returning. These were the youngest ones, most of them too young to drive, and so they were chauffeured by grown-ups. They jumped out of cars shouting, "See you! Thanks! Call me tomorrow, hear?" Keys jingled. Front doors blinked open and blinked shut again. The cars moved on.

Sarah's skirt had the same whispery sound as the Tuckers' lawn sprinkler, which was still revolving slowly in a patch of ivy.

When they reached the house, Macon let Edward out for one last run. He tried to get the cat to come in, but she stayed hunched on the kitchen window ledge glaring down at him, owlish and stubborn; so he let her be. He moved through the rooms turning off lights. By the time he came upstairs Sarah was already in bed, propped against the headboard with a glass of club soda. "Have some," she said, holding out the glass. But he said no, he was tired; and he undressed and slid under the covers.

The tinkling of Sarah's ice cubes took on some meaning in his mind. It seemed that with every tinkle, he fell deeper. Finally he opened a door and traveled down an aisle and stepped into the witness stand. They asked him the simplest of questions. "What color were the wheels?" "Who brought the bread?" "Were the shutters closed or open?" He honestly couldn't remember. He tried but he couldn't remember. They took him to the scene of the crime, a winding road like something in a fairy tale. "Tell us all you know," they said. He didn't know a thing. By now it was clear from their faces that he wasn't merely a witness; they suspected him. So he racked his brain, but still he came up empty. "You have to see my side of this!" he cried. "I put it all out of my mind; I worked to put it out! Now I can't bring it back."

"Not even to defend yourself?" they asked.

He opened his eyes. The room was dark, and Sarah breathed softly next to him. The clock radio said it was midnight. The midnight-curfew group was just returning. Hoots and laughter rang out, tires scraped a curb, and a fanbelt whinnied as someone struggled to park. Then gradually the neighborhood fell silent. It would stay that way, Macon knew, till time for the one-o'clock group. He would first hear faint strands of their music and then more laughter, car doors slamming, house doors slamming. Porch lights would switch off all along the street, gradually dimming the ceiling as he watched. In the end, he would be the only one left awake.

20

The plane to New York was a little bird of a thing, but the plane to Paris was a monster, more like a building. Inside, great crowds were cramming coats and bags into overhead compartments, stuffing suitcases under seats, arguing, calling for stewardesses. Babies were crying and mothers were snapping at children. Steerage could not have been worse than this, Macon felt.

He took his place next to a window and was joined almost immediately by an elderly couple speaking French. The man sat next to Macon and gave him a deep, unsmiling nod. Then he said something to his wife, who passed him a canvas bag. He unzipped it and sorted through its contents. Playing cards, an entire tin of Band-aids, a stapler, a hammer, a light bulb . . . Macon was fascinated. He kept sliding his eyes to the right to try and see more. When a wooden mousetrap tumbled out, he began to wonder if the man might be some sort of lunatic; but of course even a mousetrap could be explained, given a little thought. Yes, what he was witnessing, Macon decided, was just one answer to the traveler's eternal choice: Which was better? Take all you own, and struggle to carry it?

Or travel light, and spend half your trip combing the shops for what you've left behind? Either way had its drawbacks.

He glanced up the aisle, where more passengers were arriving. A Japanese man festooned with cameras, a nun, a young girl in braids. A woman with a little red vanity kit, her hair a dark tent, her face a thin triangle.

Muriel.

First he felt a kind of flush sweep through him—that flood of warmth that comes when someone familiar steps forth from a mass of strangers. And then: *Oh, my God*, he thought, and he actually looked around for some means of escape.

She walked toward him in a graceful, picky way, watching her feet, and then when she was next to him she raised her eyes and he saw that she'd known all along he was there. She wore a white suit that turned her into one of those black-white-and-red women he used to admire on movie screens as a child.

"I'm going to France," she told him.

"But you can't!" he said.

The French couple peered at him curiously, the wife sitting slightly forward so as to see him better.

More passengers arrived behind Muriel. They muttered and craned around her, trying to edge past. She stood in the aisle and said, "I'm going to walk along the Seine."

The wife made a little O with her mouth.

Then Muriel noticed the people behind her and moved on.

Macon wasn't even sure it was possible to walk along the Seine.

As soon as the aisle was cleared he half stood and peered over the back of his seat, but she had vanished. The French couple turned to him, eyes expectant. Macon settled down again.

Sarah would find out about this. She would just somehow know. She had always said he had no feelings and this would confirm it—that he could tell her good-bye so fondly and then fly off to Paris with Muriel.

Well, it was none of his doing and he'd be damned if he'd assume the blame.

By the time it was dark they were airborne, and some kind of order had emerged inside the plane. It was one of those flights as fully programmed as a day in kindergarten. Safety film, drinks, headphones, dinner, movie. Macon turned down all he was offered and studied Julian's file folder instead. Most of the material was ridiculous. Sam'n'Joe's Hotel, indeed! He wondered if Julian had made it up to tease him.

A woman passed wearing white and he glanced at her surreptitiously, but it was no one he knew.

Just before the end of the movie, he got out his shaving kit and went to use one of the lavatories near the rear. Unfortunately other people had had the same idea. Both doors were locked, and he was forced to wait in the aisle. He felt someone arrive at his side. He looked and there was Muriel.

He said, "Muriel, what in—"

"You don't own this plane!" she told him.

Heads turned.

"And you don't own Paris, either," she said.

She was standing very close to him, face to face. She gave off a scent that barely eluded him; it was not just her perfume, no, but her house; yes, that was it—the smell inside her closet, the tantalizing, unsettling smell of other people's belongings. Macon pressed his left temple. He said, "I don't understand any of this. I don't see how you knew which flight to take, even."

"I called your travel agent."

"Becky? You called Becky? What must she have thought?"

"She thought I was your editorial assistant."

"And how could you afford the fare?"

"Oh, some I borrowed from Bernice and then some from

my sister, she had this money she earned at . . . and I did everything economy-style, I took a train to New York instead of a plane—"

"Well, *that* wasn't smart," Macon said. "It probably cost you the same, in the long run, or maybe even more."

"No, what I did was—"

"But the point is, why, Muriel? Why are you doing this?"

She lifted her chin. (Her chin could get so sharp, sometimes.) "Because I felt like it," she said.

"You felt like spending five days alone in a Paris hotel? That's what it will be, Muriel."

"You need to have me around," she said.

"Need you!"

"You were falling to pieces before you had me."

A latch clicked and a man stepped out of one of the lavatories. Macon stepped inside and locked the door quickly behind him.

He wished he could just vanish. If there had been a window, he believed he would have pried it open and jumped— not because he wanted to commit any act so definite as suicide but because he wanted to erase it all; oh, Lord, just go back and erase all the untidy, unthinking things he'd been responsible for in his life.

If she had read even a one of his guidebooks, she'd have known not to travel in white.

When he emerged, she was gone. He went back to his seat. The French couple drew in their knees to let him slide past; they were transfixed by the movie screen, where a blonde wearing nothing but a bath towel was pounding on a front door. Macon got out *Miss MacIntosh* just for something to pin his mind to. It didn't work, though. Words flowed across his vision in a thin, transparent stream, meaningless. He was conscious only of Muriel somewhere behind him. He felt wired to her. He caught himself wondering what she made of this—the darkened plane, the invisible ocean beneath her, the murmur of half-real voices all around her. When he turned off his reading light and shut his eyes, he imagined he could sense that she was still awake. It was a feeling in the air—something alert, tense, almost vibrating.

By morning he was resolved. He used a different lavatory, toward the front. For once he was glad to be in such a large crowd. When they landed he was almost the first one off, and he cleared Immigration quickly and darted through the airport. The airport was Charles de Gaulle, with its space-age pods of seats. Muriel would be thoroughly lost. He exchanged his money in haste. Muriel must still be at Baggage Claims. He knew she would carry lots of baggage.

There was no question of waiting for a bus. He hailed a cab and sped off, feeling wonderfully lightweight all of a sudden. The tangle of silvery highways struck him as actually pleasant. The city of Paris, when he entered, was as wide and pale and luminous as a cool gray stare, and he admired the haze that hung over it. His cab raced down misty boulevards, turned onto a cobbled street, lurched to a stop. Macon sifted through his envelopes of money.

Not till he was entering his hotel did he recall that his travel agent knew exactly where he was staying.

It wasn't a very luxurious hotel—a small brown place where mechanical things tended to go wrong, as Macon had discovered on past visits. This time, according to a sign in the lobby, one of the two elevators was not marching. The bellman led him into the other, then up to the third floor and down a carpeted corridor. He flung open a door, loudly exclaiming in French as if overcome by such magnificence. (A bed, a bureau, a chair, an antique TV.) Macon burrowed into one of his envelopes. "Thank you," he said, offering his tip.

Once he was alone, he unpacked and he hung up his suit

coat. Then he went to the window. He stood looking out over the rooftops; the dust on the glass made them seem removed in time, part of some other age.

How would she manage alone in such an unaccustomed place?

He thought of the way she navigated a row of thrift shops —the way she cruised a street, deft and purposeful, greeting passersby by name. And the errands she took the neighbors on: chauffeuring Mr. Manion to the reflexologist who dissolved his kidney stones by massaging his toes; Mr. Runkle to the astrologer who told him when he'd win the million-dollar lottery; Mrs. Carpaccio to a certain tiny grocery near Johns Hopkins where the sausages hung from the ceiling like strips of flypaper. The places Muriel knew!

But she didn't know Paris. And she was entirely on her own. She didn't even have a credit card, probably carried very little money, might not have known to change what she did carry into francs. Might be wandering helpless, penniless, unable to speak a word of the language.

By the time he heard her knock, he was so relieved that he rushed to open the door.

"Your room is bigger than mine is," she said. She walked past him to the window. "I have a better view, though. Just think, we're really in Paris! The bus driver said it might rain but I told him I didn't care. Rain or shine, it's Paris."

"How did you know what bus to take?" he asked her.

"I brought along your guidebook."

She patted her pocket.

"Want to go to Chez Billy for breakfast?" she asked. "That's what your book recommends."

"No, I don't. I can't," he said. "You'd better leave, Muriel."

"Oh. Okay," she said. She left.

Sometimes she would do that. She'd press in till he felt trapped, then suddenly draw back. It was like a tug of war

644

where the other person all at once drops the rope, Macon thought. You fall flat on the ground; you're so unprepared. You're so empty-feeling.

He decided to call Sarah. At home it was barely dawn, but it seemed important to get in touch with her. He went over to the phone on the bureau and picked up the receiver. It was dead. He pressed the button a few times. Typical. He dropped his key in his pocket and went down to the lobby.

The lobby telephone was housed in an ancient wooden booth, very genteel. There was a red leather bench to sit on. Macon hunched over and listened to the ringing at the other end, far away. "Hello?" Sarah said.

"Sarah?"

"Who is this?"

"It's Macon."

"Macon?"

She took a moment to absorb that. "Macon, where are you?" she asked. "What's the matter?"

"Nothing's the matter. I just felt like talking to you."

"What? What time is it?"

"I know it's early and I'm sorry I woke you but I wanted to hear your voice."

"There's some kind of static on the line," she said.

"It's clear at this end."

"You sound so thin."

"That's because it's an overseas call," he said. "How's the weather there?"

"How's who?"

"The weather! Is it sunny?"

"I don't know. All the shades are down. I don't think it's even light yet."

"Will you be gardening today?"

"What?"

"Gardening!"

645

"Well, I hadn't thought. It depends on whether it's sunny, I guess."

"I wish I were there," he said. "I could help you."

"You hate to garden!"

"Yes, but . . ."

"Macon, are you all right?"

"Yes, I'm fine," he said.

"How was the flight over?"

"Oh, the flight, well, goodness! Well, I don't know; I guess I was so busy reading I didn't really notice," he said.

"Reading?" she said. Then she said, "Maybe you've got jet lag."

"Yes, maybe I do," he told her.

Fried eggs, scrambled eggs, poached eggs, omelets. He walked blindly down the sidewalk, scribbling in the margins of his guidebook. He did not go near Chez Billy. *It's puzzling*, he wrote, *how the French are so tender in preparing their food but so rough in serving it*. In the window of a restaurant, a black cat closed her eyes at him. She seemed to be gloating. She was so much at home, so sure of her place.

Displays of crushed velvet, scattered with solid gold chains and watches no thicker than poker chips. Women dressed as if for the stage: elaborate hairdos, brilliant makeup, strangely shaped trousers that had nothing to do with the human anatomy. Old ladies in little-girl ruffles and white tights and Mary Janes. Macon descended the steps to the Métro; he ostentatiously dropped his canceled ticket into a tiny receptacle marked PAPIERS. Then he turned to glare at all the others who flung their tickets on the floor, and as he turned he thought he saw Muriel, her white face glimmering in the crowd, but he must have been mistaken.

In the evening he returned to his hotel—footsore, leg muscles aching—and collapsed on his bed. Not two minutes later he heard a knock. He groaned and rose to open the door. Muriel stood there with her arms full of clothes. "Look," she said, pushing past him. "See what-all I bought." She dumped the clothes on the bed. She held them up one by one: a shiny black cape, a pair of brown jodhpurs, a bouffant red net evening dress sprinkled with different-sized disks of glass like the reflectors on bicycles. "Have you lost your senses?" Macon asked. "What must all this have cost?"

"Nothing! Or next to nothing," she said. "I found a place that's like the granddaddy of all garage sales. A whole city of garage sales! This French girl was telling me about it where I went to have my breakfast. I complimented her hat and she told me where she got it. I took a subway train to find it; your book's really helpful about the subways; and sure enough, there's everything there. Tools and gadgets too, Macon. Old car batteries, fuse boxes . . . and if you say something's too expensive, they'll bring the price down till it's cheap enough. I saw this leather coat I would have killed for but that never did get cheap enough; the man wanted thirty-five francs."

"Thirty-five francs!" Macon said. "I don't know how you could get any cheaper than that. Thirty-five francs is four dollars or so."

"Oh, really? I thought francs and dollars were about the same."

"Lord, no."

"Well, then these things were *super* bargains," Muriel said. "Maybe I'll try again tomorrow."

"But how will you get all this stuff on the plane?"

"Oh, I'll figure out some way. Now let me take it back to my room so we can go eat."

He stiffened. He said, "No, I can't."

"What harm would it do to eat supper with me, Macon? I'm someone from home! You've run into me in Paris! Can't we have a bite together?"

647

When she put it that way, it seemed so simple.

They went to the Burger King on the Champs-Elysées; Macon wanted to recheck the place anyhow. He ordered two "Woppaires." "Careful," he warned Muriel, "these are not the Whoppers you're used to. You'll want to scrape the extra pickle and onion off." But Muriel, after trying hers, said she liked it the way it was. She sat next to him on a hard little seat and licked her fingers. Her shoulder touched his. He was amazed, all at once, that she really was here.

"Who's looking after Alexander?" he asked her.

"Oh, different people."

"What different people? I hope you haven't just parked him, Muriel. You know how insecure a child that age can—"

"Relax. He's fine. Claire has him in the daytime and then Bernice comes in and cooks supper and any time Claire has a date with the General the twins will keep him or if the twins can't do it then the General says Alexander can . . . ."

Singleton Street rose up in front of Macon's eyes, all its color and confusion.

After supper Muriel suggested they take a walk, but Macon said he was tired. He was exhausted, in fact. They returned to their hotel. In the elevator Muriel asked, "Can I come to your room a while? My TV set only gets snow."

"We'd better say good night," he told her.

"Can't I just come in and keep you company?"

"No, Muriel."

"We wouldn't have to *do* anything," she said.

The elevator stopped at his floor. He said, "Muriel. Don't you understand my position? I've been married to her forever. Longer than you've been alive, almost. I can't change now. Don't you see?"

She just stood in her corner of the elevator with her eyes on his face. All her makeup had worn off and she looked young and sad and defenseless.

"Good night," he said.

He got out, and the elevator door slid shut.

He went to bed immediately but couldn't sleep after all, and ended up switching on the TV. They were showing an American western, dubbed. Rangy cowboys spoke a fluid, intricate French. Disaster followed disaster—tornadoes, Indians, droughts, stampedes. The hero stuck in there, though. Macon had long ago noticed that all adventure movies had the same moral: Perseverance pays. Just once he'd like to see a hero like himself—not a quitter, but a man who did face facts and give up gracefully when pushing onward was foolish.

He rose and switched the set off again. He tossed and turned a long time before he slept.

Large hotels, small hotels, dingy hotels with their wallpaper flaking, streamlined hotels with king-sized American beds and Formica-topped American bureaus. Dim café windows with the proprietors displayed like mannequins, clasping their hands behind their backs and rocking from heel to toe. *Don't fall for prix fixe. It's like a mother saying, "Eat, eat"—all those courses forced on you . . .*

In the late afternoon Macon headed wearily back to his own hotel. He was crossing the final intersection when he saw Muriel up ahead. Her arms were full of parcels, her hair was flying out, and her spike-heeled shoes were clipping along. "Muriel!" he called. She turned and he ran to catch up with her.

"Oh, Macon, I've had the nicest day," she said. "I met these people from Dijon and we ended up eating lunch together and they told me about . . . Here, can you take some of these? I think I overbought."

He accepted several of her parcels—crumpled, used-looking bags stuffed with fabrics. He helped her carry them into the hotel and up to her room, which seemed even smaller than it was because of the piles of clothing everywhere. She dumped her burdens on the bed and said, "Let me show you, now, where is it . . . ."

"What's this?" Macon asked. He was referring to an oddly shaped soft drink bottle on the bureau.

"Oh, I found that in the fridge," she said. "They have this little fridge in the bathroom, Macon, and it's just full of soft drinks, and wine and liquor too."

"Muriel, don't you know those cost an arm and a leg? They'll put it on your bill, don't you know that? Now, that fridge is called a mini-bar, and here's what you use it for: In the morning, when they wheel in the continental breakfast, they bring a pitcher of hot milk for some strange reason and you just take that pitcher and stick it in the mini-bar so later you can have a glass of milk. Otherwise, Lord knows how you'd get your calcium in this country. And don't eat the rolls; you know that, don't you? Don't start your day with carbohydrates, especially under the strain of travel. You're better off taking the trouble to go to some café for eggs."

"Eggs, ugh," Muriel said. She was stepping out of her skirt and trying on another—one she'd just bought, with long fringes at the hem. "I *like* the rolls," she said. "And I like the soft drinks, too."

"Well, I don't know how you can say that," he said. He picked up the bottle. "Just look at the brand name: Pschitt. If that's not the most suspicious-sounding . . . and there's another kind called Yukkie, Yukkery, something like that—"

"That's my favorite. I already finished those off," Muriel said. She was pinning her hair on top of her head. "Where we having dinner tonight?"

"Well, I don't know. I guess it's time to try someplace fancy."

"Oh, goody!"

650

He moved what appeared to be an antique satin bedjacket and sat down to watch her put her lipstick on.

They went to a restaurant lit with candles, although it wasn't quite dark yet, and were seated next to a tall, curtained window. The only other customers were American—four American business types, plainly enjoying themselves over four large platters of snails. (Sometimes Macon wondered if there really was any call for his books.)

"Now, what do I want?" Muriel said, studying the menu. "If I ask them what something is in English, do you think they'll be able to tell me?"

"Oh, you don't have to bother doing that," Macon said. "Just order Salade Niçoise."

"Order what?"

"I thought you said you'd read my guide! Salade Niçoise. It's the one safe dish. I've been all through France eating nothing but, day in and day out."

"Well, that sounds kind of monotonous," Muriel said.

"No, no. Some places put green beans in it, some don't. And at least it's low-cholesterol, which is more than you can say for—"

"I think I'll just ask the waiter," Muriel told him. She laid her menu aside. "Do you suppose they call them French windows in France?"

"What? I wouldn't have the slightest idea," he said. He looked toward the window, which was paned with deep, greenish glass. Outside, in an overgrown courtyard, a pitted stone cherub was cavorting in a fountain.

The waiter spoke more English than Macon had expected. He directed Muriel toward a cream of sorrel soup and a special kind of fish. Macon decided to go for the soup as well, rather than sit idle while Muriel had hers. "There," Muriel said. "Wasn't he nice?"

"That was a rare exception," Macon said.

She batted at the hem of her skirt. "Durn fringe! I keep thinking something's crawling up my leg," she said. "Where you going tomorrow, Macon?"

"Out of Paris altogether. Tomorrow I start on the other cities."

"You're leaving me here alone?"

"This is high-speed travel, Muriel. Not fun. I'm waking up at crack of dawn."

"Take me anyway."

"I can't."

"I haven't been sleeping so good," she said. "I get bad dreams."

"Well, then you certainly don't want to go gallivanting off to more new places."

"Last night I dreamed about Dominick," she said. She leaned toward him across the table, two spots of color high on her cheekbones. "I dreamed he was mad at me."

"Mad?"

"He wouldn't talk to me. Wouldn't look at me. Kept kicking something on the sidewalk. Turned out he was mad because I wouldn't let him use the car anymore. I said, 'Dommie, you're dead. You *can't* use the car. I'd let you if I could, believe me.'"

"Well, don't worry about it," Macon said. "It was just a travel dream."

"I'm scared it means he's mad for real. Off wherever he's at."

"He's not," Macon told her. "He wouldn't be mad."

"I'm scared he is."

"He's happy as a lark."

"You really think so?"

"Sure! He's up there in some kind of motor heaven, polishing a car all his own. And it's always spring and the sun is always shining and there's always some blonde in a halter top to help him with the buffing."

"You really think that might be true?" Muriel asked.

"Yes, I do," he said. And the funny thing was that he did, just at that moment. He had a vivid image of Dominick in a sunlit meadow, a chamois skin in his hand and a big, pleased, cocky grin on his face.

She said at the end of the evening that she wished he would come to her room—couldn't he? to guard against bad dreams? —and he said no and told her good night. And then he felt how she drew at him, pulling deep strings from inside him, when the elevator creaked away with her.

In his sleep he conceived a plan to take her along tomorrow. What harm would it do? It was only a day trip. Over and over in his scattered, fitful sleep he picked up his phone and dialed her room. It was a surprise, when he woke in the morning, to find he hadn't invited her yet.

He sat up and reached for the phone and remembered only then—with the numb receiver pressed to his ear—that the phone was out of order and he'd forgotten to report it. He wondered if it were something he could repair himself, a cord unplugged or something. He rose and peered behind the bureau. He stooped to hunt for a jack of some kind.

And his back went out.

No doubt about it—that little twang! in a muscle to the left of his spine. The pain was so sharp it snagged his breath. Then it faded. Maybe it was gone for good. He straightened, a minimal movement. But it was enough to bring the pain zinging in again.

He lowered himself to the bed inch by inch. The hard part was getting his feet up, but he set his face and accomplished that too. Then he lay pondering what to do next.

Once he had had this happen and the pain had vanished

in five minutes and not returned it. It had been only a freaky thing like a foot cramp.

But then, once he'd stayed flat in bed for two weeks and crept around like a very old man for another month after that.

He lay rearranging his agenda in his mind. If he canceled one trip, postponed another . . . Yes, possibly what he'd planned for the next three days could be squeezed into two instead, if only he were able to get around by tomorrow.

He must have gone back to sleep. He didn't know for how long. He woke to a knock and thought it was breakfast, though he'd left instructions for none to be brought today. But then he heard Muriel. "Macon? You in there?" She was hoping he hadn't left Paris yet; she was here to beg again to go with him. He knew that as clearly as if she'd announced it. He was grateful now for the spasm that gripped him as he turned away from her voice. Somehow that short sleep had cleared his head, and he saw that he'd come perilously close to falling in with her again. *Falling in*: That was the way he put it to himself. What luck that his back had stopped him. Another minute—another few seconds—and he might have been lost.

He dropped into sleep so suddenly that he didn't even hear her walk away.

When he woke again it was much later, he felt, although he didn't want to go through the contortions necessary to look at his watch. A wheeled cart was passing his room and he heard voices—hotel employees, probably—laughing in the corridor. They must be so comfortable here; they must all know each other so well. There was a knock on his door, then a jingle of keys. A small, pale chambermaid poked her face in and said, "*Pardon, monsieur.*" She started to retreat but then stopped and asked him something in French, and he gestured toward his back and winced. "Ah," she said, entering, and she said something else very rapidly. (She would be telling him about *her* back.) He said, "If you could just help me up, please," for he had decided he had no choice but to go call Julian. She seemed to understand what he meant and came over to the bed. He turned onto his stomach and then struggled up on one arm—the only way he could manage to rise without excruciating pain. The chambermaid took his other arm and braced herself beneath his weight as he stood. She was much shorter than he, and pretty in a fragile, meek way. He was conscious of his unshaven face and his rumpled pajamas. "My jacket," he told her, and they proceeded haltingly to the chair where his suit jacket hung. She draped it around his shoulders. Then he said, "Downstairs? To the telephone?" She looked over at the phone on the bureau, but he made a negative movement with the flat of his hand—a gesture that cost him. He grimaced. She clucked her tongue and led him out into the corridor.

Walking was not particularly difficult; he felt hardly a twinge. But the elevator jerked agonizingly and there was no way he could predict it. The chambermaid uttered soft sounds of sympathy. When they arrived in the lobby she led him to the telephone booth and started to seat him, but he said, "No, no, standing's easier. Thanks." She backed out and left him there. He saw her talking to the clerk at the desk, shaking her head in pity; the clerk shook his head, too.

Macon worried Julian wouldn't be in his office yet, and he didn't know his home number. But the phone was answered on the very first ring. "Businessman's Press." A woman's voice, confusingly familiar, threading beneath the hiss of long distance.

"Um—" he said. "This is Macon Leary. To whom am I—"

"Oh, Macon."

"Rose?"

"Yes, it's me."

"What are *you* doing there?"

"I work here now."

"Oh, I see."

"I'm putting things in order. You wouldn't believe the state this place is in."

"Rose, my back has gone out on me," Macon said.

"Oh, no, of all times! Are you still in Paris?"

"Yes, but I was just about to start my day trips and there are all these plans I have to change—appointments, travel reservations—and no telephone in my room. So I was wondering if Julian could do it from his end. Maybe he could get the reservations from Becky and—"

"I'll take care of it myself," Rose said. "Don't you bother with a thing."

"I don't know when I'm going to get to the other cities, tell him. I don't have any idea when I'll be—"

"We'll work it out. Have you seen a doctor?"

"Doctors don't help. Just bed rest."

"Well, rest then, Macon."

He gave her the name of his hotel, and she repeated it briskly and then told him to get on back to bed.

When he emerged from the phone booth the chambermaid had a bellboy there to help him, and between the two of them he made it to his room without much trouble. They were very solicitous. They seemed anxious about leaving him alone, but he assured them he would be all right.

All that afternoon he lay in bed, rising twice to go to the bathroom and once to get some milk from the mini-bar. He wasn't really hungry. He watched the brown flowers on the wallpaper; he thought he had never known a hotel room so intimately. The side of the bureau next to the bed had a streak in the woodgrain that looked like a bony man in a hat.

At suppertime he took a small bottle of wine from the mini-bar and inched himself into the armchair to drink it. Even the motion of raising the bottle to his lips caused him pain, but he thought the wine would help him sleep. While he was sitting there the chambermaid knocked and let herself in. She asked him, evidently, whether he wanted anything to eat, but he thanked her and said no. She must have been on her way home; she carried a battered little pocketbook.

Later there was another knock, after he had dragged himself back to bed, and Muriel said, "Macon? Macon?" He kept absolutely silent. She went away.

The air grew fuzzy and then dark. The man on the side of the bureau faded. Footsteps crossed the floor above him.

He had often wondered how many people died in hotels. The law of averages said some would, right? And some who had no close relatives—say one of his readers, a salesman without a family—well, what was done about such people? Was there some kind of potters' field for unknown travelers?

He could lie in only two positions—on his left side or on his back—and switching from one to the other meant waking up, consciously deciding to undertake the ordeal, plotting his strategy. Then he returned to a fretful semiconsciousness.

He dreamed he was seated on an airplane next to a woman dressed all in gray, a very narrow, starched, thin-lipped woman, and he tried to hold perfectly still because he sensed she disapproved of movement. It was a rule of hers; he knew that somehow. But he grew more and more uncomfortable, and so he decided to confront her. He said, "Ma'am?" She turned her eyes on him, mild, mournful eyes under finely arched brows. "Miss MacIntosh!" he said. He woke in a spasm of pain. He felt as if a tiny, cruel hand had snatched up part of his back and wrung it out.

When the waiter brought his breakfast in the morning, the chambermaid came along. She must keep grueling hours, Macon thought. But he was glad to see her. She and the waiter fussed over him, mixing his hot milk and coffee, and the waiter helped him into the bathroom while the chambermaid changed his sheets. He thanked them over and over; "*Merci*," he said, clumsily. He wished he knew the French for, "I don't know why you're being so kind." After they left he ate all of his rolls, which the chambermaid had thoughtfully buttered and spread with strawberry jam. Then he turned on the TV for company and got back in bed.

He was sorry about the TV when he heard the knock on the door, because he thought it was Muriel and she would hear. But it seemed early for Muriel to be awake. And then a key turned in the lock, and in walked Sarah.

He said, "Sarah?"

She wore a beige suit, and she carried two pieces of matched luggage, and she brought a kind of breeze of efficiency with her. "Now, everything's taken care of," she told him. "I'm going to make your day trips for you." She set down her suitcases, kissed his forehead, and picked up a glass from his breakfast table. As she went off to the bathroom she said, "We've rescheduled the other cities and I start on them tomorrow."

"But how did you get here so soon?" he asked.

She came out of the bathroom; the glass was full of water. "You have Rose to thank for that," she said, switching off the TV. "Rose is just a wizard. She's revamped that entire office. Here's a pill from Dr. Levitt."

"You know I don't take pills," he said.

"This time you do," she told him. She helped him rise up on one elbow. "You're going to sleep as much as you can, so your back has a chance to heal. Swallow."

The pill was tiny and very bitter. He could taste it even after he'd lain down again.

"Is the pain bad?" she asked him.

"Kind of."

"How've you been getting your meals?"

"Well, breakfast comes anyway, of course. That's about it."

"I'll ask about room service," she told him, picking up the phone. "Since I'll be gone so . . . What's the matter with the telephone?"

658

"It's dead."

"I'll go tell the desk. Can I bring you anything while I'm out?"

"No, thank you."

When she left, he almost wondered if he'd imagined her. Except that her suitcases sat next to his bed, sleek and creamy —the same ones she kept on the closet shelf at home.

He thought about Muriel, about what would happen if she were to knock now. Then he thought about two nights ago, or was it three, when she had strolled in with all her purchases. He wondered if she'd left any traces. A belt lost under the bed, a glass disk fallen off her cocktail dress? He began to worry about it seriously. It seemed to him almost inevitable; of course she'd left something. The only question was, what. And where.

Groaning, he rolled over and pushed himself upright. He struggled off the bed and then sagged to his knees to peer beneath it. There didn't seem to be anything there. He got to his feet and tilted over the armchair to feel around the edges of the cushion. Nothing there either. Actually she hadn't gone anywhere near the armchair, to his recollection; nor had she gone to the bureau, but even so he slid out the drawers one by one to make sure. His own belongings—just a handful— occupied one drawer. The others were empty, but the second one down had a sprinkling of pink face powder. It wasn't Muriel's, of course, but it looked like hers. He decided to get rid of it. He tottered into the bathroom, dampened a towel, and came back to swab the drawer clean. Then he saw that the towel had developed a large pink smear, as if a woman wearing too much makeup had wiped her face with it. He folded the towel so the smear was concealed and laid it in the back of the drawer. No, too incriminating. He took it out again and hid it beneath the armchair cushion. That didn't seem right either. Finally he went into the bathroom and washed the towel by hand, scrubbing it with a bar of soap till the spot was completely gone. The pain in his back was constant, and beads of sweat stood out on his forehead. At some point he decided he was acting very peculiar; in fact it must be the pill; and he dropped the wet towel in a heap on the floor and crawled back into bed. He fell asleep at once. It wasn't a normal sleep; it was a kind of burial.

He knew Sarah came in but he couldn't wake up to greet her. And he knew she left again. He heard someone knock, he heard lunch being brought, he heard the chambermaid whisper, "*Monsieur?*" He remained in his stupor. The pain was muffled but still present—just covered up, he thought; the pill worked like those inferior room sprays in advertisements, the ones that only mask offending odors. Then Sarah came back for the second time and he opened his eyes. She was standing over the bed with a glass of water. "How do you feel?" she asked him.

"Okay," he said.

"Here's your next pill."

"Sarah, those things are deadly."

"They help, don't they?"

"They knock me out," he said. But he took the pill.

She sat down on the edge of the mattress, careful not to jar him. She still wore her suit and looked freshly groomed, although she must be bushed by now. "Macon," she said quietly.

"Hmm."

"I saw that woman friend of yours."

He tensed. His back seized up.

"She saw me, too," she said. "She seemed very surprised."

"Sarah, this is not the way it looks," he told her.

"What is it then, Macon? I'd like to hear."

"She came over on her own. I didn't even know till just before the plane took off, I swear it! She followed me. I told her I didn't want her along. I told her it was no use."

She kept looking at him. "You didn't know till just before the plane took off," she said.

"I swear it," he said.

He wished he hadn't taken the pill. He felt he wasn't in full possession of his faculties.

"Do you believe me?" he asked her.

"Yes, I believe you," she said, and then she got up and started uncovering his lunch dishes.

He spent the afternoon in another stupor, but he was aware of the chambermaid's checking on him twice, and he was almost fully awake when Sarah came in with a bag of groceries. "I thought I'd make you supper myself," she told him. "Fresh fruit and things; you always complain you don't get enough fresh fruit when you travel."

"That's very nice of you, Sarah."

He worked himself around till he was half sitting, propped against a pillow. Sarah was unwrapping cheeses. "The phone's fixed," she said. "You'll be able to call for your meals and all while I'm out. Then I was thinking: After I've finished the trips, if your back is better, maybe we could do a little sightseeing on our own. Take some time for ourselves, since we're here. Visit a few museums and such."

"Fine," he said.

"Have a second honeymoon, sort of."

"Wonderful."

He watched her set the cheeses on a flattened paper bag. "We'll change your plane ticket for a later date," she said. "You're reserved to leave tomorrow morning; no chance you could manage that. I left my own ticket open-ended. Julian said I should. Did I tell you where Julian is living?"

"No, where?"

"He's moved in with Rose and your brothers."

"He's what?"

"I took Edward over to Rose's to stay while I was gone,

661

and there was Julian. He sleeps in Rose's bedroom; he's started playing Vaccination every night after supper."

"Well, I'll be damned," Macon said.

"Have some cheese."

He accepted a slice, changing position as little as possible.

"Funny, sometimes Rose reminds me of a flounder," Sarah said. "Not in looks, of course . . . She's lain on the ocean floor so long, one eye has moved to the other side of her head."

He stopped chewing and stared at her. She was pouring two glasses of cloudy brown liquid. "Apple cider," she told him. "I figured you shouldn't drink wine with those pills."

"Oh. Right," he said.

She passed him a glass. "A toast to our second honeymoon," she said.

"Our second honeymoon," he echoed.

"Twenty-one more years together."

"Twenty-one!" he said. It sounded like such a lot.

"Or would you say twenty."

"No, it's twenty-one, all right. We were married in nineteen—"

"I mean because we skipped this past year."

"Oh," he said. "No, it would still be twenty-one."

"You think so?"

"I consider last year just another stage in our marriage," he said. "Don't worry: It's twenty-one."

She clinked her glass against his.

Their main dish was a potted meat that she spread on French bread, and their dessert was fruit. She washed the fruit in the bathroom, returning with handfuls of peaches and strawberries; and meanwhile she kept up a cozy patter that made him feel he was home again. "Did I mention we had a letter from the Averys? They might be passing through Baltimore later this summer. Oh, and the termite man came."

"Ah."

"He couldn't find anything wrong, he said."

"Well, that's a relief."

"And I've almost finished my sculpture and Mr. Armistead says it's the best thing I've done."

"Good for you," Macon said.

"Oh," she said, folding the last paper bag, "I know you don't think my sculptures are important, but—"

"Who says I don't?" he asked.

"I know you think I'm just this middle-aged lady playing artist—"

"Who says?"

"Oh, I know what you think! You don't have to pretend with me."

Macon started to slump against his pillow, but was brought up short by a muscle spasm.

She cut a peach into sections, and then she sat on the bed and passed him one of the sections. She said, "Macon. Just tell me this. Was the little boy the attraction?"

"Huh?"

"Was the fact that she had a child what attracted you to that woman?"

He said, "Sarah, I swear to you, I had no idea she was planning to follow me over here."

"Yes, I realize that," she said, "but I was wondering about the child question."

"What child question?"

"I was remembering the time you said we should have another baby."

"Oh, well, that was just . . . I don't know what that was," he said. He handed her back the peach; he wasn't hungry anymore.

"I was thinking maybe you were right," Sarah said.

"What? No, Sarah; Lord, that was a terrible idea."

"Oh, I know it's scary," she told him. "I admit I'd be scared to have another."

"Exactly," Macon said. "We're too old."

"No, I'm talking about the, you know, world we'd be bringing him into. So much evil and danger. I admit it: I'd be frantic any time we let him out on the street."

Macon saw Singleton Street in his mind, small and distant like Julian's little green map of Hawaii and full of gaily drawn people scrubbing their stoops, tinkering with their cars, splashing under fire hydrants.

"Oh, well, you're right," he said. "Though really it's kind of . . . heartening, isn't it? How most human beings do try. How they try to be as responsible and kind as they can manage."

"Are you saying yes, we can have a baby?" Sarah asked.

Macon swallowed. He said, "Well, no. It seems to me we're past the time for that, Sarah."

"So," she said, "her little boy wasn't the reason."

"Look, it's over with. Can't we close the lid on it? I don't cross-examine *you*, do I?"

"But I don't have someone following me to Paris!" she said.

"And what if you did? Do you think I'd hold you to blame if someone just climbed on a plane without your knowing?"

"Before it left the ground," she said.

"Pardon? Well, I should hope so!"

"Before it left the ground, you saw her. You could have walked up to her and said, 'No. Get off. Go this minute. I want nothing more to do with you and I never want to see you again.' "

"You think I own the airline, Sarah?"

"You could have stopped her if you'd really wanted," Sarah said. "You could have taken steps."

And then she rose and began to clear away their supper.

She gave him his next pill, but he let it stay in his fist a while because he didn't want to risk moving. He lay with his eyes closed, listening to Sarah undress. She ran water in the bathroom, slipped the chain on the door, turned off the lights. When she got into bed it stabbed his back, even though she settled carefully, but he gave no sign. He heard her breathing soften almost at once. She must have been exhausted.

He reflected that he had not taken steps very often in his life, come to think of it. Really never. His marriage, his two jobs, his time with Muriel, his return to Sarah—all seemed to have simply befallen him. He couldn't think of a single major act he had managed of his own accord.

Was it too late now to begin?

Was there any way he could learn to do things differently?

He opened his hand and let the pill fall among the bedclothes. It was going to be a restless, uncomfortable night, but anything was better than floating off on that stupor again.

In the morning, he negotiated the journey out of bed and into the bathroom. He shaved and dressed, spending long minutes on each task. Creeping around laboriously, he packed his bag. The heaviest thing he packed was *Miss MacIntosh, My Darling,* and after thinking that over a while, he took it out again and set it on the bureau.

Sarah said, "Macon?"

"Sarah. I'm glad you're awake," he said.

"What are you doing?"

"I'm packing to leave."

She sat up. Her face was creased down one side.

"But what about your back?" she asked. "And I've got all those appointments! And we were going to take a second honeymoon!"

"Sweetheart," he said. He lowered himself cautiously till he was sitting on the bed. He picked up her hand. It stayed lifeless while she watched his face.

"You're going back to that woman," she said.

665

"Yes, I am," he said.

"Why, Macon?"

"I just decided, Sarah. I thought about it most of last night. It wasn't easy. It's not the easy way out, believe me."

She sat staring at him. She wore no expression.

"Well, I don't want to miss the plane," he said.

He inched to a standing position and hobbled into the bathroom for his shaving kit.

"You know what this is? It's all due to that pill!" Sarah called after him. "You said yourself it knocks you out!"

"I didn't take the pill."

There was a silence.

She said, "Macon? Are you just trying to get even with me for the time I left you?"

He returned with the shaving kit and said, "No, sweetheart."

"I suppose you realize what your life is going to be like," she said. She climbed out of bed. She stood next to him in her nightgown, hugging her bare arms. "You'll be one of those mismatched couples no one invites to parties. No one will know what to make of you. People will wonder whenever they meet you, 'My God, what does he see in her? Why choose someone so inappropriate? It's grotesque, how does he put up with her?' And her friends will no doubt be asking the same about you."

"That's probably true," Macon said. He felt a mild stirring of interest; he saw now how such couples evolved. They were not, as he'd always supposed, the result of some ludicrous lack of perception, but had come together for reasons that the rest of the world would never guess.

He zipped his overnight bag.

"I'm sorry, Sarah. I didn't want to decide this," he said.

He put his arm around her painfully, and after a pause she let her head rest against his shoulder. It struck him that even this moment was just another stage in their marriage. There would probably be still other stages in their thirtieth year, fortieth year—forever, no matter what separate paths they chose to travel.

He didn't take the elevator; he felt he couldn't bear the willy-nilliness of it. He went down the stairs instead. He managed the front door by backing through it, stiffly.

Out on the street he found the usual bustle of a weekday morning—shopgirls hurrying past, men with briefcases. No taxis in sight. He set off for the next block, where his chances were better. Walking was fairly easy but carrying his bag was torture. Lightweight though it was, it twisted his back out of line. He tried it in his left hand, then his right. And after all, what was inside it? Pajamas, a change of underwear, emergency supplies he never used . . . He stepped over to a building, a bank or office building with a low stone curb running around its base. He set the bag on the curb and hurried on.

Up ahead he saw a taxi with a boy just stepping out of it, but he discovered too late that hailing it was going to be a problem. Raising either arm was impossible. So he was forced to run in an absurd, scuttling fashion while shouting bits of French he'd never said aloud before: "*Attendez! Attendez, monsieur!*"

The taxi was already moving off and the boy was just slipping his wallet back into his jeans, but then he looked up and saw Macon. He acted fast; he spun and called out something and the taxi braked. "*Merci beaucoup,*" Macon panted, and the boy, who had a sweet, pure face and shaggy yellow hair, opened the taxi door for him and gently assisted him in. "Oof!" Macon said, seized by a spasm. The boy shut the door and then, to Macon's surprise, lifted a hand in a formal good-bye. The taxi moved off. Macon told the driver where he was going and sank back into his seat. He patted his inside pocket, checking passport, plane ticket. He unfolded his handkerchief and wiped his forehead.

Evidently his sense of direction had failed him, as usual. The driver was making a U-turn, heading back where Macon had just come from. They passed the boy once again. He had a jaunty, stiff-legged way of walking that seemed familiar.

If Ethan hadn't died, Macon thought, wouldn't he have grown into such a person?

He would have turned to give the boy another look, except that he couldn't manage the movement.

The taxi bounced over the cobblestones. The driver whistled a tune between his teeth. Macon found that bracing himself on one arm protected his back somewhat from the jolts. Every now and then, though, a pothole caught him off guard.

And if dead people aged, wouldn't it be a comfort? To think of Ethan growing up in heaven—fourteen years old now instead of twelve—eased the grief a little. Oh, it was their immunity to time that made the dead so heartbreaking. (Look at the husband who dies young, the wife aging on without him; how sad to imagine the husband coming back to find her so changed.) Macon gazed out the cab window, considering the notion in his mind. He felt a kind of inner rush, a racing forward. The real adventure, he thought, is the flow of time; it's as much adventure as anyone could wish. And if he pictured Ethan still part of that flow—in some other place, however unreachable—he believed he might be able to bear it after all.

The taxi passed Macon's hotel—brown and tidy, strangely homelike. A man was just emerging with a small anxious dog on his arm. And there on the curb stood Muriel, surrounded by suitcases and string-handled shopping bags and cardboard cartons overflowing with red velvet. She was frantically waving down taxis—first one ahead, then Macon's own. "*Arrêtez!*" Macon cried to the driver. The taxi lurched to a halt. A sudden flash of sunlight hit the windshield, and spangles flew across the glass. The spangles were old water spots, or maybe the markings of leaves, but for a moment Macon thought they were something else. They were so bright and festive, for a moment he thought they were confetti.

BREATHING LESSONS

ONE

1

Maggie and Ira Moran had to go to a funeral in Deer Lick, Pennsylvania. Maggie's girlhood friend had lost her husband. Deer Lick lay on a narrow country road some ninety miles north of Baltimore, and the funeral was scheduled for ten-thirty Saturday morning; so Ira figured they should start around eight. This made him grumpy. (He was not an early-morning kind of man.) Also Saturday was his busiest day at work, and he had no one to cover for him. Also their car was in the body shop. It had needed extensive repairs and Saturday morning at opening time, eight o'clock exactly, was the soonest they could get it back. Ira said maybe they'd just better not go, but Maggie said they had to. She and Serena had been friends forever. Or nearly forever: forty-two years, beginning with Miss Kimmel's first grade.

They planned to wake up at seven, but Maggie must have set the alarm wrong and so they overslept. They had to dress in a hurry and rush through breakfast, making do with faucet coffee and cold cereal. Then Ira headed off for the store on foot to leave a note for his customers, and Maggie walked to the body shop. She was wearing her best dress—blue and white sprigged, with cape sleeves—and crisp black pumps, on account of the funeral. The pumps were only medium-heeled but slowed her down some anyway; she was more used to crepe soles. Another problem was that the crotch of her panty hose had somehow slipped to about the middle of her thighs, so she had to take shortened, unnaturally level steps like a chunky little wind-up toy wheeling along the sidewalk.

Luckily, the body shop was only a few blocks away. (In this part of town things were intermingled—small frame houses like theirs sitting among portrait photographers' studios, one-woman beauty parlors, driving schools, and podiatry clinics.) And the weather was perfect—a warm, sunny day in September, with just enough breeze to cool her face. She patted down her bangs where they tended to frizz out like a forelock. She hugged her dress-up purse under her arm. She turned left at the corner and there was Harbor Body and Fender, with the peeling green garage doors already hoisted up and the cavernous interior smelling of some sharp-scented paint that made her think of nail polish.

She had her check all ready and the manager said the keys were in the car, so in no time she was free to go. The car was parked toward the rear of the shop, an elderly gray-blue Dodge. It looked better than it had in years. They had straightened the rear bumper, replaced the mangled trunk lid, ironed out a half-dozen crimps here and there, and covered over the dapples of rust on the doors. Ira was right: no need to buy a new car after all. She slid behind the wheel. When she turned the ignition key, the radio came on—Mel Spruce's *AM Baltimore*, a call-in talk show. She let it run, for the moment. She adjusted the seat, which had been moved back for someone taller, and she tilted the rearview mirror downward. Her own face flashed toward her, round and slightly shiny, her blue eyes quirked at the inner corners as if she were worried about something when in fact she was only straining to see in the gloom. She shifted gears and sailed smoothly toward the front of the shop, where the

676

manager stood frowning at a clipboard just outside his office door.

Today's question on AM *Baltimore* was: "What Makes an Ideal Marriage?" A woman was phoning in to say it was common interests. "Like if you both watch the same kind of programs on TV," she explained. Maggie couldn't care less what made an ideal marriage. (She'd been married twenty-eight years.) She rolled down her window and called, "Bye now!" and the manager glanced up from his clipboard. She glided past him—a woman in charge of herself, for once, lipsticked and medium-heeled and driving an undented car.

A soft voice on the radio said, "Well, I'm about to remarry? The first time was purely for love? It was genuine, true love and it didn't work at all. Next Saturday I'm marrying for security."

Maggie looked over at the dial and said, "Fiona?"

She meant to brake, but accelerated instead and shot out of the garage and directly into the street. A Pepsi truck approaching from the left smashed into her left front fender—the only spot that had never, up till now, had the slightest thing go wrong with it.

Back when Maggie played baseball with her brothers, she used to get hurt but say she was fine, for fear they would make her quit. She'd pick herself up and run on without a limp, even if her knee was killing her. Now she was reminded of that, for when the manager rushed over, shouting, "What the . . .? Are you all right?" she stared straight ahead in a dignified way and told him, "Certainly. Why do you ask?" and drove on before the Pepsi driver could climb out of his truck, which was probably just as well considering the look on his face. But in fact her fender was making a very upsetting noise, something like a piece of tin dragging over gravel, so as soon as she'd turned the corner and the two men—one scratching his head, one waving his arms—had disappeared from her rearview mirror, she came to a stop. Fiona was not on the radio anymore. Instead a woman with a raspy tenor was comparing her five husbands. Maggie cut the motor and got out. She could see what was causing the trouble. The fender was crumpled inward so the tire was hitting against it; she was surprised the wheel could turn, even. She squatted on the curb, grasped the rim of the fender in both hands, and tugged. (She remembered hunkering low in the tall grass of the outfield and stealthily, wincingly peeling her jeans leg away from the patch of blood on her knee.) Flakes of gray-blue paint fell into her lap. Someone passed on the sidewalk behind her but she pretended not to notice and tugged again. This time the fender moved, not far but enough to clear the tire, and she stood up and dusted off her hands. Then she climbed back inside the car but for a minute simply sat there. "Fiona!" she said again. When she restarted the engine, the radio was advertising bank loans and she switched it off.

Ira was waiting in front of his store, unfamiliar and oddly dashing in his navy suit. A shock of ropy black, gray-threaded hair hung over his forehead. Above him a metal sign swung in the breeze: SAM'S FRAME SHOP. PICTURE FRAMING. MATTING. YOUR NEEDLEWORK PROFESSIONALLY DISPLAYED. Sam was Ira's father, who had not had a thing to do with the business since coming down with a "weak heart" thirty years before. Maggie always put "weak heart" in quotation marks. She made a point of ignoring the apartment windows above the shop, where Sam spent his cramped, idle, querulous days with Ira's two sisters. He would probably be standing there watching. She parked next to the curb and slid over to the passenger seat.

Ira's expression was a study as he approached the car. Starting out pleased and approving, he rounded the hood and drew up short when he came upon the left fender. His long, bony, olive face grew longer. His eyes, already so narrow you couldn't be sure if they were black or merely dark brown, turned to puzzled, downward-slanting slits. He opened the door and got in and gave her a sorrowful stare.

"There was an unexpected situation," Maggie told him.

"Just between here and the body shop?"

"I heard Fiona on the radio."

"That's five blocks! Just five or six blocks."

"Ira, Fiona's getting married."

He gave up thinking of the car, she was relieved to see. Something cleared on his forehead. He looked at her a moment and then said, "Fiona who?"

"Fiona your daughter-in-law, Ira. How many Fionas do we know? Fiona the mother of your only grandchild, and now she's up and marrying some total stranger purely for security."

Ira slid the seat farther back and then pulled away from the curb. He seemed to be listening for something—perhaps for the sound of the wheel hitting. But evidently her tug on the fender had done the trick. He said, "Where'd you hear this?"

"On the radio while I was driving."

"They'd announce a thing like that on the radio?"

"She telephoned it in."

"That seems kind of . . . self-important, if you want my honest opinion," Ira said.

"No, she was just—and she said that Jesse was the only one she'd ever truly loved."

"She said this on the *radio*?"

"It was a talk show, Ira."

"Well, I don't know why everyone has to go spilling their guts in public these days," Ira said.

"Do you suppose Jesse could have been listening?" Maggie asked. The thought had just occurred to her.

"Jesse? At this hour? He's doing well if he's up before noon."

Maggie didn't argue with that, although she could have. The fact was that Jesse was an early riser, and anyhow, he worked on Saturdays. What Ira was implying was that he was shiftless. (Ira was much harder on their son than Maggie was. He didn't see half as many good points to him.) She faced forward and watched the shops and houses sliding past, the few pedestrians out with their dogs. This had been the driest summer in memory and the sidewalks had a chalky look. The air hung like gauze. A boy in front of Poor Man's Grocery was tenderly dusting his bicycle spokes with a cloth.

"So you started out on Empry Street," Ira said.

"Hmm?"

"Where the body shop is."

"Yes, Empry Street."

"And then cut over to Daimler . . ."

He was back on the subject of the fender. She said, "I did it driving out of the garage."

"You mean right there? Right at the body shop?"

"I went to hit the brake but I hit the gas instead."

"How could that happen?"

"Well, Fiona came on the radio and I was startled."

"I mean the brake isn't something you have to think about, Maggie. You've been driving since you were sixteen years old. How could you mix up the brake with the gas pedal?"

"I just did, Ira. All right? I just got startled and I did. So let's drop it."

"I mean a brake is more or less *reflex*."

"If it means so much to you I'll pay for it out of my salary."

Now it was his turn to hold his tongue. She saw him start to speak and then change his mind. (Her salary was laughable. She tended old folks in a nursing home.)

If they'd had more warning, she thought, she would have cleaned the car's interior before they set out. The dashboard was littered with parking-lot stubs. Soft-drink cups and paper napkins covered the floor at her feet. Also there were loops of black and red wire sagging beneath the glove compartment; nudge them accidentally as you crossed your legs and you'd disconnect the radio. She considered that to be Ira's doing. Men just generated wires and cords and electrical tape everywhere they went, somehow. They might not even be aware of it.

They were traveling north on Belair Road now. The scenery grew choppy. Stretches of playgrounds and cemeteries were broken suddenly by clumps of small businesses—liquor stores, pizza parlors, dark little bars and taverns dwarfed by the giant dish antennas on their roofs. Then another playground would open out. And the traffic was heavier by the minute. Everyone else was going somewhere festive and Saturday-morningish, Maggie was certain. Most of the back seats were stuffed with children. It was the hour for gymnastics lessons and baseball practice.

"The other day," Maggie told Ira, "I forgot how to say 'car pool.' "

"Why would you need to remember?" Ira asked.

"Well, that's my point."

"Pardon?"

"It shows you how time has passed, is what I'm saying. I wanted to tell one of my patients her daughter wouldn't be visiting. I said, 'Today's her day for, um,' and I couldn't think of the words. I could not think of 'car pool.' But it seems like just last week that Jesse had a game or hockey camp, Daisy had a Brownie meeting . . . Why, I used to spend all Saturday behind the wheel!"

"Speaking of which," Ira said, "was it another vehicle you hit? Or just a telephone pole?"

Maggie dug in her purse for her sunglasses. "It was a truck," she said.

"Good grief. You do it any damage?"

"I didn't notice."

"You didn't notice."

"I didn't stop to look."

She put on her sunglasses and blinked. Everything turned muted and more elegant.

"You left the scene of an accident, Maggie?"

"It wasn't an accident! It was only one of those little, like, kind of things that just happen. Why make such a big deal of it?"

"Let me see if I've got this straight," Ira said. "You zoomed out of the body shop, slammed into a truck, and kept on going."

"No, the truck slammed into *me*."

"But you were the one at fault."

"Well, yes, I suppose I was, if you insist on holding someone to blame."

"And so then you just drove on away."

"Right."

He was silent. Not a good silence.

"It was a great big huge Pepsi truck," Maggie said. "It was practically an armored tank! I bet I didn't so much as scratch it."

"But you never checked to make sure."

"I was worried I'd be late," Maggie said. "You're the one who insisted on allowing extra travel time."

"You realize the body-shop people have your name and address, don't you? All that driver has to do is ask them. We're going to find a policeman waiting for us on our doorstep."

"Ira, will you drop it?" Maggie asked. "Don't you see I have a lot on my mind? I'm heading toward the funeral of my oldest, dearest friend's husband; no telling what Serena's dealing with right now, and here I am, a whole state away. And then on top of that I have to hear it on the radio that Fiona's getting married, when it's plain as the nose on your face she and Jesse still love each other. They've always loved each other; they never stopped; it's just that they can't, oh, connect, somehow. And besides that, my one and only grandchild is all at once going to have to adjust to a brand-new stepfather. I feel like we're just flying apart! All my friends and relatives just flying off from me like the . . . expanding universe or something! Now we'll never see that child, do you realize that?"

"We never see her anyhow," Ira said mildly. He braked for a red light.

"For all we know, this new husband could be a molester," Maggie said.

"I'm sure Fiona would choose better than that, Maggie."

She shot him a look. (It wasn't like him to say anything good about Fiona.) He was peering up at the traffic light. Squint lines radiated from the corners of his eyes. "Well, of course she would *try* to choose well," Maggie said carefully, "but even the most sensible person on God's earth can't predict every single problem, can she? Maybe he's somebody smooth and suave. Maybe he'll treat Leroy just fine till he's settled into the family."

The light changed. Ira drove on.

"Leroy," Maggie said reflectively. "Do you think we'll ever get used to that name? Sounds like a boy's name. Sounds like a football player. And the way they pronounce it: *Lee*-roy. Country."

"Did you bring that map I set out on the breakfast table?" Ira asked.

"Sometimes I think we should just start pronouncing it our way," Maggie said. "Le-*roy*." She considered.

"The map, Maggie. Did you bring it?"

"It's in my purse. Le *Rwah*," she said, gargling the R like a Frenchman.

"It's not as if we still had anything to do with her," Ira said.

"We could, though, Ira. We could visit her this very afternoon."

"Huh?"

"Look at where they live: Cartwheel, Pennsylvania. It's practically on the road to Deer Lick. What we could do," she said, digging through her purse, "is go to the funeral, see, and . . . Oh, where is that map? Go to the funeral and then head back down Route One to . . . You know, I don't think I brought that map after all."

"Great, Maggie."

"I think I left it on the table."

"I asked you when we were setting out, remember? I said,

'Are you going to bring the map, or am I?' You said, 'I am. I'll just stick it in my purse.' "

"Well, I don't know why you're making such a fuss about it," Maggie said. "All we've got to do is watch the road signs; anyone could manage that much."

"It's a little more complicated than that," Ira said.

"Besides, we have those directions Serena gave me over the phone."

"Maggie. Do you honestly believe any directions of Serena's could get us where we'd care to go? Ha! We'd find ourselves in Canada someplace. We'd be off in Arizona!"

"Well, you don't have to get so excited about it."

"We would never see home again," Ira said.

Maggie shook her billfold and a pack of Kleenex from her purse.

"Serena's the one who made us late for her own wedding reception, remember that?" Ira said. "At that crazy little banquet hall we spent an hour locating."

"Really, Ira. You always act like women are such flibber-tigibbets," Maggie said. She gave up searching through her purse; evidently she had mislaid Serena's directions as well. She said, "It's Fiona's own good I'm thinking of. She'll need us to baby-sit."

"Baby-sit?"

"During the honeymoon."

He gave her a look that she couldn't quite read.

"She's getting married next Saturday," Maggie said. "You can't take a seven-year-old on a honeymoon."

He still said nothing.

They were out beyond the city limits now and the houses had thinned. They passed a used-car lot, a scratchy bit of woods, a shopping mall with a few scattered early-bird cars parked on a concrete wasteland. Ira started whistling. Maggie stopped fiddling with her purse straps and grew still.

There were times when Ira didn't say a dozen words all day, and even when he did talk you couldn't guess what he was feeling. He was a closed-in, isolated man—his most serious flaw. But what he failed to realize was, his whistling could tell the whole story. For instance—an unsettling example—after a terrible fight in the early days of their marriage they had more or less smoothed things over, patted them into place again, and then he'd gone off to work whistling a song she couldn't identify. It wasn't till later that the words occurred to her. *I wonder if I care as much,* was the way they went, *as I did before.* . . .

But often the association was something trivial, something circumstantial—"This Old House" while he tackled a minor repair job, or "The Wichita Lineman" whenever he helped bring in the laundry. *Do, do, that voodoo* . . . he whistled, unknowingly, five minutes after circling a pile of dog do on the sidewalk. And of course there were times when Maggie had no idea what he was whistling. This piece right now, say: something sort of croony, something they might play on WLIF. Well, maybe he'd merely heard it while shaving, in which case it meant nothing at all.

A Patsy Cline song; that's what it was. Patsy Cline's "Crazy."

She sat up sharply and said, "Perfectly sane people baby-sit their grandchildren, Ira Moran."

He looked startled.

"They keep them for months. Whole summers," she told him.

He said, "They don't pay drop-in visits, though."

"Certainly they do!"

"Ann Landers claims drop-in visits are inconsiderate," he said.

Ann Landers, his personal heroine.

"And it's not like we're blood relatives," he said. "We're not even Fiona's in-laws anymore."

685

"We're Leroy's grandparents till the day we die," Maggie told him.

He didn't have any answer for that.

This stretch of road was such a mess. Things had been allowed to just happen—a barbecue joint sprouting here, a swim-pool display room there. A pickup parked on the shoulder overflowed with pumpkins: ALL U CAN CARRY $1.50, the hand-lettered sign read. The pumpkins reminded Maggie of fall, but in fact it was so warm now that a line of moisture stood out on her upper lip. She rolled down her window, recoiled from the hot air, and rolled it up again. Anyway, enough of a breeze came from Ira's side. He drove one-handed, with his left elbow jutting over the sill. The sleeves of his suit had rucked up to show his wristbones.

Serena used to say Ira was a mystery. That was a compliment, in those days. Maggie wasn't even dating Ira, she was engaged to someone else, but Serena kept saying, "How can you resist him? He's such a mystery. He's so mysterious." "I don't have to resist him. He's not after me," Maggie had said. Although she had wondered. (Serena was right. He was such a mystery.) But Serena herself had chosen the most open-faced boy in the world. Funny old Max! Not a secret in him. "This here is my happiest memory," Max had said once. (He'd been twenty at the time, just finishing his freshman year at UNC.) "Me and these two fraternity brothers, we go out partying. And I have a tad bit too much to drink, so coming home I pass out in the back seat and when I wake up they've driven clear to Carolina Beach and left me there on the sand. Big joke on me: Ha-ha. It's six o'clock in the morning and I sit up and all I can see is sky, layers and layers of hazy sky that just kind of turn into sea lower down, without the least dividing line. So I stand up and fling off my clothes and go racing into the surf, all by my lonesome. Happiest day of my life."

What if someone had told him then that thirty years later

he'd be dead of cancer, with that ocean morning the clearest picture left of him in Maggie's mind? The haze, the feel of warm air on bare skin, the shock of the first cold, briny-smelling breaker—Maggie might as well have been there herself. She was grateful suddenly for the sunlit clutter of billboards jogging past; even for the sticky vinyl upholstery plastered to the backs of her arms.

Ira said, "Who would she be marrying, I wonder."

"What?" Maggie asked. She felt a little dislocated.

"Fiona."

"Oh," Maggie said. "She didn't say."

Ira was trying to pass an oil truck. He tilted his head to the left, peering for oncoming traffic. After a moment he said, "I'm surprised she didn't announce that too, while she was at it."

"All she said was, she was marrying for security. She said she'd married for love once before and it hadn't worked out."

"Love!" Ira said. "She was seventeen years old. She didn't know the first thing about love."

Maggie looked over at him. What *was* the first thing about love? she wanted to ask. But he was muttering at the oil truck now.

"Maybe this time it's an older man," she said. "Someone sort of fatherly. If she's marrying for security."

"This guy knows perfectly well I'm trying to pass and he keeps spreading over into my lane," Ira told her.

"Maybe she's just getting married so she won't have to go on working."

"I didn't know she worked."

"She got a job, Ira. You know that! She told us that! She got a job at a beauty parlor when Leroy started nursery school."

Ira honked at the oil truck.

"I don't know why you bother sitting in a room with people if you can't make an effort to listen," she said.

Ira said, "Maggie, is something wrong with you today?"

"What do you mean?"

"How come you're acting so irritable?"

"I'm not irritable," she said. She pushed her sunglasses higher. She could see her own nose—the small, rounded tip emerging below the nosepiece.

"It's Serena," he said.

"Serena?"

"You're upset about Serena and that's why you're snapping my head off."

"Well, of course I'm upset," Maggie said. "But I'm certainly not snapping your head off."

"Yes, you are, and it's also why you're going on and on about Fiona when you haven't given a thought to her in years."

"That's not true! How do you know how often I think about Fiona?"

Ira swung out around the oil truck at last.

By now, they had hit real country. Two men were splitting logs in a clearing, watched over by a gleaming black dog. The trees weren't changing color yet, but they had that slightly off look that meant they were just about to. Maggie gazed at a weathered wooden fence that girdled a field. Funny how a picture stayed in your mind without your knowing it. Then you see the original and you think, Why! It was there all along, like a dream that comes drifting back in pieces halfway through the morning. That fence, for instance. So far they were retracing the road to Cartwheel and she'd seen that fence on her spy trips and unconsciously made it her own. "Rickrack," she said to Ira.

"Hmm?"

"Don't they call that kind of fence 'rickrack'?"

He glanced over, but it was gone.

She had sat in her parked car some distance from Fiona's mother's house, watching for the teeniest, briefest glimpse of Leroy. Ira would have had a fit if he'd known what she was up to. This was back when Fiona first left, following a scene that Maggie never liked to recall. (She thought of it as That Awful Morning and made it vanish from her mind.) Oh, those days she'd been like a woman possessed; Leroy was not but a baby then, and what did Fiona know about babies? She'd always had Maggie to help her. So Maggie drove to Cartwheel on a free afternoon and parked the car and waited, and soon Fiona stepped forth with Leroy in her arms and set off in the other direction, walking briskly, her long blonde hair swinging in sheets and the baby's face a bright little button on her shoulder. Maggie's heart bounded upward, as if she were in love. In a way, she *was* in love—with Leroy and Fiona both, and even with her own son as he had looked while clumsily cradling his daughter against his black leather jacket. But she didn't dare show herself—not yet, at least. Instead she drove home and told Jesse, "I went to Cartwheel today."

His face flew open. His eyes rested on her for one startled, startling instant before he looked away and said, "So?"

"I didn't talk to her, but I could tell she misses you. She was walking all alone with Leroy. Nobody else."

"Do you think I care about that?" Jesse asked. "What do you think *I* care?"

The next morning, though, he borrowed the car. Maggie was relieved. (He was a loving, gentle, warmhearted boy, with an uncanny gift for drawing people toward him. This would be settled in no time.) He stayed gone all day—she phoned hourly from work to check—and returned as she was cooking supper. "Well?" she asked.

"Well, what?" he said, and he climbed the stairs and shut himself in his room.

She realized then that it would take a little longer than she had expected.

Three times—on Leroy's first three birthdays—she and Ira had made conventional visits, prearranged grandparent visits with presents; but in Maggie's mind the real visits were her spy trips, which continued without her planning them as if long, invisible threads were pulling her northward. She would think she was heading to the supermarket but she'd find herself on Route One instead, already clutching her coat collar close around her face so as not to be recognized. She would hang out in Cartwheel's one playground, idly inspecting her fingernails next to the sandbox. She would lurk in the alley, wearing Ira's sister Junie's bright-red wig. At moments she imagined growing old at this. Maybe she would hire on as a crossing guard when Leroy started school. Maybe she'd pose as a Girl Scout leader, renting a little Girl Scout of her own if that was what was required. Maybe she'd serve as a chaperon for Leroy's senior prom. Well. No point in getting carried away. She knew from Jesse's dark silences, from the listlessness with which Fiona pushed the baby swing in the playground, that they surely couldn't stay apart much longer. Could they?

Then one afternoon she shadowed Fiona's mother as she wheeled Leroy's stroller up to Main Street. Mrs. Stuckey was a slatternly, shapeless woman who smoked cigarettes. Maggie didn't trust her as far as she could throw her, and rightly so, for look at what she did: parked Leroy outside the Cure-Boy Pharmacy and left her there while she went in. Maggie was horrified. Leroy could be kidnapped! She could be kidnapped by any passerby. Maggie approached the stroller and squatted down in front of it. "Honey?" she said. "Want to come away with your granny?" The child stared at her. She was, oh, eighteen months or so by then, and her face had seemed surprisingly grown up. Her legs had lost their infant chubbiness. Her eyes were the same milky blue as Fiona's and slightly flat, blank, as if she didn't know who Maggie was. "It's Grandma," Maggie said, but Leroy began squirming and craning all around. "Mom-Mom?" she said. Unmistakably, she was looking toward the door where Mrs. Stuckey had disappeared. Maggie stood up and walked away quickly. The rejection felt like a physical pain, like an actual wound to the chest. She didn't make any more spy trips.

When she'd driven along here in springtime, the woods had been dotted with white dogwood blossoms. They had lightened the green hills the way a sprinkle of baby's breath lightens a bouquet. And once she'd seen a small animal that was something other than the usual—not a rabbit or a raccoon but something slimmer, sleeker—and she had braked sharply and adjusted the rearview mirror to study it as she left it behind. But it had already darted into the underbrush.

"Depend on Serena to make things difficult," Ira was saying now. "She could have phoned as soon as Max died, but no, she waits till the very last minute. He dies on Wednesday, she calls late Friday night. Too late to contact Triple A about auto routes." He frowned at the road ahead of him. "Um," he said. "You don't suppose she wants me to be a pallbearer or something, do you?"

"She didn't mention it."

"But she told you she needed our help."

"I think she meant moral support," Maggie said.

"Maybe pallbearing is moral support."

"Wouldn't that be physical support?"

"Well, maybe," Ira said.

They sailed through a small town where groups of little shops broke up the pastures. Several woman stood next to a mailbox, talking. Maggie turned her head to watch them. She had a left-out, covetous feeling, as if they were people she knew.

"If she wants me to be a pallbearer I'm not dressed right," Ira said.

"Certainly you're dressed right."

"I'm not wearing a black suit," he said.

"You don't own a black suit."

"I'm in navy."

"Navy's fine."

"Also I've got that trick back."

She glanced at him.

"And it's not as if I was ever very close to him," he said.

Maggie reached over to the steering wheel and laid a hand on his. "Never mind," she told him. "I bet anything she wants us just to be sitting there."

He gave her a rueful grin, really no more than a tuck of the cheek.

How peculiar he was about death! He couldn't handle even minor illness and had found reasons to stay away from the hospital the time she had her appendix out; he claimed he'd caught a cold and might infect her. Whenever one of the children fell sick he'd pretended it wasn't happening. He'd told her she was imagining things. Any hint that he wouldn't live forever—when he had to deal with life insurance, for instance—made him grow set-faced and stubborn and resentful. Maggie, on the other hand, worried she *would* live forever—maybe because of all she'd seen at the home.

And if she were the one who died first, he would probably pretend that that hadn't happened, either. He would probably just go on about his business, whistling a tune the same as always.

What tune would he be whistling?

They were crossing the Susquehanna River now and the lacy, Victorian-looking superstructure of the Conowingo power plant soared on their right. Maggie rolled down her window and leaned out. She could hear the distant rush of water; she was almost breathing water, drinking in the spray that rose like smoke from far below the bridge.

"You know what just occurred to me," Ira said, raising his voice. "That artist woman, what's-her-name. She was bringing a bunch of paintings to the shop this morning."

Maggie closed her window again. She said, "Didn't you turn on your answering machine?"

"What good would that do? She'd already arranged to come in."

"Maybe we could stop off somewhere and phone her."

"I don't have her number with me," Ira said. Then he said, "Maybe we could phone Daisy and ask her to do it."

"Daisy would be at work by now," Maggie told him.

"Shoot."

Daisy floated into Maggie's mind, trim and pretty, with Ira's dark coloring and Maggie's small bones. "Oh, dear," Maggie said. "I hate to miss her last day at home."

"She isn't home anyhow; you just told me so."

"She will be later on, though."

"You'll see plenty of her tomorrow," Ira pointed out. "Good and plenty."

Tomorrow they were driving Daisy to college—her freshman year, her first year away. Ira said, "All day cooped up in a car, you'll be sick to death of her."

"No, I won't! I would never get sick of Daisy!"

"Tell me that tomorrow," Ira said.

"Here's a thought," Maggie said. "Skip the reception."

"What reception?"

"Or whatever they call it when you go to somebody's house after the funeral."

"Fine with me," Ira said.

"That way we could still get home early even if we stopped off at Fiona's."

"Lord God, Maggie, are you still on that Fiona crap?"

"If the funeral were over by noon, say, and we went straight from there to Cartwheel—"

Ira swerved to the right, careening onto gravel. For a moment she thought it was some kind of tantrum. (She often had a sense of inching closer and closer to the edge of his temper.) But no, he'd pulled up at a gas station, an old-fashioned kind of place, white clapboard, with two men in overalls sitting on a bench in front. "Map," he said briefly, getting out of the car.

Maggie rolled down her window and called after him, "See if they have a snack machine, will you?"

He waved and walked toward the bench.

Now that the car was stopped, the heat flowed through the roof like melting butter. She felt the top of her head grow hot; she imagined her hair turning from brown to some metallic color, brass or copper. She let her fingers dangle lazily out the window.

If she could just get Ira to Fiona's, the rest was easy. He was not immune, after all. He had held that child on his knee. He had answered Leroy's dovelike infant coos in the same respectful tone he'd used with his own babies. "Is that so. You don't say. Well, I believe now that you mention it I did hear something of the sort." Till Maggie (always so gullible) had had to ask, "What? What did she tell you?" Then he'd give her one of his wry, quizzical looks; and so would the baby, Maggie sometimes fancied.

No, he wasn't immune, and he would set eyes on Leroy and remember instantly how they were connected. People had to be reminded, that was all. The way the world was going now, it was so easy to forget. Fiona must have forgotten how much in love she had been at the start, how she had trailed after Jesse and that rock band of his. She must have put it out of her mind on purpose, for she was no more immune than Ira. Maggie had seen the way her face fell when they arrived for Leroy's first birthday and Jesse turned out not to be with them. It was pride at work now; injured pride. "But remember?" Maggie would ask her. "Remember those early days when all you cared about was being near each other? Remember how you'd walk everywhere together, each with a hand in the rear pocket of the other's jeans?" That had seemed sort of tacky at the time, but now it made her eyes fill with tears.

Oh, this whole day was so terribly sad, the kind of day when you realized that everyone eventually got lost from everyone

694

else; and she had not written to Serena for over a year or even heard her voice till Serena phoned last night crying so hard she was garbling half her words. At this moment (letting a breeze ripple through her fingers like warm water), Maggie felt that the entire business of time's passing was more than she could bear. Serena, she wanted to say, just think: all those things we used to promise ourselves we'd never, ever do when we grew up. We promised we wouldn't mince when we walked barefoot. We promised we wouldn't lie out on the beach tanning instead of swimming, or swimming with our chins high so we wouldn't wet our hairdos. We promised we wouldn't wash the dishes right after supper because that would take us away from our husbands; remember that? How long since you saved the dishes till morning so you could be with Max? How long since Max even noticed that you didn't?

Ira came toward her, opening out a map. Maggie removed her sunglasses and blotted her eyes on her sleeves. "Find what you wanted?" she called, and he said, "Oh . . ." and disappeared behind the map, still walking. The back of the paper was covered with photos of scenic attractions. He reached his side of the car, refolded the map, and got in. "Wish I could've called Triple A," he told her. He started the engine.

"Well, I wouldn't worry," she said. "We've got loads of extra time."

"Not really, Maggie. And look how the traffic is picking up. Every little old lady taking her weekend drive."

A ridiculous remark; the traffic was mostly trucks. They pulled out in front of a moving van, behind a Buick and another oil truck, or perhaps the same truck they had passed a while back. Maggie replaced her sunglasses.

TRY JESUS, YOU WON'T REGRET IT, a billboard read. And BUBBA MCDUFF'S SCHOOL OF COSMETOLOGY. They entered Pennsylvania and the road grew smooth for a few hundred yards, like a good intention, before settling back to the same old scabby, stippled surface. The views were long and curved and green—a small child's drawing of farm country. Distinct black cows grazed on the hillsides. BEGIN ODOMETER TEST, Maggie read. She sat up straighter. Almost immediately a tiny sign flashed by: 0.1 MI. She glanced at their odometer. "Point eight exactly," she told Ira.

"Hmm?"

"I'm testing our odometer."

Ira loosened the knot of his tie.

Two tenths of a mile. Three tenths. At four tenths, she felt they were falling behind. Maybe she was imagining things, but it seemed to her that the numeral lagged somewhat as it rolled upward. At five tenths, she was almost sure of it. "How long since you had this checked?" she asked Ira.

"Had what checked?"

"The odometer."

"Well, never," he said.

"Never! Not once? And you accuse *me* of poor auto maintenance!"

"Look at that," Ira said. "Some ninety-year-old lady they've let out loose on the highway. Can't even see above her steering wheel."

He veered around the Buick, which meant that he completely bypassed one of the mileage signs. "Darn," Maggie said. "You made me miss it."

He didn't respond. He didn't even look sorry. She pinned her eyes far ahead, preparing for the seven tenths marker. When it appeared she glanced at the odometer and the numeral was just *creeping* up. It made her feel itchy and edgy. Oddly enough, though, the next numeral came more quickly. It might even have been too quick. Maggie said, "Oh-oh."

"What's the matter?"

"This is making me a nervous wreck," she said. She was watching for the road sign and monitoring the odometer dial,

696

both at once. The six rolled up on the dial several seconds ahead of the sign, she could swear. She tsked. Ira looked over at her. "Slow down," she told him.

"Huh?"

"Slow down! I'm not sure we're going to make it. See, here the seven comes, rolling up, up . . . and where's the sign? Where's the *sign*? Come on, sign! We're losing! We're too far ahead! We're—"

The sign popped into view. "Ah," she said. The seven settled into place at exactly the same instant, so precisely that she almost heard it click.

"Whew!" she said. She sank back in her seat. "That was too close for comfort."

"They do set all our gauges at the factory, you know," Ira said.

"Sure, years and years ago," she told him. "I'm exhausted."

Ira said, "I wonder how long we should keep to Route One?"

"I feel I've been wrung through a wringer," Maggie said.

She made little plucking motions at the front of her dress.

Now collections of parked trucks and RVs appeared in clearings at random intervals—no humans around, no visible explanation for anybody's stopping there. Maggie had noticed this on her earlier trips and never understood it. Were the drivers off fishing, or hunting, or what? Did country people have some kind of secret life?

"Another thing is their banks," she told Ira. "All these towns have banks that look like itty-bitty brick houses, have you noticed? With yards around them, and flower beds. Would you put your faith in such a bank?"

"No reason not to."

"I just wouldn't feel my money was secure."

"Your vast wealth," Ira teased her.

"I mean it doesn't seem professional."

"Now, according to the map," he said, "we could stay on

697

Route One a good deal farther up than Oxford. Serena had us cutting off at Oxford, if I heard you right, but . . . Check it for me, will you?"

Maggie took the map from the seat between them and opened it, one square at a time. She was hoping not to have to spread it out completely. Ira would get after her for refolding it wrong. "Oxford," she said. "Is that in Maryland or Pennsylvania?"

"It's in Pennsylvania, Maggie. Where Highway Ten leads off to the north."

"Well, then! I distinctly remember she told us to take Highway Ten."

"Yes, but if we . . . Have you been listening to a word I say? If we stayed on Route One, see, we could make better time, and I think there's a cutoff further up that would bring us directly to Deer Lick."

"Well, she must have had a reason, Ira, for telling us Highway Ten."

"A reason? Serena? Serena Gill have a reason?"

She shook out the map with a crackle. He always talked like that about her girlfriends. He acted downright jealous of them. She suspected he thought women got together on the sly and gossiped about their husbands. Typical: He was so self-centered. Although sometimes it did happen, of course.

"Did that service station have a snack machine?" she asked him.

"Just candy bars. Stuff you don't like."

"I'm dying of hunger."

"I could have got you a candy bar, but I thought you wouldn't eat it."

"Didn't they have potato chips or anything? I'm starving."

"Baby Ruths, Fifth Avenues . . ."

She made a face and went back to the map.

"Well, I would say take Highway Ten," she told him.

"I could swear I saw a later cutoff."

"Not really," she said.

"Not really? What does that mean? Either there's a cutoff or there isn't."

"Well," she said, "to tell the truth, I haven't quite located Deer Lick yet."

He flicked on his turn signal. "We'll find you someplace to eat and I'll take another look at the map," he said.

"Eat? I don't want to eat!"

"You just said you were starving to death."

"Yes, but I'm on a diet! All I want is a snack!"

"Fine. We'll get you a snack, then," he said.

"Really, Ira, I hate how you always try to undermine my diets."

"Then order a cup of coffee or something. I need to look at the map."

He was driving down a paved road that was lined with identical new ranch houses, each with a metal toolshed out back in the shape of a tiny red barn trimmed in white. Maggie wouldn't have thought there'd be any place to eat in such a neighborhood, but sure enough, around the next bend they found a frame building with a few cars parked in front of it. A dusty neon sign glowed in the window: NELL'S GROCERY & CAFE. Ira parked next to a Jeep with a Judas Priest sticker on the bumper. Maggie opened her door and stepped out, surreptitiously hitching up the crotch of her panty hose.

The grocery smelled of store bread and waxed paper. It reminded her of a grade-school lunchroom. Here and there women stood gazing at canned goods. The café lay at the rear— one long counter, with faded color photos of orange scrambled eggs and beige link sausages lining the wall behind it. Maggie and Ira settled on adjacent stools and Ira flattened his map on the counter. Maggie watched the waitress cleaning a griddle. She sprayed it with something, scraped up thick gunk with a spatula, and sprayed again. From behind she was a large white rectangle, her gray bun tacked down with black bobby pins. "What you going to order?" she asked finally, not turning around.

Ira said, "Just coffee for me, please," without looking up from his map. Maggie had more trouble deciding. She took off her sunglasses and peered at the color photos. "Well, coffee too, I guess," she said, "and also, let me think, I ought to have a salad or something, but—"

"We don't serve any salads," the waitress said. She set aside her spray bottle and came over to Maggie, wiping her hands on her apron. Her eyes, netted with wrinkles, were an eerie light green, like old beach glass. "The onliest thing I could offer is the lettuce and tomato from a sandwich."

"Well, maybe just a sack of those taco chips from the rack, then," Maggie said happily. "Though I know I shouldn't." She watched the waitress pour two mugs of coffee. "I'm trying to lose ten pounds by Thanksgiving. I've been working on the same ten pounds forever, but this time I'm determined."

"Shoot! You don't need to lose weight," the woman said, setting the mugs in front of them. The red stitching across her breast pocket read *Mabel*, a name Maggie had not heard since her childhood. What had become of all the Mabels? She tried to picture giving a new little baby that name. Meanwhile the woman was telling her, "I despise how everybody tries to look like a toothpick nowadays."

"That's what Ira says; he likes me the weight I am now," Maggie said. She glanced over at Ira but he was deep in his map, or else just pretending to be. It always embarrassed him when she took up with outsiders. "But then anytime I go to buy a dress it hangs wrong, you know? Like they don't expect me to have a bustline. I lack willpower is the problem. I crave salty things. Pickly things. Hot spices." She accepted the sack of taco chips and held it up, demonstrating.

"How about me?" Mabel asked. "Doctor says I'm so over-weight my legs are going."

"Oh, you are not! Show me where you're overweight!"

"He says it wouldn't be so bad if I was in some other job but waitressing; it gets to my veins."

"Our daughter's been working as a waitress," Maggie said. She tore open the sack of taco chips and bit into one. "Some-times she's on her feet for eight hours straight without a break. She started out in sandals but switched to crepe soles soon enough, I can tell you, even though she swore she wouldn't."

"You are surely not old enough to have a daughter that grown up," Mabel said.

"Oh, she's still a teenager; this was just a summer job. Tomorrow she leaves for college."

"College! A smarty," Mabel said.

"Oh, well, *I* don't know," Maggie said. "She did get a full scholarship, though." She held out the sack. "You want some?"

Mabel took a handful. "Mine are all boys," she told Maggie. "Studying came about as natural to them as flying."

"Yes, our boy was that way."

" 'Why aren't you doing your homework?' I'd ask them. They'd have a dozen excuses. Most often they claimed the teacher didn't assign them any, which of course was an out-and-out story."

"That's just exactly like Jesse," Maggie said.

"And their daddy!" Mabel said. "He was forever taking up for them. Seemed they were all in cahoots and I was left out in the cold. What I wouldn't give for a daughter, I tell you!"

"Well, daughters have their drawbacks too," Maggie said. She could see that Ira wanted to break in with a question (he'd placed a finger on the map and was looking at Mabel expec-tantly), but once he got his answer he'd be ready to leave, so she made him hold off a bit. "For instance, daughters have more secrets. I mean you think they're talking to you, but it's small

701

talk. Daisy, for instance: She's always been so quiet and obedient. Then up she pops with this scheme to go away to school. I had no idea she was plotting that! I said, 'Daisy? Aren't you happy here at home?' I mean of course I knew she was planning on college, but I notice University of Maryland is good enough for other people's children. 'What's wrong with closer to Baltimore?' I asked her, but she said, 'Oh, Mom, you knew all along I was aiming for someplace Ivy League.' I knew no such thing! I had no idea! And since she got the scholarship, why, she's changed past recognition. Isn't that so, Ira. Ira says—" she said, rushing on (having regretted giving him the opening), "Ira says she's just growing up. He says it's just growing pains that make her so picky and critical, and only a fool would take it to heart so. But it's difficult! It's so difficult! It's like all at once, every little thing we do is wrong; like she's hunting up good reasons not to miss us when she goes. My hair's too curly and I talk too much and I eat too many fried foods. And Ira's suit is cut poorly and he doesn't know how to do business."

Mabel was nodding, all sympathy, but Ira of course thought Maggie was acting overemotional. He didn't say so, but he shifted in his seat; that was how she knew. She ignored him. "You know what she told me the other day?" she asked Mabel. "I was testing out this tuna casserole. I served it up for supper and I said, 'Isn't it delicious? Tell me honestly what you think.' And Daisy said—"

Tears pricked her eyelids. She took a deep breath. "Daisy just sat there and studied me for the longest time," she said, "with this kind of . . . fascinated expression on her face, and then she said, 'Mom? Was there a certain conscious point in your life when you decided to settle for being ordinary?' "

She meant to go on, but her lips were trembling. She laid aside her chips and fumbled in her purse for a Kleenex. Mabel clucked. Ira said, "For God's sake, Maggie."

"I'm sorry," she told Mabel. "It got to me."

702

"Well, sure it did," Mabel said soothingly. She slid Maggie's coffee mug a little closer to her. "Naturally it did!"

"I mean, to *me* I'm not ordinary," Maggie said.

"No indeedy!" Mabel said. "You tell her, honey! You tell her that. You tell her to stop thinking that way. Know what I said to Bobby, my oldest? This was over a tuna dish too, come to think of it; isn't that a coincidence. He announces he's sick to death of foods that are mingled together. I say to him, 'Young man,' I say, 'you can just get on up and leave this table. Leave this house, while you're at it. Find a place of your own,' I say, 'cook your own durn meals, see how you can afford prime rib of beef every night.' And I meant it, too. He thought I was only running my mouth, but he saw soon enough I was serious; I set all his clothes on the hood of his car. Now he lives across town with his girlfriend. He didn't believe I would really truly make him move out."

"But that's just it; I don't want her to move out," Maggie said. "I like to have her at home. I mean look at Jesse: He brought his wife and baby to live with us and I loved it! Ira thinks Jesse's a failure. He says Jesse's entire life was ruined by a single friendship, which is nonsense. All Don Burnham did was tell Jesse he had singing talent. Call that ruining a life? But you take a boy like Jesse, who doesn't do just brilliantly in school, and whose father's always at him about his shortcomings; and you tell him there's this one special field where he shines— well, what do you expect? Think he'll turn his back on that and forget it?"

"Well, of course not!" Mabel said indignantly.

"Of course not. He took up singing with a hard-rock band. He dropped out of high school and collected a whole following of girls and finally one particular girl and then he married her; nothing wrong with that. Brought her to live in our house because he wasn't making much money. I was thrilled. They had a darling little baby. Then his wife and baby moved out on account of this awful scene, just up and left. It was nothing but an argument really, but you know how those can escalate. I said, 'Ira, go after her; it's your fault she went.' (Ira was right in the thick of that scene and I blame him to this day.) But Ira said no, let her do what she liked. He said let them just go on and go, but I felt she had ripped that child from my flesh and left a big torn spot behind."

"Grandbabies," Mabel said. "Don't get me started."

Ira said, "Not to change the subject, but—"

"Oh, Ira," Maggie told him, "just take Highway Ten and shut up about it."

He gave her a long, icy stare. She buried her nose in her Kleenex, but she knew what kind of stare it was. Then he asked Mabel, "Have you ever been to Deer Lick?"

"Deer Lick," Mabel said. "Seems to me I've heard of it."

"I was wondering where we'd cut off from Route One to get there."

"Now, that I wouldn't know," Mabel told him. She asked Maggie, "Honey, can I pour you more coffee?"

"Oh, no, thank you," Maggie said. In fact, her mug was untouched. She took a little sip to show her appreciation.

Mabel tore the bill off a pad and handed it to Ira. He paid in loose change, standing up to root through his pockets. Maggie, meanwhile, placed her damp Kleenex in the empty chip sack and made a tidy package of it so as not to be any trouble. "Well, it was nice talking to you," she told Mabel.

"Take care, sweetheart," Mabel said.

Maggie had the feeling they ought to kiss cheeks, like women who'd had lunch together.

She wasn't crying anymore, but she could sense Ira's disgust as he led the way to the parking lot. It felt like a sheet of something glassy and flat, shutting her out. He ought to have married Ann Landers, she thought. She slid into the car. The seat was so hot it burned through the back of her dress. Ira got in too and slammed the door behind him. If he had married

Ann Landers he'd have just the kind of hard-nosed, sensible wife he wanted. Sometimes, hearing his grunt of approval as he read one of Ann's snappy answers, Maggie felt an actual pang of jealousy.

They passed the ranch houses once again, jouncing along the little paved road. The map lay between them, crisply folded. She didn't ask what he'd decided about routes. She looked out the window, every now and then sniffing as quietly as possible.

"Six and half years," Ira said. "No, seven now, and you're still dragging up that Fiona business. Telling total strangers it was all my fault she left. You just have to blame someone for it, don't you, Maggie."

"If someone's to blame, why, yes, I do," Maggie told the scenery.

"Never occurred to you it might be your fault, did it."

"Are we going to go through this whole dumb argument again?" she asked, swinging around to confront him.

"Well, who brought it up, I'd like to know?"

"I was merely stating the facts, Ira."

"Who asked for the facts, Maggie? Why do you feel the need to pour out your soul to some waitress?"

"Now, there is nothing wrong with being a waitress," she told him. "It's a perfectly respectable occupation. Our own daughter's been working as a waitress, must I remind you."

"Oh, great, Maggie; another of your logical progressions."

"One thing about you that I really cannot stand," she said, "is how you act so superior. We can't have just a civilized back-and-forth discussion; oh, no. No, you have to make a point of how illogical I am, what a whifflehead I am, how you're so cool and above it all."

"Well, at least I don't spill my life story in public eating places," he told her.

"Oh, just let me out," she said. "I cannot bear your company another second."

"Gladly," he said, but he went on driving.

"Let me out, I tell you!"

He looked over at her. He slowed down. She picked up her purse and clutched it to her chest.

"Are you going to stop this car," she asked, "or do I have to jump from a moving vehicle?"

He stopped the car.

Maggie got out and slammed the door. She started walking back toward the café. For a moment it seemed that Ira planned just to sit there, but then she heard him shift gears and drive on.

The sun poured down a great wash of yellow light, and her shoes made little cluttery sounds on the gravel. Her heart was beating extra fast. She felt pleased, in a funny sort of way. She felt almost drunk with fury and elation.

She passed the first of the ranch houses, where weedy flowers waved along the edge of the front yard and a tricycle lay in the driveway. It certainly was quiet. All she could hear was the distant chirping of birds—their *chink! chink! chink!* and *video! video! video!* in the trees far across the fields. She'd lived her entire life with the hum of the city, she realized. You'd think Baltimore was kept running by some giant, ceaseless, underground machine. How had she stood it? Just like that, she gave up any plan for returning. She'd been heading toward the café with some vague notion of asking for the nearest Trailways stop, or maybe hitching a ride back home with a reliable-looking trucker; but what was the point of going home?

She passed the second ranch house, which had a mailbox out front shaped like a covered wagon. A fence surrounded the property—just whitewashed stumps linked by swags of white-washed chain, purely ornamental—and she stopped next to one of the stumps and set her purse on it to take inventory. The trouble with dress-up purses was that they were so small. Her everyday purse, a canvas tote, could have kept her going for weeks. ("You give the line 'Who steals my purse steals trash' a whole new meaning," her mother had once remarked.) Still, she had the basics: a comb, a pack of Kleenex, and a lipstick. And in her wallet, thirty-four dollars and some change and a blank check. Also two credit cards, but the check was what mattered. She would go to the nearest bank and open the largest account the check would safely cover—say three hundred dollars. Why, three hundred dollars could last her a long time! Long enough to find work, at least. The credit cards, she supposed, Ira would very soon cancel. Although she might try using them just for this weekend.

She flipped through the rest of the plastic windows in her wallet, passing her driver's license, her library card, a school photo of Daisy, a folded coupon for Affinity shampoo, and a color snapshot of Jesse standing on the front steps at home. Daisy was double-exposed—it was all the rage last year—so her precise, chiseled profile loomed semitransparent behind a full-face view of her with her chin raised haughtily. Jesse wore his mammoth black overcoat from Value Village and a very long red fringed neck scarf that dangled below his knees. She was struck—she was almost injured—by his handsomeness. He had taken Ira's one drop of Indian blood and transformed it into something rich and stunning: high polished cheekbones, straight black hair, long black lusterless eyes. But the look he gave her was veiled and impassive, as haughty as Daisy's. Neither one of them had any further need of her.

She replaced everything in her purse and snapped it shut. When she started walking again her shoes felt stiff and uncomfortable, as if her feet had changed shape while she was standing. Maybe they'd swollen; it was a very warm day. But even the weather suited her purposes. This way, she could camp out if she had to. She could sleep in a haystack. Providing haystacks still existed.

Tonight she'd phone Serena and apologize for missing the funeral. She would reverse the charges; she could do that, with

Serena. Serena might not want to accept the call at first because Maggie had let her down—Serena was always so quick to take offense—but eventually she'd give in and Maggie would explain. "Listen," she would say, "right now I wouldn't mind going to *Ira's* funeral." Or maybe that was tactless, in view of the circumstances.

The café lay just ahead, and beyond that was a low cinderblock building of some sort and beyond that, she guessed, at least a semblance of a town. It would be one of those scrappy little Route One towns, with much attention given to the requirements of auto travel. She would register at a no-frills motel, the room scarcely larger than the bed, which she pictured, with some enjoyment, as sunken in the middle and covered with a worn chenille spread. She would shop at Nell's Grocery for foods that didn't need cooking. One thing most people failed to realize was that many varieties of canned soup could be eaten cold straight from the tin, and they made a fairly balanced meal, too. (A can opener: She musn't forget to buy one at the grocery.)

As for employment, she didn't have much hope of finding a nursing home in such a town. Maybe something clerical, then. She knew how to type and keep books, although she wasn't wonderful at it. She'd had a little experience at the frame shop. Maybe an auto-parts store could use her, or she could be one of those women behind the grille at a service station, embossing credit card bills and handing people their keys. If worst came to worst she could punch a cash register. She could wait tables. She could scrub floors, for heaven's sake. She was only forty-eight and her health was perfect, and in spite of what some people might think, she was capable of anything she set her mind to.

She bent to pick a chicory flower. She stuck it in the curls above her left ear.

Ira thought she was a klutz. Everybody did. She had developed a sort of clownish, pratfalling reputation, somehow. In the nursing home once, there'd been a crash and a tinkle of glass, and the charge nurse had said, "Maggie?" Just like that! Not even checking first to make sure! And Maggie hadn't been anywhere near; it was someone else entirely. But that just went to show how people viewed her.

She had assumed when she married Ira that he would always look at her the way he'd looked at her that first night, when she stood in front of him in her trousseau negligee and the only light in the room was the filmy shaded lamp by the bed. She had unbuttoned her top button and then her next-to-top button, just enough to let the negligee slip from her shoulders and hesitate and fall around her ankles. He had looked directly into her eyes, and it seemed he wasn't even breathing. She had assumed that would go on forever.

In the parking lot in front of Nell's Grocery & Café two men stood next to a pickup, talking. One was fat and ham-faced and the other was thin and white and wilted. They were discussing someone named Doug who had come out all over in swelters. Maggie wondered what a swelter was. She pictured it as a combination of a sweat and a welt. She knew she must make an odd sight, arriving on foot out of nowhere so dressed up and citified. "Hello!" she cried, sounding like her mother. The men stopped talking and stared at her. The thin one took his cap off finally and looked inside it. Then he put it back on his head.

She could step into the café and speak to Mabel, ask if she knew of a job and a place to stay; or she could head straight for town and find something on her own. In a way, she preferred to fend for herself. It would be sort of embarrassing to confess she'd been abandoned by her husband. On the other hand, maybe Mabel knew of some marvelous job. Maybe she knew of the perfect boardinghouse, dirt cheap, with kitchen privileges, full of kindhearted people. Maggie supposed she ought to at least inquire.

She let the screen door slap shut behind her. The grocery was familiar now and she moved through its smells comfortably. At the lunch counter she found Mabel leaning on a wadded-up dishcloth and talking to a man in overalls. They were almost whispering. "Why, *you* can't do nothing about it," Mabel was saying. "What do they think *you* can do about it?"

Maggie felt she was intruding. She hadn't counted on having to share Mabel with someone else. She shrank back before she was seen; she skulked in the crackers-and-cookies aisle, hoping for her rival to depart.

"I been over it and over it," the man said creakily. "I still can't see what else I could have done."

"Good gracious, no."

Maggie picked up a box of Ritz crackers. There used to be a kind of apple pie people made that contained no apples whatsoever, just Ritz crackers. What would that taste like, she wondered. It didn't seem to her there was the remotest chance it could taste like apple pie. Maybe you soaked the crackers in cider or something first. She looked on the box for the recipe, but it wasn't mentioned.

Now Ira would be starting to realize she was gone. He would be noticing the empty rush of air that comes when a person you're accustomed to is all at once absent.

Would he go on to the funeral without her? She hadn't thought of that. No, Serena was more Maggie's friend than Ira's. And Max had been just an acquaintance. To tell the truth, Ira didn't have any friends. It was one of the things Maggie minded about him.

He'd be slowing down. He'd be trying to decide. Maybe he had already turned the car around.

He would be noticing how stark and upright a person feels when he's suddenly left on his own.

Maggie set down the Ritz crackers and drifted toward the fig newtons.

One time a number of years ago, Maggie had fallen in love, in a way, with a patient at the nursing home. The very notion was comical, of course. In love! With a man in his seventies! A man who had to ride in a wheelchair if he went any distance at all! But there you are. She was fascinated by his austere white face and courtly manners. She liked his stiff turns of speech, which gave her the feeling he was keeping his own words at a distance. And she knew what pain it caused him to dress so formally each morning, his expression magnificently disengaged as he worked his arthritic, clublike hands into the sleeves of his suit coat. Mr. Gabriel, his name was. "Ben" to everyone else, but "Mr. Gabriel" to Maggie, for she guessed how familiarity alarmed him. And she was diffident about helping him, always asking his permission first. She was careful not to touch him. It was a kind of reverse courtship, you might say. While the others treated him warmly and a little condescendingly, Maggie stood back and allowed him his reserve.

In the office files, she read that he owned a nationally prom-inent power-tool company. Yes, she could see him in that position. He had a businessman's crisp authority, a business-man's air of knowing what was what. She read that he was widowed and childless, without any close relations except for an unmarried sister in New Hampshire. Until recently he had lived by himself, but shortly after his cook started a minor grease fire in the kitchen he'd applied for admission to the home. His concern, he wrote, was that he was becoming too disabled to escape if his house burned down. Concern! You had to know the man to know what the word concealed: a morbid, obsessive dread of fire, which had taken root with that small kitchen blaze and grown till not even live-in help, and finally not even round-the-clock nursing care, could reassure him. (Maggie had ob-served his stony, fixed stare during fire drills—the only occasions on which he seemed truly to be a patient.)

Oh, why was she reading his file? She wasn't supposed to.

711

Strictly speaking, she shouldn't read even his medical record. She was nothing but a geriatric nursing assistant, certified to bathe her charges and feed them and guide them to the toilet.

And even in her imagination, she had always been the most faithful of wives. She had never felt so much as tempted. But now thoughts of Mr. Gabriel consumed her, and she spent hours inventing new ways to be indispensable to him. He always noticed, and he always thanked her. "Imagine!" he told a nurse. "Maggie's brought me tomatoes from her own backyard." Maggie's tomatoes were subject to an unusual ailment: They were bulbous, like collections of little red rubber jack balls that had collided and mashed together. This problem had persisted for several years, through several varieties of hybrids. Maggie blamed the tiny plot of city soil she was forced to confine them to (or was it the lack of sun?), but often she sensed, from the amused and tolerant looks they drew, that other people thought it had something to do with Maggie herself—with the knobby, fumbling way she seemed to be progressing through her life. Yet Mr. Gabriel noticed nothing. He declared her tomatoes smelled like a summer's day in 1944. When she sliced them they resembled doilies—scalloped around the edges, full of holes between intersections—but all he said was: "I can't tell you how much this means to me." He wouldn't even let her salt them. He said they tasted glorious, just as they were.

Well, she wasn't stupid. She realized that what appealed to her was the image he had of her—an image that would have staggered Ira. It would have staggered anyone who knew her. Mr. Gabriel thought she was capable and skillful and efficient. He believed that everything she did was perfect. He said as much, in so many words. And this was during a very unsatisfactory period in her life, when Jesse was just turning adolescent and negative and Maggie seemed to be going through a quarrelsome spell with Ira. But Mr. Gabriel never guessed any of that. Mr. Gabriel saw someone collected, moving serenely around his room straightening his belongings.

At night she lay awake and concocted dialogues in which Mr. Gabriel confessed that he was besotted with her. He would say he knew that he was too old to attract her physically, but she would interrupt to tell him he was wrong. This was a fact. The mere thought of laying her head against his starched white shoulder could turn her all warm and melting. She would promise to go anywhere with him, anywhere on earth. Should they take Daisy too? (Daisy was five or six at the time.) Of course they couldn't take Jesse; Jesse was no longer a child. But then Jesse would think she loved Daisy better, and she certainly couldn't have that. She wandered off on a sidetrack, imagining what would happen if they did take Jesse. He would lag a few steps behind, wearing one of his all-black outfits, laboring under his entire stereo system and a stack of record albums. She started giggling. Ira stirred in his sleep and said, "Hmm?" She sobered and hugged herself—a competent, adventurous woman, with infinite possibilities.

Star-crossed, that's what they were; but she seemed to have found a way to be star-crossed differently from anyone else. How would she tend Mr. Gabriel and still go out to a job? He refused to be left alone. And what job would she go to? Her only employment in all her life had been with the Silver Threads Nursing Home. Fat chance they'd give her a letter of reference after she'd absconded with one of their patients.

Another sidetrack: What if she didn't abscond, but broke the news to Ira in a civilized manner and calmly made new arrangements? She could move into Mr. Gabriel's room. She could rise from his bed every morning and be right there at work; no commute. At night when the nurse came around with the pills, she'd find Maggie and Mr. Gabriel stretched out side by side, staring at the ceiling, with their roommate, Abner Scopes, in the bed along the opposite wall.

Maggie gave another snicker.

This was turning out all skewed, somehow.

Like anyone in love, she constantly found reasons to mention his name. She told Ira everything about him—his suits and ties, his gallantry, his stoicism. "I don't know why you can't act that keen about my father; he's family," Ira said, missing the point entirely. Ira's father was a whiner, a user. Mr. Gabriel was nothing like him.

Then one morning the home held another fire drill. The alarm bell jangled and the code blared over the loudspeaker: "Dr. Red in Room Two-twenty." This happened in the middle of activity hour—an inconvenient time because the patients were so scattered. Those with any manual dexterity were down in the Crafts Room, knotting colored silk flowers. Those too crippled—Mr. Gabriel, for instance—were taking an extra session of P.T. And of course the bedridden were still in their rooms. They were the easy ones.

The rule was that you cleared the halls of all obstructions, shut stray patients into any room available, and tied red cloths to the doorknobs to show which rooms were occupied. Maggie closed off 201 and 203, where her only bedridden patients lay. She attached red cloths from the broom closet. Then she coaxed one of Joelle Barrett's wandering old ladies into 202. There was an empty tray cart next to 202 and she set that inside as well, after which she dashed off to seize Lottie Stein, who was inching along in her walker and humming tunelessly. Maggie put her in 201 with Hepzibah Murray. Then Joelle arrived, wheeling Lawrence Dunn and calling, "Oops! Tillie's out!" Tillie was the one Maggie had just stashed in 202. That was the trouble with these drills. They reminded her of those pocket-sized games where you tried to get all the silver BBs into their nooks at once. She captured Tillie and slammed her back in 202. Disturbing sounds were coming from 201. That would be a fight between Lottie and Hepzibah; Hepzibah hated having outsiders in her room. Maggie should have dealt with it, and she should also have gone to the aid of Joelle, who was having quite a struggle with Lawrence, but there was something more important on her mind. She was thinking, of course, about Mr. Gabriel.

By now, he would be catatonic with fear.

She left her corridor. (You were never supposed to do that.) She zipped past the nurses' station, down the stairs, and made a right-angle turn. The P.T. room lay at the far end of the hall. Both of its swinging doors were shut. She raced toward them, rounding first a folding chair and then a canvas laundry cart, neither of which should have been there. But all at once she heard footsteps, the squeak of rubber soles. She stopped and looked around. Mrs. Willis! Almost certainly it was Mrs. Willis, her supervisor; and here Maggie was, miles from her proper station.

She did the first thing that came to mind. She vaulted into the laundry cart.

Absurd, she knew it instantly. She was cursing herself even as she sank among the crumpled linens. She might have got away with it, though, except that she'd set the cart to rolling. Somebody grabbed it and drew it to a halt. A growly voice said, "What in the world?"

Maggie opened her eyes, which she had closed the way small children do in one last desperate attempt to make herself invisible. Bertha Washington, from the kitchen, stood gaping down at her.

"Hi, there," Maggie said.

"Well, I never!" Bertha said. "Sateen, come look at who-all's waiting for the laundry man."

Sateen Bishop's face arrived next to Bertha's, breaking into a smile. "You goofball, Maggie! What will you get up to next? Most folks just takes baths," she said.

"This was a miscalculation," Maggie told them. She stood up, batting away a towel that draped one shoulder. "Ah, well, I guess I'd better be—"

But Sateen said, "Off we goes, girl."

"Sateen! No!" Maggie cried.

Sateen and Bertha took hold of the cart, chortling like maniacs, and tore down the hall. Maggie had to hang on tight or she would have toppled backward. She careened along, dodging as she approached the bend, but the women were quicker on their feet than they looked. They swung her around handily and started back the way they'd come. Maggie's bangs lifted off her forehead in the breeze. She felt like a figurehead on a ship. She clutched the sides of the cart and called, half laughing, "Stop! Please stop!" Bertha, who was overweight, snorted and thudded beside her. Sateen made a *sissing* sound through her teeth. They rattled toward the P.T. room just as the all-clear bell sounded—a hoarse burr over the loudspeaker. Instantly the doors swung open and Mr. Gabriel emerged in his wheelchair, propelled by Mrs. Inman. Not the physical therapist, not an assistant or a volunteer, but Mrs. Inman herself, the director of nursing for the entire home. Sateen and Bertha pulled up short. Mr. Gabriel's jaw dropped.

Mrs. Inman said, "Ladies?"

Maggie laid a hand on Bertha's shoulder and climbed out of the cart. "Honestly," she told the two women. She batted down the hem of her skirt.

"Ladies, are you aware that we've been having a fire drill?"

"Yes, ma'am," Maggie said. She had always been scared to death of stern women.

"Are you aware of the seriousness of a fire drill in a nursing home?"

Maggie said, "I was just—"

"Take Ben to his room, please, Maggie. I'll speak with you in my office later."

"Yes, ma'am," Maggie said.

She wheeled Mr. Gabriel toward the elevator. When she leaned forward to press the button, her arm brushed his shoulder, and he jerked away from her. She said, "Excuse me." He didn't respond.

In the elevator he was silent, although that could have been because a doctor happened to be riding with them. But even after they arrived on the second floor and parted company with the doctor, Mr. Gabriel said nothing.

The hall had that hurricane-swept appearance it always took on after a drill. Every door was flung open and patients were roving distractedly and the staff was dragging forth the objects that didn't belong in the rooms. Maggie wheeled Mr. Gabriel into 206. His roommate hadn't returned yet. She parked the chair. Still he sat silent.

"Oh, land," she said, giving a little laugh.

His eyes slid slowly to her face.

Maybe he could view her as a sort of *I Love Lucy* type—madcap, fun-loving, full of irrepressible high spirits. That was one way to look at it. Actually, Maggie had never liked *I Love Lucy*. She thought the plots were so engineered—that dizzy woman's failures just built-in, just guaranteed. But maybe Mr. Gabriel felt differently.

"I came downstairs to find you," she said.

He watched her.

"I was worried," she told him.

So worried you took a joyride in a laundry cart, his glare said plainly.

Then Maggie, stooping to set the brake on his wheelchair, was struck by the most peculiar thought. It was the lines alongside his mouth that caused it—deep crevices that pulled the corners down. Ira had those lines. On Ira they were fainter, of course. They showed up only when he disapproved of something. (Usually Maggie.) And Ira would give her that same dark, sober, judging gaze.

Why, Mr. Gabriel was just another Ira, was all. He had Ira's craggy face and Ira's dignity, his aloofness, that could still to this day exert a physical pull on her. He was even supporting that unmarried sister, she would bet, just as Ira supported *his* sisters and his deadbeat father: a sign of a noble nature, some might say. All Mr. Gabriel was, in fact, was Maggie's attempt

717

to find an earlier version of Ira. She'd wanted the version she had known at the start of their marriage, before she'd begun disappointing him.

She hadn't been courting Mr. Gabriel; she'd been courting Ira.

Well, she helped Mr. Gabriel out of his wheelchair and into the armchair next to his bed, and then she left to check the other patients, and life went on the same as ever. In fact, Mr. Gabriel still lived at the home, although they didn't talk as much as they used to. Nowadays he seemed to prefer Joelle. He was perfectly friendly, though. He'd probably forgotten all about Maggie's ride in the laundry cart.

But Maggie remembered, and sometimes, feeling the glassy sheet of Ira's disapproval, she grew numbly, wearily certain that there was no such thing on this earth as real change. You could change husbands, but not the situation. You could change *who*, but not *what*. We're all just spinning here, she thought, and she pictured the world as a little blue teacup, revolving like those rides at Kiddie Land where everyone is pinned to his place by centrifugal force.

She picked up a box of fig newtons and read the nutrition panel on the back. "Sixty calories each," she said out loud, and Ira said, "Ah, go ahead and splurge."

"Stop undermining my diet," she told him. She replaced the box on the shelf, not turning.

"Hey, babe," he said, "care to accompany me to a funeral?"

She shrugged and didn't answer, but when he hung an arm around her shoulders she let him lead her out to the car.

718

2

To find any place in Deer Lick, you just stopped at the one traffic light and looked in all four directions. Barbershop, two service stations, hardware, grocery, three churches—everything revealed itself at a glance. The buildings were set about as demurely as those in a model-railroad village. Trees were left standing, and the sidewalks ended after three blocks. Peer down any cross street; you'd see greenery and cornfields and even, in one case, a fat brown horse dipping his nose into a pasture.

Ira parked on the asphalt next to Fenway Memorial Church, a grayish-white frame cube with a stubby little steeple like a witch's hat. There were no other cars on the lot. He'd guessed right, as it turned out: Continuing on Route One had been quicker, which wasn't all that fortunate, since it meant they'd arrived in Deer Lick thirty minutes early. Still, Maggie had expected to find some sign of the other mourners.

"Maybe it's the wrong day," she said.

"It couldn't be. 'Tomorrow,' Serena told you. No way you could mix *that* up."

"You think we should go on in?"

"Sure, if it's not locked."

When they got out of the car, Maggie's dress stuck to the

back of her legs. She felt shellacked. Her hair was knotted from the wind, and the waistband of her panty hose had folded over on itself so it was cutting into her stomach.

They climbed a set of wooden steps and tried the door. It swung open with a grudging sound. Immediately inside lay a long, dim room, uncarpeted, the raftered ceiling towering above dark pews. Massive floral arrangements stood on either side of the pulpit, which Maggie found reassuring. Only weddings and funerals called for such artificial-looking bouquets.

"Hello?" Ira tried.

His voice rang back.

They tiptoed up the aisle, creaking the floorboards. "Do you suppose there's a . . . side or something?" Maggie whispered.

"Side?"

"I mean a groom's side and a bride's side? Or rather—" Her mistake sent her into a little fit of giggles. To tell the truth, she hadn't had much experience with funerals. No one really close to her had died yet, knock on wood. "I mean," she said, "does it make any difference where we sit?"

"Just not in the front row," Ira told her.

"Well, of course not, Ira. I'm not a total fool."

She dropped into a right-hand pew midway up the aisle and slid over to make room for him. "You'd think at least some kind of music would be playing," she said.

Ira checked his watch.

Maggie said, "Maybe next time you should follow Serena's directions."

"What, and wander some cow path half the morning?"

"It's better than being the first people here."

"I don't mind being first," Ira said.

He reached into the left pocket of his suit coat. He brought out a deck of cards secured with a rubber band.

"Ira Moran! You're not playing cards in a house of worship!"

He reached into his right pocket and brought out another deck.

"What if someone comes?" Maggie asked.

"Don't worry; I have lightning reflexes," he told her.

He removed the rubber bands and shuffled the two decks together. They rattled like machine-gun fire.

"Well," Maggie said, "I'm just going to pretend that I don't know you." She gathered the straps of her purse and slid out the other end of the pew.

Ira laid down cards where she'd been sitting.

She walked over to a stained-glass window. IN MEMORY OF VIVIAN DEWEY, BELOVED HUSBAND AND FATHER, a plaque beneath it read. A husband named Vivian! She stifled a laugh. She was reminded of a thought she'd often had back in the sixties when the young men wore their hair so long: Wouldn't it feel creepy to run your fingers through your lover's soft, trailing tresses?

Churches always put the most unseemly notions in her head.

She continued toward the front, her heels clicking sharply as if she knew where she was going. She stood on tiptoe beside the pulpit to smell a waxy white flower she couldn't identify. It didn't have any scent at all, and it gave off a definite chill. In fact, she was feeling a little chilly herself. She turned and walked back down the center aisle toward Ira.

Ira had his cards spread across half the length of the pew. He was shifting them around and whistling between his teeth. "The Gambler," that was the name of the song. Disappointingly obvious. *You've got to know when to hold them, know when to fold them* . . . The form of solitaire he played was so involved it could last for hours, but it started simply and he was rearranging the cards almost without hesitation. "This is the part that's dull," he told Maggie. "I ought to have an amateur work this part, the way the old masters had their students fill in the backgrounds of their paintings."

She shot him a glance; she hadn't known they'd done that. It sounded to her like cheating. "Can't you put that five on the six?" she asked.

"Butt out, Maggie."

She wandered on down the aisle, swinging her purse loosely from her fingers.

What kind of church was this? The sign outside hadn't said. Maggie and Serena had grown up Methodist, but Max was some other denomination and after they married, Serena had switched over. She was married Methodist, though. Maggie had sung at her wedding; she'd sung a duet with Ira. (They were just starting to date then.) The wedding had been one of Serena's wilder inventions, a mishmash of popular songs and Kahlil Gibran in an era when everyone else was still clinging to "O Promise Me." Well, Serena had always been ahead of her time. No telling what kind of funeral she would put on.

Maggie pivoted at the door and walked back toward Ira. He had left his pew and was leaning over it from the pew behind so he could study the full array of cards. He must have reached the interesting stage by now. Even his whistling was slower. *You never count your money when you're sitting at the table* . . . From here he looked like a scarecrow: coat-hanger shoulders, spriggy black cowlick, his arms set at wiry angles.

"Maggie! You came!" Serena called from the doorway.

Maggie turned, but all she saw was a silhouette against a blur of yellow light. She said, "Serena?"

Serena rushed toward her, arms outstretched. She wore a black shawl that completely enveloped her, with long satiny fringes swinging at the hem, and her hair was black too, untouched by gray. When Maggie hugged her she got tangled in the tail of hair that hung down straight between Serena's shoulder blades. She had to shake her fingers loose, laughing slightly, as she stepped back. Serena could have been a Spanish señora, Maggie always thought, with her center part and her full, oval face and vivid coloring.

"And Ira!" Serena was saying. "How are you, Ira?"

Ira stood up (having somehow spirited his cards out of sight), and she kissed his cheek, while he endured it. "Mighty sad to hear about Max," he told her.

"Well, thank you," Serena said. "I'm so grateful to you for making the trip; you have no idea. All Max's relatives are up at the house and I'm feeling outnumbered. Finally I slipped away; told them I had things to see to at the church ahead of time. Did you two eat breakfast?"

"Oh, yes," Maggie said. "But I wouldn't mind finding a bathroom."

"I'll take you. Ira?"

"No, thanks."

"We'll be back in a minute, then," Serena said. She hooked her arm through Maggie's and steered her down the aisle. "Max's cousins came from Virginia," she said, "and his brother George, of course, and George's wife and daughter, and Linda's been here since Thursday with the grandchildren. . . ."

Her breath smelled of peaches, or maybe that was her perfume. Her shoes were sandals with leather straps that wound halfway up her bare brown legs, and her dress (Maggie was not surprised to see) was a vibrant red chiffon with a rhinestone sunburst at the center of the V neckline. "Maybe it's a blessing," she was saying. "All this chaos keeps my mind off things."

"Oh, Serena, has it been just terrible?" Maggie asked.

"Well, yes and no," Serena said. She was leading Maggie through a little side door to the left of the entrance, and then down a flight of narrow stairs. "I mean it went on so long, Maggie; in an awful way it was kind of a relief, at first. He'd been sick since February, you know. Only back then we didn't realize. February is such a sick month anyhow: colds and flu and leaky roofs and the furnace breaking down. So we didn't put two and two together at the time. He was feeling off a little, was all he said. Touch of this, touch of that . . . Then he turned yellow. Then his upper lip disappeared. I mean, nothing you can report to a doctor. You can't exactly phone a doctor and say . . . but I looked at him one morning and I thought, 'My Lord, he's so old! His whole face is different.' And by that time it was April, when normal people feel wonderful."

They were crossing an unlit, linoleum-floored basement overhung with pipes and ducts. They picked their way between long metal tables and folding chairs. Maggie felt right at home. How often had she and Serena traded secrets in one or another Sunday-school classroom? She thought she could smell the coated paper that was used for Bible-study leaflets.

"One day I came back from the grocery store," Serena said, "and Max wasn't there. It was a Saturday, and when I'd left he was working in the yard. Well, I didn't think much about it, started putting away the groceries—"

She ushered Maggie into a bathroom tiled in white. Her voice took on an echo. "Then all at once I look out the window and there's this totally unknown woman leading him by the hand. She was sort of . . . hovering; you could tell she thought he was handicapped or something. I went running out. She said, 'Oh! Is he yours?'"

Serena leaned back against a sink, arms folded, while Maggie entered a booth. "Was he mine!" Serena said. "Like when a neighbor comes dragging your dog who's dripping garbage from every whisker and she asks, 'Is he yours?' But I said yes. Turns out this woman found him wandering Dunmore Road with a pair of pruning shears, and he didn't seem to know where he was headed. She asked if she could help and all he said was: 'I'm not certain. I'm not certain.' But he recognized me when he saw me. His face lit up and he told her, 'There's Serena.' So I took him inside and sat him down. I asked him what had happened and he said it was the oddest feeling. He said that out of the blue, he just seemed to be walking on Dunmore Road. Then when the woman turned him back toward where he'd come from he said he saw our house, and he knew it was ours, but at the same time it was like it had nothing to do with him. He said it was like he had stepped outside his own life for a minute."

MARCY + DAVE, read the chalked words above the toilet

paper dispenser. SUE HARDY WEARS A PADDED BRA. Maggie tried to adjust to this new version of Max—vague and bewildered and buckling at the knees, no doubt, like one of her patients at the home. But what she came up with was the Max she'd always known, a hefty football-player type with a prickle of glinting blond hair and a broad, good-natured, freckled face; the Max who'd run naked into the surf at Carolina Beach. She'd seen him only a few times in the past ten years, after all; he was not the world's best at holding down a job and had moved his family often. But he had struck her as the type who stays boyish forever. It was hard to imagine him aging.

She flushed the toilet and emerged to find Serena considering one of her sandals, twisting her foot this way and that. "Have you ever done such a thing?" Serena asked her. "Stepped outside your own life?"

Maggie said, "Well, not that I can recall," and turned on the hot water.

"What would it be like, I wonder," Serena said. "Just to look around you one day and have it all amaze you—where you'd arrived at, who you'd married, what kind of person you'd grown into. Say you suddenly came to while you were—oh, say, out shopping with your daughter—but it was your seven- or eight-year-old self observing all you did. 'Why!' you'd say. 'Can this be me? Driving a car? Taking charge? Nagging some young woman like I knew what I was doing?' You'd walk into your house and say, 'Well, I don't think all that much of my taste.' You'd go to a mirror and say, 'Goodness, my chin is starting to slope just the way my mother's did.' I mean you'd be looking at things without their curtains. You'd say, 'My husband isn't any Einstein, is he?' You'd say, 'My daughter certainly could stand to lose some weight.' "

Maggie cleared her throat. (All those observations were disconcertingly true. Serena's daughter, for instance, could stand to lose a *lot* of weight.) She reached for a paper towel and said, "I thought on the phone you said he died of cancer."

"He did," Serena said. "But it was everywhere before we knew about it. Every part of him, even his brain."

"Oh, Serena."

"One day he was out selling radio ads the same as always, and next day he was flat on his back. Couldn't walk right, couldn't see right; everything he did was one-sided. He kept saying he smelled cookies. He'd say, 'Serena, when will those cookies be done?' I haven't baked cookies in years! He'd say, 'Bring me one, Serena, as soon as they're out of the oven.' So I would make a batch and then he'd look surprised and tell me he wasn't hungry."

"I wish you'd called me," Maggie said.

"What could you have done?"

Well, nothing, really, Maggie thought. She couldn't even say for certain that she knew what Serena was going through. Every stage of their lives, it seemed, Serena had experienced slightly ahead of Maggie; and every stage she'd reported on in her truthful, startling, bald-faced way, like some foreigner who didn't know the etiquette. Talk about stripping the curtains off! It was Serena who'd told Maggie that marriage was not a Rock Hudson–Doris Day movie. It was Serena who'd said that motherhood was much too hard and, when you got right down to it, perhaps not worth the effort. Now this: to have your husband die. It made Maggie nervous, although she knew it wasn't catching.

She frowned into the mirror and caught sight of the squinched blue chicory flower lolling above one ear. She plucked it off and dropped it in the wastebasket. Serena hadn't mentioned it—sure proof of her distracted state of mind.

"At first I wondered, 'How are we going to do this?' " Serena said. " 'How will the two of us manage?' Then I saw that it was only me who would manage. Max was just assuming that I would see him through it. Did the tax people threaten to audit us; did the car need a new transmission? That was *my* affair; Max had left it all behind him. He'd be dead by the time the audit rolled around, and he didn't have any further use for a car. Really it's laughable, when you stop to think. Isn't there some warning about your wishes coming true? 'Be careful what you set your heart on'—isn't there some such warning? Here I'd vowed since I was a child that I wouldn't be dependent on a man. You'd never find *me* waiting around for some man to give me the time of day! I wanted a husband who'd dote on me and stick to me like glue, and that's exactly what I got. Exactly. Max hanging on to the sight of me and following me with his eyes around the room. When he had to go to the hospital finally, he begged me not to leave him and so I stayed there day and night. But I started feeling mad at him. I remembered how I'd always been after him to exercise and take better care of his health, and he'd said exercise was nothing but a fad. Claimed jogging gave people coronaries. To hear him talk, the sidewalks were just littered with the piled-up corpses of joggers. I'd look at him in his bed and I'd say, 'Well, which do you prefer, Max: sudden death in a snazzy red warm-up suit or lying here stuck full of needles and tubes?' I said that, right out loud! I acted horrible to him."

"Oh, well," Maggie said unhappily, "I'm sure you didn't intend—"

"I intended every word," Serena said. "Why do you always have to gloss things over, Maggie? I acted horrible. Then he died."

"Oh, dear," Maggie said.

"It was nighttime, Wednesday night. I felt someone had lifted a weight off my chest, and I went home and slept twelve hours straight. Then Thursday Linda came down from New Jersey and that was nice; her and our son-in-law and the kids. But I kept feeling I ought to be doing something. There was something I was forgetting. I ought to be over at the hospital; that was it. I felt so restless. It was like that trick we used to try as children, remember? Where we'd stand in a doorway and press the backs of both hands against the frame and then when we stepped forward our hands floated up on their own as if all that pressure had been, oh, stored for future use; operating retroactively. And then Linda's kids started teasing the cat. They dressed the cat in their teddy bear's pajamas and Linda didn't even notice. She's never kept them properly in line. Max and I used to bite our tongues not to point that out. Anytime they'd come we wouldn't say a word but we'd give each other this look across the room: just trade a look, you know how you do? And all at once I had no one to trade looks with. It was the first I'd understood that I'd truly lost him."

She drew her tail of hair over one shoulder and examined it. The skin beneath her eyes was shiny. In fact, she was crying, but she didn't seem to realize that. "So I drank a whole bottle of wine," she said, "and then I phoned everyone I ever used to know, all the friends we had when Max and I were courting. You, and Sissy Parton, and the Barley twins—"

"The Barley twins! Are they coming?"

"Sure, and Jo Ann Dermott and Nat Abrams, whom she finally did end up marrying, you'll be interested to hear—"

"I haven't thought of Jo Ann in years!"

"She's going to read from *The Prophet*. You and Ira are singing."

"We're what?"

"You're singing 'Love Is a Many Splendored Thing.' "

"Oh, have mercy, Serena! Not 'Love Is a Many Splendored Thing.' "

"You sang it at our wedding, didn't you?"

"Yes, but—"

"That was what they were playing when Max first told me how he felt about me," Serena said. She lifted a corner of her

728

shawl and delicately blotted the shiny places beneath her eyes. "October twenty-second, nineteen fifty-five. Remember? The Harvest Home Ball. I came with Terry Simpson, but Max cut in."

"But this is a funeral!" Maggie said.

"So?"

"It's not a . . . request program," Maggie said.

Over their heads, a piano began thrumming the floorboards. Chord, chord, chord was plunked forth like so many place settings. Serena flung her shawl across her bosom and said, "We'd better get back up there."

"Serena," Maggie said, following her out of the bathroom, "Ira and I haven't sung in public since your wedding!"

"That's all right. I don't expect anything professional," Serena said. "All I want is a kind of rerun, like people sometimes have on their golden anniversaries. I thought it would make a nice touch."

"Nice touch! But you know how songs, well, age," Maggie said, winding after her among the tables. "Why not just some consoling hymns? Doesn't your church have a choir?"

At the foot of the stairs, Serena turned. "Look," she said. "All I'm asking is the smallest, simplest favor, from the closest friend I've had in this world. Why, you and I have been through everything together! Miss Kimmel's first grade! Miss van Deeter! Long division! Our weddings and our babies! You helped me put my mother in the nursing home. I sat up with you that time that Jesse got arrested."

"Yes, but—"

"Last night I started thinking and I said to myself, 'What am I holding this funeral for? Hardly anyone will come; we haven't lived here long enough. Why, we're not even burying him; I'm flinging his ashes on the Chesapeake next summer. We're not even going to have his casket at the service. What's the point of sitting in that church,' I said, 'listening to Mrs.

Filbert tinkle out gospel hymns on the piano? "Stumbling up the Path of Righteousness" and "Death Is Like a Good Night's Sleep." I don't even know Mrs. Filbert! I'd rather have Sissy Parton. I'd rather have "My Prayer" as played by Sissy Parton at our wedding.' So then I thought, Why not all of it? Kahlil Gibran? 'Love Is a Many Splendored Thing'?"

"Not everyone would understand, though," Maggie said. "People who weren't at the wedding, for instance."

Or even people who *were* at the wedding, she thought privately. Some of those guests had worn fairly puzzled expressions.

"Let them wonder, then," Serena said. "It's not for them I'm doing it." And she spun away and started up the stairs.

"Also there's Ira," Maggie called, following her. The fringe of Serena's shawl swatted her in the face. "Of course I'd move the earth for you, Serena, but I don't think Ira would feel comfortable singing that song."

"Ira has a nice tenor voice," Serena said. She turned at the top of the stairs. "And yours is like a silver bell; remember how people always told you that? High time you stopped keeping it a secret."

Maggie sighed and followed her up the aisle. No use pointing out, she supposed, that that bell was nearly half a century old by now.

Several other guests had arrived in Maggie's absence. They dotted the pews here and there. Serena bent to speak to a hatted woman in a slim black suit. "Sugar?" she said.

Maggie stopped short behind her and said, "Sugar Tilghman?"

Sugar turned. She had been the class beauty and was beautiful still, Maggie supposed, although it was hard to tell through the heavy black veil descending from her hat. She looked more like a widow than the widow herself. Well, she always had viewed clothes as costumes. "There you are!" she said. She rose to press her cheek against Serena's. "I am so, so sorry for your loss," she said. "Except they call me Elizabeth now."

"Sugar, you remember Maggie," Serena said.

"Maggie Daley! What a surprise."

Sugar's cheek was smooth and taut beneath the veil. It felt like one of those netted onions in a grocery store.

"If this is not the saddest thing," she said. "Robert would have come with me but he had a meeting in Houston. He said to send you his condolences, though. He said, 'Seems like only yesterday we were trying to find our way to their wedding reception.' "

"Yes, well, that's what I want to discuss with you," Serena said. "Remember at our wedding? Where you sang a solo after the vows?"

" 'Born to Be with You,' " Sugar said. She laughed. "You two marched out to it; I can see you still. The march took longer than the song, and at the finish all we heard was your high heels."

"Well," Serena said, "I'd like you to sing it again today."

Shock made Sugar's face appear to emerge from the netting. She was older-looking than Maggie had first realized. "Do what?" she said.

"Sing."

Sugar raised her eyebrows at Maggie. Maggie looked away, refusing to conspire. It was true the pianist was playing "My Prayer." But that couldn't be Sissy Parton, could it? That plump-backed woman with dimpled elbows like upside-down valentines? Why, she resembled any ordinary church lady.

"I haven't sung for twenty years or more," Sugar said. "I couldn't sing even then! All I was doing was showing off."

"Sugar, it's the last favor I'll ever ask of you," Serena said.

"Elizabeth."

"Elizabeth, one song! Among friends! Maggie and Ira are singing."

"No, wait—" Maggie said.

Sugar said, "And besides: 'Born to Be with You.' "

"What's wrong with it, I'd like to know?" Serena asked.

"Have you thought about the lyrics? *By your side, satisfied?* You want to hear that at a funeral?"

"Memorial service," Serena said, though she'd been calling it a funeral herself up till now.

"What's the difference?" Sugar asked.

"Well, it's not like there was a coffin present."

"What's the *difference*, Serena?"

"It's not like I'm by his side in the coffin or anything! It's not like I'm being ghoulish or anything! I'm by his side in a spiritual sense, is all I'm saying."

Sugar looked at Maggie. Maggie was trying to remember the words to "My Prayer." In a funeral context, she thought (or in a memorial-service context), even the blandest lines could take on a different aspect.

"You'd be the laughingstock of this congregation," Sugar said flatly.

"What do I care about that?"

Maggie left them and walked on up the aisle. She was alert to the people she passed now; they could be old-time friends. But no one looked familiar. She stopped at Ira's pew and gave him a nudge. "I'm back," she told him. He moved over. He was reading his pocket calendar—the part that listed birthstones and signs of the zodiac.

"Am I imagining things," he asked when she'd settled next to him, "or is that 'My Prayer' I'm hearing?"

"It's 'My Prayer,' all right," Maggie said. "And it's not just any old pianist, either. It's Sissy Parton."

"Who's Sissy Parton?"

"Honestly, Ira! You remember Sissy. She played at Serena's wedding."

"Oh, yes."

"Where you and I sang 'Love Is a Many Splendored Thing,' " Maggie said.

"How could I forget *that*," he said.

"Which Serena wants us to sing again today."

Ira didn't even change expression. He said, "Too bad we can't oblige her."

"Sugar Tilghman won't sing, either, and Serena's giving her fits. I don't think she'll let us out of this, Ira."

"Sugar Tilghman's here?" Ira said. He turned and looked over his shoulder.

Boys had always been fascinated by Sugar.

"She's sitting back there in the hat," Maggie told him.

"Did Sugar sing at their wedding?"

"She sang 'Born to Be with You.' "

Ira faced forward again and thought a moment. He must have been reviewing the lyrics. Eventually, he gave a little snort.

Maggie said, "Do you recall the words to 'Love Is a Many Splendored Thing'?"

"No, and I don't intend to," Ira said.

A man paused in the aisle next to Maggie. He said, "How you doing, Morans?"

"Oh, Durwood," Maggie said. She told Ira, "Move over and let Durwood have a seat."

"Durwood. Hi, there," Ira said. He slid down a foot.

"If I'd known you were coming too, I'd have hitched a ride," Durwood said, settling next to Maggie. "Peg had to take the bus to work."

"Oh, I'm sorry; we should have thought," Maggie said. "Serena must have phoned everyone in Baltimore."

"Yes, I noticed old Sugar back there," Durwood said. He slipped a ballpoint pen from his breast pocket. He was a rumpled, quiet man, with wavy gray hair that he wore just a little too long. It trailed thinly over the tops of his ears and lay in wisps on the back of his collar, giving him the look of someone down on his luck. In high school Maggie had not much liked him, but over the years he'd stayed on in the neighborhood and married a Glen Burnie girl and raised a family, and now she saw more of him than anyone else she'd grown up with. Wasn't it funny how that happened, she thought. She couldn't remember now why they hadn't been close to begin with.

Durwood was patting all his pockets, hunting something. "You wouldn't have a piece of paper, would you?" he said.

All she found was her shampoo coupon. She gave him that and he laid it on a hymnbook. Clicking his pen point, he frowned into space. "What are you writing?" Maggie asked.

"I'm trying to think of the words to 'I Want You, I Need You, I Love You.' "

Ira groaned.

The church was filling now. A family settled in the pew just in front of theirs, the children arranged by height so that the line of round blond heads slanted upward like a question. Serena flitted from guest to guest, no doubt pleading and cajoling. The fringes of her shawl had gathered a row of dust mice from somewhere. "My Prayer" played over and over, turning dogged.

Now that she knew how many people from her past were sitting here, Maggie wished she'd given more thought to her appearance. She could have worn powder, for instance, or foundation of some kind—something to make her face less rosy. Maybe she'd have tried painting brown hollows on her cheeks, the way the magazines were always recommending. Also she'd have chosen a younger dress, an eye-catching dress like Serena's. Except that she didn't own such a dress. Serena had always been more flamboyant—the only girl in their school with pierced ears. She had teetered on the edge of downright gaudy, but had somehow brought it off.

How gloriously Serena had defied the stodgy times they'd grown up in! In third grade she'd worn ballet-style shoes, paper-thin, with a stunning spray of sequins across each toe, and the other girls (in their sensible brown tie oxfords and thick wool knee socks) had bitterly envied the tripping way she walked and the dancer-like grace of her bare legs, which came out in goose

734

bumps and purple splotches at every recess period. She had brought adventurous lunches to the stewy-smelling cafeteria: one time, tiny silver sardines still in their flat silver tin. (She ate the tails. She ate the little bones. "Mm-mm! Crunch, crunch," she said, licking off each finger.) Every year on Parents' Day she proudly, officiously ushered around her scandalous mother, Anita, who wore bright-red, skin-tight toreador pants and worked in a bar. And she never hesitated to admit that she had no father. Or no father who was married, at any rate. Not married to her mother, at any rate.

In high school she had evolved her own personal fashion statement—rayon and machine embroidery and slinky blouses from the Philippines, when the other girls were wearing crinolines. You'd see the other girls wafting through the corridors, their skirts standing out like frilled lampshades; and then in their midst Serena's sultry, come-hither, plum-colored sheath handed down from Anita.

But wasn't it odd that the boys she went out with were never the sultry types themselves? They were not the dark Lotharios you would expect but the sunny innocents like Max. The plaid-shirt boys, the gym-sneaker boys: Those were the ones she'd gravitated toward. Maybe she'd coveted everydayness, more than she ever let on. Was that possible? Well, of course it was, but Maggie hadn't guessed it at the time. Serena had made such a point of being different. She was so thorny and spiky, so quick to get her hackles up and order you out of her sight forever. (How many times had she and Maggie stopped speaking—Serena swishing past as grandly as a duchess?) Even now, enfolding a funeral guest in her dramatic shawl, she gave off a rich, dark glow that made the people around her seem faded.

Maggie looked down at her hands. Lately, when she took a pinch of skin from the back of a hand and released it, she noticed the skin would stay pleated for moments afterward.

Durwood muttered to himself and scribbled phrases on her

735

coupon. Then he muttered something else, staring at the hymnal rack in front of him. Maggie felt a clutch of anxiety. She placed her fingertips together and whispered, " 'Love is a many splendored thing, it's the April rose that only grows in the—' "

"I am not going to sing that song, I tell you," Ira said.

Maggie wasn't, either, but she had a sense of being borne along by something. All through this church, she imagined, middle-aged people were mumbling sentimental phrases from the fifties. *Wondrously, love can see . . .* and *More than the buds on the May-apple tree . . .*

Why did popular songs always focus on romantic love? Why this preoccupation with first meetings, sad partings, honeyed kisses, heartbreak, when life was also full of children's births and trips to the shore and longtime jokes with friends? Once Maggie had seen on TV where archaeologists had just unearthed a fragment of music from who knows how many centuries B.C., and it was a boy's lament for a girl who didn't love him back. Then besides the songs there were the magazine stories and the novels and the movies, even the hair-spray ads and the pantyhose ads. It struck Maggie as disproportionate. Misleading, in fact.

A slim blade of black knelt at Durwood's elbow. It was Sugar Tilghman, blowing at a swatch of net to free it from her lipstick. "If I'd known I was expected to provide the entertainment I never would have come," she said. "Oh, Ira. I didn't see you there."

"How you doing, Sugar," Ira said.

"Elizabeth."

"Pardon?"

"The Barley twins have the right idea," Sugar said. "They flat-out refuse to go along with this."

"Isn't that just like them," Maggie said. The Barley twins had always acted so snobbish, preferring each other to anybody else.

"And Nick Bourne wouldn't even come to the funeral."

"Nick Bourne?"

"Said it was too long a drive."

"*I* don't recall Nick at the wedding," Maggie said.

"Well, he was in the chorus, right?"

"Oh, yes, I guess he was."

"And the chorus sang 'True Love,' remember? But if the Barley twins won't join in and Nick Bourne's not coming, there wouldn't be but the four of us, so she's going to skip the chorus part."

"You know," Durwood said, "I never understood why 'True Love' went so high on the charts. That was a really boring tune, when you think about it."

"And then 'Born to Be with You,' " Sugar said. "Wasn't it funny about Serena? Sometimes she kind of overdid. She'd take some run-of-the-mill pop song like 'Born to Be with You' that all the rest of us liked okay, and she would make so much of it, it would start to look weird. It would start to look bizarre. Things always got so exaggerated, with Serena."

"Like her wedding reception," Durwood said.

"Oh, her wedding reception! Her receiving line with just that mother of hers and one fat twelve-year-old girl cousin and Max's parents."

"Max's parents looked miserable."

"They never did approve of her."

"They thought she was sort of cheap."

"They kept asking who her people were."

"Better not to have a receiving line at all," Durwood said. "Shoot, better just to elope. I don't know why she went to so much trouble."

"Well, anyhow," Sugar said, "I told Serena I'd sing today if she insisted, but she'd have to make it some other piece. Something more appropriate. I mean I know we're supposed to be humoring the bereaved, but there are limits. And Serena said, well, all right, so long as it came from the time when they were first dating. Nineteen fifty-five, fifty-six, she said; nothing later."

" 'The Great Pretender,' " Durwood said suddenly. "Now, there was a song. Remember, Ira? Remember 'The Great Pretender'?"

Ira put on a soulful look and crooned, "O-o-o-o-o-o-oh, yes . . ."

"Why not sing that?" Durwood asked Sugar.

"Oh, be serious," Sugar said.

"Sing 'Davy Crockett,' " Ira suggested.

He and Durwood started competing: "Sing 'Yellow Rose of Texas.' "

"Sing 'Hound Dog.' "

"Sing 'Papa Loves Mambo.' "

"Will you be serious for a minute?" Sugar said. "I'm going to get up there and open my mouth and nothing's going to come out."

"Or how about 'Heartbreak Hotel'?" Ira asked.

"Ssh, everybody. They're starting," Maggie said. She had glimpsed the family approaching from the rear. Sugar rose hastily and returned to her seat, while Serena, who was bending over two women who could only be the Barley twins, settled next to them in a pew that was nowhere near the front and went on whispering. No doubt she still hoped to talk them into singing. Both twins wore their yellow hair in the short, curly, caplike style they'd favored in high school, Maggie saw, but the backs of their necks were scrawny as chicken necks and their fussy pink ruffles gave them a Minnie Pearl look.

An usher led the family up the aisle: Serena's daughter, Linda, fat and freckled, and Linda's bearded husband and two little boys in grownup suits, their expressions self-consciously solemn. Behind them came a fair-haired man, most likely the brother, and various other people, severely, somberly dressed.

Several had Max's wide face, which gave Maggie a start. She seemed to have drifted away from the reason for this ceremony, and now all at once she remembered: Max Gill had actually gone and died. The striking thing about death, she thought, was its eventfulness. It made you see you were leading a real life. Real life at last! you could say. Was that why she read the obituaries each morning, hunting familiar names? Was that why she carried on those hushed, awed conversations with the other workers when one of the nursing home patients was carted away in a hearse?

The family settled in the frontmost pew. Linda glanced back at Serena, but Serena was too busy arguing with the Barley twins to notice. Then the piano fell silent, and a door near the altar opened and a lean, bald-headed minister appeared in a long black robe. He crossed behind the pulpit. He seated himself in a dark wooden armchair and arranged the skirt of his robe fastidiously over his trousers.

"That's not Reverend Connors, is it?" Ira whispered.

"Reverend Connors is *dead*," Maggie told him.

She was louder than she'd meant to be. The row of blond heads in front of her swiveled.

Now the piano trudged off on "True Love." Evidently Sissy was filling in for the chorus. Serena was giving the Barley twins a pointed, accusing glare, but they faced stubbornly forward and pretended not to notice.

Maggie remembered Grace Kelly and Bing Crosby singing "True Love" in a movie. They'd been perched on a yacht or a sailboat or something. Both of them were dead too, come to think of it.

If the minister found the music surprising, he gave no sign. He waited till the last note had faded and then he stood and said, "Turning now to the Holy Word . . ." His voice was high-pitched and stringy. Maggie wished he were Reverend Connors. Reverend Connors had shaken the rafters. And she didn't think he'd read any Holy Word at Serena's wedding, at least not that she could recollect.

This man read a psalm, something about a lovely dwelling place, which came as a relief to Maggie because in her experience, most of the Book of Psalms tended to go on in a sort of paranoid way about enemies and evil plots. She pictured Max reclining in a lovely dwelling place with Grace Kelly and Bing Crosby, his crew cut glinting against the sunlit sails. He would be telling them one of his jokes. He could tell jokes for hours, one after the other. Serena used to say, "All right already, Gill, enough." They'd often called each other by their last names— Max using Serena's maiden name even after they were married. "Watch it there, Palermo." Maggie could hear him now. It had made the two of them look more amiable than other married couples. They'd seemed like easygoing buddies, unaware of that dark, helpless, angry, confined feeling that Maggie's own marriage descended to from time to time.

In fact, if Serena believed that marriage was not a Doris Day movie, she had certainly never proved it in public, for her grownup life had looked from outside like the cheeriest of domestic comedies: Serena ironic and indulgent and Max the merry good-time guy. They had appeared to remain focused exclusively upon each other even after becoming parents; Linda had seemed more or less extraneous. Maggie envied that. So what if Max was a bit of a failure in the outside world? "If I just didn't feel I had to *carry* him; always be the one to carry the household," Serena had confided once. But then she had turned breezy and waved a hand, clanging her bangle bracelets. "Oh, well! But he's my sweetie, right?" she'd said, and Maggie had agreed. He was as sweet as they came.

(And she remembered, if Serena didn't, how she and Serena had spent the summer after fifth grade spying on the gracious Guilford home of the man who was Serena's father, and how they had cunningly shadowed his teenaged sons and his ladylike

740

wife. "I could bring that woman's world crashing around her ears," Serena had said. "I could knock on her door and she would go, 'Why, hello, dear, whose little girl are you?' and I could tell her." But she had said this while hidden behind one of the two complacent stone lions that guarded the front walk, and she had made no move to show herself. And then she had whispered, "I will *never* be like her, I tell you." A stranger would think she meant the wife, but Maggie knew better: She meant her mother. "Mrs." Palermo—love's victim. A woman whose every trait—even the tilted, off-center way she carried her waterfall of black curls—hinted at permanent injuries.)

The minister seated himself, orchestrating his robe. Sissy Parton weighed in with a few ominous notes. She looked toward the congregation and Durwood said, "Me?" right out loud. The blond heads swiveled again. Durwood rose and headed up the aisle. Apparently you were expected to remember on your own when your song was due. Never mind that you had to cast your thoughts back twenty-nine years.

Durwood struck a pose beside the piano, resting one arm on the lid. He nodded at Sissy. The he started off in a throbbing bass: "Hold me close. Hold me tight . . ."

A lot of parents had forbidden that song in their houses. All this wanting and needing really didn't sound very nice, they had said. So Maggie and her classmates had had to go to Serena's, or to Oriole Hi Fidelity, where you could still, in those days, pile into a listening booth and play records all afternoon without making a purchase.

And now she recalled why she hadn't liked Durwood; his operatic tremolo brought it all back. Once upon a time he'd been considered quite a catch, with his wavy dark hair and his deep-brown eyes and that habit he had of beseechingly crinkling his brow. He'd sung "Believe Me if All Those Endearing Young Charms" in the high school auditorium on every conceivable occasion, always the same song, the same theatrical gestures, the same fifties crooner style, where the voice breaks with feeling. Sometimes Durwood's voice broke so extremely that the first syllable of a line was silent, and even on the second syllable he kicked in a touch late, while the plump, bespectacled music teacher gazed up at him mistily from her piano. "Dreamboat," his entry in the yearbook had read. "Man I'd Most Like to Be Shipwrecked With," he'd been voted in the school paper. He'd asked Maggie for a date and Maggie had said no and her girlfriends had told her she was crazy. "You turned down Durwood? Durwood Clegg?"

"He's too soft," she'd said, and they had repeated the word and passed it among themselves for consideration. "Soft," they'd murmured tentatively.

He was too pliant, she meant; too supplicating. She failed to see the appeal. For if Serena had made her resolutions about who not to be, why, so had Maggie; and in order not to be her mother, she planned to avoid any man remotely like her father—the person she loved best in the world. No one mild and clumsy for Maggie, thank you; no one bumbling and well-meaning and sentimental, who would force her to play the heavy. You'd never find *her* sitting icily erect while her husband, flushed with merriment, sang nonsense songs at the dinner table.

So Maggie had refused Durwood Clegg and had watched with no regrets as he went on to date Lu Beth Parsons instead. She could see Lu Beth as clear as day this very minute, clearer than Peg, whom he'd ended up marrying. She could see Durwood's khaki trousers with the Ivy League buckle in back buckled up ("attached," that signified; "going steady") and his buttondown shirt and natty brown loafers decorated with bobbing leather acorns. But of course this morning he was wearing a suit—baggy and unfashionable, inexpensive, husbandly. For a moment he shifted back and forth like those trick portraits that change expression according to where you're standing: the old lady-killer Durwood meaningfully lingering on *darling, you're*

742

all that I'm living for, with his eyebrows quirked, but then the present-day, shabby Durwood searching for the next stanza on Maggie's shampoo coupon, which he held at arm's length, with his forehead wrinkled, as he tried to make out the words.

The blond children in front were tittering. They probably found this whole event hilarious. Maggie had an urge to slam the nearest one flat over the head with a hymnbook.

When Durwood finished singing, someone mistakenly clapped—just two sharp explosions—and Durwood nodded in a grimly relieved way and returned to his seat. He settled next to Maggie with a sigh. His face was filmed with sweat and he fanned himself with the coupon. Would it seem mercenary if she asked for it back? Twenty-five cents off, at double-coupon rates . . .

Jo Ann Dermott stepped up to the pulpit with a small book covered in tooled leather. She had been a gawky girl, but middle age had filled out her corners or something. Now she was willowy and attractive in a fluid, pastel dress and subtle makeup. "At Max's and Serena's wedding," she announced, "I read Kahlil Gibran on marriage. Today, at this sadder occasion, I'll read what he says about death."

At the wedding, she had pronounced Gibran with a hard G. Today the G was soft. Maggie had no idea which was correct.

Jo Ann started reading in a level, teacher-like voice, and immediately Maggie was overcome by nervousness. It took her a moment to realize why: She and Ira were next on the program. Just the cadence of *The Prophet* had reminded her.

At the wedding they'd sat on folding chairs behind the altar, and Jo Ann had sat in front of the altar with Reverend Connors. When Jo Ann began reading, Maggie had felt that breathless flutter high in her chest that foretold stage fright. She had taken a deep, trembly breath, and then Ira had unobtrusively set a hand at the small of her back. That had steadied her. When it was time for them to sing, they had begun at the same split

743

second, on exactly the same note, as if they were meant for each other. Or so Maggie had viewed it at the time.

Jo Ann closed her book and returned to her pew. Sissy flipped pages of sheet music, the puffed flesh swinging from her valentine elbows. She flounced a bit on the bench, and then she played the opening bars of "Love Is a Many Splendored Thing."

Maybe if Maggie and Ira stayed seated, Sissy would just go on playing. She would cover for them as she had covered for the chorus.

But the piano notes died away and Sissy glanced back toward the congregation. Her hands remained on the keys. Serena turned too and, knowing exactly where to find Maggie, gave her a fond, expectant look in which there was not the slightest suspicion that Maggie would let her down.

Maggie stood up. Ira just sat there. He might be anyone— a total stranger, someone who merely happened to have chosen the same pew.

So Maggie, who had never sung a solo in her life, clutched the seat ahead of her and called out, " 'Love!' "

A bit squeakily.

The piano sailed into it. The blond children pivoted and stared up into her face.

" '. . . is a many splendored thing,' " she quavered.

She felt like an orphaned, abandoned child, with her back held very straight and her round-toed pumps set resolutely together.

Then there was a stirring at her side, not her right side, where Ira sat, but her left, where Durwood sat. Durwood hastily unfolded himself as if all at once reminded of something. " 'It's the April rose,' " he sang, " 'that only grows . . .' " This near, his voice had a resonant sound. She thought of sheets of vibrating metal.

" 'Love is Nature's way of giving . . .' " they sang together.

744

They knew all the words straight through, which Maggie found surprising, because earlier she had forgotten what it was that makes a man a king. " 'It's the golden crown,' " she sang confidently. You had to sort of *step forth*, she decided, and trust that the words would follow. Durwood carried the melody and Maggie went along with it, less quavery now although she could have used a little more volume. It was true that her voice had once been compared to a bell. She had sung in the choir for years, at least till the children came along and things got complicated; and she had taken real joy in rounding out a note just right, like a pearl or a piece of fruit that hung in the air a moment before it fell away. Though age had certainly not helped. Did anyone else hear the thread of a crack running through her high notes? Hard to tell; the congregation faced decorously forward, except for those confounded little blonds.

She thought time had gone into one of its long, slow, taffy-like stretches. She was acutely conscious of each detail of her surroundings. She felt the fabric of Durwood's sleeve just brushing her arm, and she heard Ira absentmindedly twanging a rubber band. She saw how accepting and uninterested her audience was, taking it for granted that this song would of course be sung and then some other song after that. " 'Then your fingers touched my silent heart,' " she sang, and she remembered how she and Serena had giggled over that line when they sang it themselves—oh, long before that fateful Harvest Home Ball—because where else was your heart but in your chest? Weren't they saying the lover had touched their *chests*? Serena was facing the pulpit but her head had a listening stillness to it. Her tail of hair was gathered into one of those elastic arrangements secured by two red plastic marbles, the kind of thing very young girls wore. Like a very young girl, she had summoned all her high-school friends around her—no one from a later time, no one from the dozen small towns Max had lugged her to during their marriage, for they hadn't stayed in any of those places long enough. Maggie decided that that was the saddest thing about this whole event.

The song came to an end. Maggie and Durwood sat down.

Sissy Parton moved directly into "Friendly Persuasion," but the Barley twins, who used to harmonize as closely as the Lennon Sisters, stayed seated. Serena seemed resigned by now; she didn't even give them a look. Sissy played just one stanza, and then the minister rose and said, "We are gathered here today to mourn a grievous loss."

Maggie felt she had turned to liquid. She was so exhausted that her knees were shaking.

The minister had a lot to say about Max's work for the Furnace Fund. He didn't seem to know him personally, however. Or maybe that was all Max had amounted to, in the end: a walking business suit, a firm handshake. Maggie switched her attention to Ira. She wondered how he could sit there, so impervious. He'd have let her slog through that entire song alone; she knew that. She could have stumbled and stuttered and broken down; he would have watched as coolly as if she had nothing to do with him. Why not? he would say. What obligated him to sing some corny fifties song at a semi-stranger's funeral? As usual, he'd be right. As usual, he'd be forcing Maggie to do the giving in.

She made up her mind that when the funeral was over, she would stride off in her own direction. She would certainly not drive back with him to Baltimore. Maybe she'd hitch a ride with Durwood. Gratitude rushed over her at the thought of Durwood's kindness. Not many people would have done what he had done. He was a gentle, sympathetic, softhearted man, as she should have realized from the start.

Why, if she had accepted that date with Durwood she'd be a whole different person now. It was all a matter of comparison. Compared to Ira she looked silly and emotional; anybody would have. Compared to Ira she talked too much and laughed too much and cried too much. Even ate too much! Drank too much! Behaved so sloppily and mawkishly!

She'd been so intent on not turning into her mother, she had gone and turned into her father.

The minister sat down with an audible groan. There was a rustle of linen a few pews back and then here came Sugar Tilghman, bearing her black straw hat as smoothly as a loaded tray. She tip-tapped up front to Sissy and bent over her, conferring. They murmured together. Then Sugar straightened and took a stance beside the piano with her hands held just the way their choir leader used to insist—loosely clasped at waist level, no higher—and Sissy played a bar of music that Maggie couldn't immediately name. An usher approached Serena and she rose and accepted his arm and let him escort her down the aisle, eyes lowered.

Sugar sang, " 'When I was just a little girl . . .' "

Another usher crooked his arm toward Serena's daughter, and one by one the family members filed out. Up front, Sugar gathered heart and swung gustily into the chorus:

> *Que sera sera,*
> *Whatever will be will be.*
> *The future's not ours to see,*
> *Que sera sera.*

3

When they stepped out of the church it was like stepping out of a daytime movie—that sudden shock of sunshine and birdsong and ordinary life that had been going on without them. Serena was hugging Linda. Linda's husband stood awkwardly by with the children, looking like a visitor who hoped to be invited in. And all around the churchyard, members of the class of '56 were recognizing each other. "Is that you?" they asked. And, "How long has it been?" And, "Can you believe this?" The Barley twins told Maggie she hadn't changed a bit. Jo Ann Dermott announced that everyone had changed, but only for the better. Wasn't it odd, she said, how much younger they were than their parents had been at the very same age. Then Sugar Tilghman appeared in the doorway and asked the crowd at large what other song she possibly could have sung. "I mean I know it wasn't perfect," she said, "but look what I had to choose from! Was it just too absolutely inappropriate?"

They all swore it wasn't.

Maggie said, "Durwood, I owe you the world for coming to my rescue."

"My pleasure," he told her. "Here's your coupon, by the way. None the worse for wear."

This wasn't quite true; it was limp around the edges and slightly damp. Maggie dropped it into her purse.

Ira stood near the parking lot with Nat Abrams. He and Nat had been a couple of classes ahead of the others; they were the outsiders. Not that Ira seemed to mind. He looked perfectly at ease, in fact. He was discussing auto routes. Maggie overheard snatches of "Triple A" and "Highway Ten." You would think the man was obsessed.

"Funny little place, isn't it?" Durwood said, gazing around him.

"Funny?"

"You couldn't even call it a town."

"Well, it is kind of small," Maggie said.

"I wonder if Serena will be staying on here."

They both looked over at Serena, who seemed to be trying to put her daughter back together. Linda's face was streaming with tears, and Serena had set her at a distance and was patting down various parts of her clothes. "Doesn't she still have relatives in Baltimore?" Durwood asked.

"None that claim her," Maggie said.

"I thought she had that mother."

"Her mother died a few years ago."

"Aw, really?" Durwood said.

"She got one of those diseases, some muscular something."

"Us boys were all just, like, fixated on her, once upon a time," Durwood said.

This startled Maggie, but before she could comment she saw Serena heading toward them. She had her shawl clasped tightly around her. "I want to thank you both for singing," she said. "It meant a lot to me."

"That Ira is just so stubborn I could spit," Maggie said, and Durwood said, "Beautiful service, Serena."

"Oh, be honest, you thought it was crazy," Serena said. "But you were nice to humor me. Everyone's been so nice!"

749

Her lips took on a blurred look. She drew a knot of Kleenex from her V neckline and pressed it first to one eye and then to the other. "Sorry," she said. "I keep changing moods. I feel like, I don't know, a TV screen in a windstorm. I'm so changeable."

"Most natural thing in the world," Durwood assured her.

Serena blew her nose and then tucked the Kleenex away again. "Anyhow," she said. "A neighbor's setting out some refreshments back at the house. Can you all come? I need to have people around me right now."

"Well, certainly," Maggie told her, and Durwood said, "Wouldn't miss it, Serena," both at the same time. "Just let me get my car," Durwood said.

"Oh, never mind that; we're all walking. It's just over there through the trees, and anyway there's not a lot of parking space."

She took Maggie's elbow, leaning slightly. "It did go well, didn't it?" she said. She steered her toward the road, while Durwood dropped behind with Sugar Tilghman. "I'm so glad I had the idea. Reverend Orbison threw a fit, but I said, 'Isn't this for me? Isn't a memorial service meant to comfort the living?' So he said yes, he guessed it was. And that's not the end of it, either! Wait till you see the surprise I've got up at the house."

"Surprise? What kind?" Maggie asked.

"*I'm* not telling," Serena said.

Maggie started chewing her lower lip.

They turned onto a smaller street, keeping to the shoulder because there wasn't a sidewalk. The houses here had a distinctly Pennsylvanian air, Maggie thought. They were mostly tall stone rectangles, flat-faced, set close to the road, with a meager supply of narrow windows. She imagined spare wooden furniture inside, no cushions or frills or modern conveniences, which of course was silly because a television antenna was strapped to every chimney.

The other guests were following in a leisurely parade—the

750

women tiptoeing through the gravel in their high heels, the men strolling with their hands in their pockets. Ira brought up the rear between Nat and Jo Ann. He gave no sign of minding this change in plans; or if he had at some earlier point, Maggie had luckily missed it.

"Durwood was wondering if you'd be staying on here," she told Serena. "Any chance you might move back to Baltimore?"

"Oh," Serena said, "Baltimore seems so far away by now. Who would I know anymore?"

"Me and Ira, for one thing," Maggie said. "Durwood Clegg. The Barley twins."

The Barley twins were walking just behind them, clinging to each other's arms. Both wore clip-on sunglasses over their regular glasses.

"Linda has been after me to move to New Jersey," Serena said. "Get an apartment close to her and Jeff."

"That would be nice."

"Well, I'm not so sure," Serena said. "Seems anytime we spend a few days together I begin to realize we haven't got a thing in common."

"But if you lived close by you wouldn't be spending days together," Maggie said. "You'd be dropping in and out. You'd be leaving when the conversation ran down. And besides, you'd see more of your grandchildren."

"Oh, well, grandchildren. I've never felt they had all that much to do with me."

"You wouldn't say that if someone kept them away from you," Maggie told her.

"How's *your* grandchild, Maggie?"

"I have no idea," Maggie said. "Nobody tells me a thing. And Fiona's getting married again; I found that out purely by accident."

"Is that so! Well, it'll be good for Larue to have a man around."

"Leroy," Maggie said. "But see, Fiona's true love is still

751

Jesse. She's said as much, in so many words. There's just something gone wrong between them temporarily. It would be a terrible mistake for her to marry someone else! And then poor little Leroy . . . oh, I hate to think of all that child has been through. Living in that run-down house, secondhand smoking—"

"Smoking! A six-year-old?"

"Seven-year-old. But it's her grandmother who smokes."

"Well, then," Serena said.

"But it's Leroy's lungs getting coated with tar."

"Oh, Maggie, let her go," Serena said. "Let it all go! That's what I say. I was watching Linda's boys this morning, climbing our back fence, and first I thought, Oh-oh, better call them in; they're bound to rip those sissy little suits, and then I thought, Nah, forget it. It's not *my* affair, I thought. Let them go."

"But I don't want to let go," Maggie said. "What kind of talk is that?"

"You don't have any choice," Serena told her. She stepped over a branch that lay across their path. "That's what it comes down to in the end, willy-nilly: just pruning and disposing. Why, you've been doing that all along, right? You start shucking off your children from the day you give birth; that's the whole point. A big, big moment is when you can look at them and say, 'Now if I died they could get along without me. I'm free to die,' you say. 'What a relief!' Discard, discard! Throw out the toys in the basement. Move to a smaller house. Menopause delighted me."

"Menopause!" Maggie said. "You've been through menopause?"

"Gladly," Serena told her.

"Oh, Serena!" Maggie said, and she stopped short, nearly causing the Barley twins to bump into her.

"Well, goodness," Serena said, "why should that bother you?"

752

"But I remember when we first got our periods," Maggie said. "Remember how we all waited? Remember," she said, turning to the Barley twins, "how that was once the only thing we talked about? Who had started and who had not? What it must feel like? How on earth we'd keep it secret from our husbands when we married?"

The Barley twins nodded, smiling. Their eyes were invisible behind their dark glasses.

"And now she's gone and stopped," Maggie told them.

"*We* haven't stopped," Jeannie Barley caroled.

"She's gone through change of life!" Maggie cried.

"Wonderful; announce it to the world," Serena said. She linked arms with Maggie and they resumed walking. "Believe me, I barely gave it a thought. 'Well, good,' I told myself. 'Just one more thing to let go of.' "

Maggie said, "I don't feel I'm letting go; I feel they're taking things away from me. My son's grown up and my daughter's leaving for college and they're talking at the nursing home about laying off some of the workers. It's something to do with the new state regulations—they're going to hire on more professionals and lay off people like me."

"So? That job was always beneath you anyway," Serena said. "You were a straight-A student, remember? Or near about."

"It is not beneath me, Serena; I love it. You sound just like my mother. I love that job!"

"Then go back to school and get to be a professional yourself," Serena said.

Maggie gave up on her. She was too tired, all at once, to argue.

They turned in through a little gate, onto a flagstone path. Serena's house was newer than the others—raw brick, one story, modern and compact. Someone stood at the front window, drawing back a curtain to gaze out, but when the guests ap-

753

proached she dropped the curtain and vanished. She reappeared at the door, a buttressed and corseted woman in a stiff navy dress. "Oh, you poor thing!" she cried to Serena. "You come right on in. Everybody, come in! There's lots to eat and drink. Anyone want to freshen up?"

Maggie did. She followed the woman's directions and passed through the living room, which was filled with heavy furniture in a wagon-wheel motif, and down a short hall to the bedroom. The decor seemed purely Max's doing: a bedspread patterned with multicolored license plates, a beer stein collection lining the bookshelf. On the bureau, a photo of Linda in cap and gown stood next to a bronze cowboy boot stuffed with pencils and gnawed plastic swizzle sticks. But someone had hung guest towels in the bathroom and set out a bowl of rosette-shaped soaps. Maggie washed up, using the bar of Ivory she found in a cabinet beneath the sink. She dried her hands on a grayish bath towel draped behind the shower curtain, and then she peered into the mirror. The walk had not done anything for her appearance. She tried to flatten her bangs down. She stood sideways to the mirror and sucked in her stomach. Meanwhile the Barley twins were discussing Linda's photograph: "Isn't it a pity she got Max's looks and not Serena's." Nat Abrams said, "Would this be the line for the john?" and Maggie called, "Just coming out."

She emerged to find Ira waiting with Nat; now their topic was gas mileage. She returned to the living room. The guests were gathered in the dining alcove, where platters of food covered a table—sandwiches and cakes and drinks. Sissy Parton's husband was serving as bartender. Maggie recognized him by his violent pink hair, the color of freshly cut cedarwood. It hadn't dimmed in the slightest. She went over to him and said, "Hello, Michael."

"Maggie Daley! Nice singing," he said. "But what became of Ira?"

"Oh, well . . ." she said vaguely. "Could I have a gin and tonic, please?"

He made her one, pouring the gin with a flourish. "I hate these affairs," he told her. "This is my second funeral this week."

"Who else died?" Maggie asked.

"Oh, an old poker buddy. And last month my Aunt Linette, and the month before that . . . I tell you, first I went to all my kids' school plays, and no sooner was I done with those than we start on this."

A stranger came up and asked him for a Scotch. Maggie started circulating through the living room. She didn't hear much talk of Max. People were discussing the World Series, the prevalence of crime, the proper depth for tulip bulbs. Two women Maggie had never seen before were assembling a composite portrait of some couple they both knew. "*He* was a bit of a drinker," one said.

"Yes, but he adored her."

"Oh, he'd never have managed without her."

"Were you at that Easter brunch they gave?"

"Was I there! The one with the chocolate centerpiece?"

"It was a present from him to her, she said. He'd surprised her with it that morning."

"A hollow chocolate rabbit. He'd filled it with rum."

"*She* didn't know he'd filled it with rum."

"He said he'd wanted it to be like those Swiss candies they fill with liqueurs."

"Rum seeped out the bottom."

"Little melty holes in the chocolate."

"Worst mess you ever saw, all across the tablecloth."

"Lucky it was only one of those Hallmark paper tablecloths for holidays."

Back in the dining alcove, the Barley twins were talking with Michael. They had flipped up their clip-on shades, which stuck out above their glasses like the perky antennas of some sharp-faced, cute little creatures from outer space, and they were nodding earnestly, in unison. Jo Ann and Sugar were discussing mixed marriages—the consuming interest of Jo Ann's life for years before her wedding to Nat and evidently afterward as well. "But tell me the truth," Sugar was saying. "Doesn't it sometimes seem to you like *every* marriage is mixed?" And Serena's two little grandsons were surreptitiously bombarding each other with bits of cake. It looked good: angel food. Maggie thought about trying a slice but then she remembered her diet. She had a virtuous, empty feeling in the center of her rib cage. She traveled around the table surveying what was offered, resisting even the bowl of Fritos. "The dump salad is mine," Serena's neighbor said at her elbow.

"Dump salad?"

"You take a packet of orange Jell-O powder, a can of crushed pineapple, a carton of Cool Whip . . ."

Some woman in a bouffant hairdo said hello and the neighbor turned to greet her, leaving Maggie with the gritty feeling of Jell-O powder on her teeth.

Serena was over by the buffet, beneath an oil painting of a dead bird with a basket of olive-drab fruit. Linda and her husband stood next to her. "When all these people leave, Mom," Linda was saying, "we're taking you out to dinner, anyplace your heart desires." She spoke a little above normal volume, as if Serena were hard of hearing. "We're going to buy you a real meal," she said.

"Oh, well, there's so much food right here in the house," Serena said. "And I'm honestly not all that hungry anyhow."

Her son-in-law said, "Now, Mother Gill, just tell us your favorite restaurant." Jeff, that was it. Maggie couldn't think of his last name.

Serena said, "Um . . ." She glanced around, as if hoping for a suggestion. Her eyes brushed Maggie and traveled on. Finally she said, "Oh, well, maybe the Golden Chopsticks. That's a good place."

"What kind is it, Chinese?"

"Well, yes, but they also have—"

"Oh, I just don't care for Chinese food," Linda said. "Not Chinese or Japanese, either one, I'm sorry to say."

"Or any other Oriental," Jeff pointed out. "You don't like Thai food either."

"No, that's true. Or Filipino or Burmese."

Serena said, "But—"

"And you can't eat Indian; don't forget Indian," Jeff said.

"No; Indian has those spices."

"Spices affect her digestion," Jeff told Serena.

"I guess I'm just sensitive or something," Linda said.

"Same goes for Mexican."

"But we don't have any Mexican," Serena said. "We don't have any of those places."

Linda said, "What I'd like to know is how the Mexicans themselves can stand all those spicy seasonings."

"They can't," Jeff told her. "They come down with this awful condition that coats the insides of their mouths like plates of armor."

Serena blinked. "Well," she said, "what kind of restaurant did you two have in mind?"

"We thought maybe that steak house off of Route One," Jeff told her.

"MacMann's? Oh."

"That is, if it's all right with you."

"Well, MacMann's is kind of . . . noisy, isn't it?" Serena asked.

"I never thought it was noisy," Linda said.

"I mean it's always so noisy and crowded."

"Just take it or leave it, Mom," Linda told her, raising her chin. "We were only trying to be nice, for God's sake."

Maggie, standing just outside their little circle, waited for Serena to toss her one of her wry, eye-rolling expressions. But Serena didn't even glance at her. She seemed shrunken, somehow; she had lost her dash. She lifted her drink to her lips and sipped reflectively.

Then Max's brother called, "Serena? You ready for this?"

He was gesturing toward a mildewed black leatherette case that stood on the coffee table. It looked familiar; Maggie couldn't think why. Serena brightened. She turned to Maggie and said, "That there is my surprise."

"What is it?" Maggie asked.

"We're going to show a movie of my wedding."

Of course: a film projector. Maggie hadn't seen one of those in years. She watched as Max's brother unsnapped the silver clasps. Meanwhile Serena moved away to lower the window shades. "We'll use this biggest shade for the screen," she called. "Oh, I hope the film hasn't just disintegrated or bleached out or whatever it is that old film does."

"You mean your and *Max's* wedding?" Maggie asked, following her.

"His uncle Oswald took it."

"I don't remember a camera at the wedding."

"I was thinking back over the songs last night and I all at once remembered. 'If it's still in one piece,' I said to myself, 'wouldn't it be fun to watch?' "

Fun? Maggie wasn't so sure. But she wouldn't have missed it, all the same; so she found herself a seat on the rug. She set down her glass and curled her legs to one side. A very old lady was sitting in a chair next to her, but at this level all Maggie saw were her thick beige cotton ankles melting over the tops of her shoes.

Now the guests had got wind of what was about to take place. Serena's classmates were settling around the projector, while the others started flowing distractedly in different directions, like something under a microscope. A few edged toward the door, mentioning baby-sitters and appointments elsewhere, promising Serena they would keep in touch. Several returned to the bar, and since Michael had deserted, they began mixing their own drinks. Michael was in the living room now, and so was Nat. Ira wasn't anywhere that Maggie could see. Nat was asking Sugar, "Am I in this, do you think?"

"You are if you sang at the wedding."

"Well, I didn't," he said glumly.

With just a little stretch of the imagination, Maggie thought, this could be Mr. Alden's civics class. (You had to overlook the old lady, who had remained contentedly seated with her tinkling cup of tea.) She glanced around and saw a semicircle of graying men and women, and there was something so worn down about them, so benign and unassuming, that she felt at that moment they were as close to her as family. She wondered how she could have failed to realize that they would have been aging along with her all these years, going through more or less the same stages—rearing their children and saying goodbye to them, marveling at the wrinkles they discovered in the mirror, watching their parents turn fragile and uncertain. Somehow, she had pictured them still fretting over Prom Night.

Even the sound of the projector came straight from Mr. Alden's class—the clickety-click as the reels started spinning and a square of flawed, crackled light was cast upon the window shade. What would Mr. Alden say if he could see them all together again? He was probably dead by now. And anyway, this movie wasn't showing how democracy worked or how laws were born, but—

Why, Sissy! Sissy Parton! Young and slender and prim, wearing a tight chignon encircled with artificial daisies like a French maid's frill. She was playing the piano, her wrists so gracefully arched that you could believe it was only the delicacy of her touch that caused the film to remain soundless. Above the white choir robe, the Peter Pan collar of her blouse was just visible, a pale salmon pink (in real life a deep rose, Maggie recalled). She lifted her head and looked purposefully toward a

759

certain point, and the camera followed her gaze and the screen was suddenly filled with a double row of ridiculously clean-cut young people in pleated robes. They sang silently, their mouths perfect ovals. They resembled the carolers on a Christmas card. It was Serena who identified the tune. " 'True love,' " she sang, " 'true—' " And then she broke off to say, "Oh! Would you look? Mary Jean Bennett! I never even thought to invite her. I forgot all about her. Does anybody know where Mary Jean lives now?"

No one answered, although several, in low, dreamy murmurs, carried on with " '. . for you and I have a guardian angel . . .' "

"There's Nick Bourne, the rat," Serena said. "He claimed it was too far to come to the funeral."

She was sitting on the arm of a chair, craning her neck toward the movie. In profile she looked commanding, almost glorious, Maggie thought, with that silver line of light from the screen running down her large, straight nose and the curve of her lips.

Maggie herself stood in the front row of the chorus, next to Sugar Tilghman. Her hair was in tiny squiggles all over her head; it made her face look too big. Oh, this was humiliating. But no doubt the others felt the same way. She distinctly heard Sugar groan. And when the camera switched to Durwood, with his wet, black, towering pompadour like the crest on the top of a Dairy Queen cone, he gave a sharp bark of laughter. This younger Durwood strode over to the piano with his robe flapping behind him. He assumed his position and paused importantly. Then he embarked on a silent "I Want You, I Need You, I Love You" with his eyes closed more often than open, his left arm gesturing so passionately that once he swatted a lily in a papier-mâché vase. Maggie wanted to laugh but she held it in. So did everyone else, although the old lady said, "Well! My goodness," and rattled her teacup. A couple of people were humming along with this song too, which Maggie thought was charitable of them.

Next the camera swung dizzyingly to Jo Ann Dermott at the front of the church. She gripped the edges of the pulpit and read from a book that the audience couldn't see. Since she wasn't in the chorus, her dress was completely exposed—stiff, square-shouldered, full-skirted, more matronly than anything she would ever wear again. Her lowered eyes looked naked. No one could hum along with *The Prophet*, so the reading just went on and on in total silence. Out in the dining alcove the other guests talked and laughed and clinked ice cubes. "Good Lord, fast-forward it, someone," Jo Ann said, but evidently Max's brother didn't know how (if you *could* fast-forward these old films), and so they had to sit through it.

Then the camera swooped again and there was Sissy playing the piano, with one damp curl plastered to her forehead. Maggie and Ira, side by side, stood watching Sissy gravely. (Ira was a boy, a mere child.) They drew a breath. They started singing. Maggie was slightly bunchy in her robe—she'd been fighting her extra ten pounds even then—and Ira had a plucked, fledgling look. Had he really worn his hair that short? In those days, he'd seemed totally unreadable. His unreadability was his greatest attraction. He'd reminded her of those math geniuses who don't need to write out the process but simply arrive at the answer.

He was twenty-one when that movie was filmed. Maggie was nineteen. Where they'd met, she had no idea, because at the time it hadn't mattered. They had probably passed each other in the halls in high school, maybe even elementary school. He might have visited her house, hanging out with her brothers. (He and her brother Josh were nearly the same age.) Certainly he'd sung with her at church; she knew that much. His family were members there, and Mr. Nichols, always short on male voices, had somehow talked Ira into joining the choir. But he hadn't lasted long. About the time he graduated from high school, he quit. Or maybe it was the year after. Maggie hadn't noticed exactly when it was he'd stopped appearing.

Her boyfriend in high school had been a classmate named Boris Drumm. He was short and dark, with rough skin and a frizz of cropped black hair—manly even at that age, everything she'd been looking for. It was Boris who taught Maggie to drive, and one of his exercises involved her speeding alone across the Sears, Roebuck parking lot till he loomed suddenly in front of the car to test her braking skills. Her clearest picture of him, to this day, was the determined stance he had taken in her path: arms straight out, feet wide apart, jaw set. Rock-hard, he'd seemed. Indestructible. She had had the feeling she could run him over, even, and he'd have bobbed up again untouched, like one of those plastic toy men weighted with lead at the base.

He planned on attending a college in the Midwest after graduation, but it was understood that as soon as he got his degree he and Maggie would marry. Meanwhile Maggie would live at home and go to Goucher. She wasn't much looking forward to it; it was her mother's idea. Her mother, who had taught English before she married, filled out all the application forms and even wrote Maggie's essay for her. It was very important to her that her children should rise in the world. (Maggie's father installed garage doors and had not had any college at all.) So Maggie resigned herself to four years at Goucher. In the meantime, to help with tuition, she took a summer job washing windows.

This was at the Silver Threads Nursing Home, which hadn't yet officially opened. It was a brand-new, modern building off Erdman Avenue, with three long wings and one hundred and eighty-two windows. Each of the larger windows had twelve panes of glass; the smaller windows had six. And in the left-hand corner of each pane was a white paper snowflake reading KRYSTAL KLEER MFG. CO. These snowflakes clung to the glass with a force that Maggie had never seen before or since. Whatever substance held them on, she thought later, should have been adopted by NASA. If you peeled off the top layer of paper a lower, fuzzy layer remained, and if you soaked that in hot water and then scraped it with a razor blade there were still gray shreds of rubbery glue, and after those were gone the whole pane, of course, was a mess, fingerprinted and streaky, so it had to be sprayed with Windex and buffed with a chamois skin. For one whole summer, from nine in the morning till four in the afternoon, Maggie scraped and soaked and scraped again. The tips of her fingers were continually sore. She felt her nails had been driven back into their roots. She didn't have anyone to talk to while she worked, because she was the only window-washer they'd hired. Her sole company was the radio, playing "Moonglow" and "I Almost Lost My Mind."

In August the home started admitting a few patients, although not all the work was finished yet. Of course they were settled in those rooms where the windows were fully scraped, but Maggie got in the habit of taking a break from time to time and going visiting. She would stop at one bed or another to see how people were doing. "Could you move my water pitcher a little closer, doll?" a woman would ask, or, "Would you mind pulling that curtain?" While performing these tasks, Maggie felt valuable and competent. She began attracting a following of those patients who were mobile. Someone in a wheelchair would discover which room she was working in and suddenly there'd be three or four patients sitting around her talking. Their style of conversation was to ignore her presence and argue heatedly among themselves. (Was it the blizzard of '88 or the blizzard of '89? And which number counted more in the blood pressure reading?) But they conveyed an acute awareness of their audience; she knew it was all for her benefit. She would laugh at appropriate moments or make sounds of sympathy, and the old people would take on gratified expressions.

No one in her family understood when she announced that

she wanted to forget about college and become an aide in the nursing home instead. Why, an aide was no better than a servant, her mother pointed out; no better than a chambermaid. And here Maggie had such a fine mind and had graduated at the top of her class. Did she want to be just ordinary? Her brothers, who had made the same kind of choice themselves (three were involved in some phase of the construction business, while the fourth welded locomotives at the Mount Clare railyards), claimed they had been looking to her to go further. Even her father wondered half audibly whether she knew what she was doing. But Maggie remained firm. What did she want with college? What did she want with those pointless, high-flown bits of information like the ones she'd learned in high school— *Ontogeny recapitulates phylogeny* and *Synecdoche is the use of the part to symbolize the whole*? She enrolled in a Red Cross training program, which in those days was all that was needed, and took a job at Silver Threads.

So there she was, eighteen and a half years old, working among old people and living with two elderly parents and her one unmarried brother, who was elderly himself, in a way. Boris Drumm had to earn his own school expenses, so he came back to Baltimore only at Christmas and spent the other holidays selling menswear in a shop near his campus. He wrote lengthy letters describing how his studies were altering his perceptions of the universe. The world was so full of injustice! he wrote. He had never realized. Writing back was hard because Maggie had very little to report. She didn't run into many of their friends anymore. Some had gone away to college, and when they returned they had changed. Some had married, which caused an even bigger change. Pretty soon the only people she saw regularly were Sugar and the Barley twins—just because they still sang in the choir—and, of course, Serena, her best friend. But Boris had never thought much of Serena, so Maggie seldom mentioned her in her letters.

764

Serena worked in a lingerie shop, clerking. She brought home translucent, lacy underwear in colors that made no sense. (Wouldn't a bright-red bra advertise itself through almost any piece of clothing you owned?) Modeling a black nightgown with a see-through bodice, she announced that she and Max were marrying in June, after he had finished his freshman year at UNC. UNC was a deal he had made with his parents. He had promised to try one year of college and then if he really, truly hated it they would let him drop out. What they were hoping, of course, was that he would meet a nice Southern girl and get over his infatuation with Serena. Not that they would admit it.

Max said that after they were married she could quit her job at the lingerie shop and never work again, Serena said; and also, she said (languorously lowering a black lace strap and admiring her own creamy shoulder), he was pleading with her to accompany him to the Blue Hen Motel the next time he came home. They wouldn't *do* anything, he said; just be together. Maggie was impressed and envious. It sounded very romantic to her. "You're going, aren't you?" she asked, but Serena said, "What do you think: I'm insane? I'd have to be out of my mind."

"But, Serena—" Maggie began. She was about to say that this was nothing like Anita's situation, nothing whatsoever, but Serena's fierce expression stopped her.

"*I'm* no sucker," Serena said.

Maggie wondered what she herself would do if Boris ever invited her to the Blue Hen Motel. She didn't think that would occur to him, though. Maybe it was just because she was forced to rely on his long, stuffy letters for any sense of him these days, but lately Boris had begun to seem less . . . crisp, you might say; less hard-edged. In his letters now he was talking about entering law school after college and then going into politics. Only in politics, he said, did you have the power to right the world's wrongs. But it was funny: Maggie had never seen politicians as powerful. She saw them as beggars. They were always begging for votes, altering themselves to satisfy their public, behaving spinelessly and falsely in a pathetic bid for popularity. She hated to think that Boris was that way.

She wondered if Serena ever had second thoughts about Max. No, probably not. Serena and Max seemed perfectly suited. Serena was so lucky.

Maggie's nineteenth birthday—Valentine's Day, 1957—fell on a Thursday, which was choir practice night. Serena brought a cake and after practice she passed out slices, along with paper cups of ginger ale, and everyone sang "Happy Birthday." Old Mrs. Britt, who really should have retired from singing years before but no one had the heart to suggest it, looked around her and sighed. "Isn't it sad," she said, "how the young folks are drifting away. Why, Sissy hardly comes at all since she married, and Louisa's moving to Montgomery County, and now I hear the Moran boy's gone and got himself killed."

"Killed?" Serena said. "How did that happen?"

"Oh, one of those freak training accidents," Mrs. Britt said. "I don't know the details."

Sugar, whose fiancé was at Camp Lejeune, said, "Lord, Lord, all I want is for Robert to come back safe and in one piece"—as if he were off waging hand-to-hand combat someplace, which of course he wasn't. (It happened to be one of those rare half-minutes in history when the country was not engaged in any serious hostilities.) Then Serena offered seconds on the birthday cake, but everyone had to go home.

That night in bed Maggie started thinking about the Moran boy, for some reason. Although she hadn't known him well, she found she had a clear mental picture of him: a sloucher, tall and high-cheekboned, with straight, oily black hair. She should have guessed he was doomed to die young. He'd been the only boy in the choir who didn't horse around while Mr. Nichols was talking to them. He had had an air of self-possession. She remembered too that he drove a car that ran on pure know-how, on junkyard parts and friction tape. Now that she thought of it, she believed she could envision his hands on the steering wheel. They were tanned and leathery, unusually wide across the base of the thumb, and the creases of his knuckles were deeply ingrained with mechanic's grease. She saw him in an army uniform with knife-sharp creases down the front of the trousers—a man who drove headlong to his death without even changing expression.

It was her first inkling that her generation was part of the stream of time. Just like the others ahead of them, they would grow up and grow old and die. Already there was a younger generation prodding them from behind.

Boris wrote and said he would try his very best to come home for spring vacation. Maggie wished he wouldn't sound so effortful. He had none of Ira Moran's calm assurance.

Serena got an engagement ring with a diamond shaped like a heart. It was dazzling. She began to plan and replan a great involved wedding production scheduled for the eighth of June, a date toward which she moved majestically, like a ship, with all her girlfriends fluttering in her wake. Maggie's mother said it was absurd to make such a fuss about a wedding. She said that people who lived for their weddings experienced a big letdown afterward, and then she said, changing her tone, "That poor, sad child, going to such lengths; I have to say I pity her." Maggie was shocked. (Pity! It seemed to her that Serena was already beginning her life, while she, Maggie, waited on a side rail.) Meanwhile Serena chose an ivory lace wedding dress but then changed her mind and decided white satin would be better, and she selected first an assortment of sacred music and then an assortment of secular music, and she notified all her friends that her kitchen would have a strawberry motif.

Maggie tried to remember what she knew of Ira Moran's family. They must be devastated by their loss. His mother, she seemed to recall, was dead. His father was a vague, seedy man with Ira's stooped posture, and there had been some sisters—two or three, perhaps. She could point exactly to which pew they'd always occupied in church, but now that she thought to look, she found they weren't there anymore. She watched for them all the rest of February and most of March, but they never showed up.

Boris Drumm came home for spring break and accompanied her to church that Sunday. Maggie stood in the choir section looking down at where he sat, between her father and her brother Elmer, and it occurred to her that he fit in very well. Too well. Like all the men in her family, he assumed a sort of hangdog expression during hymns and muttered them rather than sang them, or perhaps merely mouthed the words, letting his eyes skate to one side as if hoping not to be noticed. Only Maggie's mother actually sang, jutting her chin forward and enunciating clearly.

After Sunday dinner with her family, Maggie and Boris went out on the porch. Maggie lazily toed the porch swing back and forth while Boris discussed his political aspirations. He said he figured he would start small, maybe just get on the school board or something. Then he would work up to senator. "Hmm," Maggie said. She swallowed a yawn.

Then Boris gave a little cough and asked if she had ever thought of going to nursing school. That might be a good plan, he said, if she was so all fired up about taking care of old people. Probably this too had some connection with his career; senators' wives didn't empty bedpans. She said, "But I don't want to be a nurse."

"You were always so smart at your studies, though," he told her.

"I don't want to stand at a nursing station filling out forms; I want to deal with folks!" Maggie said.

Her voice was sharper than she had intended. He drew away.

"Sorry," she said.

She felt too big. She was taller than he when they were seated, especially when he hunkered down, as he was doing now.

He said, "Is something troubling you, Maggie? You haven't seemed yourself all spring vacation."

"Well, I'm sorry," she said, "but I've had a . . . loss. A very close friend of mine has passed away."

She didn't feel she was exaggerating. It did seem, by now, that she and Ira had been close. They just hadn't consciously understood that.

"Well, why didn't you say so?" Boris asked. "Who was it?"

"No one you knew."

"You can't be sure of that! Who was it?"

"Oh, well," she said, "his name was Ira."

"Ira," Boris said. "You mean Ira Moran?"

She nodded, keeping her eyes down.

"Skinny guy? Couple of classes ahead of us?"

She nodded.

"Wasn't he part Indian or something?"

She hadn't been aware of this but it sounded right. It sounded perfect.

"Of course I knew him," Boris said. "Just to say hello to, I mean. I mean, he wasn't actually a friend or anything. I didn't realize he was your friend, either."

Where does she *get* these characters, his beetled expression was saying. First Serena Palermo and now a red Indian.

"He was one of my favorite people," she said.

"He was? Oh. Is that right. Well. Well, you have my condolences, Maggie," Boris said. "I just wish you'd told me earlier." He considered a minute. He said, "How did it happen, anyway?"

"It was a training accident," Maggie said.

"Training?"

769

"In boot camp."

"I didn't even know he'd enlisted," Boris said. "I thought he worked in his father's frame shop. Isn't that where I got our prom photo framed? Sam's Frame Shop? Seems to me Ira was the one who waited on me."

"Really?" Maggie said, and she thought of Ira behind a counter, another image to add to her small collection. "Well, he did," she said. "Enlist, I mean. And then he had this accident."

"I'm sorry to hear that," Boris said.

A few minutes later she told him she'd prefer to spend the rest of the day alone, and Boris said that of course he understood.

That night in bed she started crying. Speaking of Ira's death out loud was what had done it. She hadn't mentioned it before, not even to Serena, who would say, "What are you talking about? You barely knew the guy."

She and Serena were growing apart, Maggie realized. She cried harder, blotting her tears on the hem of her sheet.

The next day Boris went back to school. Maggie had the morning off and so she was the one who drove him to the bus station. She felt lonesome after she had said goodbye. It suddenly seemed very sad that he had come all this way just to see her. She wished she had been nicer to him.

At home, her mother was spring cleaning. She had already rolled up the carpets and laid down the sisal mats for summer, and now she stripped the curtains from the windows with a snapping sound. A bleak white light gradually filled the house. Maggie climbed the stairs to her room and flung herself on her bed. For the rest of her life, probably, she was doomed to live on unmarried in this tedious, predictable family.

After a few minutes, she got up and went to her parents' room. She took the yellow pages from under the telephone. *Frames*, no. *Picture frames*, yes. *Sam's Frame Shop*. She had thought she just wanted to see it in print, but eventually she scribbled the address on a memo pad and took it back to her room.

She owned no black-bordered stationery, so she chose the plainest of what she'd been given for graduation—white with a single green fern in one corner. *Dear Mr. Moran,* she wrote.

> *I used to sing in the choir with your son and I had to*
> *let you know how sad I am to hear of his death. I'm*
> *not writing just out of politeness. I thought Ira was the*
> *most wonderful person I've ever met. There was some-*
> *thing special about him and I wanted to tell you that*
> *as long as I live, I'm going to remember him fondly.*
>
> With deepest sympathy,
Margaret M. Daley

She sealed and addressed the envelope and then, before she could change her mind, she walked to the corner and dropped it in the mailbox.

At first she didn't think about Mr. Moran's answering, but later on, at work, it occurred to her that he might. Of course: People were supposed to answer sympathy notes. Maybe he would say something personal about Ira that she could store up and treasure. Maybe he would say that Ira had mentioned her name. That wasn't completely impossible. Or, seeing how she had been one of the few who had properly valued his son, he might even send her some little memento—maybe an old photo. She would love a photo. She wished now she had thought to ask for one.

Since she'd mailed the letter Monday, it would probably reach Ira's father Tuesday. So his answer could come on Thursday. She hurried through her work Thursday morning in a fever of impatience. At lunch hour she phoned home, but her mother said the mail hadn't arrived yet. (She also said, "Why? What are you expecting?" which was the kind of thing that made

Maggie long to get married and move out.) At two she phoned again, but her mother said there'd been nothing for her.

That evening, walking to choir practice, she counted up the days once more and realized that Mr. Moran might not have received her letter on Tuesday after all. She hadn't mailed it till nearly noon, she remembered. This made her feel better. She started walking faster, waving at Serena when she spotted her on the steps of the church.

Mr. Nichols was late, and the choir members joked and gossiped while they waited for him. They were all a little heady now that spring was here—even old Mrs. Britt. The church windows were open and they could hear the neighborhood children playing out on the sidewalk. The night air smelled of newly cut grass. Mr. Nichols, when he arrived, wore a sprig of lavender in his buttonhole. He must have bought it from the street vendor, who had only that morning appeared with his cart for the first time that year. "Sorry, ladies and gentlemen," Mr. Nichols said. He set his briefcase on a pew and rooted through it for his notes.

The church door opened again and in walked Ira Moran.

He was very tall and somber, in a white shirt with the sleeves rolled up and slim black trousers. He wore a stern expression that lengthened his chin, as if there were something lumpy in his mouth. Maggie felt her heart stop. She felt icy at first and then overheated, but she stared through him blankly with dry, wide eyes, keeping her thumb in place in the hymnbook. Even in that first moment, she knew he wasn't a ghost or a mirage. He was as real as the gummy varnished pews, not so flawlessly assembled as she had pictured but more intricately textured— more physical, somehow; more complicated.

Mr. Nichols said, "Oh, Ira. Glad to see you."

"Thanks," Ira said. Then he filed through the folding chairs toward the rear, where the men sat, and he took a seat. But Maggie saw how his gaze first skimmed the women in front, resting finally on her. She could tell he knew about the letter. She felt a flush pass over her face. Ordinarily graceful out of pure caution, pure timidity, she had been caught in an error so clumsy that she didn't believe she could ever again meet another person's eyes.

She sang numbly, standing and sitting as ordered. She sang "Once to Every Man and Nation" and "Shall We Gather at the River." Then Mr. Nichols had the men do "Shall We Gather at the River" on their own, and then he asked the accompanist to repeat a certain passage. While this was going on, Maggie leaned toward Mrs. Britt and whispered, "Wasn't that the Moran boy? The one who came in late?"

"Why, yes, I believe it was," Mrs. Britt said pleasantly.

"Didn't you tell us he'd been killed?"

"I did?" Mrs. Britt asked. She looked surprised and sat back in her chair. A moment later, she sat forward again and said, "That was the *Rand* boy who was killed. Monty Rand."

"Oh," Maggie said.

Monty Rand had been a little pale dishcloth of a person with an incongruously deep bass voice. Maggie had never much liked him.

After choir practice she gathered her belongings as quickly as possible and was first out the door, scuttling down the sidewalk with her purse hugged to her chest, but she hadn't even reached the corner when she heard Ira behind her. "Maggie?" he called.

She slowed beneath a streetlight and then stopped, not looking around. He came up next to her. His legs made a shadow like scissors on the sidewalk.

"Mind if I walk your way?" he said.

"Do what you like," she told him shortly. He fell into step beside her.

"So how've you been?" he asked.

"I'm okay."

"You're out of school now, right?"

773

She nodded. They crossed a street.

"Got a job?" he asked.

"I work at the Silver Threads Nursing Home."

"Oh. Well, good."

He started whistling the last hymn they had practiced: "Just a Closer Walk with Thee." He sauntered beside her with his hands in his pockets. They passed a couple kissing at a bus stop. Maggie cleared her throat and said, "Silly me! I mixed you up with the Rand boy."

"Rand?"

"Monty Rand; he got killed in boot camp and I thought they said it was you."

She still didn't look at him, although he was near enough so she could smell his fresh-ironed shirt. She wondered who had ironed it. One of his sisters, probably. What did that have to do with anything? She tightened her hold on her purse and walked faster, but Ira kept up with her. She was conscious of his dark, hooked presence at her elbow.

"So now will you write to *Monty's* father?" he asked her.

When she risked a sidelong glance she saw the humorous pleat at the corner of his mouth.

"Go ahead and laugh," she told him.

"I'm not laughing."

"Go ahead! Tell me I made a fool of myself."

"Do you hear me laughing?"

They had reached her block now. She could see her house up ahead, part of a string of row houses, the porch glowing orange beneath the bugproof light. This time when she stopped she looked directly into his face, and he returned the look without a hint of a smile, keeping his hands shoved in his pockets. She hadn't expected his eyes to be so narrow. He could have been Asian, rather than Indian.

"Your father must have split his sides," she said.

"No, he was just . . . he just asked me what it could mean."

774

She tried to think what words she had used in the letter. Special, she'd written. Oh, Lord. And worse yet: wonderful. She wished she could disappear.

"I remember you from choir practice," Ira said. "You're Josh's sister, right? But I guess we never really knew each other."

"No, of course not," she said. "Goodness! We were total strangers." She tried to sound brusque and sensible.

He studied her a moment. Then he said, "So do you think we might get to know each other now?"

"Well," she said, "I do go out with someone."

"Really? Who?"

"Boris Drumm," she said.

"Oh, yes."

She looked off toward her house. She said, "We'll probably get married."

"I see," he said.

"Well, goodbye," she told him.

He lifted a hand in silence, thought a moment, and then turned and walked away.

That Sunday, though, he came to sing with the choir at the morning service. Maggie felt relieved, almost lightweight with relief, as if she'd been given a second chance, and then her heart sank when he just melted into the crowd again after church. But Thursday night he was at choir practice again and he walked her home when it was over. They talked about trivial subjects—Mrs. Britt's splintery voice, for instance. Maggie grew more comfortable. When they reached her house she saw her neighbor's dog out front, peeing on Maggie's mother's one rose-bush, with the neighbor standing there watching; so she called, "Hey, lady! Get your dog out of our yard, you hear?" She was joking; it was the rough style of humor she had picked up from her brothers. But Ira didn't know that and he looked taken aback. Then Mrs. Wright laughed and said, "You and who else going to make me, kid?" and Ira relaxed. But Maggie felt she'd been clumsy once again, and she murmured a hasty good night and went inside.

Soon enough it became a pattern—Thursday nights and Sunday mornings. People started to notice. Maggie's mother said, "Maggie? Does Boris know about this new friendship of yours?" and Maggie snapped, "Of course he knows"—a lie, or at best a half-truth. (Maggie's mother thought Boris was God's gift to women.) But Serena said, "Good for you! High time you dumped Mr. Holier-than-Thou."

"I haven't dumped him!"

"Why not?" Serena asked. "When you compare him to Ira! Ira's so mysterious."

"Well, he *is* part Indian, of course," Maggie said.

"And you have to admit he's attractive."

Oh, Jesse was not the only one who'd been swayed by a single friend! Certainly Serena had more than a little to do with all that happened afterward.

She asked Maggie and Ira to sing a duet at her wedding, for instance. Out of the blue (for Ira had never been thought to have a particularly striking voice), she took it into her head that they should sing "Love is a Many Splendored Thing" before the exchange of vows. So of course they had to practice; so of course he had to come to her house. They commiserated with each other and they clucked over Serena's musical taste, but it never occurred to them to refuse her. Maggie's mother kept tip-tapping in and out with folded laundry that had no business in the living room. " 'Once,' " they sang, " 'on a high and windy hill,' " and then Maggie sputtered into laughter, but Ira remained sober. Maggie seemed to be turning into someone else, those days—someone giddy and unstable and accident-prone. Sometimes she imagined that that sympathy note had thrown her permanently off balance.

She knew by then that Ira ran his father's frame shop single-handed—Sam's "weak heart" had got to him the day after Ira's high-school graduation—and that he lived above the shop with his father and his two much older sisters, one of whom was a little slow and the other just shy or retiring or something. He wanted to go to college, though, if he could ever scrape together the money. He'd had hopes since childhood of becoming a doctor. He told her this in a neutral tone; he didn't seem discouraged about the way his life was turning out. Then he said maybe she'd like to come home with him sometime and meet his sisters; they didn't get to talk to very many people. But Maggie said, "No!" and then flushed and said, "Oh, I guess I'd better not," and pretended not to notice his amusement. She was afraid she'd run into his father. She wondered if his sisters knew about the letter too, but she didn't want to ask.

Never, not once in all this time, did he act any more than mildly friendly. When necessary he would take her arm—just to steer her through a crowd, say—and his hand felt firm and warm on her bare skin; but as soon as they'd passed the crowd he would release her. She wasn't even sure what he thought of her. She wasn't sure what she thought of him, either. And after all, there was Boris to consider. She went on writing Boris regularly—if anything, a little more often than usual.

Serena's wedding rehearsal was a Friday evening. It wasn't a very formal rehearsal. Max's parents, for instance, didn't even bother attending, although Serena's mother showed up with her hair in a million pink rollers. And events happened out of order, with Maggie (standing in for the bride, for good luck) coming down the aisle ahead of all the musical selections because Max had a trainload of relatives to meet in half an hour. She walked alongside Anita, which was one of Serena's more peculiar innovations. "Who else could give me away?" Serena asked. "You surely don't imagine my father would do it." Anita herself, however, didn't seem so happy with this arrangement. She teetered and staggered in her spike-heeled shoes and dug her long red nails into Maggie's wrist in order to keep her balance. At the altar Max slung an arm around Maggie and said, shoot, maybe he'd just settle for her instead; and Serena, sitting in a center pew, called, "That'll be quite enough of that, Max Gill!" Max was the same freckled, friendly, overgrown boy he'd always been. It was hard for Maggie to picture him married.

After the vows Max left for Penn Station and the rest of them practiced the music. They all performed in a fairly amateurish style, Maggie thought, which was fine with her because she and Ira didn't sound their best that night. They started off raggedly, and Maggie forgot that they had planned to split up the middle verse. She sailed right into the first two lines along with Ira, then stopped in confusion, then missed her own cue and fell into a fit of giggles. At that moment, the laughter not yet faded from her face, she saw Boris Drumm in the foremost pew. He wore a baffled, rumpled frown, as if someone had just awakened him.

Well, she'd known he was due home for the summer, but he hadn't told her which day. She pretended not to recognize him. She and Ira finished their song, and then she reverted to Serena's role and marched back up the aisle, minus Max, so Sugar could practice the timing on "Born to Be with You." After that Serena clapped her hands and shouted, "Okay, gang!" and they prepared to leave, all talking at once. They were thinking of going out for pizza. They swarmed toward Maggie, who waited at the rear of the church, but Boris stayed where he was, facing forward. He would be expecting Maggie to join him. She studied the back of his head, which was block-like and immobile. Serena handed her her purse and said, "You've got company, I see." Right behind Serena was Ira. He stopped in front of Maggie and looked down at her. He said, "Will you be going for pizza?"

Maggie said, "I guess not."

He nodded, blank-faced, and left. But he walked in a different direction from the others, as if he didn't feel they would welcome him without Maggie. Which of course was nonsense.

Maggie went back up the aisle and sat next to Boris, and they kissed. She said, "How was your trip?" and he said, "Who was that you were singing with?" at exactly the same instant. She pretended she hadn't heard. "How was your trip?" she asked again, and he said, "Wasn't that Ira Moran?"

"Who, the one singing?" she asked.

"That was Ira Moran! You told me he was dead!"

"It was a misunderstanding," she said.

"I heard you say it, Maggie."

"I mean I misunderstood that he was dead. He was only, um, wounded."

"Ah," Boris said. He turned that over in his mind.

"It was only a flesh wound, was all," Maggie told him. "A scalp wound." She wondered if the two terms contradicted each other. She riffled quickly through various movies she had seen.

"So then what? He just comes walking in one day?" Boris asked. "I mean he just pops up, like some kind of ghost? How did it happen, exactly?"

"Boris," Maggie said, "I fail to comprehend why you keep dwelling on this in such a tiresome fashion."

"Oh. Well. Sorry," Boris said.

(Had she really sounded so authoritative? She found it hard to imagine, looking back.)

On the morning of the wedding, Maggie got up early and walked to Serena's apartment—the second floor of a formstone row house—to help her dress. Serena seemed unruffled but her mother was all in a dither. Anita's habit when she was nervous was to speak very fast and with practically no punctuation, like someone in a hard-sell commercial. "Why she won't roll her hair like everybody else when I told her way last week I said hon nobody wears long hair anymore you ought to go to the beauty shop and get you a nice little flip to peek out under your veil . . ." She was rushing around the shabby, sparsely equipped

779

kitchen in a dirty pink satin bathrobe, with a cigarette dangling from her lips. She was making a great clatter but not much was getting accomplished. Serena, lazy and nonchalant in one of Max's big shirts, said, "Take it easy, Mom, will you?" She told Maggie, "Mom thinks we ought to change the whole ceremony."

"Change it how?" Maggie asked.

"She doesn't have any bridesmaids!" Anita said. "She doesn't have a maid of honor even and what's worse there's no kind of masculine person to walk her down the aisle!"

"She's upset she has to walk me down the aisle," Serena told Maggie.

"Oh if only your uncle Maynard would come and do it instead!" Anita cried. "Maybe we should move the wedding up a week and give him another chance because the way you have it now is all cockeyed it's too oddball I can just picture how those hoity-toity Gills will be scrupulizing me and smirking amongst themselves and besides that last perm I got scorched the tip-ends of my hair I can't walk down the aisle."

"Let's go get me dressed," Serena told Maggie, and she led her away.

In Serena's room, which was really just half of Anita's room curtained off with a draggled aqua bed sheet, Serena sat down at her vanity table. She said, "I thought of giving her a belt of whiskey, but I worried it might backfire."

Maggie said, "Serena, are you sure you ought to be marrying Max?"

Serena squawked and wheeled to face her. She said, "Maggie Daley, don't you start with me! I've already got my wedding cake frosted."

"But I mean how do you know? How can you be certain you chose the right man?"

"I can be certain because I've come to the end of the line," Serena said, turning back to the mirror. Her voice was at normal level now. She patted on liquid foundation, expertly dotting her chin and forehead and cheeks. "It's just *time* to marry, that's all," she said. "I'm so tired of dating! I'm so tired of keeping up a good front! I want to sit on the couch with a regular, normal husband and watch TV for a thousand years. It's going to be like getting out of a girdle; that's exactly how I picture it."

"What are you saying?" Maggie asked. She was almost afraid of the answer. "Are you telling me you don't really love Max?"

"Of course I love him," Serena said. She blended the dots into her skin. "But I've loved other people as much. I loved Terry Simpson our sophomore year—remember him? But it wasn't time to get married then, so Terry is not the one I'm marrying."

Maggie didn't know what to think. Did everybody feel that way? Had the grownups been spreading fairy tales? "The minute I saw Eleanor," her oldest brother had told her once, "I said, 'That girl is going to be my wife someday.' " It hadn't occurred to Maggie that he might simply have been ready for a wife, and therefore had his eye out for the likeliest prospect.

So there again, Serena had managed to color Maggie's view of things. "We're not in the hands of fate after all," she seemed to be saying. "Or if we are, we can wrest ourselves free any time we care to."

Maggie sat down on the bed and watched Serena applying her rouge. In Max's shirt, Serena looked casual and sporty, like anybody's girl next door. "When this is over," she told Maggie, "I'm going to dye my wedding dress purple. Might as well get some use out of it."

Maggie gazed at her thoughtfully.

The wedding was due to start at eleven, but Anita wanted to get to the church much earlier, she said, in case of mishaps. Maggie rode with them in Anita's ancient Chevrolet. Serena drove because Anita said she was too nervous, and since Serena's skirt billowed over so much of the seat, Maggie and Anita sat in back. Anita was talking nonstop and sprinkling cigarette ashes across the lap of her shiny peach mother-of-the-bride dress. "Now that I think of it Serena I can't imagine why you're holding your reception in the Angels of Charity building which is so damn far away and every time I've tried to find it I've gotten all turned around and had to ask directions from passing strangers . . . ."

They came to the Alluring Lingerie Shop, and Serena double-parked and heaved her cascades of satin out of the car in order to go model her dress for Mrs. Knowlton, her employer. While they waited for her, Anita said, "Honestly you'd suppose if you can rent a man to come tend your bar or fix your toilet or check on why your door won't lock it wouldn't be any problem at all to engage one for the five eentsy minutes it takes to walk your daughter down the aisle don't you agree?"

"Yes, ma'am," Maggie said, and she dug absently into a hole in the vinyl seat and pulled out a wad of cotton batting.

"Sometimes I think she's trying to show me up," Anita said.

Maggie didn't know how to answer that.

Finally Serena returned to the car, bearing a wrapped gift. "Mrs. Knowlton told me not to open this till our wedding night," she said. Maggie blushed and slid her eyes toward Anita. Anita merely gazed out the window, sending two long streamers of smoke from her nostrils.

In the church, Reverend Connors led Serena and her mother to a side room. Maggie went to wait for the other singers. Mary Jean was already there, and soon Sissy arrived with her husband and her mother-in-law. No Ira, though. Well, there was plenty of time. Maggie took her long white choir robe from its hanger and slipped it over her head, losing herself in its folds, and then of course she emerged all tousled and had to go off to comb her hair. But even when she returned, Ira was not to be seen.

The first of the guests had arrived. Boris sat in one of the pews, uncomfortably close. He was listening to a lady in a spotted veil and he was nodding intelligently, respectfully, but Maggie felt there was something tense about the set of his head. She looked toward the entrance. Other people were straggling in now, her parents and the Wrights next door and Serena's old baton teacher. No sign of the long, dark shape that was Ira Moran.

After she had let him walk off alone the night before, he must have decided to vanish altogether.

"Excuse me," she said. She bumped down the row of folding chairs and hurried through the vestibule. One of her full sleeves caught on the knob of the open door and yanked her up short in a foolish way, but she shook herself loose before anybody noticed, she thought. She paused on the front steps. "Well, hi!" an old classmate said. "Um . . . ." Maggie murmured, and she shaded her eyes and looked up and down the street. All she saw were more guests. She felt a moment's impatience with them; they seemed so frivolous. They were smiling and greeting each other in that gracious style they used only at church, and the women turned their toes out fastidiously as they walked, and their white gloves glinted in the sunlight.

In the doorway, Boris said, "Maggie?"

She didn't turn around. She ran down the steps with her robe flowing behind her. The steps were the wide, exceptionally shallow sort unsuited for any normal human stride; she was forced to adopt a limping, uneven rhythm. "Maggie!" Boris cried, so she had to run on after reaching the sidewalk. She shouldered her way between guests and then was past them, skimming down the street, ballooning white linen like a sailboat in a wind.

Sam's Frame Shop was only two blocks from the church, but they were long blocks and it was a warm June morning. She was damp and breathless when she arrived. She pulled open the plate-glass door and stepped into a close, cheerless interior with a worn linoleum floor. L-shaped samples of mold-ings hung from hooks on a yellowing pegboard wall, and the counter was painted a thick, cold gray. Behind this counter stood a bent old man in a visor, with shocks of white hair poking every which way. Ira's father.

She was surprised to find him there. The way she'd heard it, he never set foot in the shop anymore. She hesitated, and he said, "Can I help you, miss?"

She had always thought Ira had the darkest eyes she'd ever seen, but this man's eyes were darker. She couldn't even tell where they were focused; she had the fleeting notion that he might be blind.

"I was looking for Ira," she told him.

"Ira's not working today. He's got some kind of event."

"Yes, a wedding; he's singing at a wedding," she said. "But he hasn't shown up yet, so I came to get him."

"Oh?" Sam said. He moved his head closer to her, leading with his nose, not lessening in the least his impression of a blind man. "You wouldn't be Margaret, would you?" he asked.

"Yes, sir," she said.

He thought that over. He gave an abrupt, wheezy chuckle.

"Margaret M. Daley," he said.

She stood her ground.

"So you assumed Ira was dead," he said.

"Is he here?" she asked.

"He's upstairs, dressing."

"Could you call him, please?"

"How did you suppose he'd died?" he asked her.

"I mistook him for someone else. Monty Rand," she said, mumbling the words. "Monty got killed in boot camp."

"Boot camp!"

"Could you call Ira for me, please?"

"You'd never find Ira in boot camp," Sam told her. "Ira's got dependents, just as much as if he was married. Not that he

784

ever could be married in view of our situation. My heart has been acting up on me for years and one of his sisters is not quite right in the head. Why, I don't believe the army would have him even if he volunteered! Then me and the girls would have to go on welfare; we'd be a burden on the government. 'Get along with you,' those army folks would tell him. 'Go on back to them that need you. We've got no use for you here.' "

Maggie heard feet running down a set of stairs somewhere— a muffled, drumming sound. A door opened in the pegboard wall behind the counter and Ira said, "Pop—"

He stopped and looked at her. He wore a dark, ill-fitting suit and a stiff white shirt, with a navy tie dangling unknotted from his collar.

"We'll be late for the wedding," she told him.

He shot back a cuff and checked his watch.

"Come on!" she said. It wasn't only the wedding she was thinking of. She felt there was something dangerous about staying around Ira's father.

And sure enough, Sam said, "Me and your little friend here was just discussing you going into the army."

"Army?"

"*Ira* couldn't join the army, I told her. He's got us."

Ira said, "Well, anyhow, Pop, I ought to be back from this thing in a couple of hours."

"You really have to take that long? That's most of the morning!" Sam turned to Maggie and said, "Saturday's our busiest day at work."

Maggie wondered why, in that case, the shop was empty. She said, "Yes, well, we should be—"

"In fact, if Ira joined the army we'd just have to close this place up," Sam said. "Sell it off lock, stock, and barrel, when it's been in the family for forty-two years come October."

"What are you talking about?" Ira asked him. "Why would I want to join the army?"

"Your little friend here thought you'd gone into the army and got yourself killed," Sam told him.

"Oh," Ira said. Now the danger must have dawned on him too, for this time it was he who said, "We should be going."

"She thought you'd blown yourself up in boot camp," Sam told him. He gave another of his wheezy chuckles. There was something mole-like and relentless about that way he led with his nose, Maggie felt. "Ups and writes me a letter of condolence," he said. "Ha!" He told Maggie, "Gave me quite a start. I had this half-second or so where I thought, Wait a minute. Has Ira *passed*? First I knew of it, if so. And first I'd heard of you. First I'd heard of any girl, matter of fact, in years. I mean it's not like he has any friends anymore. His chums at school were that brainy crowd that went away to college and by now they've all lost touch with him and he doesn't see a soul his own age. 'Look here!' I told him. 'A girl at last!' After I'd withstood the shock. 'Better grab her while you got the chance,' I told him."

"Let's go," Ira said to Maggie.

He lifted a hinged section of the counter and stepped through it, but Sam went on talking. "Trouble is, now you know she can manage fine without you," he said.

Ira paused, still holding up the hinged section.

"She writes a little note of condolence and then continues with her life, as merry as pie," Sam told him.

"What did you expect her to do, throw herself in my grave?"

"Well, you got to admit she bore up under her grief mighty well. Writes me a nice little note, sticks a postage stamp in one corner, then carries on with her girlfriend's wedding arrangements."

"Right," Ira said, and he lowered the counter and came over to Maggie. Was he totally impenetrable? His eyes were flat, and his hand, when he took her arm, was perfectly steady.

"You're wrong," Maggie told Sam.

"Huh?"

"I wasn't doing fine without him! I was barely existing."

"No need to get all het up about it," Sam said.

"And for your information, there's any number of girls who think he's perfectly wonderful and I am not the only one and also it's ridiculous to say he can't get married. You have no right; anyone can get married if they want to."

"He wouldn't dare!" Sam told her. "He's got me and his sisters to think of. You want us all in the poorhouse? Ira? Ira, you wouldn't dare to get married!"

"Why not?" Ira asked calmly.

"You've got to think of me and your sisters!"

"I'm marrying her anyhow," Ira said.

Then he opened the door and stood back to let Maggie walk through it.

On the stoop outside, they stopped and he put his arms around her and drew her close. She could feel the narrow bones of his chest against her cheek and she heard his heart beating in her ear. His father must have been able to see everything through the plate-glass door, but even so Ira bent his head and kissed her on the lips, a long, warm, searching kiss that turned her knees weak.

Then they started off toward the church, although first there was a minor delay because the hem of her choir robe caught her up short. Ira had to open the door once again (not even glancing at his father) and set her loose.

But to look at Serena's movie, would you guess what had come just before? They seemed an ordinary couple, maybe a bit mismatched as to height. He was too tall and thin and she was too short and plump. Their expressions were grave but they certainly didn't look as if anything earth-shattering had recently taken place. They opened and closed their mouths in silence while the audience sang for them, poking gentle fun, intoning melodramatically. " 'Love is Nature's way of giving, a reason

787

to be living . . .' " Only Maggie knew how Ira's hand had braced the small of her back.

Then the Barley twins leaned into each other and sang the processional, their faces raised like baby birds' faces; and the camera swung from them to Serena all in white. Serena sailed down the aisle with her mother hanging on to her. Funny: From this vantage neither one of them seemed particularly unconventional. Serena stared straight ahead, intent. Anita's makeup was a little too heavy but she could have been anybody's mother, really, anxious-looking and outdated in her tight dress. "Look at you!" someone told Serena, laughing. Meanwhile the audience sang, " 'Though I don't know many words to say . . .' "

But then the camera jerked and swooped and there was Max, waiting next to Reverend Connors in front of the altar. One by one, the singers trailed off. Sweet Max, pursing his chapped lips and squinting his blue eyes in an attempt to seem fittingly dignified as he watched Serena approaching. Everything about him had faded except for his freckles, which stood out like metal spangles across his broad cheeks.

Maggie felt tears welling up. Several people blew their noses.

No one, she thought, had suspected back then that it would all turn out to be so serious.

But of course the mood brightened again, because the song went on too long and the couple had to stand in position, with Reverend Connors beaming at them, while the Barley twins wound down. And by the time the vows were exchanged and Sugar rose to sing the recessional, most of the people in the audience were nudging each other expectantly. For who could forget what came next?

Max escorted Serena back down the aisle far too slowly, employing a measured, hitching gait that he must have thought appropriate. Sugar's song was over and done with before they had finished exiting. Serena tugged at Max's elbow, spoke ur-

788

gently in his ear, traveled almost backward for the last few feet as she towed him into the vestibule. And then once they were out of sight, what a battle there'd been! The whispers, rising to hisses, rising to shouts! "If you'd stayed through the goddamn rehearsal," Serena had cried, "instead of tearing off to Penn Station for your never-ending relatives and leaving me to practice on my own so you had no idea how fast to walk me—" The congregation had remained seated, not knowing where to look. They'd grinned sheepishly at their laps, and finally broke into laughter.

"Serena, honey," Max had said, "pipe down. For Lord's sake, Serena, everyone can hear you, Serena, honey pie . . ."

Naturally none of this was apparent from the movie, which was finished anyhow except for a few scarred numerals flashing by. But all around the room people were refreshing other people's recollections, bringing the scene back to life. "And then she stalked out—"

"Slammed the church door—"

"Shook the whole building, remember?"

"Us just staring back toward the vestibule wondering how to behave—"

Someone flipped a window shade up: Serena herself. The room was filled with light. Serena was smiling but her cheeks were wet. People were saying, "And then, Serena . . ." and, "Remember, Serena?" and she was nodding and smiling and crying. The old lady next to Maggie said, "Dear, dear Maxwell," and sighed, perhaps not even aware of the others' merriment.

Maggie rose and collected her purse. She wanted Ira; she felt lost without Ira. She looked around for him but saw only the others, meaningless and bland. She threaded her way to the dining alcove, but he wasn't among the guests who stood picking over the platters of food. She walked down the hall and peeked into Serena's bedroom.

And there he was, seated at the bureau. He'd pulled a chair

up close and moved Linda's graduation picture out of the way so he could spread a solitaire layout clear across the polished surface. One angular brown hand was poised above a jack, preparing to strike. Maggie stepped inside and shut the door. She set her purse down and wrapped her arms around him from behind. "You missed a good movie," she said into his hair. "Serena showed a film of her wedding."

"Isn't that just like her," Ira said. He placed the jack on a queen. His hair smelled like coconut—its natural scent, which always came through sooner or later no matter what shampoo he used.

"You and I were singing our duet," she said.

"And I suppose you got all teary and nostalgic."

"Yes, I did," she told him.

"Isn't that just like *you*," he said.

"Yes, it is," she said, and she smiled into the mirror in front of them. She felt she was almost boasting, that she'd made a kind of proclamation. If she was easily swayed, she thought, at least she had chosen who would sway her. If she was locked in a pattern, at least she had chosen what that pattern would be. She felt strong and free and definite. She watched Ira scoop up a whole row of diamonds, ace through ten, and lay them on the jack. "We looked like children," she told him. "Like infants. We were hardly older than Daisy is now; just imagine. And thought nothing of deciding then and there who we'd spend the next sixty years with."

"Mmhmm," Ira said.

He pondered a king, while Maggie laid her cheek on the top of his head. She seemed to have fallen in love again. In love with her own husband! The convenience of it pleased her— like finding right in her pantry all the fixings she needed for a new recipe.

"Remember the first year we were married?" she asked him. "It was awful. We fought every minute."

"Worst year of my life," he agreed, and when she moved

790

around to the front he sat back slightly so she could settle on his lap. His thighs beneath her were long and bony—two planks of lumber. "Careful of my cards," he told her, but she could feel he was getting interested. She laid her head on his shoulder and traced the stitching of his shirt pocket with one finger.

"That Sunday we invited Max and Serena to dinner, remember? Our very first guests. We rearranged the furniture five times before they got there," she said. "I'd go out in the kitchen and come back to find you'd shifted all the chairs into corners, and I'd say, 'What have you *done?*' and shift them all some other way, and by the time the Gills arrived, the coffee table was upside down on the couch and you and I were having a shouting quarrel."

"We were scared to death, is what it was," Ira said. He had his arms around her now; she felt his amused, dry voice vibrating through his chest. "We were trying to act like grownups but we didn't know if we could pull it off."

"And then our first anniversary," Maggie said. "What a fiasco! Mother's etiquette book said it was either the paper anniversary or the clock anniversary, whichever I preferred. So I got this bright idea to construct your gift from a kit I saw advertised in a magazine: a working clock made out of paper."

"*I* don't remember that."

"That's because I never gave it to you," Maggie said.

"What happened to it?"

"Well, I must have put it together wrong," Maggie said. "I mean I followed all the directions, but it never really acted like it was supposed to. It dragged, it stopped and started, one edge curled over, there was a ripple under the twelve where I'd used too much glue. It was . . . makeshift, amateur. I was so ashamed of it, I threw it in the trash."

"Why, sweetheart," he said.

"I was afraid it was a symbol or something, I mean a symbol of our marriage. We were makeshift ourselves, is what I was afraid of."

He said, "Shoot, we were just learning back then. We didn't know what to do with each other."

"We know now," she whispered. Then she pressed her mouth into one of her favorite places, that nice warm nook where his jaw met his neck.

Meanwhile her fingers started traveling down to his belt buckle.

Ira said, "Maggie?" but he made no move to stop her. She straightened up to loosen his belt and unzip his fly.

"We can sit right here in this chair," she whispered. "No one will ever guess."

Ira groaned and pulled her against him. When he kissed her his lips felt smooth and very firm. She thought she could hear her own blood flooding through her veins; it made a rushing sound, like a seashell.

"Maggie Daley!" Serena said.

Ira started violently and Maggie jumped up from his lap. Serena stood frozen with one hand on the doorknob. She was gaping at Ira, at his open zipper and his shirttail flaring out.

Well, it could have gone in either direction, Maggie figured. You never knew with Serena. Serena could have just laughed it off. But maybe the funeral had been too much for her, or the movie afterward, or just widowhood in general. At any rate, she said, "I don't believe this. I do not believe it."

Maggie said, "Serena—"

"In my own house! My bedroom!"

"I'm sorry; please, we're both so sorry . . . ." Maggie said, and Ira, hastily righting his clothes, said, "Yes, we honestly didn't—"

"You always were impossible," Serena told Maggie. "I suspect it's deliberate. No one could act so goofy purely by chance. I haven't forgotten what happened with my mother at the nursing home. And now this! At a funeral gathering! In the bedroom I shared with my husband!"

"It was an accident, Serena. We never meant to—"

"An accident!" Serena said. "Oh, just go."

"What?"

"Just leave," she said, and she wheeled and walked away.

Maggie picked up her purse, not looking at Ira. Ira collected his cards. She went through the doorway ahead of him and they walked down the hall to the living room. People stood back a little to let them pass. She had no idea how much they had heard. Probably everything; there was something hushed and thrilled about them. She opened the front door and then turned around and said, "Well, bye now!"

"Goodbye," they murmured. "Bye, Maggie, bye, Ira . . ."

Outside, the sunlight was blinding. She wished they'd driven over from the church. She took hold of Ira's hand when he offered it and picked her way along the gravel next to the road, fixing her eyes on her pumps, which had developed a thin film of dust.

"Well," Ira said finally, "we certainly livened up *that* little gathering."

"I feel just terrible," Maggie said.

"Oh, it'll blow over," Ira told her. "You know how she is." Then he gave a snort and said, "Just look on the bright side. As class reunions go—"

"But it wasn't a class reunion; it was a funeral," Maggie said. "A memorial service. I went and ruined a memorial service! She probably thinks we were showing off or something, taunting her now that she's a widow. I feel terrible."

"She'll forgive us," he told her.

A car swished by and he changed places with her, setting her to the inside away from the traffic. Now they walked slightly apart, not touching. They were back to their normal selves. Or almost back. Not entirely. Some trick of light or heat blurred Maggie's vision, and the stony old house they were passing seemed to shimmer for a moment. It dissolved in a gentle, radiant haze, and then it regrouped itself and grew solid again.

TWO

For the past several months now, Ira had been noticing the human race's wastefulness. People were squandering their lives, it seemed to him. They were splurging their energies on petty jealousies or vain ambitions or long-standing, bitter grudges. It was a theme that emerged wherever he turned, as if someone were trying to tell him something. Not that he needed to be told. Didn't he know well enough all he himself had wasted?

He was fifty years old and had never accomplished one single act of consequence. Once he had planned to find a cure for some major disease and now he was framing petit point instead.

His son, who couldn't carry a tune, had dropped out of high school in hopes of becoming a rock star. His daughter was one of those people who fritter themselves away on unnecessary worries; she chewed her fingernails to nubbins and developed blinding headaches before exams and agonized so over her grades that their doctor had warned of ulcers.

And his wife! He loved her, but he couldn't stand how she refused to take her own life seriously. She seemed to believe it was a sort of practice life, something she could afford to play around with as if they offered second and third chances to get it right. She was always making clumsy, impetuous rushes toward nowhere in particular—side trips, random detours.

Like today, for instance: this Fiona business. Fiona was no longer any relation, not their daughter-in-law and not even an acquaintance, in Ira's opinion. But here Maggie sat, trailing a hand out the window as they whizzed down Route One toward home, and what did she return to (just when he was hoping she'd forgotten) but her whim to pay Fiona a visit. Bad enough they'd lost their Saturday to Max Gill's funeral—a kind of side trip in itself—but now she wanted to plunge off in a whole new direction. She wanted to swing by Cartwheel, Pennsylvania, just so she could offer to baby-sit while Fiona went on her honeymoon. A completely pointless proposal; for Fiona did have a mother, didn't she, who'd been tending Leroy all along and surely could be counted on for the next little bit as well. Ira pointed that out. He said, "What's the matter with what's-her-name? Mrs. Stuckey?"

"Oh, Mrs. *Stuckey*," Maggie said, as if that were answer enough. She brought in her hand and rolled up the window. Her face glowed in the sunlight, round and pretty and intense. The breeze had ruffled her hair so it stood out in loops all over her head. It was a hot, gasoline-smelling breeze and Ira wasn't sorry to have lost it. However, this constant opening and shutting of the window was getting on his nerves. She operated from second to second, he thought. She never looked any distance ahead. A spasm of irritation darted raggedly through his temples.

Here was a woman who had once let a wrong number consume an entire evening. "Hello?" she'd said into the phone, and a man had said, "Laverne, stay right there safe in your house. I just talked to Dennis and he's coming to fetch you." And then had hung up. Maggie cried, "Wait!"—speaking into a dead receiver; typical. Whoever it was, Ira had told her, deserved what he got. If Dennis and Laverne never managed to connect, why, that was their problem, not hers. But Maggie had gone on and on about it. " 'Safe,' " she moaned. " 'Safe in the house,' he told me. Lord only knows what that poor Laverne is going through." And she had spent the evening dialing all possible variations of their own number, every permutation of every digit, hoping to find Laverne. But never did, of course.

Cartwheel, Pennsylvania, was so close it could practically reach out and grab them, to hear her talk. "It's on that cutoff right above the state line. I forget the name," she was saying. "But I couldn't see it anywhere on that map you got at the service station."

No wonder she'd been so little help navigating; she'd been hunting Cartwheel instead.

Traffic was surprisingly sparse for a Saturday. Mostly it was trucks—small, rusty trucks carrying logs or used tires, not the sleek monsters you'd see on I-95. They were traveling through farm country at this point, and each truck as it passed left another layer of dust on the wan, parched, yellowing fields that lined the road.

"Here's what we'll do," Maggie told him. "Stop by Fiona's just for an instant. A teeny, eeny instant. Not accept even a glass of iced tea. Make her our offer and go."

"That much you could handle by telephone," Ira said.

"No, I couldn't!"

"Telephone when we get back to Baltimore, if you're so set on baby-sitting."

"That child is not but seven years old," Maggie told him, "and she must just barely remember us. We can't take her on for a week just cold! We have to let her get reacquainted first."

"How do you know it's a week?" Ira asked.

She was riffling through her purse now. She said, "Hmm?"

"How do you know the honeymoon will last a week, Maggie?"

"Well, I *don't* know. Maybe it's two weeks. Maybe even a month, I don't know."

He wondered, all at once, if this whole wedding was a

myth—something she'd invented for her own peculiar reasons. He wouldn't put it past her.

"And besides!" he said. "We could never stay away that long. We've got jobs."

"Not away: in Baltimore. We'd take her back down to Baltimore."

"But then she'd be missing school," he said.

"Oh, that's no problem. We'll let her go to school near us," Maggie said. "Second grade is second grade, after all, the same all over."

Ira had so many different arguments against that that he was struck speechless.

Now she dumped her purse upside down in her lap. "Oh, dear," she said, studying her billfold, her lipstick, her comb, and her pack of Kleenex. "I wish I'd brought that map from home."

It was another form of wastefulness, Ira thought, to search yet again through a purse whose contents she already knew by heart. Even Ira knew those contents by heart. And it was wasteful to continue caring about Fiona when Fiona obviously had no feeling for them, when she had made it very clear that she just wanted to get on with her life. Hadn't she stated that, even? "I just want to get on with my life"—it had a familiar ring. Maybe she had shouted it during that scene before she left, or maybe later during one of those pathetic visits they used to pay after the divorce, with Leroy bashful and strange and Mrs. Stuckey a single accusatory eye glaring around the edge of the living room door. Ira winced. Waste, waste, and more waste, all for nothing. The long drive and the forced conversation and the long drive home again, for absolutely nothing.

And it was wasteful to devote your working life to people who forgot you the instant you left their bedsides, as Ira was forever pointing out. Oh, it was also admirably selfless, he supposed. But he didn't know how Maggie endured the impermanence, the lack of permanent results—those feeble, senile patients who confused her with a long-dead mother or a sister who'd insulted them back in 1928.

It was wasteful too to fret so over the children. (Who were no longer children anyhow—not even Daisy.) Consider, for instance, the cigarette papers that Maggie had found last spring on Daisy's bureau. She had picked them up while she was dusting and come running to Ira. "What'll we do? What are we going to do?" she had wailed. "Our daughter's smoking marijuana; this is one of the telltale clues they mention in that pamphlet that the school gives out." She'd got Ira all involved and distressed; that happened more often than he liked to admit. Together they had sat up far into the night, discussing ways of dealing with the problem. "Where did we go wrong?" Maggie cried, and Ira hugged her and said, "There now, dear heart. I promise you we'll see this thing through." All for nothing yet again, it turned out. Turned out the cigarette papers were for Daisy's flute. You slid them under the keys whenever they started sticking, Daisy explained offhandedly. She hadn't even bothered to take umbrage.

Ira had felt ridiculous. He'd felt he had spent something scarce and real—hard currency.

Then he thought of how a thief had once stolen Maggie's pocketbook, marched right into the kitchen where she was shelving groceries and stolen it off the counter as bold-faced as you please; and she took after him. She could have been killed! (The efficient, the streamlined thing to do was to shrug and decide she was better off without that pocketbook—had never cared for it anyhow, and surely could spare the few limp dollars in the billfold.) It was February and the sidewalks were sheets of glare ice, so running was impossible. Ira, returning from work, had been astonished to see a young boy shuffling toward him at a snail's pace with Maggie's red pocketbook dangling from his shoulder, and behind him Maggie herself came jogging along

inch by inch with her tongue between her teeth as she concentrated on her footing. The two of them had resembled those
mimes who can portray a speedy stride while making no progress
at all. In fact, it had looked sort of comical, Ira reflected now.
His lips twitched. He smiled.

"What," Maggie ordered.

"You were crazy to go after that pocketbook thief," he told
her.

"Honestly, Ira. How does your mind work?"

Exactly the question he might have asked her.

"Anyhow, I did get it back," she said.

"Only by chance. What if he'd been armed? Or a little
bigger? What if he hadn't panicked when he saw me?"

"You know, come to think of it, I believe I dreamed about
that boy just a couple of nights ago," Maggie said. "He was
sitting in this kitchen that was kind of our kitchen and kind of
not our kitchen, if you know what I mean. . . ."

Ira wished she wouldn't keep telling her dreams. It made
him feel fidgety and restless.

Maybe if he hadn't gotten married. Or at least had not had
children. But that was too great a price to pay; even in his
darkest moods he realized that. Well, if he had put his sister
Dorrie in an institution, then—something state-run that
wouldn't cost too much. And told his father, "I will no longer
provide your support. Weak heart or not, take over this goddamn
shop of yours and let me get on with my original plan if I can
cast my mind back far enough to remember what it was." And
made his other sister venture into the world to find employment.
"You think we're not *all* scared?" he would ask her. "But we
go out anyway and earn our keep, and so will you."

But she would die of terror.

He used to lie in bed at night when he was a little boy and
pretend he was seeing patients. His drawn-up knees were his
desk and he'd look across his desk and ask, kindly, "What seems
to be the trouble, Mrs. Brown?" At one point he had figured

he might be an orthopedist, because bonesetting was so immediate. Like furniture repair, he had thought. He had imagined that the bone would make a clicking sound as it returned to its rightful place, and the patient's pain would vanish utterly in that very instant.

"Hoosegow," Maggie said.

"Pardon?"

She scooped up her belongings and poured them back in her purse. She set the purse on the floor at her feet. "The cutoff to Cartwheel," she told him. "Wasn't it something like Hoosegow?"

"I wouldn't have the faintest idea."

"Moose Cow. Moose Lump."

"I'm not going there, whatever it's called," Ira told her.

"Goose Bump."

"I would just like to remind you," he said, "about those other visits. Remember how they turned out? Leroy's second birthday, when you phoned ahead to arrange things, *telephoned*, and still Fiona somehow forgot you were coming. They went off to Hershey Park and we had to wait on the doorstep forever and finally turn around and come home."

Carrying Leroy's gift, he didn't say: a gigantic, blankly smiling Raggedy Ann that broke his heart.

"And her third birthday, when you brought her that kitten unannounced even though I warned you to check with Fiona beforehand, and Leroy started sneezing and Fiona said she couldn't keep it. Leroy cried all afternoon, remember? When we left, she was still crying."

"She could have taken shots for that," Maggie said, stubbornly missing the point. "Lots of children take allergy shots and they have whole housefuls of pets."

"Yes, but Fiona didn't want her to. She didn't want us interfering, and she really didn't want us visiting, either, which is why I said we shouldn't go there anymore."

Maggie cut her eyes over at him in a quick, surmising way.

Probably she was wondering if he knew about those other trips, the ones she had made on her own. But if she had cared about keeping them secret you'd think she would have filled the gas tank afterward.

"What I'm saying is—" he said.

"I know what you're saying!" she cried. "You don't have to keep hammering at it!"

He drove in silence for a while. A row of dotted lines stitched down the highway ahead of him. Dozens of tiny birds billowed up from a grove of trees and turned the blue sky cindery, and he watched them till they disappeared.

"My Grandma Daley used to have a picture in her parlor," Maggie said. "A little scene carved in something yellowish like ivory, or more likely celluloid. It showed this old couple sitting by the fireplace in their rocking chairs, and the title was etched across the bottom of the frame: 'Old Folks at Home.' The woman was knitting and the man was reading an enormous book that you just knew was the Bible. And you knew there must be grown children away someplace; I mean that was the whole idea, that the old folks were left at home while the children went away. But they were so *extremely* old! They had those withered-apple faces and potato-sack bodies; they were people you would classify in an instant and dismiss. I never imagined that I would be an Old Folk at Home."

"You're plotting to have that child come live with us," Ira said. It hit him with a thump, as clearly as if she had spoken the words. "That's what you've been leading to. Now that you're losing Daisy you're plotting for Leroy to come and fill her place."

"I have no such intention!" Maggie said—too quickly, it seemed to him.

"Don't think I don't see through you," he told her. "I suspected all along there was something fishy about this baby-sitting business. You're counting on Fiona to agree to it, now that she's all caught up with a brand-new husband."

804

"Well, that just shows how little you know, then, because I have no earthly intention of keeping Leroy for good. All I want to do is drop in on them this afternoon and make my offer, which might just incidentally cause Fiona to reconsider a bit about Jesse."

"Jesse?"

"Jesse our son, Ira."

"Yes, Maggie, I know Jesse's our son, but I can't imagine what you think she could reconsider. They're finished. She walked out on him. Her lawyer sent him those papers to sign and he signed them every one and sent them back."

"And has never, ever been the same since," Maggie said. "He or Fiona, either. But anytime he makes a move to reconcile, she is passing through a stage where she won't speak to him, and then when *she* makes a move he has slammed off somewhere with hurt feelings and doesn't know she's trying. It's like some awful kind of dance, some out-of-sync dance where every step's a mistake."

"Well? So?" Ira said. "I would think that ought to tell you something."

"Tell me what?"

"Tell you those two are a lost cause, Maggie."

"Oh, Ira, you just don't give enough credit to luck," Maggie said. "Good luck or bad luck, either one. Watch out for that car in front of you."

She meant the red Chevy—an outdated model, big as a barge, its finish worn down to the color of a dull red rubber eraser. Ira was already watching it. He didn't like the way it kept drifting from side to side and changing speeds.

"Honk," Maggie instructed him.

Ira said, "Oh, I'll just—"

He would just get past the fellow, he was going to say. Some incompetent idiot; best to put such people far behind you. He pressed the accelerator and checked the rearview mirror, but at the same time Maggie reached over to jab his horn. The long, insistent blare startled him. He seized Maggie's hand and returned it firmly to her lap. Only then did he realize that the Chevy driver, no doubt equally startled, had slowed sharply just feet ahead. Maggie made a grab for the dashboard. Ira had no choice; he swerved right and plowed off the side of the road.

Dust rose around them like smoke. The Chevy picked up speed and rounded a curve and vanished.

"Jesus," Ira said.

Somehow their car had come to a stop, although he couldn't recall braking. In fact, the engine had died. Ira was still gripping the wheel, and the keys were still swinging from the ignition, softly jingling against each other.

"You just had to butt in, Maggie, didn't you," he said.

"Me? You're blaming this on me? What did I do?"

"Oh, nothing. Only honked the horn when I was the one driving. Only scared that fellow so he lost what last few wits he had. Just once in your life, Maggie, I wish you would manage not to stick your nose in what doesn't concern you."

"And if I didn't, who would?" she asked him. "And how can you say it doesn't concern me when here I sit in what's known far and wide as the death seat? And also, it wasn't my honking that caused the trouble; it was that crazy driver, slowing down for no apparent reason."

Ira sighed. "Anyway," he said. "Are you all right?"

"I could just strangle him!" she said.

He supposed that meant she was fine.

He restarted the engine. It coughed a couple of times and then took hold. He checked for traffic and pulled out onto the highway again. After the gravelly roadside, the pavement felt too frictionless, too easy. He noticed how his hands were shaking on the steering wheel.

"That man was a maniac," Maggie said.

"Good thing we had our seat belts fastened."

806

"We ought to report him."

"Oh, well. So long as no one was hurt."

"Go faster, will you, Ira?"

He glanced over at her.

"I want to get his license number," she said. Her tangled curls gave her the look of a wild woman.

Ira said, "Now, Maggie. When you think about it, it was really as much our doing as his."

"How can you say that? When he was driving by fits and starts and wandering every which way; have you forgotten?"

Where did she find the energy? he wondered. How come she had so much to expend? He was hot and his left shoulder ached where he'd slammed against his seat belt. He shifted position, relieving the pressure of the belt across his chest.

"You don't want him causing a serious accident, do you?" Maggie asked.

"Well, no."

"Probably he's been drinking. Remember that public-service message on TV? We have a civic duty to report him. Speed up, Ira."

He obeyed, mostly out of exhaustion.

They passed an electrician's van that had passed them earlier and then, as they crested a hill, they caught sight of the Chevy just ahead. It was whipping right along as if nothing had happened. Ira was surprised by a flash of anger. Damn fool driver. And who said it had to be a man? More likely a woman, strewing chaos everywhere without a thought. He pressed harder on the accelerator. Maggie said, "Good," and rolled down her window.

"What are you doing?" he asked.

"Go faster."

"What did you open your window for?"

"Hurry, Ira! We're losing him."

"Be funny if we got a ticket for this," Ira said.

But he let the speedometer inch up to sixty-five, to sixty-eight. They drew close behind the Chevy. Its rear window was so dusty that Ira had trouble seeing inside. All he could tell was that the driver wore a hat of some kind and sat very low in the seat. There didn't seem to be any passengers. The license plate was dusty too—a Pennsylvania plate, navy and yellow, the yellow mottled with gray as if mildewed.

"Y two eight—" Ira read out.

"Yes, yes, I have it," Maggie said. (She was the type who could still reel off her childhood telephone number.) "Now let's pass him," she told Ira.

"Oh, well . . ."

"You see what kind of driver he is. I think we ought to pass."

Well, that made sense. Ira veered left.

Just as they came alongside the Chevy, Maggie leaned out her window and pointed downward with her index finger. "Your wheel!" she shouted. "Your wheel! Your front wheel is falling off!"

"Good grief," Ira said.

He checked the mirror. Sure enough, the Chevy had slowed and was moving toward the shoulder.

"Well, he believed you," he said.

He had to admit it was sort of a satisfaction.

Maggie twisted around in her seat, gazing out the rear window. Then she turned to Ira. There was a stricken look on her face that he couldn't account for. "Oh, Ira," she said.

"Now what."

"He was old, Ira."

Ira said, "These goddamn senior-citizen drivers . . ."

"Not only was he old," she said. "He was black."

"So?"

"I didn't see him clearly till I'd said that about the wheel," she said. "He didn't mean to run us off the road! I bet he doesn't even know it happened. He had this wrinkled, dignified face

808

and when I told him about the wheel his mouth dropped open but still he remembered to touch the brim of his hat. His hat! His gray felt hat like my grandfather wore!"

Ira groaned.

Maggie said, "Now he thinks we played a trick on him. He thinks we're racist or something and lied about his wheel to be cruel."

"He doesn't think any such thing," Ira said. "As a matter of fact, he has no way of knowing his wheel *isn't* falling off. How would he check it? He'd have to watch it in motion."

"You mean he's still sitting there?"

"No, no," Ira said hastily. "I mean he's probably back on the road by now but he's traveling a little slower, just to make sure it's all right."

"I wouldn't do that," Maggie said.

"Well, you're not him."

"He wouldn't do that, either. He's old and confused and alone and he's sitting there in his car, too scared to drive another inch."

"Oh, Lord," Ira said.

"We have to go back and tell him."

Somehow, he'd known that was coming.

"We won't say we deliberately lied," Maggie said. "We'll tell him we just weren't sure. We'll ask him to make a test drive while we watch, and then we'll say, 'Oops! Our mistake. Your wheel is fine; we must have misjudged.' "

"Where'd you get this 'we' business?" Ira asked. "I never told him it was loose in the first place."

"Ira, I'm begging you on bended knee, please turn around and go rescue that man."

"It is now one-thirty in the afternoon," Ira said. "With luck we could be home by three. Maybe even two-thirty. I could open the shop for a couple of hours, which may not be much but it's better than nothing."

"That poor old man is sitting in his car staring straight in front of him not knowing what to do," Maggie said. "He's still hanging on to the steering wheel. I can see him as plain as day."

So could Ira.

He slowed as they came to a large, prosperous-looking farm. A grassy lane led toward the barn, and he veered onto that without signaling first, in order to make the turn seem more sudden and more exasperated. Maggie's sunglasses scooted the length of the dashboard. Ira backed up, waited for a stream of traffic that all at once materialized, and then spun out onto Route One again, this time heading north.

Maggie said, "I knew you couldn't be heartless."

"Just imagine," Ira told her. "All up and down this highway, other couples are taking weekend drives together. They're traveling from Point A to Point B. They're holding civilized discussions about, I don't know, current events. Disarmament. Apartheid."

"He probably thinks we belong to the Ku Klux Klan," Maggie said. She started chewing her lip the way she always did when she was worried.

"No stops, no detours," Ira said. "If they take any break at all, it's for lunch in some classy old inn. Someplace they researched ahead of time, where they even made reservations."

He was starving, come to think of it. He hadn't eaten a thing at Serena's.

"It was right about here," Maggie said, perking up. "I recognize those silos. It was just before those mesh-looking silos. There he is."

Yes, there he was, not sitting in his car after all but walking around it in a wavery circle—a stoop-shouldered man the color of a rolltop desk, wearing one of those elderly suits than seem longer in front than in back. He was studying the tires of the Chevy, which might have been abandoned years ago; it had a settled, resigned appearance. Ira signaled and made a U-turn, arriving neatly behind so the two cars' bumpers almost touched. He opened the door and stepped out. "Can we help?" he called.

Maggie got out too but seemed willing for once to let Ira do the talking.

"It's my wheel," the old man said. "Lady back up the road a ways pointed out my wheel was falling off."

"That was us," Ira told him. "Or my wife, at least. But you know, I believe she might have been wrong. That wheel seems fine to me."

The old man looked at him directly now. He had a skull-like, deeply lined face, and the whites of his eyes were so yellow they were almost brown. "Oh, well, surely, *seems* fine," he said. "When the car is setting stark still like it is."

"But I mean even before," Ira told him. "Back when you were still on the road."

The old man appeared unconvinced. He prodded the tire with the toe of his shoe. "Anyhow," he said. "Mighty nice of you folks to stop."

Maggie said, "Nice! It's the least we could do." She stepped forward. "I'm Maggie Moran," she said. "This is my husband, Ira."

"My name's Mr. Daniel Otis," the old man said, touching the brim of his hat.

"Mr. Otis, see, I had this sort of, like, mirage as we were driving past your car," Maggie said. "I thought I noticed your wheel wobbling. But then the very next instant I said, 'No, I believe I imagined it.' Didn't I, Ira? Just ask Ira. 'I believe I made that driver stop for no good reason,' I told him."

"They's all kindly explanations why you might have seen it wobble," Mr. Otis said.

"Why, certainly!" Maggie cried. "Heat waves, maybe, rippling above the pavement. Or maybe, I don't know—"

"Might have been a sign, too," Mr. Otis said.

"Sign?"

"Might have been the Lord was trying to warn me."

"Warn you about what?"

"Warn me my left front wheel was fixing to drop off."

Maggie said, "Well, but—"

"Mr. Otis," Ira said. "I think it's more likely my wife just made a mistake."

"Now, you can't know that."

"An understandable mistake," Ira said, "but all the same, a mistake. So what we ought to do is, you get into your car and drive it just a few yards down the shoulder. Maggie and I will watch. If your wheel's not loose, you're free and clear. If it is, we'll take you to a service station."

"Oh, why, I appreciate that," Mr. Otis said. "Maybe Buford, if it ain't too much trouble."

"Pardon?"

"Buford Texaco. It's up ahead a piece; my nephew works there."

"Sure, anywhere," Ira said, "but I'm willing to bet—"

"In fact, if it ain't too much trouble you might just go on and carry me there right now," Mr. Otis said.

"Now?"

"I don't relish driving a car with a wheel about to drop off."

"Mr. Otis," Ira said. "We'll test the wheel. That's what I've been telling you."

"I'll test it," Maggie said.

"Yes, Maggie will test it. Maggie? Honey, maybe I should be the one."

"Shoot, yes; it's way too risky for a lady," Mr. Otis told her.

Ira had been thinking of the risk to the Chevy, but he said, "Right. You and Mr. Otis watch; I'll drive."

"No, sir, I can't allow you to do that," Mr. Otis said. "I appreciate it, but I can't allow it. Too much danger. You folks just carry me to the Texaco, please, and my nephew will come fetch the car with the tow truck."

Ira looked at Maggie. Maggie looked back at him helplessly. The sounds of traffic whizzing past reminded him of those TV thrillers where spies rendezvoused in modern wastelands, on the edges of superhighways or roaring industrial complexes.

"Listen," Ira said. "I'll just come right out with this—"

"Or don't carry me! Don't," Mr. Otis cried. "I already inconvenienced you-all enough, I know that."

"The fact is, we feel responsible," Ira told him. "What we said about your wheel wasn't so much a mistake as a plain and simple, um, exaggeration."

"Yes, we made it up," Maggie said.

"Aw, no," Mr. Otis said, shaking his head, "you just trying to stop me from worrying."

"A while back you kind of, like, more or less, slowed down too suddenly in front of us," Maggie said, "and caused us to run off the road. Not intending to, I realize, but—"

"I did that?"

"Not intending to," Maggie assured him.

"And besides," Ira said, "you probably slowed because we accidentally honked. So it's not as if—"

"Oh, I declare. Florence, that's my niece, she is all the time after me to turn in my driver's license, but I surely never expected—"

"Anyhow, I did a very inconsiderate thing," Maggie told him. "I said your wheel was falling off when really it was fine."

"Why, I call that a very *Christian* thing," Mr. Otis said. "When I had caused you to run off the road! You folks been awful nice about this."

"No, see, really the wheel was—"

"Many would've let me ride on to my death," Mr. Otis said.

"The wheel was fine!" Maggie told him. "It wasn't wobbling in the slightest."

Mr. Otis tipped his head back and studied her. His lowered eyelids gave him such a haughty, hooded expression that it seemed he might finally have grasped her meaning. But then he said, "Naw, that can't be right. Can it? Naw. I tell you: Now that I recollect, that car was driving funny all this morning. I knew it and yet *didn't* know it, you know? And I reckon it must've hit you-all the same way—kindly like you half glimpsed it out of the corner of your vision so you were moved to say what you did, not understanding just why."

That settled it; Ira took action. "Well, then," he said, "nothing to do but test it. Keys inside?" And he strode briskly to the Chevy and opened the door and slid in.

"Aw, now!" Mr. Otis cried. "Don't you go risking your neck for *me*, mister!"

"He'll be all right," Maggie told him.

Ira gave Mr. Otis a reassuring wave.

Even though the window was open, the Chevy was pulsing with heat. The clear plastic seat cover seemed to have partially melted, and there was a strong smell of overripe banana. No wonder: The remains of a bag lunch sat on the passenger seat—a crumpled sack, a banana peel, and a screw of cellophane.

Ira turned the key in the ignition. When the engine roared up he leaned out toward Maggie and Mr. Otis and said, "Watch carefully."

They said nothing. For two people who looked so little alike, they wore oddly similar expressions: wary and guarded, as if braced for the worst.

Ira put the car in gear and started rolling along the shoulder. He felt he was driving something that stood out too far on all sides—a double bed, for instance. Also, there was a rattle in the exhaust system.

After a few yards, he braked and cocked his head out the window. The others had not moved from where they stood; they'd merely turned their faces in his direction.

"Well?" he called.

There was a pause. Then Mr. Otis said, "Yessir, seem like I did see a bit of a jiggling motion to it."

"You did?" Ira asked.

He quirked an eyebrow at Maggie.

"But you didn't," he said.

"Well, I'm not certain," Maggie told him.

"Excuse me?"

"Maybe I just imagined it," she said, "but I thought there was a little, sort of, I don't know . . ."

Ira shifted gears and backed up with a jolt. When he was alongside them once more he said, "Now I want you both to watch very, very closely."

He drove farther this time, a dozen yards or so. They were forced to follow him. He glanced in the side-view mirror and saw Maggie scurrying along with her arms folded beneath her bosom. He stopped the car and climbed out to face them.

"Oh, that wheel is loose, all right," Mr. Otis called as he arrived.

Ira said, "Maggie?"

"It reminded me of a top, just before it stops spinning and falls over," Maggie said.

"Now listen here, Maggie—"

"I know! I know!" she said. "But I can't help it, Ira; I really saw it wobble. And also it looked kind of squashy."

"Well, that's a whole different problem," Ira said. "The tire may be underinflated. But that wheel is on tight as a drum, I swear it. I could feel it. I can't believe you're doing this, Maggie."

"Well, I'm sorry," she said stubbornly, "but I refuse to say I didn't see what I saw with my own two eyes. I just think we're going to have to take him to that Texaco."

Ira looked at Mr. Otis. "You got a lug wrench?" he asked.

"A . . . sir?"

"If you've got a lug wrench, I could tighten that wheel myself."

"Oh, why . . . Is a lug wrench like a ordinary wrench?"

"You probably have one in your trunk," Ira told him, "where you keep your jack."

"Oh! But where do I keep my jack, I wonder," Mr. Otis said.

"In your trunk," Ira repeated doggedly, and he reached inside the car for the keys and handed them over. He was keeping his face as impassive as possible, but inwardly he felt the way he felt anytime he stopped by Maggie's nursing home: utterly despairing. He couldn't see how this Mr. Otis fellow made it from day to day, bumbling along as he did.

"Lug wrench, lug wrench," Mr. Otis was murmuring. He unlocked the trunk and flung the lid up. "Now let me just . . ."

At first glance, the trunk's interior seemed a solid block of fabric. Blankets, clothes, and pillows had been packed inside so tightly that they had congealed together. "Oh, me," Mr. Otis said, and he plucked at a corner of a graying quilt, which didn't budge.

"Never mind," Ira told him. "I'll get mine."

He walked back to the Dodge. It suddenly seemed very well kept, if you overlooked what Maggie had done to the left front fender. He took his keys from the ignition and unlocked the trunk and opened it.

Nothing.

Where once there'd been a spare tire, tucked into the well beneath the floor mat, now there was an empty space. And not a sign of the gray vinyl pouch in which he kept his tools.

He called, "Maggie?"

She turned lazily from her position by the Chevy and tilted her head in his direction.

"What happened to my spare tire?" he asked.

"It's on the car."

"*On* the car?"

She nodded vigorously.

"You mean it's in use?"

816

"Right."

"Then where's the original tire?"

"It's getting patched at the Exxon back home."

"Well, how did . . . ?"

No, never mind; better not get sidetracked. "So where are the tools, then?" he called.

"What tools?"

He slammed the lid down and walked back to the Chevy. There was no point shouting; he could see his lug wrench was not going to be anywhere within reach. "The tools you changed the tire with," he told her.

"Oh, I didn't change the tire. A man stopped and helped me."

"Did he use the tools in the trunk?"

"I guess so, yes."

"Did he put them back?"

"Well, he must have," Maggie said. She frowned, evidently trying to recall.

"They're not there, Maggie."

"Well, I'm sure he didn't steal them, if that's what you're thinking. He was a very nice man. He wouldn't even accept any money; he said he had a wife of his own and—"

"I'm not saying he stole them; I'm just asking where they are."

Maggie said, "Maybe on the . . ." and then mumbled something further, he wasn't sure what.

"Pardon?"

"I said, maybe on the corner of Charles Street and Northern Parkway!" she shouted.

Ira turned to Mr. Otis. The old man was watching him with his eyes half closed; he appeared to be falling asleep on his feet.

"I guess we'll have to unpack your trunk," Ira told him.

Mr. Otis nodded several times but made no move to begin.

"Shall we just unload it?" Ira asked.

"Well, we could do that," Mr. Otis said doubtfully.

There was a pause.

Ira said, "Well? Shall we start?"

"We could start if you like," Mr. Otis told him, "but I'd be very much surprised if we was to find a wheel wrench."

"Everybody has a wheel wrench. Lug wrench," Ira said. "It comes with the car."

"I never saw it."

"Oh, Ira," Maggie said. "Can't we just drive him to the Texaco and get his nephew to fix it properly?"

"And how do you think he would do that, Maggie? He'd take a wrench and tighten the lug nuts, not that they need it."

Mr. Otis, meanwhile, had managed to remove a single item from the trunk: a pair of flannel pajama bottoms. He held them up and considered them.

Maybe it was the dubious expression on his face, or maybe it was the pajamas themselves—crinkled and withered, trailing a frazzled drawstring—but at any rate, Ira all at once gave in. "Oh, what the hell," he said. "Let's just go to the Texaco."

"Thank you, Ira," Maggie told him sweetly.

And Mr. Otis said, "Well, if you sure it ain't too much trouble."

"No, no . . . ." Ira passed a hand across his forehead. "So I guess we'd better lock up the Chevy," he said.

Maggie said, "What Chevy?"

"That's what kind of car this is, Maggie."

"Ain't hardly no point locking it with a wheel about to fly off," Mr. Otis said.

Ira had a brief moment when he wondered if this whole situation might be Mr. Otis's particularly passive, devilish way of getting even.

He turned and walked back to his own car. Behind him he heard the Chevy's trunk lid clanging shut and the sound of their feet on the gravel, but he didn't wait for them to catch up.

Now the Dodge was as hot as the Chevy, and the chrome shaft of the gearshift burned his fingers. He sat there with the motor idling while Maggie helped Mr. Otis settle in the back seat. She seemed to know by instinct that he would require assistance; he had to be folded across the middle in some complicated fashion. The last of him to enter was his feet, which he gathered to him by lifting both knees with his hands. Then he let out a sigh and took his hat off. In the mirror Ira saw a bony, plated-looking scalp, with two cottony puffs of white hair snarling above his ears.

"I surely do appreciate this," Mr. Otis said.

"Oh, no trouble!" Maggie told him, flouncing onto the front seat.

Speak for yourself, Ira thought sourly.

He waited for a cavalcade of motorcyclists to pass (all male, unhelmeted, swooping by in long S-curves, as free as birds), and then he pulled onto the highway. "So whereabouts are we headed?" he asked.

"Oh, why, you just drive on past the dairy farm and make a right," Mr. Otis told him. "It ain't but three, four miles."

Maggie craned around in her seat and said, "You must live in this area."

"Back-air a ways on Dead Crow Road," Mr. Otis told her. "Or used to, till last week. Lately I been staying with my sister Lurene."

Then he started telling her about his sister Lurene, who worked off and on at the K Mart when her arthritis wasn't too bad; and that of course led to a discussion of Mr. Otis's own arthritis, the sneaky slow manner it had crept up on him and the other things he had thought it was first and how the doctor had marveled and made over his condition when Mr. Otis finally thought to consult him.

"Oh, if you had seen what I have seen," Maggie said. "People in the nursing home where I work just knotted over; don't

I know it." She had a tendency to fall into other people's rhythms of speech while she was talking to them. Close your eyes and you could almost fancy she was black herself, Ira thought.

"It's a evil, mean-spirited ailment; no two ways about it," Mr. Otis said. "This here is the dairy farm, mister. You want to take your next right."

Ira slowed down. They passed a small clump of cows moonily chomping and staring, and then they turned onto a road not two full lanes wide. The pavement was patchy, with hand-painted signs tilting off the grassy embankment: DANGER LIVE-STOCK MAY BE LOOSE and SLOW THIS MEANS YOU and HOUNDS AND HORSES CROSSING.

Now Mr. Otis was explaining how arthritis had forced him to retire. He used to be a roofer, he said, down home in North Carolina. He used to walk those ridgepoles as nimble as a squirrel and now he couldn't manage the lowest rung of a ladder.

Maggie made a clucking sound.

Ira wondered why Maggie always had to be inviting other people into their lives. She didn't feel a mere husband was enough, he suspected. Two was not a satisfactory number for her. He remembered all the strays she had welcomed over the years—her brother who spent a winter on their couch when his wife fell in love with her dentist, and Serena that time that Max was in Virginia hunting work, and of course Fiona with her baby and her mountains of baby equipment, her stroller and her playpen and her wind-up infant swing. In his present mood, Ira thought he might include their own children as well, for weren't Jesse and Daisy also outsiders—interrupting their most private moments, wedging between the two of them? (Hard to believe that some people had children to hold a marriage *together*.) And neither one had been planned for, at least not quite so soon. In the days before Jesse was born, Ira had still had hopes of going back to school. It was supposed to be the next thing in line, after paying off his sister's medical bills and his

820

father's new furnace. Maggie would keep on working full time. But then she found out she was pregnant, and she had to take leave from her job. And after that Ira's sister developed a whole new symptom, some kind of seizures that required hospitalization; and a moving van crashed into the shop one Christmas Eve and damaged the building. Then Maggie got pregnant with Daisy, another surprise. (Had it been unwise, perhaps, to leave matters of contraception to someone so accident-prone?) But that was eight years after Jesse, and Ira had more or less abandoned his plans by then anyhow.

Sometimes—on a day like today, say, this long, hot day in this dusty car—he experienced the most crushing kind of tiredness. It was an actual weight on his head, as if the ceiling had been lowered. But he supposed that everybody felt that way, now and again.

Maggie was telling Mr. Otis the purpose of their trip. "My oldest, closest friend just lost her husband," she was saying, "and we had to go to his funeral. It was the saddest occasion."

"Oh, gracious. Well, now, I want to offer my sincere condolences," Mr. Otis said.

Ira slowed behind a round-shouldered, humble-looking car from the forties, driven by an old lady so hunched that her head was barely visible above the steering wheel. Route One, the nursing home of highways. Then he remembered that this wasn't Route One anymore, that they had drifted sideward or maybe even backward, and he had a dreamy, floating sensation. It was like that old spell during a change of seasons when you momentarily forget what stage the year is going through. Is it spring, or is it fall? Is the summer just beginning, or is it coming to an end?

They passed a modern, split-level house with two plaster statues in the yard: a Dutch boy and girl bobbing delicately toward each other so their lips were almost touching. Then a trailer park and assorted signs for churches, civic organizations,

Al's Lawn and Patio Furnishings. Mr. Otis sat forward with a grunt, clutching the back of the seat. "Right up-air is the Texaco," he said. "See it?"

Ira saw it: a small white rectangle set very close to the road. Mylar balloons hovered high above the pumps—three to each pump, red, silver, and blue, twining lazily about one another.

He turned onto the concrete apron, carefully avoiding the signal cord that stretched across it, and braked and looked back at Mr. Otis. But Mr. Otis stayed where he was; it was Maggie who got out. She opened the rear door and set a hand beneath the old man's elbow while he uncurled himself. "Now, just where is your nephew?" she asked.

Mr. Otis said, *"Somewheres about."*

"Are you sure of that? What if he's not working today?"

"Why, he must be working. Ain't he?"

Oh, Lord, they were going to prolong this situation forever. Ira cut the engine and watched the two of them walking across the apron.

Over by the full-service island, a white boy with a stringy brown ponytail listened to what they asked and then shook his head. He said something, waving an arm vaguely eastward. Ira groaned and slid down lower in his seat.

Then here came Maggie, clicking along, and Ira took heart; but when she reached the car all she did was lean in through the passenger window. "We have to wait a minute," she told him.

"What for?"

"His nephew's out on a call but he's expected back in no time."

"Then why can't we just leave?" Ira asked.

"I couldn't do that! I wouldn't rest easy. I wouldn't know how it came out."

"What do you mean, how it came out? His wheel is perfectly fine, remember?"

"It wobbled, Ira. I saw it wobble."

He sighed.

"And maybe his nephew won't show up for some reason," she said, "so Mr. Otis will be stranded here. Or maybe it will cost money. I want to make sure he's not out any money."

"Look here, Maggie—"

"Why don't you fill the tank? Surely we could use some gas."

"We don't have a Texaco credit card," he told her.

"Pay cash. Fill the tank and by then I bet Lamont will be pulling into the station."

"Lamont," already. Next thing you knew, she'd have adopted the boy.

He restarted the engine, muttering, and drew up next to the self-serve island and got out. They had an older style of pump here that Baltimore no longer used—printed flip-over numerals instead of LED, and a simple pivot arrangement to trip the switch. Ira had to readjust, cast his mind back a couple of years in order to get the thing going. Then while the gas flowed into the tank he watched Maggie settle Mr. Otis on a low, white-washed wall that separated the Texaco from someone's vegetable garden. Mr. Otis had his hat back on and he was hunkered under it like a cat under a table, peering forth reflectively, chewing on a mouthful of air, as old men were known to do. He was ancient, and yet probably not so many years older than Ira himself. It was a thought to give you pause. Ira heard the jolt as the gas cut off, and he turned back to the car. Overhead, the balloons rustled against each other with a sound that made him think of raincoats.

While he was paying inside the station he noticed a snack machine, so he walked over to the others to see if they wanted something. They were deep in conversation, Mr. Otis going on and on about someone named Duluth. "Maggie, they've got potato chips," Ira said. "The kind you like: barbecue."

823

Maggie waved a hand at him. "I think you were absolutely justified," she told Mr. Otis.

"And bacon rinds!" Ira said. "You hardly ever find bacon rinds these days."

She gave him a distant, abstracted look and said, "Have you forgotten I'm on a diet?"

"How about you, then, Mr. Otis?"

"Oh, why, no, thank you, sir; thank you kindly, sir," Mr. Otis said. He turned to Maggie and went on: "So anyways, I axes her, 'Duluth, how can you hold me to count for that, woman?' "

"Mr. Otis's wife is mad at him for something he did in her dream," Maggie told Ira.

Mr. Otis said, "Here I am just as unaware as a babe and I come down into the kitchen, I axes, 'Where my breakfast?' She say, 'Fix it yourself.' I say, 'Huh?' "

"That is just so unfair," Maggie told him.

Ira said, "Well, I believe I'll have a snack," and he walked back toward the station, hands stuffed into his pockets, feeling left out.

Dieting too, he thought; dieting was another example of Maggie's wastefulness. The water diet and the protein diet and the grapefruit diet. Depriving herself meal after meal when in Ira's opinion she was just exactly right as she was—not even what you'd call plump; just a satisfying series of handfuls, soft, silky breasts and a creamy swell of bottom. But since when had she ever listened to Ira? He dropped coins glumly into the snack machine and punched the key beneath a sack of pretzels.

When he got back, Maggie was saying, "I mean think if we all did that! Mistook our dreams for real life. Look at me: Two or three times a year, near-about, I dream this neighbor and I are kissing. This totally bland neighbor named Mr. Simmons who looks like a salesman of something, I don't know, insurance or real estate or something. In the daytime I don't give him a thought, but at night I dream we're kissing and I long for him to unbutton my blouse, and in the morning at the bus stop I'm so embarrassed I can't even meet his eyes but then I see he's just the same as ever, bland-faced man in a business suit."

"For God's sake, Maggie," Ira said. He tried to picture this Simmons character, but he had no idea who she could be talking about.

"I mean what if I was held to blame for that?" Maggie asked. "Some thirty-year-old . . . kid I don't have the faintest interest in! I'm not the one who designed that dream!"

"No, indeed," Mr. Otis said. "And anyways, this here of Duluth's was Duluth's dream. It weren't even me that dreamed it. She claim I was standing on her needlepoint chair, her chair seat she worked forever on, so she order me off but when I stepped down I was walking on her crocheted shawl and her embroidered petticoat, my shoes was dragging lace and ruffles and bits of ribbon. 'If that ain't just like you,' she tell me in the morning, and I say, 'What did I do? Show me what I did. Show me where I ever trompled on a one of them things.' She say, 'You are just a mowing-down type of man, Daniel Otis, and if I knew I'd have to put up with you so long I'd have made a more thoughtful selection when I married.' So I say, 'Well, if that's how you feel, I'm leaving,' and she say, 'Don't forget your things,' and off I go."

"Mr. Otis has been living in his car these last few days and moving around among relatives," Maggie told Ira.

"Is that right," Ira said.

"So it matters quite a heap to me that my wheel not pop off," Mr. Otis added.

Ira sighed and sat down on the wall next to Maggie. The pretzels were the varnished kind that stuck in his teeth, but he was so hungry that he went on eating them.

Now the ponytailed boy walked toward them, so direct and purposeful in his tap-heeled leather boots that Ira stood up again, imagining they had some business to discuss. But all the boy did was coil the air hose that had been hissing on the concrete all this time without their noticing. In order not to look indecisive, Ira went on over to him anyhow. "So!" he said. "What's the story on this Lamont?"

"He's out," the boy told him.

"No chance we could get you to come, I guess. Run you over to the highway in our car and get you to look at Mr. Otis here's wheel for us."

"Nope," the boy said, hanging the hose on its hook.

Ira said, "I see."

He returned to the wall, and the boy walked back to the station.

"I think it might be Moose Run," Maggie was telling Mr. Otis. "Is that the name? This cutoff that leads into Cartwheel."

"Now, I don't know about no Moose Run," Mr. Otis said, "but I have heard tell of Cartwheel. Just can't say right off exactly how you'd get there. See, they's so many places hereabouts that sound like towns, call theyselves towns, but really they ain't much more than a grocery store and a gas pump."

"That's Cartwheel, all right," Maggie said. "One main street. No traffic lights. Fiona lives on a skinny little road that doesn't even have a sidewalk. Fiona's our daughter-in-law. Ex-daughter-in-law, I suppose I should say. She used to be our son Jesse's wife, but now they're divorced."

"Yes, that is how they do nowadays," Mr. Otis said. "Lamont is divorced too, and my sister Florence' girl Sally. I don't know why they bother getting married."

Just as if his own marriage were in perfect health.

"Have a pretzel," Ira said. Mr. Otis shook his head absently but Maggie dug down deep in the bag and came up with half a dozen.

"Really it was all a misunderstanding," she told Mr. Otis. She bit into a pretzel. "They were perfect for each other. They

826

even looked perfect: Jesse so dark and Fiona so blond. It's just that Jesse was working musician's hours and his life was sort of, I don't know, unsteady. And Fiona was so young, and inclined to fly off the handle. Oh, I used to just ache for them. It broke Jesse's heart when she left him; she took their little daughter and went back home to her mother. And Fiona's heart was broken too, I know, but do you think she would say so? And now they're so neatly divorced you would think they had never been married."

All true, as far as it went, Ira reflected; but there was a lot she'd left out. Or not left out so much as slicked over, somehow, like that image of their son—the "musician" plying his trade so busily that he was forced to neglect his "wife" and his "daughter." Ira had never thought of Jesse as a musician; he'd thought of him as a high-school dropout in need of permanent employment. And he had never thought of Fiona as a wife but rather as Jesse's teenaged sidekick—her veil of gleaming blond hair incongruous above a skimpy T-shirt and tight jeans—while poor little Leroy had not been much more than their pet, their stuffed animal won at a carnival booth.

He had a vivid memory of Jesse as he'd looked the night he was arrested, back when he was sixteen. He'd been picked up for public drunkenness with several of his friends—a onetime occurrence, as it turned out, but Ira had wanted to make sure of that and so, intending to be hard on him, he had insisted Maggie stay home while he went down alone to post bail. He had sat on a bench in a public waiting area and finally there came Jesse, walking doubled over between two officers. Evidently his wrists had been handcuffed behind his back and he had attempted, at some point, to step through the circle of his own arms so as to bring his hands in front of him. But he had given up or been interrupted halfway through the maneuver, and so he hobbled out lopsided, twisted like a sideshow freak with his wrists trapped between his legs. Ira had experienced the most complicated mingling of emotions at the sight: anger at his son and anger at the authorities too, for exhibiting Jesse's humiliation, and a wild impulse to laugh and an aching, flooding sense of pity. Jesse's jacket sleeves had been pushed up his forearms in the modern style (something boys never did in Ira's day) and that had made him seem even more vulnerable, and so had his expression, once he was unlocked and could stand upright, although it was a fiercely defiant expression and he wouldn't acknowledge Ira's presence. Now when Ira thought of Jesse he always pictured him as he'd been that night, that same combination of infuriating and pathetic. He wondered how Maggie pictured him. Maybe she delved even farther into the past. Maybe she saw him at age four or age six, a handsome, uncommonly engaging little kid with no more than the average kid's problems. At any rate, she surely didn't view him as he really was.

No, nor their daughter, either, he thought. Maggie saw Daisy as a version of Maggie's mother—accomplished, efficient—and she fluttered around her, looking inadequate. She had fluttered ever since Daisy was a little girl with an uncannily well-ordered room and a sheaf of color-coded notebooks for her homework. But Daisy was pitiable too, in her way. Ira saw that clearly, even though she was the one he felt closer to. She seemed to be missing out on her own youth—had never even had a boyfriend, so far as Ira could tell. Whenever Jesse got into mischief as a child Daisy had taken on a pinch-faced expression of disapproval, but Ira would almost rather she had joined in the mischief herself. Wasn't that how it was supposed to work? Wasn't that how it worked in other families, those jolly, noisy families Ira used to watch wistfully when he was a little boy? Now she was packed for college—had been packed for weeks—and had no clothes left but the throwaways that she wasn't taking with her; and she walked around the house looking bleak and joyless as a nun in her limp, frayed blouses and faded skirts. But Maggie thought she was admirable. "When I was her age I hadn't even begun to decide what I wanted to be," she said. Daisy wanted to be a quantum physicist. "I'm just so impressed with that," Maggie said, till Ira said, "Maggie, just what is a quantum physicist?"—honestly wanting to know. "Do you have the foggiest inkling?" he asked. Then Maggie thought he was belittling her and she said, "Oh, I admit I'm not scientific! I never said I was scientific! I'm just a geriatric nursing assistant, I admit it!" and Ira said, "All I meant was— Jesus! All I meant was—" and Daisy poked her head in the door and said, "Would you please, please not have another one of your blowups; I'm trying to read."

"Blowup!" Maggie cried. "I make the simplest little remark—"

And Ira told Daisy, "Listen here, miss, if you're so easily disturbed as all that, you can just go read in the library."

So Daisy had withdrawn, pinch-faced once again, and Maggie had buried her head in her hands.

"Same old song and dance"—that was how Jesse had once referred to marriage. This was one morning when Fiona had left the breakfast table in tears, and Ira had asked Jesse what was wrong. "You know how it is," Jesse had answered. "Same old song and dance as always." Then Ira (who had asked not out of empty curiosity but as a means of implying *This matters, son; pay her some heed*) had wondered what that "you know" signified. Was Jesse saying that Ira's marriage and his own had anything in common? Because if so, he was way out of line. They were two entirely different institutions. Ira's marriage was as steady as a tree; not even he could tell how wide and deep the roots went.

Still, Jesse's phrase had stuck in his memory: same old song and dance. Same old arguments, same recriminations. The same jokes and affectionate passwords, yes, and abiding loyalty and gestures of support and consolations no one else knew how to offer; but also the same old resentments dragged up year after year, with nothing ever totally forgotten: the time Ira didn't act happy to hear Maggie was pregnant, the time Maggie failed to defend Ira in front of her mother, the time Ira refused to visit Maggie in the hospital, the time Maggie forgot to invite Ira's family to Christmas dinner.

And the unvaryingness—ah, Lord; who could blame Jesse for chafing against that? Probably the boy had been watching his parents sideways all the years of his childhood, swearing *he* would never put up with such a life: plugging along day after day, Ira heading to his shop every morning, Maggie to the nursing home. Probably those afternoons that Jesse had spent helping out at the shop had been a kind of object lesson. He must have recoiled from it—Ira sitting endlessly on his high wooden stool, whistling along with his easy-listening radio station as he measured a mat or sawed away at his miter box. Women came in asking him to frame their cross-stitched homilies and their amateur seascapes and their wedding photos (two serious people in profile gazing solely at each other). They brought in illustrations torn from magazines—a litter of puppies or a duckling in a basket. Like a tailor measuring a half-dressed client, Ira remained discreetly sightless, appearing to form no judgment about a picture of a sad-faced kitten tangled in a ball of yarn. "He wants a pastel-colored mat of some kind, wouldn't you say?" the women might ask. (They often used personal pronouns, as if the pictures were animate.)

"Yes, ma'am," Ira would answer.

"Maybe a pale blue that would pick up the blue of his ribbon."

"Yes, we could do that."

And through Jesse's eyes he would see himself all at once as a generic figure called The Shopkeeper: a drab and obsequious man of indeterminate age.

Above the shop he could usually hear the creak, pause,

creak of his father's rocking chair, and the hesitant footsteps of one of his sisters crossing the living room floor. Their voices, of course, weren't audible, and for this reason Ira had fallen into the habit of imagining that his family never spoke during the day—that they were keeping very still till Ira came. He was the backbone of their lives; he knew that. They depended on him utterly.

In his childhood he had been extraneous—a kind of afterthought, half a generation younger than his sisters. He had been so much the baby that he'd called every family member "honey," because that was how all those grownups or almost-grownups addressed him and he'd assumed it was a universal term. "I need my shoes tied, honey," he would tell his father. He didn't have the usual baby's privileges, though; he was never the center of attention. If any of them could be said to occupy that position it was his sister Dorrie—mentally handicapped, frail and jerky, bucktoothed, awkward—although even Dorrie had a neglected air and tended to sit by herself on the outskirts of a room. Their mother suffered from a progressive disease that killed her when Ira was fourteen, that left him forever afterward edgy and frightened in the presence of illness; and anyhow she had never shown much of a talent for mothering. She devoted herself instead to religion, to radio evangelists and inspirational pamphlets left by door-to-door missionaries. Her idea of a meal was saltines and tea, for all of them. She never got hungry like ordinary mortals or realized that others could be hungry, but simply took in sustenance when the clock reminded her. If they wanted real food it was up to their father, for Dorrie was not capable of anything complicated and Junie was subject to some kind of phobia that worsened over the years till she refused to leave the house for so much as a quart of milk. Their father had to see to that when he was finished down at the shop. He would trudge upstairs for the grocery list, trudge out again, return with a few tin cans, and putter around the kitchen with the girls. Even after Ira was old enough, his assistance was not required. He was the interloper, the one rude splash of color in a sepia photograph. His family gave him a wide berth while addressing him remotely and kindly. "You finish your homework, honey?" they would ask, and they asked this even in the summer and over the Christmas holidays.

Then Ira graduated—had already paid his deposit at the University of Maryland, with dreams of going on to medical school—and his father suddenly abdicated. He just . . . imploded, was how Ira saw it. Declared he had a weak heart and could not continue. Sat down in his platform rocker and stayed there. Ira took over the business, which wasn't easy because he'd never played the smallest part in it up till then. All at once he was the one his family turned to. They relied on him for money and errands and advice, for transportation to the doctor and news of the outside world. It was, "Honey, is this dress out of style?" and, "Honey, can we afford a new rug?" In a way, Ira felt gratified, especially at the beginning, when this seemed to be just a temporary, summer-vacation state of affairs. He was no longer on the sidelines; he was central. He rooted through Dorrie's bureau drawers for the mate to her favorite red sock; he barbered Junie's graying hair; he dumped the month's receipts into his father's lap, all in the knowledge that he, Ira, was the only one they could turn to.

But summer stretched into fall, and first the university granted him a semester's postponement and then a year's postponement, and then after a while the subject no longer came up.

Well, face it, there were worse careers than cutting forty-five-degree angles in strips of gilded molding. And he did have Maggie, eventually—dropping into his lap like a wonderful gift out of nowhere. He did have two normal, healthy children. Maybe his life wasn't exactly what he had pictured when he was eighteen, but whose was? That was how things worked, most often.

Although he knew that Jesse didn't see it that way.

No compromises for Jesse Moran, no, sir. No modifications, no lowering of sights for Jesse. "I refuse to believe that I will die unknown," he had said to Ira once, and Ira, instead of smiling tolerantly as he should have, had felt slapped in the face.

Unknown.

Maggie said, "Ira, did you happen to notice a soft-drink machine inside the station?"

He looked at her.

"Ira?"

He pulled himself together and said, "Why, yes, I think so."

"With diet soft drinks?"

"Um . . ."

"I'll go check," Maggie said. "Those pretzels made me thirsty. Mr. Otis? Want something to drink?"

"Oh, no, I'm doing all right," Mr. Otis told her.

She tripped off toward the building, her skirt swinging. Both men watched her go.

"A fine, fine lady," Mr. Otis said.

Ira let his eyes close briefly and rubbed the ache in his forehead.

"A real angel of mercy." Mr. Otis said.

In stores sometimes Maggie would bring her selections to a clerk and say, "I suppose you expect me to pay for these," in the fake-tough tone that her brothers used when they were joking. Ira always worried she had overstepped, but the clerk would laugh and say something like: "Well, that thought had occurred to me." So the world was not as Ira had perceived it, evidently. It was more the way Maggie perceived it. She was the one who got along in it better, collecting strays who stuck to her like lint and falling into heart-to-heart talks with total strangers. This Mr. Otis, for instance: his face alight with enthusiam, his eyes stretched into crepe-edged triangles. "She puts me in mind of the lady with the chimney," he was telling Ira. "I knew it was someone; just couldn't think who."

"Chimney?"

"White lady I did not know from Adam," Mr. Otis said. "She was leaking round her chimney she say and she call me to come give a estimate. But I misstepped somehow and fell right off her roof while I was walking about. Only knocked the wind out as it happened, but Lordy, for a while there I thought I was a goner, laid there on the ground not able to catch my breath, and this lady she insist on driving me to the hospital. On the way, though, my breath come back to me and so I say, 'Mrs., let's not go after all, they'll only take my life savings to say I got nothing wrong with me,' so she say fine but then has to buy me a cup of coffee and some hash browns at McDonald's, which happen to lie next to a Toys R Us, so she axes would I mind if we run in afterwards and bought a little red wagon for her nephew whose birthday it was tomorrow? And I say no and in fact she buy two, one for my niece's son Elbert also, and next to that is this gardening place—"

"Yes, that is Maggie, all right," Ira said.

"Not a straight-line kind of person."

"No indeedy," Ira said.

That seemed to use up all their topics of conversation. They fell silent and focused on Maggie, who was returning with a soft-drink can held at arm's length. "Darn thing just bubbled up all over me," she called cheerfully. "Ira? Want a sip?"

"No, thanks."

"Mr. Otis?"

"Oh, why, no, I don't believe I do, thanks anyhow."

She settled between them and tipped her head back for a long, noisy swig.

Ira started wishing for a game of solitaire. All this idleness was getting to him. Judging from the way those balloons were bobbing about, though, he guessed his cards might blow away, and so he tucked his hands in his armpits and slouched lower on the wall.

They sold balloons like that at Harborplace, or next to it. Lone, grim men stood on street corners with trees of Mylar lozenges floating overhead. He remembered how entranced his sister Junie had been when she first saw them. Poor Junie: in a way more seriously handicapped than Dorrie, even—more limited, more imprisoned. Her fears confounded them all, because nothing very dreadful had ever befallen her in the outside world, at least not so far as anyone knew. In the beginning they tried to point that out. They said useless things like: "What's the worst that could happen?" and "*I'll* be with you." Then gradually they stopped. They gave up on her and let her stay where she was.

Except for Maggie, that is. Maggie was too obstinate to give up. And after years of failed attempts, one day she conceived the notion that Junie might be persuaded to go out if she could go in costume. She bought Junie a bright-red wig and a skin-tight dress covered with poppies and a pair of spike-heeled patent-leather shoes with ankle straps. She plastered Junie's face with heavy makeup. To everyone's astonishment, it worked. Giggling in a terrified, unhappy way, Junie allowed Maggie and Ira to lead her to the front stoop. The next day, slightly farther. Then finally to the end of the block. Never without Ira, though. She wouldn't do it with just Maggie; Maggie was not a blood relation. (Ira's father, in fact, wouldn't even call Maggie by name but referred to her as "Madam." "Will Madam be coming too, Ira?"—a title that exactly reflected the mocking, skeptical attitude he had assumed toward her from the start.)

"You see what's at work here," Maggie said of Junie. "When she's in costume it's not she who's going out; it's someone else. Her real self is safe at home."

Evidently she was right. Clinging to Ira's arm with both hands, Junie walked to the pharmacy and requested a copy of

Soap Opera Digest. She walked to the grocery store and placed an order for chicken livers in an imperious, brazen manner as if she were another kind of woman entirely—a flamboyant, maybe even trampish woman who didn't care what people thought of her. Then she collapsed into giggles again and asked Ira how she was doing. Well, Ira was pleased at her progress, of course, but after a while the whole thing got to be a nuisance. She wanted to venture this place and that, and always it was such a production—the preparations, the dress and the makeup, the assurances he was forced to offer. And those ridiculous heels hampered her so. She walked like someone navigating a freshly mopped floor. Really it would have been simpler if she'd gone on staying home, he reflected. But he was ashamed of himself for the thought.

Then she got this urge to visit Harborplace. She had watched on TV when Harborplace first opened and she had somehow come to the conclusion that it was one of the wonders of the world. So naturally, after she'd gained some confidence, nothing would do but that she must see it in person. Only Ira didn't want to take her. To put it mildly, he was not a fan of Harborplace. He felt it was un-Baltimorean—in fact, a glorified shopping mall. And parking would be bound to cost an arm and a leg. Couldn't she settle for somewhere else? No, she couldn't, she said. Couldn't just Maggie take her, then? No, she needed Ira. He knew she needed him; how could he suggest otherwise? And then their father wanted to come too, and then Dorrie, who was so excited that she already had her "suitcase" (a Hutzler's coat box) packed for the occasion. Ira had to set his teeth and agree to it.

They scheduled the trip for a Sunday—Ira's only day off. Unfortunately, it turned out to be a misty, lukewarm morning, with showers predicted for afternoon. Ira suggested a postponement but no one would hear of it, not even Maggie, who had become as fired up as the others. So he drove them all downtown, where by some miracle he found a parking spot on the street, and they got out and started walking. It was so foggy that buildings just a few yards away were invisible. When they reached the corner of Pratt and Light streets and looked across to Harborplace they couldn't even see the pavilions; they were merely denser patches of gray. The traffic signal, turning green, was the one little pinprick of color. And nobody else was in sight except for a single balloon man, who took shape eerily on the opposite corner as they approached.

It was the balloons that snagged Junie's attention. They seemed made of liquid metal; they were silver-toned and crushy, puckered around the edges like sofa cushions. Junie cried, "Oh!" She stepped up onto the curb, gaping all the while. "What *are* those?" she cried.

"Balloons, of course," Ira said. But when he tried to lead her past, she craned back to look at them and so did Dorrie, who was hanging on his other arm.

He could see what the problem was. TV had kept Junie informed of the world's important developments but not the trivial ones, like Mylar; so those were what stopped her in her tracks. It was perfectly understandable. At that moment, though, Ira just didn't feel like catering to her. He didn't want to be there at all, and so he rushed them forward and around the first pavilion. Junie's hand was like a claw on his arm. Dorrie, whose left leg had been partially paralyzed after her latest seizure, leaned on his other arm and hobbled grotesquely, her Hutzler's coat box slamming against her hip at every step. And behind them, Maggie murmured encouragement to his father, whose breathing was growing louder and more effortful.

"But those are not any balloons *I* have had experience of!" Junie said. "What material is that? What do they call it?"

By then they had reached the promenade around the water's edge, and instead of answering, Ira gazed pointedly toward the view. "Isn't this what you were dying to see?" he reminded her.

But the view was nothing but opaque white sheets and a fuzzy-edged *U.S.S. Constellation* riding on a cloud, and Harborplace was a hulking, silent concentration of vapors.

Well, the whole trip ended in disaster, of course. Junie said everything had looked better on TV, and Ira's father said his heart was flapping in his chest, and then Dorrie somehow got her feelings hurt and started crying and had to be taken home before they'd set foot inside a pavilion. Ira couldn't remember now what had hurt her feelings, but what he did remember, so vividly that it darkened even this glaringly sunlit Texaco, was the sensation that had come over him as he stood there between his two sisters. He'd felt suffocated. The fog had made a tiny room surrounding them, an airless, steamy room such as those that house indoor swimming pools. It had muffled every sound but his family's close, oppressively familiar voices. It had wrapped them together, locked them in, while his sisters' hands dragged him down the way drowning victims drag down whoever tries to rescue them. And Ira had thought, *Ah, God, I have been trapped with these people all my life and I am never going to be free.* And he had known then what a failure he'd been, ever since the day he took over his father's business.

Was it any wonder he was so sensitive to waste? He had given up the only serious dream he'd ever had. You can't get more wasteful than that.

"Lamont!" Maggie said.

She was looking toward a revolving yellow light over by the gas pumps—a tow truck, towing nothing. It stopped with a painful screeching sound and the engine died. A black man in a denim jacket swung out of the cab.

"That's him, all right," Mr. Otis said, rising by inches from his seat.

Lamont walked to the rear of the truck and examined something. He kicked a tire and then started toward the cab. He was not as young as Ira had expected—no mere boy but a solidly

838

built, glowering man with plum-black skin and a heavy way of walking.

"Well, hey there!" Mr. Otis called.

Lamont halted and looked over at him. "Uncle Daniel?" he said.

"How you been, son?"

"What *you* doing here?" Lamont asked, approaching.

When he reached the wall, Maggie and Ira stood up, but Lamont didn't glance in their direction. "Ain't you gone back to Aunt Duluth yet?" he asked Mr. Otis.

"Lamont, I'm going to need that truck of yourn," Mr. Otis said.

"What for?"

"Believe my left front wheel is loose."

"What? Where's it at?"

"Out on Route One. This here fellow kindly give me a lift."

Lamont briefly skimmed Ira with his eyes.

"We just happened to be driving past," Ira told him.

"Hmm," Lamont said in an unfriendly tone, and then, turning again to his uncle, "Now let's see what you telling me. Your car is out on the highway someplace . . ."

"It was Mrs. here caught on to it," Mr. Otis said, and he gestured toward Maggie, who beamed up at Lamont trustfully. A slender thread of soft-drink foam traced her upper lip; it made Ira feel protective.

"I won't offer you my hand," she told Lamont. "This Pepsi has just fizzed all over me."

Lamont merely studied her, with the corners of his mouth pulled down.

"She lean out her window and call, 'Your wheel!' " Mr. Otis said. " 'Your front wheel is falling off!' "

"Really that was a fabrication," Maggie told Lamont. "I made it up."

Sweet Jesus.

839

Lamont said, "Say what?"

"I fibbed," Maggie said blithely. "We admitted as much to your uncle, but I don't know, it was kind of hard to convince him."

"You saying you told him a lie?" Lamont asked.

"Right."

Mr. Otis smiled self-consciously down at his shoes.

"Well, actually—" Ira began.

"It was after he almost stopped dead in front of us," Maggie said. "We had to veer off the road, and I was so mad that as soon as we caught up with him I said that about his wheel. But I didn't know he was old! I didn't know he was helpless!"

"Helpless?" Mr. Otis asked, his smile growing less certain.

"And besides, then it did seem his wheel was acting kind of funny," Maggie told Lamont. "So we brought him here to the Texaco."

Lamont looked no more threatening than he'd seemed all along, Ira was relieved to see. In fact, he dismissed the two of them entirely. He turned instead to his uncle. "Hear that?" he asked. "See there? Now it comes to you running folks off the road."

"Lamont, I'll tell you the truth," Mr. Otis said. "I do believe when I think back on it that wheel has not been acting properly for some days now."

"Didn't I say you ought to give up driving? Didn't we all say that? Didn't Florence beg you to hand in your license? Next time you might not be so lucky. Some crazy white man going to shoot your head off next time."

Mr. Otis appeared to shrink, standing there quietly with his hat brim shielding his face.

"If you'd've stayed home with Aunt Duluth where you belong, none of this wouldn't be happening," Lamont told him. "Cruising about on the interstate! Sleeping here and there like some hippie!"

840

"Well, I had thought I was driving real cautious and careful," Mr. Otis said.

Ira cleared his throat. "So about the wheel—" he said.

"You just got to go on back home and make up," Lamont told Mr. Otis. "Quit drawing this thing out and apologize to Aunt Duluth and get that rust heap out of folkses' way."

"I can't apologize! I ain't done nothing to be sorry for," Mr. Otis said.

"What's the difference, man? Apologize even so."

"See, I *couldn't* have done it; it was only in her dream. Duluth went and had this dream, see—"

"You been married fifty-some years to that woman," Lamont said, "and half of those years the two of you been in a snit about something. She ain't speaking to you or you ain't speaking to her or she moves out or you moves out. Shoot, man, one time you both moves out and leaves your house standing empty. Plenty would give their right arms for a nice little house like you-all's, and what do you do? Leave it stand empty while you off careening about in your Chevy and Aunt Duluth's sleeping on Florence's couch discommoding her family."

A reminiscent smile crossed Mr. Otis's face. "It's true," he said. "I had thought I was leaving her, that time, and she thought she was leaving me."

"You two act like quarrelsome children," Lamont told him.

"Well, at least I'm still married, you notice!" Mr. Otis said. "At least I'm still married, unlike some certain others I could name!"

Ira said, "Well, at any rate—"

"Even worse than children," Lamont went on, as if he hadn't heard. "Children at least got the time to spare, but you two are old and coming to the end of your lives. Pretty soon one or the other of you going to die and the one that's left behind will say, 'Why did I act so ugly? That was who it *was*; that person was

who I was with; and here we threw ourselves away on spitefulness,' you'll say."

"Well, it's probably going to be me that dies first," Mr. Otis
said, "so I just ain't going to worry about that."

"I'm serious, Uncle."

"*I'm* serious. Could be what you throw away is all that really
counts; could be that's the whole point of things, wouldn't that
be something? Spill it! Spill it all, I say! No way *not* to spill it.
And anyhow, just look at the times we had. Maybe that's what
I'll end up thinking. 'My, we surely did have us a time. We
were a real knock-down, drag-out, heart-and-soul type of couple,' I'll say. Something to reflect on in the nursing home."

Lamont rolled his eyes heavenward.

Ira said, "Well, not to change the subject, but is this wheel
business under control now?"

Both men looked over at him. "Oh," Mr. Otis said finally.
"I reckon you two will want to be moving on."

"Only if you're sure you're all right," Maggie told him.

"He'll be fine," Lamont said. "Get on and go."

"Yes, don't you give me another thought," Mr. Otis said.
"Let me squire you to your car." And he walked off between
the two of them. Lamont stayed behind, looking disgusted.

"That boy is just so cranky," Mr. Otis told Ira. "I don't
know who he takes after."

"You think he'll be willing to help you?"

"Oh, surely. He just want to rant and carry on some first."

They reached the Dodge, and Mr. Otis insisted on opening
Maggie's door for her. It took longer than if she had done it
herself; he had to get positioned just right and gain some le-
verage. Meanwhile he was saying to Ira, "And it ain't like he
had room to criticize. A divorced man! Handing out advice like
a expert!"

He closed the door after Maggie with a loose, ineffectual
sound so that she had to reopen it and give it a good slam. "A

842

man who ups and splits at the first little setback," he told Ira. "Lives alone all pruned and puckerish, drying out like a raisin. Sets alone in front of the TV, night after night, and won't go courting nobody new for fear she'll do him like his wife did."

"Tsk!" Maggie said, looking up at him through her window. "That is always so sad to see."

"But do you think *he* sees it?" Mr. Otis asked. "Naw." He followed Ira around to the driver's side of the car. "He believe that's just a regular life," he told Ira.

"Well, listen," Ira said as he slid behind the wheel. "If there's any kind of expense with the tow truck I want to hear about it, understand?" He shut the door and leaned out the window to say, "I'd better give you our address."

"There won't be no expense," Mr. Otis said, "but I appreciate the thought." He tipped his hat back slightly and scratched his head. "You know I used to have this dog," he said. "Smartest dog I ever owned. Bessie. She just loved to chase a rubber ball. I would throw it for her and she would chase it. Anytime the ball landed on a kitchen chair, though, Bessie would poke her nose through the spindles of the chair-back and whine and moan and whimper, never dreaming she could just walk around and grab the ball from in front."

Ira said, "Um . . ."

"Puts me in mind of Lamont," Mr. Otis said.

"Lamont."

"Blind in spots."

"Oh! Yes, Lamont!" Ira said. He was relieved to find the connection.

"Well, I don't want to hold you up," Mr. Otis told him, and he offered Ira his hand. It felt very light and fragile, like the skeleton of a bird. "You-all take care driving now, hear?" He bent forward to tell Maggie, "Take care!"

"You too," she told him. "And I hope things work out with Duluth."

843

"Oh, they will, they will. Sooner or later." He chuckled and stepped back as Ira started the engine. Like a host seeing off his guests, he stood there gazing after them till they pulled out onto the road and he disappeared from Ira's rearview mirror.

"Well!" Maggie said, bouncing into a more comfortable position in her seat. "So anyhow . . ."

As if that whole excursion had been only a little hiccup in the midst of some long story she was telling.

Ira turned on the radio but all he could find was the most local kind of news—crop prices, a fire in a Knights of Columbus building. He turned it off. Maggie was rooting through her purse. "Now, where on earth?" she said.

"What're you looking for?"

"My sunglasses."

"On the dashboard."

"Oh, right."

She reached for them and perched them on the end of her nose. Then she rotated her face, staring all around as if testing their effectiveness. "Doesn't the sunlight bother your eyes?" she asked him finally.

"No, I'm fine."

"Maybe *I* should drive."

"No, no . . ."

"I haven't taken a single turn this whole day," she said.

"That's all right. Thanks anyhow, sweetheart."

"Well, you just let me know if you change your mind," she told him, and she sank back in her seat and gazed out at the view.

Ira cocked an elbow on the window ledge. He started whistling a tune.

Maggie stiffened and looked over at him.

"You just think I'm some sort of harum-scarum lady driver," she told him.

"Huh?" he said.

"You're just wondering what kind of fool you are even to consider allowing me behind the wheel."

He blinked. He had assumed the subject was concluded. "Lord, Maggie," he said, "why do you always take things so personally?"

"I just do, that's why," she told him, but she spoke without heat, as if uninterested in her own words, and then returned to studying the scenery.

Once they were back on Route One, Ira picked up speed. Traffic had grown heavier, but it was moving briskly. The farms gave way to patches of commercial land—a mountain of bald tires, a stepped, angular cliff of cinder blocks, a field of those windowed enclosures that fit over the beds of pickup trucks and turn them into campers. Ira wasn't sure what those were called. It bothered him; he liked to know the names of things, the specific, accurate term that would sum an object up.

"Spruce Gum," Maggie said.

"Pardon?"

She was twisted around in her seat, gazing behind her. She said, "Spruce Gum! That was the cutoff to Fiona's! We just now passed it."

"Oh, yes, Spruce Gum," he said. It did ring a bell.

"Ira," Maggie said.

"Hmm?"

"It's not so far out of the way."

He glanced at her. She had her hands pressed together, her face set toward him, her mouth bunched up a little as if she were willing certain words from him (the way she used to will the right answer out of Jesse when she was drilling him on his multiplication tables).

"Is it?" she said.

"No," he said.

She misunderstood him; she drew in a breath to start arguing. But he said, "No, I guess it's not."

"What: You mean you'll take me there?"

"Well," he said. And then he said, "Oh, well, we've already pretty much shot the day, right?" And he flicked his blinker on and looked for a place to turn the car around.

"Thank you, Ira," she told him, and she slid over as far as her seat belt allowed and planted a little brush stroke of a kiss below his ear.

Ira said, "Hmf," but he sounded more grudging than he really felt.

After he'd reversed the car in a lumberyard, he headed back up Route One and took a left onto Spruce Gum Road. They were facing into the sun now. Dusty shafts of light filmed the windshield. Maggie pushed her glasses higher on her nose, and Ira flipped his visor down.

Was it the haze on the windshield that made him think again of their trip to Harborplace? At any rate, for some reason he suddenly remembered why Dorrie had started crying that day.

Standing at the water's edge, hemmed in by fog, she had been moved to open her suitcase and show him its contents. None of what she'd brought was much different from any other time. There were the usual two or three comic books, he recalled, and probably a snack for her sweet tooth—a squashed Hostess cupcake perhaps, with the frosting smashed into the cellophane—and of course the rhinestone hatband that had once belonged to their mother. And finally her greatest treasure: a fan magazine with Elvis Presley on the cover. *King of Rock*, the title read. Dorrie worshiped Elvis Presley. Ordinarily Ira humored her, even bought her posters whenever he came across them, but on that particular morning he was feeling so burdened, he just hadn't had the patience. "Elvis," Dorrie said happily, and Ira said, "For God's sake, Dorrie, don't you know the guy is dead and buried?"

Then she had stopped smiling and her eyes had filled with

tears, and Ira had felt pierced. Everything about her all at once saddened him—her skimpy haircut and her chapped lips and her thin face that was so homely and so sweet, if only people would see. He put an arm around her. He hugged her bony little body close and gazed over her head at the *Constellation* floating in the fog. The tops of the masts had dwindled away and the ropes and chains had dissolved and the old ship had looked its age for once, swathed in clouds of mist you could mistake for the blurring of time. And Junie had pressed close to his other side and Maggie and Sam had watched steadfastly, waiting for him to say what to do next. He had known then what the true waste was; Lord, yes. It was not his having to support these people but his failure to notice how he loved them. He loved even his worn-down, defeated father, even the memory of his poor mother who had always been so pretty and never realized it because anytime she approached a mirror she had her mouth drawn up lopsided with shyness.

But then the feeling had faded (probably the very next instant, when Junie started begging to leave) and he forgot what he had learned. And no doubt he would forget again, just as Dorrie had forgotten, by the time they reached home, that Elvis Presley was no longer King of Rock.

THREE

1

Maggie had a song that she liked to sing with Ira when they were traveling. "On the Road Again," it was called—not the Willie Nelson chestnut but a blues-sounding piece from one of Jesse's old Canned Heat albums, stomping and hard-driving. Ira did the beat: "Boom-da-da, boom-da-da, boom-da-da, boom! boom!" Maggie sang the melody. " 'Take a hint from me, Mama, please! don't you cry no more,' " she sang. The telephone poles appeared to be flashing by in rhythm. Maggie felt rangy and freewheeling. She tipped her head back against the seat and swirled one ankle, keeping time.

In the old days, when she'd driven this road alone, the countryside had seemed unwelcoming—enemy territory. Among these woods and stony pastures her only grandchild was being held hostage, and Maggie (smothered in scarves, or swathed in an anonymous trench coat, or half obscured by Junie's bubbly red wig) had driven as if slipping between something. She'd had a sense of slithering, evading. She had fixed her mind on that child and held her face firmly before her: a bright baby face as round as a penny, eyes that widened with enthusiasm whenever Maggie walked into the room, dimpled fists revving up at the sight of her. I'm coming, Leroy! Don't forget me! But then over and over again those trips had proved so unsatisfactory, ending with that last awful time, when Leroy had twisted in her stroller and called, "Mom-Mom?"—hunting her other grandmother, her lesser grandmother, her *pretender* grandmother; and Maggie had finally given up and limited herself thereafter to the rare official visits with Ira. And even those had stopped soon enough. Leroy had begun to fade and dwindle, till one day she was no larger than somebody at the wrong end of a telescope—still dear, but very far removed.

Maggie thought of last summer when her old cat, Pumpkin, had died. His absence had struck her so intensely that it had amounted to a presence—the lack of his furry body twining between her ankles whenever she opened the refrigerator door, the lack of his motorboat purr in her bed whenever she woke up at night. Stupidly, she had been reminded of the time Leroy and Fiona had left, although of course there was no comparison. But here was something even stupider: A month or so later, when cold weather set in, Maggie switched off the basement dehumidifier as she did every year and even *that* absence had struck her. She had mourned in the most personal way the silencing of the steady, faithful whir that used to thrum the floorboards. What on earth was wrong with her? she had wondered. Would she spend the rest of her days grieving for every loss equally—a daughter-in-law, a baby, a cat, a machine that dries the air out?

Was this how it felt to grow old?

Now the fields were a brassy color, as pretty as a picture on a calendar. They held no particular significance. Maybe it helped that Ira was with her—an ally. Maybe it was just that sooner or later, even the sharpest pain became flattened.

" 'But I ain't going down that long old lonesome road all by myself,' " she sang automatically, and Ira sang, "Boom-da-da, boom-da-da—"

If Fiona remarried she would most likely acquire a new mother-in-law. Maggie hadn't considered that. She wondered if Fiona and this woman would be close. Would they spend their every free moment together, as cozy as two girlfriends?

"And suppose she has another baby!" Maggie said.

Ira broke off his boom-das to ask, "Huh?"

"I saw her through that whole nine months! What will she do without me?"

"Who're you talking about?"

"Fiona, of course. Who do you think?"

"Well, I'm sure she'll manage somehow," Ira said.

Maggie said, "Maybe, and maybe not." She turned away from him to look out at the fields again. They seemed unnaturally textureless. "I drove her to her childbirth classes," she said. "I drilled her in her exercises. I was her official labor coach."

"So now she knows all about it," Ira said.

"But it's something you have to repeat with each pregnancy," Maggie told him. "You have to keep at it."

She thought of how she had kept at Fiona, whom pregnancy had turned lackadaisical and vague, so that if it hadn't been for Maggie she'd have spent her entire third trimester on the couch in front of the TV. Maggie would clap her hands briskly— "Okay!"—and snap off the *Love Boat* rerun and fling open the curtains, letting sunshine flood the dim air of the living room and the turmoil of rock magazines and Fresca bottles. "Time for your pelvic squats!" she would cry, and Fiona would shrink and raise one arm to shield her eyes from the light.

"Pelvic squats, good grief," she would say. "Abdominal humps. It all sounds so gross." But she would heave to her feet, sighing. Even in pregnancy, her body was a teenager's—slender and almost rubbery, reminding Maggie of those scantily clad girls she'd glimpsed on beaches who seemed to belong to a completely different species from her own. The mound of the baby was a separate burden, a kind of package jutting out in front of her. "Breathing lessons—really," she said, dropping to the floor with a thud. "Don't they reckon I must know how to breathe by now?"

"Oh, honey, you're just lucky they offer such things," Maggie told her. "*My* first pregnancy, there wasn't a course to be found, and I was scared to death. I'd have loved to take lessons! And afterward: I remember leaving the hospital with Jesse and thinking, 'Wait. Are they going to let me just walk off with him? I don't know beans about babies! I don't have a license to do this. Ira and I are just amateurs.' I mean you're given all these lessons for the unimportant things—piano-playing, typing. You're given years and years of lessons in how to balance equations, which Lord knows you will never have to do in normal life. But how about parenthood? Or marriage, either, come to think of it. Before you can drive a car you need a state-approved course of instruction, but driving a car is nothing, nothing, compared to living day in and day out with a husband and raising up a new human being."

Which had not been the most reassuring notion, perhaps; for Fiona had said, "Jiminy," and dropped her head in her hands.

"Though I'm certain you'll do fine," Maggie said in a hurry, "And of course you have me here to help you."

"Oh, jiminy," Fiona said.

Ira turned down a little side road called Elm Lane—a double string of tacky one-story cottages with RVs in most of the driveways and sometimes a sloping tin trailer out back. Maggie asked him, "Who will wake up in the night now and bring her the baby to nurse?"

"Her husband, one would hope," Ira said. "Or maybe she'll keep the baby in *her* room this time, the way you should have had her do last time." Then he gave his shoulders a slight shake, as if ridding himself of something, and said, "What baby? Fi-

854

ona's not having a baby; she's just getting married, or so you claim. Let's put first things first here."

Well, but first things weren't put first the time before; Fiona had been two months pregnant when she married Jesse. Not that Maggie wanted to remind him of that. Besides, her thoughts were on something else now. She was caught by an unexpected, piercingly physical memory of bringing the infant Leroy in to Fiona for her 2 a.m. feeding—that downy soft head wavering on Maggie's shoulder, that birdlike mouth searching the bend of Maggie's neck inside her bathrobe collar, and then the close, sleep-smelling warmth of Jesse's and Fiona's bedroom. "Oh," she said without meaning to, and then, "Oh!" For there in Mrs. Stuckey's yard (hard-packed earth, not really a yard at all) stood a wiry little girl with white-blond hair that stopped short squarely at her jawline. She had just let go of a yellow Frisbee, which sailed shuddering toward their car and landed with a thump on the hood as Ira swung into the driveway.

"That's not—" Maggie said. "Is that—?"

"Must be Leroy," Ira told her.

"It's not!"

But of course, it had to be. Maggie was forced to make such a leap across time, though—from the infant on her shoulder to this gawky child, all in two seconds. She was experiencing some difficulty. The child dropped her hands to her sides and stared at them. Frowning gave her forehead a netted look. She wore a pink tank top with some kind of red stain down the front, berry juice or Kool-Aid, and baggy shorts in a blinding Hawaiian print. Her face was so thin it was triangular, a cat's face, and her arms and legs were narrow white stems.

"Maybe it's a neighbor girl," Maggie told Ira—a last-ditch effort.

He didn't bother replying.

As soon as he switched the ignition off, Maggie opened the door and stepped out. She called "Leroy?"

"What."

"Are you Leroy?"

The child deliberated a moment, as if uncertain, and then nodded.

"So," Maggie said. "Well, hi there!" she cried.

Leroy went on staring. She didn't seem one grain less suspicious.

Actually, Maggie reflected (already adjusting to new developments), this was one of the most interesting ages. Seven and a half—old enough to converse with but not yet past willing to admire a grownup, provided the grownup played her cards right. Cagily, Maggie rounded the car and approached the child with her purse in both hands, resisting the urge to fling out her arms for a hug. "I guess you must not remember me," she said, stopping a measured distance away.

Leroy shook her head.

"Why, sweetie, I'm your grandma!"

"You are?" Leroy said. She reminded Maggie of someone peering through a veil.

"Your other grandma. Your Grandma Moran."

It was crazy to have to introduce herself to her own flesh and blood. And crazier still, Maggie thought, that Jesse would have needed to do the same thing. He had not laid eyes on his daughter since—when? Since just after he and Fiona split up —before Leroy was a year old, even. What a sad, partitioned life they all seemed to be living!

"I'm from your father's side of the family," she told Leroy, and Leroy said, "Oh."

So at least she did know she had a father.

"And this is your grandpa," Maggie said.

Leroy shifted her gaze to Ira. In profile, her nose was seen to be tiny and extremely pointed. Maggie could have loved her for her nose alone.

Ira was out of the car by now, but he didn't come over to

Leroy immediately. Instead he reached for the Frisbee on the hood. Then he crossed the yard to them, meanwhile studying the Frisbee and turning it around and around in his hands as if he'd never seen one before. (Wasn't this just like him? Allowing Maggie to rush in while he hung back all reserved, but you notice he did tag along, and would share the benefit of anything she accomplished.) When he arrived in front of Leroy he tossed the Frisbee toward her lightly, and both her hands came up like two skinny spiders to grab it.

"Thanks," she said.

Maggie wished *she* had thought of the Frisbee.

"We don't seem familiar at all?" she asked Leroy.

Leroy shook her head.

"Why! I was standing by when you were born, I'll have you know. I was waiting in the hospital for you to be delivered. You stayed with us the first eight or nine months of your life."

"I did?"

"You don't remember staying with us?"

"How could she, Maggie?" Ira asked.

"Well, she might," Maggie said, for she herself had a very clear memory of a scratchy-collared dress she used to hate being stuffed into as an infant. And besides, you would think all that loving care had to have left some mark, wouldn't you? She said, "Or Fiona might have told her about it."

"She told me I lived in Baltimore," Leroy said.

"That was us," Maggie said. "Your parents lived with us in your daddy's old boyhood room in Baltimore."

"Oh."

"Then you and your mother moved away."

Leroy rubbed her calf with the instep of her bare foot. She was standing very straight, militarily straight, giving the impression she was held there only by a sense of duty.

"We visited on your birthdays afterward, remember that?"

"Nope."

"She was just a little thing, Maggie," Ira said.

"We came for your first three birthdays," Maggie persisted. (Sometimes you could snag a memory and reel it in out of nowhere, if you used the proper hook.) "But your second birthday you were off at Hershey Park, and so we didn't get to see you."

"I've been to Hershey Park six times," Leroy said. "Mindy Brant has only been twice."

"Your third birthday, we brought you a kitten."

Leroy tilted her head. Her hair wafted to one side—corn silk, lighter than air. "A tiger kitten," she said.

"Right."

"Stripy all over, even on its tummy."

"You do remember!"

"That was you-all brought me that kitten?"

"That was us," Maggie said.

Leroy looked back and forth between the two of them. Her skin was delicately freckled, as if dusted with those sugar sprinkles people put on cakes. That must come from the Stuckey side. Maggie's family never freckled, and certainly Ira's didn't, with their Indian connections. "And then what happened?" she was asking.

"What happened when?"

"What happened to the kitten! You must've took it back."

"Oh, no, honey, we didn't take it back. Or rather, we did but only because you turned out to be allergic. You started sneezing and your eyes got teary."

"And after that, what?" Leroy asked.

"Well, I wanted to visit again," Maggie said, "but your grandpa told me we shouldn't. I wanted to with all my heart, but your grandpa told me—"

"I meant, what did you do with the kitten," Leroy said.

"Oh. The kitten. Well. We gave it to your grandpa's two sisters, your . . . great-aunts, I suppose they'd be; goodness."

"So have they still got it?"

"No, actually it was hit by a car," Maggie said.

"Oh."

"It wasn't used to traffic and somehow it slipped out when someone left the door open."

Leroy stared ahead, fixedly. Maggie hoped she hadn't upset her. She said, "So tell me! Is your mother home?"

"My mother? Sure."

"Could we see her, maybe?"

Ira said, "Maybe she's busy."

"No, she's not busy," Leroy said, and she turned and started toward the house. Maggie didn't know if they were supposed to follow or not. She looked over at Ira. He was standing there slouched with his hands in his trouser pockets, so she took her cue from him and stayed where she was.

"Ma!" Leroy called, climbing the two front steps. Her voice had a certain mosquito quality that went with her thin face. "Ma? You in there?" She opened the screen door. "Hey, Ma!"

Then all at once there was Fiona leaning in the doorway, one arm outstretched to keep the screen door from banging shut again. She wore cut-off denim shorts and a T-shirt with some kind of writing across it. "No need to shout," she said. At that moment she saw Maggie and Ira. She stood up straighter.

Maggie moved forward, clutching her purse. She said, "How are you, Fiona?"

"Well . . . fine," Fiona said.

And then she looked beyond them. Oh, Maggie was not mistaken about that. Her eyes swept the yard furtively and alighted on the car for just the briefest instant. She was wondering if Jesse had come too. She still cared enough to wonder.

Her eyes returned to Maggie.

"I hope we're not disturbing you," Maggie said.

"Oh, um, no, . . ."

"We were just passing through and thought we'd stop by and say hello."

Fiona lifted her free arm and smoothed her hair off her

859

forehead with the back of her hand—a gesture that exposed the satiny white inner surface of her wrist, that made her seem distracted, at a loss. Her hair was still fairly long but she had done something to it that bushed it out more; it didn't hang in sheets now. And she had gained a bit of weight. Her face was slightly broader across the cheekbones, the hollow of her collarbone was less pronounced, and although she was translucently pale, as always, she must have started using makeup, for Maggie detected a half-moon of powdered shadow on each eyelid—that rose-colored shadow that seemed to be so popular lately, that made women look as if they were suffering from a serious cold.

Maggie climbed the steps and stood next to Leroy, continuing to hold her purse in a way that implied she wasn't expecting so much as a handshake. She was able now to read the writing on Fiona's shirt: LIME SPIDERS, it said—whatever that meant. "I heard you on the radio this morning." she said.

"Radio," Fiona said, still distracted.

"On AM Baltimore."

"Baltimore," Fiona said.

Leroy, meanwhile, had ducked under her mother's arm and then turned so she was facing Maggie, side by side with Fiona, gazing up with the same unearthly clear-aqua eyes. There wasn't a trace of Jesse in that child's appearance. You'd think at least his coloring would have won out.

"I told Ira, 'Why not just stop off and visit,' " Maggie said. "We were up this way anyhow, for Max Gill's funeral. Remember Max Gill? My friend Serena's husband? He died of cancer. So I said, 'Why not stop off and visit Fiona. We wouldn't stay but a minute.' "

"It feels funny to see you," Fiona said.

"Funny?"

"I mean . . . Come inside, why don't you?"

"Oh, I know you must be busy," Maggie said.

860

"No, I'm not busy. Come on in."

Fiona turned and led the way into the house. Leroy followed, with Maggie close behind. Ira took a little longer. When Maggie looked over her shoulder she found him kneeling in the yard to tie his shoe, a slant of hair falling over his forehead. "Well, come on, Ira," she told him.

He rose in silence and started toward her. Her annoyance changed to something softer. Sometimes Ira took on a gangling aspect, she thought, like a bashful young boy not yet comfortable in public.

The front door opened directly into the living room, where the sun slipping through the venetian blinds striped the green shag rug. Heaps of crocheted cushions tumbled across a couch upholstered in a fading tropical print. The coffee table bore sliding stacks of magazines and comic books, and a green ceramic ashtray shaped like a rowboat. Maggie remembered the ashtray from earlier visits. She remembered staring at it during awkward pauses and wondering if it could float, in which case it would make a perfect bathtub toy for Leroy. Now that came back to her, evidently having lurked all these years within some cupboard in her brain.

"Have a seat," Fiona said, plumping a cushion. She asked Ira, "So how're you doing?" as he ducked his head in the doorway.

"Oh, passably," he told her.

Maggie chose the couch, hoping Leroy would sit there too. But Leroy dropped to the rug and stretched her reedy legs out in front of her. Fiona settled in an armchair, and Ira remained standing. He circled the room, pausing at a picture of two basset puppies nestled together in a hatbox. With the tip of one finger, he traced the gilded molding that lined the frame.

"Would you like some refreshments?" Fiona asked.

Maggie said, "No, thank you."

"Maybe a soda or something."

"We're not thirsty, honestly."

Leroy said, "I could use a soda."

"You're not who I was asking." Fiona told her.

Maggie wished she'd brought Leroy some sort of present. They had so little time to make connections; she felt pushed and anxious. "Leroy," she said too brightly, "is Frisbee a big interest of yours?"

"Not really," Leroy told her bare feet.

"Oh."

"I'm still just learning," Leroy said. "I can't make it go where I want yet."

"Yes, that's the tricky part, all right," Maggie said.

Unfortunately, she had no experience with Frisbees herself. She looked hopefully at Ira, but he had moved on to some kind of brown metal appliance that stood in the corner—a box fan, perhaps, or a heater. She turned back to Leroy. "Does it glow in the dark?" she asked after a pause.

Leroy said, "Huh?"

"Excuse me," Fiona reminded her.

"Excuse me?"

"Does your Frisbee glow in the dark? Some do, I believe."

"Not this one," Leroy said.

"Ah!" Maggie cried. "Then maybe we should buy you one that does."

Leroy thought about that. Finally she asked, "Why would I want to play Frisbee in the dark?"

"Good question," Maggie said.

She sat back, spent, wondering where to go from there. She looked again at Ira. He was hunkered over the appliance now, inspecting the controls with total concentration.

Well, no point avoiding this forever. Maggie made herself smile. She tilted her head receptively and said, "Fiona, we were so surprised to hear about your wedding plans."

"My what?"

"Wedding plans."

"Is that supposed to be a joke?"

"Joke?" Maggie asked. She faltered. "Aren't you getting married?"

"Not that I'm aware of."

"But I heard it on the radio!"

Fiona said, "What is this radio business? I don't know what you're talking about."

"On WNTK," Maggie said. "You called in and said—"

"The station I listen to is WXLR," Fiona told her.

"No, this was—"

"*Excellent Rock Around the Clock.* A Brittstown station."

"This was WNTK," Maggie said.

"And they claimed I was getting married?"

"*You* claimed it. You called in and claimed your wedding was next Saturday."

"Not me," Fiona said.

There was a kind of alteration of rhythm in the room.

Maggie experienced a surge of relief, followed by acute embarrassment. How could she have been so sure? What on earth had got into her, not even to question that the voice she'd heard was Fiona's? And on such a staticky, inadequate radio; she'd known perfectly well how inadequate it was, with those dinky little auto speakers that didn't begin to approach high fidelity.

She braced herself for Ira's I-told-you-so. He still seemed absorbed in the appliance, though, which was nice of him.

"I guess I made a mistake," she said finally.

"I guess you did," Fiona said.

And Leroy said, "Married!" and uttered a little hiss of amusement and wiggled her toes. Each toenail, Maggie saw, bore the tiniest dot of red polish, almost completely chipped off.

"So who was the lucky guy?" Fiona asked.

"You didn't say," Maggie told her.

"What: I just came on the air and announced my engagement?"

"It was a call-in talk show," Maggie said. She spoke slowly;

she was rearranging her thoughts. All at once Fiona was not getting married. There was still a chance, then! Things could still be worked out! And yet in some illogical way Maggie continued to believe the wedding really had been planned, so that she wondered at the girl's inconsistency. "People called in to discuss their marriages with the host," she said.

Fiona knit her pale brows, as if considering the possibility that she might have been one of them.

She was so pretty, and Leroy was so endearingly spiky and unusual; Maggie felt how thirsty her eyes were, drinking them in. It was like the early days with her children, when every neck-crease, every knuckle-dent, could send her into a reverie. Look at Fiona's hair shining like ribbons, like bands of crinkle gift ribbon! Look at the darling little gold studs in Leroy's earlobes!

Ira, speaking into the grille of the appliance, said, "This thing really do much good?" His voice rang back at them tinnily.

"So far as I know," Fiona said.

"Fairly energy-efficient?"

She lifted both hands, palms up. "Beats me."

"How many BTUs does it give off?"

"That's just something Mom runs in the wintertime to keep her feet warm," Fiona said. "I never have paid it much heed, to tell the truth."

Ira leaned farther forward to read a decal on the appliance's rear.

Maggie seized on a change of subject. She said, "How *is* your mother, Fiona?"

"Oh, she's fine. Right now she's at the grocery store."

"Wonderful," Maggie said. Wonderful that she was fine, she meant. But it was also wonderful that she was out. She said, "And you're looking well too. You're wearing your hair a little fuller, aren't you?"

"It's crimped," Fiona said. "I use this special iron, like; you know bigger hair has a slimming effect."

"Slimming! You don't need slimming."

"I most certainly do. I put on seven pounds over this past summer."

"Oh, you didn't, either. You couldn't have! Why you're just a—"

Just a twig, she was going to say; or just a stick. But she got mixed up and combined the two words: "You're just a twick!"

Fiona glanced at her sharply, and no wonder; it had sounded vaguely insulting. "Just skin and bones, I mean," Maggie said, fighting back a giggle. She remembered now how fragile their relationship had been, how edgy and defensive Fiona had often seemed. She folded her hands and placed her feet carefully together on the green shag rug.

So Fiona was not getting married after all.

"How's Daisy?" Fiona asked.

"She's doing well."

Leroy said, "Daisy who?"

"Daisy Moran," Fiona said. Without further explanation, she turned back to Maggie. "All grown up by now, I bet."

"Daisy is your aunt. Your daddy's little sister," Maggie told Leroy. "Yes; tomorrow she leaves for college," she said to Fiona.

"College! Well, she always was a brain."

"Oh, no . . . but it's true she won a full scholarship."

"Little bitty Daisy," Fiona said. "Just think."

Ira had finished with the appliance, finally. He moved on to the coffee table. The Frisbee rested on a pile of comic books, and he picked it up and examined it all over again. Maggie stole a peek at him. He still had not said, "I told you so," but she thought she detected something noble and forbearing in the set of his spine.

"You know, I'm in school myself, in a way," Fiona said.

"Oh? What kind of school?"

"I'm studying electrolysis."

"Why, that's lovely, Fiona," Maggie said.

She wished she could shake off this fulsome tone of voice.

865

It seemed to belong to someone else entirely—some elderly, matronly, honey-sweet woman endlessly marveling and exclaiming.

"The beauty parlor where I'm a shampoo girl is paying for my course," Fiona said. "They want their own licensed operator. They say I'm sure to make heaps of money."

"That's just lovely!" Maggie said. "Then maybe you can move out and find a place of your own."

And leave the pretender grandma behind, was what she was thinking. But Fiona gave her a blank look.

Leroy said, "Show them your practice kit, Ma."

"Yes, show us," Maggie said.

"Oh, you don't want to see that," Fiona said.

"Yes, we do. Don't we, Ira?"

Ira said, "Hmm? Oh, absolutely." He held the Frisbee up level, like a tea tray, and gave it a meditative spin.

"Well, then, wait a sec," Fiona said, and she got up and left the room. Her sandals made a dainty slapping sound on the wooden floor of the hallway

"They're going to hang a sign in the beauty parlor window," Leroy told Maggie. "Professionally painted with Ma's name."

"Isn't that something!"

"It's a genuine science, Ma says. You've got to have trained experts to teach you how to do it."

Leroy's expression was cocky and triumphant. Maggie resisted the urge to reach down and cup the complicated small bones of her knee.

Fiona returned, carrying a rectangular yellow kitchen sponge and a short metal rod the size of a ballpoint pen. "First we practice with a dummy instrument," she said. She dropped onto the couch beside Maggie. "We're supposed to work at getting the angle exactly, perfectly right."

She set the sponge on her lap and gripped the rod between her fingers. There was a needle at its tip, Maggie saw. For some

866

reason she had always thought of electrolysis as, oh, not quite socially mentionable, but Fiona was so matter-of-fact and so skilled, targeting one of the sponge's pores and guiding the needle into it at a precisely monitored slant; Maggie couldn't help feeling impressed. This was a highly technical field, she realized—maybe something like dental hygiene. Fiona said, "We travel into the follicle, see, easy, easy . . ." and then she said, "Oops!" and raised the heel of her hand an inch or two. "If this was a real person I'd have been leaning on her eyeball," she said. "Pardon me, lady," she told the sponge. "I didn't mean to smush you." Mottled black lettering was stamped across the sponge's surface: STABLER'S DARK BEER. MADE WITH MOUNTAIN SPRING WATER.

Ira stood over them now, with the Frisbee dangling from his fingers. He asked, "Does the school provide the sponge?"

"Yes, it's included in the tuition," Fiona said.

"They must get it free," he reflected. "Courtesy of Stabler's. Interesting."

"Stabler's? Anyhow, first we practice with the dummy and then with the real thing. Us students all work on each other: eyebrows and mustache and such. This girl that's my partner, Hilary, she wants me to do her bikini line."

Ira pondered that for a moment and then backed off in a hurry.

"You know these high-cut swimsuits nowadays, they show everything you've got," Fiona told Maggie.

"Oh, it's becoming impossible!" Maggie cried. "I'm just making do with my old suit till the fashions change."

Ira cleared his throat and said, "Leroy, what would you say to a game of Frisbee."

Leroy looked up at him.

"I could show you how to make it go where you want," he told her.

She took so long deciding that Maggie felt a pang for Ira's

sake, but finally she said, "Well, okay," and unfolded herself from the floor. "Tell about the professionally painted sign," she told Fiona. Then she followed Ira out of the room. The screen door made a sound like a harmonica chord before it banged shut.

So.

This was the first time Maggie had been alone with Fiona since that awful morning. For once the two of them were free of Ira's hampering influence and the hostile, suspicious presence of Mrs. Stuckey. Maggie edged forward on the couch. She clasped her hands tightly; she pointed her knees intimately in Fiona's direction.

"The sign's going to read FIONA MORAN," Fiona was saying. "LICENSED ELECTROLOGIST. PAINLESS REMOVAL OF SUPERFLUOUS HAIR."

"I can't wait to see it," Maggie said.

She thought about that last name: Moran. If Fiona really hated Jesse, would she have kept his name all these years?

"On the radio," she said, "you told the man you were marrying for security."

"Maggie, I swear to you, the station I listen to is—"

"WXLR," Maggie said. "Yes, I know. But I just had it in my head that that was you, and so I . . ."

She watched Fiona set the sponge and needle in the rowboat ashtray.

"Anyway," she said. "Whoever it was who called, she said the first time she'd married for love and it hadn't worked out. So this time she was aiming purely for security."

"Well, what a ninny," Fiona said. "If marriage was such a drag when she loved the guy, what would it be like when she didn't?"

"Exactly," Maggie said. "Oh, Fiona, I'm so glad that wasn't you!"

"Shoot, I don't even have a steady boyfriend," Fiona said.

868

"You don't?"

But Maggie found the phrasing of that a bit worrisome. She said, "Does that mean . . . you have someone not steady?"

"I just barely get to date at all," Fiona said.

"Well! What a pity," Maggie said. She put on a sympathetic expression.

"This one guy? Mark Derby? I went out with him for about three months, but then we had a fight. I bashed his car in after I had borrowed it, was the reason. But it really wasn't my fault. I was starting to make a left turn, when these teenage boys came up from behind and passed me on the left and so of course I hit them. Then they had the nerve to claim it was all my doing; they claimed I had my right-turn signal on instead of my left."

"Well, anyone who'd get mad about *that* you don't want to date anyhow," Maggie told her.

"I said, 'I had my left-turn signal on. Don't you think I know my left from my right?' "

"Of course you do," Maggie said soothingly. She lifted her left hand and flicked an imaginary turn signal, testing. "Yes, left is down and right is . . . or maybe it's the not the same in every model of car."

"It's exactly the same," Fiona told her. "At least, I think it is."

"Then maybe it was the windshield wipers," Maggie said. "I've done that, lots of times: switched on my wipers instead of my blinkers."

Fiona considered. Then she said, "No, because *something* was lit up. Otherwise they wouldn't say I was signaling a right turn."

"One time I had my mind elsewhere and I went for my blinkers and shifted gears instead," Maggie said. She started laughing. "Going along about sixty miles an hour and shifted into reverse. Oh, Lord." She pulled the corners of her mouth down, recollecting herself. "Well," she told Fiona, "I'd say you're better off without the man."

"What man? Oh. Mark," Fiona said. "Yes, it's not like we were in love or anything. I only went out with him because he asked me. Plus my mom is friends with his mom. He has the nicest mother; real sweet-faced woman with a little bit of a stammer. I always feel a stammer shows sincerity of feeling, don't you?"

Maggie said, "Why, c-c-certainly I do."

It took Fiona a second to catch on. Then she laughed. "Oh, you're such a card," she said, and she tapped Maggie's wrist. "I'd forgotten what a card you are."

"So is that the end of it?" Maggie asked.

"End of what?"

"This . . . thing with Mark Derby. I mean suppose he asks you out again?"

"No way," Fiona said. "Him and his precious Subaru; no way would I go out with him."

"That's very wise of you," Maggie told her.

"Shoot! I'd have to be a moron."

"*He* was a moron, not to appreciate you," Maggie said.

Fiona said, "Hey. How's about a beer."

"Oh, I'd love a beer!"

Fiona jumped up, tugging down her shorts, and left the room. Maggie sank lower on the couch and listened to the sounds drifting in through the window—a car swishing past and Leroy's throaty chuckle. If this house were hers, she thought, she would get rid of all this clutter. You couldn't see the surface of the coffee table, and the layers of sofa cushions nudged her lower back uncomfortably.

"Only thing we've got is Bud Light—is that okay?" Fiona asked when she returned. She was carrying two cans and a sack of potato chips.

"It's perfect; I'm on a diet," Maggie said.

She accepted one of the cans and popped the tab, while

Fiona settled next to her on the couch. "I ought to go on a diet," Fiona said. She ripped open the cellophane sack. "Snack foods are my biggest downfall."

"Oh, mine too," Maggie said. She took a sip of her beer. It was crisp-tasting and bitter; it brought memories flooding in the way the smell of a certain perfume will. How long had it been since she'd last had a beer? Maybe not since Leroy was a baby. Back then (she recalled as she waved away the potato chips), she sometimes drank as many as two or three cans a day, keeping Fiona company because beer was good for her milk supply, they'd heard. Now that would probably be frowned upon, but at the time they had felt dutiful and virtuous, sipping their Miller High Lifes while the baby drowsily nursed. Fiona used to say she could feel the beer zinging directly to her breasts. She and Maggie would start drinking when Maggie came home from work—midafternoon or so, just the two of them. They would grow all warm and confiding together. By the time Maggie got around to fixing supper she would be feeling, oh, not drunk or anything but filled with optimism, and then later at the table she might act a bit more talkative than usual. It was nothing the others would notice, though. Except perhaps for Daisy. "Really, Mom. Honestly," Daisy would say. But then, she was always saying that.

As was Maggie's mother, come to think of it. "Honestly, Maggie." She had stopped by late one afternoon and caught Maggie lounging on the couch, a beer balanced on her midriff, while Fiona sat next to her singing "Dust in the Wind" to the baby. "How have you let things get so *common*?" Mrs. Daley had asked, and Maggie, looking around her, had all at once wondered too. The cheap, pulpy magazines scattered everywhere, the wadded wet diapers, the live-in daughter-in-law—it did look common. How had it happened?

"I wonder if Claudine and Peter ever married," Maggie said now, and she took another sip of her beer.

"Claudine? Peter?" Fiona asked.

"On that soap opera we used to watch. Remember? His sister Natasha was trying to split them up."

"Oh, Lord, Natasha. She was one mean lady," Fiona said. She dug deep into the sack of potato chips.

"They had just got engaged when you left us," Maggie said. "They were planning to throw a big party and then Natasha found out about it—remember?"

"She looked kind of like this girl I always detested in elementary school," Fiona said.

"Then you left us," Maggie said.

Fiona said, "Actually, now that you mention it she must not have managed to split them up after all, because a couple of years later they had this baby that was kidnapped by a demented airline stewardess."

"At first I couldn't believe you had really gone for good," Maggie said. "Whole months passed by when I'd come home and switch on the TV and check what was happening with Claudine and Peter, just so I could fill you in when you got back."

"Anyhow," Fiona said. She set her beer on the coffee table.

"Silly of me, wasn't it? Wherever you had gone, you surely would have been near a TV. It's not like you had abandoned civilization. But I don't know; maybe I just wanted to keep up with the story for my own sake, so that after you came back we could carry on like before. I was positive you'd be coming back."

"Well, anyhow. What's past is past," Fiona said.

"No, it's not! People are always saying that, but what's past is never past; not entirely," Maggie told her. "Fiona, this is a marriage we're talking about. You two had so much sunk into it; such an exhausting amount was sunk in. And then one day you quarreled over nothing whatsoever, no worse than any other time, and off you went. As easy as that! Shrugged your shoulders and walked away from it! How could that be possible?"

"It just was, all right?" Fiona said. "Jiminy! Do we have to

872

keep rehashing this?" And she reached for her beer can and drank, tipping her head far back. She wore rings on every one of her fingers, Maggie saw—some plain silver, some set with turquoise stones. That was new. But her nails were still painted the pearly pink that had always seemed her special color, that could bring her instantly to mind whenever Maggie caught sight of it somewhere.

Maggie rotated her own can thoughtfully, meanwhile stealing sideways peeks at Fiona.

"I wonder where Leroy's got to," Fiona said.

Another evasion. It was obvious where she'd got to; she was right outside the window. "Give her a little more spin, now," Ira was saying, and Leroy called, "Watch out, here comes a killer!"

"On the radio you said your first marriage was real, true love," Maggie told Fiona.

"Look. How many times—"

"Yes, yes," Maggie said hastily, "that wasn't you; I understand. But still, something about what the girl on the radio was saying . . . I mean it's like she was speaking for more than just herself. It's like she was talking about what the whole *world* was doing. 'Next Saturday I'm marrying for security,' she said, and I just suddenly had this sense that the world was sort of drying up or withering away or something, getting small and narrow and pinched. I felt so—I don't know—so unhopeful, all of a sudden. Fiona, maybe I shouldn't mention this, but last spring Jesse brought this young woman he'd met to supper—oh, no one important! not anybody important!—and I thought to myself, Well, she's all very well and good, I suppose, but she's not the real thing. I mean she's only second best, I thought. We're only making do here. Oh, why is everyone settling for less? is what I thought. And I feel the same way about what's-his-name, Mark Derby. Why bother dating someone merely because he asks you, when you and Jesse love each other so much?"

"You call it love when he signed that lawyer's papers without a word and sent them back, not putting up the slightest token of a fight?" Fiona asked. "When he's two or three or even four months late with his support check and then mails it without a letter or a note, not even my full name on the envelope but only F. Moran?"

"Well, that's pure pride, Fiona. Both of you are way too—"

"And when he hasn't laid eyes on his daughter since her fifth birthday? Try explaining that to a child. 'Oh, he's just proud, Leroy, honey—' "

"Fifth birthday?" Maggie said.

"Here she keeps wondering why all the other kids have fathers. Even the kids whose parents are divorced—at least they get to see their fathers on weekends."

"He visited on her fifth birthday?" Maggie asked.

"Look at that! He didn't even bother telling you."

"What: He just showed up? Or what?"

"He showed up out of the blue in a car packed to the teeth with the most unsuitable presents you ever saw," Fiona said. "Stuffed animals and dolls, and a teddy bear so big he had to strap it in the front seat like a human because it wouldn't fit through the rear door. It was much too big for a child to cuddle, not that Leroy would have wanted to. She isn't a cuddly type of person. She's more the sporty type. He should have brought her athletic equipment; he should have brought her—"

"But, Fiona, how was he to know that?" Maggie asked. She felt an ache beginning inside her; she grieved for her son with his carful of wrongheaded gifts that he must have spent his last penny on, because heaven knows he wasn't well off. She said, "He was trying his best, after all. He just didn't realize."

"Of course he didn't realize! He didn't have the faintest idea; the last time he visited, she was still a baby. So here he comes with this drink-and-wet doll that cries 'Mama,' and when he catches sight of Leroy in her dungarees he stops short; you can see he's not pleased. He says, 'Who *is* that?' He says, 'But she's so—' I had had to run fetch her from the neighbor's and quick smooth down her hair on the way through the alley. In the alley I told her, 'Tuck your shirt in, honey. Here, let me lend you my barrette,' and Leroy stood still for it, which she wouldn't do ordinarily, believe me. And when I had fastened the barrette I said, 'Stand back and let me look at you,' and she stood back and licked her lips and said, 'Am I okay? Or not.' I said, 'Oh, honey, you're beautiful,' and then she walks into the house and Jesse says, 'But she's so—' "

"He was surprised she had grown, that's all it was," Maggie said.

"I could have cried for her," Fiona said.

"Yes," Maggie said gently. She knew how that felt.

Fiona said, " 'She's so what, Jesse?' I ask him. 'She's so what? How dare you come tromping in here telling me she's so something or other when the last time you sent us a check was December? And instead you waste your money on this trash, this junk,' I tell him, 'this poochy-faced baby doll when the only doll she'll bother with is G. I. Joe.' "

"Oh, Fiona," Maggie said.

"Well, what did he expect?"

"Oh, why does this always happen between you two? He loves you, Fiona. He loves you both. He's just the world's most inept at showing it. If you knew what it must have cost him to make that trip! I can't tell you how often I've asked him, I've said, 'Are you planning to let your daughter just drift on out of your life? Because that's what she's bound to do, Jesse; I'm warning you,' and he said, 'No, but I don't . . . but I can't figure how to . . . I can't stand to be one of those artificial fathers,' he said, 'with those busywork visits to zoos and small-talk suppers at McDonald's.' And I said, 'Well, it's better than nothing, isn't it?' and he said, 'No, it is not better than nothing.

It's not at all. And what do *you* know about the subject, anyhow?'—that way he does, you've seen how he does, where he acts so furious but if you look at his eyes you'll notice these sudden dark rings beneath them that he used to get when he was just a little fellow trying not to cry."

Fiona ducked her head. She started tracing the rim of her beer can with one finger.

"On Leroy's first birthday," Maggie said, "he was all set to come with us and visit, I told you that. I said, 'Jesse, I really feel it would mean a lot to Fiona if you came,' and he said, 'Well, maybe I will, then. Yes,' he said, 'I could do that, I guess,' and he asked me about fifty times what kind of present a year-old baby might enjoy. Then he went shopping all Saturday and brought back one of those shape-sorter boxes, but Monday after work he exchanged it for a woolen lamb because, he said, he didn't want to seem like he was pushing her intellectually or anything. 'I don't want to be like Grandma Daley, always popping up with these educational toys,' he said, and then on Thursday—her birthday was a Friday that year, remember?—he asked me exactly how you had phrased your invitation. 'I mean,' he said, 'did it sound to you like maybe she was expecting me to stay on over the weekend? Because if so then I might borrow Dave's van and drive up separately from you and Dad.' And I said, 'Well, you could do that, Jesse. Yes, what a good idea; why don't you.' He said, 'But how did she word it, is what I'm asking,' and I said, 'Oh, I forget,' and he said, 'Think.' I said, 'Well, as a matter of fact . . .' I said, 'Um, in fact, she didn't actually word it any way, Jesse, not directly straight out,' and he said, 'Wait. I thought she told you it would mean a lot to her if I came.' I said, 'No, it was me who said that, but I know it's true. I know it would mean a great deal to her.' He said, 'What's going on here? You told me clearly that it was Fiona who said that.' I said, 'I never told you any such thing! Or at least I don't think I did; unless maybe perhaps by accident I—' He said, 'Are you saying she didn't ask for me?'

'Well, I just know she would have,' I told him, 'if the two of you were not so all-fired careful of your dignity. I just know she wanted to, Jesse—' But by then he was gone. Slammed out of the house and vanished, did not come home all Thursday night, and Friday we had to set off without him. I was so disappointed."

"*You* were disappointed!" Fiona said. "You had promised you would be bringing him. I waited, I dressed up, I got myself a make-over at the beauty parlor. Then you turn into the driveway and he's not with you."

"Well, I told him when we got home," Maggie said, "I told him, 'We tried our best, Jesse, but it wasn't us Fiona dressed up for, you can be certain. It was you, and you should have seen her face when you didn't get out of the car.'"

Fiona slapped a sofa cushion with the flat of her palm. She said, "I might have known you would do that."

"Do what?"

"Oh, make me look pitiful in front of Jesse."

"I didn't make you look pitiful! I merely said—"

"So then he calls me on the phone. I knew that was why he called me. Says, 'Fiona? Hon?' I could hear it in his voice that he was sorry for me. I knew what you must have told him. I say, 'What do you want? Are you calling for a reason?' He says, 'No, um, no reason . . .' I say, 'Well, then, you're wasting your money, aren't you?' and I hang up."

"Fiona, for Lord's sake," Maggie said. "Didn't it occur to you he might have called because he missed you?"

Fiona said, "Ha!" and took another swig of beer.

"I wish you could have seen him the way I saw him," Maggie said. "After you left, I mean. He was a wreck! A shambles. His most cherished belonging was your tortoiseshell soapbox."

"My what?"

"Don't you remember your soapbox, the one with the tortoiseshell lid?"

"Well, yes."

"He would open it sometimes and draw a breath of it," Maggie said. "I saw him! I promise! The day you left, that evening, I found Jesse in the bedroom with his nose buried deep in your soapbox and his eyes closed."

"Well, what in the world?" Fiona said.

"I believe he must have inherited some of my sense of smell," Maggie told her.

"You're talking about that little plastic box. The one I used to keep my face soap in."

"Then as soon as he saw me he hid it behind his back," Maggie said. "He was embarrassed I had caught him. He always liked to act so devil-may-care; you know how he acted. But a few days later, when your sister came for your things, I couldn't find your soapbox anywhere. She was packing up your cosmetic case, is how I happened to think of it, so I said, 'Let's see, now, somewhere around . . .' but that soapbox seemed to have vanished. And I couldn't ask Jesse because he had walked out as soon as your sister walked in, so I started opening his bureau drawers and that's where I found it, in his treasure drawer among the things he never throws away—his old-time baseball cards and the clippings about his band. But I didn't give it to your sister. I just shut the drawer again. In fact, I believe he has kept that soapbox to this day, Fiona, and you can't tell me it's because he feels sorry for you. He wants to remember you. He goes by smell, just the way I do; smell is what brings a person most clearly to his mind."

Fiona gazed down at her beer can. That eye shadow was oddly attractive, Maggie realized. Sort of peach-like. It gave her lids a peach's pink blush.

"Does he still look the same?" Fiona asked finally.

"The same?"

"Does he still look like he used to?"

"Why, yes."

Fiona gave a sharp sigh.

There was a moment of quiet, during which Leroy said, "Durn! Missed." A car passed, trailing threads of country music. *I've had some bad times, lived through some sad times . . .*

"You know," Fiona said, "there's nights when I wake up and think, How could things have gotten so twisted? They started out perfectly simple. He was just this boy I was crazy about and followed anyplace his band played, and everything was so straightforward. When he didn't notice me at first, I sent him a telegram, did he ever mention that? *Fiona Stuckey would like to go with you to Deep Creek Lake,* that's what it said, because I knew he was planning to drive there with his friends. And so he took me along, and that's where it all began. Wasn't that straightforward? But then, I don't know, everything sort of folded over on itself and knotted up, and I'm not even sure how it happened. There's times I think, Shoot, maybe I ought to just fire off another telegram. *Jesse,* I'd say, *I love you still, and it begins to seem I always will.* He wouldn't even have to answer; it's just something I want him to know. Or I'll be down in Baltimore at my sister's and I'll think, Why not drop by and visit him? Just walk in on him? Just see what happens?"

"Oh, you ought to," Maggie said.

"But he'd say, 'What are *you* doing here?' Or some such thing. I mean it's bound and determined to go wrong. The whole cycle would just start over again."

"Oh, Fiona, isn't it time somebody broke that cycle?" Maggie asked. "Suppose he did say that; not that I think he would. Couldn't you for once stand your ground and say, 'I'm here because I want to see you, Jesse'? Cut through all this to-and-fro, these hurt feelings and these misunderstandings. Say, 'I'm here because I've missed you. So there!' "

"Well, maybe I should do that," Fiona said slowly.

"Of course you should."

"Maybe I should ride back down with you."

"With us?"

"Or maybe not."

"You're talking about . . . this afternoon?"

"No, maybe not; what am I saying? Oh, Lord. I knew I shouldn't drink in the daytime; it always makes my head so muzzy—"

"But that's a wonderful idea!" Maggie said.

"Well, if Leroy came with me, for instance; if we just made a little visit. I mean visiting you two, not Jesse. After all, you're Leroy's grandparents, right? What could be more natural? And then spent the night at my sister's place—"

"No, not at your sister's. Why there? We have plenty of room at our house."

There was a crunch of gravel outside—the sound of a car rolling up. Maggie tensed, but Fiona didn't seem to hear. "And then tomorrow after lunch we could catch the Greyhound bus," she was saying, "or let's see, midafternoon at the latest. The next day's a working day and Leroy has school, of course—"

A car door clunked shut. A high, complaining voice called, "Leroy?"

Fiona straightened. "Mom," she said, looking uneasy.

The voice said, "Who's that you got with you, Leroy?" And then, "Why. Mr. Moran."

What Ira answered, Maggie had no idea. All that filtered through the venetian blinds was a brief rumble.

"My, my," Mrs. Stuckey said. "Isn't this . . . ." something or other.

"It's Mom," Fiona told Maggie.

"Oh, how nice; we'll get to see her after all," Maggie said unhappily.

"She is going to have a fit."

"A fit?"

"She would kill me if I was to go and visit you."

Maggie didn't like the uncertain sound of that verb construction.

The screen door opened and Mrs. Stuckey plodded in—a

880

gray, scratchy-haired woman wearing a ruffled sundress. She was lugging two beige plastic shopping bags, and a cigarette drooped from her colorless, cracked lips. Oh, Maggie had never understood how such a woman could have given birth to Fiona—finespun Fiona. Mrs. Stuckey set the bags in the center of the shag rug. Even then, she didn't glance up. "One thing I despise," she said, removing her cigarette, "is these new-style plastic grocery bags with the handles that cut your fingers in half."

"How are you, Mrs. Stuckey?" Maggie asked.

"Also they fall over in the car trunk and spill their guts out," Mrs. Stuckey said. "I'm all right, I suppose."

"We just stopped by for a second," Maggie said. "We had to go to a funeral in Deer Lick."

"Hmm," Mrs. Stuckey said. She took a drag of her cigarette. She held it like a foreigner, pinched between her thumb and her index finger. If she had calculated outright, she could not have chosen a more unbecoming dress. It completely exposed her upper arms, which were splotched and doughy.

Maggie waited for Fiona to mention the trip to Baltimore, but Fiona was fiddling with her largest turquoise ring. She slid it up past her first knuckle, twisted it, and slid it down again. So Maggie had to be the one. She said, "I've been trying to talk Fiona into coming home with us for a visit."

"Fat chance of that," Mrs. Stuckey said.

Maggie looked over at Fiona. Fiona went on fiddling with her ring.

"Well, she's thinking she might do it," Maggie said finally.

Mrs. Stuckey drew back from her cigarette to glare at the long tube of ash at its tip. Then she stubbed it out in the rowboat, perilously close to the yellow sponge. A strand of smoke wound toward Maggie.

"Me and Leroy might go just for the weekend," Fiona said faintly.

"For the what?"

"For the weekend."

Mrs. Stuckey stooped for the grocery bags and started wading out of the room, bending slightly at the knees so her arms looked too long for her body. At the door she said, "I'd sooner see you lying in your casket."

"But, Mom!"

Fiona was on her feet now, following her into the hallway. She said, "Mom, the weekend's half finished anyhow. We're talking about just one single night! One night at Leroy's grandparents' house."

"And Jesse Moran would be nowhere about, I suppose," Mrs. Stuckey said at a distance. There was a crash—presumably the grocery bags being dumped on a counter.

"Oh, Jesse might be *around* maybe, but—"

"Yah, yah," Mrs. Stuckey said on an outward breath.

"Besides, so what if he is? Don't you think Leroy should get to know her daddy?"

Mrs. Stuckey's answer to that was just a mutter, but Maggie heard it clearly. "Anyone whose daddy is Jesse Moran is better off staying strangers."

Well! Maggie felt her face grow hot. She had half a mind to march out to the kitchen and give Mrs. Stuckey what for. "Listen," she would say. "You think there haven't been times I've cursed your daughter? She hurt my son to the bone. There were times I could have wrung her neck, but have you ever heard me speak a word against her?"

In fact, she even stood up, with a sudden, violent motion that creaked the sofa springs, but then she paused. She smoothed down the front of her dress. The gesture served to smooth her thoughts as well, and instead of heading for the kitchen she collected her purse and went off to find a bathroom, clamping her lips very tightly. Please, God, don't let the bathroom lie on the other side of the kitchen. No, there it was—the one open door at the end of the hall. She caught the watery green of a shower curtain.

After she had used the toilet, she turned on the sink faucet and patted her cheeks with cool water. She bent closer to the mirror. Yes, definitely she had a flustered look. She would have to get hold of herself. She hadn't finished even that one beer, but she thought it might be affecting her. And it was essential just now to play her cards right.

For instance, about Jesse. Although she had failed to mention it to Fiona, Jesse lived in an apartment uptown now, and therefore they couldn't merely assume that he would happen by while Fiona was visiting. He would have to be expressly invited. Maggie hoped he hadn't made other plans. Saturday: That could mean trouble. She checked her watch. Saturday night he might very well be singing with his band, or just going out with his friends. Sometimes he even dated—no one important, but still . . .

She flushed the toilet, and under cover of the sound she slipped out of the bathroom and opened the door next to it. This room must be Leroy's. Dirty clothes and comic books lay everywhere. She closed the door again and tried the one opposite. Ah, a grownup's room. A decorous white candlewick bedspread, and a telephone on the nightstand.

"After all you done to free yourself, you want to go back to that boy and get snaggled up messy as ever," Mrs. Stuckey said, clattering tin cans.

"Who says I'm getting snaggled? I'm just paying a weekend visit."

"He'll have you running circles around him just like you was before."

"Mom, I'm twenty-five years old. I'm not that same little snippet I used to be."

Maggie closed the door soundlessly behind her and went over to lift the receiver. Oh, dear, no push buttons. She winced each time the dial made its noisy, rasping return to home base. The voices in the kitchen continued, though. She relaxed and pressed the receiver to her ear.

One ring. Two rings.

It was a good thing Jesse was working today. For the last couple of weeks, the phone in his apartment had not been ringing properly. He could call other people all right, but he never knew when someone might be calling him. "Why don't you get it fixed? Or buy a new one; they're dirt cheap these days," Maggie had said, but he said, "Oh, I don't know, it's kind of a gas. Anytime I pass the phone I just pick it up at random. I say, 'Hello?' Twice I've actually found a person on the other end." Maggie had to smile now, remembering that. There was something so . . . oh, so *lucky* about Jesse. He was so fortunate and funny and haphazard.

"Chick's Cycle Shop," a boy said.

"Could I speak to Jesse, please?"

The receiver at the other end clattered unceremoniously against a hard surface. "Jess!" the boy called, moving off. There was a silence, overlaid by the hissing sound of long distance.

Of course this was stealing, if you wanted to get picky about it—using someone else's phone to call out of state. Maybe she ought to leave a couple of quarters on the nightstand. Or would that be considered an insult? With Mrs. Stuckey, there was no right way to do a thing.

Jesse said, "Hello."

"Jesse?"

"Ma?"

His voice was Ira's voice, but years younger.

"Jesse, I can't talk long," she whispered.

"What? Speak up, I can barely hear you."

"I can't," she said.

"What?"

She cupped the mouthpiece with her free hand. "I was wondering," she said. "Do you think you could come to supper tonight?"

"Tonight? Well, I was sort of planning on—"

884

"It's important," she said.

"How come?"

"Well, it just is," she said, playing for time.

She had a decision to make, here. She could pretend it was on Daisy's account, for Daisy's going away. (That was safe enough. In spite of their childhood squabbles he was fond of Daisy, and had asked her only last week whether she would forget him after she left.) Or she could tell him the truth, in which case she might set in motion another of those ridiculous scenes.

But hadn't she just been saying it was time to cut through all that?

She took a deep breath. She said, "I'm having Fiona and Leroy to dinner."

"You're what?"

"Don't hang up! Don't say no! This is your only daughter!" she cried in a rush.

And then glanced anxiously toward the door, fearing she'd been too loud.

"Now, slow down, Ma," Jesse said.

"Well, we're up here in Pennsylvania," she said more quietly, "because we happened to be going to a funeral. Max Gill died—I don't know if Daisy's had a chance to tell you. And considering that we were in the neighborhood . . . and Fiona told me in so many words that she wanted very much to see you."

"Oh, Ma. Is this going to be like those other times?"

"What other times?"

"Is this like when you said she phoned and I believed you and phoned her back—"

"She did phone then! I swear it!"

"Somebody phoned, but you had no way of knowing who. An anonymous call. You didn't tell me that part, did you?"

Maggie said, "The telephone rang, I picked it up. I said,

'Hello?' No answer. It was just a few months after she left; who else could it have been? I said, 'Fiona?' She hung up. If it wasn't Fiona, why did she hang up?"

"Then all you tell me is: 'Jesse, Fiona called today,' and I break my neck getting to the phone and make a total fool of myself. I say, 'Fiona? What did you want?' and she says, 'To whom am I speaking, please?' I say, 'Goddamn it, Fiona, you know perfectly well this is Jesse,' and she says, 'Don't you use that language with me, Jesse Moran,' and I say, 'Now, look here. It wasn't me who called *you*, may I remind you,' and she says, 'But it was you, Jesse, because here you are on the line, aren't you,' and I say, 'But goddamn it—' "

"Jesse," Maggie said, "Fiona says she sometimes thinks of sending you another telegram."

"Telegram?"

"Like the first one. You remember the first one."

"Yes," Jesse said. "I remember."

"You never told me about that. But at any rate," she hurried on, "the telegram would read, *Jesse, I love you still, and it begins to seem I always will.*"

A moment passed.

Then he said, "You just don't quit, do you?"

"You think I'd make such a thing up?"

"If she really wanted to send it, then what stopped her?" he asked. "Why didn't I ever get it? Hmm?"

"How could I make it up when I didn't even know about the first one, Jesse? Answer me that! And I'm quoting her exactly; for once I'm able to tell you exactly how she worded it. I remember because it was one of those unintentional rhymes. You know the way things can rhyme when you don't want them to. It's so ironic, because if you did want them to, you'd have to rack your brain for days and comb through special dictionaries. . . ."

She was babbling whatever came to mind, just to give Jesse

886

time to assemble a response. Was there ever anyone so scared of losing face? Not counting Fiona, of course.

Then she imagined she heard some change in the tone of his silence—a progression from flat disbelief to something less certain. She let her voice trail off. She waited.

"If I did happen to come," he said finally, "what time would you be serving supper?"

"You'll do it? You will? Oh, Jesse, I'm so glad! Let's say six-thirty," she told him. "Bye!" and she hung up before he could proceed to some further, more resistant stage.

She stood beside the bed a moment. In the front yard, Ira called, "Whoa, there!"

She picked up her purse and left the room.

Fiona was kneeling in the hallway, rooting through the bottom of a closet. She pulled out a pair of galoshes and threw them aside. She reached in again and pulled out a canvas tote bag.

"Well, I talked to Jesse," Maggie told her.

Fiona froze. The tote bag was suspended in midair.

"He's really pleased you're coming," Maggie said.

"Did he say that?" Fiona asked.

"He certainly did."

"I mean in so many words?"

Maggie swallowed. "No," she said, because if there was a cycle to be broken here, she herself had had some part in it; she knew that. She said, "He just told me he'd be there for supper. But anyone could hear how pleased he was."

Fiona studied her doubtfully.

"He said, 'I'll be there!' " Maggie told her.

Silence.

" 'I'll be there right after work, Ma! You can count on me!' " Maggie said. " 'Goddamn! I wouldn't miss it for the world!' "

"Well," Fiona said finally.

Then she unzipped the tote bag.

"If I were traveling alone I'd make do with just a toothbrush," she told Maggie. "But once you've got a kid, you know how it is. Pajamas, comics, storybooks, coloring books for the car . . . and she has to have her baseball glove, her everlasting baseball glove. You never know when you might rustle up a game, she says."

"No, that's true, you never do," Maggie said, and she laughed out loud for sheer happiness.

2

Ira had a way, when he was truly astonished, of getting his face sort of locked in one position. Here Maggie had worried he'd be angry, but no, he just took a step backward and stared at her and then his face locked, blank and flat like something carved of hardwood.

He said, "Fiona's what?"

"She's coming for a visit," Maggie said. "Won't that be nice?"

No reaction.

"Fiona and Leroy, both," Maggie told him.

Still no reaction.

Maybe it would have been better if he'd got angry.

She moved past him, keeping her smile. "Leroy, honey, your mother wants you," she called. "She needs you to help her pack."

Leroy was less easily surprised than Ira, evidently. She said, "Oh. Okay," and give the Frisbee an expert flip in Ira's direction before skipping toward the house. The Frisbee ricocheted off Ira's left knee and landed in the dirt. He gazed down at it absently.

"We should have cleaned the car out," Maggie told him.

"If I'd known we would be riding so many passengers today . . ."

She went over to the Dodge, which was blocked now by a red Maverick that must be Mrs. Stuckey's. You could tell the Dodge had recently traveled some distance. It had a beaten-down, dusty look. She opened a rear door and tsked. A stack of library books slumped across the back seat, and a crocheted sweater that she had been hunting for days lay there all squinched and creased, no doubt from being sat upon by Otis. The floor was cobbled with cloudy plastic lids from soft-drink cups. She reached in to gather the books—major, important novels by Dostoevsky and Thomas Mann. She had checked them out in a surge of good intentions at the start of the summer and was returning them unread and seriously overdue. "Open the trunk, will you?" she asked Ira.

He moved slowly toward the trunk and opened it, not changing his expression. She dumped in the books and went back for the sweater.

"How could this happen?" Ira asked her.

"Well, we were discussing her soapbox, see, and—"

"Her what? I mean it came about so quickly. So all of a sudden. I leave you alone for a little game of Frisbee and the next thing I know you're out here with beer on your breath and a whole bunch of unexpected houseguests."

"Why, Ira, I would think you'd be glad," she told him. She folded the sweater and laid it in the trunk.

"But it's like the second I shut the door behind me, you two got down to business," he said. "How do you accomplish these things?"

Maggie started collecting soft-drink lids from the floor of the car. "You can close the trunk now," she told him.

She carried a fistful of lids around to the rear of the house and dropped them in a crumpled garbage can. The cover was only a token cover, a battered metal beret that she replaced crookedly on top. And the house's siding was speckled with

890

mildew, and rust stains trailed from a fuel tank affixed beneath the window.

"How long will they be staying?" Ira asked when she returned.

"Just till tomorrow."

"We have to take Daisy to college tomorrow, did you forget?"

"No, I didn't forget."

"Aha," he said. "Your fiendish plot: Throw Jesse and Fiona together on their own. I know you, Maggie Moran."

"You don't necessarily know me at all," she told him.

If things went the way she hoped they would this evening, she would have no need of plots for tomorrow.

She opened the front door on her side of the Dodge and sank onto the seat. Inside, the car was stifling. She blotted her upper lip on the hem of her skirt.

"So how do we present this?" Ira asked. " 'Surprise, surprise, Jesse boy! Here's your ex-wife, here's your long-lost daughter. Never mind that you legally parted company years ago; *we've* decided you're getting back together now.' "

"Well, for your information," she said, "I've already told him they're coming, and he'll be at our house for supper."

Ira bent to look in on her. He said, "You told him?"

"Right."

"How?" he asked.

"By phone, of course."

"You phoned him? You mean just now?"

"Right."

"And he'll be there for supper?"

"Right."

He straightened up and leaned against the car. "I don't get it," he said finally.

"What's to get?"

"There's something too simple about it."

All she could see of him was his midsection—a hollow-looking white shirt wilting over a belt. Wouldn't he be baking? This metal must radiate heat like a flatiron. Although it was true that the air had grown cooler now and the sun was slightly less direct, already starting to slip behind a faraway scribble of trees.

"I'm worried about that Maverick," she said, speaking to Ira's belt buckle.

"Hmm?"

"Mrs. Stuckey's Maverick. I'd hate to ask her to move it, and I'm not sure we have room to get around it."

That caught him, as she'd guessed it would—a question of logistics. He left, abruptly; she felt the car rock. He wandered off to check the Maverick's position, and Maggie tipped her head back against the seat and closed her eyes.

Why was Ira so negative about Jesse? Why did he always have that skeptical twist to his voice when he discussed him? Oh, Jesse wasn't perfect—good heavens, no—but he had all kinds of endearing qualities. He was so generous and affectionate. And if he lost his temper easily, why, he regained it easily too, and had never been known to bear a grudge, which was more than you could say for Ira.

Was it plain old envy—a burdened, restrained man's envy of someone who was constitutionally carefree?

When Jesse was just a baby Ira was always saying, "Don't pick him up every time he cries. Don't feed him every time he's hungry. You'll spoil him."

"Spoil him?" Maggie had asked. "Feeding him when he's hungry is spoiling him? That's nonsense."

But she had sounded more confident than she'd felt. *Was* she spoiling him? This was her very first experience with an infant. She had been the youngest in her family and never had the casual contact with babies that some of her friends had had. And Jesse was such a puzzling baby—colicky, at the start, giving no hint of the merry little boy he would later turn out to be.

892

He had flown into tiny, red-faced rages for no apparent reason in the middle of the night. Maggie had had to walk him end-lessly, wearing an actual path in the rug around the dining room table. Was it possible, she had wondered, that this baby just plain didn't like her? Where was it written that a child was always compatible with his parents? When you thought about it, it was amazing that so many families got along as well as they did. All they had to rely on was luck—the proper personality genes turning up like dice. And in Jesse's case, maybe the luck had been poor. She felt he was chafing against his parents. They were too narrow, too sedate, too conservative.

Once, carrying a squalling Jesse down the aisle of a city bus, Maggie had been surprised to feel him suddenly relax in her arms. He had hushed, and she had looked at his face. He was staring at a dressed-up blonde in one of the seats. He started smiling at her. He held out his arms. His kind of person, at last! Unfortunately, though, the blonde was reading a magazine and she never gave him so much as a glance.

And then the minute he discovered other children—all of whom instantly loved him—why, he hit the streets running and was hardly seen at home anymore. But that, too, Ira found fault with, for Jesse missed his curfews, forgot to appear for dinner, neglected his schoolwork in favor of a pickup basketball game in the alley. Mr. Moment-by-Moment, Ira used to call him. And Maggie had to admit the name was justified. Were some people simply born without the ability to link one moment to the next? If so, then Jesse was one of them: a disbeliever in consequences, mystified by others' habit of holding against him things that had happened, why, hours ago! days ago! way last week, even! He was genuinely perplexed that someone could stay angry at something he himself had immediately forgotten.

Once when he was eleven or twelve he'd been horsing around with Maggie in the kitchen, punching his catcher's mitt while he teased her about her cooking, and the telephone rang and he answered and said, "Huh? Mr. Bunch?" Mr. Bunch was his sixth-grade teacher, so Maggie assumed the call was for Jesse and she turned back to her work. Jesse said, "Huh?" He said, "Wait a minute! You can't blame *me* for that!" Then he slammed the phone down, and Maggie, glancing over, saw those telltale dark rings beneath his eyes. "Jesse? Honey? What's the matter?" she had asked. "Nothing," he told her roughly, and he walked out. He left his catcher's mitt on the table, worn and deeply pocketed and curiously alive. The kitchen echoed.

But not ten minutes later she noticed him in the front yard with Herbie Albright, laughing uproariously, crashing through the little boxwood hedge as he'd been told not to a hundred times.

Yes, it was his laughter that she pictured when she thought of him—his eyes lit up and dancing, his teeth very white, his head thrown back to show the clean brown line of his throat. (And why was it that Maggie remembered the laughter while Ira remembered the tantrums?) In a family very nearly without a social life, Jesse was intensely, almost ridiculously social, knee-deep in friends. Classmates came home with him from school every afternoon, and sometimes as many as seven or eight stayed over on weekends, their sleeping bags taking up all the floor space in his room, their cast-off jackets and six-guns and model airplane parts spilling out into the hallway. In the morning when Maggie went to wake them for pancakes the musky, wild smell of boy hung in the doorway like curtains, and she would blink and back off and return to the safety of the kitchen, where little Daisy, swathed to her toes in one of Maggie's aprons, stood on a chair earnestly stirring batter.

He took up running one spring and ran like a maniac, throwing himself into it the way he did with everything that interested him, however briefly. This was when he was fifteen and not yet licensed to drive, so he sometimes asked Maggie for a lift to his favorite track, the Ralston School's cedar-chip-carpeted oval in the woods out in Baltimore County. Maggie would wait for him in the car, reading a library book and glancing up from time to time to check his progress. She could always spot him, even when the track was crowded with middle-aged ladies in sweat suits and Ralston boys in numbered uniforms. Jesse wore tattered jeans and a black T-shirt with the sleeves ripped off, but it wasn't only his clothes that identified him; it was his distinctive style of running. His gait was free and open, as if he were holding nothing in reserve for the next lap. His legs flew out and his arms made long reaching motions, pulling in handfuls of the air in front of him. Every time Maggie located him, her heart would pinch with love. Then he would vanish into the forested end of the track and she would go back to her book.

But one day he didn't come out of the forest. She waited but he didn't appear. And yet the others came, even the slowest, even the silly-looking Swedish-walker people with their elbows pumping like chicken wings. She got out of the car finally and went over to the track, shading her eyes. No Jesse. She followed the bend of the oval into the woods, her crepe-soled work shoes sinking into the cedar chips so her calf muscles felt weighted. People pounded past her, glancing over momentarily, giving her the impression they were leaving their faces behind. In the woods to her left, she noticed a flash of white. It was a girl in a white shirt and shorts, lying on her back in the leaves, and Jesse was lying on top of her. He was fully clothed but, yes, smack on top of her, and the girl's white arms were twined around his neck. "Jesse, I have to be getting home soon," Maggie called. Then she turned and walked back toward the car, feeling plain and clumsy. A moment later cedar chips crunched behind her and Jesse overtook her and sped past, his amazingly long gym shoes landing deftly, plop-plop, and his muscular brown arms scooping the air.

So then it was girls, girls, girls—a jostling parade of girls, all of them fair and slender and pretty, with soft, unformed faces and a tidy style of dressing. They called him on the phone and sent letters reeking of perfume and sometimes simply arrived on the doorstep, treating Maggie with a deference that made her feel ancient. They paid her vivacious compliments—"Oh, Mrs. Moran, I love that blouse!"—meanwhile searching behind her for Jesse. Maggie had to fight down the urge to bristle, to bar their entrance. Who would know better than she how deviously girls could behave? Why, a boy didn't stand a chance! But then Jesse would saunter out, not even rearranging his face at the sight of them, making no effort whatsoever, his T-shirt giving off the yeasty smell of fresh sweat and his hair obscuring his eyes. The girls would grow positively swaybacked with perkiness, and Maggie knew it was they who didn't stand a chance. She felt rueful and proud, both. She was ashamed of herself for feeling proud, and to make up for it she acted especially kind to every girl who came. Sometimes she acted so kind that the girls continued to visit her for months after Jesse had dropped them. They'd sit in the kitchen and confide in her, not just about Jesse but about other things as well, problems with their parents and such. Maggie enjoyed that. Usually Daisy would be sitting there too, her head bent over her homework, and Maggie had the feeling they were all three part of a warm community of females, a community she had missed out on when she was growing up with her brothers.

Was it about that time that the music began? Loud music, with a hammering beat. One day it just flooded the house, as if Jesse's turning adolescent had opened a door through which the drums and electric guitars suddenly poured in. Let him merely duck into the kitchen for a sandwich and the clock radio would start blaring out "Lyin' Eyes." Let him dash up to his room for his catcher's mitt and his stereo would swing into "Afternoon Delight." And of course he never turned anything off again, so long after he'd left the house the music would still be playing. Maybe he intended it that way. It was his signature, his footprint on their lives. "I'll be out in the world now, but don't forget me," he was saying, and there they sat, two stodgy grownups and a prim little girl, while "When Will I Be Loved" jangled through the emptiness he left behind him.

Then he stopped liking what his classmates liked and he claimed the Top Forty was dentist music, elevator music. ("Oh," Maggie said sadly, for she had enjoyed that music—or some of it, at least.) The songs that filled the house grew whining and slippery or downright ill-tempered, and they were sung by scroungy, beatnik-looking groups dressed in rags and tags and bits of military uniforms. (Meanwhile the old albums filtered downstairs to line the shelf beneath the living room hi-fi, each new stage Jesse entered adding to Maggie's collection of castoffs, which she sometimes played secretly when she was all alone in the house.)

And then he started writing his own songs, with peculiar modern names like "Microwave Quartet" and "Cassette Recorder Blues." A few of these he sang for Maggie when Ira wasn't around. He had a nasal, deadpan style of singing that was more like talking. To Maggie it sounded very professional, very much like what you might hear on the radio, but then, of course, she was only his mother. Although his friends were impressed, too; she knew that. His friend Don Burnham, whose second cousin had come this close to being hired as a roadie for the Ramones, said Jesse was good enough to form a group of his own and sing in public.

This Don Burnham was a perfectly nice, well-raised boy who had transferred to Jesse's school at the start of eleventh grade. When Jesse first brought him home, Don had made conversation with Maggie (not something you would take for granted, in a boy that age) and sat politely through Daisy's exhibit of her state-capitals postcard collection. "Next time I come," he'd told Maggie out of the blue, "I'll bring you my

Doonesbury scrapbook." Maggie had said, "Oh, why, I'll look forward to that." But the next time he came he had his acoustic guitar along, and Jesse sang one of his songs for him while Don strummed beneath it. *Seems like this old world is on fast forward nowadays* . . . Then Don told Jesse he ought to sing in public, and from that moment ever afterward (or so it seemed in retrospect), Jesse was gone.

He formed a band called Spin the Cat—he and a bunch of older boys, high-school dropouts mostly. Maggie had no idea where he'd found them. He began to dress more heavily, as if for combat; he wore black denim shirts and black jeans and crumpled leather motorcycle boots. He came in at all hours smelling of beer and tobacco or, who knows, maybe worse than tobacco. He developed a following of a whole new type of girl, crisper and flashier, who didn't bother making up to Maggie or sitting in her kitchen. And in the spring it emerged that he hadn't attended school in some time, and would not be promoted from junior year to senior.

Seventeen and a half years old and he'd thrown away his future, Ira said, all for a single friendship. Never mind that Don Burnham wasn't even part of Jesse's band, and had passed smoothly on to senior year himself. In Ira's version of things, Don's one piece of advice had landed with a *ping!* and life had never been the same again. Don was some kind of providential instrument, fate's messenger. In Ira's version of things.

Shape up or ship out, Ira told Jesse. Earn the missing credits in summer school, or otherwise find a job and move to his own apartment. Jesse said he'd had a bellyful of school. He would be glad to get a job, he said, and he couldn't wait to move to his own apartment, where he could come and go as he pleased, with nobody breathing down his neck. Ira said, "Good riddance," and went upstairs without another word. Jesse left the house, tramping across the porch in his motorcycle boots. Maggie started crying.

898

How could Ira imagine Jesse's life? Ira was one of those people who are born competent. Everything came easy to him. There was no way he could fully realize how Jesse used to feel plodding off to school every morning—his shoulders already hunched against defeat, his jacket collar standing up crooked, and his hands shoved deep in his pockets. What it must be like to be Jesse! To have a perfectly behaved younger sister, and a father so seamless and infallible! Really his only saving grace was his mother, his harum-scarum klutzy mother, Maggie said to herself. She was making one of her wry private jokes but she meant it, all the same. And she wished he'd taken more from her. Her ability to see the best in things, for instance. Her knack for accepting, for adapting.

But no. Slit-eyed and wary, all his old light-heartedness gone, Jesse prowled the city in search of work. He was hoping for a job in a record store. He didn't even have pocket money (at this point that band of his still played for free—for the "exposure," was how they put it) and was forced to borrow bus fare from Maggie. And each day he came back glummer than the day before, and each evening he and Ira fought. "If you showed up for your interviews dressed like a normal person—" Ira told him.

"A place puts that much stock in appearance, I wouldn't want to work there anyhow," Jesse said.

"Fine, then you'd better learn how to dig ditches, because that's the only job where they *don't* put stock in appearance."

Then Jesse would slam out of the house once again, and how flat things seemed after he left! How shallow, how lacking in spirit! Maggie and Ira gazed at each other bleakly across the living room. Maggie blamed Ira; he was too harsh. Ira blamed Maggie; she was too soft.

Sometimes, deep down inside, Maggie blamed herself too. She saw now that there was a single theme to every decision she had made as a parent: The mere fact that her children were children, condemned for years to feel powerless and bewildered and confined, filled her with such pity that to add any further hardship to their lives seemed unthinkable. She could excuse anything in them, forgive them everything. She would have made a better mother, perhaps, if she hadn't remembered so well how it felt to be a child.

She dreamed that Jesse was dead—that in fact he had died years ago, back when he was still a sunny, prankish little boy, and she had somehow failed to realize it. She dreamed she was sobbing uncontrollably; there was no way to survive such a loss. Then she saw in the crowd on deck (for she was taking a boat trip, all at once) a child who resembled Jesse, standing with his parents, whom she had never seen before. He glanced over at her and looked quickly away, but she could tell that he thought she seemed familiar. She smiled at him. He glanced at her again and then looked away again. She edged a few inches closer, meanwhile pretending to study the horizon. He had come back to life in another family; that was how she explained it to herself. He wasn't hers now, but never mind, she would start over. She would win him to her side. She felt his eyes alight on her once more and she sensed how puzzled he was, half remembering her and half not; and she knew it meant that underneath, he and she would always love each other.

Now, at this point Daisy was nine years old, or just about to turn nine—enough of a child still, you would think, to keep Maggie fully occupied. But the fact was that at that very moment, Daisy took it into her head to start growing away too. She had always been a bit precocious. In her infancy Ira had called her Lady-Baby, because she was so mature and reserved, her small face a knot of opinion. At thirteen months she had undertaken her own toilet training. In first grade she had set her alarm for an hour earlier than anyone else in the household and slipped downstairs each morning to sort through the laundered clothes for a proper outfit. (She could iron better than

Maggie even then, and liked to look neat as a pin and color-coordinated.) And now she seemed to have leapt ahead to that stage where the outside world took precedence over family. She had four very serious, like-minded friends, including one, Lavinia Murphy, whose mother was perfect. Perfect Mrs. Murphy headed the PTA and the Bake Sale and (since she didn't work) was free to drive the little girls to every kind of cultural event, and she hosted wonderful slumber parties, with treasure hunts. The spring of '78, Daisy practically lived with the Murphys. Maggie would come home from work and call, "Daisy?" but all she found was a silent house and a note on the front-hall bookshelf.

Then one afternoon the house wasn't silent after all but murmury and conspiratorial, she could sense it the moment she entered, and upstairs, Jesse's bedroom door was closed. She knocked. After a startled pause, Jesse called, "Just a second." She heard rustles and whispers. When he came out he had a girl in tow. Her long blond hair was rumpled and her lips had a bruised look. She sidled past Maggie with her eyes downcast and descended the stairs behind Jesse. Maggie heard the front door open; she heard Jesse saying goodbye in a low voice. As soon as he came back upstairs (unashamedly heading straight to Maggie), she told him that the mother of that girl, whoever she was, would be horrified to know her daughter had been alone with a boy in his bedroom. Jesse said, "Oh, no, her mom lives in Pennsylvania somewhere. Fiona stays with her sister, and her sister doesn't mind."

"Well, I do," Maggie said.

Jesse didn't argue with that, and the girl stopped coming around. Or at least she was out of sight when Maggie returned from work each day. Though Maggie had a feeling; she picked up certain clues. She noticed that Jesse was gone more than ever, that he returned abstracted, that his brief spells at home were marked by long private conversations on the upstairs telephone and it was always the same girl's voice—soft and questioning—when Maggie happened to lift the receiver.

He found a job in an envelope factory, finally, something to do with shipping, and started looking for an apartment. The only trouble was, the rents were so high and his paycheck was so puny. Good, Ira said. Now maybe he would have to face a few hard facts. Maggie wished Ira would just shut up. "Don't worry," she told Jesse. "Something will come along." That was toward the end of June. In July he was still living at home. And one Wednesday evening in August, he caught Maggie alone in the kitchen and informed her, very calmly and directly, that he seemed to have got this girl he knew in trouble.

The air in the room grew oddly still. Maggie wiped her hands on her apron.

She said, "Is it that Fiona person?"

He nodded.

"So now what?" Maggie asked. She was as cool as he was; she surprised herself. This seemed to be happening to someone else. Or maybe she had expected it without knowing. Maybe it was something that had been heading their way all along, like a glacier bearing down on them.

"Well," Jesse said, "that's what I needed to discuss with you. I mean, what I want and what she wants are two different things."

"What is it you want?" Maggie asked, thinking she knew.

"I want her to keep the baby."

For a moment, that didn't register. Even the word itself—"baby"—seemed incongruous on Jesse's lips. It seemed almost, in an awful way, cute.

She said, "Keep it?"

"I thought I'd start hunting an apartment for the three of us."

"You mean get married?"

"Right."

902

"But you're not even eighteen years old," Maggie said. "And I bet the girl isn't, either. You're too young."

"My birthday's in two weeks, Ma, and Fiona's is not long after. And she doesn't like school anyway; half the time she skips class and hangs out with me instead. Besides, I've always looked forward to having a kid. It's exactly what I've been needing: something of my own."

"Something of your own?"

"I'll just have to find a better-paying job, is all."

"Jesse, you've got a whole family of your own! What are you talking about?"

"But it's not the same," Jesse said. "I've just never felt . . . I don't know. So anyhow, I've been looking for a job that pays more money. See, a baby takes a lot of equipment and such. I've written down a list from Dr. Spock."

Maggie stared at him. The only question she could come up with was: "Where on earth did you get hold of a Dr. Spock?"

"At the bookstore; where else?"

"You went into a bookstore and bought a baby-care book?"

"Sure."

That seemed the biggest surprise of all. She couldn't picture it.

"I've learned a lot," he told her. "I think Fiona ought to breast-feed."

"Jesse—"

"I found these plans in *Home Hobby Journal* for building a cradle."

"Honey, you don't know how hard it is. You're children yourselves! You can't take on a baby."

"I'm asking you, Ma. I'm serious," Jesse said. And he did have that sharply etched look to his lips that he always got when he felt strongly about something.

"But just what are you asking me?" Maggie said.

"I want you to go and talk to Fiona."

"What? Talk about what?"

"Tell her you think she should keep it."

"You mean she wants to put it up for adoption," Maggie said. "Or else . . . um . . . stop the pregnancy."

"Well, that's what she says, but—"

"Which?" Maggie asked.

"The second thing."

"Ah."

"But she doesn't really want that. I know she doesn't," he said. "It's just that she's so stubborn. She expects the worst of me, seems like. She takes it for granted I'm going to, like, ditch her or something. Well, first off, she didn't even tell me about it—can you believe it? Hid it from me! Went through weeks of worrying and never breathed a hint of it even though she saw me every day, near about. And then when the test came out positive, what does she do? Asks me for the money to get rid of the baby. I say, 'Huh? To do what? Now, hold on a sec,' I tell her. 'Aren't you skipping over a few of the usual steps here? Whatever happened to "What do *you* think, Jesse?" and "Which decision are we two going to settle on?" Aren't you going to offer me a chance?' I ask her. She says, 'Chance for what?' 'Well, what about marriage?' I ask her. 'What about me taking on my proper responsibilities, for God's sake?' She says, 'Don't do me any favors, Jesse Moran.' I say, 'Favors? You're talking about my son, here.' She says, 'Oh, I have no illusions'—that is how she talks when she gets on her high horse. 'I have no illusions,' she says. 'I knew what you were when I first laid eyes on you. Footloose and fancy-free,' she says, 'lead singer in a hard-rock band. You don't have to explain yourself to me.' I felt I'd been, like, stenciled or something. I mean where did she get this picture of me? Not from anything that happened in real life, I can tell you. So I say, 'No, I will *not* give you the money; no, sir, no way,' and she says, 'I might have known to expect that'—purposely misunderstanding. I hate when people do that, purposely acting so wronged and martyred. 'I might have figured,' she says, 'that I couldn't count on you for the simplest little abortion fee.' Says the word right out, kind of like she cracked the air with it; I honestly couldn't speak for a second. I say, 'Goddammit, Fiona—' and she says, 'Oh, fine, great, just cuss at me too on top of everything else,' and I say—"

"Jesse. Honey," Maggie said. She rubbed her left temple. She had a sense that she was losing track of some important thread here. "I really think that if Fiona has made up her mind—" she said.

"She's got an appointment the first thing Monday morning, at this clinic over on Whitside Avenue. Monday is her sister's day off; her sister's going with her. See there? She doesn't invite *me* to go with her. And I have talked to her till I'm blue in the face. There's nothing more I can say. So here's what I'm asking: You be the one. You go to the clinic and stop her."

"Me?"

"You always get along so well with my girlfriends. You can do it; I know you can. Tell her about my job. I'm quitting at the envelope factory. I've applied at this computer store, where they'll train me to fix computers, pay me while I'm learning. They said I have a good chance of getting hired. And also Dave in the band, his mother owns a house in Waverly near the stadium and the whole top floor's an apartment that'll be vacant by November, cheap as dirt, Dave says, with a little room for the baby. You're supposed to let the baby sleep in a separate room from its parents; I've been reading up on that. You'd be amazed how much I know! I've decided I'm for pacifiers. Some people don't like the looks of them, but if you give a baby a pacifier he won't suck his thumb later on. Also, it is absolutely not true that pacifiers push their front teeth out of line."

He hadn't talked so much in months, but the sad part was that the more he talked, the younger he seemed. His hair was tangled where he'd run his fingers through it, and his body was all sharp angles as he tore around the kitchen. Maggie said, "Jesse, honey, I know you're going to make a wonderful father someday, but the fact of the matter is, this really has to be the girl's decision. It's the girl who has to go through the pregnancy."

"Not alone, though. I would support her. I would comfort her. I would take care of her. I want to do this, Ma."

She didn't know what more to say, and Jesse must have realized that. He stopped his pacing. He stood squarely in front of her. He said, "Look. You're my only hope. All I'm asking is, you let her know how I feel. Then she can decide whichever way she likes. What could be the harm in that?"

"But why can't *you* let her know how you feel?" Maggie said.

"Don't you think I've tried? I've talked till I'm blue in the face. But everything I say seems to come out wrong. She takes offense, I take offense; we just get all tangled in knots, somehow. By now we're used up. We're worn down into the ground."

Well, she certainly knew what that felt like.

"Couldn't you just consider it?" he asked.

She tilted her head.

"Just consider the possibility?"

"Oh," she said, "the *possibility*, maybe . . ."

He said, "Yes! That's all I'm asking! Thanks, Ma. Thanks a million."

"But, Jesse—"

"And you won't tell Dad yet, will you?"

"Well, not for the time being," she said lamely.

"You can picture what *he* would say," he said.

Then he gave her one of his quick hugs, and he was gone.

For the next few days she felt troubled, indecisive. Examples came to mind of Jesse's fickleness—how (like most boys his age) he kept moving on to new stages and new enthusiasms, leaving the old ones behind. You couldn't leave a wife and baby behind!

But then other pictures came too: for instance, the year they'd all got the flu except for Jesse, and he had had to take care of them. She had glimpsed him blurrily through a haze of fever; he had sat on the edge of the bed and fed her a bowl of chicken soup, spoonful by spoonful, and when she fell asleep between swallows he had waited without complaint until she jerked awake, and then he fed her another spoonful.

"You haven't forgotten, have you?" Jesse asked now whenever he met up with her. And, "You won't go back on your promise, will you?"

"No, no . . ." she would say. And then, "What promise?" What had she let herself in for, exactly? He tucked a slip of paper into her palm one evening—an address on Whitside Avenue. The clinic, she supposed. She dropped it in her skirt pocket. She said, "Now you realize I can't—" But Jesse had already evaporated, dexterous as a cat burglar.

Ira was in a good mood those days, because he'd heard about the computer job. It had come through, as Jesse had foreseen, and he was due to start training in September. "This is more like it," Ira told Maggie. "This is something with a future. And who knows? Maybe after a bit he'll decide to go back to school. I'm sure they'll want him to finish school before they promote him."

Maggie was quiet, thinking.

She had to work on Saturday, so that kept her mind off things, but Sunday she sat a long time on the porch. It was a golden hot day and everyone seemed to be out walking infants. Carriages and strollers wheeled past, and men lunged by with babies in backpacks. Maggie wondered if a backpack was one of the pieces of equipment Jesse considered essential. She would bet it was. She cocked her head toward the house, listening. Ira was watching a ball game on TV and Daisy was away at Mrs. Perfect's. Jesse was still asleep, having come in late from playing at a dance in Howard County. She'd heard him climb

907

the stairs a little after three, singing underneath his breath. *Girlie if I could I would put you on defrost . . .*

"Music is so different now," she had said to Jesse once. "It used to be 'Love Me Forever' and now it's 'Help Me Make It Through the Night.' "

"Aw, Ma," he had said, "don't you get it? In the old days they just hid it better. It was always 'Help Me Make It Through the Night.' "

A line came to her from a song that was popular back when Jesse was a little boy. *I must think of a way*, it went, tactfully, tentatively, *into your heart . . .*

When Jesse was a little boy he liked to tell her stories while she cooked; he seemed to believe she needed entertaining. "Once there was a lady who never fed her children anything but doughnuts," he might begin, or, "Once there was a man who lived on top of a Ferris wheel." All of his stories were whimsical and inventive, and now that she considered, she saw that they had had in common the theme of joyousness, of the triumph of sheer fun over practicality. He strung one particular story out for weeks, something about a retarded father who bought an electric organ with the grocery money. The retarded part came from his aunt Dorrie, she supposed. But the way he told it, the father's handicap was a kind of virtue. The father said, "What do we need food for anyhow? I like better for my children to hear nice music." Maggie laughed when she repeated the story to Ira, but Ira hadn't seen the humor. He took offense first on Dorrie's account (he didn't like the word "retarded") and then on his own. Why was it the father who was retarded? Why not the mother, was probably what he meant— much more realistic, given Maggie's shortcomings. Or maybe he didn't mean that at all, but Maggie imagined he did, and it developed into a quarrel.

They had quarreled over Jesse ever since he was born, it seemed now, always taking the same stances. Ira criticized,

Maggie excused. Ira claimed that Jesse wouldn't keep a civil tongue in his head, refused to wipe that obstinate expression off his face, acted hopelessly inept when helping out at the shop. He just had to come into his own, Maggie said. For some it took longer than for others. "Decades longer?" Ira asked. She said, "Have a little patience, Ira." (A switch. Ira was the one with the patience. Maggie was the rusher-in.)

How was it that she had never realized the power of the young back when she was young herself? She saw it now as a missed opportunity. In her girlhood she'd been so easily cowed; she hadn't dreamed that children were capable of setting up such storms in a family.

She and Ira tried to keep their own storms private, but no doubt Jesse overheard at least a little. Or maybe he just sensed how they felt; for more and more, as he entered his teens, it was to Maggie that he offered his few crumbs of conversation, while he grew steadily more distant from Ira. By the time he told her about the baby, Maggie felt fairly distant from Ira herself. They'd been through too many arguments, rehashed the subject of Jesse too many thousand times. It wasn't merely her promise that kept Maggie from telling Ira about the baby; it was battle fatigue. Ira would hit the roof! And rightly so, of course.

But she thought of how Jesse had nudged her lips with the soup spoon, coaxing her to eat. Sometimes, at the height of her fever, she had wakened to hear thin, sad, faraway music emerging from the earphones on his head, and she had been convinced that they were the sounds of his innermost thoughts made clear to her at long last.

Monday morning she went to work as usual at seven but begged off sick at a quarter till nine and drove to Whitside Avenue. The clinic was a remodeled store of some kind, with a curtained plate-glass window. She spotted it first not by its street number but by the knot of picketers outside. There were

909

three women, several children, and a small, dapper man. THIS CLINIC MURDERS THE INNOCENT, one sign said, and another showed a blown-up photo of a beautiful smiling baby with GIVE HER A CHANCE printed in white across her mop of black curls. Maggie parked in front of an insurance agency next door. The picketers glanced over at her and then went back to watching the clinic.

A car drew up and a girl in jeans got out, followed by a young boy. The girl bent to say something to the driver, after which she waved and the car moved on. The couple walked briskly toward the clinic, while the picketers swarmed around them. "God sees what you're about to do!" one woman called, and another blocked the girl's path, but she veered away. "Where is your conscience?" the man shouted after her. She and the boy vanished behind the door. The picketers straggled back to their places. They were discussing something heatedly; they appeared to be disagreeing. Maggie had the impression that some of them felt they should have been more forceful.

A few minutes later, a woman alighted from a taxi. She was maybe Maggie's age, very well dressed and all by herself. The picketers seemed to feel they had to make up for past defeats. They circled her; they had so much to say that it came to Maggie's ears as a garble of bee sounds. They pressed pamphlets on her. The largest of the women put an arm around her shoulders. The patient, if that was what she was, cried, "Let go of me!" and jabbed an elbow into the picketer's rib cage. Then she was gone too. The picketer bent over—in pain, Maggie thought at first, but she was merely lifting one of the children. They returned to their original positions. In this heat, they moved so slowly that their indignation looked striven-for and counterfeit.

Maggie rooted through her purse for a piece of paper to fan herself with. She would have liked to get out of the car, but then where would she stand? Alongside the picketers?

Footsteps approached, a double set, and she glanced up to see Fiona and a slightly older girl, who must have been her sister.

She had worried she wouldn't recognize Fiona, having caught sight of her only the once. But she knew her right off—the long fair hair, the pale face with nothing yet written upon it. She wore jeans and a bright, shrimp-pink T-shirt. As it happened, Maggie had a prejudice against shrimp pink. She thought it was lower-class. (Oh, how strange it was to remember now that she had once viewed Fiona as lower-class! She had imagined there was something cheap and gimcrack about her; she had mistrusted the bland pallor of her face, and she had suspected that her sister's too-heavy makeup concealed the same unhealthy complexion. Pure narrow-mindedness! Maggie could admit that now, having come to see Fiona's good points.)

At any rate, she got out of the car. She walked over to them and said, "Fiona?"

The sister murmured, "Told you they'd try something." She must have thought Maggie was a picketer. And Fiona walked on, eyelids lowered so they were two white crescents.

"Fiona, I'm Jesse's mother," Maggie said.

Fiona slowed and looked at her. The sister came to a stop.

"I won't interfere if you're certain you know what you're doing," Maggie said, "but, Fiona, have you considered every angle?"

"Not all that many *to* consider," the sister said bluntly. "She's seventeen years old."

Fiona allowed herself to be led away then, still gazing at Maggie over her shoulder.

"Have you talked about it with Jesse?" Maggie asked. She ran after them. "Jesse wants this baby! He told me so."

The sister called back, "Is he going to bear it? Is he going to walk it at night and change its diapers?"

"Yes, he is!" Maggie said. "Well, not bear it, of course . . ."

They had reached the picketers by now. A woman held out one of the pamphlets. On the front was a color photo of an unborn baby who seemed a good deal past the embryo stage, in fact almost ready to be delivered. Fiona shrank away. "Leave her alone," Maggie told the woman. She said, "Fiona, Jesse really cares about you. You have to believe me."

"I have seen enough of Jesse Moran to last me a lifetime," the sister said. She shoved past a fat woman with two toddlers and an infant in a sling.

"You're just saying that because you have him cast in this certain role," Maggie told her, "this rock-band member who got your little sister pregnant. But it's not so simple! It's not so cut-and-dried! He bought a Dr. Spock book—did he mention that, Fiona? He's already researched pacifiers and he thinks you ought to breast-feed."

The fat woman said to Fiona, "All the angels in heaven are crying over you."

"Listen," Maggie told the woman. "Just because *you've* got too many children is no reason to wish the same trouble on other people."

"The angels call it murder," the woman said.

Fiona flinched. Maggie said, "Can't you see you're upsetting her?" They had reached the door of the clinic now, but the dapper little man was barring their way. "Get out of here," Maggie told him. "Fiona! Just think it over! That's all I ask of you."

The man held his ground, which gave Fiona time to turn to Maggie. She looked a little teary. "Jesse doesn't care," she said.

"Of course he cares!"

"He says to me, 'Don't worry, Fiona, I won't let you down.' Like I am some kind of obligation! Some charitable cause!"

"He didn't mean it that way. You're misreading him. He honestly wants to marry you."

"And live on what money?" the sister asked. She had a braying, unpleasant voice, much deeper than Fiona's. "He doesn't even have a decent-paying job."

"He's getting one! Computers! Opportunity for advancement!" Maggie said. She was forced to speak so telegraphically because Fiona's sister had somehow cleared the door of picketers and was tugging it open. A woman held a postcard in front of Fiona's face: the curly-haired baby again. Maggie batted it aside. "At least come home with me so you and Jesse can talk it over," she told Fiona. "That won't commit you to anything."

Fiona hesitated. Her sister said, "For God's sake, Fiona," but Maggie seized her advantage. She took Fiona by the wrist and led her back through the crowd, keeping up a steady stream of encouragement. "He says he's building a cradle; he's already got the plans. It's enough to break your heart. Leave her alone, dammit! Do I have to call the police? Who gave you the right to pester us?"

"Who gave her the right to murder her baby?" a woman called.

"She has every right in the world! Fiona, this is a natural-born caretaker we're talking about here. You should have seen him during the Hong Kong flu."

"The what?"

"Or Bangkok, or Sing Sing, or one of those flus . . . Anyway, it's nothing to do with charity. He wants this baby more than anything."

Fiona peered into her face. She said, "And he's building a . . . ?"

"He's building a cradle. A beautiful one, with a hood," Maggie said. If it turned out not to have a hood she could always say she had been mistaken.

Fiona's sister scurried alongside them, her heels clicking busily. She said, "Fiona, if you don't get back in there this instant I am washing my hands of this whole affair, I tell you.

Fiona, they have scheduled you!" And the picketers milled uncertainly a few feet behind. Fiona's wrist was smooth and impossibly thin, like a stalk of bamboo. Maggie released it, reluctantly, in order to open the car door. "Climb in," she said. "Buzz off," she told the picketers. And to the sister she said, "Nice meeting you."

The picketers dropped back. One said, "Now look, uh . . ."

"We have constitutional permission to do this, I'll have you know," Maggie said. The woman looked confused.

"I hunt up a clinic," Fiona's sister said, "I take her to be tested. I make the appointment, I sacrifice a perfectly good day off when I could have gone to Ocean City with my boyfriend—"

"You could still do that," Maggie said, checking her watch.

She hurried around to the driver's side, fearful that Fiona would try to escape, but when she got in, Fiona was sitting there limply with her head tipped back and her eyes closed. Her sister bent in through the open window. "Fiona, just tell me this much," she said. "If Jesse Moran was so hot for this baby, how come it wasn't him who came down here to fetch you?"

Fiona raised her lids and looked over at Maggie. "Well, he tried," Maggie told her. "He's been trying for days, you know he has, but somehow you're always at cross-purposes."

Fiona closed her eyes again. Maggie started the car and drove off.

The strange part was that having won—at least temporarily—she didn't feel a bit triumphant. Just worn out. And slightly confused, to tell the truth. How was it things had ended up this way, when all along she'd been telling Jesse he was nowhere near old enough? Oh, Lord. What had she gone and done? She glanced secretly at Fiona. Fiona's skin seemed slick, almost glazed. "Are you feeling ill?" Maggie asked her.

"I believe I might upchuck," Fiona said, barely moving her lips.

"You want me to stop the car?"

"Let's just get there."

Maggie drove more carefully, as if transporting a basket of eggs.

In front of the house she parked, got out, and came around to help Fiona from her seat. Fiona was a dead weight. She leaned heavily against Maggie. But she had a young smell— fresh-ironed cotton and those sugary beginner cosmetics you find in dime stores—and that gave Maggie some reassurance. Oh, this girl was not bad at heart! She was barely older than Daisy; she was an ordinary, open-faced child bewildered by what had happened to her.

They crossed the sidewalk slowly and climbed the steps to the porch. Their shoes made a hollow sound on the floorboards. "Sit here," Maggie said, and she helped Fiona into the chair where she herself had sat all yesterday afternoon. "You need the air," she said. "Take deep, deep breaths. I'm going to go find Jesse."

Fiona closed her eyes.

Inside, the rooms were cool and dark. Maggie climbed the stairs to Jesse's room and knocked on his door. She poked her head in. "Jesse?" she said.

"Mmf."

His window shades were lowered so she could barely make out the shapes of the furniture. His bed was a tangle of twisted sheets. "Jesse, I've brought Fiona," she said. "Could you come down to the porch?"

"Huh?"

"Could you come down to the porch and talk with Fiona?"

He stirred a little and raised his head, so she knew she could leave him. She went back downstairs and into the kitchen, where she poured a glass of iced tea from a pitcher in the refrigerator. She put the glass on a china plate, encircled it with saltine crackers, and carried it out to Fiona. "Here," she said. "Take little bites of these saltines. Take tiny sips of tea."

Fiona was already looking better, sitting upright now in her chair, and she said, "Thank you," when Maggie laid the plate on her knees. She nibbled at a corner of a cracker. Maggie settled in a rocker next to her.

"When I was expecting Daisy," Maggie said, "I lived on tea and saltines for two solid months. It's a wonder we didn't both get malnutrition. I was so sick with Daisy I thought I would die, but with Jesse I never had a moment's discomfort. Isn't that funny? You'd think it would have been the other way around."

Fiona set down her cracker. "I should've stayed at the clinic," she said.

"Oh, honey," Maggie said. She felt suddenly depressed. She had an instantaneous, chillingly clear vision of how Ira's face would look when he learned what she had done. "Fiona, it's not too late," she said. "You're only here to discuss it all, right? You're not committed to a thing." Although even as she spoke she saw the clinic receding steadily. This was something like rushing toward a jump rope, she imagined. Miss that split second where entry is possible and you've flubbed up everything. She reached out and touched Fiona's arm. "And after all," she said, "you do love each other, don't you? Don't you love each other?"

"Yes, but maybe if we got married he would start to hold it against me," Fiona said. "I mean, he's a lead singer! He'll probably want to go to England or Australia or some such after he gets famous. And meanwhile, his band has just barely started earning any money. Where would we live? How would we work this?"

"At first you could live here with us," Maggie said. "Then in November you can move to an apartment Jesse knows about in Waverly. Jesse has it all figured out."

Fiona stared toward the street. "If I had stayed on at the clinic everything would be over by now," she said after a minute.

"Oh, Fiona. Please. Oh, tell me I didn't do wrong!" Maggie said. She looked around for Jesse. What was keeping him? It shouldn't be up to her to carry on this courtship. "Wait here," she said. She got up and hurried into the house. "Jesse!" she cried. But he didn't answer, and she heard the shower running. That boy would insist on showering first if the house were on fire, she thought. She ran upstairs and pounded on the bathroom door. "Jesse, are you coming?" she called.

He cut the water off. "What?" he said.

"Come out, I tell you!"

No answer. But she heard the shower curtain screech across the rod.

She went into his bedroom and snapped up both window shades. She wanted to find his Dr. Spock book. It would serve as a kind of selling point till he came downstairs; or at least it would provide a topic of conversation. But she couldn't find it—just dirty clothes, French-fry cartons, records left out of their jackets. She looked for the cradle plans then. What would they be—blueprints? Not a sign of them. Well, of course, he'd have taken them to the basement, where Ira kept his tools. She tore back down the stairs, calling toward the porch as she passed, "He's on his way!" (She could picture Fiona getting up and leaving.) Through the kitchen, down a set of narrow wooden steps, over to Ira's workbench. No plans there, either. Ira's tools hung neatly on the backboard, each matching its own painted outline—a sure sign Jesse had not been near them. On the workbench itself were two squares of sandpaper and a sheaf of doweling rods still bound together by rubber bands, part of a drying rack that Ira had promised to build into a corner of the back porch. She seized the doweling rods and raced back up the basement steps. "Look," she told Fiona, slamming out the screen door. "Jesse's cradle."

Fiona lowered her glass. She accepted the rods and gazed at them. "Cradle?" she said doubtfully.

917

"It's going to have . . . spindles; that's what they are," Maggie said. "Antique style."

You would think those rods could be read, the way Fiona studied them.

Then Jesse came out, bringing with him the fragrance of shampoo. His hair was wet and tousled and his skin was radiant. He said, "Fiona? You didn't go through with it?" and she lifted her face, still holding the rods like a kind of scepter, and said, "Well, all right, Jesse, if you want. I guess we could get married if you want."

Then Jesse wrapped his arms around her and dropped his head to her shoulder, and something about that picture—his dark head next to her blond one—reminded Maggie of the way she used to envision marriage before she was married herself. She had thought of it as more different than it really was, somehow, more of an alteration in people's lives—two opposites drawn together with a dramatic crashing sound. She had supposed that when she was married all her old problems would fall away, something like when you go on vacation and leave a few knotty tasks incomplete as if you'd never have to come back and face them. And of course, she had been wrong. But watching Jesse and Fiona, she could almost believe that that early vision was the right one. She slipped into the house, shutting the screen door very softly behind her, and she decided everything was going to work out after all.

They were married in Cartwheel, in Mrs. Stuckey's living room. Just family attended. Ira was grim-faced and silent, Maggie's mother sat stiff with outrage, and Maggie's father seemed befuddled. Only Mrs. Stuckey showed the proper festive attitude. She wore a fuchsia corduroy pantsuit and a corsage as big as her head, and before the ceremony she told everybody that her one regret was that Mr. Stuckey had not lived to see this day. Although maybe, she said, he was here in spirit; and then she went on at some length about her personal theory of ghosts. (They were the completions of the dead's intended gestures, their unfinished plans still hanging in the air—something like when you can't remember what it was you went to the kitchen for and so you pantomime the motion, a twist of the wrist perhaps, and that reminds you you had come out to turn the dripping faucet off. So wasn't there a chance that Mr. Stuckey was right here in the living room, having dreamed of walking both his precious daughters down the aisle someday?) Then she said that to her mind, marriage was just as educational as high school and maybe more so. "I mean I dropped out of school myself," she said, "and have never once regretted it." Fiona's sister rolled her eyes. But it was a good thing Mrs. Stuckey felt that way, since Fiona wouldn't turn eighteen till January and required parental permission for a marriage license.

Fiona herself wore a beige, loose-waisted dress that she and Maggie had gone shopping for together, and Jesse looked very distinguished in a suit and tie. He looked like a grownup, in fact. Daisy acted shy around him, and kept hanging on to Maggie's arm and looking over at him. "What's the matter with you? Straighten up," Maggie told her. She was feeling very irritable, for some reason. She worried that Ira was going to be angry at her forever. He seemed to be holding her solely accountable for this entire situation.

After the wedding, Jesse and Fiona went to Ocean City for a week. Then they came home to Jesse's room, where Maggie had moved in an extra bureau and exchanged his old bunks for a double bed from J. C. Penney. The house grew more crowded, of course, but it was a pleasant sort of crowdedness, cheerful and expectant. Fiona seemed to fit right in; she was so agreeable, so ready to let Maggie take charge—more so than Maggie's own children had ever been. Jesse set off happily every morning for his computer job, and returned every evening with some new baby-care gadget—a pack of bunny-shaped diaper pins or an ingenious spouted training cup. He was reading up on childbirth and kept embracing different theories, each more peculiar than the last. (For instance, at one point he proposed that the delivery take place underwater, but he couldn't find a doctor who would agree to it.)

Daisy and her friends forgot Mrs. Perfect entirely and camped in Maggie's living room—five dumbstruck, enchanted little girls reverently eyeing Fiona's stomach. And Fiona played up to them, sometimes inviting them to her room to admire her growing layette, after which she might seat them one by one at the mirror and experiment with their hair. (Her sister was a beautician and had taught Fiona everything she knew, Fiona said.) Then in the evening, if Jesse's band had an engagement somewhere, he and Fiona would go out together and not return till 2 or 3 a.m., and Maggie, half waking, would hear their whispers on the stairs. The lock on their bedroom door would click stealthily and Maggie would sink back into sleep, contented.

Even Ira seemed resigned, after he'd got over the shock. Oh, at first he was so disgusted that Maggie had feared he would walk out of the house forever. For days he had not spoken, and when Jesse entered the room he would leave. But gradually he came around. He was most comfortable, Maggie thought, when he could act tolerant and long-suffering, and surely he had the opportunity for that now. Here all his apprehensions had been confirmed: His son had got a girl in trouble and his wife had meddled unforgivably and now the girl was living in Jesse's bedroom among the Iggy Pop posters. He could sigh and say, "Didn't I tell you? Didn't I always warn you?" (Or at least he could give that impression; not that he said it aloud.) Fiona drifted past him into the bathroom every morning, wearing her fluffy pink robe and her big pink powder-puff slippers and carrying her tortoiseshell soapbox, and Ira flattened himself against the wall as if she were twice as big as she was. But he treated her with unfailing courtesy. He even taught her his complicated brand of solitaire, when the boredom of sitting at home got to be too much for her, and he lent her his Mariner's Library books—a whole row of memoirs by people who had sailed alone around the world and such. He had been trying to press them on his children for years. ("As far as I'm concerned," Fiona told Maggie, "those books are just more of that 'How I took Route So-and-so' that men always think is so fascinating." But she didn't let on to Ira.) And by November, when the Waverly apartment was supposed to become available, Ira didn't ask why they weren't moving out.

Nor did Maggie; she carefully avoided the subject. In fact, for all she knew, the apartment had fallen through somehow. Maybe the current tenants had changed their plans. At any rate, Jesse and Fiona said nothing about leaving. Fiona followed Maggie around now the way the children had followed her when they were tiny. She trailed her from room to room, asking fractious questions. "Why do I feel so logy?" she asked, and, "Am I ever going to have anklebones again?" She had started attending childbirth classes and wanted Maggie to go with her to the labor room. Jesse, she said, might pass out or something. Maggie said, "Why, Jesse's dying to go with you," but Fiona said, "I don't want him to see me like that! He isn't even kin."

Nor was Maggie, Maggie could have said. Although it seemed she really was, in some ways.

In Jesse's company, Fiona began to take on an aggrieved and nagging tone. She complained about the unfairness—how Jesse got to go off to work every day while she sat home growing fatter. She should have stayed in school after all, she said, at least through fall semester; but no, no, Jesse had to have things his way: homebody wife, the Little Mother act. When she spoke like this there was something old-ladyish in her voice, and Jesse when he answered sounded sullen. "Have you heard one word I've been saying?" Fiona would ask, and Jesse would say, "I heard, I heard." What was it that struck Maggie as so familiar? It was a tune, almost. It was the tune of the arguments Jesse used to have with his parents; that was it. Jesse and Fiona were more like a boy and his mother than husband and wife.

But Fiona wasn't feeling well; no wonder she was snappish. That early-pregnancy sleepiness never left her, even in her seventh and eighth months, when most women were bundles of energy. Jesse would say, "Put on your clothes! We're booked at the Granite Tavern tonight and they're paying us real money," and she would say, "Oh, I don't know; maybe I'll let you go on without me."

"Without you?" he would ask. "You mean alone?" And his face would get all hurt and surprised. But he would go. Once, he didn't even eat supper—just left the minute she told him she wasn't coming with him, although it was barely 6 p.m. Then Fiona didn't eat, either, but sat there at the table playing with her food, a tear slipping down her cheek from time to time, and afterward she put on the hooded windbreaker that didn't button over her stomach anymore and she went for a long, long walk. Or she might have gone to visit her sister; Maggie had no idea. At eight or so Jesse phoned and Maggie had to tell him she was out someplace. "What do you mean, out?" he asked.

"Just out, Jesse. I'm sure she'll be coming back soon."

"She said she was too tired to go out. She couldn't come to the Granite Tavern because she was too tired."

"Oh, maybe she—"

But he had already hung up, a metallic clunk in her ear.

Well, these things happened. (Didn't Maggie know they happened?) And the next morning Jesse and Fiona were fine—had reconciled at some point and acted more loving than ever. Maggie had been anxious for no reason, it turned out.

*   *   *

The baby was due in early March, but on February first Fiona woke up with a backache. Maggie was excited the instant she heard. "This is it, I bet," she told Fiona.

"It can't be!" Fiona said. "I'm not ready."

"Of course you're ready. You've got your layette; your suitcase is packed—"

"But Jesse hasn't built the cradle yet."

It was true. Whatever other equipment he'd laid in, that cradle had not materialized. Maggie said, "Never mind; he can do it while you're in the hospital."

"This is a plain old backache anyhow," Fiona said. "I've had this feeling often, before I was pregnant, even."

At noon, though, when Maggie phoned from work, Fiona sounded less certain. "I'm getting these cramps, like, in my stomach," she said. "Can you please come home early?"

"I'll be there," Maggie told her. "Have you called Jesse yet?"

"Jesse? No."

"Why don't you call him."

"Okay, but promise you'll come home? Start right now."

"I'm on my way."

She arrived to find Jesse timing Fiona's contractions, using an official-looking stopwatch he'd bought especially for this occasion. He was jubilant. "We're moving right along!" he told Maggie.

Fiona looked scared. She kept giving little moans, not during the contractions but between them. "Hon, I don't think you're breathing right," Jesse told her.

Fiona said, "Lay off about my breathing! I'll breathe any way I choose."

"Well, I just want you to be comfortable. Are you comfortable? Is the baby moving?"

"I don't know."

"Is he moving or isn't he? Fiona? You must have some idea."

"I don't know, I tell you. No. He's not."

"The baby isn't moving," Jesse told Maggie.

"Don't worry. He's just getting ready," Maggie said.

"Something must be wrong."

"Nothing's wrong, Jesse. Believe me."

But he didn't believe her, which is why they ended up leaving for the hospital far too early. Maggie drove. Jesse said he might crash the car if he drove, but then he spent the whole trip protesting every move Maggie made. "What possessed you to get behind a bus? Switch lanes. Not now, for God's sake! Check your rearview mirror. Oh, God, we'll all be killed and they'll have to cut the baby out of her stomach in the middle of Franklin Street."

Fiona shrieked at this, which so unnerved Maggie that she slammed on the brakes and threw all three of them against the windshield. Jesse said, "Let us out! Better we go by foot! Let her give birth on the sidewalk!"

"Fine," Maggie said. "Get out of the car."

Fiona said, "What?"

"Now, Ma, just cool it," Jesse said. "No need to get hysterical. Depend on Ma to fall apart in any little emergency," he told Fiona.

They rode the rest of the way in silence, and Maggie left them at the hospital entrance and went off to park.

When she located them in Admissions, Fiona was just settling into a wheelchair. "I want my mother-in-law to come with me," she told the nurse.

"Only Daddy can come with you," the nurse said. "Grandma has to stay in the waiting room."

Grandma?

"I don't want Daddy, I want Grandma!" Fiona cried, sounding about six years old.

"Here we go now," the nurse said. She wheeled her away. Jesse followed, wearing that hurt, undefended expression Maggie had seen so often lately.

Maggie went to the waiting room, which was the size of a football field. A vast expanse of beige carpeting was broken up by clustered arrangements of beige vinyl couches and chairs. She settled on an empty couch and chose a ruffle-edged magazine from the beige wooden end table. "How to Keep the Zing! in Your Marriage," the first article was called. It instructed her to be unpredictable; greet her husband after work wearing nothing but a black lace apron. Ira would think she had lost her mind. Not to mention Jesse and Fiona and the five enchanted little girls. She wished she had thought to bring her knitting. She wasn't that much of a knitter—her stitches had a way of galloping along for a few inches and then squinching up in tight little puckers, reminding her of a car that bucks and stalls—but lately she had thrown herself into a purple football jersey for the baby. (It was going to be a boy; everybody assumed so, and only boys' names had been considered.)

She set the magazine aside and went over to the flank of pay phones that lined one wall. First she dialed the number at home. When no one answered—not even Daisy, who was usually back from school by three—she checked her watch and discovered it was barely two o'clock. She had thought it was much later. She dialed Ira's work number. "Sam's Frame Shop," he answered.

"Ira?" she said. "Guess what—I'm at the hospital."

"You are? What's wrong?"

"Nothing's wrong. Fiona's having her baby."

"Oh," he said. "I thought you'd crashed the car or something."

"You want to come wait with me? It's going to be a while yet."

"Well, maybe I should go home to watch Daisy," Ira said.

Maggie sighed. "Daisy's at school," she told him. "And anyhow, she hasn't needed watching in years."

"You'll want someone to put supper on, though."

She gave up on him. (Lord forbid her deathbed should be

in a hospital; he would probably not attend it.) She said, "Well, suit yourself, Ira, but I would think you'd want to see your own grandchild."

"I'll see him soon enough, won't I?" Ira asked.

Maggie glimpsed Jesse across the waiting room. "I have to go now," she said, and she hung up. "Jesse?" she said, hurrying toward him. "What's the news?"

"Everything's fine. Or so they claim."

"How's Fiona?"

"She's scared," he said, "and I try to calm her down, but those hospital people keep shooing me out. Anytime someone official comes they ask me to leave."

So much for modern developments, Maggie thought. Men were still being shielded from everything truly important.

Jesse went back to Fiona but kept Maggie posted, reappearing every half hour or so to speak knowingly of stages and centimeters. "It's going pretty fast now," he said once, and another time, "Many people believe that an eight-months baby is more at risk than a seven-months baby, but that's an old wives' tale. It's just a superstition." His hair stood up in thick tufts, like wind-tossed grass. Maggie restrained herself from reaching out to smooth it. Unexpectedly, he reminded her of Ira. However different the two might be in other ways, they both had this notion that reading up on something, getting equipped for something, would put them in control.

She considered going home for a while (it was nearly five o'clock) but she knew she would only fret and pace, so she stayed where she was and kept in touch by telephone. Daisy reported that Ira was fixing a pancake supper. "No green vegetable?" Maggie asked. "Where's the green vegetable?" Ira got on the phone to assure her that he was serving spiced crab-apple rings on the side. "Spiced crab-apple rings are not green, Ira," Maggie said. She felt herself growing weepy. She ought to be at home supervising her family's nutrition; she ought to be storming the labor room to comfort Fiona; she ought to take Jesse in her arms and rock him because he was nothing but a child still, much too young for what was happening to him. But here she stood, clutching a salty-smelling receiver in a public phone hutch. Her stomach felt all knotted and tight. It hadn't been so long since she was a patient in the labor room herself, and her muscles recalled it exactly.

She told Ira goodbye and went through the doors where Jesse kept disappearing. She traveled down a corridor, hoping for, oh, at least a nursery full of newborns to cheer her up. She passed another, smaller waiting room, perhaps leading to some lab or private office. An elderly couple sat there on two molded plastic chairs, and across from them sat a burly man in paint-spattered coveralls. As Maggie slowed to glance in, a nurse called, "Mr. Plum?" and the elderly man rose and went toward a back room, leaving behind a brand new magazine. Maggie breezed in as if she had a perfect right to be there and scooped up the magazine, at the same time performing a clumsy half-curtsy to show the old woman she meant no intrusion. She settled beside the man in coveralls. Never mind that this was just another ladies' magazine; at least the pages still gave off a shellacked, unused smell and the movie stars spilling their secrets were wearing up-to-date hairdos. She skimmed an article about a new kind of diet. You picked one favorite food and ate all you wanted, three times a day, nothing else besides. Maggie would have chosen beef-and-bean burritos from Lexington Market.

In the back room, the nurse said, "Now, Mr. Plum, I'm giving you this jar for urine."

"My what?"

"Urine."

"How's that?"

"It's for urine!"

"Speak up—I can't hear you."

927

"*Urine*, I said! You take this jar home! You collect all your urine! For twenty-four hours! You bring the jar back!"

In the chair across from Maggie, the wife gave an embarrassed titter. "He's deaf as a doorknob," she told Maggie. "Has to have everything shouted out for all and sundry to hear."

Maggie smiled and shook her head, not knowing how else to respond. Then the man in coveralls stirred. He placed his great, furry fists on his knees. He cleared his throat. "You know," he said, "it's the funniest thing. I can catch that nurse's voice all right but I don't understand a single word she's saying."

Maggie's eyes filled with tears. She dropped her magazine and groped in her purse for a Kleenex, and the man said, "Lady? You okay?"

She couldn't tell him it was his kindness that had undone her—such delicacy, in such an unlikely-looking person—and so she said, "It's my son, he's having a baby. I mean my son's wife is."

The man and the old woman waited, their faces prepared to take on the proper look of shock and pity as soon as they heard the bad part. And she couldn't tell them, "It's all my fault, I set everything pell-mell in motion not once considering the consequences," so instead she said, "It's months and months too early, it's nowhere near her due date . . ."

The man clicked his tongue. His forehead furrowed upon itself like cloth. The old woman said, "Oh, my stars, you must be worried sick. But don't you give up hope, because my nephew Brady's wife, Angela . . ."

And that was why, when Jesse passed down the corridor from the delivery room a few minutes later, he found his mother in a little side cubicle surrounded by a huddle of strangers. They were patting her and murmuring consolations—an old woman, a workman of some sort, a nurse with a clipboard, and a stooped old man clutching a gigantic empty jar. "Ma?" Jesse said, stepping in. "The baby's here, and both of them are fine."

"Praise Jesus!" the old woman shouted, flinging her hands toward the ceiling.

"The only trouble is," Jesse said, eyeing the woman dubiously, "it's a girl. I wasn't counting on a girl, somehow."

"You would let a thing like that bother you?" the old woman demanded. "At a moment such as this? That child was snatched from the jaws of death!"

"From . . . ?" Jesse said. Then he said, "No, it's just a superstition that an eight-months—"

"Let's get out of here," Maggie said, and she fought her way free of the huddle to grab his arm and steer him away.

How that baby took over the house! Her cries of fury and her mourning-dove coos, her mingled smells of powder and ammonia, her wheeling arms and legs. She had Fiona's coloring but Jesse's spirit and his feistineess (no Lady-Baby this time). Her small, fine features were scrunched very close together low down in her face, so when Fiona combed her bit of hair into a sprout on top of her head she resembled a Kewpie doll; and like a doll she was trundled everywhere by the enchanted little girls, who would have cut school if permitted, just to lug her about by the armpits and shake her rattle too close to her eyes and hang over her, breathing heavily, while Maggie bathed her. Even Ira showed some interest, although he pretended not to. "Let me know when she's big enough to play baseball," he said, but as early as the second week, Maggie caught him taking sidelong peeks into the bureau drawer where Leroy slept, and by the time she had learned to sit up, the two of them were deep in those exclusive conversations of theirs.

And Jesse? He was devoted—always offering to help out, sometimes making a nuisance of himself, to hear Fiona tell it. He walked Leroy during her fussy spells, and he left his warm bed to burp her and then carry her back to Maggie's room after the two o'clock feeding. And once, when Maggie took Fiona shopping, he spent a whole Saturday morning solely in charge, returning Leroy none the worse for wear, although the careful way he had dressed her—with her overall straps mistakenly clamping down her collar, severely mashing the double row of ruffles—made Maggie feel sad, for some reason. He claimed that he had never wanted a boy at all; or if he had, he couldn't remember why. "Girls are perfect," he said. "Leroy is perfect. Except, you know . . ."

"Except?" Maggie asked.

"Well, it's just that . . . shoot, before she was born I had this sort of, like, anticipation. And now I've got nothing to anticipate, you know?"

"Oh, that'll pass," Maggie said. "Don't worry."

But later, to Ira, she said, "I never heard of a father getting postpartum blues."

Maybe if the mother didn't, the father did; was that the way it worked? For Fiona herself was cheerful and oblivious. Often as she flitted around the baby she seemed more like one of the enchanted little girls than like a mother. She paid too much heed to Leroy's appurtenances, Maggie felt—to her frilly clothes, her ribboned sprout of hair. Or maybe it just seemed so. Maybe Maggie was jealous. It was true that she hated to relinquish the baby when she went off to work every morning. "How can I leave her?" she wailed to Ira. "Fiona doesn't know the first little bit about child care."

"Well, only one way she's ever going to learn," Ira said. And so Maggie left, hanging back internally, and called home several times a day to see how things were going. But they were always going fine.

In the nursing home one afternoon she heard a middle-aged visitor talking to his mother—a vacant, slack-jawed woman in a wheelchair. He told her how his wife was, how the kids were. His mother smoothed her lap robe. He told her how his job

930

was. His mother plucked at a bit of lint and flicked it onto the floor. He told her about a postcard that had come for her at the house. The church was holding an Easter bazaar and they wanted her to check off which task she would volunteer for. This struck the son as comical, in view of his mother's disabilities. "They offered you your choice," he said, chuckling. "You could clerk at the needlework booth or you could tend the babies." His mother's hands grew still. She raised her head. Her face lit up and flowered. "Oh!" she cried softly. "I'll tend the babies!"

Maggie knew just how she felt.

Leroy was a long, thin infant, and Fiona worried she was outgrowing the bureau drawer she slept in. "When are you going to get started on that cradle?" she asked Jesse, and Jesse said, "Any day now."

Maggie said, "Maybe we should just buy a crib. A cradle's for a newborn; she wouldn't fit it for long."

But Fiona said, "No, I set my heart on a cradle." She told Jesse. "You promised."

"I don't remember promising."

"Well, you did," she said.

"All right! I'll get to it! Didn't I tell you I would?"

"You don't have to shout at me," she said.

"I'm not shouting."

"Yes, you are."

"Am not."

"Are too."

"Children! Children!" Maggie said, pretending she was joking.

But only pretending.

Once, Fiona spent the night at her sister's, snatching up the baby and stomping out after a fight. Or not a fight exactly but a little misunderstanding: The band was playing at a club in downtown Baltimore and Fiona planned to come along, as usual, till Jesse worried aloud that Leroy had a cold and shouldn't be left. Fiona said Maggie would tend her just fine and Jesse said a baby with a cold needed her mother and then Fiona said it was amazing how he was so considerate of that baby but so inconsiderate of his wife and then Jesse said . . .

Well.

Fiona left and did not come back until morning; Maggie feared she was gone for good, endangering that poor sick baby, who needed much more nursing than Fiona could provide. She must have been planning to desert them all along, in fact. Why, just look at her soapbox! Wasn't it odd that for almost a year now she had borne off to the bathroom twice daily a tortoiseshell soapbox, a tube of Aim toothpaste (*not* the Morans' brand), and a toothbrush in a plastic cylinder? And that her toilet supplies were continually stored in a clear vinyl travel case on the bureau? She might as well be a guest. She had never meant to settle in permanently.

"Go after her," Maggie told Jesse, but Jesse asked, "Why should I? She's the one who walked out." He was at work when Fiona returned the next day, wan and puffy-eyed. Strands of her uncombed hair mingled with the fake-fur trim of her windbreaker hood, and Leroy was wrapped clumsily in a garish daisy-square afghan that must have belonged to the sister.

What Maggie's mother said was true: The generations were sliding downhill in this family. They were descending in every respect, not just in their professions and their educations but in the way they reared their children and the way they ran their households. ("How have you let things get so *common*?" Maggie heard again in her memory.) Mrs. Daley stood over the sleeping Leroy and pleated her lips in disapproval. "They would put an infant in a bureau drawer? They would let her stay in here with you and Ira? What can they be thinking of? It must be that Fiona person. Really, Maggie, that Fiona is so . . . Why, she isn't even a Baltimore girl! Anyone who would pronounce Wicomico as Weeko-Meeko! And what is that racket I'm hearing?"

Maggie tilted her head to listen. "It's Canned Heat," she decided.

"Candide? I'm not asking the name of it; I mean why is it playing? When you children were small I played Beethoven and Brahms, I played all of Wagner's operas!"

Yes, and Maggie could still recall her itch of boredom as Wagner's grandiose weight crashed through the house. And her frustration when, beginning some important story with "Me and Emma went to—" she had been cut short by her mother. (" 'Emma and I,' if you please.") She had sworn never to do that to her own children, preferring to hear what it was they had to say and let the grammar take care of itself. Not that it had done so, at least not in Jesse's case.

Maybe her own downhill slide was deliberate. If so, she owed Jesse an apology. Maybe he was just carrying out her secret scheme for revolution, and would otherwise—who knows?—have gone on to be a lawyer like Mrs. Daley's father.

Well, too late now.

Leroy learned to crawl and she crawled right out of her bureau drawer, and the next day Ira came home with a crib. He assembled it, without comment, in his and Maggie's bedroom. Without comment, Fiona watched from the doorway. The skin beneath her eyes had a sallow, soiled look.

On a Saturday in September, they celebrated Ira's father's birthday. Maggie had made it a tradition to spend his birthday at the Pimlico Race Track—all of them together, even though it meant closing the frame shop. They would take a huge picnic lunch and a ten-dollar bill for each person to bet with. In times past the whole family had squeezed into Ira's car, but of course that was no longer possible. This year they had Jesse and Fiona (who had been away on their honeymoon the year before), and

933

Leroy too, and even Ira's sister Junie decided she might brave the trip. So Jesse borrowed the van that his band used to transport their instruments. SPIN THE CAT was lettered across its side, the S and the C striped like tigers' tails. They loaded the back with picnic hampers and baby supplies, and then they drove to the shop to pick up Ira's father and sisters. Junie wore her usual going-out costume, everything cut on the bias, and carried a parasol that wouldn't collapse, which caused some trouble when she climbed in. And Dorrie was hugging her Hutzler's coat box, which caused even more trouble. But everyone acted good-natured about it—even Ira's father, who always said he was way too old to make a fuss over birthdays.

It was a beautiful day, the kind that starts out cool until sunlight gently warms your outer layers and then your inner layers. Daisy was trying to get them to sing "Camptown Races," and Ira's father wore a grudging, self-conscious smile. This was how families ought to be, Maggie thought. And in the bus that carried them in from the parking lot—a bus they half filled, if you counted the picnic hampers balanced on empty seats and the diaper bag and folded stroller blocking the aisle—she felt sorry for their fellow passengers who sat alone or in pairs. Most of them had a workaday attitude. They wore sensible clothes and stern, purposeful expressions, and they were here to win. The Morans were here to celebrate.

They spread out over one whole row of bleachers, parking Leroy alongside in her stroller. Then Mr. Moran, who prided himself on his knowledge of horseflesh, went off to the paddocks to size things up, and Ira went too, to keep him company. Jesse found a couple he knew—a man in motorcycle gear and a slip of a girl in fringed buckskin pants—and disappeared with them; he wasn't much of a gambler. The women settled down to select their horses by the ring of their names, which was a method that seemed to work about as well as any other. Maggie favored one called Infinite Mercy, but Junie disagreed. She said that didn't sound to her like a horse with enough fight to it.

Because of the baby, who was teething or something and acted a little fretful, they staggered their trips to the betting windows. Fiona went first with Ira's sisters, while Maggie stayed behind with Leroy and Daisy. Then the others came back and Maggie and Daisy went, Daisy bristling with good advice. "What you do," she said, "is put two dollars to show. That's safest." But Maggie said, "If I'd wanted *safe* I'd be sitting at home," and bet all ten dollars on Number Four to win. (In the past she'd argued for the family to pool every bit of their money and head straight for the fifty-dollar-minimum window, a dangerous and exciting spot she'd never so much as approached, but she knew by now not to bother trying.) Along the way they ran into Ira and his father, who were discussing statistics. The jockeys' weights, their previous records, the horses' fastest times and what kind of turf they did best on—there was plenty to consider, if you cared. Maggie bet her ten dollars and left, while Daisy joined the men, and the three of them stood deliberating.

"This kid is wearing me out," Fiona said when Maggie got back. Leroy evidently didn't want to be carried and she kept straining toward the ground, which was littered with beer-can tabs and cigarette butts. Dorrie, who was supposed to be helping, had opened her coat box instead and was laying an orderly row of marshmallows from one end of the bleacher to the other. Maggie said, "Here, I'll take her, poor lamb," and she bore Leroy off to the railing to admire the horses, which were just assembling at the starting gate with skittery, mincing steps. "What do horses say?" Maggie asked. "*Nicker*-nicker-nicker!" she supplied. Ira and his father returned, still arguing. Their subject now was the sheet of racing tips that Mr. Moran had purchased from a man with no teeth. "Which ones did you vote for?" Maggie asked them.

"You don't *vote*, Maggie," Ira told her. The horses took off, looking somehow quaint and toylike. They galloped past with a sound that reminded her of a flag ruffling in the wind. Then, just like that, the race was finished. "So soon!" Maggie lamented. She never could get over how quickly it all happened; there was hardly anything to watch. "Really baseball gives a better sense of time," she told the baby.

The results lit up the electric billboard: Number Four was nowhere to be seen. That struck Maggie as a relief, in a way. She wouldn't need to make any more choices. In fact, the only person who came out ahead was Mr. Moran. He had won six dollars on Number Eight, a horse his tip sheet had recommended. "See there?" he asked Ira. Daisy hadn't bet at all; she was saving for a race she felt surer of.

Maggie gave the baby to Daisy and started unpacking their lunch. "There's ham on rye, turkey on white, roast beef on whole wheat," she announced. "There's chicken salad, deviled eggs, potato salad, and cole slaw. Peaches, fresh strawberries, and melon balls. Don't forget to save room for the birthday cake." The people nearby were munching on junk food bought right there at the track. They stared curiously at the hampers, each one of which Daisy had lined with a starched checkered cloth tucked into little pleats around the edges. Maggie passed out napkins. "Where's Jesse?" she asked, searching the crowd.

"I have no idea," Fiona said. Somehow, she had ended up with Leroy again. She jiggled her sharply against her shoulder, while Leroy screwed up her face and made fussing noises. Well, Maggie could have predicted as much. You don't use such a rapid rhythm with a baby; shouldn't Fiona have learned that by now? Wouldn't simple instinct have informed her? Maggie felt an edgy little poke of irritation in the small of her back. To be fair, it wasn't Fiona who annoyed her so much as the fussing—Leroy's jagged "eh, eh." If Maggie weren't loading paper plates she could have taken over herself, but as it was, all she could do was make suggestions. "Try putting her in the stroller, Fiona. Maybe she'll fall asleep."

"She won't fall asleep; she'll just climb out again," Fiona said. "Oh, where is Jesse?"

"Daisy, go look for your brother," Maggie commanded.

"I can't; I'm eating."

"Go anyway. For goodness' sake, I can't do everything."

"Is it my fault he went off with his dumb friends some-where?" Daisy asked. "I just got started on my sandwich."

"Now listen, young lady . . . Ira?"

But Ira and his father had left again for the betting windows. Maggie said, "Oh, for— Dorrie, could you please go and hunt Jesse for me?"

"Well, but I am dealing out these here marshmallows," Dorrie said.

The marshmallows traveled in a perfect, unbroken row the length of their bleacher, like a dotted line. As a result, none of them could sit down. People kept pausing at the far end, mean-ing to take a seat, but then they saw the marshmallows and moved on. Maggie sighed. Behind her back, a bugle call floated on the clear, still air, but Maggie, facing the bleachers, went on searching the crowd for Jesse. Then Junie nudged a few of Dorrie's marshmallows out of line and sat down very suddenly, clutching her parasol with both hands. "Maggie," she mur-mured, "I am feeling just so, I don't know, all at once. . . ."

"Take a deep breath," Maggie said briskly. This happened, from time to time. "Remind yourself you're here as someone else."

"I believe I'm going to faint," Junie said, and without warn-ing she swung her spike-heeled sandals up and lay down flat upon the bleacher. The parasol remained in both her hands, ris-ing from her chest as if planted there. Dorrie rushed distractedly around her, trying to retrieve as many marshmallows as possible.

"Daisy, is that your brother up there with those people?" Maggie asked.

Daisy said, "Where?" but Fiona was quicker. She wheeled and said, "It most certainly is." Then she shrieked, "Jesse Moran! You get your ass on down here!"

Her voice was that stringy, piercing kind. Everybody stared. Maggie said, "Oh, well, I wouldn't—"

"You hear me?" Fiona shrieked, and Leroy started crying in earnest.

"There's no need to shout, Fiona," Maggie said.

Fiona said, "What?"

She glared at Maggie, ignoring the squalling baby. It was one of those moments when Maggie just wanted to back up and start over. (She had always felt paralyzed in the presence of an angry woman.) Meanwhile Jesse, who couldn't have missed hearing his name, began to thread his way toward them. Maggie said, "Oh, here he comes!"

"You're telling me not to shout at my own husband?" Fiona asked.

She was shouting even now. She had to, over the cries of the baby. Leroy's face was red, and spikes of damp hair were plastered to her forehead. She looked sort of homely, to be frank. Maggie felt an urge to walk off from this whole group, pretend they had nothing to do with her; but instead she made her voice go light and she said, "No, I only meant he wasn't that far from us, you see—"

"You meant nothing of the sort," Fiona said, squeezing the baby too tightly. "You're trying to *run* us, just like always; trying to run our lives."

"No, really, Fiona—"

"What's up?" Jesse asked breezily, arriving among them.

"Ma and Fiona are having a fight," Daisy said. She took a dainty nibble from her sandwich.

"We are not!" Maggie cried. "I merely suggested—"

"A fight?" Ira said. "What?"

He and Mr. Moran were all at once standing in the aisle behind Jesse. "What's going on here?" he asked above Leroy's cries.

Maggie told him, "Nothing's going on! For Lord's sake, all I said was—"

938

"Can't you folks be left to your own devices for even a minute?" Ira asked. "And why is Junie lying down like that? How do these things happen so *fast*?"

Unfair, unfair. To hear him talk, you would think they had such scenes every day. You would think that Ira himself was in line for the Nobel Peace Prize. "For your information," Maggie told him, "I was just standing here minding my own business—"

"You have never once in all the time I've known you managed to mind your own business," Fiona said.

"Now cool it, Fiona," Jesse said.

"And you!" Fiona screeched, turning on him. "You think this baby is just mine? How come I always get stuck with her while you go off with your buddies, answer me that!"

"Those weren't my buddies; they were only—"

"He was drinking with them too," Daisy murmured, with her eyes on her sandwich.

"Well, big deal," Jesse told her.

"Drinking from this silver flat kind of bottle that belonged to that girl."

"So what if I was, Miss Goody-Goody?"

"Now listen," Ira said. "Let's just all sit down a minute and get ahold of ourselves. We're blocking people's view."

He sat, setting an example. Then he looked behind him.

"My marshmallows!" Dorrie squawked.

"You can't leave your marshmallows here, Dorrie. No one has room to sit."

"You messed up my marshmallows!"

"I believe I'm going to be ill," Junie said, speaking upward into the spokes of her parasol.

Leroy's crying had reached the stage where she had to fight for each breath.

Ira stood up again, dusting off the seat of his pants. He said, "Now listen, folks—"

"Will you stop calling us *folks*?" Fiona demanded.

939

Ira halted, looking startled.

Maggie felt a tug on her sleeve and turned. It was Mr. Moran, who had at some point worked around behind her. He held up a ticket. "What?" she asked.

"I won."

"Won what?"

"I won that last race! My horse came in first."

"Oh, the race," she said. "Well, isn't that . . ."

But her attention veered toward Fiona, who was reeling off a list of wrongs that she seemed to have been saving up for Jesse all these months. ". . . knew from the start I'd be a fool to marry you; didn't I say so? But you were so gung-ho, you and your pacifiers and your Dr. Spock . . ."

The people in the bleachers behind them were gazing point-edly in different directions, but they sent each other meaningful glances and small, secret smiles. The Morans had turned into spectacles. Maggie couldn't bear it. She said, "Please! Can't we just sit down?"

"You and your famous cradle," Fiona told Jesse, "that you didn't build one stick of after you promised, you swore to me—"

"I never swore to you! Where do you keep coming up with this cradle business from?"

"You swore on the Bible," Fiona told him.

"Well, good God Almighty! I mean, maybe it crossed my mind once to build one, but I'd have had to be crazy to go through with it. I can see it now: Dad standing there criticizing every little hammer blow, letting me know what a hopeless clod I am, and you'd be agreeing with him just like always, I bet, by the time I was finished. No way would I let myself in for that!"

"Well, you bought the wood, didn't you?"

"What wood?"

"You bought those long wooden rods."

"Rods? For a cradle? I never bought any rods."

940

"Your mother told me—"

"How would I use rods to build a cradle?"

"Spindles, she told me."

They both looked at Maggie. Coincidentally, the baby paused just then for a deep, hiccuping breath. A bass voice rumbled over the loudspeaker, announcing that Misappropriation had been scratched.

Ira cleared his throat and said, "Are you talking about doweling rods? Those were mine."

"Ira, no," Maggie wailed, because there was still a chance they could smooth things over, if only he wouldn't insist on spelling out every boring little fact. "They were the spindles for your cradle," she told Jesse. "You already had the blueprints. Right?"

"What blueprints? All I said was—"

"If I remember correctly," Ira interrupted in his stuffy way, "those rods were purchased for the drying rack I built on the back porch. You've all seen that drying rack."

"Drying rack," Fiona said. She continued looking at Maggie.

"Oh, well," Maggie said, "this cradle business is so silly, isn't it? I mean, it's like the dime-store necklace that relatives start quarreling over after the funeral. It's just a . . . And besides, Leroy couldn't even use a cradle anymore! She's got that nice crib Ira bought."

Leroy remained quiet, still hiccuping, gazing at Maggie intently.

"I married you for that cradle," Fiona told Jesse.

"Well, that's just plain ridiculous!" Maggie said. "For a cradle! I never heard such a—"

"Maggie, enough," Ira said.

She stopped, with her mouth open.

"If you married Jesse for a cradle," Ira told Fiona, "you were sadly mistaken."

"Oh, Ira!" Maggie cried.

"Shut up, Maggie. She had no business telling you that," Ira said to Fiona. "It's Maggie's weakness: She believes it's all right to alter people's lives. She thinks the people she loves are better than they really are, and so then she starts changing things around to suit her view of them."

"That's not one bit true," Maggie said.

"But the fact is," Ira told Fiona calmly, "Jesse is not capable of following through with *anything*, not even a simple cradle. He's got some lack; I know he's my son, but he's got some lack, and you might as well face up to it. He's not a persevering kind of person. He lost that job of his a month ago and he hangs out every day with his pals instead of looking for work."

Maggie and Fiona, together, said, "What?"

"They found out he wasn't a high school graduate," Ira told them. And then, as an afterthought: "He's seeing another girl too."

Jesse said, "What are you talking about? That girl is just a friend."

"I don't know her name," Ira said, "but she belongs to a rock group called Babies in Trouble."

"We're just good friends, I tell you! That girl is Dave's girl!"

Fiona seemed to be made of china. Her face was dead white and still; her pupils were black pinpoints.

"If you knew this all along," Maggie demanded of Ira, "why didn't you say something?"

"I didn't feel right about it. I for one don't hold with changing people's worlds around," Ira said. And then (just as Maggie was getting ready to hate him) his face sagged and he dropped wearily onto the bleacher. "I shouldn't have done it now, either," he said.

He had dislodged a whole section of marshmallows, but Dorrie, who could be sensitive to atmospheres, merely bent in silence to collect them.

Fiona held out her palm. "Give me the keys," she told Jesse.

"Huh?"

"The keys to the van. Hand them over."

"Where are you going?" Jesse asked her.

"I don't know! How would I know? I just have to get out of here."

"Fiona, I only ever talked to that girl because she didn't think I was some kind of clod like everyone else seems to do. You've got to believe me, Fiona."

"The keys," Fiona said.

Ira said, "Let her have them, Jesse."

"But—"

"We'll take a bus."

Jesse reached into the rear pocket of his jeans. He brought out a cluster of keys attached to a miniature black rubber gym shoe. "So will you be at the house? Or what," he said.

"I have no idea," Fiona told him, and she snapped the keys out of his grasp.

"Well, where will you be? At your sister's?"

"Anywhere. None of your business. I don't know where. I just want to get on with my life," she said.

And she hoisted the baby higher on her hip and stalked off, leaving behind the diaper bag and the stroller and her paper plate of lunch with the potato salad turning a pathetic shade of ivory.

"She'll come around," Maggie told Jesse. Then she said, "I will never forgive you for this, Ira Moran."

She felt another tug on her sleeve and she turned. Ira's father was still holding up his ticket. "I was right to buy that tip sheet," he said. "What does Ira know about tip sheets?"

"Nothing," Maggie said furiously, and she started rewrapping Fiona's sandwich.

All around her she heard murmuring, like ripples widening across a pond:

"What'd he say?"

943

"Tip sheet."

"What'd she say?"

"Nothing."

"She did say something, I saw her lips move."

"She said, 'Nothing.' "

"But I thought I saw—"

Maggie straightened and faced the rows of people on the bleachers. "I said, 'Nothing,' is what I said," she called out clearly.

Somebody sucked in a breath. They all looked elsewhere.

It was amazing, Ira often said, how people fooled themselves into believing what they wanted to. (How Maggie fooled herself, he meant.) He said it when Maggie threatened to sue the Police Department that time they charged Jesse with Drunk and Disorderly. He said it when she swore that Spin the Cat sounded better than the Beatles. And he said it again when she refused to accept that Fiona was gone for good.

That evening after the races Maggie sat up late with Jesse, pretending to be knitting although she ripped out as much as she added. Jesse drummed his fingers on the arm of his chair. "Can't you sit still for once?" Maggie asked him, and then she said, "Maybe you should try calling her sister again."

"I already tried three times, for God's sake. They must be just letting it ring."

"Maybe you should go in person."

"That would be worse," Jesse said. "Pounding on the door while they hid inside and listened. I bet they'd be laughing and looking over at each other and making these goggly eyes."

"They wouldn't do that!"

"I guess I'll take the van back to Dave," Jesse said.

He rose to leave. Maggie didn't try to stop him, because she figured he was secretly going to the sister's place after all.

The van had been parked out front when they returned from Pimlico. For one relieved moment, everyone assumed Fiona was in the house. And the keys were on top of the bookcase just inside the door, where the family always left keys and stray gloves and notes saying when they'd be back. But there wasn't any note from Fiona. In the room she shared with Jesse, the unmade bed had a frozen look. Every hillock of the sheets appeared to have hardened. In Maggie's and Ira's room the crib was empty and desolate. However, this couldn't be a permanent absence. Nothing was packed; nothing was missing. Even Fiona's toilet articles still sat on the bureau in their travel case. "See there?" Maggie told Jesse, because he was worried too, she could tell; and she pointed to the travel case. "Oh. Right," he said, reassured. She crossed the hall to the bathroom and found the usual fleet of rubber ducks and tugboats. "You people," she said happily. Emerging, passing Jesse's room once more, she found him standing in front of the bureau with his eyes half shut and his nose buried deep in Fiona's soapbox. She understood him perfectly. Smells could bring a person back clearer than pictures, even; didn't she know that?

When the night stretched on and Jesse didn't return, she told herself that he must have found Fiona. They must be having a nice long talk. She ripped out all her garbled rows of knitting and rewound her ball of yarn and went to bed. In the dark, Ira mumbled, "Jesse back yet?"

"No, nor Fiona, either one," she said.

"Oh, well, Fiona," he said. "Fiona's gone for good."

There was a sudden clarity to his voice. It was the voice of someone talking in his sleep, which made his words seem oracular and final. Maggie felt a clean jolt of anger. Easy for *him* to say! He could toss off people without a thought.

It struck her as very significant that Ira's idea of entertainment was those interminable books about men who sailed the Atlantic absolutely alone.

He was right, though: In the morning, Fiona was still missing. Jesse came down to breakfast with that same stunned expression on his face. Maggie hated to ask, but finally she said, "Honey? You didn't find her?"

"No," he said shortly, and then he requested the marmalade in a way that shut off all further questions.

Not till that afternoon did the notion of foul play occur to her. How could they have missed it? Of course: No one traveling with an infant would leave behind all Fiona had left—the diaper bag, the stroller, the pink plastic training cup Leroy liked to drink her juice from. Someone must have kidnapped them, or worse: shot them during a street crime. The police would have to be notified this instant. She said as much to Ira, who was reading the Sunday paper in the living room. Ira didn't even look up. "Spare yourself the embarrassment, Maggie," he said quietly.

"Embarrassment?"

"She's walked out of her own free will. Don't bother the police with this."

"Ira, young mothers do not walk out with just their purses. They pack. They have to! Think," she said. "Remember all she took with her on a simple trip to Pimlico. You know what I suspect? I suspect she came back here, parked the van, carried Leroy to the grocery store for teething biscuits—I heard her say yesterday morning she was low on teething biscuits—and stepped smack into a holdup scene. You've read how robbers always choose women and children for hostages! It's more effective that way. It gets results."

Ira regarded her almost absently over the top of his paper, as if he found her just marginally interesting.

"Why, she's even left behind her soap! Her toothbrush!" she told Ira.

"Her travel case," Ira pointed out.

"Yes, and if she'd gone of her own free will—"

"Her travel case, Maggie, like she'd use in a hotel. But now she's back at, I don't know, her sister's or her mother's, where her real belongings are, and she doesn't need a travel case."

"Oh, that's nonsense," Maggie said. "And just look at her closet. It's full of clothes."

"Are you sure of that?"

"Of course. It's the first thing I checked."

"Are you sure there's nothing missing? Her favorite sweater? That jacket she's so keen on?"

Maggie considered a moment. Then she stood up and went down the hall to Jesse's room.

Jesse lay on the bed, fully dressed, with his arms folded behind his head. He glanced over at her as she entered. "Excuse me a moment," she told him, and she opened the door of his closet.

Fiona's clothes hung inside, all right, but not her windbreaker or that big striped duster she liked to wear around the house. There were only two or three skirts (she hardly ever wore skirts), a few blouses, and a ruffled dress that she'd always claimed made her look fat. Maggie spun around and went to Fiona's bureau. Jesse watched from the bed. She jerked open a drawer and found a single pair of blue jeans (artificially whitened with bleach, a process that was no longer stylish) and below them two turtlenecks from last winter and below those a pair of maternity slacks with an elastic panel in front. It was like the layers in an archaeological dig. Maggie had the fleeting fantasy that if she delved farther she would find cheerleader sweaters, then grade-school pinafores, then Fiona's baby clothes. She smoothed the layers down again and shut the drawer.

"But where would she be?" she asked Jesse.

It seemed for a long while that he wasn't going to answer. Finally, though, he said, "I guess her sister's."

"You said you didn't find her there."

"I didn't go there."

947

She thought that over. Then she said, "Oh, Jesse."

"I'll be damned if I make a fool of myself."

"Jesse, honey—"

"If I have to beg her then I'd sooner not have her," he said.

And he turned over with his face to the wall, ending the conversation.

It was two or three days afterward that Fiona's sister called. She said, "Mrs. Moran?" in that braying voice that Maggie instantly recognized. "This is Crystal Stuckey," she said. "Fiona's sister?"

"Oh, yes!"

"And I want to know if you'll be home for the next little bit so we can come by and pick up her things."

"Yes, of course, come right away," Maggie said. Because Jesse was home too, as it happened—lying on his bed again. She went to find him as soon as she'd hung up. "That was Fiona's sister," she said. "Christina?"

He slid his eyes toward her. "Crystal," he said.

"Crystal. They're coming to get her things."

He sat up slowly and swung his boots over the side of the bed.

"I'll go out and do some shopping," Maggie told him.

"What? No, wait."

"You'll have the place to yourselves."

"Wait, don't go. How will I—? Maybe we'll need you."

"Need me? What for?"

"I don't want to say the wrong thing to her," he said.

"Honey, I'm sure you won't say the wrong thing."

"Ma. Please," he said.

So she stayed, but she went to her own room, out of the way. Her room was at the front of the house, which was why, when a car drove up, she was able to draw aside the curtain and see who was coming. It was Crystal and a beefy young man, no doubt the famous boyfriend Fiona was always referring to.

That was whom Crystal had meant by "we"; Fiona was nowhere in evidence. Maggie dropped the curtain. She heard the doorbell ring; she heard Jesse shout, "Coming!" and clatter down the stairs two at a time. Then, after a pause, she heard a brief mumble. The door slammed shut again. Had he kicked them out, or what? She lifted the curtain once more and peered down, but it was Jesse she saw, not the guests—Jesse tearing off down the sidewalk, shrugging himself into his black leather jacket as he went. In the downstairs hall, Crystal called, "Mrs. Moran?"—her voice less braying now, more tentative.

"Just a minute," Maggie said.

Crystal and her boyfriend had brought cartons from the liquor store, and Maggie helped fill them. Or tried to help. She slid a blouse from a hanger and folded it slowly, regretfully, but Crystal said, "You can just give those blouses to the veterans. Don't bother with nothing synthetic, Fiona told me. She's living back at home now and she hasn't got much closet room."

Maggie said, "Ah," and laid the blouse aside. She felt a twinge of envy. Wouldn't it be wonderful to save only what was first-class and genuine and pure, and walk out on everything else! When Crystal and the boyfriend drove off, all they left behind was the chaff.

Then Jesse found a job at a record store and stopped lying around on his bed so much of the time; and Daisy and the enchanted little girls returned to Mrs. Perfect. Maggie was on her own again. Just like that, she was deprived of all the gossip and eventfulness and the peeks into other households that children can provide. It was then she started making her spy trips to Cartwheel, not that those were ever very satisfying; or sometimes after work she would choose to walk to the frame shop rather than continue sitting in an empty house. But then she would wonder why she had come, for Ira was usually too busy to talk with her and anyhow, he said, he'd be home in just a couple of hours, wouldn't he? What was it she was hanging about for?

So she would climb the stairs to his family's apartment, and she'd pass a bit of time listening to his sisters recount the latest soap opera or his father list his aches and pains. In addition to his so-called weak heart, Mr. Moran suffered from arthritis and his vision was failing. He was over eighty, after all. The men in that family had traditionally fathered their children so late in life that when Mr. Moran talked about his great-grandfather, he was referring to a man who'd been born in the 1700s. That had never struck Maggie before, but now it seemed positively creepy. What an elderly, faltering atmosphere she lived in! Her mornings at the nursing home, her afternoons at the Morans', her evenings with Ira's solitaire games . . . She drew her sweater more tightly around her and clucked at news of her father-in-law's indigestion. "Used to be I could eat anything," he told her. "What has happened here?" He peered at her with his glintless eyes, as if expecting an answer. Lately his upper lids had developed heavy, pouched folds; his Cherokee grandmother emerged more clearly year by year. "Rona never had the remotest inkling," he told Maggie. Rona was Ira's mother. "She died before she went through all this," he said. "Wrinkles and gnarls and creaky joints and heartburn—she missed out on it."

"Well, but she had other pains," Maggie reminded him. "Maybe worse ones."

"It's like she didn't live a real life," he said, not listening. "I mean all of life, the whole messy kit and caboodle that comes at the end."

He sounded peevish; he seemed to think his wife had got away with something. Maggie clucked again and patted his hand. It felt the way she imagined an eagle's foot would feel.

Eventually she would go back downstairs to Ira, coax him to close shop a few minutes early and walk her home. He would slouch along in a kind of dark fog, something inward-turned in his gaze. When they passed the Larkin sisters' house, Maggie always glanced toward it and then looked quickly away. In the old days, wheeling Leroy homeward in her stroller, they would find a rocking horse waiting hopefully on the Larkins's front porch. It would have appeared by magic at the top of the steps where earlier there'd been nothing: a tiny, faded wooden animal with a bashful smile and long black lowered lashes. But now there was no sign of it; even those two ancient ladies knew somehow that the Morans hadn't managed to keep their family together.

Oh, how would Fiona summon the constant vigilance that child required? It wasn't merely a matter of feeding her and changing her. Leroy was one of those dauntless babies who fling themselves brazenly off stair landings and chair edges, trusting someone will be there to catch them. Fiona was nowhere near alert enough. And she had hardly any sense of smell, Maggie had noticed. Why, Maggie could scent a fire before it started, almost. Maggie could walk through a mall and unerringly detect the smell of foods improperly handled—a musty, etherish sharpness not unlike the smell of a child with a fever. Everybody else would be oblivious, but, "Stop!" Maggie would call, holding up a palm as the others drifted toward a sandwich stand. "Not there! Anywhere but there!"

She had so much to offer, if only someone would take it.

It seemed pointless to cook a real supper now. Jesse was always out and Daisy most often ate at Mrs. Perfect's, or if forced to eat at home would sulk so that it wasn't worth having her around. So Maggie just heated a couple of frozen dinners or a can of soup. Sometimes she didn't even do that. One evening, when she had sat two hours at the kitchen table staring into space instead of making the trip to the frame shop, Ira walked in and said, "What's for supper?" and she said, "I can't deal with supper! I mean look at this!" and she waved at the can of soup in front of her. "Two and three quarters servings," she read out. "What do they expect, I have two and three quarters people to feed? Or three, and I'll just give one of them less? Or maybe I'm supposed to save the rest for another meal, but do you know how long it would take me to come out even? First I'd have an extra three quarters of a serving and then six quarters and then nine. I'd have to open four cans of soup before I had leftovers that weren't in fractions. Four cans, I tell you! Four cans of the same single flavor!"

She started crying, letting the tears roll down her cheeks luxuriously. She felt the way she had felt as a child when she knew she was behaving unreasonably, knew she was shocking the grownups and acting like a perfect horror, but all at once *wanted* to behave unreasonably and even took some pleasure in it.

Ira might have turned on his heel and walked out; she was half expecting that. Instead, he sank into the chair across from her. He put his elbows on the table and lowered his head into his hands.

Maggie stopped crying. She said, "Ira?"

He didn't answer.

"Ira, what is it?" she asked him.

She rose and bent over him and hugged him. She squatted next to him and tried to peer up into his face. Had something happened to his father? To one of his sisters? Was he just so disgusted with Maggie that he couldn't endure it? What *was* it?

The answer seemed to arrive through his back—through the ripple of knobby vertebrae down his C-shaped, warm, thin back. Her fingers felt the answer first.

He was just as sad as Maggie was, and for just the same reasons. He was lonely and tired and lacking in hope and his son had not turned out well and his daughter didn't think much of him, and he still couldn't figure where he had gone wrong.

He let his head fall against her shoulder. His hair was thick and rough, strung through with threads of gray that she had never noticed before, that pierced her heart in a way that her own few gray hairs never had. She hugged him tightly and nuzzled her face against his cheekbone. She said, "It will be all right. It will be all right."

And it was, eventually. Don't ask her why. Well, for one thing, Jesse really liked his new job, and he seemed bit by bit to recover some of his old spirit. And then Daisy announced at last that Mrs. Perfect was "too tennis-y" and returned to her place in the family. And Maggie gave up her spy trips, as if Leroy and Fiona had been put to rest in her mind somehow. But none of those reasons was the most important one. It was more to do with Ira, she believed—that moment with Ira in the kitchen. Although they never referred to it afterward, and Ira didn't act any different, and life continued just the same as always.

She straightened in her seat and peered through the windshield, looking for the others. They should be about ready by now. Yes, here came Leroy, just backing out of the house with a suitcase bigger than she was. Ira thudded among things in the trunk and whistled a cheerful tune. "King of the Road," that's what he was whistling. Maggie got out to open the rear door. It seemed to her now that unknowingly, she'd been aiming ever since she woke up this morning toward this single purpose: bringing Leroy and Fiona home at last.

3

The way Mrs. Stuckey's car was parked behind theirs, they had just enough room to maneuver around it. Or so Ira claimed. Maggie thought he was wrong. "You could manage if the mailbox wasn't there," she said, "but it is there, and you are going to hit it when you veer out."

"Only if I were deaf, dumb, and blind," Ira said.

In the back seat, Fiona gave a small sigh.

"Look," Ira told Maggie. "You go stand beside the mailbox. Let me know when I come close. All I have to do is swing into the yard a few feet, take a sharp right back onto the driveway—"

"I'm not going to be responsible for that! You'll hit the mailbox and blame me."

"Maybe we should just ask Mom to move the Maverick," Fiona suggested.

Maggie said, "Oh, well," and Ira said, "No, I'm sure we can make it."

Neither one of them wanted Mrs. Stuckey marching out all put-upon.

"All right, then you get behind the wheel," Ira told Maggie, "and I'll direct you."

"Then I'll be the one to hit the mailbox, and I'll still get blamed."

"Maggie. There's a good ten feet between the mailbox and the Maverick. So once you're past the Maverick you just nip back onto the driveway and you're free and clear. I'll tell you when."

Maggie thought that over. She said, "Promise you won't yell if I hit the mailbox?"

"You won't hit the mailbox."

"Promise, Ira."

"Lord above! Fine, I promise."

"And you won't look up at the heavens, or make that hissing noise through your teeth—"

"Maybe I should just go get Mom," Fiona said.

"No, no, this is a cinch," Ira told her. "Any imbecile could handle it; believe me."

Maggie didn't like the sound of that.

Ira climbed out of the car and went to stand by the mailbox. Maggie slid over on the seat. She gripped the steering wheel with both hands and checked the rearview mirror. It was angled wrong, set for Ira's height instead of hers, and she reached up to adjust it. The top of Leroy's head flashed toward her, gleaming dully like the back of a watch case, followed by Ira's lean figure with his elbows cocked and his hands jammed into his rear pockets. The mailbox was a little Quonset hut beside him.

The driver's seat had been set for Ira also, way too far back, but Maggie figured it wouldn't matter for such a short distance. She shifted into reverse. Ira called, "Okay, bring her hard to your left . . ."

How come he always referred to difficult tasks as feminine? This car was not a she until it had to perform some complicated maneuver. It was the same for stubborn screws and tight jar lids, and for bulky pieces of furniture as they were being moved.

She swung onto the packed dirt yard and around the Maverick, proceeding perhaps a bit too fast but still in control. Then she reached with her foot for the brake. There wasn't one. Or there was, but it was positioned wrong, closer than she had expected considering that the seat was moved back. Her foot hit the shaft instead of the pedal and the car raced on unimpeded. Ira shouted, "What the—?" Maggie, with her gaze still fixed on the rearview mirror, saw the blur as he dove for cover. *Whap!* the mailbox said when she hit it. Leroy said, "Golly," in an awed tone of voice.

Maggie shifted into Park and poked her head out the window. Ira was hauling himself up from the dirt. He dusted off his hands. He said, "You just had to prove you were right about that mailbox, Maggie, didn't you."

"You promised, Ira!"

"Left taillight is smashed all to hell," he said, bending to examine it. He prodded something. There was a clinking sound. Maggie pulled her head in and faced forward.

"He promised he wouldn't say a word," she told Fiona and Leroy. "Watch how he goes back on that."

Fiona absently patted Leroy's bare knee.

"Smashed to smithereens," Ira called.

"You promised you wouldn't make a fuss!"

He grunted; she saw that he was righting the mailbox. From here, it didn't even look dented. "I don't suppose we need to tell your mother about this," Maggie said to Fiona.

"She already knows," Leroy said. "She's watching from the house."

It was true there was a suspicious slant to one of the venetian blind slats. Maggie said, "Oh, this day has seemed just so . . . I don't know . . ." and she slid down in her seat till she was more or less sitting on her shoulder blades.

Then Ira appeared in the window. "Try your lights," he told her.

"Hmm?"

"Your lights. I want to see if she works or not."

There he went with that "she" again. Maggie reached out wearily, not bothering to sit up straight, and pulled the knob.

"Just as I thought," Ira called from the rear. "No left taillight."

"I don't want to hear about it," Maggie told the ceiling.

Ira reappeared at the window and motioned for her to move over. "We'll be ticketed for this—what do you bet?" he said, opening the door and getting in.

"I really couldn't care less," she said.

"Late as we're running now," he said (another reproach), "it'll be dark before we're halfway home, and the state police are going to nail us for driving without a taillight."

"Stop off and get it fixed, then," Maggie said.

"Oh, well, you know those highway service stations," Ira told her. He shifted gears, pulled forward a little, and then backed smoothly out of the driveway. It didn't seem to cause him any difficulty whatsoever. "They charge an arm and a leg for something I could pick up almost free at Rudy's Auto Supply," he said. "I'm just going to take my chances."

"You could always explain your wife was a blithering idiot."

He didn't argue with that.

As they started down the road, Maggie glanced at the mailbox, which was standing at a slight tilt but otherwise seemed fine. She twisted in her seat till she was looking at Fiona and Leroy—their pale, staring faces unsettlingly alike. "You two all right?" she asked them.

"Sure," Leroy answered for both of them. She was hugging her baseball glove to her chest.

Ira said, "Bet you didn't expect us to have a wreck before we'd left your driveway, did you?"

"Didn't expect you to go asking for a wreck, either," Fiona told him.

Ira glanced over at Maggie with his eyebrows raised.

By now the sun had dropped out of sight and the sky had lost its color. All the pastures were turning up their undersides in a sudden breeze. Leroy said, "How long is this trip going to take us anyhow?"

"Just an hour or so," Fiona told her. "You remember how far it is to Baltimore."

Maggie said, "Leroy remembers Baltimore?"

"From visiting my sister."

"Oh. Of course," Maggie said.

She watched the scenery for a while. Something about the fading light gave the little houses a meek, defeated look. Finally she forced herself to ask, "How *is* your sister, Fiona?"

"She's fine, considering," Fiona said. "You knew she lost her husband."

"I didn't realize she was married, even."

"Well, no, I guess you wouldn't," Fiona said. "She married her boyfriend? Avery? And he died not six weeks later in a construction accident."

"Oh, poor Crystal," Maggie said. "What is happening here? Everyone's losing their husbands. Did I tell you we've just come from Max Gill's funeral?"

"Yes, but I don't think I knew him," Fiona said.

"You must have known him! He was married to my friend Serena that I went to school with. The Gills. I'm positive you met them."

"Well, those people were old, though," Fiona said. "Or not old, maybe, but you know. Crystal and Avery, they were barely back from their honeymoon. When you've been married only six weeks everything is still perfect."

And later it is not, was her implication. Which Maggie couldn't argue with. Still, it saddened her to realize they all took such a thing for granted.

A stop sign loomed ahead and Ira slowed and then turned onto Route One. After the country roads they had been traveling, Route One seemed more impressive. Trucks were streaming toward them, a few with their headlights already on. Someone had set a hand-lettered signboard on the porch of a little café: SUPPER NOW BEING SERVED. Good farm food, no doubt—corn on the cob and biscuits. Maggie said, "I suppose we should stop for groceries on the way home. Leroy, are you starved?"

Leroy nodded emphatically.

"I haven't had a thing but chips and pretzels since morning," Maggie said.

"That and a beer in broad daylight," Ira reminded her.

Maggie pretended not to hear him. "Leroy," she said, "tell me what your favorite food is."

Leroy said, "Oh, I don't know."

"There must be something."

Leroy poked a fist into the palm of her baseball glove.

"Hamburgers? Hot dogs?" Maggie asked. "Charcoaled steaks? Or how about crabs?"

Leroy said, "Crabs in their shells, you mean? Ick!"

Maggie felt suddenly at a loss.

"She's partial to fried chicken," Fiona said. "She asks Mom to fix that all the time. Don't you, Leroy?"

"Fried chicken! Perfect," Maggie said. "We'll pick up the makings on our way into town. Won't that be nice?"

Leroy remained silent, and no wonder; Maggie knew how chirpy and artificial she sounded. An old person, trying too hard. But if only Leroy could see that Maggie was still young underneath, just peering out from behind an older face mask!

Now all at once Ira cleared his throat. Maggie tensed. Ira said, "Um, Fiona, Leroy . . . you heard we're taking Daisy to college tomorrow."

"Yes, Maggie told me," Fiona said. "I can't believe it: eentsy little Daisy."

"I mean, we two are going to be driving her. We're starting early in the morning."

"Not *that* early," Maggie said quickly.

"Well, eight or nine o'clock, Maggie."

"What's your point?" Fiona asked Ira. "You don't think we ought to be visiting?"

Maggie said, "Good heavens, no! He didn't mean that at all."

"Well, it sounded to me like he did," Fiona said.

Ira said, "I just wanted to be sure you knew what you were getting into. That it would have to be such a short stay, I mean."

"That's no problem, Ira," Maggie told him. "If she wants she can go on over to her sister's in the morning."

"Well, fine then, but it's getting dark and we're not even halfway home. I would think—"

"Maybe we better just stop right here and go on back where we came from," Fiona said.

"Oh, no, Fiona!" Maggie cried. "We had this all settled!"

"I can't remember now why I said we'd come in the first place," Fiona said. "Lord! What must I have been thinking of?"

Maggie unbuckled her seat belt and twisted around so she was facing Fiona. "Fiona, please," she said. "It's only for a little while, and it's been so long since we've seen Leroy. I've got all these things I want to show her. I want her to meet Daisy and I was planning to take her by the Larkin sisters'; they won't believe how she's grown."

"Who're the Larkin sisters?" Leroy asked.

"These two old ladies; they used to set out their rocking horse for you to ride on."

Fiona said, "I don't remember that."

"We'd pass by their porch and it would be empty, and then when we turned around to come home the horse would be sitting there waiting."

"I don't remember a thing about it," Fiona said.

Leroy said, "Me neither."

"Well, of course *you* wouldn't," Fiona told her. "You were just a baby. You didn't live there hardly any time at all."

This struck Maggie as unfair. She said, "Well, goodness, she was nearly a year old when you left, Fiona."

"She was not! She was barely seven months."

"That's not right; she had to have been, oh, eight months at least. If you left in September—"

"Seven months, eight months, what's the difference?" Ira asked. "Why make a federal case of it?" He found Leroy's face in the mirror and said, "I bet you don't remember how your grandma tried to teach you to say 'Daddy,' either."

"I did?" Maggie asked.

"It was going to be a surprise for his birthday," Ira told Leroy. "She would clap her hands and you were supposed to say 'Daddy' on cue. But when she clapped her hands all you'd do was laugh. You thought it was some kind of game."

Maggie tried to picture that. Why did her memories never coincide with Ira's? Instead they seemed to dovetail—one moment his to recall and the next hers, as if they had agreed to split their joint life between them. (Illogically, she always worried about whether she had behaved right during those moments she had forgotten.)

"So did it work, or not?" Leroy was asking Ira.

"Work?"

"Did I learn to say 'Daddy'?"

"Well, no, actually," Ira said. "You were way too little to be talking yet."

"Oh."

Leroy seemed to be digesting that. Then she sat forward so she was practically nose to nose with Maggie. Her eyes had darker blue specks in them, as if even they were freckled. "I am going to get to see him, aren't I?" she said. "He's not giving a concert or anything, is he?"

"Who?" Maggie asked, although of course she knew.

"My . . . Jesse."

"Well, certainly you are. You'll see him at supper after he

961

gets off work. He loves fried chicken, just like you. It must be genetic."

"The thing of it is—" Ira began.

Maggie said, "What do you like for dessert, Leroy?"

"The thing of it is," Ira said, "this is Saturday night. What if Jesse has other plans and he can't make supper?"

"But he *can* make supper, Ira; I already told you that."

"Or if he has to leave right after. I mean what are we doing here, Maggie? We don't have any toys anymore or any sports equipment and our TV is on the blink. We don't have anything to keep a child occupied. And would you please face forward and fasten your seat belt? You're making me nervous."

"I'm just trying to figure out what to buy for dessert," Maggie said. But she turned around and reached for her seat belt. "Your daddy's favorite dessert is mint chocolate chip ice cream," she told Leroy.

"Oh, mine too," Leroy said.

Fiona said, "What are you talking about? You hate mint chocolate chip."

"I love it," Leroy told her.

"You absolutely do not!"

"Yes, I do, Ma. It was only when I was little I didn't like it."

"Well, you must have been little just last week, then, missy."

Maggie said hastily, "What other flavors do you like, Leroy?"

"Well, fudge ripple, for instance," Leroy said.

"Oh, what a coincidence! Jesse is crazy about fudge ripple."

Fiona rolled her eyes. Leroy said, "Really? I think fudge ripple is just excellent."

"I have seen you go without any dessert whatsoever if the only choice was mint chocolate chip ice cream," Fiona told Leroy.

"You don't know every little thing about me!" Leroy cried.

Fiona said, "Geeze, Leroy," and slumped down low in her seat with her arms tightly folded.

962

They were in Maryland now, and Maggie imagined that the country here looked different—more luxurious. The hillsides, emptied of livestock, had turned a deep, perfect green, and in the faded light the long white fences gave off a moony glimmer. Ira was whistling "Sleepytime Gal." Maggie couldn't think why, for a second. Did it signify he was tired, or what? But then she realized he must still have his mind on Leroy's baby days. That was the song they used to sing her to sleep with—he and Maggie, harmonizing. Maggie leaned her head against the back of the seat and silently followed the lyrics as he whistled.

When you're a stay-at-home, play-at-home, eight-o'clock
Sleepytime gal . . .

All at once she looked down at her wrist and saw that she wore two watches. One was her regular watch, a little Timex, and the other was a big old chunky man's watch with a wide leather band. In fact, it belonged to her father, but it had been lost or broken years ago. The face was a rectangle, pinkish, and the numerals were a pale blue that would glow in the dark. She cupped her hand over her wrist and bent close, making a little cave of darkness so she could see the numbers light up. Her fingers smelled of bubble gum. Beside her, Serena said, "Just another five minutes, that's all I ask. If nothing happens by then, I promise we can go."

Maggie raised her head and stared through the leaves at the two stone lions across the street. Between them lay a white sidewalk, curving across an immaculate lawn and arriving finally at a stately brick colonial house, and within that house lived the man who was Serena's father. The front door was the kind without a window, without even those tiny glass panes that are placed too high to be useful. Maggie wondered how Serena could stare so intently at something so blank and ungiving. They were crouched uncomfortably among the twisted branches of a rhododendron bush. Maggie said, "That's what you told me half an hour ago. No one's going to come."

Serena laid a hand on her arm, hushing her. The door was swinging open. Mr. Barrett stepped out and then turned back to say something. His wife appeared, tugging at her gloves. She wore a slim brown dress with long sleeves, and Mr. Barrett's suit was almost the same shade of brown. Neither Maggie nor Serena had ever seen him in anything but a suit, not even on weekends. He was like a dollhouse doll, Maggie thought—one of those jointed plastic figures with the clothes painted on, nonremovable, and a clean-cut, anonymous face. He shut the door and took his wife's elbow and they moved down the side-walk, their heels gritty-sounding. When they passed between the stone lions they seemed to be looking directly at Maggie and Serena; Maggie could see the needles of silver in Mr. Barrett's crew cut. But his expression told her nothing, and neither did his wife's. They turned sharply to their left and headed toward a long blue Cadillac parked at the curb. Serena let her breath out. Maggie felt a sense of frustration that was almost suffocating. How sealed off these people were! You could study them all day and still not know them. (Or any other married couple either, maybe.) There were moments—the first time they had made love, say, or say a conversation they'd once had when one of them woke up frightened in the middle of the night—that nobody else in the world had any inkling of.

Maggie turned to Serena and said, "Oh, Serena, I'm so sorry for your loss." Serena wore her red funeral dress and she was blotting her tears on the fringe of her black shawl. "Dear heart, I am so sorry," Maggie said, and when she woke up, she was crying too. She thought she was home in bed and Ira was asleep beside her, his breath as steady as tires hissing past on a pavement and his warm bare arm supporting her head, but that was the back of the car seat she felt. She sat up and brushed at her eyes with her fingertips.

The light had slipped yet another notch downward into dusk and they had reached that long, tangled commercial stretch just above Baltimore. Blazing signs streaked by, HI-Q PLUMBING SUPPLIES and CECIL'S GRILL and EAT EAT EAT. Ira was just a gray profile, and when Maggie turned to see Leroy and Fiona she found all the color washed out of them except for what flashed across their faces from the neon. "I must have been asleep," she told them, and they nodded. She asked Ira, "How much further?"

"Oh, another fifteen minutes or so. We're already inside the Beltway."

"Don't forget we need to stop at a grocery store."

She was cross with herself for missing out on part of the conversation. (Or hadn't there been any? That would be worse.) Her head felt cottony and nothing seemed completely real. They passed a house with a lighted, glassed-in porch on which drum sets were displayed, smaller drums stacked on top of larger, some gold-spangled like a woman's lamé evening gown and all of them glittering with chrome, and she wondered if she were dreaming again. She turned to follow the house with her eyes. The drums grew smaller but stayed eerily bright, like fish in an aquarium.

"I had the weirdest dream," she said after a moment.

"Was I in it?" Leroy wanted to know.

"Not that I can remember. But you might have been."

"Last week my friend Valerie dreamed I had died," Leroy said.

"Ooh, don't even say such a thing!"

"She dreamed I got run over by a tractor trailer," Leroy said with satisfaction.

Maggie swiveled to catch Fiona's eye. She wanted to assure her that such a dream meant nothing, or maybe she wanted the assurance for herself. But Fiona wasn't listening. She was gazing at the clutter of convenience stores and pizza parlors.

"Mighty Value Supermarket," Ira said. He flicked his left turn signal on.

Maggie said, "Mighty what? I never heard of it."

"It's handy, is what counts," Ira told her. He was delayed by a stream of oncoming traffic, but finally he found an opening and darted across the street and into a lot littered with abandoned shopping carts. He parked beside a panel truck and switched off the engine.

Leroy said she wanted to come too. Maggie said, "Well, of course," and then Ira, who had just started to slouch down behind the wheel, straightened and opened his door as if he'd been planning to go with them all along. This made Maggie smile. (Don't try and tell *her* he didn't care about his grandchild!) Fiona said, "Well, I certainly don't want to sit here by myself," and she stepped out of the car to follow them. She had never been fond of grocery shopping, as Maggie recalled.

The Mighty Value turned out to be one of those vast, cold, white, shiny places with rank upon rank of checkout counters, most of them closed. Some syrupy love song was playing over the loudspeaker. Against her will, Maggie slowed down, keeping time with the music. She drifted past the fruits and vegetables, dreamily swinging her pocketbook, while the others went ahead. Leroy took a run with an empty cart and then hopped on the back and coasted until she caught up with Ira, who had already reached the poultry counter. He turned and smiled at her. From Maggie's angle his profile looked sharp and wolfish—hungry, really. It was something about the way he jutted his face toward Leroy. Maggie bypassed Fiona and arrived next to him. She slipped her arm through his and lightly brushed her cheek against his shoulder.

"Dark meat or white?" Ira was asking Leroy.

"Dark," Leroy said promptly. "Me and Ma like drumsticks."

"Us too," Ira told her, and he picked out a pack and dropped it into her cart.

"And sometimes me and Ma eat thighs, but we don't think wings are worth the bother," Leroy said.

"Me and Ma" this, "me and Ma" that—how long had it been since Maggie herself was so central to anyone's world? And this "Ma" was only Fiona, fragile-boned Fiona sashaying up the aisle in her cut-off shorts.

Humming along with the loudspeaker music, Ira placed a pack of thighs on top of the drumsticks in the cart. "Now for the ice cream," he said. Leroy coasted away on the cart and Maggie and Ira followed. Maggie still had her arm linked through Ira's. Fiona trailed behind.

In the freezer section they had no trouble deciding on fudge ripple, but then there were so many different fudge ripples to choose from: Mighty Value's house brand and the standard brands and then the fancy, foreign-sounding brands that Ira called "designer desserts." He was opposed to designer desserts on principle; he wanted to get the Mighty Value. Fiona, who had discovered the Hair Care section, offered no opinion, but Leroy said that she and Ma had always favored Breyer's. And Maggie voted to go all out and choose something foreign. They could have discussed it forever, except that by now the loudspeaker was playing "Tonight You Belong to Me," and halfway through the song Ira began muttering along with it. " 'Way down,' " he rumbled absently, " 'by the stream . . .' " So then Maggie couldn't resist chiming in on that airy little soprano part: " 'How sweet, it will seem . . .' "

It started as a spoof, but it developed into a real production. " 'Once more, just to dream, in the moonlight!' " Their voices braided together on the chorus and then sailed apart, only to reunite and twine around each other once again. Fiona forgot the box of hair dye she was studying; Leroy clasped her hands admiringly under her chin; an old woman paused in the aisle to smile at them. It was the old woman who brought Maggie back to earth. All at once she imagined some deception in this

967

scene, some lie that she and Ira were collaborating in with their compliant harmonizing and the romantic gaze they trained upon each other. She broke off in the middle of a solo line. "Patience and Prudence," she informed Leroy briskly. "Nineteen fifty-seven."

"Fifty-six," Ira said.

Maggie said, "Whatever."

They turned their attention back to the ice cream.

In the end they decided on Breyer's, with chocolate sauce from the shelf above the freezer. "Hershey's chocolate sauce, or Nestlé's?" Ira asked.

"I'll leave it up to you two."

"Or here's a Mighty Value brand. What do you say we go for that?"

"Just not Brown Cow," Leroy told him. "I can't abide Brown Cow."

"Definitely not Brown Cow," Ira said.

"Brown Cow smells like candle wax," Leroy told Maggie.

Maggie said, "Ah." She looked down at Leroy's pointy little face and smiled.

Fiona asked Maggie, "Have you ever considered using a mousse?"

"A what?"

"A styling mousse. On your hair."

"Oh, on my hair," Maggie said. She had thought they were talking about some kind of ice-cream sauce. "Why, no, I don't believe I have."

"A lot of our beauticians recommend it."

Was Fiona recommending it to Maggie? Or maybe she was only speaking generally. "Just what would it do for a person?" Maggie asked.

"Well, in your case it would give your hair a little, I don't know, a little shape or something. It would kind of organize it."

968

"I'll buy some," Maggie decided.

She picked up a silvery container, along with a bottle of Affinity shampoo since she still had that coupon. (*Brings back the fullness that time has taken away,* a display card promised.) Then they all went to the express lane, rushed along by Maggie because it was after six, according to her watch, and she had told Jesse six-thirty. Ira said, "Do you have enough money? I could go get the car while you're paying."

She nodded, and he left them. Leroy laid their purchases neatly on the counter. The customer in front of them was buying nothing but breads. Rye bread, white bread, biscuits, whole wheat rolls. Maybe he was trying to fatten up his wife. Say he was the jealous type, and his wife was very thin and beautiful. The customer departed, taking his breads with him. Leroy said, "Double bags, please," in a bossy, experienced voice. The boy at the cash register grunted without looking. He was muscular and good-looking, deeply tanned, and he wore a gold razor blade on a chain inside the open collar of his shirt. What on earth could that mean? He rang up their items swiftly, his fingers stabbing the keys. Last came the shampoo. Maggie dug through her purse for the coupon and handed it to him. "Here," she said, "this is for you."

He took it and turned it over. He read it narrowly, not quite moving his lips. Then he gave it back to her. He said, "Well, uh, thanks," and then, "That'll be sixteen forty-three."

Maggie felt confused, but she counted out the money and picked up the bag. As they left the register she asked Fiona, "Does Mighty Value not accept coupons, or what?"

"Coupons? I wouldn't know," Fiona said.

"Maybe it's expired," Maggie said. She shifted her grocery bag in order to peer at the expiration date. But the print was covered over at right angles by Durwood Clegg's heavy blue script: *Hold me close, hold me tight, make me thrill with delight . . .*

Maggie's face grew hot. She said, "Well! Of all the conceit!"

"Pardon?" Fiona asked, but Maggie didn't answer. She screwed up the coupon and dropped it into the grocery bag.

Outside, it was much darker now. The air was a deep, transparent blue and insects were flitting around the lights high above the parking lot. Ira leaned against the car by the curb. "You want to put the groceries in the trunk?" he asked Maggie, but she said, "No, I'll just hold them." She suddenly felt old and weary. It seemed they would never reach home. She got into the car and sat down hard, with the grocery bag slumped any which way on her knees.

St. Michael the Archangel. Charlie's Fine Liquors. Used-car dealers, one after the other. Gatch Memorial Church. Dead Man's Fingers Crab House. HAPPY HOUR NITELY, with red and blue neon bubbles fizzing above a neon cocktail glass. Cemeteries and shabby frame houses and fast-food restaurants and empty playgrounds. They took a right off Belair Road—finally, finally leaving Route One—and headed down their own street. The frame houses grew more numerous. Their windows were squares of yellow light, some gauzy with curtains and some fully exposed, revealing ornate decorative lamps or china figurines meticulously centered on the sills. For no good reason, Maggie was reminded of rides she had taken with Ira during their courtship, driving past houses where every other couple in the world, it seemed, had a space to be alone in. What she would have given, back then, for even the smallest of those houses, even just four walls and a bed! She felt a sweet, sad fullness in her chest now, remembering that long-ago ache.

They passed the Seeing Eye Palmistry Parlor, really just a private home with a sign propped in the living room window. A girl was sitting out on the steps, maybe waiting her turn; she had a small, heart-shaped face and she was dressed all in black except for her purple suede shoes, which showed up clearly in the light from the porch. A man trudged down the sidewalk with a little girl riding his shoulders and clutching two handfuls of his hair. It seemed the scenery had grown more intimate, more specific. Maggie turned toward Leroy and said, "I don't suppose any of this is familiar."

"Oh, I've seen it," Leroy said.

"You have?"

"Only in passing," Fiona corrected her quickly.

"When was that?"

Leroy looked at Fiona, who said, "We might have driven by here once or twice."

Maggie said, "Is that so."

In front of their own house, Ira parked. It was one of those houses that appear to be mostly front porch, at least from the street—squat and low-browed, not at all impressive, as Maggie was the first to admit. She wished at least the lights were on. That would have made it seem more welcoming. But every window was dark. "Well!" she said, too heartily. She opened her door and got out of the car, clutching the groceries. "Come on in, everyone!"

There was something befuddled about the way they milled around on the sidewalk. They had been traveling for too long. When Ira started up the steps, he accidentally banged Fiona's suitcase against the railing, and he fumbled awhile with the key before he got the door unlocked.

They entered the musty, close darkness of the front hallway. Ira flipped on the light. Maggie called, "Daisy?" without a hope that Daisy would answer. Clearly the house was deserted. She shifted the grocery bag to her left hip and picked up the notepad that lay on top of the bookcase. *Gone to say goodbye to Lavinia,* Daisy's precise italics read. "She's at Mrs. Perfect's," Maggie told Ira. "Well, she'll be back! How long can it take to say goodbye? She'll be back in no time!"

This was all for Leroy's benefit, to show that Daisy really existed—that there was more to this house than old people.

Leroy was circling the hallway, with her baseball glove

tucked under one arm. She was squinting up at the photographs that covered the walls. "Who's that?" she asked, pointing to one.

Ira as a young father stood in dappled sunlight, awkwardly holding a baby. "That's your grandpa, holding your daddy," Maggie told her.

Leroy said, "Oh," and moved on at once. Probably she had hoped it was Jesse holding Leroy. Maggie cast her eyes around the room to see if she could locate such a picture. You could hardly make out the wallpaper pattern for all the photos that hung here, each framed professionally by Ira and each mat and molding different, like a sample of something. There was Jesse as a toddler, as a little boy on a scooter, as a thumbtack-sized face among rows of other faces in fifth grade. But no picture of Jesse as a grownup, Maggie realized; not even as a teenager. And certainly not as a father. They had run out of wall space by then. Besides, Maggie's mother was always saying how trashy it was to display one's family photographs anywhere but a bedroom.

Fiona was pushing her suitcase toward the stairs, leaving two long thin scratches on the floorboards behind her. "Oh, don't bother with that," Maggie told her. "Ira will carry it up for you later."

How must Fiona feel, returning after so long—walking across the porch where she'd decided to keep her baby, passing through the front door that she had so often slammed out of in a huff? She looked drawn and dispirited. The sudden light had crumpled the skin around her eyes. She abandoned her suitcase and pointed to a photo high on the wall. "There I happen to be," she told Leroy. "In case you're interested."

She meant her bridal photo. Maggie had forgotten that. A wedding present from Crystal, who had brought a camera to the ceremony, it showed a coltish young girl in a wrinkled dress. The frame was a black plastic diploma frame that must have come from Woolworth's. Leroy studied the photo without expression. Then she moved into the living room, where Ira was switching on lamps.

Maggie took the groceries out to the kitchen, with Fiona close behind. "So where is he?" Fiona asked in a low voice.

"Well, he's probably . . ." Maggie said. She flicked on the overhead light and glanced at the clock. "I told him we'd eat at six-thirty and it's barely that now and you know how he loses track of time, so don't worry—"

Fiona said, "I'm not worried! Who says I'm worried? I don't care if he comes or he doesn't."

"No, of course not," Maggie said soothingly.

"I just brought Leroy to visit you two. I don't care if he comes."

"Well, of course you don't."

Fiona sat down heavily in a kitchen chair and threw her purse on the table. Like the most formal of guests, she was carrying that purse with her from room to room; some things never changed. Maggie sighed and began unpacking the groceries. She put the ice cream in the freezer, and then she slit open both packs of chicken and dumped them into a bowl. "What kind of vegetables does Leroy like?" she asked.

Fiona said, "Hmm? Vegetables?" She didn't seem to have her mind on the question. She was gazing at the wall calendar, which still showed the month of August. Oh, this wasn't a very organized house, not that Fiona had any right to complain. The counters seemed to collect stray objects on their own. The cupboards were filled with dusty spice bottles and cereal boxes and mismatched dishes. Drawers sagged open, exposing a jumble of belongings. One drawer caught Maggie's eye, and she went over to riffle through the layers of papers stuffed inside. "Now, somewhere here," she said, "I could almost swear . . ."

She came across a PTA announcement. A torn-out recipe for something called Amazin' Raisin Pie. A packet of get-well cards that she'd been hunting since the day she bought them. And then, "Aha," she said, holding up a flier.

"What is it?"

"Picture of Jesse as a grownup. For Leroy."

She brought it over to Fiona: a darkly photocopied photo of the band. Lorimer was sitting in front with his drums and Jesse stood behind, his arms draped loosely around the necks of the other two, Dave and what's-his-name. All wore black. Jesse had his eyebrows knitted in a deliberate scowl. SPIN THE CAT was printed in furry, tiger-striped letters beneath their picture, and a blank space at the bottom allowed for a specific time and place to be written in by hand.

"Of course it doesn't do him justice," Maggie said. "These rock groups always try to look so, I don't know, so surly; have you noticed? Maybe I should just show her the snapshot I carry in my wallet. He isn't smiling there, either, but at least he's not frowning."

Fiona took the flier to study it more closely. "How funny," she said. "Everyone's just the same."

"Same?"

"I mean they were always going to be *going* somewhere; didn't you always think so? They had such high-and-mighty plans. And they used to keep changing so, changing their views of music. Why, one time Leroy asked me just what kind of songs her daddy played, new wave or punk or heavy metal or what, exactly—I think she wanted to impress her friends—and I said, 'Lordy, by now it could be anything; I wouldn't have the foggiest notion.' But just look at them."

"Well? So?" Maggie said. "What's to look at?"

"Lorimer's still got his hair fixed in that silly shag haircut with the tail down the back of his neck that I was always dying to chop off," Fiona said. "They're still wearing the same style of clothes, even. Same old-fashioned Hell's Angels style of clothing."

"Old-fashioned?" Maggie asked.

"You could picture how they'll get to be forty and still playing together on weekends when their wives will let them, playing for Rotary Club get-togethers and such."

It bothered Maggie to hear this, but she didn't let on. She turned back to her bowl of chicken.

Fiona said, "Who was it he brought to dinner?"

"Pardon?"

"You said he brought this woman to dinner one time."

Maggie glanced over at her. Fiona was still holding the photo, gazing at it with a bemused expression. "Nobody important," Maggie said.

"Well, who?"

"Just some woman he'd met someplace; we've been through a lot of those. Nobody long-term."

Fiona set the photo down on the table, but she went on looking at it.

Out in the living room, ragged music started thrumming forth from the hi-fi. Evidently Leroy had found one of Jesse's castoffs. Maggie heard *Hey hey* and *Every day* and a familiar twanging of strings, although she couldn't say who was playing. She took a carton of buttermilk from the refrigerator and poured it over the chicken. A headache was tightening the skin of her forehead. Now that she thought of it, she realized it had been nagging at her for some time.

"I'm going to call Jesse," she told Fiona suddenly.

She went over to the wall telephone and lifted the receiver. There wasn't any dial tone. Instead she heard a ringing at the other end. "Ira must be using the extension," she said, and she hung up again. "Well, so anyhow. Vegetables. Which vegetables will Leroy eat?"

"She likes tossed salad," Fiona said.

"Oh, dear, I should've bought lettuce."

"Maggie," Ira said, entering the kitchen, "what did you do to my answering machine?"

"Me? I didn't do anything."

"You most certainly did."

"I did not! I already told you about that little mishap last evening, but then I put a new message on."

He crooked his finger, beckoning her to the telephone. "Try it," he told her.

"What for?"

"Try dialing the shop."

She shrugged and came over to the phone. After she dialed, the phone at the other end rang three times. Something clicked. "Well, here goes," Maggie's own voice said, faraway and tinny. "Let's see: Press Button A, wait for the red . . . oh, shoot."

Maggie blinked.

"I must be doing something wrong," her voice continued. Then, in the falsetto she often used when she was clowning around with her children: "Who, me? Do something wrong? Little old perfect me? I'm shocked at the very suggestion!"

There was a ribbony shriek, like a tape on fast forward, followed by a beep. Maggie hung up. She said, "Well . . . um . . ."

"God knows what my customers thought," Ira told her.

"Maybe no one called," she said hopefully.

"I don't even know how you managed it! That machine is supposed to be foolproof."

"Well, it only goes to show: You can't trust the simplest product nowadays," she told him. She lifted the receiver again and started dialing Jesse's number. While his telephone rang and rang, she twined the cord nervously between her fingers. She was conscious of Fiona watching them, seated at the table with her chin resting on her cupped hand.

"Who're you calling?" Ira asked.

She pretended not to hear.

"Who's she calling, Fiona?"

"Well, Jesse, I think," Fiona told him.

"Did you forget his phone won't ring?"

976

Maggie looked up at him. "Oh!" she said.

She replaced the receiver and then gazed at it regretfully.

"Oh, well," Fiona said, "maybe he's on his way. It's Saturday night, after all; how late does he work?"

"Not late at all," Ira told her.

"*Where* does he work, come to think of it?"

"Chick's Cycle Shop. He sells motorcycles."

"Wouldn't they be closed by now?"

"Of course they're closed. They close at five."

"Then why bother calling?"

"No, no, she was calling his apartment," Ira said.

Fiona said, "His—"

Maggie went back to the bowl of chicken. She stirred it around in the buttermilk. She took a flattened brown paper bag from one of the drawers and poured some flour into it.

"Jesse has an apartment?" Fiona asked Ira.

"Why, yes."

Maggie measured in baking powder, salt, and pepper.

"An apartment away from here?"

"Up on Calvert Street."

Fiona thought that over.

Maggie said, "Here's something I always wanted to ask you, Fiona!" Her voice had somehow taken on that chirpy tone again. "Remember just a few months after you left?" she asked. "When Jesse phoned you and said you'd phoned him first and you said you hadn't? Well, had you, or hadn't you? Was it you who phoned our house and I said, 'Fiona?' and you hung up?"

"Oh, goodness . . ." Fiona said vaguely.

"I mean it had to be, or why else would the person hang up when I said your name?"

"I really don't recollect," Fiona said, and then she reached for her purse and rose. Walking in an airy, aimless way, as if she hardly noticed she was leaving, she wandered out of the kitchen, calling, "Leroy? Where'd you get to?"

977

"See there?" Maggie told Ira.

"Hmm?"

"It was her. I knew it all along."

"She didn't say it was."

"Oh, Ira, you are so obtuse sometimes," she said.

She closed the brown paper bag and shook it, mixing the seasonings. You can't have things both ways, she should have told Fiona. You can't laugh at him for staying the same and also object when he changes. Why, of course he had moved! Did Fiona imagine he had sat here waiting for her all these years?

And yet Maggie knew how she felt, somehow. You have this picture of a person; you have him tucked away in your mind in this certain fixed position.

She looked again at the band photo on the table. They had all been so enthusiastic once, she thought. So much energy had been invested. She remembered those early rehearsals in Lorimer's parents' garage, and the months and months when they'd been thrilled to perform for free, even, and the night that Jesse had come home triumphantly waving a ten-dollar bill—his share of their first paycheck.

"Is that Daisy?" Ira asked.

"What?"

"I thought I heard the front door."

"Oh!" Maggie said. "Maybe it's Jesse."

"Don't count on it," he told her.

But only Jesse would sling the door back against the bookcase that way. Maggie dusted off her hands. "Jesse?" she called.

"Here I am."

She hurried out to the hall, and Ira followed more slowly. Jesse stood just inside the door. He was looking toward the living room, where Leroy was poised like some startled small animal with her hands pressed together in front of her and one foot drawn up behind her. Jesse said, "Well, hi."

"Hi," Leroy said.

"How're you doing?"

"I'm okay."

He looked over at Maggie. Maggie said, "Hasn't she grown?" His long black eyes returned to Leroy.

Now Maggie moved toward him, willing him further into the house. (He always seemed on the verge of leaving.) She took his arm and said, "I'm frying up some chicken; it'll be a few more minutes. You two can sit in here and get acquainted."

But he had never been easily led. He was wearing a knitted jersey, and beneath the thin cloth she felt his resistance—the steely muscle above his elbow. His boots remained rooted to the floor. He was going to take his own sweet time at this.

"So what're you listening to?" he asked Leroy.

"Oh, just some record."

"You a Dead fan?"

"Dead? Um, sure."

"You want some better album, then," he said. "This one here is too popular with the masses."

"Oh, yeah, well," she said. "I was just thinking that myself."

He glanced at Maggie again. He was holding his face in a way that caused his chin to lengthen, just as Ira always did when he was trying to keep back a smile.

"She's athletic too," Maggie told him. "Brought along her baseball glove."

"That so?" he asked Leroy.

She nodded. The toe of her raised foot pointed daintily downward, ballet style.

Then something clattered upstairs and Fiona called, "Maggie, where—?"

She arrived on the landing. They all looked up at her.

"Oh," she said.

And she began to descend the stairs very smoothly and quietly, with one hand trailing along the banister. The only sound was the slapping of her sandals against her bare heels.

Jesse said, "Good to see you, Fiona."

She reached the hall and looked up at him. "It's good to see you too," she said.

"Done something new to your hair, haven't you?"

She lifted a hand, with her eyes still on his face, and touched the ends of her hair. "Oh! Maybe so," she told him.

Maggie said, "Well, I guess I'd better get back to—"

And Ira said, "Need help in the kitchen, Maggie?"

"Yes, please!" she sang out happily.

Fiona told Jesse, "I was just upstairs hunting my soapbox."

Maggie hesitated.

"Soapbox?" Jesse asked.

"I tried your bureau drawer, but it's empty. All I found was mothballs. Did you take my soapbox with you when you moved to your apartment?"

"What soapbox are you talking about?"

"My tortoiseshell soapbox! The one you kept."

Jesse looked over at Maggie. Maggie said, "You remember her soapbox."

"Well, no, I can't say as I do," Jesse said, and he grabbed hold of his forelock the way he always did when he was puzzled.

"You kept it after she left," Maggie told him. "I saw you with it. There was a bar of soap inside, remember? That clear kind of soap you can see through."

"*Oh*, yes," Jesse said, letting go of his forelock.

"You remember it?"

"Sure."

Maggie relaxed. She flashed a bracing smile at Leroy, who had lowered her foot to the floor now and was looking uncertain.

"So where is it?" Fiona asked. "Where's my soapbox, Jesse?"

"Well, uh, didn't your sister take it?"

"No."

"I thought she packed it up along with your other things."

"No," Fiona said. "You had it in your bureau."

Jesse said, "Gosh, Fiona. In that case maybe it's thrown out by now. But look, if it means so much to you, then I'd be glad to—"

"But you kept it, because it reminded you of me," Fiona told him. "It smelled like me! You closed your eyes and held my soapbox to your nose."

Jesse's gaze swiveled to Maggie again. He said, "Ma? Is that what you told her?"

"You mean it's not true?" Fiona asked him.

"You said I went around sniffing soapboxes, Ma?"

"You did!" Maggie said. Although she hated having to repeat it to his face. She had never meant to shame him. She turned to Ira (who was wearing exactly the shocked, reproachful expression she had expected) and said, "He kept it in his top drawer."

"Your treasure drawer," Fiona told Jesse. "Do you suppose I'd come all the way down here like any ordinary . . . groupie if your mother hadn't told me that? I didn't have to come! I was getting along just fine! But your mother says you hung on to my soapbox and wouldn't let Crystal pack it, you closed your eyes and took this big whiff, you've kept it to this day, she said, you've never let it go, you sleep with it under your pillow at night."

Maggie cried, "I never said—!"

"What do you think I am? Some kind of loser?" Jesse asked Fiona.

"Now, listen," Ira said.

Everyone seemed glad to turn to him.

"Let me get this straight," he said. "You're talking about a plastic soapbox."

"My plastic soapbox," Fiona told him, "that Jesse sleeps every night with."

"Well, there seems to be some mistake," Ira said. "How would Maggie even know such a thing? Jesse has his own apartment now. All he sleeps with that I've ever heard of is an auto greeter."

"A what?"

"Oh, never mind."

"What's an auto greeter?"

There was a pause. Then Ira said, "You know: the person who stands at the door when you go in to buy a car. She makes you give your name and address before she'll call a salesman."

"She? You mean a woman?"

"Right."

"Jesse sleeps with a woman?"

"Right."

Maggie said, "You just had to spoil things, Ira, didn't you."

"No," Ira told her, "it's the simple truth that's spoiled things, Maggie, and the truth is, Jesse's involved with somebody else now."

"But that woman's no one important! I mean they're not engaged or married or anything! She's no one he really cares about!"

She looked to Jesse to back her up, but he was studiously examining the toe of his left boot.

"Oh, Maggie, admit it," Ira said. "This is the way things *are*. This is how he's going to be. He never was fit husband material! He passes from girlfriend to girlfriend and he can't seem to hold the same job for longer than a few months; and every job he loses, it's somebody else's fault. The boss is a jerk, or the customers are jerks, or the other workers are—"

"Now, hold on," Jesse began, while Maggie said, "Oh, why do you always, always exaggerate, Ira! He worked in the record shop a full year, have you forgotten that?"

"Everyone in Jesse's acquaintance," Ira finished calmly, "by some magical coincidence ends up being a jerk."

Jesse turned and walked out of the house.

It made things more disturbing, somehow, that he didn't slam the door but let it click shut very gently behind him.

Maggie said, "He'll be back." She was speaking to Fiona,

982

but when Fiona didn't respond (her face was almost wooden; she was staring after Jesse), she told Leroy instead. "You saw how glad he was to see you, didn't you?"

Leroy just gaped.

"He's upset at what Ira said about him, is all," Maggie told her. And then she said, "Ira, I will never forgive you for this."

"Me!" Ira said.

Fiona said, "Stop it."

They turned.

"Just stop, both of you," she said. "I'm tired to death of it. I'm tired of Jesse Moran and I'm tired of the two of you, repeating your same dumb arguments and niggling and bickering, Ira forever so righteous and Maggie so willing to be wrong."

"Why . . . Fiona?" Maggie said. Her feelings were hurt. Maybe it was silly of her, but she had always secretly believed that outsiders regarded her marriage with envy. "We're not bickering; we're just discussing," she said. "We're compiling our two views of things."

Fiona said, "Oh, forget it. I don't know why I thought anything would be any different here." And she stepped into the living room and hugged Leroy, whose eyes were wide and startled. She said, "There, there, honey," and she buried her face in the crook of Leroy's neck. Plainly, Fiona herself was the one who needed consoling.

Maggie glanced at Ira. She looked elsewhere.

"Soapbox?" Ira asked. "How could you invent such a story?"

She didn't answer. (Anything she said might look like bickering.) Instead she walked away from him. She headed toward the kitchen in what she hoped was a dignified silence, but Ira followed, saying, "Look here, Maggie, you can't keep engineering other people's lives this way. Face facts! Wake up and smell the coffee!"

Ann Landers's favorite expression: Wake up and smell the coffee. She hated it when he quoted Ann Landers. She went over to the counter and started dropping chicken parts into the paper bag.

"Soapbox!" Ira marveled to himself.

"You want peas with your chicken?" she asked. "Or green beans."

But Ira said, "I'm going to go wash up." And he left.

So here she was alone. Well! She brushed a tear from her lashes. She was in trouble with everybody in this house, and she deserved to be; as usual she had acted pushy and meddle-some. And yet it hadn't seemed like meddling while she was doing it. She had simply felt as if the world were the tiniest bit out of focus, the colors not quite within the lines—something like a poorly printed newspaper ad—and if she made the smallest adjustment then everything would settle perfectly into place.

"Stupid!" she told herself, rattling the chicken parts in the bag. "Stupid old nosy-bones!" She slammed a skillet onto the stove and poured in too much oil. She twisted a knob savagely and then stood back and waited for the burner to heat. Now look: Droplets of oil were dotted across the front of her best dress, over the mound of her stomach. She was clumsy and fat-stomached and she didn't even have the sense to wear an apron while she was cooking. Also she had paid way too much for this dress, sixty-four dollars at Hecht's, which would scandalize Ira if he knew. How could she have been so greedy? She dabbed at her nose with the back of her hand. Took a deep breath. Well. Anyhow.

The oil wasn't hot enough yet, but she started adding the chicken. Unfortunately, there was quite of lot of it. Too much, it appeared now. (Unless they could coax Jesse back before suppertime.) She had to push the pieces too close together in order to fit in the last few drumsticks.

Peas, or green beans? That still hadn't been settled. She wiped her hands on a dishtowel and went out to the living room to check. "Leroy," she said, "what would—?"

But the living room was empty. Leroy's record had a worn

984

sound now, as if it were playing for the second or third time. "Truckin', got my chips cashed in . . ." an assortment of men sang doggedly. No one sat on the sofa or in either of the armchairs.

Maggie crossed the hallway to the front porch and called, "Leroy? Fiona?"

No answer. Four vacant rockers faced out toward the streetlight.

"Ira?"

"Upstairs," he called, his voice muffled-sounding.

She turned away from the door. Fiona's suitcase, thank goodness, still stood at the foot of the stairs; so she couldn't have gone far. "Ira, is Leroy with you?" Maggie called.

He appeared on the landing with a towel draped around his neck. Still drying his face, he looked down at her.

"I can't find her," she told him. "I can't find either one of them."

"Did you look on the porch?"

"Yes."

He came downstairs, carrying the towel. "Well, maybe they went out back," he said.

She followed him through the front door and around the side of the house. The night air was warm and humid. A gnat or mosquito whined in her ear and she waved it away. Who would want to be out here at this hour? Not Leroy or Fiona, evidently. The backyard, when they reached it, was a small, empty square of darkness.

"They've gone," Ira told her.

"Gone? You mean for good?"

"They must have."

"But their suitcase is still in the hall."

"Well, it was pretty heavy," he said, and he took her arm and steered her up the back porch steps. "If they were traveling on foot, they most likely didn't want to carry it."

"On foot," she said.

In the kitchen, the chicken was crackling away. Maggie paid no attention, but Ira turned the burner down.

"If they're on foot, we can catch them," Maggie said.

"Wait, Maggie—"

Too late; she was off. She sped through the hall again, out the door, down the steps to the street. Fiona's sister lived somewhere west of here, near Broadway. They would have turned left, therefore. Shading her eyes beneath the glare of the streetlight, Maggie peered up the stretch of deserted sidewalk. She saw a white cat walking alone in that high-bottomed, hesitant manner that cats take on in unfamiliar surroundings. A moment later a girl with long dark hair flew out of an alley and scooped it up, crying "Turkey! *There* you are!" She vanished with a flounce of her skirt. A car passed, leaving behind a scrap of a ball game: ". . . no outs and the bases loaded and it's hot times on Thirty-third Street tonight, folks . . ." The sky glowed a grayish pink over the industrial park.

Ira came up and set a hand on her shoulder. "Maggie, honey," he said.

But she shook him off and started back toward the house.

When she was upset she lost all sense of direction, and she concentrated now on her path like a blind man, reaching out falteringly to touch the little boxwood hedge by the walk, stumbling twice as she climbed the steps to the porch. "Sweetheart," Ira said behind her. She crossed the hallway to the foot of the stairs. She laid Fiona's suitcase flat and knelt to unfasten the latches.

Inside she found a pink cotton nightgown and a pair of child's pajamas and some lacy bikini underpants—none of these folded but scrunched instead like wrung-out dishcloths. And beneath those, a zippered cosmetics case, two stacks of tattered comic books, half a dozen beauty magazines, a box of dominoes, and a giant, faded volume of horse stories. All objects Fiona and Leroy could easily do without. What they couldn't do without—Fiona's purse and Leroy's baseball glove—had gone with them.

Sifting through these layers of belongings while Ira stood mute behind her, Maggie had a sudden view of her life as circular. It forever repeated itself, and it was entirely lacking in hope.

4

There was an old man in Maggie's nursing home who believed that once he reached heaven, all he had lost in his lifetime would be given back to him. "Oh, yes, what a good idea!" Maggie had said when he told her about it. She had assumed he meant intangibles—youthful energy, for instance, or that ability young people have to get swept away and impassioned. But then as he went on talking she saw that he had something more concrete in mind. At the Pearly Gates, he said, Saint Peter would hand everything to him in a gunnysack: The little red sweater his mother had knit him just before she died, that he had left on a bus in fourth grade and missed with all his heart ever since. The special pocketknife his older brother had flung into a cornfield out of spite. The diamond ring his first sweetheart had failed to return to him when she broke off their engagement and ran away with the minister's son.

Then Maggie thought of what she might find in her own gunnysack—the misplaced compacts, single earrings, and umbrellas, some of which she hadn't noticed losing at the time but recollected weeks or months afterward. ("Didn't I used to have a . . . ?" "Whatever became of my . . . ?") Objects freely given up, even, which later she wished back again—for example, those 1950s skirts she had donated to Goodwill, now that lower hem-

988

lines were once more in fashion. And she had said, "Oh, yes," again, but a shade less certainly, for it didn't seem that she had suffered losses quite as bitter as the old man's.

Now, though (sorting leftover fried chicken into plastic containers for Ira's lunches), she reconsidered that gunnysack, and this time it bulged much fuller. She remembered a green dress that her brother Josh's wife, Natalie, had admired one day. Maggie had said, "Take it, it matches your eyes," for it truly did, and she had been glad for Natalie to have it; she had loved her like a sister. But then Josh and Natalie had divorced and Natalie moved away and didn't keep in touch anymore, as if she'd divorced Maggie as well, and now Maggie wanted that dress returned. It used to move so fluidly when she walked! It was one of those dresses that go anywhere, that feel right for every occasion.

And she would like that funny little kitten, Thistledown, who'd been Ira's very first present to her in their courting days. She was a jokey, mischievous creature, forever battling imaginary enemies with her needle teeth and soft gray paws, and Maggie and Ira used to spend hours playing with her. But then Maggie had unintentionally murdered the poor thing by running her mother's dryer without checking inside first, and when she'd gone to pull the clothes out there was Thistle, as limp and frowsy and boneless as her namesake, and Maggie had cried and cried. After that there had been a whole string of other cats—Lucy and Chester and Pumpkin—but now all at once Maggie wanted Thistle back again. Surely Saint Peter allowed animals in that gunnysack, didn't he? Would he allow all the lean, unassuming dogs of Mulraney Street, those part-this-part-thats whose distant voices had barked her to sleep every night of her childhood? Would he allow the children's little gerbil, tirelessly plodding the years away on his wire treadmill till Maggie set him free out of pity and Pumpkin caught him and ate him?

And that corny key chain she used to have, a metal disk

that rotated on an axle, with LOVES ME on one side and LOVES ME NOT on the other. Boris Drumm had given her that, and when Jesse got his license she had sentimentally passed it on to him. She had dropped it into his palm after chauffeuring him home from his driver's test, but unfortunately the car was still in gear and it had started rolling as she climbed out. "Oh, great going, Ma," Jesse had said, reaching for the brake; and something about his lofty amusement had made her see him for the first time as a man. But now he carried his keys in a little leather case—snakeskin, she believed. She would like that key chain back again. She could actually feel it between her fingers—the lightweight, cheap metal and the raised lettering, the absentminded spin she used to give it as she stood talking with Boris: Loves me, loves me not. And once again she saw Boris rising up before her car as she practiced braking. Why, all he'd been trying to say was: Here I am! Pay me some notice!

Also, her clear brown bead necklace that looked something like dark amber. Antique plastic, the girl at the thrift shop had called it. A contradiction in terms, you would think; but Maggie had loved that necklace. So had Daisy, who in her childhood often borrowed it, along with a pair of Maggie's high-heeled shoes, and finally lost it in the alley out back of the house. She had worn it jumping rope on a summer evening and come home in tears because it had vanished. Definitely that would be in the gunnysack. And the summer evening as well, why not—the children smelling of sweat and fireflies, the warm porch floorboards sticking slightly to your chair rockers, the voices ringing from the alley: "Call *that* a strike?" and "Miss Mary Mack, Mack, Mack, dressed all in black, black, black . . ."

She stowed the containers of chicken at the front of the refrigerator, where Ira couldn't overlook them, and she pictured Saint Peter's astonishment as he watched what spilled forth: a bottle of wind, a box of fresh snow, and one of those looming moonlit clouds that used to float overhead like dirigibles as Ira walked her home from choir practice.

The dishes in the draining rack were dry by now and she stacked them and put them in the cupboard. Then she fixed herself a big bowl of ice cream. She wished they had bought mint chocolate chip. Fudge ripple was too white-tasting. She climbed the stairs, digging her spoon in. At the door to Daisy's room, she paused. Daisy was kneeling on the floor, fitting books into a carton. "Want some ice cream?" Maggie asked her.

Daisy glanced up and said, "No, thanks."

"All you had for supper was a drumstick."

"I'm not hungry," Daisy said, and she pushed a lock of hair off her forehead. She was wearing clothes that she wouldn't be taking with her—baggy jeans and a blouse with a torn button-hole. Her room already seemed uninhabited; the knickknacks that usually sat on her shelves had been packed for weeks.

"Where are your stuffed animals?" Maggie said.

"In my suitcase."

"I thought you were leaving them home."

"I was, but I changed my mind," Daisy said.

She had been quiet all through supper. Maggie could tell she was anxious about tomorrow. It was like her not to talk about it, though. You had to read the signs—her lack of appetite and her decision to bring her stuffed animals after all. Maggie said, "Well, honey, you let me know if you want any help."

"Thanks, Mom."

Maggie went on down the hall to the bedroom she shared with Ira. Ira was sitting tailor-fashion on the bed, laying out a game of solitaire. He had taken off his shoes and rolled his shirt sleeves up. "Care for some ice cream?" Maggie asked him.

"No, thanks."

"I shouldn't have any, either," she said. "But travel is such a strain, somehow. I feel I've burned a million calories just sitting in that car."

In the mirror above the bureau, though, she was positively obese. She set her ice cream on the dresser scarf and leaned forward to study her face, sucking in her cheeks to give herself a hollow look. It didn't work. She sighed and moved away. She went into the bathroom for her nightgown. "Ira," she called, her voice echoing off the tiles, "do you suppose Serena is still mad at us?"

She had to peer around the door to catch his answer: a shrug.

"I was thinking I might phone to see how she's doing," she told him, "but I'd hate for her to hang up on me."

She unbuttoned her dress and pulled it over her head and tossed it onto the toilet lid. Then she stepped out of her shoes. "Remember when I helped her put her mother in the nursing home?" she asked. "That time, she didn't speak for months and whenever I tried to call she'd bang the receiver down. I hated when she did that. That thunk on the other end of the line. It made me feel so small. It made me feel we were back in third grade."

"That's because she was *behaving* like a third-grader," Ira said.

Maggie came out in her slip to take another spoonful of ice cream. "And I don't even know why she got so upset," she told Ira's reflection in the mirror. "It was a perfectly honest mistake! I had the best intentions in the world! I said to her mother, 'Listen,' I said, 'you want to make a hit with the other residents? Want to show the staff right off that you're not just another bland old lady?' I mean this was Anita! Who used to wear the red toreador pants! I couldn't have them underestimating her, could I? That's why I told Serena we shouldn't take her in till Sunday evening, Halloween, and that's why I sewed that clown suit on my own machine and went all the way out Eastern Avenue to a what-do-you-call-it. What's it called?"

"Theatrical supply house," Ira said, dealing out another row of cards.

"Theatrical supply house, for white greasepaint. How was I to know they'd thrown the costume party on Saturday that year?"

She brought her ice cream over to the bed and settled down, propping her pillow against the headboard. Ira was frowning at his layout. "You would think I had deliberately plotted to make her a laughingstock," Maggie told him, "the way Serena carried on."

Whom she was picturing in her mind, though, was not Serena just then but Anita: her painted face, her red yarn hair, the triangles Maggie had lipsticked beneath her eyes which made them seem unnaturally bright or even teary, just like a real circus clown's. And then her chin quivering and denting inward as she sat in her wheelchair, watching Maggie leave.

"I was a coward," Maggie said suddenly, setting down her bowl. "I should have stayed and helped Serena get her changed. But I felt so foolish; I felt I'd made such a mess of things. I just said, 'Bye now!' and walked out, and the last I saw of her she was sitting there in a fright wig like somebody . . . inappropriate and senile and pathetic, with everyone around her dressed in normal clothing."

"Oh, honey, she adjusted to the place just fine, in the end," Ira said. "Why make such a big deal of it?"

"Because you didn't see how she looked, Ira. And also she was wearing one of those Poseys, you know? One of those Posey restraining devices because she couldn't sit upright on her own anymore. A clown suit and a Posey! I was dumb, I tell you."

She was hoping Ira would continue contradicting her, but all he did was lay a jack of clubs on a queen.

"I don't know why I kid myself that I'm going to heaven," Maggie told him.

Silence.

"So shall I call her, or not?"

"Call who?"

"Serena, Ira. Who have we been talking about here?"

"Sure, if you like," he said.

"But suppose she hangs up on me?"

"Then think of all you'll save on the phone bill."

She made a face at him.

She took the telephone from the nightstand and set it in her lap. Pondered it for a moment. Lifted the receiver. Tactfully, Ira bent lower over his cards and started whistling. (He was so polite about privacy, although as Maggie knew from experience you could overhear quite a lot while pretending to be absorbed in your song.) She punched in Serena's number very slowly and deliberately, as if that would help their conversation.

Serena's telephone gave two short rings instead of one long. Maggie thought of that as rural and slightly backward. *Breep-breep*, it said. *Breep-breep*.

Serena said, "Hello?"

"Serena?"

"Yes?"

"It's me."

"Oh, hi."

Maybe she hadn't realized yet who "me" was. Maggie cleared her throat. She said, "It's Maggie."

"Hi, Maggie."

Maggie relaxed against her pillow and stretched her legs out. She said, "I called to see how you were doing."

"Just fine!" Serena said. "Or, well, I don't know. Not so hot, to tell the truth. I keep walking up and down, walking from one room to another. Can't seem to stay in one place."

"Isn't Linda there?"

"I sent her away."

"What for?"

"She got on my nerves."

"On your nerves! How?"

"Oh, this way and that. I forget. They took me out to dinner and . . . I admit it was partly my fault. I was acting sort of contrary. I didn't like the restaurant and I couldn't stand the people who were eating there. I kept thinking how good it would feel to be alone, to have the house to myself. But now here I am and it's so quiet. It's like I'm wrapped in cotton or something. I was thrilled to hear the phone ring."

"I wish you lived closer," Maggie said.

Serena said, "I don't have anyone to tell about the trivia, what the plumbing's up to and how the red ants have come back in the kitchen."

"You can tell *me*," Maggie said.

"Well, but they're not your red ants too, don't you see? I mean you and I are not in this together."

"Oh," Maggie said.

There was a pause.

What was it Ira was whistling? Something from that record Leroy had played this evening; the lyrics were on the tip of Maggie's tongue. He scooped up a run of diamonds and shifted them to a king.

"You know," Serena said, "whenever Max went on a business trip we'd have so much to tell each other when he came home. He would talk and talk, and *I* would talk and talk, and then, you know what we'd do?"

"What?"

"We'd have a great big horrible fight."

Maggie laughed.

"And then we'd patch it up, and then we'd go to bed together," Serena said. "Crazy, wasn't it? And now I keep thinking: If Max were resurrected this minute, hale and hearty, would we still have our horrible fight just the same?"

"Well, I guess you would," Maggie said.

She wondered how it would feel to know she had seen Ira for the very last time on this earth. She supposed she would have trouble believing it. For several months, maybe, she would half expect him to come sauntering in again just as he had sauntered into choir practice that first spring evening thirty years ago.

"Um, also, Serena," she said, "I want to apologize for what happened after the funeral."

"Oh, forget it."

"No, really, both of us feel just terrible."

She hoped Serena couldn't hear Ira in the background; it made her apology seem insincere. *Lately it occurs to me*, he was whistling cheerily, *what a long, strange trip it's been . . .*

"Forget it; I flew off the handle," Serena told her. "Widow's nerves, or something. Pure silliness. I'm past the stage now where I can discard old friends without a thought; I can't afford it."

"Oh, don't say that!"

"What, you *want* me to discard you?"

"No, no . . ."

"Just joking," Serena told her. "Maggie, thanks for calling. I mean it. It was good to hear your voice."

"Anytime," Maggie said.

"Bye."

"Bye."

Serena hung up. A moment later, so did Maggie.

This ice cream wasn't even edible anymore. She had let it turn to soup. Also she was feeling overstuffed. She looked down at herself—at the bodice of her slip stretched tight across her breasts. "I'm an elephant," she told Ira.

He said, "Not again."

"Seriously."

He tapped his upper lip with a forefinger and studied his cards.

Well. She rose and went into the bathroom, stripping as she walked, and took her nightgown from its hook. When she dropped it over her head it shook itself out around her, loose and cool and weightless. "Whew!" she said. She washed her face and brushed her teeth. A trail of underclothes led from bedroom to bathroom; she picked them up and stuffed them into the hamper.

Sometimes, after an especially trying day, she felt an urge to burn everything she had worn.

Then while she was arranging her dress on a hanger, she was struck by a thought. She looked over at Ira. She looked away. She hung the dress in her closet, next to her one silk blouse.

"Goodness," she said, turning toward him again. "Wasn't Cartwheel dinky."

"Mm."

"I'd forgotten how dinky," she said.

"Mmhmm."

"I bet their school is dinky too."

No response.

"Do you suppose the Cartwheel school offers a good education?"

"I really couldn't say," Ira said.

She closed the closet door firmly. "Well, *I* can say," she told him. "It must be a full year behind the schools in Baltimore. Maybe two."

"And naturally Baltimore's schools are superb," Ira said.

"Well, at least they're better than Cartwheel's."

He raised an eyebrow at her.

"I mean most likely," Maggie said.

He picked up a card, moved it onto another, then changed his mind and moved it back again.

"Here's what we could do," Maggie said. "Write and ask Fiona if she's given any thought to Leroy's education. Offer to enroll her down here in Baltimore and let Leroy live with us nine months of the year."

"No," Ira said.

"Or even twelve months, if it works out that way. You know

how attached children get to their classmates and such. She might not want to leave."

"Maggie, look at me."

She faced him, hands on her hips.

"No," he said.

There were a lot of arguments she could have mentioned. All kinds of arguments!

But she didn't, somehow. She dropped her hands and wandered over to the window.

It was a warm, deep, quiet night, with just enough breeze to set the shade-pull swinging. She raised the shade higher and leaned out, pressing her forehead against the gritty screen. The air smelled of rubber tires and grass. Snatches of adventure music drifted up from the Lockes' TV next door. Across the street, the Simmonses were climbing their front steps, the husband jingling his house keys. *They* would not be going to bed yet; no chance of that. They were one of those happily childless young couples with eyes for only each other, and no doubt they were returning from dinner in a restaurant and now would . . . do what? Put on some romantic music, maybe, something with violins, and sit conversing graciously on their spotless white love seat, each raising a wineglass made of that thin, extra-breakable crystal that doesn't even have a lip around the rim. Or maybe they would dance. She had seen them dancing on their front porch once—the wife in spike heels, with her hair swept up in an igloo shape, the husband holding her slightly apart in a formal, admiring way.

Maggie spun around and returned to the bed. "Oh, Ira," she said, dropping down beside him, "what are we two going to live for, all the rest of our lives?"

She had dislodged a stack of his cards, but he kindly refrained from straightening them and instead reached out one arm and drew her in. "There, now, sweetheart," he said, and he settled her next to him. Still holding her close, he transferred a four of spades to a five, and Maggie rested her head against his chest and watched. He had arrived at the interesting part of the game by now, she saw. He had passed that early, superficial stage when any number of moves seemed possible, and now his choices were narrower and he had to show real skill and judgment. She felt a little stir of something that came over her like a flush, a sort of inner buoyancy, and she lifted her face to kiss the warm blade of his cheekbone. Then she slipped free and moved to her side of the bed, because tomorrow they had a long car trip to make and she knew she would need a good night's sleep before they started.